AGATHA CHRISTIE

Murderers Abroad

Five Complete Novels

AGATHA CHRISTIE

Murderers Abroad
Five Complete Novels

THE MYSTERY OF THE BLUE TRAIN
MURDER IN MESOPOTAMIA
THEY CAME TO BAGHDAD
SO MANY STEPS TO DEATH
PASSENGER TO FRANKFURT

AVENEL BOOKS
New York

Copyright © 1989 by Agatha Christie Ltd.

This omnibus was originally published in separate volumes under the titles: *The Mystery of the Blue Train* copyright 1928 by Dodd, Mead and Company, Inc., Copyright renewed; *Murder in Mesopotamia* copyright 1935, 1936 by Agatha Christie Mallowan, Copyright renewed; *They Came to Baghdad* copyright 1951 by Agatha Christie Limited, Copyright renewed © 1979 by Agatha Christie Limited; *So Many Steps to Death* copyright 1954, © 1955 by Agatha Christie, Copyright renewed; *Passenger to Frankfurt* copyright © 1970 by Agatha Christie Limited.

This 1989 edition is published by Avenel Books, distributed by Crown Publishers, Inc., 225 Park Avenue South, New York, New York 10003, by arrangement with GP Putnam's Sons.

Printed and bound in the United States of America

Library of Congress Cataloging-in-Publication Data

Christie, Agatha, 1890–1976.
    Agatha Christie—murderers abroad.
      p. cm.
    Contents: Murder in Mesopotamia—They came to Baghdad—Passenger to Frankfurt—The mystery of the blue train—So many steps to death.
    1. Detective and mystery stories, English.   I. Title: Murderers abroad.
PR6005.H66A74   1989
823'.912—dc20   89-33440
                                                              CIP

ISBN 0-517-69043-8

h g f e d c b a

CONTENTS

THE MYSTERY OF THE BLUE TRAIN

Dedicated to
Two Distinguished Members
of the O.F.D.
CARLOTTA and PETER

Contents

1

The Man with the White Hair

IT WAS CLOSE on midnight when a man crossed the Place de la Concorde. In spite of the handsome fur coat which garbed his meager form, there was something essentially weak and paltry about him.

A little man with a face like a rat. A man, one would say, who could never play a conspicuous part, or rise to prominence in any sphere. And yet, in leaping to such a conclusion, an onlooker would have been wrong. For this man, negligible and inconspicuous as he seemed, played a prominent part in the destiny of the world. In an Empire where rats ruled, he was the king of the rats.

Even now, an Embassy awaited his return. But he had business to do first —business of which the Embassy was not officially cognizant. His face gleamed white and sharp in the moonlight. There was the least hint of a curve in the thin nose. His father had been a Polish Jew, a journeyman tailor. It was business such as his father would have loved that took him abroad tonight.

He came to the Seine, crossed it, and entered one of the less reputable quarters of Paris. Here he stopped before a tall, dilapidated house and made his way up to an apartment on the fourth floor. He had barely time to knock before the door was opened by a woman who had evidently been awaiting his arrival. She gave him no greeting, but helped him off with his overcoat and then led the way into the tawdrily furnished sitting room. The electric light was shaded with dirty pink festoons, and it softened, but could not disguise, the girl's face with its mask of crude paint. Could not disguise, either, the broad Mongolian cast of her countenance. There was no doubt of Olga Demiroff's profession, nor of her nationality.

"All is well, little one?"

"All is well, Boris Ivanovitch."

He nodded murmuring: "I do not think I have been followed."

5

But there was anxiety in his tone. He went to the window, drawing the curtains aside slightly, and peering carefully out. He started away violently.

"There are two men—on the opposite pavement. It looks to me——" He broke off and began gnawing at his nails—a habit he had when anxious.

The Russian girl was shaking her head with a slow, reassuring action.

"They were here before you came."

"All the same, it looks to me as though they were watching this house."

"Possibly," she admitted indifferently.

"But then——"

"What of it? Even if they *know*—it will not be *you* they will follow from here."

A thin, cruel smile came to his lips.

"No," he admitted, "that is true."

He mused for a minute or two and then observed.

"This damned American—he can look after himself as well as anybody."

"I suppose so."

He went again to the window.

"Tough customers," he muttered, with a chuckle. "Known to the police, I fear. Well, well, I wish Brother Apache good hunting."

Olga Demiroff shook her head.

"If the American is the kind of man they say he is, it will take more than a couple of cowardly apaches to get the better of him." She paused. "I wonder——"

"Well?"

"Nothing. Only twice this evening a man has passed along this street—a man with white hair."

"What of it?"

"This. As he passed those two men, he dropped his glove. One of them picked it up and returned it to him. A threadbare device."

"You mean—that the white-haired man is—their employer?"

"Something of the kind."

The Russian looked alarmed and uneasy.

"You are sure—the parcel is safe? It has not been tampered with? There has been too much talk . . . much too much talk."

He gnawed his nails again.

"Judge for yourself."

She bent to the fireplace, deftly removing the coals. Underneath, from among the crumpled balls of newspaper, she selected from the very middle an oblong package wrapped round with grimy newspaper, and handed it to the man.

"Ingenious," he said, with a nod of approval.

"The apartment has been searched twice. The mattress on my bed was ripped open."

"It is as I said," he muttered. "There has been too much talk. This haggling over the price—it was a mistake."

He had unwrapped the newspaper. Inside was a small brown paper parcel. This in turn he unwrapped, verified the contents, and quickly wrapped it up once more. As he did so, an electric bell rang sharply.

"The American is punctual," said Olga, with a glance at the clock.

She left the room. In a minute she returned ushering in a stranger, a big, broad-shouldered man whose transatlantic origin was evident. His keen glance went from one to the other.

"M. Krassnine?" he inquired politely.

"I am he," said Boris. "I must apologize for—for the unconventionality of this meeting place. But secrecy is urgent. I—I cannot afford to be connected with this business in any way."

"Is that so?" said the American politely.

"I have your word, have I not, that no details of this transaction will be made public? That is one of the conditions of—sale."

The American nodded.

"That has already been agreed upon," he said indifferently. "Now, perhaps, you will produce the goods."

"You have the money—in notes?"

"Yes," replied the other.

He did not, however, make any attempt to produce it. After a moment's hesitation, Krassnine gestured toward the small parcel on the table.

The American took it up and unrolled the wrapping paper. The contents he took over to a small electric lamp and submitted them to a very thorough examination. Satisfied, he drew from his pocket a thick leather wallet and extracted from it a wad of notes. These he handed to the Russian, who counted them carefully.

"All right?"

"I thank you, Monsieur. Everything is correct."

"Ah!" said the other. He slipped the brown paper parcel negligently into his pocket. He bowed to Olga. "Good evening, Mademoiselle. Good evening, M. Krassnine."

He went out, shutting the door behind him. The eyes of the two in the room met. The man passed his tongue over his dry lips.

"I wonder—will he ever get back to his hotel?" he muttered.

By common accord, they both turned to the window. They were just in time to see the American emerge into the street below. He turned to the left and marched along at a good pace without once turning his head. Two shadows stole from a doorway and followed noiselessly. Pursuers and pursued vanished into the night. Olga Demiroff spoke.

"He will get back safely," she said. "You need not fear—or hope—whichever it is."

"Why do you think he will be safe?" asked Krassnine curiously.

"A man who has made as much money as he has could not possibly be a fool," said Olga. "And talking of money——"

She looked significantly at Krassnine.

"Eh?"

"My share, Boris Ivanovitch."

With some reluctance, Krassnine handed over two of the notes. She nodded her thanks, with a complete lack of emotion, and tucked them away in her stocking.

"That is good," she remarked, with satisfaction.

He looked at her curiously.

"You have no regrets, Olga Vassilovna?"

"Regrets? For what?"

"For what has been in your keeping. There are women—most women, I believe, who go mad over such things."

She nodded reflectively.

"Yes, you speak truth there. Most women have that madness. I—have not. I wonder now——" She broke off.

"Well?" asked the other curiously.

"The American will be safe with them—yes, I am sure of that. But afterward——"

"Eh? What are you thinking of?"

"He will give them, of course, to some woman," said Olga thoughtfully. "I wonder what will happen then. . . ."

She shook herself impatiently and went over to the window. Suddenly she uttered an exclamation and called to her companion.

"See, he is going down the street now—the man I mean."

They both gazed down together. A slim, elegant figure was progressing along at a leisurely pace. He wore an opera hat and a cloak. As he passed a street lamp, the light illumined a thatch of thick white hair.

2

M. le Marquis

THE MAN WITH the white hair continued on his course, unhurried, and seemingly indifferent to his surroundings. He took a side turning to the right and another one to the left. Now and then he hummed a little air to himself.

Suddenly he stopped dead and listened intently. He had heard a certain sound. It might have been the bursting of a tire or it might have been—a shot. A curious smile played round his lips for a minute. Then he resumed his leisurely walk.

On turning a corner he came upon a scene of some activity. A representa-

tive of the law was making notes in a pocketbook, and one or two late passersby had collected on the spot. To one of these the man with the white hair
made a polite request for information.

"Something has been happening, yes?"

"Mais oui, Monsieur. Two apaches set upon an elderly American gentleman."

"They did him no injury?"

"No, indeed." The man laughed. "The American, he had a revolver in his
pocket, and before they could attack him, he fired shots so closely round
them that they took alarm and fled. The police, as usual, arrived too late."

"Ah!" said the inquirer.

He displayed no emotion of any kind.

Placidly and unconcernedly he resumed his nocturnal strolling. Presently
he crossed the Seine and came into the richer areas of the city. It was some
twenty minutes later that he came to a stop before a certain house in a quiet
but aristocratic thoroughfare.

The shop, for shop it was, was a restrained and unpretentious one.
D. Papopolous, dealer in antiques, was so known to fame that he needed no
advertisement, and indeed most of his business was not done over a counter.
M. Papopolous had a very handsome apartment of his own overlooking the
Champs Élysées, and it might reasonably be supposed that he would have
been found there and not at his place of business at such an hour, but the man
with the white hair seemed confident of success as he pressed the obscurely
placed bell, having first given a quick glance up and down the deserted street.

His confidence was not misplaced. The door opened and a man stood in the
aperture. He wore gold rings in his ears and was of a swarthy cast of countenance.

"Good evening," said the stranger. "Your master is within?"

"The master is here, but he does not see chance visitors at this time of
night," growled the other.

"I think he will see me. Tell him that his friend M. le Marquis is here."

The man opened the door a little wider and allowed the visitor to enter.

The man who gave his name as M. le Marquis had shielded his face with
his hand as he spoke. When the manservant returned with the information
that M. Papopolous would be pleased to receive the visitor a further change
had taken place in the stranger's appearance. The manservant must have been
very unobservant or very well trained for he betrayed no surprise at the small
black satin mask which hid the other's features. Leading the way to a door at
the end of the hall, he opened it and announced in a respectful murmur: *"M.
le Marquis."*

The figure which rose to receive this strange guest was an imposing one.
There was something venerable and patriarchal about M. Papopolous. He
had a high domed forehead and a beautiful white beard. His manner had in it
something ecclesiastical and benign.

"My dear friend," said M. Papopolous.

He spoke in French and his tones were rich and unctuous.

"I must apologize," said the visitor, "for the lateness of the hour."

"Not at all. Not at all," said M. Papopolous—"an interesting time of night. You have had, perhaps, an interesting evening?"

"Not personally," said M. le Marquis.

"Not personally," repeated M. Papopolous, "no, no, of course not. And there is news, eh?"

He cast a sharp glance sideways at the other, a glance that was not ecclesiastical or benign in the least.

"There is no news. The attempt failed. I hardly expected anything else."

"Quite so," said M. Papopolous; "anything crude——"

He waved his hand to express his intense distaste for crudity in any form. There was indeed nothing crude about M. Papopolous nor about the goods he handled. He was well known in most European courts, and kings called him Demetrius in a friendly manner. He had the reputation for the most exquisite discretion. That, together with the nobility of his aspect, had carried him through several very questionable transactions.

"The direct attack——" said M. Papopolous. He shook his head. "It answers sometimes—but very seldom."

The other shrugged his shoulders.

"It saves time," he remarked, "and to fail costs nothing—or next to nothing. The other plan—will not fail."

"Ah," said M. Papopolous, looking at him keenly.

The other nodded slowly.

"I have great confidence in your—er—reputation," said the antique dealer.

M. le Marquis smiled gently.

"I think I may say," he murmured, "that your confidence will not be misplaced."

"You have unique opportunities," said the other, with a note of envy in his voice.

"I make them," said M. le Marquis.

He rose and took up the cloak which he had thrown carelessly on the back of a chair.

"I will keep you informed, M. Papopolous, through the usual channels, but there must be no hitch in your arrangements."

M. Papopolous was pained.

"There is *never* a hitch in my arrangements," he complained.

The other smiled, and without any further word of adieu he left the room, closing the door behind him.

M. Papopolous remained in thought for a moment stroking his venerable white beard, and then moved across to a second door which opened inward. As he turned the handle, a young woman, who only too clearly had been leaning against it with her ear to the keyhole, stumbled headlong into the room. M. Papopolous displayed neither surprise nor concern. It was evidently all quite natural to him.

"Well, Zia?" he asked.

"I did not hear him go," explained Zia.

She was a handsome young woman, built on Junoesque lines, with dark flashing eyes and such a general air of resemblance to M. Papopolous that it was easy to see they were father and daughter.

"It is annoying," she continued vexedly, "that one cannot see through a keyhole and hear through it at the same time."

"It has often annoyed me," said M. Papopolous, with great simplicity.

"So that is M. le Marquis," said Zia slowly. "Does he always wear a mask, Father?"

"Always."

There was a pause.

"It is the rubies, I suppose?" asked Zia.

Her father nodded.

"What do you think, my little one?" he inquired, with a hint of amusement in his beady black eyes.

"Of M. le Marquis?"

"Yes."

"I think," said Zia slowly, "that it is a very rare thing to find a well-bred Englishman who speaks French as well as that."

"Ah!" said M. Papopolous, "so that is what you think."

As usual, he did not commit himself, but he regarded Zia with benign approval.

"I thought, too," said Zia, "that his head was an odd shape."

"Massive," said her father—"a trifle massive. But then that effect is always created by a wig."

They both looked at each other and smiled.

3

Heart of Fire

RUFUS VAN ALDIN passed through the revolving doors of the Savoy, and walked to the reception desk. The desk clerk smiled a respectful greeting.

"Pleased to see you back again, Mr. Van Aldin," he said.

The American millionaire nodded his head in a casual greeting.

"Everything all right?" he asked.

"Yes, sir. Major Knighton is upstairs in the suite now."

Van Aldin nodded again.

"Any mail?" he vouchsafed.

"They have all been sent up, Mr. Van Aldin. Oh! wait a minute."

He dived into a pigeonhole, and produced a letter.

"Just come this minute," he explained.

Rufus Van Aldin took the letter from him, and as he saw the handwriting, a woman's flowing hand, his face was suddenly transformed. The harsh contours of it softened, and the hard line of his mouth relaxed. He looked a different man. He walked across to the lift with the letter in his hand and the smile still on his lips.

In the drawing room of his suite, a young man was sitting at a desk nimbly sorting correspondence with the ease born of long practice. He sprang up as Van Aldin entered.

"Hallo, Knighton!"

"Glad to see you back, sir. Had a good time?"

"So so!" said the millionaire unemotionally. "Paris is rather a one-horse city nowadays. Still—I got what I went over for."

He smiled to himself rather grimly.

"You usually do, I believe," said the secretary, laughing.

"That's so," agreed the other.

He spoke in a matter-of-fact manner, as one stating a well-known fact. Throwing off his heavy overcoat, he advanced to the desk.

"Anything urgent?"

"I don't think so, sir. Mostly the usual stuff. I have not quite finished sorting it out."

Van Aldin nodded briefly. He was a man who seldom expressed either blame or praise. His methods with those he employed were simple; he gave them a fair trial and dismissed promptly those who were inefficient. His selections of people were unconventional. Knighton, for instance, he had met casually at a Swiss resort two months previously. He had approved of the fellow, looked up his war record, and found in it the explanation of the limp with which he walked. Knighton had made no secret of the fact that he was looking for a job, and indeed diffidently asked the millionaire if he knew of any available post. Van Aldin remembered, with a grim smile of amusement, the young man's complete astonishment when he had been offered the post of secretary to the great man himself.

"But—but I have no experience of business," he had stammered.

"That doesn't matter a cuss," Van Aldin had replied. "I have got three secretaries already to attend to that kind of thing. But I am likely to be in England for the next six months, and I want an Englishman who—well, knows the ropes—and can attend to the social side of things for me."

So far, Van Aldin had found his judgment confirmed. Knighton had proved quick, intelligent, and resourceful, and he had a distinct charm of manner.

The secretary indicated three or four letters placed by themselves on the top of the desk.

"It might perhaps be as well, sir, if you glanced at these," he suggested. "The top one is about the Colton agreement——"

But Rufus Van Aldin held up a protesting hand.

"I am not going to look at a durned thing tonight," he declared. "They can all wait till the morning. Except this one," he added, looking down at the letter he held in his hand. And again that strange transforming smile stole over his face.

Richard Knighton smiled sympathetically.

"Mrs. Kettering?" he murmured. "She rang up yesterday and today. She seems very anxious to see you at once, sir."

"Does she, now!"

The smile faded from the millionaire's face. He ripped open the envelope which he held in his hand and took out the enclosed sheet. As he read it his face darkened, his mouth set grimly in the line which Wall Street knew so well, and his brows knit themselves ominously. Knighton turned tactfully away, and went on opening letters and sorting them. A muttered oath escaped the millionaire, and his clenched fist hit the table sharply.

"I'll not stand for this," he muttered to himself. "Poor little girl, it's a good thing she has her old father behind her."

He walked up and down the room for some minutes, his brows drawn together in a scowl. Knighton still bent assiduously over the desk. Suddenly Van Aldin came to an abrupt halt. He took up his overcoat from the chair where he had thrown it.

"Are you going out again, sir?"

"Yes; I'm going round to see my daughter."

"If Colton's people ring up——"

"Tell them to go to the devil," said Van Aldin.

"Very well," said the secretary unemotionally.

Van Aldin had his overcoat on by now. Cramming his hat upon his head, he went toward the door. He paused with his hand upon the handle.

"You are a good fellow, Knighton," he said. "You don't worry me when I am rattled."

Knighton smiled a little, but made no reply.

"Ruth is my only child," said Van Aldin, "and there is no one on this earth who knows quite what she means to me."

A faint smile irradiated his face. He slipped his hand into his pocket.

"Care to see something, Knighton?"

He came back toward the secretary.

From his pocket he drew out a parcel carelessly wrapped in brown paper. He tossed off the wrapping and disclosed a big, shabby, red velvet case. In the center of it were some twisted initials surmounted by a crown. He snapped the case open, and the secretary drew in his breath sharply. Against the slightly dingy white of the interior, the stones glowed like blood.

"My God! sir," said Knighton. "Are they—are they real?"

Van Aldin laughed a quiet little cackle of amusement.

"I don't wonder at your asking that. Among these rubies are the three largest in the world. Catherine of Russia wore them, Knighton. That center one there is known as Heart of Fire. It's perfect—not a flaw in it."

"But," the secretary murmured, "they must be worth a fortune."

"Four or five hundred thousand dollars," said Van Aldin nonchalantly, "and that is apart from the historical interest."

"And you carry them about—like that, loose in your pocket?"

Van Aldin laughed amusedly.

"I guess so. You see, they are my little present for Ruthie."

The secretary smiled discreetly.

"I can understand now Mrs. Kettering's anxiety over the telephone," he murmured.

But Van Aldin shook his head. The hard look returned to his face.

"You are wrong there," he said. "She doesn't know about these; they are my little surprise for her."

He shut the case, and began slowly to wrap it up again.

"It's a hard thing, Knighton," he said, "how little one can do for those one loves. I can buy a good portion of the earth for Ruth, if it would be any use to her, but it isn't. I can hang these things round her neck and give her a moment or two's pleasure, maybe, but——"

He shook his head.

"When a woman is not happy in her home——"

He left the sentence unfinished. The secretary nodded discreetly. He knew, none better, the reputation of the Hon. Derek Kettering. Van Aldin sighed. Slipping the parcel back in his coat pocket, he nodded to Knighton and left the room.

4

In Curzon Street

THE HON. MRS. Derek Kettering lived in Curzon Street. The butler who opened the door recognized Rufus Van Aldin at once and permitted himself a discreet smile of greeting. He led the way upstairs to the big double drawing-room on the first floor.

A woman who was sitting by the window started up with a cry.

"Why, Dad, if that isn't too good for anything! I've been telephoning Major Knighton all day to try and get hold of you, but he couldn't say for sure when you were expected back."

Ruth Kettering was twenty-eight years of age. Without being beautiful, or in the real sense of the word even pretty, she was striking looking because of her coloring. Van Aldin had been called Carrots and Ginger in his time, and Ruth's hair was almost pure auburn. With it went dark eyes and very black lashes—the effect somewhat enhanced by art. She was tall and slender, and moved well. At a careless glance it was the face of a Raphael Madonna. Only if one looked closely did one perceive the same line of jaw and chin as in Van Aldin's face, bespeaking the same hardness and determination. It suited the man, but suited the woman less well. From her childhood upward Ruth Van Aldin had been accustomed to having her own way, and anyone who had ever stood up against her soon realized that Rufus Van Aldin's daughter never gave in.

"Knighton told me you'd phoned him," said Van Aldin. "I only got back from Paris half an hour ago. What's all this about Derek?"

Ruth Kettering flushed angrily.

"It's unspeakable. It's beyond all limits," she cried. "He—he doesn't seem to listen to anything I say."

There was bewilderment as well as anger in her voice.

"He'll listen to me," said the millionaire grimly.

Ruth went on.

"I've hardly seen him for the last month. He goes about everywhere with that woman."

"With what woman?"

"Mirelle. She dances at the Parthenon, you know."

Van Aldin nodded.

"I was down at Leconbury last week. I—I spoke to Lord Leconbury. He was awfully sweet to me, sympathized entirely. He said he'd give Derek a good talking to."

"Ah!" said Van Aldin.

"What do you mean by 'Ah!', Dad?"

"Just what you think I mean, Ruthie. Poor old Leconbury is a washout. Of course he sympathized with you, of course he tried to soothe you down. Having got his son and heir married to the daughter of one of the richest men in the States, he naturally doesn't want to mess the thing up. But he's got one foot in the grave already, everyone knows that, and anything he may say will cut darned little ice with Derek."

"Can't *you* do anything, Dad?" urged Ruth, after a minute or two.

"I might," said the millionaire. He waited a second reflectively, and then went on. "There are several things I might do, but there's only one that will be any real good. How much pluck have you got, Ruthie?"

She stared at him. He nodded back at her.

"I mean just what I say. Have you got the grit to admit to all the world that you've made a mistake? There's only one way out of this mess, Ruthie. Cut your losses and start afresh."

"You mean——"

"Divorce."

"Divorce!"

Van Aldin smiled dryly.

"You say that word, Ruth, as though you'd never heard it before. And yet your friends are doing it all around you every day."

"Oh! I know that. But——"

She stopped, biting her lip. Her father nodded comprehendingly.

"I know, Ruth. You're like me, you can't bear to let go. But I've learned, and you've got to learn, that there are times when it's the only way. I might find ways of whistling Derek back to you, but it would all come to the same in the end. *He's no good,* Ruth; he's rotten through and through. And mind you, I blame myself for ever letting you marry him. But you were kind of set on having him, and he seemed in earnest about turning over a new leaf—and well, I'd crossed you once, honey . . ."

He did not look at her as he said the last words. Had he done so, he might have seen the swift color that came up in her face.

"You did," she said in a hard voice.

"I was too durned softhearted to do it a second time. I can't tell you how I wish I had, though. You've led a poor kind of life for the last few years, Ruth."

"It has not been very—agreeable," agreed Mrs. Kettering.

"That's why I say to you that this thing has got to *stop!*" He brought his hand down with a bang on the table. "You may have a hankering after the fellow still. *Cut it out.* Face facts. Derek Kettering married you for your money. That's all there is to it. Get rid of him, Ruth."

Ruth Kettering looked down at the ground for some moments, then she said, without raising her head:

"Supposing he doesn't consent?"

Van Aldin looked at her in astonishment.

"He won't have a say in the matter."

She flushed and bit her lip.

"No—no—of course not. I only meant——"

She stopped. Her father eyed her keenly.

"What did you mean?"

"I meant——" She paused, choosing her words carefully. "He mayn't take it lying down."

The millionaire's chin shot out grimly.

"You mean he'll fight the case? Let him! But, as a matter of fact, you're wrong. He won't fight. Any solicitor he consults will tell him he hasn't a leg to stand upon."

"You don't think"—she hesitated—"I mean—out of sheer spite against me —he might try to make it awkward?"

Her father looked at her in some astonishment.

"Fight the case, you mean?"

He shook his head.

"Very unlikely. You see, he would have to have something to go upon."

Mrs. Kettering did not answer. Van Aldin looked at her sharply.

"Come, Ruth, out with it. There's something troubling you—what is it?"

"Nothing, nothing at all."

But her voice was unconvincing.

"You are dreading the publicity, eh? Is that it? You leave it to me. I'll put the whole thing through so smoothly that there will be no fuss at all."

"Very well, Dad, if you really think it's the best thing to be done."

"Got a fancy for the fellow still, Ruth? Is that it?"

"No."

The word came with no uncertain emphasis. Van Aldin seemed satisfied. He patted his daughter on the shoulder.

"It will be all right, little girl. Don't you worry any. Now let's forget all about this. I have brought you a present from Paris."

"For me? Something very nice?"

"I hope you'll think so," said Van Aldin, smiling.

He took the parcel from his coat pocket and handed it to her. She unwrapped it eagerly, and snapped open the case. A long-drawn "Oh!" came from her lips. Ruth Kettering loved jewels—always had done so.

"Dad, how—how wonderful!"

"Rather in a class by themselves, aren't they?" said the millionaire, with satisfaction. "You like them, eh?"

"Like them? Dad, they're unique. How did you get hold of them?"

Van Aldin smiled.

"Ah! that's my secret. They had to be bought privately, of course. They are rather well known. See that big stone in the middle? You have heard of it, maybe; that's the historic 'Heart of Fire.' "

"Heart of Fire!" repeated Mrs. Kettering.

She had taken the stones from the case and was holding them against her breast. The millionaire watched her. He was thinking of the series of women who had worn the jewels. The heartaches, the despairs, the jealousies. "Heart of Fire," like all famous stones, had left behind it a trail of tragedy and violence. Held in Ruth Kettering's assured hand, it seemed to lose its potency of evil. With her cool, equable poise, this woman of the western world seemed a negation to tragedy or heart-burnings. Ruth returned the stones to their case; then, jumping up, she flung her arms round her father's neck.

"Thank you, thank you, thank you, Dad! They are wonderful! You do give me the most marvelous presents always."

"That's all right," said Van Aldin, patting her shoulder. "You are all I have, you know, Ruthie."

"You will stay to dinner, won't you, Father?"

"I don't think so. You were going out, weren't you?"

"Yes, but I can easily put that off. Nothing very exciting."

"No," said Van Aldin. "Keep your engagement. I have got a good deal to attend to. See you tomorrow, my dear. Perhaps if I phone you, we can meet at Galbraiths'?"

Messrs. Galbraith, Galbraith, Cuthbertson, & Galbraith were Van Aldin's London solicitors.

"Very well, Dad." She hesitated. "I suppose it—this—won't keep me from going to the Riviera?"

"When are you off?"

"On the fourteenth."

"Oh, that will be all right. These things take a long time to mature. By the way, Ruth, I shouldn't take those rubies abroad if I were you. Leave them at the bank."

Mrs. Kettering nodded.

"We don't want to have you robbed and murdered for the sake of 'Heart of Fire,' " said the millionaire jocosely.

"And yet you carried it about in your pocket loose," retorted his daughter, smiling.

"Yes——"

Something, some hesitation, caught her attention.

"What is it, Dad?"

"Nothing." He smiled. "Thinking of a little adventure of mine in Paris."

"An adventure?"

"Yes, the night I bought these things."

He made a gesture toward the jewel case.

"Oh, do tell me."

"Nothing to tell, Ruthie. Some apache fellows got a bit fresh and I shot at them and they got off. That's all."

She looked at him with some pride.

"You're a tough proposition, Dad."

"You bet I am, Ruthie."

He kissed her affectionately and departed. On arriving back at the Savoy, he gave a curt order to Knighton.

"Get hold of a man called Goby; you'll find his address in my private book. He's to be here tomorrow morning at half past nine."

"Yes, sir."

"I also want to see Mr. Kettering. Run him to earth for me if you can. Try his Club—at any rate, get hold of him somehow, and arrange for me to see him here tomorrow morning. Better make it latish, about twelve. His sort aren't early risers."

The secretary nodded in comprehension of these instructions. Van Aldin gave himself into the hands of his valet. His bath was prepared, and as he lay luxuriating in the hot water, his mind went back over the conversation with his daughter. On the whole he was well satisfied. His keen mind had long since accepted the fact that divorce was the only possible way out. Ruth had agreed to the proposed solution with more readiness than he had hoped for. Yet, in spite of her acquiescence, he was left with a vague sense of uneasiness.

Something about her manner, he felt, had not been quite natural. He frowned to himself.

"Maybe I'm fanciful," he muttered, "and yet—I bet there's something she has not told me."

5

A Useful Gentleman

RUFUS VAN ALDIN had just finished the sparse breakfast of coffee and dry toast, which was all he ever allowed himself, when Knighton entered the room.

"Mr. Goby is below, sir, waiting to see you."

The millionaire glanced at the clock. It was just half past nine.

"All right," he said curtly. "He can come up."

A minute or two later, Mr. Goby entered the room. He was a small, elderly man, shabbily dressed, with eyes that looked carefully all around the room, and never at the person he was addressing.

"Good morning, Goby," said the millionaire. "Take a chair."

"Thank you, Mr. Van Aldin."

Mr. Goby sat down with his hands on his knees, and gazed earnestly at the radiator.

"I have got a job for you."

"Yes, Mr. Van Aldin?"

"My daughter is married to the Hon. Derek Kettering, as you may perhaps know."

Mr. Goby transferred his gaze from the radiator to the left-hand drawer of the desk, and permitted a deprecating smile to pass over his face. Mr. Goby knew a great many things, but he always hated to admit the fact.

"By my advice, she is about to file a petition for divorce. That, of course, is a solicitor's business. But, for private reasons, I want the fullest and most complete information."

Mr. Goby looked at the cornice and murmured:

"About Mr. Kettering?"

"About Mr. Kettering."

"Very good, sir."

Mr. Goby rose to his feet.

"When will you have it ready for me?"

"Are you in a hurry, sir?"

"I'm always in a hurry," said the millionaire.

Mr. Goby smiled understandingly at the fender.

"Shall we say two o'clock this afternoon, sir?" he asked.

"Excellent," approved the other. "Good morning, Goby."

"Good morning, Mr. Van Aldin."

"That's a very useful man," said the millionaire as Goby went out and his secretary came in. "In his own line he's a specialist."

"What is his line?"

"Information. Give him twenty-four hours and he would lay the private life of the Archbishop of Canterbury bare for you."

"A useful sort of chap," said Knighton, with a smile.

"He has been useful to me once or twice," said Van Aldin. "Now then, Knighton, I'm ready for work."

The next few hours saw a vast quantity of business rapidly transacted. It was half past twelve when the telephone bell rang, and Mr. Van Aldin was informed that Mr. Kettering had called. Knighton looked at Van Aldin, and interpreted his brief nod.

"Ask Mr. Kettering to come up, please."

The secretary gathered up his papers and departed. He and the visitor passed each other in the doorway, and Derek Kettering stood aside to let the other go out. Then he came in, shutting the door behind him.

"Good morning, sir. You are very anxious to see me, I hear."

The lazy voice with its slightly ironic inflection roused memories in Van Aldin. There was charm in it—there had always been charm in it. He looked piercingly at his son-in-law. Derek Kettering was thirty-four, lean of build, with a dark, narrow face, which had even now something indescribably boyish in it.

"Come in," said Van Aldin curtly. "Sit down."

Kettering flung himself lightly into an armchair. He looked at his father-in-law with a kind of tolerant amusement.

"Not seen you for a long time, sir," he remarked pleasantly. "About two years, I should say. Seen Ruth yet?"

"I saw her last night," said Van Aldin.

"Looking very fit, isn't she?" said the other lightly.

"I didn't know you had had much opportunity of judging," said Van Aldin dryly.

Derek Kettering raised his eyebrows.

"Oh, we sometimes meet at the same nightclub, you know," he said airily.

"I am not going to beat about the bush," Van Aldin said curtly. "I have advised Ruth to file a petition for divorce."

Derek Kettering seemed unmoved.

"How drastic!" he murmured. "Do you mind if I smoke, sir?"

He lit a cigarette, and puffed out a cloud of smoke as he added nonchalantly:

"And what did Ruth say?"

"Ruth proposes to take my advice," said her father.

"Does she really?"

"Is that all you have got to say?" demanded Van Aldin sharply.

Kettering flicked his ash into the grate.

"I think, you know," he said, with a detached air, "that she's making a great mistake."

"From your point of view she doubtless is," said Van Aldin grimly.

"Oh, come now," said the other; "don't let's be personal. I really wasn't thinking of myself at the moment. I was thinking of Ruth. You know my poor old Governor really can't last much longer; all the doctors say so. Ruth had better give it a couple more years, then I shall be Lord Leconbury, and she can be châtelaine of Leconbury, which is what she married me for."

"I won't have any of your darned impudence," roared Van Aldin.

Derek Kettering smiled at him quite unmoved.

"I agree with you. It's an obsolete idea," he said. "There's nothing in a title nowadays. Still, Leconbury is a very fine old place, and, after all, we are one of the oldest families in England. It will be very annoying for Ruth if she divorces me to find me marrying again, and some other woman queening it at Leconbury instead of her."

"I am serious, young man," said Van Aldin.

"Oh, so am I," said Kettering. "I am in very low water financially; it will put me in a nasty hole if Ruth divorces me, and, after all, if she has stood it for ten years, why not stand it a little longer? I give you my word of honor that the old man can't possibly last out another eighteen months, and, as I said before, it's a pity Ruth shouldn't get what she married me for."

"You suggest that my daughter married you for your title and position?"

Derek Kettering laughed a laugh that was not all amusement.

"You don't think it was a question of a love match?" he asked.

"I know," said Van Aldin slowly, "that you spoke very differently in Paris ten years ago."

"Did I? Perhaps I did. Ruth was very beautiful, you know—rather like an angel or a saint, or something that had stepped down from a niche in a church. I had fine ideas, I remember, of turning over a new leaf, of settling down and living up to the highest traditions of English home life with a beautiful wife who loved me."

He laughed again, rather more discordantly.

"But you don't believe that, I suppose?" he said.

"I have no doubt at all that you married Ruth for her money," said Van Aldin unemotionally.

"And that she married me for love?" asked the other ironically.

"Certainly," said Van Aldin.

Derek Kettering stared at him for a minute or two, then he nodded reflectively.

"I see you believe that," he said. "So did I at the time. I can assure you, my dear father-in-law, I was very soon undeceived."

"I don't know what you are getting at," said Van Aldin, "and I don't care. You have treated Ruth darned badly."

"Oh, I have," agreed Kettering lightly, "but she's tough, you know. She's your daughter. Underneath the pink-and-white softness of her she's as hard as granite. You have always been known as a hard man, so I have been told, but Ruth is harder than you are. You, at any rate, love one person better than yourself. Ruth never has and never will."

"That is enough," said Van Aldin. "I asked you here so that I could tell you fair and square what I meant to do. My girl has got to have some happiness, and remember this, I am behind her."

Derek Kettering got up and stood by the mantelpiece. He tossed away his cigarette. When he spoke, his voice was very quiet.

"What exactly do you mean by that, I wonder?" he said.

"I mean," said Van Aldin, "that you had better not try to defend the case."

"Oh," said Kettering. "Is that a threat?"

"You can take it any way you please," said Van Aldin.

Kettering drew a chair up to the table. He sat down fronting the millionaire.

"And supposing," he said softly, "that, just for argument's sake, I did defend the case?"

Van Aldin shrugged his shoulders.

"You have not got a leg to stand upon, you young fool. Ask your solicitors, they will soon tell you. Your conduct has been notorious, the talk of London."

"Ruth has been kicking up a row about Mirelle, I suppose. Very foolish of her. I don't interfere with her friends."

"What do you mean?" said Van Aldin sharply.

Derek Kettering laughed.

"I see you don't know everything, sir," he said. "You are, perhaps naturally, prejudiced."

He took up his hat and stick and moved toward the door.

"Giving advice is not much in my line." He delivered his final thrust. "But, in this case, I should advise most strongly perfect frankness between father and daughter."

He passed quickly out of the room and shut the door behind him just as the millionaire sprang up.

"Now, what the hell did he mean by that?" said Van Aldin as he sank back into his chair again.

All his uneasiness returned in full force. There was something here that he had not yet got to the bottom of. The telephone was by his elbow; he seized it, and asked for the number of his daughter's house.

"Hallo! Hallo! Is that Mayfair 81907? Mrs. Kettering in? Oh, she's out, is she? Yes, out to lunch. What time will she be in? You don't know? Oh, very good; no, there's no message."

He slammed the receiver down again angrily. At two o'clock he was pacing the floor of his room waiting expectantly for Goby. The latter was ushered in at ten minutes past two.

"Well?" barked the millionaire sharply.

But little Mr. Goby was not to be hurried. He sat down at the table, produced a very shabby pocketbook, and proceeded to read from it in a monotonous voice. The millionaire listened attentively, with an increasing satisfaction. Goby came to a full stop, and looked attentively at the wastepaper basket.

"Um!" said Van Aldin. "That seems pretty definite. The case will go through like winking. The hotel evidence is all right, I suppose?"

"Cast iron," said Mr. Goby, and looked malevolently at a gilt armchair.

"And financially he's in very low water. He's trying to raise a loan now, you say? Has already raised practically all he can upon his expectations from his father. Once the news of the divorce gets about, he won't be able to raise another cent, and not only that, his obligations can be bought up and pressure can be put upon him from that quarter. We have got him, Goby; we have got him in a cleft stick."

He hit the table a bang with his fist. His face was grim and triumphant.

"The information," said Mr. Goby in a thin voice, "seems satisfactory."

"I have got to go round to Curzon Street now," said the millionaire. "I am much obliged to you, Goby. You are the goods all right."

A pale smile of gratification showed itself on the little man's face.

"Thank you, Mr. Van Aldin," he said; "I try to do my best."

Van Aldin did not go direct to Curzon Street. He went first to the City, where he had two interviews which added to his satisfaction. From there he took the tube to Down Street. As he was walking along Curzon Street, a figure came out of No. 160, and turned up the street toward him, so that they passed each other on the pavement. For a moment, the millionaire had fancied it might be Derek Kettering himself; the height and build were not unlike. But as they came face to face, he saw that the man was a stranger to him. At least—no, not a stranger; his face awoke some call of recognition in the millionaire's mind, and it was associated definitely with something unpleasant. He cudgeled his brains in vain, but the thing eluded him. He went on, shaking his head irritably. He hated to be baffled.

Ruth Kettering was clearly expecting him. She ran to him and kissed him when he entered.

"Well, Dad, how are things going?"

"Very well," said Van Aldin; "but I have got a word or two to say to you, Ruth."

Almost insensibly he felt the change in her; something shrewd and watchful replaced the impulsiveness of her greeting. She sat down in a big armchair.

"Well, Dad?" she asked. "What is it?"

"I saw your husband this morning," said Van Aldin.

"You saw Derek?"

"I did. He said a lot of things, most of which were darned cheek. Just as he was leaving, he said something that I didn't understand. He advised me to be sure that there was perfect frankness between father and daughter. What did he mean by that, Ruthie?"

Mrs. Kettering moved a little in her chair.

"I—I don't know, Dad. How should I?"

"Of course you know," said Van Aldin. "He said something else, about his having his friends and not interfering with yours. What did he mean by that?"

"I don't know," said Ruth Kettering again.

Van Aldin sat down. His mouth set itself in a grim line.

"See here, Ruth. I am not going into this with my eyes closed. I am not at all sure that that husband of yours doesn't mean to make trouble. Now, he can't do it, I am sure of that. I have got the means to silence him, to shut his mouth for good and all, but I have got to know if there's any need to use those means. What did he mean by your having your own friends?"

Mrs. Kettering shrugged her shoulders.

"I have got lots of friends," she said uncertainly. "I don't know what he meant, I am sure."

"You do," said Van Aldin.

He was speaking now as he might have spoken to a business adversary.

"I will put it plainer. Who is the man?"

"What man?"

"*The* man. That's what Derek was driving at. Some special man who is a friend of yours. You needn't worry, honey, I know there is nothing in it, but we have got to look at everything as it might appear to the Court. They can twist these things about a good deal, you know. I want to know who the man is, and just how friendly you have been with him."

Ruth didn't answer. Her hands were kneading themselves together in intense nervous absorption.

"Come, honey," said Van Aldin in a softer voice. "Don't be afraid of your old Dad. I was not too harsh, was I, even that time in Paris?—By gosh!"

He stopped, thunderstruck.

"That's who it was," he murmured to himself. "I thought I knew his face."

"What are you talking about, Dad? I don't understand."

The millionaire strode across to her and took her firmly by the wrist.

"See here, Ruth, have you been seeing that fellow again?"

"What fellow?"

"The one we had all that fuss about years ago. You know who I mean well enough."

"You mean"—she hesitated—"you mean the Comte de la Roche?"

"Comte de la Roche!" snorted Van Aldin. "I told you at the time that the man was no better than a swindler. You had entangled yourself with him then very deeply, but I got you out of his clutches."

"Yes, you did," said Ruth bitterly. "And I married Derek Kettering."

"You wanted to," said the millionaire sharply.

She shrugged her shoulders.

"And now," said Van Aldin slowly, "you have been seeing him again—after all I told you. He has been in the house today. I met him outside, and couldn't place him for the moment."

Ruth Kettering had recovered her composure.

"I want to tell you one thing, Dad; you are wrong about Armand—the Comte de la Roche, I mean. Oh, I know there were several regrettable incidents in his youth—he has told me about them; but—well, he has cared for me always. It broke his heart when you parted us in Paris, and now——"

She was interrupted by the snort of indignation her father gave.

"So you fell for that stuff, did you? You, a daughter of mine! My God!"

He threw up his hands.

"That women can be such darned fools!"

6

Mirelle

DEREK KETTERING EMERGED from Van Aldin's suite so precipitantly that he collided with a lady passing across the corridor. He apologized, and she accepted his apologies with a smiling reassurance and passed on, leaving with him a pleasant impression of a soothing personality and rather fine gray eyes.

For all his nonchalance, his interview with his father-in-law had shaken him more than he cared to show. He had a solitary lunch, and after it, frowning to himself a little, he went around to the sumptuous flat that housed the lady known as Mirelle. A trim Frenchwoman received him with smiles.

"But enter then, Monsieur. Madame reposes herself."

He was ushered into the long room with its Eastern setting which he knew so well. Mirelle was lying on the divan, supported by an incredible number of cushions, all in varying shades of amber, to harmonize with the yellow ochre of her complexion. The dancer was a beautifully made woman, and if her face, beneath its mask of yellow, was in truth somewhat haggard, it had a bizarre charm of its own, and her orange lips smiled invitingly at Derek Kettering.

He kissed her, and flung himself into a chair.

"What have you been doing with yourself? Just got up, I suppose?"

The orange mouth widened into a long smile.

"No," said the dancer. "I have been at work."

She flung out a long, pale hand toward the piano, which was littered with untidy music scores.

"Ambrose has been here. He has been playing me the new Opera."

Kettering nodded without paying much attention. He was profoundly uninterested in Claud Ambrose and the latter's operatic setting of Ibsen's *Peer Gynt.* So was Mirelle, for that matter, regarding it merely as a unique opportunity for her own presentation as Anitra.

"It is a marvellous dance," she murmured. "I shall put all the passion of the desert into it. I shall dance hung over with jewels—ah! and, by the way, *mon ami,* there is a pearl that I saw yesterday in Bond Street—a black pearl."

She paused, looking at him invitingly.

"My dear girl," said Kettering, "it's no use talking of black pearls to me. At the present minute, as far as I am concerned, the fat is in the fire."

She was quick to respond to his tone. She sat up, her big black eyes widening.

"What is that you say, Dereek? What has happened?"

"My esteemed father-in-law," said Kettering, "is preparing to go off the deep end."

"Eh?"

"In other words, he wants Ruth to divorce me."

"How stupid!" said Mirelle. "Why should she want to divorce you?"

Derek Kettering grinned.

"Mainly because of you, *chérie!*" he said.

Mirelle shrugged her shoulders.

"That is foolish," she observed in a matter-of-fact voice.

"Very foolish," agreed Derek.

"What are you going to do about it?" demanded Mirelle.

"My dear girl, what can I do? On the one side, the man with unlimited money; on the other side, the man with unlimited debts. There is no question as to who will come out on top."

"They are extraordinary, these Americans," commented Mirelle. "It is not as though your wife were fond of you."

"Well," said Derek, "what are we going to do about it?"

She looked at him inquiringly. He came over and took both her hands in his.

"Are you going to stick to me?"

"What do you mean? After——"

"Yes," said Kettering. "After, when the creditors come down like wolves on the fold. I am damned fond of you, Mirelle; are you going to let me down?"

She pulled her hands away from him.

"You know I adore you, Dereek."

He caught the note of evasion in her voice.

"So that's that, is it? The rats will leave the sinking ship."

"Ah, Dereek!"

"Out with it," he said violently. "You will fling me over; is that it?"

She shrugged her shoulders.

"I am fond of you, *mon ami*—indeed I am fond of you. You are very charming—*un beau garçon,* but *ce n'est pas pratique.*"

"You are a rich man's luxury, eh? Is that it?"

"If you like to put it that way."

She leaned back on the cushions, her head flung back.

"All the same, I am fond of you, Dereck."

He went over to the window and stood there some time looking out, with his back to her. Presently the dancer raised herself on her elbow and stared at him curiously.

"What are you thinking of, *mon ami?*"

He grinned at her over his shoulder, a curious grin, that made her vaguely uneasy.

"As it happened, I was thinking of a woman, my dear."

"A woman, eh?"

Mirelle pounced on something that she could understand.

"You are thinking of some other woman, is that it?"

"Oh, you needn't worry; it is purely a fancy portrait. 'Portrait of a lady with gray eyes.' "

Mirelle said sharply, "When did you meet her?"

Derek Kettering laughed, and his laughter had a mocking, ironical sound.

"I ran into the lady in the corridor of the Savoy Hotel."

"Well! what did she say?"

"As far as I can remember, I said, 'I beg your pardon,' and she said, 'It doesn't matter,' or words to that effect."

"And then?" persisted the dancer.

Kettering shrugged his shoulders.

"And then—nothing. That was the end of the incident."

"I don't understand a word of what you are talking about," declared the dancer.

"Portrait of a lady with gray eyes," murmured Derek reflectively. "Just as well I am never likely to meet her again."

"Why?"

"She might bring me bad luck. Women do."

Mirelle slipped quickly from her couch, and came across to him, laying one long, snakelike arm round his neck.

"You are foolish, Dereck," she murmured. "You are very foolish. You are *beau garçon,* and I adore you, but I am not made to be poor—no, decidedly I am not made to be poor. Now listen to me; everything is very simple. You must make it up with your wife."

"I am afraid that's not going to be actually in the sphere of practical politics," said Derek dryly.

"How do you say? I do not understand."

"Van Aldin, my dear, is not taking any. He is the kind of man who makes up his mind and sticks to it."

"I have heard of him," nodded the dancer. "He is very rich, is he not? Almost the richest man in America. A few days ago, in Paris, he bought the most wonderful ruby in the world—'Heart of Fire' it is called."

Kettering did not answer. The dancer went on musingly:

"It is a wonderful stone—a stone that should belong to a woman like me. I love jewels, Dereek; they say something to me. Ah! to wear a ruby like 'Heart of Fire.' "

She gave a little sigh, and then became practical once more.

"You don't understand these things, Dereek; you are only a man. Van Aldin will give these rubies to his daughter, I suppose. Is she his only child?"

"Yes."

"Then when he dies, she will inherit all his money. She will be a rich woman."

"She is a rich woman already," said Kettering dryly. "He settled a couple of million on her at her marriage."

"A couple of million! But that is immense. And if she died suddenly, eh? That would all come to you?"

"As things stand at present," said Kettering slowly, "it would. As far as I know she has not made a will."

"*Mon Dieu!*" said the dancer. "If she were to die, what a solution that would be."

There was a moment's pause, and then Derek Kettering laughed outright.

"I like your simple, practical mind, Mirelle, but I am afraid what you desire won't come to pass. My wife is an extremely healthy person."

"*Eh, bien!*" said Mirelle; "there are accidents."

He looked at her sharply but did not answer.

She went on.

"But you are right, *mon ami,* we must not dwell on possibilities. See now, my little Dereek, there must be no more talk of this divorce. Your wife must give up the idea."

"And if she won't?"

The dancer's eyes widened to slits.

"I think she will, my friend. She is one of those who would not like the publicity. There are one or two pretty stories that she would not like her friends to read in the newspapers."

"What do you mean?" asked Kettering sharply.

Mirelle laughed, her head thrown back.

"*Parbleu!* I mean the gentleman who calls himself the Comte de la Roche. I know all about him. I am Parisienne, you remember. He was her lover before she married you, was he not?"

Kettering took her sharply by the shoulders.

"That is a damned lie," he said, "and please remember that, after all, you are speaking of my wife."

Mirelle was a little sobered.

"You are extraordinary, you English," she complained. "All the same, I dare say that you may be right. The Americans are so cold, are they not? But you will permit me to say, *mon ami,* that she was *in love with him* before she married you, and her father stepped in and sent the Comte about his business. And the little Mademoiselle, she wept many tears! But she obeyed. Still, you must know as well as I do, Dereek, that it is a very different story now. She sees him nearly every day, and on the fourteenth she goes to Paris to meet him."

"How do you know all this?" demanded Kettering.

"Me? I have friends in Paris, my dear Dereek, who know the Comte intimately. It is all arranged. She is going to the Riviera, so she says, but in reality the Comte meets her in Paris and—who knows! Yes, yes, you can take my word for it, it is all arranged."

Derek Kettering stood motionless.

"You see," purred the dancer, "if you are clever, you have her in the hollow of your hand. You can make things very awkward for her."

"Oh, for God's sake be quiet," cried Kettering. "Shut your cursed mouth!"

Mirelle flung herself down again on the divan with a laugh. Kettering caught up his hat and coat and left the flat, banging the door violently. And still the dancer sat on the divan and laughed softly to herself. She was not displeased with her work.

7

Letters

MRS. SAMUEL HARFIELD presents her compliments to Miss Katherine Grey and wishes to point out that under the circumstances Miss Grey may not be aware——

Mrs. Harfield, having written so far fluently, came to a dead stop, held up by what has proved an insuperable difficulty to many other people—namely, the difficulty of expressing oneself fluently in the third person.

After a minute or two of hesitation, Mrs. Harfield tore up the sheet of notepaper and started afresh.

DEAR MISS GREY—Whilst fully appreciating the adequate way you discharged your duties to my Cousin Emma (whose recent death has indeed been a severe blow to us all), I cannot but feel——

Again Mrs. Harfield came to a stop. Once more the letter was consigned to the wastepaper basket. It was not until four false starts had been made that Mrs. Harfield at last produced an epistle that satisfied her. It was duly sealed and stamped and addressed to Miss Katherine Grey, Little Crampton, St. Mary Mead, Kent, and it lay beside that lady's plate on the following morning at breakfast time in company with a more important looking communication in a long blue envelope.

Katherine Grey opened Mrs. Harfield's letter first. The finished production ran as follows:

DEAR MISS GREY—My husband and I wish to express our thanks to you for your services to my poor cousin, Emma. Her death has been a great blow to us, though we were, of course, aware that her mind has been failing for some time past. I understand that her latter testamentary dispositions have been of a most peculiar character, and they would not hold good, of course, in any court of law. I have no doubt that, with your usual good sense, you have already realized this fact. If these matters can be arranged privately it is always so much better, my husband says. We shall be pleased to recommend you most highly for a similar post and hope that you will also accept a small present. Believe me, dear Miss Grey, yours cordially,
                                   MARY ANNE HARFIELD.

Katherine Grey read the letter through, smiled a little, and read it a second time. Her face as she laid the letter down after the second reading was distinctly amused. Then she took up the second letter. After one brief perusal she laid it down and stared very straight in front of her. This time she did not smile. Indeed, it would have been hard for anyone watching her to guess what emotions lay behind that quiet, reflective gaze.

Katherine Grey was thirty-three. She came of good family, but her father had lost all his money, and Katherine had had to work for her living from an early age. She had been just twenty-three when she had come to old Mrs. Harfield as companion.

It was generally recognized that old Mrs. Harfield was "difficult." Companions came and went with startling rapidity. They arrived full of hope and they usually left in tears. But from the moment Katherine Grey set foot in Little Crampton, ten years ago, perfect peace had reigned. No one knows how these things come about. Snake charmers, they say, are born, not made. Katherine Grey was born with the power of managing old ladies, dogs, and small boys, and she did it without any apparent sense of strain.

At twenty-three she had been a quiet girl with beautiful eyes. At thirty-three she was a quiet woman, with those same gray eyes, shining steadily out on the world with a kind of happy serenity that nothing could shake. More-over, she had been born with, and still possessed, a sense of humor.

As she sat at the breakfast table, staring in front of her, there was a ring at the bell, accompanied by a very energetic rat-a-tat-tat at the knocker. In another minute the little maidservant opened the door and announced rather breathlessly:

"Dr. Harrison."

The big, middle-aged doctor came bustling in with the energy and breezi-ness that had been foreshadowed by his onslaught on the knocker.

"Good morning, Miss Grey."

"Good morning, Dr. Harrison."

"I dropped in early," began the doctor, "in case you should have heard from one of those Harfield cousins. Mrs. Samuel, she calls herself—a per-fectly poisonous person."

Without a word, Katherine picked up Mrs. Harfield's letter from the table and gave it to him. With a good deal of amusement she watched his perusal of it, the drawing together of the bushy eyebrows, the snorts and grunts of violent disapproval. He dashed it down again on the table.

"Perfectly monstrous," he fumed. "Don't you let it worry you, my dear. They're talking through their hat. Mrs. Harfield's intellect was as good as yours or mine, and you won't get anyone to say the contrary. They wouldn't have a leg to stand upon, and they know it. All that talk of taking it into court is pure bluff. Hence this attempt to get round you in a hole-and-corner way. And look here, my dear, don't let them get round you with soft soap either. Don't get fancying it's your duty to hand over the cash, or any tom-foolery of conscientious scruples."

"I'm afraid it hasn't occurred to me to have scruples," said Katherine. "All these people are distant relatives of Mrs. Harfield's husband, and they never came near her or took any notice of her in her lifetime."

"You're a sensible woman," said the doctor. "I know, none better, that you've had a hard life of it for the last ten years. You're fully entitled to enjoy the old lady's savings, such as they were."

Katherine smiled thoughtfully.

"Such as they were," she repeated. "You've no idea of the amount, Doc-tor?"

"Well—enough to bring in five hundred a year or so, I suppose."

Katherine nodded.

"That's what I thought," she said. "Now read this."

She handed him the letter she had taken from the long blue envelope. The doctor read and uttered an exclamation of utter astonishment.

"Impossible," he muttered. "Impossible."

"She was one of the original shareholders in Mortaulds. Forty years ago she must have had an income of eight or ten thousand a year. She has never, I am sure, spent more than four hundred a year. She was always terribly careful about money. I always believed that she was obliged to be careful about every penny."

"And all the time the income has accumulated at compound interest. My dear, you're going to be a very rich woman."

Katherine Grey nodded.

"Yes," she said, "I am."

She spoke in a detached, impersonal tone, as though she were looking at the situation from outside.

"Well," said the doctor, preparing to depart, "you have all my congratulations." He flicked Mrs. Samuel Harfield's letter with his thumb. "Don't worry about that woman and her odious letter."

"It really isn't an odious letter," said Miss Grey tolerantly. "Under the circumstances, I think it's really quite a natural thing to do."

"I have the gravest suspicions of you sometimes," said the doctor.

"Why?"

"The things that you find perfectly natural."

Katherine Grey laughed.

Doctor Harrison retailed the great news to his wife at lunchtime. She was very excited about it.

"Fancy old Mrs. Harfield—with all that money. I'm glad she left it to Katherine Grey. That girl's a saint."

The doctor made a wry face.

"Saints I always imagine must have been difficult people. Katherine Grey is too human for a saint."

"She's a saint with a sense of humor," said the doctor's wife, twinkling. "And, though I don't suppose you've ever noticed the fact, she's extremely good looking."

"Katherine Grey?" The doctor was honestly surprised. "She's got very nice eyes, I know."

"Oh, you men!" cried his wife. "Blind as bats. Katherine's got all the makings of a beauty in her. All she wants is clothes!"

"Clothes? What's wrong with her clothes? She always looks very nice."

Mrs. Harrison gave an exasperated sigh, and the doctor rose preparatory to starting on his rounds.

"You might look in on her, Polly," he suggested.

"I'm going to," said Mrs. Harrison promptly.

She made her call about three o'clock.

"My dear, I'm so glad," she said warmly, as she squeezed Katherine's hand. "And every one in the village will be glad too."

"It's very nice of you to come and tell me," said Katherine. "I hoped you would come in because I wanted to ask about Johnnie."

"Oh! Johnnie. Well——"

Johnnie was Mrs. Harrison's youngest son. In another minute she was off, retailing a long history in which Johnnie's adenoids and tonsils bulked largely. Katherine listened sympathetically. Habits die hard. Listening had been her portion for ten years now. "My dear, I wonder if I ever told you about that naval ball at Portsmouth? When Lord Charles admired my gown?" And composedly, kindly, Katherine would reply: "I rather think you have, Mrs. Harfield, but I've forgotten about it. Won't you tell it me again?" And then the old lady would start off full swing, with numerous details. And half of Katherine's mind would be listening, saying the right things mechanically when the old lady paused. . . .

Now, with that same curious feeling of duality to which she was accustomed, she listened to Mrs. Harrison.

At the end of half an hour, the latter recalled herself suddenly.

"I've been talking about myself all this time," she exclaimed. "And I came here to talk about you and your plans."

"I don't know that I've got any yet."

"My dear—you're not going to stay on *here.*"

Katherine smiled at the horror in the other's tone.

"No; I think I want to travel. I've never seen much of the world, you know."

"I should think not. It must have been an awful life for you cooped up here all these years."

"I don't know," said Katherine. "It gave me a lot of freedom."

She caught the other's gasp, and reddened a little.

"It must sound foolish—saying that. Of course, I hadn't much freedom in the downright physical sense——"

"I should think not," breathed Mrs. Harrison, remembering that Katherine had seldom had that useful thing as a "day off."

"But, in a way, being tied physically gives you lots of scope mentally. You're always free to think. I've had a lovely feeling always of mental freedom."

Mrs. Harrison shook her head.

"I can't understand that."

"Oh! you would if you'd been in my place. But, all the same, I feel I want a change. I want—well, I want things to happen. Oh! not to me—I don't mean that. But to be in the midst of things, exciting things—even if I'm only the looker-on. You know, things don't happen in St. Mary Mead."

"They don't indeed," said Mrs. Harrison, with fervor.

"I shall go to London first," said Katherine. "I have to see the solicitors, anyway. After that, I shall go abroad, I think."

"Very nice."

"But, of course, first of all——"

"Yes?"

"I must get some clothes."

"Exactly what I said to Arthur this morning," cried the doctor's wife. "You know, Katherine, you could look possibly positively beautiful if you tried."

Miss Grey laughed unaffectedly.

"Oh! I don't think you could ever make a beauty out of me," she said sincerely. "But I shall enjoy having some really good clothes. I'm afraid I'm talking about myself an awful lot."

Mrs. Harrison looked at her shrewdly.

"It must be quite a novel experience for you," she said dryly.

Katherine went to say good-bye to old Miss Viner before leaving the village. Miss Viner was two years older than Mrs. Harfield, and her mind was mainly taken up with her own success in outliving her dead friend.

"You wouldn't have thought I'd have outlasted Jane Harfield, would you?" she demanded triumphantly of Katherine. "We were at school together, she and I. And here we are, she taken, and I left. Who would have thought it?"

"You've always eaten brown bread for supper, haven't you?" murmured Katherine mechanically.

"Fancy your remembering that, my dear. Yes; if Jane Harfield had had a slice of brown bread every evening and taken a little stimulant with her meals she might be here today."

The old lady paused, nodding her head triumphantly; then added in sudden remembrance:

"And so you've come into a lot of money, I hear? Well, well. Take care of it. And you're going up to London to have a good time? Don't think you'll get married, though, my dear, because you won't. You're not the kind to attract the men. And, besides, you're getting on. How old are you now?"

"Thirty-three," Katherine told her.

"Well," remarked Miss Viner doubtfully, "that's not so very bad. You've lost your first freshness, of course."

"I'm afraid so," said Katherine, much entertained.

"But you're a very nice girl," said Miss Viner kindly. "And I'm sure there's many a man might do worse than take you for a wife instead of one of these flibbertigibbets running about nowadays showing more of their legs than the Creator ever intended them to. Good-bye, my dear, and I hope you'll enjoy yourself, but things are seldom what they seem in this life."

Heartened by these prophecies, Katherine took her departure. Half the village came to see her off at the station, including the little maid of all work, Alice, who brought a stiff wired nosegay and cried openly.

"There ain't a many like her," sobbed Alice when the train had finally departed. "I'm sure when Charlie went back on me with that girl from the Dairy, nobody could have been kinder than Miss Grey was, and though particular about the brasses and the dust, she was always one to notice when you'd give a thing an extra rub. Cut myself in little pieces for her, I would, any day. A real lady, that's what I call her."

Such was Katherine's departure from St. Mary Mead.

8

Lady Tamplin Writes a Letter

"WELL," SAID LADY Tamplin, "well."

She laid down the continental *Daily Mail* and stared out across the blue waters of the Mediterranean. A branch of golden mimosa, hanging just above her head, made an effective frame for a very charming picture. A golden-haired, blue-eyed lady in a very becoming negligee. That the golden hair owed something to art, as did the pink-and-white complexion, was undeniable, but the blue of the eyes was Nature's gift, and at forty-four Lady Tamplin could still rank as a beauty.

Charming as she looked, Lady Tamplin was, for once, not thinking of herself. That is to say, she was not thinking of her appearance. She was intent on graver matters.

Lady Tamplin was a well-known figure on the Riviera, and her parties at the Villa Marguerite were justly celebrated. She was a woman of considerable experience, and had had four husbands. The first had been merely an indiscretion, and so was seldom referred to by the lady. He had had the good sense to die with commendable promptitude, and his widow thereupon espoused a rich manufacturer of buttons. He too had departed for another sphere after three years of married life—it was said after a congenial evening with some boon companions. After him came Viscount Tamplin, who had placed Rosalie securely on those heights where she wished to tread. She had retained her title when she married for a fourth time. This fourth venture had been undertaken for pure pleasure. Mr. Charles Evans, an extremely good-looking young man of twenty-seven, with delightful manners, a keen love of sport, and an appreciation of this world's goods, had no money of his own whatsoever.

Lady Tamplin was very pleased and satisfied with life generally, but she had occasional faint preoccupations about money. The button manufacturer had left his widow a considerable fortune, but, as Lady Tamplin was wont to say, "what with one thing and another——" (one thing being the depreciation of stocks owing to the War, and the other the extravagances of the late Lord Tamplin). She was still comfortably off. But to be merely comfortably off is hardly satisfactory to one of Rosalie Tamplin's temperament.

So, on this particular January morning, she opened her blue eyes extremely wide as she read a certain item of news and uttered that noncommittal monosyllable "Well." The only other occupant of the balcony was her daughter, the Hon. Lenox Tamplin. A daughter such as Lenox was a sad thorn in Lady Tamplin's side, a girl with no kind of tact, who actually looked older than her age, and whose peculiar sardonic form of humor was, to say the least of it, uncomfortable.

"Darling," said Lady Tamplin, "just fancy."

"What is it?"

Lady Tamplin picked up the *Daily Mail,* handed it to her daughter, and indicated with an agitated forefinger the paragraph of interest.

Lenox read it without any of the signs of agitation shown by her mother. She handed back the paper.

"What about it?" she asked. "It is the sort of thing that is always happening. Cheese-paring old women are always dying in villages and leaving fortunes of millions to their humble companions."

"Yes, dear, I know," said her mother, "and I dare say the fortune is not anything like as large as they say it is; newspapers are so inaccurate. But even if you cut it down by half——"

"Well," said Lenox, "it has not been left to us."

"Not exactly, dear," said Lady Tamplin; "but this girl, this Katherine Grey, is actually a cousin of mine. One of the Worcestershire Greys, the Edgeworth lot. My very own cousin! Fancy!"

"Aha," said Lenox.

"And I was wondering——" said her mother.

"What there was in it for us," finished Lenox, with that sideways smile that her mother always found difficult to understand.

"Oh, darling," said Lady Tamplin, on a faint note of reproach.

It was very faint, because Rosalie Tamplin was used to her daughter's outspokenness and to what she called Lenox's uncomfortable way of putting things.

"I was wondering," said Lady Tamplin, again drawing her artistically penciled brows together, "whether—oh, good morning, Chubby darling; are you going to play tennis? How nice!"

Chubby, thus addressed, smiled kindly at her, remarked perfunctorily, "How topping you look in that peach-colored thing," and drifted past them and down the steps.

"The dear thing," said Lady Tamplin, looking affectionately after her husband. "Let me see, what was I saying? Ah!" She switched her mind back to business once more. "I was wondering——"

"Oh, for God's sake get on with it. That is the third time you have said that."

"Well, dear," said Lady Tamplin, "I was thinking that it would be very nice if I wrote to dear Katherine and suggested that she should pay us a little visit out here. Naturally, she is quite out of touch with Society. It would be nicer for her to be launched by one of her own people. An advantage for her and an advantage for us."

"How much do you think you would get her to cough up?" asked Lenox.

Her mother looked at her reproachfully and murmured.

"We should have to come to some financial arrangement, of course. What with one thing and another—the War—your poor father——"

"And Chubby now," said Lenox. "He is an expensive luxury if you like."

"She was a nice girl as I remember her," murmured Lady Tamplin, pursuing her own line of thought—"quiet, never wanted to shove herself forward, not a beauty, and never a manhunter."

"She will leave Chubby alone, then?" said Lenox.

Lady Tamplin looked at her in protest. "Chubby would never——" she began.

"No," said Lenox, "I don't believe he would; he knows a jolly sight too well which way his bread is buttered."

"Darling," said Lady Tamplin, "you have such a coarse way of putting things."

"Sorry," said Lenox.

Lady Tamplin gathered up the *Daily Mail* and her negligee, a vanity bag, and various odd letters.

"I shall write to dear Katherine at once," she said, "and remind her of the dear old days at Edgeworth."

She went into the house, a light of purpose shining in her eyes.

Unlike Mrs. Samuel Harfield, correspondence flowed easily from her pen. She covered four sheets without pause or effort, and on re-reading it found no occasion to alter a word.

Katherine received it on the morning of her arrival in London. Whether she read between the lines of it or not is another matter. She put it in her handbag and started out to keep the appointment she had made with Mrs. Harfield's lawyers.

The firm was an old-established one in Lincoln's Inn Fields, and after a few minutes' delay Katherine was shown into the presence of the senior partner, a kindly, elderly man with shrewd blue eyes and a fatherly manner.

They discussed Mrs. Harfield's will and various legal matters for some minutes, then Katherine handed the lawyer Mrs. Samuel's letter.

"I had better show you this, I suppose," she said, "though it is really rather ridiculous."

He read it with a slight smile.

"Rather a crude attempt, Miss Grey. I need hardly tell you, I suppose, that these people have no claim of any kind upon the estate, and if they endeavor to contest the will no court will uphold them."

"I thought as much."

"Human nature is not always very wise. In Mrs. Samuel Harfield's place, I should have been more inclined to make an appeal to your generosity."

"That is one of the things I wanted to speak to you about. I should like a certain sum to go to these people."

"There is no obligation."

"I know that."

"And they will not take it in the spirit it is meant. They will probably regard it as an attempt to pay them off, though they will not refuse it on that account."

"I can see that, and it can't be helped."

"I should advise you, Miss Grey, to put that idea out of your head."

Katherine shook her head. "You are quite right, I know, but I should like it done all the same."

"They will grab at the money and abuse you all the more afterward."

"Well," said Katherine, "let them if they like. We all have our own ways of enjoying ourselves. They were, after all, Mrs. Harfield's only relatives, and though they despised her as a poor relation and paid no attention to her when she was alive, it seems to me unfair that they should be cut off with nothing."

She carried her point, though the lawyer was still unwilling, and she presently went out into the streets of London with a comfortable assurance that she could spend money freely and make what plans she liked for the future. Her first action was to visit the establishment of a famous dressmaker.

A slim, elderly Frenchwoman, rather like a dreaming duchess, received her, and Katherine spoke with a certain naïveté.

"I want, if I may, to put myself into your hands. I have been very poor all my life and know nothing about clothes, but now I have come into some money and want to look really well dressed."

The Frenchwoman was charmed. She had an artist's temperament, which had been soured earlier in the morning by a visit from an Argentine meat queen, who had insisted on having those models least suited to her flamboyant type of beauty. She scrutinized Katherine with keen, clever eyes. "Yes—yes, it will be a pleasure. Mademoiselle has a very good figure; for her the simple lines will be best. She is also *très anglaise.* Some people it would offend them if I said that, but Mademoiselle, no. *Une belle Anglaise,* there is no style more delightful."

The demeanor of a dreaming duchess was suddenly put off. She screamed out direction to various mannequins. "Clothilde, Virginie, quickly, my little ones, the little *tailleur gris clair* and the *robe de soirée 'soupir d'automne.'* Marcelle, my child, the little mimosa suit of crêpe de chine."

It was a charming morning. Marcelle, Clothilde, Virginie, bored and scornful, passed slowly round, squirming and wriggling in the time-honored fashion of mannequins. The Duchess stood by Katherine and made entries in a small notebook.

"An excellent choice, Mademoiselle. Mademoiselle has great *goût.* Yes, indeed. Mademoiselle cannot do better than those little suits if she is going to the Riviera, as I suppose, this winter."

"Let me see that evening dress once more," said Katherine—"the pinky mauve one."

Virginie appeared, circling slowly.

"That is the prettiest of all," said Katherine, as she surveyed the exquisite draperies of mauve and gray and blue. "What do you call it?"

"Soupir d'automne; yes, yes, that is truly the dress of Mademoiselle."

What was there in these words that came back to Katherine with a faint feeling of sadness after she had left the dressmaking establishment?

" *'Soupir d'automne; that is truly the dress of Mademoiselle.'* " Autumn, yes, it was autumn for her. She who had never known spring or summer, and would never know them now. Something she had lost never could be given to her again. These years of servitude in St. Mary Mead—and all the while life passing by.

"I am an idiot," said Katherine. "I am an idiot. What do I want? Why, I was more contented a month ago than I am now."

She drew out from her handbag the letter she had received that morning from Lady Tamplin. Katherine was no fool. She understood the nuances of that letter as well as anybody and the reason of Lady Tamplin's sudden show of affection toward a long-forgotten cousin was not lost upon her. It was for profit and not for pleasure that Lady Tamplin was so anxious for the company of her dear cousin. Well, why not? There would be profit on both sides.

"I will go," said Katherine.

She was walking down Piccadilly at the moment, and turned into Cook's to clinch the matter then and there. She had to wait for a few minutes. The man with whom the clerk was engaged was also going to the Riviera. Everyone, she felt, was going. Well, for the first time in her life, she, too, would be doing what "everybody did."

The man in front of her turned abruptly, and she stepped into his place. She made her demand to the clerk, but at the same time half of her mind was busy with something else. That man's face—in some vague way it was familiar to her. Where had she seen him before? Suddenly she remembered. It was in the Savoy outside her room that morning. She had collided with him in the passage. Rather an odd coincidence that she should run into him twice in a day. She glanced over her shoulder, rendered uneasy by something, she knew not what. The man was standing in the doorway looking back at her. A cold shiver passed over Katherine; she had a haunting sense of tragedy, of doom impending. . . .

Then she shook the impression from her with her usual good sense and turned her whole attention to what the clerk was saying.

9

An Offer Refused

IT WAS RARELY that Derek Kettering allowed his temper to get the better of him. An easygoing insouciance was his chief characteristic, and it had stood him in good stead in more than one tight corner. Even now, by the time he had left Mirelle's flat, he had cooled down. He had need of coolness. The corner he was in now was a tighter one than he had ever been in before, and unforeseen factors had arisen with which, for the moment, he did not know how to deal.

He strolled along deep in thought. His brow was furrowed, and there was none of the easy, jaunty manner which sat so well upon him. Various possibilities floated through his mind. It might have been said of Derek Kettering that he was less of a fool than he looked. He saw several roads that he might take—one in particular. If he shrank from it, it was for the moment only. Desperate ills need desperate remedies. He had gauged his father-in-law correctly. A war between Derek Kettering and Rufus Van Aldin could end only one way. Derek damned money and the power of money vehemently to himself. He walked up St. James's Street, across Piccadilly, and strolled along it in the direction of Piccadilly Circus. As he passed the offices of Messrs. Thomas Cook & Sons his footsteps slackened. He walked on, however, still turning the matter over in his mind. Finally, he gave a brief nod of his head, turned sharply—so sharply as to collide with a couple of pedestrians who were following in his footsteps, and went back the way he had come. This time he did not pass Cook's, but went in. The office was comparatively empty, and he got attended to at once.

"I want to go to Nice next week. Will you give me particulars?"

"What date, sir?"

"The 14th. What is the best train?"

"Well, of course, *the* best train is what they call 'The Blue Train.' You avoid the tiresome Customs business at Calais."

Derek nodded. He knew all this, none better.

"The 14th," murmured the clerk; "that is rather soon. The Blue Train is nearly always all booked up."

"See if there is a berth left," said Derek. "If there is not——" He left the sentence unfinished, with a curious smile on his face.

The clerk disappeared for a few minutes, and presently returned. "That is all right, sir; still three berths left. I will book you one of them. What name?"

"Pavett," said Derek. He gave the address of his rooms in Jermyn Street.

The clerk nodded, finished writing it down, wished Derek good morning politely, and turned his attention to the next client.

"I want to go to Nice—on the 14th. Isn't there a train called the Blue Train?"

Derek looked around sharply.

Coincidence—a strange coincidence. He remembered his own half-whimsical words to Mirelle, *"Portrait of a lady with gray eyes. I don't suppose I shall ever see her again."* But he *had* seen her again, and, what was more, she proposed to travel to the Riviera on the same day as he did.

Just for a moment a shiver passed over him; in some ways he was superstitious. He had said, half-laughingly, that this woman might bring him bad luck. Suppose—suppose that should prove to be true. From the doorway he looked back at her as she stood talking to the clerk. For once his memory had not played him false. A lady—a lady in every sense of the word. Not very young, not singularly beautiful. But with something—gray eyes that might perhaps see too much. He knew as he went out of the door that in some way he was afraid of this woman. He had a sense of fatality.

He went back to his rooms in Jermyn Street and summoned his man.

"Take this check, Pavett, cash it first thing in the morning, and go around to Cook's in Piccadilly. They will have some tickets there booked in your name, pay for them, and bring them back."

"Very good, sir."

Pavett withdrew.

Derek strolled over to a side-table and picked up a handful of letters. They were of a type only too familiar. Bills, small bills and large bills, one and all pressing for payment. The tone of the demands was still polite. Derek knew how soon that polite tone would change if—if certain news became public property.

He flung himself moodily into a large, leather-covered chair. A damned hole—that was what he was in. Yes, a damned hole! And ways of getting out of that damned hole were not too promising.

Pavett appeared with a discreet cough.

"A gentleman to see you—sir—Major Knighton."

"Knighton, eh?"

Derek sat up, frowned, became suddenly alert. He said in a softer tone, almost to himself: "Knighton—I wonder what is in the wind now?"

"Shall I—er—show him in, sir?"

His master nodded. When Knighton entered the room he found a charming and genial host awaiting him.

"Very good of you to look me up," said Derek.

Knighton was nervous.

The other's keen eyes noticed that at once. The errand on which the secretary had come was clearly distasteful to him. He replied almost mechanically to Derek's easy flow of conversation. He declined a drink, and, if anything, his manner became stiffer than before. Derek appeared at last to notice it.

"Well," he said cheerfully, "what does my esteemed father-in-law want with me? You have come on his business, I take it?"

Knighton did not smile in reply.

"I have, yes," he said carefully. "I—I wish Mr. Van Aldin had chosen someone else."

Derek raised his eyebrows in mock dismay.

"Is it as bad as all that? I am not very thin skinned, I can assure you, Knighton."

"No," said Knighton; "but this——"

He paused.

Derek eyed him keenly.

"Go on, out with it," he said kindly. "I can imagine my dear father-in-law's errands might not always be pleasant ones."

Knighton cleared his throat. He spoke formally in tones that he strove to render free of embarrassment.

"I am directed by Mr. Van Aldin to make you a definite offer."

"An offer?" For a moment Derek showed his surprise. Knighton's opening words were clearly not what he had expected. He offered a cigarette to Knighton, lit one himself, and sank back in his chair, murmuring in a slightly sardonic voice:

"An offer? That sounds rather interesting."

"Shall I go on?"

"Please. You must forgive my surprise, but it seems to me that my dear father-in-law has rather climbed down since our chat this morning. And climbing down is not what one associates with strong men, Napoleons of finance, etc. It shows—I think it shows that he finds his position weaker than he thought it."

Knighton listened politely to the easy, mocking voice, but no sign of any kind showed itself on his rather stolid countenance. He waited until Derek had finished, and then he said quietly, "I will state the proposition in the fewest possible words."

"Go on."

Knighton did not look at the other. His voice was curt and matter-of-fact.

"The matter is simply this. Mrs. Kettering, as you know, is about to file a petition for divorce. If the case goes undefended you will receive one hundred thousand on the day that the decree is made absolute."

Derek, in the act of lighting his cigarette, suddenly stopped dead.

"A hundred thousand!" he said sharply. "Dollars?"

"Pounds."

There was dead silence for at least two minutes. Kettering had his brows together thinking. A hundred thousand pounds. It meant Mirelle and a continuance of his pleasant, carefree life. It meant that Van Aldin knew something. Van Aldin did not pay for nothing. He got up and stood by the chimney-piece.

"And in the event of my refusing his handsome offer?" he asked, with a cold, ironical politeness.

Knighton made a deprecating gesture.

"I can assure you, Mr. Kettering," he said earnestly, "that it is with the utmost unwillingness that I came here with this message."

"That's all right," said Kettering. "Don't distress yourself; it's not your fault. Now then—I asked you a question, will you answer it?"

Knighton also rose. He spoke more reluctantly than before.

"In the event of your refusing this proposition," he said, "Mr. Van Aldin wished me to tell you in plain words that he proposes to break you. Just that."

Kettering raised his eyebrows, but he retained his light, amused manner.

"Well, well!" he said, "I suppose he can do it. I certainly should not be able to put up much of a fight against America's man of millions. A hundred thousand! If you are going to bribe a man there is nothing like doing it thoroughly. Supposing I were to tell you that for two hundred thousand I'd do what he wanted, what then?"

"I would take your message back to Mr. Van Aldin," said Knighton unemotionally. "Is that your answer?"

"No," said Derek; "funnily enough it is not. You can go back to my father-in-law and tell him to take himself and his bribes to hell. Is that clear?"

"Perfectly," said Knighton. He got up, hesitated, and then flushed. "I—you will allow me to say, Mr. Kettering, that I am glad you have answered as you have."

Derek did not reply. When the other had left the room he remained for a minute or two lost in thought. A curious smile came to his lips.

"And that is that," he said softly.

10

On the Blue Train

"DAD!"

Mrs. Kettering started violently. Her nerves were not completely under control this morning. Very perfectly dressed in a long mink coat and a little hat of Chinese lacquer red, she had been walking along the crowded platform of Victoria deep in thought, and her father's sudden appearance and hearty greeting had an unlooked-for effect upon her.

"Why, Ruth, how you jumped!"

"I didn't expect to see you, I suppose, Dad. You said good-bye to me last night and said you had a conference this morning."

"So I have," said Van Aldin, "but you are more to me than any number of darned conferences. I came to take a last look at you, since I am not going to see you for some time."

"That is very sweet of you, Dad. I wish you were coming too."

"What would you say if I did?"

The remark was merely a joking one. He was surprised to see the quick color flame in Ruth's cheeks. For a moment he almost thought he saw dismay flash out of her eyes. She laughed uncertainly and nervously.

"Just for a moment I really thought you meant it," she said.

"Would you have been pleased?"

"Of course." She spoke with exaggerated emphasis.

"Well," said Van Aldin, "that's good."

"It isn't really for very long, Dad," continued Ruth; "you know, you are coming out next month."

"Ah!" said Van Aldin unemotionally, "sometimes I guess I will go to one of these big guys in Harley Street and have him tell me that I need sunshine and change of air right away."

"Don't be so lazy," cried Ruth; "next month is ever so much nicer than this month out there. You have got all sorts of things you can't possibly leave just now."

"Well, that's so, I suppose," said Van Aldin, with a sigh. "You had better be getting on board this train of yours, Ruth. Where is your seat?"

Ruth Kettering looked vaguely up at the train. At the door of one of the Pullman cars a thin, tall woman dressed in black was standing—Ruth Kettering's maid. She drew aside as her mistress came up to her.

"I have put your dressing-case under your seat, Madam, in case you should need it. Shall I take the rugs, or will you require one?"

"No, no, I shan't want one. Better go and find your own seat now, Mason."

"Yes, Madam."

The maid departed.

Van Aldin entered the Pullman car with Ruth. She found her seat, and Van Aldin deposited various papers and magazines on the table in front of her. The seat opposite to her was already taken, and the American gave a cursory glance at its occupant. He had a fleeting impression of attractive gray eyes and a neat traveling costume. He indulged in a little more desultory conversation with Ruth, the kind of talk peculiar to those seeing other people off by train.

Presently, as whistles blew, he glanced at his watch.

"I had best be clearing out of here. Good-bye, my dear. Don't worry, I will attend to things."

"Oh, Father!"

He turned back sharply. There had been something in Ruth's voice, something so entirely foreign to her usual manner, that he was startled. It was almost a cry of despair. She had made an impulsive movement toward him, but in another minute she was mistress of herself once more.

"Till next month," she said cheerfully.

Two minutes later the train started.

Ruth sat very still, biting her under lip and trying hard to keep the unaccustomed tears from her eyes. She felt a sudden sense of horrible desolation. There was a wild longing upon her to jump out of the train and to go back before it was too late. She, so calm, so self-assured, for the first time in her life felt like a leaf swept by the wind. If her father knew—what would he say?

Madness! Yes, just that, madness! For the first time in her life she was swept away by emotion, swept away to the point of doing a thing which even she knew to be incredibly foolish and reckless. She was enough Van Aldin's daughter to realize her own folly, and level headed enough to condemn her own action. But she was his daughter in another sense also. She had that same iron determination that would have what it wanted, and once it had made up its mind would not be balked. From her cradle she had been self-willed; the very circumstances of her life had developed that self-will in her. It drove her now remorselessly. Well, the die was cast. She must go through with it now.

She looked up, and her eyes met those of the woman sitting opposite. She had a sudden fancy that in some way this other woman had read her mind. She saw in those gray eyes understanding and—yes—compassion.

It was only a fleeting impression. The faces of both women hardened to well-bred impassiveness. Mrs. Kettering took up a magazine, and Katherine Grey looked out of the window and watched a seemingly endless vista of depressing streets and suburban houses.

Ruth found an increasing difficulty in fixing her mind on the printed page in front of her. In spite of herself, a thousand apprehensions preyed on her mind. What a fool she had been! What a fool she was! Like all cool and self-sufficient people, when she did lose her self-control she lost it thoroughly. It was too late. . . . Was it too late? Oh, for someone to speak to, for someone to advise her. She had never before had such a wish; she would have scorned the idea of relying on any judgment other than her own, but now—what was the matter with her? Panic. Yes, that would describe it best—panic. She, Ruth Kettering, was completely and utterly panic-stricken.

She stole a covert glance at the figure opposite. If only she knew someone like that, some nice, cool, calm, sympathetic creature. That was the sort of person one could talk to. But you can't, of course, confide in a stranger. And Ruth smiled to herself a little at the idea. She picked up the magazine again. Really she must control herself. After all, she had thought all this out. She had decided of her own free will. What happiness had she ever had in her life up to now? She said to herself restlessly: "Why shouldn't I be happy? No one will ever know."

It seemed no time before Dover was reached. Ruth was a good sailor. She disliked the cold, and was glad to reach the shelter of the private cabin she had telegraphed for. Although she would not have admitted the fact, Ruth was in some ways superstitious. She was of the order of people to whom coincidence appeals. After disembarking at Calais and settling herself down with her maid in her double compartment in the Blue Train, she went along to the luncheon car. It was with a little shock of surprise that she found herself set down to a small table with, opposite her, the same woman who had been her *vis-à-vis* in the Pullman. A faint smile came to the lips of both women.

"This is quite a coincidence," said Mrs. Kettering.

"I know," said Katherine; "it is odd the way things happen."

A flying attendant shot up to them with the wonderful velocity always displayed by the Compagnie Internationale des Wagons-Lits and deposited two cups of soup. By the time the omelette succeeded the soup they were chatting together in friendly fashion.

"It will be heavenly to get into the sunshine," sighed Ruth.

"I am sure it will be a wonderful feeling."

"You know the Riviera well?"

"No; this is my first visit."

"Fancy that."

"You go every year, I expect?"

"Practically. January and February in London are horrible."

"I have always lived in the country. They are not very inspiring months there either. Mostly mud."

"What made you suddenly decide to travel?"

"Money," said Katherine. "For ten years I have been a paid companion with just enough money of my own to buy myself strong country shoes; now I have been left what seems to me a fortune, though I dare say it would not seem so to you."

"Now I wonder why you say that—that it would not seem so to me."

Katherine laughed. "I don't really know. I suppose one forms impressions without thinking of it. I put you down in my own mind as one of the very rich of the earth. It was just an impression. I dare say I am wrong."

"No," said Ruth, "you are not wrong." She had suddenly become very grave. "I wish you would tell me what other impressions you formed about me?"

"I——"

Ruth swept on disregarding the other's embarrassment.

"Oh, please, don't be conventional. I want to know. As we left Victoria I looked across at you, and I had the sort of feeling that you—well, understood what was going on in my mind."

"I can assure you I am not a mind reader," said Katherine, smiling.

"No; but will you tell me, please, just what you thought." Ruth's eagerness was so intense and so sincere that she carried her point.

"I will tell you if you like, but you must not think me impertinent. I thought that for some reason you were in great distress of mind, and I was sorry for you."

"You are right. You are quite right. I am in terrible trouble. I—I should like to tell you something about it, if I may."

"Oh, dear," Katherine thought to herself, "how extraordinarily alike the world seems to be everywhere! People were always telling me things in St. Mary Mead, and it is just the same thing here, and I don't really want to hear anybody's troubles!"

She replied politely:

"Do tell me."

They were just finishing their lunch. Ruth gulped down her coffee, rose from her seat, and quite oblivious of the fact that Katherine had not begun to sip her coffee, said: "Come to my compartment with me."

They were two single compartments with a communicating door between them. In the second of them a thin maid, whom Katherine had noticed at Victoria, was sitting very upright on the seat, clutching a big scarlet morocco case with the initials R. V. K. on it. Mrs. Kettering pulled the communicating door to and sank down on the seat. Katherine sat down beside her.

"I am in trouble and I don't know what to do. There is a man whom I am fond of—very fond of indeed. We cared for each other when we were young, and we were thrust apart most brutally and unjustly. Now we have come together again."

"Yes?"

"I—I am going to meet him now. Oh! I dare say you think it is all wrong, but you don't know the circumstances. My husband is impossible. He has treated me disgracefully."

"Yes," said Katherine again.

"What I feel so badly about is this. I have deceived my father—it was he who came to see me off at Victoria today. He wishes me to divorce my husband, and, of course, he has no idea—that I am going to meet this other man. He would think it extraordinarily foolish."

"Well, don't you think it is?"

"I—I suppose it is."

Ruth Kettering looked down at her hands; they were shaking violently.

"But I can't draw back now."

"Why not?"

"I—it is all arranged, and it would break his heart."

"Don't you believe it," said Katherine robustly; "hearts are pretty tough."

"He will think I have no courage, no strength of purpose."

"It seems to me an awfully silly thing that you are going to do," said Katherine. "I think you realize that yourself."

Ruth Kettering buried her face in her hands. "I don't know—I don't know. Ever since I left Victoria I have had a horrible feeling of something—something that is coming to me very soon—that I can't escape."

She clutched convulsively at Katherine's hand.

"You must think I am mad talking to you like this, but I tell you I know something horrible is going to happen."

"Don't think it," said Katherine; "try to pull yourself together. You could send your father a wire from Paris, if you like, and he would come to you at once."

The other brightened.

"Yes, I could do that. Dear old Dad. It is queer—but I never knew until today how terribly fond of him I am." She sat up and dried her eyes with a handkerchief. "I have been very foolish. Thank you so much for letting me talk to you. I don't know why I got into such a queer, hysterical state."

She got up. "I am quite all right now. I suppose, really, I just needed someone to talk to. I can't think now why I have been making such an absolute fool of myself."

Katherine got up too.

"I am so glad you feel better," she said, trying to make her voice sound as conventional as possible. She was only too well aware that the aftermath of confidences is embarrassment. She added tactfully:

"I must be going back to my own compartment."

She emerged into the corridor at the same time as the maid was also coming out from the next door. The latter looked toward Katherine, over her shoulder, and an expression of intense surprise showed itself on her face. Katherine turned also, but by that time whoever it was who had aroused the maid's interest had retreated into his or her compartment, and the corridor was empty. Katherine walked down it to regain her own place, which was in the next coach. As she passed the end compartment the door opened and a woman's face looked out for a moment and then pulled the door to sharply. It was a face not easily forgotten, as Katherine was to know when she saw it again. A beautiful face, oval and dark, very heavily made up in a bizarre fashion. Katherine had a feeling that she had seen it before somewhere.

She regained her own compartment without other adventure and sat for some time thinking of the confidence which had just been made to her. She wondered idly who the woman in the mink coat might be, wondered also how the end of her story would turn out.

"If I have stopped anyone from making an idiot of themselves, I suppose I have done good work," she thought to herself. "But who knows? That is the kind of woman who is hard-headed and egotistical all her life, and it might be good for her to do the other sort of thing for a change. Oh, well—I don't suppose I shall ever see her again. She certainly won't want to see *me* again. That is the worst of letting people tell you things. They never do."

She hoped that she would not be given the same place at dinner. She reflected, not without humor, that it might be awkward for both of them. Leaning back with her head against a cushion she felt tired and vaguely depressed. They had reached Paris, and the slow journey round the *ceinture,* with its interminable stops and waits, was very wearisome. When they arrived at the Gare de Lyon she was glad to get out and walk up and down the platform. The keen cold air was refreshing after the steam-heated train. She observed with a smile that her friend of the mink coat was solving the possible awkwardness of the dinner problem in her own way. A dinner basket was being handed up and received through the window by the maid.

When the train started once more, and dinner was announced by a violent ringing of bells, Katherine went along to it much relieved in mind. Her *vis-à-vis* tonight was of an entirely different kind—a small man, distinctly foreign in appearance, with a rigidly waxed moustache and an egg-shaped head which he carried rather on one side. Katherine had taken in a book to dinner with her. She found the little man's eyes fixed upon it with a kind of twinkling amusement.

"I see, Madame, that you have a *Roman Policier.* You are fond of such things?"

"They amuse me," Katherine admitted.

The little man nodded with the air of complete understanding.

"They have a good sale always, so I am told. Now why is that, eh, Mademoiselle? I ask it of you as a student of human nature—why should that be?"

Katherine felt more and more amused.

"Perhaps they give one the illusion of living an exciting life," she suggested.

He nodded gravely.

"Yes; there is something in that."

"Of course, one knows that such things don't really happen," Katherine was continuing, but he interrupted her sharply.

"Sometimes, Mademoiselle! Sometimes! I who speak to you—they have happened to *me.*"

She threw him a quick, interested glance.

"Someday, who knows, *you* might be in the thick of things," he went on. "It is all chance."

"I don't think it is likely," said Katherine. "Nothing of that kind ever happens to me."

He leaned forward.

"Would you like it to?"

The question startled her, and she drew in her breath sharply.

"It is my fancy, perhaps," said the little man, as he dexterously polished one of the forks, "but I think that you have a yearning in you for interesting happenings. *Eh bien,* Mademoiselle, all through my life I have observed one thing—'All one wants one gets!' Who knows?" His face screwed itself up comically. "You may get more than you bargain for."

"Is that a prophecy?" asked Katherine, smiling as she rose from the table.

The little man shook his head.

"I never prophesy," he declared pompously. "It is true that I have the habit of being always right—but I do not boast of it. Goodnight, Mademoiselle, and may you sleep well."

Katherine went back along the train amused and entertained by her little neighbor. She passed the open door of her friend's compartment and saw the conductor making up the bed. The lady in the mink coat was standing looking out of the window. The second compartment, as Katherine saw through the communicating door, was empty, with rugs and bags heaped up on the seat. The maid was not there.

Katherine found her own bed prepared, and since she was tired, she went to bed and switched off her light about half-past nine.

She woke with a sudden start; how much time had passed she did not know. Glancing at her watch, she found that it had stopped. A feeling of intense uneasiness pervaded her and grew stronger moment by moment. At last she got up, threw her dressing-gown round her shoulders, and stepped out into the corridor. The whole train seemed wrapped in slumber. Katherine let down the window and sat by it for some minutes, drinking in the cool night air and trying vainly to calm her uneasy fears. She presently decided that she would go along to the end and ask the conductor for the right time so that she could set her watch. She found, however, that his little chair was vacant. She hesitated for a moment and then walked through into the next coach. She looked down the long, dim line of the corridor and saw, to her surprise, that a man was standing with his hand on the door of the compartment occupied by the lady in the mink coat. That is to say, she thought it was the compartment. Probably, however, she was mistaken. He stood there for a moment or two with his back to her, seeming uncertain and hesitating in his attitude. Then he slowly turned, and with an odd feeling of fatality, Katherine recognized him as the same man whom she had noticed twice before— once in the corridor of the Savoy Hotel and once in Cook's offices. Then he opened the door of the compartment and passed in, drawing it to behind him.

An idea flashed across Katherine's mind. Could this be the man of whom the other woman had spoken—the man she was journeying to meet?

Then Katherine told herself that she was romancing. In all probability she had mistaken the compartment.

She went back to her own carriage. Five minutes later the train slackened speed. There was the long plaintive hiss of the Westinghouse brake, and a few minutes later the train came to a stop at Lyons.

11

Murder

KATHERINE WAKENED THE next morning to brilliant sunshine. She went along to breakfast early, but met none of her acquaintances of the day before. When she returned to her compartment it had just been restored to its daytime appearance by the conductor, a dark man with a drooping moustache and melancholy face.

"Madame is fortunate," he said; "the sun shines. It is always a great disappointment to passengers when they arrive on a gray morning."

"I should have been disappointed, certainly," said Katherine.

The man prepared to depart.

"We are rather late, Madame," he said. "I will let you know just before we get to Nice."

Katherine nodded. She sat by the window, entranced by the sunlit panorama. The palm trees, the deep blue of the sea, the bright yellow mimosa came with all the charm of novelty to the woman who for fourteen years had known only the drab winters of England.

When they arrived at Cannes, Katherine got out and walked up and down the platform. She was curious about the lady in the mink coat, and looked up at the windows of her compartment. The blinds were still drawn down—the only ones to be so on the whole train. Katherine wondered a little, and when she re-entered the train she passed along the corridor and noticed that these two compartments were still shuttered and closed. The lady of the mink coat was clearly no early riser.

Presently the conductor came to her and told her that in a few minutes the train would arrive at Nice. Katherine handed him a tip; the man thanked her, but still lingered. There was something odd about him. Katherine, who had at first wondered whether the tip had not been big enough, was now convinced that something far more serious was amiss. His face was of a sickly pallor, he was shaking all over, and looked as if he had been frightened out of his life. He was eyeing her in a curious manner. Presently he said abruptly: "Madame will excuse me, but is she expecting friends to meet her at Nice?"

"Probably," said Katherine. "Why?"

But the man merely shook his head and murmured something that Katherine could not catch and moved away, not reappearing until the train came to rest at the station, when he started handing her belongings down from the window.

Katherine stood for a moment or two on the platform rather at a loss, but a fair young man with an ingenuous face came up to her and said rather hesitatingly:

"Miss Grey, is it not?"

Katherine said that it was, and the young man beamed upon her seraphically and murmured:

"I am Chubby, you know—Lady Tamplin's husband. I expect she mentioned me, but perhaps she forgot. Have you got your *billet de bagages?* I lost mine when I came out this year, and you would not believe the fuss they made about it. Regular French red tape!"

Katherine produced it, and was just about to move off beside him when a very gentle and insidious voice murmured in her ear:

"A little moment, Madame, if you please."

Katherine turned to behold an individual who made up for insignificance of stature by a large quantity of gold lace and uniform. The individual explained. "There were certain formalities. Madame would perhaps be so kind as to accompany him. The regulations of the police——" He threw up his arms. "Absurd, doubtless, but there it was."

Mr. Chubby Evans listened with a very imperfect comprehension, his French being of a limited order.

"So like the French," murmured Mr. Evans. He was one of those staunch patriotic Britons who, having made a portion of a foreign country their own, strongly resent the original inhabitants of it. "Always up to some silly dodge or other. They've never tackled people on the station before, though. This is something quite new. I suppose you'll have to go."

Katherine departed with her guide. Somewhat to her surprise, he led her toward a siding where a coach of the departed train had been shunted. He invited her to mount into this, and, preceding her down the corridor, held aside the door of one of the compartments. In it was a pompous-looking official personage, and with him a nondescript being who appeared to be a clerk. The pompous-looking personage rose politely, bowed to Katherine, and said:

"You will excuse me, Madame, but there are certain formalities to be complied with. Madame speaks French, I trust?"

"Sufficiently, I think, Monsieur," replied Katherine in that language.

"That is good. Pray be seated, Madame. I am M. Caux, the Commissary of Police." He blew out his chest importantly, and Katherine tried to look sufficiently impressed.

"You wish to see my passport?" she inquired. "Here it is."

The Commissary eyed her keenly and gave a little grunt.

"Thank you, Madame," he said, taking the passport from her. He cleared his throat. "But what I really desire is a little information."

"Information?"

The Commissary nodded his head slowly.

"About a lady who has been a fellow-passenger of yours. You lunched with her yesterday."

"I am afraid I can't tell you anything about her. We fell into conversation over our meal, but she is a complete stranger to me. I have never seen her before."

"And yet," said the Commissary sharply, "you returned to her compartment with her after lunch and sat talking for some time?"

"Yes," said Katherine; "that is true."

The Commissary seemed to expect her to say something more. He looked at her encouragingly.

"Yes, Madame?"

"Well, Monsieur?" said Katherine.

"You can, perhaps, give me some kind of idea of that conversation?"

"I could," said Katherine, "but at the moment I see no reason to do so."

In somewhat British fashion she felt annoyed. This foreign official seemed to her impertinent.

"No reason?" cried the Commissary. "Oh yes, Madame, I can assure you that there *is* a reason."

"Then perhaps you will give it to me."

The Commissary rubbed his chin thoughtfully for a minute or two without speaking.

"Madame," he said at last, "the reason is very simple. The lady in question was found dead in her compartment this morning."

"Dead!" gasped Katherine. "What was it—heart failure?"

"No," said the Commissary in a reflective, dreamy voice. "No—she was murdered."

"Murdered!" cried Katherine.

"So you see, Madame, why we are anxious for any information we can possibly get."

"But surely her maid——"

"The maid has disappeared."

"Oh!" Katherine paused to assemble her thoughts.

"Since the conductor had seen you talking with her in her compartment, he quite naturally reported the fact to the police, and that is why, Madame, we have detained you, in the hope of gaining some information."

"I am very sorry," said Katherine; "I don't even know her name."

"Her name is Kettering. That we know from her passport and from the labels on her luggage. If we——"

There was a knock on the compartment door. M. Caux frowned. He opened it about six inches.

"What is the matter?" he said peremptorily. "I cannot be disturbed."

The egg-shaped head of Katherine's dinner acquaintance showed itself in the aperture. On his face was a beaming smile.

"My name," he said, "is Hercule Poirot."

"Not," the Commissary stammered, "not *the* Hercule Poirot?"

"The same," said M. Poirot. "I remember meeting you once, M. Caux, at the *Sûreté* in Paris, though doubtless you have forgotten me?"

"Not at all, Monsieur, not at all," declared the Commissary heartily. "But enter, I pray of you. You know of this——"

"Yes, I know," said Hercule Poirot. "I came to see if I might be of any assistance?"

"We should be flattered," replied the Commissary promptly. "Let me present you, M. Poirot, to"—he consulted the passport he still held in his hand—"to Madame—er—Mademoiselle Grey."

Poirot smiled across at Katherine.

"It is strange, is it not," he murmured, "that my words should have come true so quickly?"

"Mademoiselle, alas! can tell us very little," said the Commissary.

"I have been explaining," said Katherine, "that this poor lady was a complete stranger to me."

Poirot nodded.

"But she talked to you, did she not?" he said gently. "You formed an impression—is it not so?"

"Yes," said Katherine thoughtfully. "I suppose I did."

"And that impression was——"

"Yes, Mademoiselle"—the Commissary jerked himself forward—"let us by all means have your impressions."

Katherine sat turning the whole thing over in her mind. She felt in a way as if she were betraying a confidence, but with that ugly word "Murder" ringing in her ears she dared not keep anything back. Too much might hang upon it. So, as nearly as she could, she repeated word for word the conversation she had had with the dead woman.

"That is interesting," said the Commissary, glancing at the other. "Eh, M. Poirot, that is interesting? Whether it has anything to do with the crime——" He left the sentence unfinished.

"I suppose it could not be suicide," said Katherine, rather doubtfully.

"No," said the Commissary, "it could not be suicide. She was strangled with a length of black cord."

"Oh!" Katherine shivered. M. Caux spread out his hands apologetically. "It is not nice—no. I think that our train robbers are more brutal than they are in your country."

"It is horrible."

"Yes, yes"—he was soothing and apologetic—"but you have great courage, Mademoiselle. At once, as soon as I saw you, I said to myself, 'Mademoiselle has great courage.' That is why I am going to ask you to do something more —something distressing, but I assure you very necessary."

Katherine looked at him apprehensively.

He spread out his hands apologetically.

"I am going to ask you, Mademoiselle, to be so good as to accompany me to the next compartment."

"Must I?" asked Katherine in a low voice.

"Someone must identify her," said the Commissary, "and since the maid has disappeared"—he coughed significantly—"you appear to be the person who has seen most of her since she joined the train."

"Very well," said Katherine quietly; "if it is necessary——"

She rose. Poirot gave her a little nod of approval.

"Mademoiselle is sensible," he said. "May I accompany you, M. Caux?"

"Enchanted, my dear M. Poirot."

They went out into the corridor, and M. Caux unlocked the door of the dead woman's compartment. The blinds on the far side had been drawn halfway up to admit light. The dead woman lay on the berth to their left, in so natural a posture that one could have thought her asleep. The bedclothes were drawn up over her, and her head was turned to the wall, so that only the red auburn curls showed. Very gently M. Caux laid a hand on her shoulder and turned the body back so that the face came into view. Katherine flinched a little and dug her nails into her palms. A heavy blow had disfigured the features almost beyond recognition. Poirot gave a sharp exclamation.

"When was that done, I wonder?" he demanded. "Before death or after?"

"The doctor says after," said M. Caux.

"Strange," said Poirot, drawing his brows together. He turned to Katherine. "Be brave, Mademoiselle; look at her well. Are you sure that this is the woman you talked to in the train yesterday?"

Katherine had good nerves. She steeled herself to look long and earnestly at the recumbent figure. Then she leaned forward and took up the dead woman's hand.

"I am quite sure," she replied at length. "The face is too disfigured to recognize, but the build and carriage and hair are exact, and besides I noticed *this*"—she pointed to a tiny mole on the dead woman's wrist—"while I was talking to her."

"Bon," approved Poirot. "You are an excellent witness, Mademoiselle. There is, then, no question as to the identity, but it is strange, all the same." He frowned down on the dead woman in perplexity.

M. Caux shrugged his shoulders.

"The murderer was carried away by rage, doubtless," he suggested.

"If she had been struck down, it would have been comprehensible," mused Poirot, "but the man who strangled her slipped up behind and caught her unawares. A little choke—a little gurgle—that is all that would be heard, and then afterward—that smashing blow on her face. Now why? Did he hope that if the face were unrecognizable she might not be identified? Or did he hate her so much that he could not resist striking that blow even after she was dead?"

Katherine shuddered, and he turned at once to her kindly.

"You must not let me distress you, Mademoiselle," he said. "To you this is all very new and terrible. To me, alas! it is an old story. One moment, I pray of you both."

They stood against the door watching him as he went quickly round the compartment. He noted the dead woman's clothes neatly folded on the end of the berth, the big fur coat that hung from a hook, and the little red lacquer hat tossed up on the rack. Then he passed through into the adjoining compartment, that in which Katherine had seen the maid sitting. Here the berth had not been made up. Three or four rugs were piled loosely on the seat; there was a hat box and a couple of suitcases. He turned suddenly to Katherine.

"You were in here yesterday," he said. "Do you see anything changed, anything missing?"

Katherine looked carefully around both compartments.

"Yes," she said, "there is something missing—a scarlet morocco case. It had the initials 'R. V. K.' on it. It might have been a small dressing case or a big jewel case. When I saw it, the maid was holding it."

"Ah!" said Poirot.

"But, surely," said Katherine. "I—of course, I don't know anything about such things, but surely it is plain enough, if the maid and the jewel case are missing?"

"You mean that it was the maid who was the thief? No, Mademoiselle; there is a very good reason against that."

"What?"

"The maid was left behind in Paris."

He turned to Poirot.

"I should like you to hear the conductor's story yourself," he murmured confidentially. "It is very suggestive."

"Mademoiselle would doubtless like to hear it also," said Poirot. "You do not object, Monsieur le Commissaire?"

"No," said the Commissary, who clearly did object very much. "No, certainly, M. Poirot, if you say so. You have finished here?"

"I think so. One little minute."

He had been turning over the rugs, and now he took one to the window and looked at it, picking something off it with his fingers.

"What is it?" demanded M. Caux sharply.

"Four auburn hairs." He bent over the dead woman. "Yes, they are from the head of Madame."

"And what of it? Do you attach importance to them?"

Poirot let the rug drop back on the seat.

"What is important? What is not? One cannot say at this stage. But we must note each little fact carefully."

They went back again into the first compartment, and in a minute or two the conductor of the carriage arrived to be questioned.

"Your name is Pierre Michel?" said the Commissary.

"Yes, Monsieur le Commissaire."

"I should like you to repeat to this gentleman"—he indicated Poirot—"the story that you told me as to what happened in Paris."

"Very good, Monsieur le Commissaire. It was after we had left the Gare de Lyon I came along to make the beds, thinking that Madame would be at dinner, but she had a dinner-basket in her compartment. She said to me that she had been obliged to leave her maid behind in Paris, so that I only need make up one berth. She took her dinner-basket into the adjoining compartment, and sat there while I made up the bed; then she told me that she did not wish to be wakened early in the morning, that she liked to sleep on. I told her I quite understood, and she wished me 'goodnight.' "

"You yourself did not go into the adjoining compartment?"

"No, Monsieur."

"Then you did not happen to notice if a scarlet morocco case was amongst the luggage there?"

"No, Monsieur, I did not."

"Would it have been possible for a man to have been concealed in the adjoining compartment?"

The conductor reflected.

"The door was half open," he said. "If a man had stood behind that door I should not have been able to see him, but he would, of course, have been perfectly visible to Madame when she went in there."

"Quite so," said Poirot. "Is there anything more you have to tell us?"

"I think that is all, Monsieur. I can remember nothing else."

"And now this morning?" prompted Poirot.

"As Madame had ordered, I did not disturb her. It was not until just before Cannes that I ventured to knock at the door. Getting no reply, I opened it. The lady appeared to be in her bed asleep. I took her by the shoulder to rouse her, and then——"

"And then you saw what had happened," volunteered Poirot. *"Très bien.* I think I know all I want to know."

"I hope, Monsieur le Commissaire, it is not that I have been guilty of any negligence," said the man piteously. "Such an affair to happen on the Blue Train! It is horrible."

"Console yourself," said the Commissary. "Everything will be done to keep the affair as quiet as possible, if only in the interests of justice. I cannot think you have been guilty of any negligence."

"And Monsieur le Commissaire will report as much to the Company?"

"But certainly, but certainly," said M. Caux impatiently. "That will do now."

The conductor withdrew.

"According to the medical evidence," said the Commissary, "the lady was probably dead before the train reached Lyons. Who then was the murderer? From Mademoiselle's story, it seems clear that somewhere on her journey she was to meet this man of whom she spoke. Her action in getting rid of the maid seems significant. Did the man join the train at Paris, and did she conceal him in the adjoining compartment? If so, they may have quarreled, and he may have killed her in a fit of rage. That is one possibility. The other, and the more likely to my mind, is that her assailant was a train robber traveling on the train; that he stole along the corridor unseen by the conductor, killed her, and went off with the red morocco case, which doubtless contained jewels of some value. In all probability he left the train at Lyons, and we have already telegraphed to the station there for full particulars of anyone seen leaving the train."

"Or he might have come on to Nice," suggested Poirot.

"He might," agreed the Commissary, "but that would be a very bold course."

Poirot let a minute or two go by before speaking, and then he said:

"In the latter case you think the man was an ordinary train robber?"

The Commissary shrugged his shoulders.

"It depends. We must get hold of the maid. It is possible that she has the red morocco case with her. If so, then the man of whom she spoke to Mademoiselle may be concerned in the case, and the affair is a crime of passion. I myself think the solution of a train robber is the more probable. These bandits have become very bold of late."

Poirot looked suddenly across to Katherine.

"And you, Mademoiselle," he said, "you heard and saw nothing during the night?"

"Nothing," said Katherine.

Poirot turned to the Commissary.

"We need detain Mademoiselle no longer, I think," he suggested.

The latter nodded.

"She will leave us her address?" he said.

Katherine gave him the name of Lady Tamplin's villa. Poirot made her a little bow.

"You permit that I see you again, Mademoiselle?" he said. "Or have you so many friends that your time will be all taken up?"

"On the contrary," said Katherine, "I shall have plenty of leisure, and I shall be very pleased to see you again."

"Excellent," said Poirot, and gave her a little friendly nod. "This shall be a *'Roman Policier' à nous.* We will investigate this affair together."

12

At the Villa Marguerite

"THEN YOU WERE really in the thick of it all!" said Lady Tamplin enviously. "My dear, how thrilling!" She opened her china blue eyes very wide and gave a little sigh.

"A real murder," said Mr. Evans gloatingly.

"Of course Chubby had no idea of anything of the kind," went on Lady Tamplin; "he simply could *not* imagine why the police wanted you. My dear, what an opportunity! I think, you know—yes, I certainly think something might be made out of this."

A calculating look rather marred the ingenuousness of the blue eyes.

Katherine felt slightly uncomfortable. They were just finishing lunch, and she looked in turn at the three people sitting around the table. Lady Tamplin, full of practical schemes; Mr. Evans, beaming with naïve appreciation, and Lenox with a queer crooked smile on her dark face.

"Marvelous luck," murmured Chubby; "I wish I could have gone along with you—and seen—all the exhibits."

His tone was wistful and childlike.

Katherine said nothing. The police had laid no injunctions of secrecy upon her, and it was clearly impossible to suppress the bare facts or try to keep them from her hostess. But she did rather wish it had been possible to do so.

"Yes," said Lady Tamplin, coming suddenly out of her reverie, "I do think something might be done. A little account, you know, cleverly written up. An eyewitness, a feminine touch: 'How I chatted with the dead woman, little thinking——' that sort of thing, you know."

"Rot!" said Lenox.

"You have no idea," said Lady Tamplin in a soft, wistful voice, "what newspapers will pay for a little tidbit! Written, of course, by someone of really unimpeachable social position. You would not like to do it yourself, I dare say, Katherine dear, but just give me the bare bones of it, and *I* will manage the whole thing for you. Mr. de Haviland is a special friend of mine. We have a little understanding together. A most delightful man—not at all reporterish. How does the idea strike you, Katherine?"

"I would much prefer to do nothing of the kind," said Katherine bluntly.

Lady Tamplin was rather disconcerted at this uncompromising refusal. She sighed and turned to the elucidation of further details.

"A very striking-looking woman, you said? I wonder now who she could have been. You didn't hear her name?"

"It was mentioned," Katherine admitted, "but I can't remember it. You see, I was rather upset."

"I should think so," said Mr. Evans; "it must have been a beastly shock."

It is to be doubted whether, even if Katherine had remembered the name, she would have admitted the fact. Lady Tamplin's remorseless cross-examination was making her restive. Lenox, who was observant in her own way, noticed this, and offered to take Katherine upstairs to see her room. She left her there, remarking kindly before she went: "You mustn't mind Mother; she would make a few pennies' profit out of her dying grandmother if she could."

Lenox went down again to find her mother and her stepfather discussing the newcomer.

"Presentable," said Lady Tamplin, "quite presentable. Her clothes are all right. That gray thing is the same model that Gladys Cooper wore in *Palm Trees in Egypt.*"

"Have you noticed her eyes—what?" interposed Mr. Evans.

"Never mind her eyes, Chubby," said Lady Tamplin tartly; "we are discussing the things that really matter."

"Oh, quite," said Mr. Evans, and retired into his shell.

"She doesn't seem to me very—malleable," said Lady Tamplin, rather hesitating to choose the right word.

"She has all the instincts of a lady, as they say in books," said Lenox, with a grin.

"Narrow-minded," murmured Lady Tamplin. "Inevitable under the circumstances, I suppose."

"I expect you will do your best to broaden her," said Lenox, with a grin, "but you will have your work cut out. Just now, you noticed, she stuck down her forefeet and laid back her ears and refused to budge."

"Anyway," said Lady Tamplin hopefully, "she doesn't look to me at all mean. Some people, when they come into money, seem to attach undue importance to it."

"Oh, you'll easily touch her for what you want," said Lenox; "and, after all, that is all that matters, isn't it? That is what she is here for."

"She is my own cousin," said Lady Tamplin, with dignity.

"Cousin, eh?" said Mr. Evans, waking up again. "I suppose I call her Katherine, don't I?"

"It is of no importance at all what you call her, Chubby," said Lady Tamplin.

"Good," said Mr. Evans; "then I will. Do you suppose she plays tennis?" he added hopefully.

"Of course not," said Lady Tamplin. "She has been a companion, I tell you. Companions don't play tennis—or golf. They might possibly play golf-croquet, but I have always understood that they wind wool and wash dogs most of the day."

"O God!" said Mr. Evans; "do they really?"

Lenox drifted upstairs again to Katherine's room. "Can I help you?" she asked rather perfunctorily.

On Katherine's disclaimer, Lenox sat on the edge of the bed and stared thoughtfully at her guest.

"Why did you come?" she said at last. "To us, I mean. We're not your sort."

"Oh, I am anxious to get into Society."

"Don't be an ass," said Lenox promptly, detecting the flicker of a smile. "You know what I mean well enough. You are not a bit what I thought you would be. I say, you *have* got some decent clothes." She sighed. "Clothes are no good to me. I was born awkward. It's a pity, because I love them."

"I love them too," said Katherine, "but it has not been much use my loving them up to now. Do you think this is nice?"

She and Lenox discussed several models with artistic fervor.

"I like you," said Lenox suddenly. "I came up to warn you not to be taken in by Mother, but I think now that there is no need to do that. You are frightfully sincere and upright and all those queer things, but you are not a fool. Oh hell! what is it now?"

Lady Tamplin's voice was calling plaintively from the hall:

"Lenox, Derek has just rung up. He wants to come to dinner tonight. Will it be all right? I mean, we haven't got anything awkward, like quails, have we?"

Lenox reassured her and came back into Katherine's room. Her face looked brighter and less sullen.

"I'm glad old Derek is coming," she said; "you'll like him."

"Who is Derek?"

"He is Lord Leconbury's son, married a rich American woman. Women are simply potty about him."

"Why?"

"Oh, the usual reason—very good-looking and a regular bad lot. Everyone goes off their head about him."

"Do you?"

"Sometimes I do," said Lenox, "and sometimes I think I would like to marry a nice curate and live in the country and grow things in frames." She paused a minute, and then added, "An Irish curate would be best, and then I should hunt."

After a minute or two she reverted to her former theme. "There is something queer about Derek. All that family are a bit potty—mad gamblers, you know. In the old days they used to gamble away their wives and their estates, and did most reckless things just for the love of it. Derek would have made a perfect highwayman—debonair and gay, just the right manner." She moved to the door. "Well, come down when you feel like it."

Left alone, Katherine gave herself up to thought. Just at present she felt thoroughly ill at ease and jarred by her surroundings. The shock of the discovery in the train and the reception of the news by her new friends jarred upon her susceptibilities. She thought long and earnestly about the murdered woman. She had been sorry for Ruth, but she could not honestly say that she had liked her. She had divined only too well the ruthless egoism that was the keynote of her personality, and it repelled her.

She had been amused and a trifle hurt by the other's cool dismissal of her when she had served her turn. That she had come to some decision, Katherine was quite certain, but she wondered now what that decision had been. Whatever it was, death had stepped in and made all decisions meaningless. Strange that it should have been so, and that a brutal crime should have been the ending of that fateful journey. But suddenly Katherine remembered a small fact that she ought, perhaps, to have told the police—a fact that had for the moment escaped her memory. Was it of any real importance? She had certainly thought that she had seen a man going into that particular compartment, but she realized that she might easily have been mistaken. It might have been the compartment next door, and certainly the man in question could be no train robber. She recalled him very clearly as she had seen him on those two previous occasions—once at the Savoy and once at Cook's office. No, doubtless she had been mistaken. He had not gone into the dead woman's compartment, and it was perhaps as well that she had said nothing to the police. She might have done incalculable harm by doing so.

She went down to join the others on the terrace outside. Through the branches of mimosa, she looked out over the blue of the Mediterranean, and, while listening with half an ear to Lady Tamplin's chatter, she was glad that she had come. This was better than St. Mary Mead.

That evening she put on the mauvy pink dress that went by the name of *soupir d'automne,* and after smiling at her reflection in the mirror, went downstairs with, for the first time in her life, a faint feeling of shyness.

Most of Lady Tamplin's guests had arrived, and since noise was the essential of Lady Tamplin's parties, the din was already terrific. Chubby rushed up to Katherine, pressed a cocktail upon her, and took her under his wing.

"Oh, here you are, Derek," cried Lady Tamplin, as the door opened to admit the last comer. "Now at last we can have something to eat. I am starving."

Katherine looked across the room. She was startled. So this—was Derek, and she realized that she was not surprised. She had always known that she would someday meet the man whom she had seen three times by such a curious chain of coincidences. She thought, too, that he recognized her. He paused abruptly in what he was saying to Lady Tamplin, and went on again as though with an effort. They all went in to dinner, and Katherine found that he was placed beside her. He turned to her at once with a vivid smile.

"I knew I was going to meet you soon," he remarked, "but I never dreamt that it would be here. It had to be, you know. Once at the Savoy and once at Cook's—never twice without three times. Don't say you can't remember me or never noticed me. I insist upon your pretending that you noticed me, anyway."

"Oh, I did," said Katherine; "but this is not the third time. It is the fourth. I saw you on the Blue Train."

"On the Blue Train!" Something undefinable came over his manner; she could not have said just what it was. It was as though he had received a check, a setback. Then he said carelessly:

"What was the rumpus this morning? Somebody had died, hadn't they?"

"Yes," said Katherine slowly; "somebody had died."

"You shouldn't die on a train," remarked Derek flippantly. "I believe it causes all sorts of legal and international complications, and it gives the train an excuse for being even later than usual."

"Mr. Kettering?" A stout American lady, who was sitting opposite, leaned forward and spoke to him with the deliberate intonation of her race. "Mr. Kettering, I do believe you have forgotten me, and I thought you such a perfectly lovely man."

Derek leaned forward, answering her, and Katherine sat almost dazed.

Kettering! That was the name, of course! She remembered it now—but what a strange, ironical situation! Here was this man whom she had seen go into his wife's compartment last night, who had left her alive and well, and now he was sitting at dinner, quite unconscious of the fate that had befallen her. Of that there was no doubt. He did not know.

A servant was leaning over Derek, handing him a note and murmuring in his ear. With a word of excuse to Lady Tamplin, he broke it open, and an expression of utter astonishment came over his face as he read; then he looked at his hostess.

"This is most extraordinary. I say, Rosalie, I am afraid I will have to leave you. The Prefect of Police wants to see me at once. I can't think what about."

"Your sins have found you out," remarked Lenox.

"They must have," said Derek; "probably some idiotic nonsense, but I suppose I shall have to push off to the Prefecture. How dare the old boy rout me out from dinner? It ought to be something deadly serious to justify that," and he laughed as he pushed back his chair and rose to leave the room.

13

Van Aldin Gets a Telegram

ON THE AFTERNOON of the 15th February a thick yellow fog had settled down on London. Rufus Van Aldin was in his suite at the Savoy and was making the most of the atmospheric conditions by working double time. Knighton was overjoyed. He had found it difficult of late to get his employer to concentrate on the matters in hand. When he had ventured to urge certain courses, Van Aldin had put him off with a curt word. But now Van Aldin seemed to be throwing himself into work with redoubled energy, and the secretary made the most of his opportunities. Always tactful, he plied the spur so unobtrusively that Van Aldin never suspected it.

Yet in the middle of this absorption in business matters, one little fact lay at the back of Van Aldin's mind. A chance remark of Knighton's, uttered by the secretary in all unconsciousness, had given rise to it. It now festered unseen, gradually reaching further and further forward into Van Aldin's consciousness, until at last, in spite of himself, he had to yield to its insistence.

He listened to what Knighton was saying with his usual air of keen attention, but in reality not one word of it penetrated his mind. He nodded automatically, however, and the secretary turned to some other paper. As he was sorting them out, his employer spoke:

"Do you mind telling me that over again, Knighton?"

For a moment Knighton was at a loss.

"You mean about this, sir?" He held up a closely written Company report.

"No, no," said Van Aldin; "what you told me about seeing Ruth's maid in Paris last night. I can't make it out. You must have been mistaken."

"I can't have been mistaken, sir; I actually spoke to her."

"Well, tell me the whole thing again."

Knighton complied.

"I had fixed up the deal with Bartheimers," he explained, "and had gone

back to the Ritz to pick up my traps preparatory to having dinner and catching the nine o'clock train from the Gare du Nord. At the reception desk I saw
a woman whom I was quite sure was Mrs. Kettering's maid. I went up to her
and asked if Mrs. Kettering was staying there."

"Yes, yes," said Van Aldin. "Of course. Naturally. And she told you that
Ruth had gone on to the Riviera and had sent her to the Ritz to await further
orders there?"

"Exactly that, sir."

"It is very odd," said Van Aldin. "Very odd, indeed, unless the woman had
been impertinent or something of that kind."

"In that case," objected Knighton, "surely Mrs. Kettering would have paid
her down a sum of money, and told her to go back to England. She would
hardly have sent her to the Ritz."

"No," muttered the millionaire; "that's true."

He was about to say something further, but checked himself. He was fond
of Knighton and liked and trusted him, but he could hardly discuss his
daughter's private affairs with his secretary. He had already felt hurt by
Ruth's lack of frankness, and this chance information which had come to him
did nothing to allay his misgivings.

Why had Ruth got rid of her maid in Paris? What possible object or motive
could she have had in so doing?

He reflected for a moment or two on the curious combination of chance.
How should it have occurred to Ruth, except as the wildest coincidence, that
the first person that the maid should run across in Paris should be her father's
secretary? Ah, but that was the way things happened. That was the way
things got found out.

He winced at the last phrase; it had arisen with complete naturalness to his
mind. Was there then "something to be found out"? He hated to put this
question to himself; he had no doubt of the answer. The answer was—he was
sure of it—Armand de la Roche.

It was bitter to Van Aldin that a daughter of his should be gulled by such a
man, yet he was forced to admit that she was in good company—that other
well-bred and intelligent women had succumbed just as easily to the Count's
fascination. Men saw through him, women did not.

He sought now for a phrase that would allay any suspicion that his secretary might have felt.

"Ruth is always changing her mind about things at a moment's notice," he
remarked, and then he added in a would-be careless tone: "The maid didn't
give any—er—reason for this change of plan?"

Knighton was careful to make his voice as natural as possible as he replied:
"She said, sir, that Mrs. Kettering had met a friend unexpectedly."

"Is that so?"

The secretary's practiced ears caught the note of strain underlying the
seemingly casual tone.

"Oh, I see. Man or woman?"

"I think she said a man, sir."

Van Aldin nodded. His worst fears were being realized. He rose from his chair, and began pacing up and down the room, a habit of his when agitated. Unable to contain his feelings any longer, he burst forth:

"There is one thing no man can do, and that is to get a woman to listen to reason. Somehow or other, they don't seem to have any kind of *sense*. Talk of woman's instinct—why, it is well known all the world over that a woman is the surest mark for any rascally swindler. Not one in ten of them knows a scoundrel when she meets one; they can be preyed on by any good-looking fellow with a soft side to his tongue. If I had my way——"

He was interrupted. A page-boy entered with a telegram. Van Aldin tore it open, and his face went a sudden chalky white. He caught hold of the back of a chair to steady himself, and waved the page-boy from the room.

"What's the matter, sir?"

Knighton had risen in concern.

"Ruth!" said Van Aldin hoarsely.

"Mrs. Kettering?"

"Killed!"

"An accident to the train?"

Van Aldin shook his head.

"No. From this it seems she has been robbed as well. They don't use the word, Knighton, but my poor girl has been murdered."

"Oh, my God, sir!"

Van Aldin tapped the telegram with his forefinger.

"This is from the police at Nice. I must go out there by the first train."

Knighton was efficient as ever. He glanced at the clock.

"Five o'clock from Victoria, sir."

"That's right. You will come with me, Knighton. Tell my man, Archer, and pack your own things. See to everything here. I want to go round to Curzon Street."

The telephone rang sharply, and the secretary lifted the receiver.

"Yes; who is it?"

Then to Van Aldin.

"Mr. Goby, sir."

"Goby? I can't see him now. No—wait, we have plenty of time. Tell them to send him up."

Van Aldin was a strong man. Already he had recovered that iron calm of his. Few people would have noticed anything amiss in his greeting to Mr. Goby.

"I am pressed for time, Goby. Got anything important to tell me?"

Mr. Goby coughed.

"The movements of Mr. Kettering, sir. You wished them reported to you."

"Yes—well?"

"Mr. Kettering, sir, left London for the Riviera yesterday morning."

"What?"

Something in his voice must have startled Mr. Goby. That worthy gentleman departed from his usual practice of never looking at the person to whom he was talking, and stole a fleeting glance at the millionaire.

"What train did he go on?" demanded Van Aldin.

"The Blue Train, sir."

Mr. Goby coughed again and spoke to the clock on the mantelpiece.

"Mademoiselle Mirelle, the dancer from the Parthenon, went by the same train."

14

Ada Mason's Story

"I CANNOT REPEAT to you often enough, Monsieur, our horror, our consternation, and the deep sympathy we feel for you."

Thus M. Carrège, the Juge d'Instruction, addressed Van Aldin. M. Caux, the Commissary, made sympathetic noises in his throat. Van Aldin brushed away horror, consternation, and sympathy with an abrupt gesture. The scene was the Examining Magistrate's room at Nice. Besides M. Carrège, the Commissary, and Van Aldin, there was a further person in the room. It was that person who now spoke.

"M. Van Aldin," he said, "desires action—swift action."

"Ah!" cried the Commissary, "I have not yet presented you. M. Van Aldin, this is M. Hercule Poirot; you have doubtless heard of him. Although he has retired from his profession for some years now, his name is still a household word as one of the greatest living detectives."

"Pleased to meet you, M. Poirot," said Van Aldin, falling back mechanically on a formula that he had discarded some years ago. "You have retired from your profession?"

"That is so, Monsieur. Now I enjoy the world."

The little man made a grandiloquent gesture.

"M. Poirot happened to be traveling on the Blue Train," explained the Commissary, "and he has been so kind as to assist us out of his vast experience."

The millionaire looked at Poirot keenly. Then he said unexpectedly:

"I am a very rich man, M. Poirot. It is usually said that a rich man labors under the belief that he can buy everything and every one. That is not true. I am a big man in my way, and one big man can ask a favor from another big man."

Poirot nodded a quick appreciation.

"That is very well said, M. Van Aldin. I place myself entirely at your service."

"Thank you," said Van Aldin. "I can only say call upon me at any time, and you will not find me ungrateful. And now, gentlemen, to business."

"I propose," said M. Carrège, "to interrogate the maid, Ada Mason. You have her here, I understand?"

"Yes," said Van Aldin. "We picked her up in Paris in passing through. She was very upset to hear of her mistress's death, but she tells her story coherently enough."

"We will have her in, then," said M. Carrège.

He rang the bell on his desk, and in a few minutes Ada Mason entered the room.

She was very neatly dressed in black, and the tip of her nose was red. She had exchanged her gray traveling gloves for a pair of black suede ones. She cast a look around the Examining Magistrate's office in some trepidation, and seemed relieved at the presence of her mistress's father. The Examining Magistrate prided himself on his geniality of manner, and did his best to put her at her ease. He was helped in this by Poirot, who acted as interpreter, and whose friendly manner was reassuring to the Englishwoman.

"Your name is Ada Mason; is that right?"

"Ada Beatrice I was christened, sir," said Mason primly.

"Just so. And we can understand, Mason, that this has all been very distressing."

"Oh, indeed it has, sir. I have been with many ladies and always given satisfaction, I hope, and I never dreamt of anything of this kind happening in any situation where I was."

"No, no," said M. Carrège.

"Naturally I have read of such things, of course, in the Sunday papers. And then I always have understood that those foreign trains——" She suddenly checked her flow, remembering that the gentlemen who were speaking to her were of the same nationality as the trains.

"Now let us talk this affair over," said M. Carrège. "There was, I understand, no question of your staying in Paris when you started from London?"

"Oh no, sir. We were to go straight through to Nice."

"Have you ever been abroad with your mistress before?"

"No, sir. I had only been with her two months, you see."

"Did she seem quite as usual when starting on this journey?"

"She was worried like and a bit upset, and she was rather irritable and difficult to please."

M. Carrège nodded.

"Now then, Mason, what was the first you heard of your stopping in Paris?"

"It was at the place they call the Gare de Lyon, sir. My mistress was thinking of getting out and walking up and down the platform. She was just going out into the corridor when she gave a sudden exclamation, and came back into her compartment with a gentleman. She shut the door between her carriage and mine, so that I didn't see or hear anything, till she suddenly opened it again and told me that she had changed her plans. She gave me some money and told me to get out and go to the Ritz. They knew her well there, she said, and would give me a room. I was to wait there until I heard from her; she would wire me what she wanted me to do. I had just time to get my things together and jump out of the train before it started off. It was a rush."

"While Mrs. Kettering was telling you this, where was the gentleman?"

"He was standing in the other compartment, sir, looking out of the window."

"Can you describe him to us?"

"Well, you see, sir, I hardly saw him. He had his back to me most of the time. He was a tall gentleman and dark; that's all I can say. He was dressed very like any other gentleman in a dark blue overcoat and a gray hat."

"Was he one of the passengers on the train?"

"I don't think so, sir; I took it that he had come to the station to see Mrs. Kettering in passing through. Of course he might have been one of the passengers; I never thought of that."

Mason seemed a little flurried by the suggestion.

"Ah!" M. Carrège passed lightly to another subject. "Your mistress later requested the conductor not to rouse her early in the morning. Was that a likely thing for her to do, do you think?"

"Oh yes, sir. The mistress never ate any breakfast and she didn't sleep well at nights, so that she liked sleeping on in the morning."

Again M. Carrège passed to another subject.

"Amongst the luggage there was a scarlet morocco case, was there not?" he asked. "Your mistress's jewel case?"

"Yes, sir."

"Did you take that case to the Ritz?"

"*Me* take the mistress's jewel case to the Ritz! Oh no, indeed, sir." Mason's tones were horrified.

"You left it behind you in the carriage?"

"Yes, sir."

"Had your mistress many jewels with her, do you know?"

"A fair amount, sir; made me a bit uneasy sometimes, I can tell you, with those nasty tales you hear of being robbed in foreign countries. They were insured, I know, but all the same it seemed a frightful risk. Why, the rubies alone, the mistress told me, were worth several hundred thousand pounds."

"The rubies! What rubies?" barked Van Aldin suddenly.

Mason turned to him.

"I think it was you who gave them to her, sir, not very long ago."

"My God!" cried Van Aldin. "You don't say she had those rubies with her? I told her to leave them at the Bank."

Mason gave once more the discreet cough which was apparently part of her stock-in-trade as a lady's maid. This time it expressed a good deal. It expressed far more clearly than words could have done, that Mason's mistress had been a lady who took her own way.

"Ruth must have been mad," muttered Van Aldin. "What on earth could have possessed her?"

M. Carrège in turn gave vent to a cough, again a cough of significance. It riveted Van Aldin's attention on him.

"For the moment," said M. Carrège, addressing Mason, "I think that is all. If you will go into the next room, Mademoiselle, they will read over to you the questions and answers, and you will sign accordingly."

Mason went out escorted by the clerk, and Van Aldin said immediately to the Magistrate:

"Well?"

M. Carrège opened a drawer in his desk, took out a letter, and handed it across to Van Aldin.

"This was found in Madame's handbag."

> CHÈRE AMIE [the letter ran]— I will obey you; I will be prudent, discreet—all those things that a lover most hates. Paris would perhaps have been unwise, but the Isles d'Or are far away from the world, and you may be assured that nothing will leak out. It is like you and your divine sympathy to be so interested in the work on famous jewels that I am writing. It will, indeed, be an extraordinary privilege to actually see and handle these historic rubies. I am devoting a special passage to "Heart of Fire." My wonderful one! Soon I will make up to you for all those sad years of separation and emptiness.—Your ever-adoring,
>
> ARMAND.

15

The Comte de la Roche

VAN ALDIN READ the letter through in silence. His face turned a dull angry crimson. The men watching him saw the veins start out on his forehead, and his big hands clench themselves unconsciously. He handed back the letter without a word. M. Carrège was looking with close attention at his desk, M. Caux's eyes were fixed upon the ceiling, and M. Hercule Poirot was tenderly brushing a speck of dust from his coat sleeve. With the greatest tact they none of them looked at Van Aldin.

It was M. Carrège, mindful of his status and his duties, who tackled the unpleasant subject.

"Perhaps, Monsieur," he murmured, "you are aware by whom—er—this letter was written?"

"Yes, I know," said Van Aldin heavily.

"Ah?" said the Magistrate inquiringly.

"A scoundrel who calls himself the Comte de la Roche."

There was a pause; then M. Poirot leaned forward, straightened a ruler on the judge's desk, and addressed the millionaire directly.

"M. Van Aldin, we are all sensible, deeply sensible, of the pain it must give you to speak of these matters, but believe me, Monsieur, it is not the time for concealments. If justice is to be done, we must know everything. If you will reflect a little minute you will realize the truth of that clearly for yourself."

Van Aldin was silent for a moment or two, then almost reluctantly he nodded his head in agreement.

"You are quite right, M. Poirot," he said. "Painful as it is, I have no right to keep anything back."

The Commissary gave a sigh of relief, and the Examining Magistrate leaned back in his chair and adjusted a pince-nez on his long thin nose.

"Perhaps you will tell us in your own words, M. Van Aldin," he said, "all that you know of this gentleman."

"It began eleven or twelve years ago—in Paris. My daughter was a young girl then, full of foolish, romantic notions, like all young girls are. Unknown to me, she made the acquaintance of this Comte de la Roche. You have heard of him, perhaps?"

The Commissary and Poirot nodded in assent.

"He calls himself the Comte de la Roche," continued Van Aldin, "but I doubt if he has any right to the title."

"You would not have found his name in the *Almanac de Gotha,*" agreed the Commissary.

"I discovered as much," said Van Aldin. "The man was a good-looking, plausible scoundrel, with a fatal fascination for women. Ruth was infatuated with him, but I soon put a stop to the whole affair. The man was no better than a common swindler."

"You are quite right," said the Commissary. "The Comte de la Roche is well known to us. If it were possible, we should have laid him by the heels before now, but *ma foi!* it is not easy; the fellow is cunning, his affairs are always conducted with ladies of high social position. If he obtains money from them under false pretenses or as the fruit of blackmail, *eh bien!* naturally they will not prosecute. To look foolish in the eyes of the world, oh no, that would never do, and he has an extraordinary power over women."

"That is so," said the millionaire heavily. "Well, as I told you, I broke the affair up pretty sharply. I told Ruth exactly what he was, and she had, perforce, to believe me. About a year afterward, she met her present husband and married him. As far as I knew, that was the end of the matter; but only a week ago, I discovered, to my amazement, that my daughter had resumed her acquaintance with the Comte de la Roche. She had been meeting him frequently in London and Paris. I remonstrated with her on her imprudence, for I may tell you gentlemen, that, on my insistence, she was preparing to bring a suit for divorce against her husband."

"That is interesting," murmured Poirot softly, his eyes on the ceiling.

Van Aldin looked at him sharply, and then went on.

"I pointed out to her the folly of continuing to see the Comte under the circumstances. I thought she agreed with me."

The Examining Magistrate coughed delicately.

"But according to this letter——" he began, and then stopped.

Van Aldin's jaw set itself squarely.

"I know. It's no good mincing matters. However unpleasant, we have got to face facts. It seems clear that Ruth had arranged to go to Paris and meet de la Roche there. After my warnings to her, however, she must have written to the Count suggesting a change of rendezvous."

"The Isles d'Or," said the Commissary thoughtfully, "are situated just opposite Hyères, a remote and idyllic spot."

Van Aldin nodded.

"My God! How could Ruth be such a fool?" he exclaimed bitterly. "All this talk about writing a book on jewels! Why, he must have been after the rubies from the first."

"There are some very famous rubies," said Poirot, "originally part of the Crown jewels of Russia; they are unique in character, and their value is almost fabulous. There has been a rumor that they have lately passed into the possession of an American. Are we right in concluding, Monsieur, that you were the purchaser?"

"Yes," said Van Aldin. "They came into my possession in Paris about ten days ago."

"Pardon me, Monsieur, but you have been negotiating for their purchase for some time?"

"A little over two months. Why?"

"These things become known," said Poirot. "There is always a pretty formidable crowd on the track of jewels such as these."

A spasm distorted the other's face.

"I remember," he said brokenly, "a joke I made to Ruth when I gave them to her. I told her not to take them to the Riviera with her, as I could not afford to have her robbed and murdered for the sake of the jewels. My God! the things one says—never dreaming or knowing they will come true."

There was a sympathetic silence, and then Poirot spoke in a detached manner.

"Let us arrange our facts with order and precision. According to our present theory, this is how they run. The Comte de la Roche knows of your purchase of these jewels. By an easy stratagem he induces Madame Kettering to bring the stones with her. He, then, is the man Mason saw in the train at Paris."

The other three nodded in agreement.

"Madame is surprised to see him, but she deals with the situation promptly. Mason is got out of the way; a dinner basket is ordered. We know from the conductor that he made up the berth for the first compartment, but he did not go into the second compartment, and that a man could quite well have been concealed from him. So far the Comte could have been hidden to a marvel. No one knows of his presence on the train except Madame; he has been careful that the maid did not see his face. All that she could say is that he was tall and dark. It is all most conveniently vague. They are alone—and the train rushes through the night. There would be no outcry, no struggle, for the man is, so she thinks, her lover."

He turned gently to Van Aldin.

"Death, Monseiur, must have been almost instantaneous. We will pass over that quickly. The Comte takes the jewel case which lies ready to his hand. Shortly afterward the train draws into Lyons."

M. Carrège nodded his approval.

"Precisely. The conductor without descends. It would be easy for our man to leave the train unseen; it would be easy to catch a train back to Paris or anywhere he pleases. And the crime would be put down as an ordinary train robbery. But for the letter found in Madame's bag, the Comte would not have been mentioned."

"It was an oversight on his part not to search that bag," declared the Commissary.

"Without doubt he thought she had destroyed that letter. It was—pardon me, Monsieur—it was an indiscretion of the first water to keep it."

"And yet," murmured Poirot, "it was an indiscretion the Comte might have foreseen."

"You mean?"

"I mean we are all agreed on one point, and that is that the Comte de la Roche knows one subject *à fond:* Women. How was it that, knowing women as he does, he did not foresee that Madame would have kept that letter?"

"Yes—yes," said the Examining Magistrate doubtfully, "there is something in what you say. But at such times, you understand, a man is not master of himself. He does not reason calmly. *Mon Dieu!*" he added, with feeling, "if our criminals kept their heads and acted with intelligence, how should we capture them?"

Poirot smiled to himself.

"It seems to me a clear case," said the other, "but a difficult one to prove. The Comte is a slippery customer, and unless the maid can identify him——"

"Which is most unlikely," said Poirot.

"True, true." The Examining Magistrate rubbed his chin. "It is going to be difficult."

"If he did indeed commit the crime——" began Poirot. M. Caux interrupted.

"If—you say *if?*"

"Yes, Monsieur le Juge, I say *if.*"

The other looked at him sharply. "You are right," he said at last, "we go too fast. It is possible that the Comte may have an alibi. Then we should look foolish."

"Ah, ça par exemple," replied Poirot, "that is of no importance whatever. Naturally, if he committed the crime he will have an alibi. A man with the Comte's experience does not neglect to take precautions. No, I said *if* for a very different reason."

"And what was that?"

Poirot wagged an emphatic forefinger. "The psychology."

"Eh?" said the Commissary.

"The psychology is at fault. The Comte is a scoundrel—yes. The Comte is a swindler—yes. The Comte preys upon women—yes. He proposes to steal Madame's jewels—again yes. Is he the kind of man to commit murder? I say *no!* A man of the type of the Comte is always a coward; he takes no risks. He plays the safe, the mean, what the English call the low-down game; but murder, a hundred times no!" He shook his head in a dissatisfied manner.

The Examining Magistrate, however, did not seem disposed to agree with him.

"The day always comes when such gentry lose their heads and go too far," he observed sagely. "Doubtless that is the case here. Without wishing to disagree with you, M. Poirot——"

"It was only an opinion," Poirot hastened to explain. "The case is, of course, in your hands, and you will do what seems fit to you."

"I am satisfied in my own mind that the Comte de la Roche is the man we need to get hold of," said M. Carrège. "You agree with me, Monsieur le Commissaire?"

"Perfectly."

"And you, M. Van Aldin?"

"Yes," said the millionaire. "Yes; the man is a thorough-paced villain, no doubt about it."

"It will be difficult to lay hands on him, I am afraid," said the Magistrate, "but we will do our best. Telegraphed instructions shall go out at once."

"Permit me to assist you," said Poirot. "There need be no difficulty."

"Eh?"

The others stared at him. The little man smiled beamingly back at them.

"It is my business to know things," he explained. "The Comte is a man of intelligence. He is at present at a villa he has leased, the Villa Marina at Antibes."

16

Poirot Discusses the Case

EVERYBODY LOOKED RESPECTFULLY at Poirot. Undoubtedly the little man had scored heavily. The Commissary laughed—on a rather hollow note.

"You teach us all our business," he cried. "M. Poirot knows more than the police."

Poirot gazed complacently at the ceiling, adopting a mock-modest air.

"What will you; it is my little hobby," he murmured, "to know things. Naturally I have the time to indulge it. I am not overburdened with affairs."

"Ah!" said the Commissary shaking his head portentously. "As for me——"

He made an exaggerated gesture to represent the cares that lay on his shoulders.

Poirot turned suddenly to Van Aldin.

"You agree, Monsieur, with this view? You feel certain that the Comte de la Roche is the murderer?"

"Why, it would seem so—yes, certainly."

Something guarded in the answer made the Examining Magistrate look at the American curiously. Van Aldin seemed aware of his scrutiny and made an effort as though to shake off some preoccupation.

"What about my son-in-law?" he asked. "You have acquainted him with the news? He is in Nice, I understand."

"Certainly, Monsieur." The Commissary hesitated, and then murmured very discreetly: "You are doubtless aware, M. Van Aldin, that M. Kettering was also one of the passengers on the Blue Train that night?"

The millionaire nodded.

"Heard it just before I left London," he vouchsafed laconically.

"He tells us," continued the Commissary, "that he had no idea his wife was traveling on the train."

"I bet he hadn't," said Van Aldin grimly. "It would have been rather a nasty shock to him if he'd come across her on it."

The three men looked at him questioningly.

"I'm not going to mince matters," said Van Aldin savagely. "No one knows what my poor girl has had to put up with. Derek Kettering wasn't alone. He had a lady with him."

"Ah?"

"Mirelle—the dancer."

M. Carrège and the Commissary looked at each other and nodded as though confirming some previous conversation. M. Carrège leaned back in his chair, joined his hands, and fixed his eyes on the ceiling.

"Ah!" he murmured again. "One wondered." He coughed. "One has heard rumors."

"The lady," said M. Caux, "is very notorious."

"And also," murmured Poirot softly, "very expensive."

Van Aldin had gone very red in the face. He leaned forward and hit the table a bang with his fist.

"See here," he cried, "my son-in-law is a damned scoundrel!"

He glared at them, looking from one face to another.

"Oh, I know," he went on. "Good looks and a charming, easy manner. It took me in once upon a time. I suppose he pretended to be broken-hearted when you broke the news to him—that is, if he didn't know it already."

"Oh, it came as a complete surprise to him. He was overwhelmed."

"Darned young hypocrite," said Van Aldin. "Simulated great grief, I suppose?"

"N—no," said the Commissary cautiously. "I would not quite say that— eh, M. Carrège?"

The Magistrate brought the tips of his fingers together, and half closed his eyes.

"Shock, bewilderment, horror—these things, yes," he declared judicially. "Great sorrow—no—I should not say that."

Hercule Poirot spoke once more.

"Permit me to ask, M. Van Aldin, does M. Kettering benefit by the death of his wife?"

"He benefits to the tune of a couple of millions," said Van Aldin.

"Dollars?"

"Pounds. I settled that sum on Ruth absolutely on her marriage. She made no will and leaves no children, so the money will go to her husband."

"Whom she was on the point of divorcing," murmured Poirot. "Ah, yes— *précisément.*"

The Commissary turned and looked sharply at him.

"Do you mean——" he began.

"I mean nothing," said Poirot. "I arrange the facts, that is all."

Van Aldin stared at him with awakening interest.

The little man rose to his feet.

"I do not think I can be of any further service to you, M. le Juge," he said politely, bowing to M. Carrège. "You will keep me informed of the course of events? It will be a kindness."

"But certainly—most certainly."

Van Aldin rose also.

"You don't want me any more at present?"

"No, Monsieur; we have all the information we need for the moment."

"Then I will walk a little way with M. Poirot. That is, if he does not object?"

"Enchanted, Monsieur," said the little man, with a bow.

Van Aldin lighted a large cigar, having first offered one to Poirot, who declined it and lit one of his own tiny cigarettes. A man of great strength of character, Van Aldin already appeared to be his everyday, normal self once more. After strolling along for a minute or two in silence, the millionaire spoke:

"I take it, M. Poirot, that you no longer exercise your profession?"

"That is so, Monsieur. I enjoy the world."

"Yet you are assisting the police in this affair?"

"Monsieur, if a doctor walks along the street and an accident happens, does he say, 'I have retired from my profession, I will continue my walk,' when there is someone bleeding to death at his feet? If I had been already in Nice, and the police had sent to me and asked me to assist them, I should have refused. But this affair, the good God thrust it upon me."

"You were on the spot," said Van Aldin thoughtfully. "You examined the compartment, did you not?"

Poirot nodded.

"Doubtless you found things that were, shall we say, suggestive to you?"

"Perhaps," said Poirot.

"I hope you see what I am leading up to?" said Van Aldin. "It seems to me that the case against this Comte de la Roche is perfectly clear, but I am not a fool. I have been watching you for this last hour or so, and I realize that for some reason of your own you don't agree with that theory?"

Poirot shrugged his shoulders.

"I may be wrong."

"So we come to the favor I want to ask you. Will you act in this matter for me?"

"For you personally?"

"That was my meaning."

Poirot was silent for a moment or two. Then he said:

"You realize what you are asking?"

"I guess so," said Van Aldin.

"Very well," said Poirot. "I accept. But in that case, I must have frank answers to my questions."

"Why, certainly. That is understood."

Poirot's manner changed. He became suddenly brusque and businesslike.

"This question of a divorce," he said. "It was you who advised your daughter to bring the suit?"

"Yes."

"When?"

"About ten days ago. I had had a letter from her complaining of her husband's behavior, and I put it to her very strongly that divorce was the only remedy."

"In what way did she complain of his behavior?"

"He was being seen about with a *very* notorious lady—the one we have been speaking of—Mirelle."

"The dancer. Ah-ha! And Madame Kettering objected? Was she very devoted to her husband?"

"I would not say that," said Van Aldin, hesitating a little.

"It was not her heart that suffered, it was her pride—is that what you would say?"

"Yes, I suppose you might put it like that."

"I gather that the marriage had not been a happy one from the beginning?"

"Derek Kettering is rotten to the core," said Van Aldin. "He is incapable of making any woman happy."

"He is, as you say in England, a bad lot. That is right, is it not?"

Van Aldin nodded.

"*Très bien!* You advise Madame to seek a divorce, she agrees; you consult your solicitors. When does M. Kettering get news of what is in the wind?"

"I sent for him myself, and explained the course of action I proposed to take."

"And what did he say?" murmured Poirot softly.

Van Aldin's face darkened at the remembrance.

"He was infernally impudent."

"Excuse the question, Monsieur, but did he refer to the Comte de la Roche?"

"Not by name," growled the other unwillingly, "but he showed himself cognizant of the affair."

"What, if I may ask, was M. Kettering's financial position at the time?"

"How do you suppose I should know that?" asked Van Aldin, after a very brief hesitation.

"It seemed likely to me that you would inform yourself on that point."

"Well—you are quite right, I did. I discovered that Kettering was on the rocks."

"And now he has inherited two million pounds! *La vie*—it is a strange thing, is it not?"

Van Aldin looked at him sharply.

"What do you mean?"

"I moralize," said Poirot. "I reflect, I speak the philosophy. But to return to where we were. Surely M. Kettering did not propose to allow himself to be divorced without making a fight for it?"

Van Aldin did not answer for a minute or two, then he said:

"I don't exactly know what his intentions were."

"Did you hold any further communications with him?"

Again a slight pause, then Van Aldin said:

"No."

Poirot stopped dead, took off his hat, and held out his hand.

"I must wish you good day, Monsieur. I can do nothing for you."

"What are you getting at?" demanded Van Aldin angrily.

"If you do not tell me the truth, I can do nothing."

"I don't know what you mean."

"I think you do. You may rest assured, M. Van Aldin, that I know how to be discreet."

"Very well, then," said the millionaire. "I'll admit that I was not speaking the truth just now. I *did* have further communication with my son-in-law."

"Yes?"

"To be exact, I sent my secretary, Major Knighton, to see him, with in- structions to offer him the sum of one hundred thousand pounds in cash if the divorce went through undefended."

"A pretty sum of money," said Poirot appreciatively; "and the answer of Monsieur your son-in-law?"

"He sent back word that I could go to hell," replied the millionaire suc- cinctly.

"Ah!" said Poirot.

He betrayed no emotion of any kind. At the moment he was engaged in methodically recording facts.

"Monsieur Kettering has told the police that he neither saw nor spoke to his wife on the journey from England. Are you inclined to believe that state- ment, Monsieur?"

"Yes, I am," said Van Aldin. "He would take particular pains to keep out of her way, I should say."

"Why?"

"Because he had got that woman with him."

"Mirelle?"

"Yes."

"How did you come to know that fact?"

"A man of mine, whom I had put on to watch him, reported to me that they had both left by that train."

"I see," said Poirot. "In that case, as you said before, he would not be likely to attempt to hold any communication with Madame Kettering."

The little man fell silent for some time. Van Aldin did not interrupt his meditation.

17

An Aristocratic Gentleman

"YOU HAVE BEEN to the Riviera before, Georges?" said Poirot to his valet the following morning.

George was an intensely English, rather wooden-faced individual.

"Yes, sir. I was here two years ago when I was in the service of Lord Edward Frampton."

"And today," murmured his master, "you are here with Hercule Poirot. How one mounts in the world!"

The valet made no reply to this observation. After a suitable pause he asked:

"The brown lounge suit, sir? The wind is somewhat chilly today."

"There is a grease spot on the waistcoat," objected Poirot. "A *morceau* of *Fillet de sole à la Jeanette* alighted there when I was lunching at the Ritz last Tuesday."

"There is no spot there now, sir," said George reproachfully. "I have removed it."

"Très bien!" said Poirot. "I am pleased with you, Georges."

"Thank you, sir."

There was a pause, and then Poirot murmured dreamily:

"Supposing, my good Georges, that you had been born in the same social sphere as your late master, Lord Edward Frampton—that, penniless yourself, you had married an extremely wealthy wife, but that that wife proposed to divorce you, with excellent reasons, what would you do about it?"

"I should endeavor, sir," replied George, "to make her change her mind."

"By peaceful or by forcible methods?"

George looked shocked.

"You will excuse me, sir," he said, "but a gentleman of the aristocracy would not behave like a Whitechapel coster. He would not do anything low."

"Would he not, Georges? I wonder now. Well, perhaps you are right."

There was a knock on the door. George went to it and opened it a discreet inch or two. A low murmured colloquy went on, and then the valet returned to Poirot.

"A note, sir."

Poirot took it. It was from M. Caux, the Commissary of Police.

"We are about to interrogate the Comte de la Roche. The Juge d'Instruction begs that you will be present."

"Quickly, my suit, Georges! I must hasten myself."

A quarter of an hour later, spick and span in his brown suit, Poirot entered the Examining Magistrate's room. M. Caux was already there, and both he and M. Carrège greeted Poirot with polite *empressement*.

"The affair is somewhat discouraging," murmured M. Caux.

"It appears that the Comte arrived in Nice the day before the murder."

"If that is true, it will settle your affair nicely for you," responded Poirot.

M. Carrège cleared his throat.

"We must not accept this alibi without very cautious inquiry," he declared. He struck the bell upon the table with his hand.

In another minute a tall dark man, exquisitely dressed, with a somewhat haughty cast of countenance, entered the room. So very aristocratic-looking was the Count, that it would have seemed sheer heresy even to whisper that his father had been an obscure corn-chandler in Nantes—which, as a matter of fact, was the case. Looking at him, one would have been prepared to swear that innumerable ancestors of his must have perished by the guillotine in the French Revolution.

"I am here, gentlemen," said the Count haughtily. "May I ask why you wish to see me?"

"Pray be seated, Monsieur le Comte," said the Examining Magistrate politely. "It is the affair of the death of Madame Kettering that we are investigating."

"The death of Madame Kettering? I do not understand."

"You were—ahem!—acquainted with the lady, I believe, Monsieur le Comte?"

"Certainly I was acquainted with her. What has that to do with the matter?"

Sticking an eyeglass in his eye, he looked coldly around the room, his glance resting longest on Poirot, who was gazing at him with a kind of simple, innocent admiration which was most pleasing to the Count's vanity. M. Carrège leaned back in his chair and cleared his throat.

"You do not perhaps know, Monsieur le Comte"—he paused—"that Madame Kettering was murdered?"

"Murdered? *Mon Dieu,* how terrible!"

The surprise and the sorrow were excellently done—so well done, indeed, as to seem wholly natural.

"Madame Kettering was strangled between Paris and Lyons," continued M. Carrège, "and her jewels were stolen."

"It is iniquitous!" cried the Count warmly; "the police should do something about these train bandits. Nowadays no one is safe."

"In Madame's handbag," continued the Judge, "we found a letter to her from you. She had, it seemed, arranged to meet you?"

The Count shrugged his shoulders and spread out his hands.

"Of what use are concealments," he said frankly. "We are all men of the world. Privately and between ourselves, I admit the affair."

"You met her in Paris and traveled down with her, I believe?" said M. Carrège.

"That was the original arrangement, but by Madame's wish it was changed. I was to meet her at Hyères."

"You did not meet her on the train at the Gare de Lyon on the evening of the 14th?"

"On the contrary, I arrived in Nice on the morning of that day, so what you suggest is impossible."

"Quite so, quite so," said M. Carrège. "As a matter of form, you would perhaps give me an account of your movements during the evening and night of the 14th."

The Count reflected for a minute.

"I dined in Monte Carlo at the Café de Paris. Afterward I went to Le

Sporting. I won a few thousands francs." He shrugged his shoulders. "I returned home at perhaps one o'clock."

"Pardon me, Monsieur, but how did you return home?"

"In my own two-seater car."

"No one was with you?"

"No one."

"You could produce witnesses in support of this statement?"

"Doubtless many of my friends saw me there that evening. I dined alone."

"Your servant admitted you on your return to your villa?"

"I let myself in with my own latch-key."

"Ah!" murmured the Magistrate.

Again he struck the bell on the table with his hand. The door opened, and a messenger appeared.

"Bring in the maid, Mason," said M. Carrège.

"Very good, Monsieur le Juge."

Ada Mason was brought in.

"Will you be so good, Mademoiselle, as to look at this gentleman. To the best of your ability was it he who entered your mistress's compartment in Paris?"

The woman looked long and searchingly at the Count, who was, Poirot fancied, rather uneasy under this scrutiny.

"I could not say, sir, I am sure," said Mason at last. "It might be and again it might not. Seeing as how I only saw his back, it's hard to say. I rather think it *was* the gentleman."

"But you are not sure?"

"No-o," said Mason unwillingly; "n-no, I am not sure."

"You have seen this gentleman before in Curzon Street?"

Mason shook her head.

"I should not be likely to see any visitors that come to Curzon Street," she explained, "unless they were staying in the house."

"Very well, that will do," said the Examining Magistrate sharply.

Evidently he was disappointed.

"One moment," said Poirot. "There is a question I would like to put to Mademoiselle, if I may?"

"Certainly, M. Poirot—certainly, by all means."

Poirot addressed himself to the maid.

"What happened to the tickets?"

"The tickets, sir?"

"Yes; the tickets from London to Nice. Did you or your mistress have them?"

"The mistress had her own Pullman ticket, sir; the others were in my charge."

"What happened to them?"

"I gave them to the conductor on the French train, sir; he said it was usual. I hope I did right, sir?"

"Oh, quite right, quite right. A mere matter of detail."

Both M. Caux and the Examining Magistrate looked at him curiously. Mason stood uncertainly for a minute or two, and then the Magistrate gave her a brief nod of dismissal, and she went out. Poirot scribbled something on a scrap of paper and handed it across to M. Carrège. The latter read it and his brow cleared.

"Well, gentlemen," demanded the Count haughtily, "am I to be detained further?"

"Assuredly not, assuredly not," M. Carrège hastened to say, with a great deal of amiability. "Everything is now cleared up as regards your own position in this affair. Naturally, in view of Madame's letter, we were bound to question you."

The Count rose, picked up his handsome stick from the corner, and, with rather a curt bow, left the room.

"And that is that," said M. Carrège. "You were quite right, M. Poirot—much better to let him feel he is not suspected. Two of my men will shadow him night and day, and at the same time we will go into the question of the alibi. It seems to me rather—er—a fluid one."

"Possibly," agreed Poirot thoughtfully.

"I asked M. Kettering to come here this morning," continued the Magistrate, "though really I doubt if we have much to ask him, but there are one or two suspicious circumstances——" He paused, rubbing his nose.

"Such as?" asked Poirot.

"Well"—the Magistrate coughed—"this lady with whom he is said to be traveling—Mademoiselle Mirelle. She is staying at one hotel and he at another. That strikes me—er—as rather odd."

"It looks," said M. Caux, "as though they were being careful."

"Exactly," said M. Carrège triumphantly; "and what should they have to be careful about?"

"An excess of caution is suspicious, eh?" said Poirot.

"*Précisément.*"

"We might, I think," murmured Poirot, "ask M. Kettering one or two questions."

The Magistrate gave instructions. A moment or two later, Derek Kettering, debonair as ever, entered the room.

"Good morning, Monsieur," said the Judge politely.

"Good morning," said Derek Kettering curtly. "You sent for me. Has anything fresh turned up?"

"Pray sit down, Monsieur."

Derek took a seat and flung his hat and stick on the table.

"Well?" he asked impatiently.

"We have, so far, no fresh data," said M. Carrège cautiously.

"That's very interesting," said Derek dryly. "Did you send for me here in order to tell me that?"

"We naturally thought, Monsieur, that you would like to be informed of the progress of the case," said the Magistrate severely.

"Even if the progress was nonexistent."

"We also wished to ask you a few questions."

"Ask away."

"You are quite sure that you neither saw nor spoke with your wife on the train?"

"I've answered that already. I did not."

"You had, no doubt, your reasons."

Derek stared at him suspiciously.

"I—did—not—know—she—was—on—the—train," he explained, spacing his words elaborately, as though to someone dull of intellect.

"That is what you say, yes," murmured M. Carrège.

A frown suffused Derek's face.

"I should like to know what you're driving at. Do you know what I think, M. Carrège?"

"What do you think, Monsieur?"

"I think the French police are vastly overrated. Surely you must have some data as to these gangs of train robbers. It's outrageous that such a thing could happen on a *train de luxe* like that, and that the French police should be helpless to deal with the matter."

"We are dealing with it, Monsieur, never fear."

"Madame Kettering, I understand, did not leave a will," interposed Poirot suddenly. His fingertips were joined together, and he was looking intently at the ceiling.

"I don't think she ever made one," said Kettering. "Why?"

"It is a very pretty little fortune that you inherit there," said Poirot—"a very pretty little fortune."

Although his eyes were still on the ceiling, he managed to see the dark flush that rose to Derek Kettering's face.

"What do you mean, and who are you?"

Poirot gently uncrossed his knees, withdrew his gaze from the ceiling, and looked the young man full in the face.

"My name is Hercule Poirot," he said quietly, "and I am probably the greatest detective in the world. You are quite sure that you did not see or speak to your wife on that train?"

"What are you getting at? Do you—do you mean to insinuate that I—I killed her?"

He laughed suddenly.

"I mustn't lose my temper; it's too palpably absurd. Why, if I killed her I should have had no need to steal her jewels, would I?"

"That is true," murmured Poirot, with a rather crestfallen air. "I did not think of that."

"If ever there were a clear case of murder and robbery, this is it," said

Derek Kettering. "Poor Ruth, it was those damned rubies did for her. It must have got about she had them with her. There has been murder done for those same stones before now, I believe."

Poirot sat up suddenly in his chair. A very faint green light glowed in his eyes. He looked extraordinarily like a sleek, well-fed cat.

"One more question, M. Kettering," he said. "Will you give me the date when you last saw your wife?"

"Let me see," Kettering reflected. "It must have been—yes over three weeks ago. I am afraid I can't give you the date exactly."

"No matter," said Poirot dryly; "that is all I wanted to know."

"Well," said Derek Kettering impatiently, "anything further?"

He looked toward M. Carrège. The latter sought inspiration from Poirot, and received it in a very faint shake of the head.

"No, M. Kettering," he said politely; "no, I do not think we need trouble you any further. I wish you good morning."

"Good morning," said Kettering. He went out, banging the door behind him.

Poirot leaned forward and spoke sharply, as soon as the young man was out of the room.

"Tell me," he said peremptorily, "when did you speak of these rubies to M. Kettering?"

"I have not spoken of them," said M. Carrège. "It was only yesterday afternoon that we learned about them from M. Van Aldin."

"Yes; but there was a mention of them in the Comte's letter."

M. Carrège looked pained.

"Naturally I did not speak of that letter to M. Kettering," he said in a shocked voice. "It would have been most indiscreet at the present juncture of affairs."

Poirot leaned forward and tapped the table.

"Then how did he know about them?" he demanded softly. "Madame could not have told him, for he has not seen her for three weeks. It seems unlikely that either M. Van Aldin or his secretary would have mentioned them; their interviews with him have been on entirely different lines, and there has not been any hint or reference to them in the newspapers."

He got up and took his hat and stick.

"And yet," he murmured to himself, "our gentleman knows all about them. I wonder now, yes, I wonder!"

18

Derek Lunches

DEREK KETTERING WENT straight to the Negresco, where he ordered a couple of cocktails and disposed of them rapidly; then he stared moodily out over the dazzling blue sea. He noted the passersby mechanically—a damned dull crowd, badly dressed, and painfully uninteresting; one hardly ever saw anything worthwhile nowadays. Then he corrected this last impression rapidly, as a woman placed herself at a table a little distance away from him. She was wearing a marvelous confection of orange and black, with a little hat that shaded her face. He ordered a third cocktail; again he stared out to sea, and then suddenly he started. A well-known perfume assailed his nostrils, and he looked up to see the orange-and-black lady standing beside him. He saw her face now, and recognized her. It was Mirelle. She was smiling that insolent, seductive smile he knew so well.

"Dereek!" she murmured. "You are pleased to see me, no?"

She dropped into a seat the other side of the table.

"But welcome me, then, stupid one," she mocked.

"This is an unexpected pleasure," said Derek. "When did you leave London?"

She shrugged her shoulders.

"A day or two ago."

"And the Parthenon?"

"I have, how do you say it?—given them the chuck!"

"Really?"

"You are not very amiable, Dereek."

"Do you expect me to be?"

Mirelle lit a cigarette and puffed at it for a few minutes before saying:

"You think, perhaps, that it is not prudent so soon?"

Derek stared at her, then he shrugged his shoulders, and remarked formally:

"You are lunching here?"

"*Mais oui*. I am lunching with you."

"I am extremely sorry," said Derek. "I have a very important engagement."

"*Mon Dieu!* But you men are like children," exclaimed the dancer. "But yes, it is the spoilt child that you act to me, ever since that day in London when you flung yourself out of my flat, you sulk. Ah! *mais c'est inouï!*"

"My dear girl," said Derek, "I really don't know what you are talking about. We agreed in London that rats desert a sinking ship, that is all that there is to be said."

In spite of his careless words, his face looked haggard and strained. Mirelle leaned forward suddenly.

"You cannot deceive me," she murmured. "I know—I know what you have done for me."

He looked up at her sharply. Some undercurrent in her voice arrested his attention. She nodded her head at him.

"Ah! have no fear; I am discreet. You are magnificent! You have a superb courage, but, all the same, it was I who gave you the idea that day, when I said to you in London that accidents sometimes happened. And you are not in danger? The police do not suspect you?"

"What the devil——"

"Hush!"

She held up a slim olive hand with one big emerald on the little finger.

"You are right; I should not have spoken so in a public place. We will not speak of the matter again, but our troubles are ended; our life together will be wonderful—wonderful!"

Derek laughed suddenly—a harsh, disagreeable laugh.

"So the rats come back, do they? Two million makes a difference—of course it does. I ought to have known that." He laughed again. "You will help me to spend that two million, won't you, Mirelle? You know how, no woman better." He laughed again.

"Hush!" cried the dancer. "What is the matter with you, Dereek? See—people are turning to stare at you."

"Me? I will tell you what is the matter. I have finished with you, Mirelle. Do you hear? Finished!"

Mirelle did not take it as he expected her to do. She looked at him for a minute or two, and then she smiled softly.

"But what a child! You are angry—you are sore, and all because I am practical. Did I not always tell you that I adored you?"

She leaned forward.

"But I know you, Dereek. Look at me—see, it is Mirelle who speaks to you. You cannot live without her, you know it. I loved you before, I will love you a hundred times more now. I will make life wonderful for you—but wonderful. There is no one like Mirelle."

Her eyes burned into his. She saw him grow pale and draw in his breath, and she smiled to herself contentedly. She knew her own magic and power over men.

"That is settled," she said softly, and gave a little laugh. "And now, De-reek, will you give me lunch?"

"No."

He drew in his breath sharply and rose to his feet.

"I am sorry, but I told you—I have got an engagement."

"You are lunching with someone else? Bah! I don't believe it."

"I am lunching with that lady over there."

He crossed abruptly to where a lady in white had just come up the steps. He addressed her a little breathlessly.

"Miss Grey, will you—will you have lunch with me? You met me at Lady Tamplin's, if you remember."

Katherine looked at him for a minute or two with those thoughtful gray eyes that said so much.

"Thank you," she said, after a moment's pause; "I should like to very much."

19

An Unexpected Visitor

THE COMTE DE la Roche had just finished *déjeuner,* consisting of an *omelette fines herbes,* an *entrecôte Bearnaise,* and a *Savarin au Rhum.* Wiping his fine black moustache delicately with his table napkin, the Comte rose from the table. He passed through the salon of the villa, noting with appreciation the few *objets d'art* which were carelessly scattered about. The Louis XV snuff box, the satin shoe worn by Marie Antoinette, and the other historic trifles were part of the Comte's *mise en scène.* They were, he would explain to his fair visitors, heirlooms in his family. Passing through on to the terrace, the Comte looked out on the Mediterranean with an unseeing eye. He was in no mood for appreciating the beauties of scenery. A fully matured scheme had been rudely brought to naught, and his plans had to be cast afresh. Stretching himself out in a basket chair, a cigarette held between his white fingers, the Comte pondered deeply.

Presently Hippolyte, his manservant, brought out coffee and a choice of liqueurs. The Comte selected some very fine old brandy.

As the manservant was preparing to depart, the Comte arrested him with a slight gesture. Hippolyte stood respectfully to attention. His countenance was hardly a prepossessing one, but the correctitude of his demeanor went far to obliterate the fact. He was now the picture of respectful attention.

"It is possible," said the Comte, "that in the course of the next few days various strangers may come to the house. They will endeavor to scrape acquaintance with you and with Marie. They will probably ask you various questions concerning me."

"Yes, Monsieur le Comte."

"Perhaps this has already happened?"

"No, Monsieur le Comte."

"There have been no strangers about the place? You are certain?"

"There has been no one, Monsieur le Comte."

"That is well," said the Comte dryly; "nevertheless they will come—I am sure of it. They will ask questions."

Hippolyte looked at his master in intelligent anticipation.

The Comte spoke slowly, without looking at Hippolyte.

"As you know, I arrived here last Tuesday morning. If the police or any other inquirer should question you, do not forget that fact. I arrived on Tuesday, the 14th—not Wednesday, the 15th. You understand?"

"Perfectly, Monsieur le Comte."

"In an affair where a lady is concerned, it is always necessary to be discreet. I feel certain, Hippolyte, that you can be discreet."

"I can be discreet, Monsieur."

"And Marie?"

"Marie also. I will answer for her."

"That is well then," murmured the Comte.

When Hippolyte had withdrawn, the Comte sipped his black coffee with a reflective air. Occasionally he frowned, once he shook his head slightly, twice he nodded it. Into the midst of these cogitations came Hippolyte once more.

"A lady, Monsieur."

"A lady?"

The Comte was surprised. Not that a visit from a lady was an unusual thing at the Villa Marina, but at this particular moment the Comte could not think who the lady was likely to be.

"She is, I think, a lady not known to Monsieur," murmured the valet helpfully.

The Comte was more and more intrigued.

"Show her out here, Hippolyte," he commanded.

A moment later a marvelous vision in orange and black stepped out on the terrace, accompanied by a strong perfume of exotic blossoms.

"Monsieur le Comte de la Roche?"

"At your service, Mademoiselle," said the Comte, bowing.

"My name is Mirelle. You may have heard of me."

"Ah, indeed, Mademoiselle, but who has not been enchanted by the dancing of Mademoiselle Mirelle? Exquisite!"

The dancer acknowledged this compliment with a brief mechanical smile.

"My descent upon you is unceremonious," she began.

"But seat yourself, I beg of you, Mademoiselle," cried the Comte, bringing forward a chair.

Behind the gallantry of his manner he was observing her narrowly. There were very few things that the Comte did not know about women. True, his experience had not lain much in ladies of Mirelle's class, who were themselves predatory. He and the dancer were, in a sense, birds of a feather. His arts, the Comte knew, would be thrown away on Mirelle. She was a Parisienne, and a shrewd one. Nevertheless, there was one thing that the Comte could recognize infallibly when he saw it. He knew at once that he was in the presence of a very angry woman, and an angry woman, as the Comte was well aware, always says more than is prudent, and is occasionally a source of profit to a level-headed gentleman who keeps cool.

"It is most amiable of you, Mademoiselle, to honor my poor abode thus."

"We have mutual friends in Paris," said Mirelle. "I have heard of you from them, but I come to see you today for another reason. I have heard of you since I came to Nice—in a different way, you understand."

"Ah?" said the Comte softly.

"I will be brutal," continued the dancer; "nevertheless, believe that I have your welfare at heart. They are saying in Nice, Monsieur le Comte, that you are the murderer of the English lady, Madame Kettering."

"I!—the murderer of Madame Kettering? Bah! But how absurd!"

He spoke more languidly than indignantly, knowing that he would thus provoke her further.

"But yes," she insisted; "it is as I tell you."

"It amuses people to talk," murmured the Comte indifferently. "It would be beneath me to take such wild accusations seriously."

"You do not understand." Mirelle bent forward, her dark eyes flashing. "It is not the idle talk of those in the streets. It is the police."

"The police—ah?"

The Comte sat up, alert once more.

Mirelle nodded her head vigorously several times.

"Yes, yes. You comprehend me—I have friends everywhere. The Prefect himself——" She left the sentence unfinished, with an eloquent shrug of the shoulders.

"Who is not indiscreet where a beautiful woman is concerned?" murmured the Count politely.

"The police believe that you killed Madame Kettering. But they are wrong."

"Certainly they are wrong," agreed the Comte easily.

"You say that, but you do not know the truth. I do."

The Comte looked at her curiously.

"You know who killed Madame Kettering? Is that what you would say, Mademoiselle?"

Mirelle nodded vehemently.

"Yes."

"Who was it?" asked the Comte sharply.

"Her husband." She bent nearer to the Comte, speaking in a low voice that vibrated with anger and excitement. "It was her husband who killed her."

The Comte leaned back in his chair. His face was a mask.

"Let me ask you, Mademoiselle—how do you know this?"

"How do I know it?" Mirelle sprang to her feet, with a laugh. "He boasted of it beforehand. He was ruined, bankrupt, dishonored. Only the death of his wife could save him. He told me so. He traveled on the same train—but she was not to know it. Why was that, I ask you? So that he might creep upon her in the night——Ah!"—she shut her eyes—"I can see it happening. . . ."

The Count coughed.

"Perhaps—perhaps," he murmured. "But surely, Mademoiselle, in that case he would not steal the jewels?"

"The jewels!" breathed Mirelle. "The jewels. Ah! Those rubies . . ."

Her eyes grew misty, a faraway light in them. The Comte looked at her curiously, wondering for the hundredth time at the magical influence of precious stones on the female sex. He recalled her to practical matters.

"What do you want me to do, Mademoiselle?"

Mirelle became alert and businesslike once more.

"Surely it is simple. You will go to the police. You will say to them that M. Kettering committed this crime."

"And if they do not believe me? If they ask for proof?" He was eyeing her closely.

Mirelle laughed softly, and drew her orange-and-black wrap closer round her.

"Send them to me, Monsieur le Comte," she said softly; "I will give them the proof they want."

Upon that she was gone, an impetuous whirlwind, her errand accomplished.

The Comte looked after her, his eyebrows delicately raised.

"She is in a fury," he murmured. "What has happened now to upset her? But she shows her hand too plainly. Does she really believe that M. Kettering killed his wife? She would like me to believe it. She would even like the police to believe it."

He smiled to himself. He had no intention whatsoever of going to the police. He saw various other possibilities; to judge by his smile, an agreeable vista of them.

Presently, however, his brow clouded. According to Mirelle, he was suspected by the police. That might be true or it might not. An angry woman of the type of the dancer was not likely to bother about the strict veracity of her statements. On the other hand, she might easily have obtained—inside information. In that case—his mouth set grimly—in that case he must take certain precautions.

He went into the house and questioned Hippolyte closely once more as to whether any strangers had been to the house. The valet was positive in his assurances that this was not the case. The Comte went up to his bedroom and crossed over to an old bureau that stood against the wall. He let down the lid of this, and his delicate fingers sought for a spring at the back of one of the pigeonholes. A secret drawer flew out; in it was a small brown paper package. The Comte took this out and weighed it in his hand carefully for a minute or two. Raising his hand to his head, with a slight grimace he pulled out a single hair. This he placed on the lip of the drawer and shut it carefully. Still carrying the small parcel in his hand, he went downstairs and out of the house to the garage, where stood a scarlet two-seater car. Ten minutes later he had taken the road for Monte Carlo.

He spent a few hours at the Casino, then sauntered out into the town. Presently he re-entered the car and drove off in the direction of Mentone. Earlier in the afternoon he had noticed an inconspicuous gray car some little distance behind him. He noticed it again now. He smiled to himself. The road was climbing steadily upward. The Comte's foot pressed hard on the accelerator. The little red car had been specially built to the Comte's design, and had a far more powerful engine than would have been suspected from its appearance. It shot ahead.

Presently he looked back and smiled; the gray car was following behind. Smothered in dust, the little red car leaped along the road. It was traveling now at a dangerous pace, but the Comte was a first-class driver. Now they were going downhill, twisting and curving unceasingly. Presently the car slackened speed, and finally came to a standstill before a Bureau de Poste. The Comte jumped out, lifted the lid of the tool chest, extracted the small brown paper parcel and hurried into the post office. Two minutes later he was driving once more in the direction of Mentone. When the gray car arrived there, the Comte was drinking English five o'clock tea on the terrace of one of the hotels.

Later, he drove back to Monte Carlo, dined there, and reached home once more at eleven o'clock. Hippolyte came out to meet him with a disturbed face.

"Ah! Monsieur le Comte has arrived. Monsieur le Comte did not telephone me, by any chance?"

The Comte shook his head.

"And yet at three o'clock I received a summons from Monsieur le Comte, to present myself to him at Nice, at the Negresco."

"Really," said the Comte; "and you went?"

"Certainly, Monsieur, but at the Negresco they knew nothing of Monsieur le Comte. He had not been there."

"Ah," said the Comte, "doubtless at that hour Marie was out doing her afternoon marketing?"

"That is so, Monsieur le Comte."

"Ah, well," said the Comte, "it is of no importance. A mistake."

He went upstairs, smiling to himself.

Once within his own room, he bolted his door and looked sharply around. Everything seemed as usual. He opened various drawers and cupboards. Then he nodded to himself. Things had been replaced almost exactly as he had left them, but not quite. It was evident that a very thorough search had been made.

He went over to the bureau and pressed the hidden spring. The drawer flew open, but the hair was no longer where he had placed it. He nodded his head several times.

"They are excellent, our French police," he murmured to himself—"excellent. Nothing escapes them."

20

Katherine Makes a Friend

ON THE FOLLOWING morning Katherine and Lenox were sitting on the terrace of the Villa Marguerite. Something in the nature of a friendship was springing up between them, despite the difference in age. But for Lenox, Katherine would have found life at the Villa Marguerite quite intolerable. The Kettering case was the topic of the moment. Lady Tamplin frankly exploited her guest's connection with the affair for all it was worth. The most persistent rebuffs that Katherine could administer quite failed to pierce Lady Tamplin's self-esteem. Lenox adopted a detached attitude, seemingly amused at her mother's maneuvers, and yet with a sympathetic understanding of Katherine's feelings. The situation was not helped by Chubby, whose naïve delight was unquenchable, and who introduced Katherine to all and sundry as:

"This is Miss Grey. You know that Blue Train business? She was in it up to the ears! Had a long talk with Ruth Kettering a few hours before the murder! Bit of luck for her, eh?"

A few remarks of this kind had provoked Katherine that morning to an unusually tart rejoinder, and when they were alone together Lenox observed in her slow drawl:

"Not used to exploitation, are you? You have a lot to learn, Katherine."

"I am sorry I lost my temper. I don't, as a rule."

"It is about time you learnt to blow off steam. Chubby is only an ass; there is no harm in him. Mother, of course, is trying, but you can lose your temper with her until Kingdom come, and it won't make any impression. She will open large, sad blue eyes at you and not care a bit."

Katherine made no reply to this filial observation, and Lenox presently went on:

"I am rather like Chubby. I delight in a good murder, and besides—well, knowing Derek makes a difference."

Katherine nodded.

"So you lunched with him yesterday," pursued Lenox reflectively. "Do you like him, Katherine?"

Katherine considered for a minute or two.

"I don't know," she said very slowly.

"He is very attractive."

"Yes, he is attractive."

"What don't you like about him?"

Katherine did not reply to the question, or at any rate not directly. "He spoke of his wife's death," she said. "He said he would not pretend that it had been anything but a bit of most marvelous luck for him."

"And that shocked you, I suppose," said Lenox. She paused, and then added in rather a queer tone of voice: "He likes you, Katherine."

"He gave me a very good lunch," said Katherine, smiling.

Lenox refused to be sidetracked.

"I saw it the night he came here," she said thoughtfully. "The way he looked at you; and you are not his usual type—just the opposite. Well, I suppose it is like religion—you get it at a certain age."

"Mademoiselle is wanted at the telephone," said Marie, appearing at the window of the salon. "M. Hercule Poirot desires to speak with her."

"More blood and thunder. Go on, Katherine; go and dally with your detective."

M. Hercule Poirot's voice came neat and precise in its intonation to Katherine's ear.

"That is Mademoiselle Grey who speaks? *Bon.* Mademoiselle, I have a word for you from M. Van Aldin, the father of Madame Kettering. He wishes very much to speak with you, either at the Villa Marguerite or at his hotel, whichever you prefer."

Katherine reflected for a moment, but she decided that for Van Aldin to come to the Villa Marguerite would be both painful and unnecessary. Lady Tamplin would have hailed his advent with far too much delight. She never lost a chance of cultivating millionaires. She told Poirot that she would much rather come to Nice.

"Excellent, Mademoiselle. I will call for you myself in an auto. Shall we say in about three-quarters of an hour?"

Punctually to the moment Poirot appeared. Katherine was waiting for him, and they drove off at once.

"Well, Mademoiselle, how goes it?"

She looked at his twinkling eyes, and was confirmed in her first impression that there was something very attractive about M. Hercule Poirot.

"This is our own Roman Policier, is it not?" said Poirot. "I made you the promise that we should study it together. And me, I always keep my promises."

"You are too kind," murmured Katherine.

"Ah, you mock yourself at me; but do you want to hear the developments of the case, or do you not?"

Katherine admitted that she did, and Poirot proceeded to sketch for her a thumbnail portrait of the Comte de la Roche.

"You think he killed her," said Katherine thoughtfully.

"That is the theory," said Poirot guardedly.

"Do you yourself believe that?"

"I did not say so. And you, Mademoiselle, what do think?"

Katherine shook her head.

"How should I know? I don't know anything about those things, but I should say that——"

"Yes," said Poirot encouragingly.

"Well—from what you say the Count does not sound the kind of man who would actually kill anybody."

"Ah! Very good," cried Poirot, "you agree with me; that is just what I have said." He looked at her sharply. "But tell me, you have met Mr. Derek Kettering?"

"I met him at Lady Tamplin's, and I lunched with him yesterday."

"A *mauvais sujet,*" said Poirot, shaking his head; "but *les femmes*—they like that, eh?"

He twinkled at Katherine and she laughed.

"He is the kind of man one would notice anywhere," continued Poirot. "Doubtless you observed him on the Blue Train?"

"Yes, I noticed him."

"In the restaurant car?"

"No. I didn't notice him at meals at all. I only saw him once—going into his wife's compartment."

Poirot nodded. "A strange business," he murmured. "I believe you said you were awake, Mademoiselle, and looked out of your window at Lyons? You saw no tall dark man such as the Comte de la Roche leave the train?"

Katherine shook her head. "I don't think I saw anyone at all," she said. "There was a youngish lad in a cap and overcoat who got out, but I don't think he was leaving the train, only walking up and down the platform. There was a fat Frenchman with a beard, in pyjamas and an overcoat, who wanted a cup of coffee. Otherwise, I think there were only the train attendants."

Poirot nodded his head several times. "It is like this, you see," he confided, "the Comte de la Roche has an alibi. An alibi, it is a very pestilential thing, and always open to the gravest suspicion. But here we are!"

They went straight up to Van Aldin's suite, where they found Knighton. Poirot introduced him to Katherine. After a few commonplaces had been exchanged, Knighton said, "I will tell Mr. Van Aldin that Miss Grey is here."

He went through a second door into an adjoining room. There was a low murmur of voices, and then Van Aldin came into the room and advanced toward Katherine with outstretched hand, giving her at the same time a shrewd and penetrating glance.

"I am pleased to meet you, Miss Grey," he said simply. "I have been wanting very badly to hear what you can tell me about Ruth."

The quiet simplicity of the millionaire's manner appealed to Katherine strongly. She felt herself in the presence of a very genuine grief, the more real for its absence of outward sign.

He drew forward a chair.

"Sit here, will you, and just tell me all about it."

Poirot and Knighton retired discreetly into the other room, and Katherine and Van Aldin were left alone together. She found no difficulty in her task. Quite simply and naturally she related her conversation with Ruth Kettering, word for word as nearly as she could. He listened in silence, leaning back in his chair, with one hand shading his eyes. When she had finished he said quietly:

"Thank you, my dear."

They both sat silent for a minute or two. Katherine felt that words of sympathy would be out of place. When the millionaire spoke, it was in a different tone:

"I am very grateful to you, Miss Grey. I think you did something to ease my poor Ruth's mind in the last hours of her life. Now I want to ask you something. You know—M. Poirot will have told you—about the scoundrel that my poor girl had got herself mixed up with. He was the man of whom she spoke to you—the man she was going to meet. In your judgment do you think she might have changed her mind after her conversation with you? Do you think she meant to go back on her word?"

"I can't honestly tell you. She had certainly come to some decision, and seemed more cheerful in consequence of it."

"She gave you no idea where she intended to meet the skunk—whether in Paris or at Hyères?"

Katherine shook her head.

"She said nothing as to that."

"Ah!" said Van Aldin thoughtfully, "and that is the important point. Well, time will show."

He got up and opened the door of the adjoining room. Poirot and Knighton came back.

Katherine declined the millionaire's invitation to lunch, and Knighton went down with her and saw her into the waiting car. He returned to find Poirot and Van Aldin deep in conversation.

"If we only knew," said the millionaire thoughtfully, "what decision Ruth came to. It might have been any of half a dozen. She might have meant to leave the train at Paris and cable to me. She may have meant to have gone on to the south of France and have an explanation with the Count there. We are in the dark—absolutely in the dark. But we have the maid's word for it that she was both startled and dismayed at the Count's appearance at the station in Paris. That was clearly not part of the preconceived plan. You agree with me, Knighton?"

The secretary started. "I beg your pardon, Mr. Van Aldin. I was not listening."

"Daydreaming, eh?" said Van Aldin. "That's not like you. I believe that girl has bowled you over."

Knighton blushed.

"She is a remarkably nice girl," said Van Aldin thoughtfully, "very nice. Did you happen to notice her eyes?"

"Any man," said Knighton, "would be bound to notice her eyes."

21

At the Tennis

SEVERAL DAYS HAD elapsed. Katherine had been for a walk by herself one morning, and came back to find Lenox grinning at her expectantly.

"Your young man has been ringing you up, Katherine!"

"Who do you call my young man?"

"A new one—Rufus Van Aldin's secretary. You seem to have made rather an impression there. You are becoming a serious breaker of hearts, Katherine. First Derek Kettering, and now this young Knighton. The funny thing is, that I remember him quite well. He was in Mother's War Hospital that she ran out here. I was only a kid of about eight at the time."

"Was he badly wounded?"

"Shot in the leg, if I remember rightly—rather a nasty business. I think the doctors messed it up a bit. They said he wouldn't limp or anything, but when he left here he was still completely dot and go one."

Lady Tamplin came out and joined them.

"Have you been telling Katherine about Major Knighton?" she asked. "Such a dear fellow! Just at first I didn't remember him—one had so many—but now it all comes back."

"He was a bit too unimportant to be remembered before," said Lenox. "Now that he is a secretary to an American millionaire, it is a very different matter."

"Darling!" said Lady Tamplin in her vague reproachful voice.

"What did Major Knighton ring up about?" inquired Katherine.

"He asked if you would like to go to the tennis this afternoon. If so, he would call for you in a car. Mother and I accepted for you with *empressement.* Whilst you dally with a millionaire's secretary, you might give me a chance with the millionaire, Katherine. He is about sixty, I suppose, so that he will be looking about for a nice sweet young thing like me."

"I should like to meet Mr. Van Aldin," said Lady Tamplin earnestly; "one has heard so much of him. Those fine rugged figures of the Western world"—she broke off—"so fascinating," she murmured.

"Major Knighton was very particular to say it was Mr. Van Aldin's invitation," said Lenox. "He said it so often that I began to smell a rat. You and Knighton would make a very nice pair, Katherine. Bless you, my children!"

Katherine laughed, and went upstairs to change her clothes.

Knighton arrived soon after lunch and endured manfully Lady Tamplin's transports of recognition.

When they were driving together toward Cannes he remarked to Katherine: "Lady Tamplin has changed wonderfully little."

"In manner or appearance?"

"Both. She must be, I suppose, well over forty, but she is a remarkably beautiful woman still."

"She is," agreed Katherine.

"I am very glad that you could come today," went on Knighton. "M. Poirot is going to be there also. What an extraordinary little man he is. Do you know him well, Miss Grey?"

Katherine shook her head. "I met him on the train on the way here. I was reading a detective novel, and I happened to say something about such things not happening in real life. Of course, I had no idea of who he was."

"He is a very remarkable person," said Knighton slowly, "and has done some very remarkable things. He has a kind of genius for going to the root of the matter, and right up to the end no one has any idea of what he is really thinking. I remember I was staying at a house in Yorkshire, and Lady Clanravon's jewels were stolen. It seemed at first to be a simple robbery, but it completely baffled the local police. I wanted them to call in Hercule Poirot, and said he was the only man who could help them, but they pinned their faith to Scotland Yard."

"And what happened?" said Katherine curiously.

"The jewels were never recovered," said Knighton dryly.

"You really do believe in him?"

"I do indeed. The Comte de la Roche is a pretty wily customer. He has wriggled out of most things. But I think he has met his match in Hercule Poirot."

"The Comte de la Roche," said Katherine thoughtfully; "so you really think he did it?"

"Of course." Knighton looked at her in astonishment. "Don't you?"

"Oh yes," said Katherine hastily; "that is, I mean, if it was not just an ordinary train robbery."

"It might be, of course," agreed the other, "but it seems to me that the Comte de la Roche fits into this business particularly well."

"And yet he has an alibi."

"Oh, alibis!" Knighton laughed; his face broke into his attractive boyish smile.

"You confess that you read detective stories, Miss Grey. You must know that anyone who has a perfect alibi is always open to grave suspicion."

"Do you think that real life is like that?" asked Katherine, smiling.

"Why not? Fiction is founded on fact."

"But is rather superior to it," suggested Katherine.

"Perhaps. Anyway, if I was a criminal I should not like to have Hercule Poirot on my track."

"No more should I," said Katherine, and laughed.

They were met on arrival by Poirot. As the day was warm he was attired in a white duck suit, with a white camellia in his buttonhole.

"Bonjour, Mademoiselle," said Poirot. "I look very English, do I not?"

"You look wonderful," said Katherine tactfully.

"You mock yourself at me," said Poirot genially, "but no matter. Papa Poirot, he always laughs the last."

"Where is Mr. Van Aldin?" asked Knighton.

"He will meet us at our seats. To tell you the truth, my friend, he is not too well pleased with me. Oh, those Americans—the repose, the calm, they know it not! Mr. Van Aldin, he would that I fly myself in the pursuit of criminals through all the byways of Nice."

"I should have thought myself that it would not have been a bad plan," observed Knighton.

"You are wrong," said Poirot; "in these matters one needs not energy but finesse. At the tennis one meets everyone. That is so important. Ah, there is Mr. Kettering."

Derek came abruptly up to them. He looked reckless and angry, as though something had arisen to upset him. He and Knighton greeted each other with some frigidity. Poirot alone seemed unconscious of any sense of strain, and chatted pleasantly in a laudable attempt to put everyone at their ease. He paid little compliments.

"It is amazing, M. Kettering, how well you speak the French," he observed —"so well that you could be taken for a Frenchman if you chose. That is a very rare accomplishment among Englishmen."

"I wish I did," said Katherine. "I am only too well aware that my French is of a painfully British order."

They reached their seats and sat down, and almost immediately Knighton perceived his employer signaling to him from the other end of the court, and went off to speak to him.

"Me, I approve of that young man," said Poirot, sending a beaming smile after the departing secretary; "and you, Mademoiselle?"

"I like him very much."

"And you, M. Kettering?"

Some quick rejoinder was springing to Derek's lips, but he checked it as though something in the little Belgian's twinkling eyes had made him suddenly alert. He spoke carefully, choosing his words.

"Knighton is a very good fellow," he said.

Just for a moment Katherine fancied that Poirot looked disappointed.

"He is a great admirer of yours, M. Poirot," she said, and she related some of the things that Knighton had said. It amused her to see the little man plume himself like a bird, thrusting out his chest, and assuming an air of mock modesty that would have deceived no one.

"That reminds me, Mademoiselle," he said suddenly, "I have a little matter of business I have to speak to you about. When you were sitting talking to that poor lady in the train, I think you must have dropped a cigarette case."

Katherine looked rather astonished. "I don't think so," she said. Poirot drew from his pocket a cigarette case of soft blue leather, with the initial K on it in gold.

"No, that is not mine," Katherine said.

"Ah, a thousand apologies. It was doubtless Madame's own. K, of course, stands for Kettering. We were doubtful, because she had another cigarette case in her bag, and it seemed odd that she should have two." He turned to Derek suddenly. "You do not know, I suppose, whether this was your wife's case or not?"

Derek seemed momentarily taken aback. He stammered a little in his reply: "I—I don't know. I suppose so."

"It is not yours by any chance?"

"Certainly not. If it were mine it would hardly have been in my wife's possession."

Poirot looked more ingenuous and childlike than ever.

"I thought perhaps you might have dropped it when you were in your wife's compartment," he explained guilelessly.

"I never was there. I have already told the police that a dozen times."

"A thousand pardons," said Poirot, with his most apologetic air. "It was Mademoiselle here who mentioned having seen you going in."

He stopped with an air of embarrassment.

Katherine looked at Derek. His face had gone rather white, but perhaps that was her fancy. His laugh, when it came, was natural enough.

"You made a mistake, Miss Grey," he said easily. "From what the police have told me, I gather that my own compartment was only a door or two away from that of my wife's—though I never suspected the fact at the time. You must have seen me going into my own compartment." He got up quickly as he saw Van Aldin and Knighton approaching.

"I'm going to leave you now," he announced. "I can't stand my father-in-law at any price."

Van Aldin greeted Katherine very courteously, but was clearly in a bad humor.

"You seem fond of watching tennis, M. Poirot," he growled.

"It is a pleasure to me, yes," cried Poirot placidly.

"It is as well you are in France," said Van Aldin. "We are made of sterner stuff in the States. Business comes before pleasure there."

Poirot did not take offense; indeed, he smiled gently and confidingly at the irate millionaire.

"Do not enrage yourself, I beg of you. Every one his own methods. Me, I have always found it a delightful and pleasing idea to combine business and pleasure together."

He glanced at the other two. They were deep in conversation, absorbed in each other. Poirot nodded his head in satisfaction, and then leaned toward the millionaire, lowering his voice as he did so.

"It is not only for pleasure that I am here, M. Van Aldin. Observe just opposite us that tall old man—the one with the yellow face and the venerable beard."

"Well, what of him?"

"That," Poirot said, "is M. Papopolous."

"A Greek, eh?"

"As you say—a Greek. He is a dealer in antiques of worldwide reputation. He has a small shop in Paris, and he is suspected by the police of being something more."

"What?"

"A receiver of stolen goods, especially jewels. There is nothing as to the recutting and resetting of gems that he does not know. He deals with the highest in Europe and with the lowest of the riff-raff of the underworld."

Van Aldin was looking at Poirot with suddenly awakened attention.

"Well?" he demanded, a new note in his voice.

"I ask myself," said Poirot, "I, Hercule Poirot"—he thumped himself dramatically on the chest—"ask myself *why is M. Papopolous suddenly come to Nice?*"

Van Aldin was impressed. For a moment he had doubted Poirot and suspected the little man of being past his job, a *poseur* only. Now, in a moment, he switched back to his original opinion. He looked straight at the little detective.

"I must apologize to you, M. Poirot."

Poirot waved the apology aside with an extravagant gesture.

"Bah!" he cried, "all that is of no importance. Now listen, M. Van Aldin; I have news for you."

The millionaire looked sharply at him, all his interest aroused.

Poirot nodded.

"It is as I say. You will be interested. As you know, M. Van Aldin, the Comte de la Roche has been under surveillance ever since his interview with the Juge d'Instruction. The day after that, during his absence, the Villa Marina was searched by the police."

"Well," said Van Aldin, "did they find anything? I bet they didn't."

Poirot made him a little bow.

"Your acumen is not at fault, M. Van Aldin. They found nothing of an incriminating nature. It was not to be expected that they would. The Comte de la Roche, as your expressive idiom has it, was not born on the preceding day. He is an astute gentleman with great experience."

"Well, go on," growled Van Aldin.

"It may be, of course, that the Comte had nothing of a compromising nature to conceal. But we must not neglect the possibility. If, then, he has something to conceal, where is it? Not in his house—the police searched thoroughly. Not on his person, for he knows that he is liable to arrest at any minute. There remains—his car. As I say, he was under surveillance. He was followed on that day to Monte Carlo. From there he went by road to Mentone, driving himself. His car is a very powerful one, it outdistanced his pursuers, and for about a quarter of an hour they completely lost sight of him."

"And during that time you think he concealed something by the roadside?" asked Van Aldin, keenly interested.

"By the roadside, no. *Ça n'est pas pratique.* But listen now—me, I have made a little suggestion to M. Carrège. He is graciously pleased to approve of it. In each Bureau de Poste in the neighborhood it has been seen to that there is someone who knows the Comte de la Roche by sight. Because, you see, Messieurs, the best way of hiding a thing is by sending it away by the post."

"Well?" demanded Van Aldin; his face was keenly alight with interest and expectation.

"Well—*voilà!*" With a dramatic flourish Poirot drew out from his pocket a loosely wrapped brown paper package from which the string had been removed.

"During that quarter of an hour's interval, our good gentleman mailed this."

"The address?" asked the other sharply.

Poirot nodded his head.

"Might have told us something, but unfortunately it does not. The package was addressed to one of these little newspaper shops in Paris where letters and parcels are kept until called for on payment of a small commission."

"Yes, but what is inside?" demanded Van Aldin impatiently.

Poirot unwrapped the brown paper and disclosed a square cardboard box. He looked around him.

"It is a good moment," he said quietly. "All eyes are on the tennis. Look, Monsieur!"

He lifted the lid of the box for the fraction of a second. An exclamation of utter astonishment came from the millionaire. His face turned as white as chalk.

"My God!" he breathed, "the rubies."

He sat for a minute as though dazed. Poirot restored the box to his pocket and beamed placidly. Then suddenly the millionaire seemed to come out of his trance; he leaned across to Poirot and wrung his hand so heartily that the little man winced with pain.

"This is great," said Van Aldin. "Great! You are the goods, M. Poirot. Once and for all, you are the goods."

"It is nothing," said Poirot modestly. "Order, method, being prepared for eventualities beforehand—that is all there is to it."

"And now, I suppose, the Comte de la Roche has been arrested?" continued Van Aldin eagerly.

"No," said Poirot.

A look of utter astonishment came over Van Aldin's face.

"But why? What more do you want?"

"The Comte's alibi is still unshaken."

"But that is nonsense."

"Yes," said Poirot; "I rather think it is nonsense, but unfortunately we have to prove it so."

"In the meantime he will slip through your fingers."

Poirot shook his head very energetically.

"No," he said, "he will not do that. The one thing the Comte cannot afford to sacrifice is his social position. At all costs he must stop and brazen it out."

Van Aldin was still dissatisfied.

"But I don't see——"

Poirot raised a hand. "Grant me a little moment, Monsieur. Me, I have a little idea. Many people have mocked themselves at the little ideas of Hercule Poirot—and they have been wrong."

"Well," said Van Aldin, "go ahead. What is this little idea?"

Poirot paused for a moment and then he said:

"I will call upon you at your hotel at eleven o'clock tomorrow morning. Until then, say nothing to anyone."

22

M. Papopolous Breakfasts

M. PAPOPOLOUS WAS at breakfast. Opposite him sat his daughter, Zia.

There was a knock at the sitting room door, and a chasseur entered with a card which he brought to Mr. Papopolous. The latter scrutinized it, raised his eyebrows, and passed it over to his daughter.

"Ah!" said M. Papopolous, scratching his left ear thoughtfully, "Hercule Poirot. I wonder now."

Father and daughter looked at each other.

"I saw him yesterday at the tennis," said M. Papopolous. "Zia, I hardly like this."

"He was very useful to you once," his daughter reminded him.

"That is true," acknowledged M. Papopolous; "also he has retired from active work, so I hear."

These interchanges between father and daughter had passed in their own language. Now M. Papopolous turned to the chasseur and said in French: *"Faites monter ce monsieur."*

A few minutes later Hercule Poirot, exquisitely attired, and swinging a cane with a jaunty air, entered the room.

"My dear M. Papopolous."

"My dear M. Poirot."

"And Mademoiselle Zia." Poirot swept her a low bow.

"You will excuse us going on with our breakfast," said M. Papopolous, pouring himself out another cup of coffee. "Your call is—ahem!—a little early."

"It is scandalous," said Poirot, "but see you, I am pressed."

"Ah!" murmured M. Papopolous, "you are on an affair then?"

"A very serious affair," said Poirot: "the death of Madame Kettering."

"Let me see," M. Papopolous looked innocently up at the ceiling, "that was the lady who died on the Blue Train, was it not? I saw a mention of it in the papers, but there was no suggestion of foul play."

"In the interests of justice," said Poirot, "it was thought best to suppress that fact."

There was a pause.

"And in what way can I assist you, M. Poirot?" asked the dealer politely.

"Voilà," said Poirot, "I shall come to the point." He took from his pocket the same box that he had displayed at Cannes, and, opening it, he took out the rubies and pushed them across the table to Papopolous.

Although Poirot was watching him narrowly, not a muscle of the old man's face moved. He took up the jewels and examined them with a kind of detached interest, then he looked across at the detective inquiringly:

"Superb, are they not?" asked Poirot.

"Quite excellent," said M. Papopolous.

"How much should you say they are worth?"

The Greek's face quivered a little.

"Is it really necessary to tell you, M. Poirot?" he asked.

"You are shrewd, M. Papopolous. No, it is not. They are not, for instance, worth five hundred thousand dollars."

Papopolous laughed, and Poirot joined with him.

"As an imitation," said Papopolous, handing them back to Poirot, "they are, as I said, quite excellent. Would it be indiscreet to ask, M. Poirot, where you came across them?"

"Not at all," said Poirot; "I have no objection to telling an old friend like yourself. They were in the possession of the Comte de la Roche."

M. Papopolous' eyebrows lifted themselves eloquently.

"Indeed," he murmured.

Poirot leaned forward and assumed his most innocent and beguiling air.

"M. Papopolous," he said, "I am going to lay my cards upon the table. The original of these jewels was stolen from Madame Kettering on the Blue Train. Now I will say to you first this: *I am not concerned with the recovery of these jewels. That is the affair of the police.* I am working not for the police but for M. Van Aldin. I want to lay hands on the man who killed Madame Kettering. I am interested in the jewels only in so far as they may lead me to the man. You understand?"

The last two words were uttered with great significance. M. Papopolous, his face quite unmoved, said quietly:

"Go on."

"It seems to me probable, Monsieur, that the jewels will change hands in Nice—may already have done so."

"Ah!" said M. Papopolous.

He sipped his coffee reflectively, and looked a shade more noble and patriarchal than usual.

"I say to myself," continued Poirot, with animation, "what good fortune! My old friend, M. Papopolous, is in Nice. He will aid me."

"And how do you think I can aid you?" inquired M. Papopolous coldly.

"I said to myself, without doubt M. Papopolous is in Nice on business."

"Not at all," said M. Papopolous, "I am here for my health—by the doctor's orders."

He coughed hollowly.

"I am desolated to hear it," replied Poirot, with somewhat insincere sympathy. "But to continue. When a Russian Grand Duke, an Austrian Archduchess, or an Italian Prince wish to dispose of their family jewels—to whom do they go? To M. Papopolous, is it not? He who is famous all over the world for the discretion with which he arranges these things."

The other bowed.

"You flatter me."

"It is a great thing, discretion," mused Poirot, and was rewarded by the fleeting smile which passed across the Greek's face. "I, too, can be discreet."

The eyes of the two men met.

Then Poirot went on speaking very slowly, and obviously picking his words with care.

"I say to myself, this: if these jewels have changed hands in Nice, M. Papopolous would have heard of it. He has knowledge of all that passes in the jewel world."

"Ah!" said M. Papopolous, and helped himself to a croissant.

"The police, you understand," said M. Poirot, "do not enter into the matter. It is a personal affair."

"One hears rumors," admitted M. Papopolous cautiously.

"Such as?" prompted Poirot.

"Is there any reason why I should pass them on?"

"Yes," said Poirot, "I think there is. You may remember, M. Papopolous, that seventeen years ago there was a certain article in your hands, left there as security by a very—er—Prominent Person. It was in your keeping and it unaccountably disappeared. You were, if I may use the English expression, in the soup."

His eyes came gently round to the girl. She had pushed her cup and plate aside, and with both elbows on the table and her chin resting on her hands was listening eagerly. Still keeping an eye on her he went on:

"I am in Paris at the time. You send for me. You place yourself in my hands. If I restore to you that—article, you say I shall earn your undying gratitude. *Eh bien!* I did restore it to you."

A long sigh came from M. Papopolous.

"It was the most unpleasant moment of my career," he murmured.

"Seventeen years is a long time," said Poirot thoughtfully, "but I believe that I am right in saying, Monsieur, that your race does not forget."

"A Greek?" murmured Papopolous, with an ironical smile.

"It was not as a Greek I meant," said Poirot.

There was a silence, and then the old man drew himself up proudly.

"You are right, M. Poirot," he said quietly. "I am a Jew. And, as you say, our race does not forget."

"You will aid me then?"

"As regards the jewels, Monsieur, I can do nothing."

The old man, as Poirot had done just now, picked his words carefully.

"I know nothing. I have heard nothing. But I can perhaps do you a good turn—that is, if you are interested in racing."

"Under certain circumstances I might be," said Poirot, eyeing him steadily.

"There is a horse running at Longchamps that would, I think, repay attention. I cannot say for certain, you understand; this news passed through so many hands."

He stopped, fixing Poirot with his eye, as though to make sure that the latter was comprehending him.

"Perfectly, perfectly," said Poirot, nodding.

"The name of the horse," said M. Papopolous, leaning back and joining the tips of his fingers together, "is the Marquis. I think, but I am not sure, that it is an English horse, eh, Zia?"

"I think so too," said the girl.

Poirot got up briskly.

"I thank you, Monsieur," he said. "It is a great thing to have what the English call a tip from the stable. *Au revoir,* Monsieur, and many thanks."

He turned to the girl.

"*Au revoir,* Mademoiselle Zia. It seems to me but yesterday that I saw you in Paris. One would say that two years had passed at most."

"There is a difference between sixteen and thirty-three," said Zia ruefully.

"Not in your case," declared Poirot gallantly. "You and your father will perhaps dine with me one night."

"We shall be delighted," replied Zia.

"Then we will arrange it," declared Poirot, "and now—*je me sauve.*"

Poirot walked along the street humming a little tune to himself. He twirled his stick with a jaunty air, once or twice he smiled to himself quietly. He turned into the first Bureau de Poste he came to and sent off a telegram. He took some time in wording it, but it was in code and he had to call upon his memory. It purported to deal with a missing scarf-pin, and was addressed to Inspector Japp, Scotland Yard.

Decoded, it was short and to the point.

Wire me everything known about man whose soubriquet is the Marquis.

23

A New Theory

IT WAS EXACTLY eleven o'clock when Poirot presented himself at Van Aldin's hotel. He found the millionaire alone.

"You are punctual, M. Poirot," he said, with a smile, as he rose to greet the detective.

"I am always punctual," said Poirot. "The exactitude—always do I observe it. Without order and method——"

He broke off. "Ah, but it is possible that I have said these things to you before. Let us come at once to the object of my visit."

"Your little idea?"

"Yes, my little idea." Poirot smiled.

"First of all, Monsieur, I should like to interview once more the maid, Ada Mason. She is here?"

"Yes, she's here."

"Ah!"

Van Aldin looked at him curiously. He rang the bell, and a messenger was dispatched to find Mason.

Poirot greeted her with his usual politeness, which was never without effect on that particular class.

"Good afternoon, Mademoiselle," he said cheerfully. "Be seated, will you not, if Monsieur permits."

"Yes, yes, sit down, my girl," said Van Aldin.

"Thank you, sir," said Mason primly, and she sat down on the extreme edge of a chair. She looked bonier and more acid than ever.

"I have come to ask you yet more questions," said Poirot. "We must get to the bottom of this affair. Always I return to the question of the man in the train. You have been shown the Comte de la Roche. You say that it is possible he was the man, but you are not sure."

"As I told you, sir, I never saw the gentleman's face. That is what makes it so difficult."

Poirot beamed and nodded.

"Precisely, exactly. I comprehend well the difficulty. Now, Mademoiselle, you have been in the service of Madame Kettering two months, you say. During that time, how often did you see your master?"

Mason reflected a minute or two, and then said:

"Only twice, sir."

"And was that near to, or far away?"

"Well once, sir, he came to Curzon Street. I was upstairs, and I looked over the banisters and saw him in the hall below. I was a bit curious like, you understand, knowing the way things—er—were." Mason finished up with her discreet cough.

"And the other time?"

"I was in the Park, sir, with Annie—one of the housemaids, sir, and she pointed out the master to me walking with a foreign lady."

Again Poirot nodded.

"Now listen, Mason, this man whom you saw in the carriage talking to your mistress at the Gare de Lyon, how do you know it was not your master?"

"The master, sir? Oh, I don't think it could have been."

"But you are not sure," Poirot persisted.

"Well—I never thought of it, sir."

Mason was clearly upset at the idea.

"You have heard that your master was also on the train. What more natural than that it should be he who came along the corridor."

"But the gentleman who was talking to the mistress must have come from outside, sir. He was dressed for the street. In an overcoat and soft hat."

"Just so, Mademoiselle, but reflect a minute. The train has just arrived at the Gare de Lyon. Many of the passengers promenade themselves upon the quay. Your mistress was about to do so, and for that purpose had doubtless put on her fur coat, eh?"

"Yes, sir," agreed Mason.

"Your master, then, does the same. The train is heated, but outside in the station it is cold. He puts on his overcoat and his hat and he walks along beside the train, and looking up at the lighted windows he suddenly sees Madame Kettering. Until then he has had no idea that she was on the train. Naturally, he mounts the carriage and goes to her compartment. She gives an exclamation of surprise at seeing him and quickly shuts the door between the two compartments since it is possible that their conversation may be of a private nature."

He leaned back in his chair and watched the suggestion slowly take effect. No one knew better than Hercule Poirot that the class to which Mason belongs cannot be hurried. He must give her time to get rid of her own preconceived ideas. At the end of three minutes she spoke:

"Well, of course, sir, it might be so. I never thought of it that way. The master is tall and dark, and just about that build. It was seeing the hat and coat that made me say it was a gentleman from outside. Yes, it might have been the master. I would not like to say either way, I am sure."

"Thank you very much, Mademoiselle. I shall not require you any further. Ah, just one thing more." He took from his pocket the cigarette case he had already shown to Katherine. "Is that your mistress's case?" he said to Mason.

"No, sir, it is not the mistress's—at least——"

She looked suddenly startled. An idea was clearly working its way to the forefront of her mind.

"Yes," said Poirot encouragingly.

"I think, sir—I can't be sure, but I think—it is a case that the mistress bought to give to the master."

"Ah," said Poirot in a noncommittal manner.

"But whether she ever did give it to him or not, I can't say, of course."

"Precisely," said Poirot, "precisely. That is all, I think, Mademoiselle. I wish you good afternoon."

Ada Mason retired discreetly, closing the door noiselessly behind her.

Poirot looked across at Van Aldin, a faint smile upon his face. The millionaire looked thunderstruck.

"You think—you think it was Derek?" he queried, "but—everything points the other way. Why, the Count has actually been caught redhanded with the jewels on him."

"No."

"But you told me——"

"What did I tell you?"

"That story about the jewels. You showed them to me."

"No."

Van Aldin stared at him.

"You mean to say you didn't show them to me."

"No."

"Yesterday—at the tennis?"

"No."

"Are you crazy, M. Poirot, or am I?"

"Neither of us is crazy," said the detective. "You ask me a question; I answer it. You say have I not shown you the jewels yesterday? I reply—no. What I showed you, M. Van Aldin, was a first-class imitation, hardly to be distinguished except by an expert from the real ones."

24

Poirot Gives Advice

IT TOOK THE millionaire some few minutes to take the thing in. He stared at Poirot as though dumbfounded. The little Belgian nodded at him gently.

"Yes," he said, "it alters the position, does it not?"

"Imitation!"

He leaned forward.

"All along, M. Poirot, you have had this idea? All along this is what you have been driving at? You never believed that the Comte de la Roche was the murderer?"

"I have had doubts," said Poirot quietly. "I said as much to you. Robbery with violence and murder"—he shook his head energetically—"no, it is difficult to picture. It does not harmonize with the personality of the Comte de la Roche."

"But you believe that he meant to steal the rubies?"

"Certainly. There is no doubt as to that. See, I will recount to you the affair as I see it. The Comte knew of the rubies and he laid his plans accordingly. He made up a romantic story of a book he was writing, so as to induce your daughter to bring them with her. He provided himself with an exact duplicate. It is clear, is it not, that substitution is what he was after. Madame, your daughter, was not an expert on jewels. It would probably be a long time before she discovered what had occurred. When she did so—well—I do not think she would prosecute the Comte. Too much would come out. He would have in his possession various letters of hers. Oh yes, a very safe scheme from the Comte's point of view—one that he has probably carried out before."

"It seems clear enough, yes," said Van Aldin musingly.

"It accords with the personality of the Comte de la Roche," said Poirot.

"Yes, but now——" Van Aldin looked searchingly at the other. "What actually happened? Tell me that, M. Poirot."

Poirot shrugged his shoulders.

"It is quite simple," he said; "someone stepped in ahead of the Comte."

There was a long pause.

Van Aldin seemed to be turning things over in his mind. When he spoke it was without beating about the bush.

"How long have you suspected my son-in-law, M. Poirot?"

"From the very first. He had the motive and the opportunity. Everyone took for granted that the man in Madame's compartment in Paris was the Comte de la Roche. I thought so, too. Then you happened to mention that you had once mistaken the Comte for your son-in-law. That told me that they were of the same height and build, and alike in coloring. It put some curious ideas in my head. The maid had only been with your daughter a short time. It was unlikely that she would know M. Kettering well by sight, since he had not been living in Curzon Street; also the man was careful to keep his face turned away."

"You believe he—murdered her," said Van Aldin hoarsely.

Poirot raised a hand quickly.

"No, no, I did not say that—but it is a possibility—a very strong possibility. He was in a tight corner, a very tight corner, threatened with ruin. This was the one way out."

"But why take the jewels?"

"To make the crime appear an ordinary one committed by train robbers. Otherwise suspicion might have fallen on him straight away."

"If that is so, what has he done with the rubies?"

"That remains to be seen. There are several possibilities. There is a man in Nice who may be able to help, the man I pointed out at the tennis."

He rose to his feet and Van Aldin rose also and laid his hand on the little man's shoulder. His voice when he spoke was harsh with emotion.

"Find Ruth's murderer for me," he said, "that is all I ask."

Poirot drew himself up.

"Leave it in the hands of Hercule Poirot," he said superbly; "have no fears. I will discover the truth."

He brushed a speck of fluff from his hat, smiled reassuringly at the millionaire, and left the room. Nevertheless, as he went down the stairs some of the confidence faded from his face.

"It is all very well," he murmured to himself, "but there are difficulties. Yes, there are great difficulties." As he was passing out of the hotel he came to a sudden halt. A car had drawn up in front of the door. In it was Katherine Grey, and Derek Kettering was standing beside it talking to her earnestly. A minute or two later the car drove off and Derek remained standing on the pavement looking after it. The expression on his face was an odd one. He gave a sudden impatient gesture of the shoulders, sighed deeply, and turned to find Hercule Poirot standing at his elbow. In spite of himself he started. The two men looked at each other, Poirot steadily and unwaveringly and Derek with a kind of lighthearted defiance. There was a sneer behind the easy mockery of his tone when he spoke, raising his eyebrows slightly as he did so.

"Rather a dear, isn't she?" he asked easily.

His manner was perfectly natural.

"Yes," said Poirot thoughtfully, "that describes Mademoiselle Katherine very well. It is very English, that phrase there, and Mademoiselle Katherine, she also is very English."

Derek remained perfectly still without answering.

"And yet she is *sympathique,* is it not so?"

"Yes," said Derek; "there are not many like her."

He spoke softly, almost as though to himself. Poirot nodded significantly.

Then he leaned toward the other and spoke in a different tone, a quiet, grave tone that was new to Derek Kettering.

"You will pardon an old man, Monsieur, if he says to you something that you may consider impertinent. There is one of your English proverbs that I would quote to you. It says that 'it is well to be off with the old love, before being on with the new.' "

Kettering turned on him angrily.

"What the devil do you mean?"

"You enrage yourself at me," said Poirot placidly. "I expected as much. As to what I mean—I mean, Monsieur, that there is a second car with a lady in it. If you turn your head you will see her."

Derek spun round. His face darkened with anger.

"Mirelle, damn her!" he muttered. "I will soon——"

Poirot arrested the movement he was about to make.

"Is it wise what you are about to do there?" he asked warningly. His eyes shone softly with a green light in them. But Derek was past noticing the warning signs. In his anger he was completely off his guard.

"I have broken with her utterly, and she knows it," cried Derek angrily.

"You have broken with her, yes, but has *she* broken with you?"

Derek gave a sudden harsh laugh.

"She won't break with two million pounds if she can help it," he murmured brutally; "trust Mirelle for that."

Poirot raised his eyebrows.

"You have the outlook cynical," he murmured.

"Have I?" There was no mirth in his sudden wide smile. "I have lived in the world long enough, M. Poirot, to know that all women are pretty much alike." His face softened suddenly. "All save one."

He met Poirot's gaze defiantly. A look of alertness crept into his eyes, then faded again. "That one," he said, and jerked his head in the direction of Cap Martin.

"Ah!" said Poirot.

This quiescence was well calculated to provoke the impetuous temperament of the other.

"I know what you are going to say," said Derek rapidly, "the kind of life I have led, the fact that I am not worthy of her. You will say that I have no right to think even of such a thing. You will say that it is not a case of giving a dog a bad name—I know that it is not decent to be speaking like this with my wife dead only a few days, and murdered at that."

He paused for breath, and Poirot took advantage of the pause to remark in his plaintive tone.

"But, indeed, I have not said anything at all."

"But you will."

"Eh?" said Poirot.

"You will say that I have no earthly chance of marrying Katherine."

"No," said Poirot, "I would not say that. Your reputation is bad, yes, but with women—never does that deter them. If you were a man of excellent character, of strict morality who had done nothing that he should not do, and —possibly everything that he should do—*eh bien!* then I should have grave doubts of your success. Moral worth, you understand, it is not romantic. It is appreciated, however, by widows."

Derek Kettering stared at him, then he swung round on his heel and went up to the waiting car.

Poirot looked after him with some interest. He saw the lovely vision lean out of the car and speak.

Derek Kettering did not stop. He lifted his hat and passed straight on.

"Ça y est," said M. Hercule Poirot, "it is time, I think, that I return *chez moi."*

He found the imperturbable George pressing trousers.

"A pleasant day, Georges, somewhat fatiguing, but not without interest," he said.

George received these remarks in his usual wooden fashion.

"Indeed, sir."

"The personality of a criminal, Georges, is an interesting matter. Many murderers are men of great personal charm."

"I always heard, sir, that Dr. Crippen was a pleasant-spoken gentleman. And yet he cut up his wife like so much mincemeat."

"Your instances are always apt, Georges."

The valet did not reply, and at that moment the telephone rang. Poirot took up the receiver.

" 'Allo—'allo—yes, yes, it is Hercule Poirot who speaks."

"This is Knighton. Will you hold the line a minute, M. Poirot? Mr. Van Aldin would like to speak to you."

There was a moment's pause, then the millionaire's voice came through.

"Is that you, M. Poirot? I just wanted to tell you that Mason came to me now of her own accord. She has been thinking it over, and she says that she is almost certain that the man at Paris was Derek Kettering. There was something familiar about him at the time, she says, but at the minute she could not place it. She seems pretty certain now."

"Ah," said Poirot, "thank you, M. Van Aldin. That advances us."

He replaced the receiver, and stood for a minute or two with a very curious smile on his face. George had to speak to him twice before obtaining an answer.

"Eh?" said Poirot. "What is that that you say to me?"

"Are you lunching here, sir, or are you going out?"

"Neither," said Poirot, "I shall go to bed and take a *tisane.* The expected has happened, and when the expected happens, it always causes me emotion."

25

Defiance

As DEREK KETTERING passed the car, Mirelle leaned out.

"Dereek—I must speak to you for a moment——"

But, lifting his hat, Derek passed straight on without stopping.

When he got back to his hotel, the concierge detached himself from his wooden pen and accosted him.

"A gentleman is waiting to see you, Monsieur."

"Who is it?" asked Derek.

"He did not give me his name, Monsieur, but he said his business with you was important, and that he would wait."

"Where is he?"

"In the little salon, Monsieur. He preferred it to the lounge he said, as being more private."

Derek nodded, and turned his steps in that direction.

The small salon was empty except for the visitor, who rose and bowed with easy foreign grace as Derek entered. As it chanced, Derek had only seen the Comte de la Roche once, but found no difficulty in recognizing that aristocratic nobleman, and he frowned angrily. Of all the consummate impertinence!

"The Comte de la Roche, is it not?" he said. "I am afraid you have wasted your time in coming here."

"I hope not," said the Comte agreeably. His white teeth glittered.

The Comte's charm of manner was usually wasted on his own sex. All men, without exception, disliked him heartily. Derek Kettering was already conscious of a distinct longing to kick the Count bodily out of the room. It was only the realization that scandal would be unfortunate just at present that restrained him. He marveled anew that Ruth could have cared, as she certainly had, for this fellow. A bounder, and worse than a bounder. He looked with distaste at the Count's exquisitely manicured hands.

"I called," said the Comte, "on a little matter of business. It would be advisable, I think, for you to listen to me."

Again Derek felt strongly tempted to kick him out, but again he refrained. The hint of a threat was not lost upon him, but he interpreted it in his own way. There were various reasons why it would be better to hear what the Comte had to say.

He sat down and drummed impatiently with his fingers on the table.

"Well," he said sharply, "what is it?"

It was not the Comte's way to come out into the open at once.

"Allow me, Monsieur, to offer you my condolences on your recent bereavement."

"If I have any impertinence from you," said Derek quietly, "you go out by that window."

He nodded his head toward the window beside the Comte, and the latter moved uneasily.

"I will send my friends to you, Monsieur, if that is what you desire," he said haughtily.

Derek laughed.

"A duel, eh? My dear Count, I don't take you seriously enough for that. But I should take a good deal of pleasure in kicking you down the Promenade des Anglais."

The Comte was not at all anxious to take offense. He merely raised his eyebrows and murmured:

"The English are barbarians."

"Well," said Derek, "what is it you have to say to me?"

"I will be frank," said the Comte, "I will come immediately to the point. That will suit us both, will it not?"

Again he smiled in his agreeable fashion.

"Go on," said Derek curtly.

The Comte looked at the ceiling, joined the tips of his fingers together, and murmured softly:

"You have come into a lot of money, Monsieur."

"What the devil has that got to do with you?"

The Comte drew himself up.

"Monsieur, my name is tarnished! I am suspected—accused—of foul crime."

"The accusation does not come from me," said Derek coldly; "as an interested party I have not expressed any opinion."

"I am innocent," said the Comte, "I swear before heaven"—he raised his hand to heaven—"that I am innocent."

"M. Carrège is, I believe, the Juge d'Instruction in charge of the case," hinted Derek politely.

The Comte took no notice.

"Not only am I unjustly suspected of a crime that I did not commit, but I am also in serious need of money."

He coughed softly and suggestively.

Derek rose to his feet.

"I was waiting for that," he said softly; "you blackmailing brute! I will not give you a penny. My wife is dead, and no scandal that you can make can touch her now. She wrote you foolish letters, I dare say. If I were to buy them from you for a round sum at this minute, I am pretty certain that you would manage to keep one or two back; and I will tell you this, M. de la Roche, blackmailing is an ugly word both in England and in France. That is my answer to you. Good afternoon."

"One moment"—the Comte stretched out a hand as Derek was turning to leave the room. "You are mistaken, Monsieur. You are completely mistaken. I am, I hope, a 'gentleman.' " Derek laughed. "Any letters that a lady might write to me I should hold sacred." He flung back his head with a beautiful air of nobility. "The proposition that I was putting before you was of quite a different nature. I am, as I said, extremely short of money, and my conscience might impel me to go to the police with certain information."

Derek came slowly back into the room.

"What do you mean?"

The Comte's agreeable smile flashed forth once more.

"Surely it is not necessary to go into details," he purred. "Seek whom the crime benefits, they say, don't they? As I said just now, you have come into a lot of money lately."

Derek laughed.

"If that is all——" he said contemptuously.

But the Comte was shaking his head.

"But it is not all, my dear sir. I should not come to you unless I had much more precise and detailed information than that. It is not agreeable, Monsieur, to be arrested and tried for murder."

Derek came close up to him. His face expressed such furious anger that involuntarily the Comte drew back a pace or two.

"Are you threatening *me?*" the young man demanded angrily.

"You shall hear nothing more of the matter," the Comte assured him.

"Of all the colossal bluffs that I have ever struck——"

The Comte raised a white hand.

"You are wrong. It is not a bluff. To convince you I will tell you this. My information was obtained from a certain lady. It is she who holds the irrefutable proof that you committed the murder."

"She? Who?"

"Mademoiselle Mirelle."

Derek drew back as though struck.

"Mirelle," he muttered.

The Comte was quick to press what he took to be his advantage.

"A bagatelle of one hundred thousand francs," he said. "I ask no more."

"Eh?" said Derek absently.

"I was saying, Monsieur, that a bagatelle of one hundred thousand francs would satisfy my—conscience."

Derek seemed to recollect himself. He looked earnestly at the Comte.

"You would like my answer now?"

"If you please, Monsieur."

"Then here it is. You can go to the devil. See?"

Leaving the Comte too astonished to speak, Derek turned on his heel and swung out of the room.

Once out of the hotel he hailed a taxi and drove to Mirelle's hotel. On inquiring, he learned that the dancer had just come in. Derek gave the concierge his card.

"Take this up to Mademoiselle and ask if she will see me."

A very brief interval elapsed, and then Derek was bidden to follow a *chasseur*.

A wave of exotic perfume assailed Derek's nostrils as he stepped over the threshold of the dancer's apartments. The room was filled with carnations, orchids, and mimosa. Mirelle was standing by the window in a peignoir of foamy lace.

She came toward him, her hands outstretched.

"Dereek—you have come to me. I knew you would."

He put aside the clinging arms and looked down on her sternly.

"Why did you send the Comte de la Roche to me?"

She looked at him in astonishment, which he took to be genuine.

"I? Send the Comte de la Roche to you? But for what?"

"Apparently—for blackmail," said Derek grimly.

Again she stared. Then suddenly she smiled and nodded her head.

"Of course. It was to be expected. It is what he would do, *ce type là*. I might have known it. No, indeed, Dereek, I did not send him."

He looked at her piercingly, as though seeking to read her mind.

"I will tell you," said Mirelle. "I am ashamed, but I will tell you. The other day, you comprehend, I was mad with rage, quite mad—" She made an eloquent gesture. "My temperament, it is not a patient one. I want to be revenged on you, and so I go to the Comte de la Roche, and I tell him to go to the police and say so and so, and so and so. But have no fear, Dereek. Not completely did I lose my head; the proofs rests with me alone. The police can do nothing without my word, you understand? And now—now?"

She nestled up close to him, looking up at him with melting eyes.

He thrust her roughly away from him. She stood there, her breast heaving, her eyes narrowing to a catlike slit.

"Be careful, Dereek, be very careful. You have come back to me, have you not?"

"I shall never come back to you," said Derek steadily.

"Ah!"

More than ever the dancer looked like a cat. Her eyelids flickered.

"So there is another woman? The one with whom you lunched that day. Eh! am I right?"

"I intend to ask that lady to marry me. You might as well know."

"That prim Englishwoman! Do you think that I will support that for one moment? Ah, no." Her beautiful lithe body quivered. "Listen, Dereek, do you remember that conversation we had in London? You said the only thing that could save you was the death of your wife. You regretted that she was so healthy. Then the idea of an accident came to your brain. And more than an accident."

"I suppose," said Derek contemptuously, "that it was this conversation that you repeated to the Comte de la Roche."

Mirelle laughed.

"Am I a fool? Could the police do anything with a vague story like that? See—I will give you a last chance. You shall give up this Englishwoman. You shall return to me. And then, *chéri,* never, never will I breathe——"

"Breathe what?"

She laughed softly. "You thought no one saw you——"

"What do you mean?"

"As I say, you thought no one saw you—but *I* saw you, Dereek, *mon ami; I saw you coming out of the compartment of Madame your wife just before the train got into Lyons that night. And* I know more than that. I know that when you came out of her compartment she was dead."

He stared at her. Then, like a man in a dream he turned very slowly and went out of the room, swaying slightly as he walked.

26

A Warning

"AND SO IT is," said Poirot, "that we are the good friends and have no secrets from each other."

Katherine turned her head to look at him. There was something in his voice, some undercurrent of seriousness, which she had not heard before.

They were sitting in the gardens of Monte Carlo. Katherine had come over with her friends, and they had run into Knighton and Poirot almost immediately on arrival. Lady Tamplin had seized upon Knighton and had overwhelmed him with reminiscences, most of which Katherine had a faint suspicion were invented. They had moved away together, Lady Tamplin with her hand on the young man's arm. Knighton had thrown a couple of glances back over his shoulder, and Poirot's eyes twinkled a little as he saw them.

"Of course we are friends," said Katherine.

"From the beginning we have been sympathetic to each other," mused Poirot.

"When you told me that a 'Roman Policier' occurs in real life."

"And I was right, was I not?" he challenged her, with an emphatic forefinger. "Here we are, plunged in the middle of one. That is natural for me—it is my *métier*—but for you it is different. Yes," he added in a reflective tone, "for you it is different."

She looked sharply at him. It was as though he were warning her, pointing out to her some menace that she had not seen.

"Why do you say that I am in the middle of it? It is true that I had that conversation with Mrs. Kettering just before she died, but now—now all that is over. I am not connected with the case any more."

"Ah, Mademoiselle, Mademoiselle, can we ever say, 'I have finished with this or that'?"

Katherine turned defiantly round to face him.

"What is it?" she asked. "You are trying to tell me something—to convey it to me rather. But I am not clever at taking hints. I would much rather that you said anything you have to say straight out."

Poirot looked at her sadly. *"Ah, mais c'est Anglais ça,"* he murmured, "everything in black and white, everything clearcut and well defined. But life, it is not like that, Mademoiselle. There are the things that are not yet, but which cast their shadow before."

He dabbed his brow with a very large silk pocket-handkerchief and murmured:

"Ah, but it is that I become poetical. Let us, as you say, speak only of facts. And, speaking of facts, tell me what you think of Major Knighton."

"I like him very much indeed," said Katherine warmly; "he is quite delightful."

Poirot sighed.

"What is the matter?" asked Katherine.

"You reply so heartily," said Poirot. "If you had said in an indifferent voice, 'Oh, quite nice,' *eh bien,* do you know I should have been better pleased."

Katherine did not answer. She felt slightly uncomfortable. Poirot went on dreamily:

"And yet, who knows? With *les femmes,* they have so many ways of concealing what they feel—and heartiness is perhaps as good a way as any other."

He sighed.

"I don't see——" began Katherine.

He interrupted her.

"You do not see why I am being so impertinent, Mademoiselle? I am an old man, and now and then—not very often—I come across someone whose welfare is dear to me. We are friends, Mademoiselle. You have said so yourself. And it is just this—I should like to see you happy."

Katherine stared very straight in front of her. She had a cretonne sunshade with her, and with its point she traced little designs in the gravel at her feet.

"I have asked you a question about Major Knighton, now I will ask you another. Do you like Mr. Derek Kettering?"

"I hardly know him," said Katherine.

"That is not an answer, that."

"I think it is."

He looked at her, struck by something in her tone. Then he nodded his head gravely and slowly.

"Perhaps you are right, Mademoiselle. See you, I who speak to you have seen much of the world, and I know that there are two things which are true. A good man may be ruined by his love for a bad woman—but the other way holds good also. A bad man may equally be ruined by his love for a good woman."

Katherine looked up sharply.

"When you say ruined——"

"I mean from his point of view. One must be wholehearted in crime as in everything else."

"You are trying to warn me," said Katherine in a low voice. "Against whom?"

"I cannot look into your heart, Mademoiselle; I do not think you would let me if I could. I will just say this. There are men who have a strange fascination for women."

"The Comte de la Roche," said Katherine, with a smile.

"There are others—more dangerous than the Comte de la Roche. They have qualities that appeal—recklessness, daring, audacity. You are fascinated, Mademoiselle; I see that, but I think that it is no more than that. I hope so. This man of whom I speak, the emotion he feels is genuine enough, but all the same——"

"Yes?"

He got up and stood looking down at her. Then he spoke in a low, distinct voice:

"You could, perhaps, love a thief, Mademoiselle, *but not a murderer.*"

He wheeled sharply away on that and left her sitting there.

He heard the little gasp she gave and paid no attention. He had said what he meant to say. He left her there to digest that last unmistakable phrase.

Derek Kettering, coming out of the Casino into the sunshine, saw her sitting alone on the bench and joined her.

"I have been gambling," he said, with a light laugh, "gambling unsuccessfully. I have lost everything—everything, that is, that I have with me."

Katherine looked at him with a troubled face. She was aware at once of something new in his manner, some hidden excitement that betrayed itself in a hundred different infinitesimal signs.

"I should think you were always a gambler. The spirit of gambling appeals to you."

"Every day and in every way a gambler? You are about right. Don't *you* find something stimulating in it? To risk all on one throw—there is nothing like it."

Calm and stolid as she believed herself to be, Katherine felt a faint answering thrill.

"I want to talk to you," went on Derek, "and who knows when I may have another opportunity? There is an idea going about that I murdered my wife—

no, please don't interrupt. It is absurd, of course." He paused for a minute or two, then went on, speaking more deliberately. "In dealing with the police and Local Authorities here I have had to pretend to—well—a certain decency. I prefer not to pretend with you. I meant to marry money. I was on the lookout for money when I first met Ruth Van Aldin. She had the look of a slim Madonna about her, and I—well—I made all sorts of good resolutions— and was bitterly disillusioned. My wife was in love with another man when she married me. She never cared for me in the least. Oh, I am not complaining; the thing was a perfectly respectable bargain. She wanted Leconbury and I wanted money. The trouble arose simply through Ruth's American blood. Without caring a pin for me, she would have liked me to be continually dancing attendance. Time and again she as good as told me that she had bought me and that I belonged to her. The result was that I behaved abominably to her. My father-in-law will tell you that, and he is quite right. At the time of Ruth's death, I was faced with absolute disaster." He laughed suddenly. "One *is* faced with absolute disaster when one is up against a man like Rufus Van Aldin."

"And then?" asked Katherine in a low voice.

"And then," Derek shrugged his shoulders, "Ruth was murdered—very providentially."

He laughed, and the sound of his laugh hurt Katherine. She winced.

"Yes," said Derek. "that wasn't in very good taste. But it is quite true. Now I am going to tell you something more. From the very first moment I saw you I knew you were the only woman in the world for me. I was—afraid of you. I thought you might bring me bad luck."

"Bad luck?" said Katherine sharply.

He stared at her. "Why do you repeat it like that? What have you got in your mind?"

"I was thinking of things that people have said to me."

Derek grinned suddenly. "They will say a lot to you about me, my dear, and most of it will be true. Yes, and worse things too—things that I shall never tell you. I have been a gambler always—and I have taken some long odds. I shan't confess to you now or at any other time. The past is done with. There is one thing I do wish you to believe. I swear to you solemnly that I did not kill my wife."

He said the words earnestly enough, yet there was somehow a theatrical touch about them. He met her troubled gaze and went on:

"I know. I lied the other day. It *was* my wife's compartment I went into."

"Ah," said Katherine.

"It's difficult to explain just why I went in, but I'll try. I did it on an impulse. You see, I was more or less spying on my wife. I kept out of sight on the train. Mirelle had told me that my wife was meeting the Comte de la Roche in Paris. Well, as far as I had seen, that was not so. I felt ashamed, and I thought suddenly that it would be a good thing to have it out with her once and for all, so I pushed open the door and went in."

He paused.

"Yes," said Katherine gently.

"Ruth was lying on the bunk asleep—her face was turned away from me—I could only see the back of her head. I could have waked her up, of course. But suddenly I felt a reaction. What, after all, was there to say that we hadn't both of us said a hundred times before? She looked so peaceful lying there. I left the compartment as quietly as I could."

"Why lie about it to the police?" asked Katherine.

"Because I'm not a complete fool. I've realized from the beginning that, from the point of view of motive, I'm the ideal murderer. If I once admitted that I had been in her compartment just before she was murdered, I'd do for myself once and for all."

"I see."

Did she see? She could not have told herself. She was feeling the magnetic attraction of Derek's personality, but there was something in her that resisted, that held back . . .

"Katherine——"

"I——"

"You know that I care for you. Do—do you care for me?"

"I—I don't know."

Weakness there. Either she knew or she did not know. If—if only——

She cast a look around desperately as though seeking something that would help her. A soft color rose in her cheeks as a tall fair man with a limp came hurrying along the path toward them—Major Knighton.

There was relief and an unexpected warmth in her voice as she greeted him.

Derek stood up scowling, his face black as a thundercloud.

"Lady Tamplin having a flutter?" he said easily. "I must join her and give her the benefit of my system."

He swung round on his heel and left them together. Katherine sat down again. Her heart was beating rapidly and unevenly, but as she sat there talking commonplaces to the quiet, rather shy man beside her, her self-command came back.

Then she realized with a shock that Knighton also was laying bare his heart, much as Derek had done, but in a very different manner.

He was shy and stammering. The words came haltingly with no eloquence to back them.

"From the first moment I saw you—I—I ought not to have spoken so soon —but Mr. Van Aldin may leave here any day, and I might not have another chance. I know you can't care for me so soon—that is impossible. I dare say it is presumption anyway on my part. I have private means, but not very much —no, please don't answer now. I know what your answer would be. But in case I went away suddenly I just wanted you to know—that I care."

She was shaken—touched. His manner was so gentle and appealing.

"There's one thing more. I just wanted to say that if—if you are ever in trouble, anything that I can do——"

He took her hand in his, held it tightly for a minute, then dropped it and walked rapidly away toward the Casino without looking back.

Katherine sat perfectly still, looking after him. Derek Kettering—Richard Knighton—two men so different—so very different. There was something kind about Knighton, kind and trustworthy. As to Derek——

Then suddenly Katherine had a very curious sensation. She felt that she was no longer sitting alone on the seat in the Casino gardens, but that someone was standing beside her, and that that someone was the dead woman, Ruth Kettering. She had a further impression that Ruth wanted—badly—to tell her something. The impression was so curious, so vivid, that it could not be driven away. She felt absolutely certain that the spirit of Ruth Kettering was trying to convey something of vital importance to her. The impression faded. Katherine got up, trembling a little. What was it that Ruth Kettering had wanted so badly to say?

27

Interview with Mirelle

WHEN KNIGHTON LEFT Katherine he went in search of Hercule Poirot, whom he found in the Rooms, jauntily placing the minimum stake on the even numbers. As Knighton joined him, the number thirty-three turned up, and Poirot's stake was swept away.

"Bad luck!" said Knighton; "are you going to stake again?"

Poirot shook his head.

"Not at present."

"Do you feel the fascination of gambling?" asked Knighton curiously.

"Not at roulette."

Knighton shot a swift glance at him. His own face became troubled. He spoke haltingly, with a touch of deference.

"I wonder, are you busy, M. Poirot? There is something I would like to ask you about."

"I am at your disposal. Shall we go outside? It is pleasant in the sunshine."

They strolled out together, and Knighton drew a deep breath.

"I love the Riviera," he said. "I came here first twelve years ago, during the War, when I was sent to Lady Tamplin's Hospital. It was like Paradise, coming from Flanders to this."

"It must have been," said Poirot.

"How long ago the War seems now!" mused Knighton.

They walked on in silence for some little way.

"You have something on your mind?" said Poirot.

Knighton looked at him in some surprise.

"You are quite right," he confessed. "I don't know how you knew it, though."

"It showed itself only too plainly," said Poirot dryly.

"I did not know that I was so transparent."

"It is my business to observe the physiognomy," the little man explained, with dignity.

"I will tell you, M. Poirot. You have heard of this dancer woman—Mirelle?"

"She who is the *chère amie* of M. Derek Kettering?"

"Yes, that is the one; and, knowing this, you will understand that M. Van Aldin is naturally prejudiced against her. She wrote to him, asking for an interview. He told me to dictate a curt refusal, which of course I did. This morning she came to the hotel and sent up her card, saying that it was urgent and vital that she should see Mr. Van Aldin at once."

"You interest me," said Poirot.

"Mr. Van Aldin was furious. He told me what message to send down to her. I ventured to disagree with him. It seemed to me both likely and probable that this woman Mirelle might give us valuable information. We know that she was on the Blue Train, and she may have seen or heard something that it might be vital for us to know. Don't you agree with me, M. Poirot?"

"I do," said Poirot dryly. "M. Van Aldin, if I may say so, behaved exceedingly foolishly."

"I am glad you take that view of the matter," said the secretary. "Now I am going to tell you something, M. Poirot. So strongly did I feel the unwisdom of Mr. Van Aldin's attitude that I went down privately and had an interview with the lady."

"Eh bien?"

"The difficulty was that she insisted on seeing Mr. Van Aldin himself. I softened his message as much as I possibly could. In fact—to be candid—I gave it in a very different form. I said that Mr. Van Aldin was too busy to see her at present, but that she might make any communication she wished to me. That, however, she could not bring herself to do, and she left without saying anything further. But I have a strong impression, M. Poirot, that that woman knows something."

"This is serious," said Poirot quietly. "You know where she is staying?"

"Yes." Knighton mentioned the name of the hotel.

"Good," said Poirot; "we will go there immediately."

The secretary looked doubtful.

"And Mr. Van Aldin?" he queried doubtfully.

"M. Van Aldin is an obstinate man," said Poirot dryly. "I do not argue with obstinate men. I act in spite of them. We will go and see the lady immediately. I will tell her that you are empowered by M. Van Aldin to act for him, and you will guard yourself well from contradicting me."

Knighton still looked slightly doubtful, but Poirot took no notice of his hesitation.

At the hotel, they were told that Mademoiselle was in, and Poirot sent up both his and Knighton's cards, with "From Mr. Van Aldin" penciled upon them.

Word came down that Mademoiselle Mirelle would receive them.

When they were ushered into the dancer's apartments, Poirot immediately took the lead.

"Mademoiselle," he murmured, bowing very low, "we are here on behalf of M. Van Aldin."

"Ah! And why did he not come himself?"

"He is indisposed," said Poirot mendaciously; "the Riviera throat, it has him in its grip, but me, I am empowered to act for him, as is Major Knighton, his secretary. Unless, of course, Mademoiselle would prefer to wait a fortnight or so."

If there was one thing of which Poirot was tolerably certain, it was that to a temperament such as Mirelle's the mere word "wait" was anathema.

"Eh bien, I will speak, Messieurs," she cried. "I have been patient. I have held my hand. And for what? That I should be insulted! Yes, insulted! Ah! Does he think to treat Mirelle like that? To throw her off like an old glove. I tell you never has a man tired of me. Always it is I who tire of them."

She paced up and down the room, her slender body trembling with rage. A small table impeded her free passage and she flung it from her into a corner, where it splintered against the wall.

"That is what I will do to him," she cried, "and that!"

Picking up a glass bowl filled with lilies she flung it into the grate, where it smashed into a hundred pieces.

Knighton was looking at her with cold British disapproval. He felt embarrassed and ill at ease. Poirot, on the other hand, with twinkling eyes was thoroughly enjoying the scene.

"Ah, it is magnificent!" he cried. "It can be seen—Madame has a temperament."

"I am an artist," said Mirelle; "every artist has a temperament. I told Dereek to beware, and he would not listen." She whirled round on Poirot suddenly. "It is true, is it not, that he wants to marry that English miss?"

Poirot coughed.

"On m'a dit," he murmured, "that he adores her passionately."

Mirelle came toward them.

"He murdered his wife," she screamed. "There—now you have it! He told me beforehand that he meant to do it. He had got to an *impasse*—zut! he took the easiest way out."

"You say that M. Kettering murdered his wife."

"Yes, yes, yes. Have I not told you so?"

"The police," murmured Poirot, "will need proof of that—er—statement."

"I tell you I saw him come out of her compartment that night on the train."

"When?" asked Poirot sharply.

"Just before the train reached Lyons."

"You will swear to that, Mademoiselle?"

It was a different Poirot who spoke now, sharp and decisive.

"Yes."

There was a moment's silence. Mirelle was panting, and her eyes, half defiant, half frightened, went from the face of one man to the other.

"This is a serious matter, Mademoiselle," said the detective. "You realize how serious?"

"Certainly I do."

"That is well," said Poirot. "Then you understand, Mademoiselle, that no time must be lost. You will, perhaps, accompany us immediately to the office of the Examining Magistrate."

Mirelle was taken aback. She hesitated, but, as Poirot had foreseen, she had no loophole for escape.

"Very well," she muttered. "I will fetch a coat."

Left alone together, Poirot and Knighton exchanged glances.

"It is necessary to act while—how do you say it?—the iron is hot," murmured Poirot. "She is temperamental; in an hour's time, maybe, she will repent, and she will wish to draw back. We must prevent that at all costs."

Mirelle reappeared, wrapped in a sand-colored velvet wrap trimmed with leopard skin. She looked not altogether unlike a leopardess, tawny and dangerous. Her eyes still flashed with anger and determination.

They found M. Caux and the Examining Magistrate together. A few brief introductory words from Poirot, and Mademoiselle Mirelle was courteously entreated to tell her tale. This she did in much the same words as she had done to Knighton and Poirot, though with far more soberness of manner.

"This is an extraordinary story, Mademoiselle," said M. Carrège slowly. He leaned back in his chair, adjusted his pince-nez, and looked keenly and searchingly at the dancer through them.

"You wish us to believe M. Kettering actually boasted of the crime to you beforehand?"

"Yes, yes. She was too healthy, he said. If she were to die it must be an accident—he would arrange it all."

"You are aware, Mademoiselle," said M. Carrège sternly, "that you are making yourself out to be an accessory before the fact?"

"Me? But not the least in the world, Monsieur. Not for a moment did I take that statement seriously. Ah no, indeed! I know men, Monsieur; they say many wild things. It would be an odd state of affairs if one were to take all they said *au pied de la lettre.*"

The Examining Magistrate raised his eyebrows.

"We are to take it, then, that you regarded M. Kettering's threats as mere idle words? May I ask, Mademoiselle, what made you throw up your engagements in London and come out to the Riviera?"

Mirelle looked at him with melting black eyes.

"I wished to be with the man I loved," she said simply. "Was it so unnatural?"

Poirot interpolated a question gently.

"Was it, then, at M. Kettering's wish that you accompanied him to Nice?"

Mirelle seemed to find a little difficulty in answering this. She hesitated perceptibly before she spoke. When she did, it was with a haughty indifference of manner.

"In such matters I please myself, Monsieur," she said.

That the answer was not an answer at all was noted by all three men. They said nothing.

"When were you first convinced that M. Kettering had murdered his wife?"

"As I tell you, Monsieur, I saw M. Kettering come out of his wife's compartment just before the train drew into Lyons. There was a look on his face —ah! at the moment I could not understand it—a look haunted and terrible. I shall never forget it."

Her voice rose shrilly, and she flung out her arms in an extravagant gesture.

"Quite so," said M. Carrège.

"Afterwards, when I found that Madame Kettering was dead when the train left Lyons, then—then I knew!"

"And still—you did not go to the police, Mademoiselle," said the Commissary mildly.

Mirelle glanced at him superbly; she was clearly enjoying herself in the role she was playing.

"Shall I betray my lover?" she asked. "Ah no; do not ask a woman to do that."

"Yet now——" hinted M. Caux.

"Now it is different. He has betrayed me! Shall I suffer that in silence . . . ?"

The Examining Magistrate checked her.

"Quite so, quite so," he murmured soothingly. "And now, Mademoiselle, perhaps you will read over the statement of what you have told us, see that it is correct, and sign it."

Mirelle wasted no time on the document.

"Yes, yes," she said, "it is correct." She rose to her feet. "You require me no longer, Messieurs?"

"At present, no, Mademoiselle."

"And Dereek will be arrested?"

"At once, Mademoiselle."

Mirelle laughed cruelly and drew her fur draperies closer about her.

"He should have thought of this before he insulted me," she cried.

"There is one little matter"—Poirot coughed apologetically—"just a matter of detail."

"Yes?"

"What makes you think Madame Kettering was dead when the train left Lyons?"

Mirelle stared.

"But she *was* dead."

"Was she?"

"Yes, of course. I——"

She came to an abrupt stop. Poirot was regarding her intently, and he saw the wary look that came into her eyes.

"I have been told so. Everybody says so."

"Oh," said Poirot, "I was not aware that the fact had been mentioned outside the Examining Magistrate's office."

Mirelle appeared somewhat discomposed.

"One hears those things," she said vaguely; "they get about. Somebody told me. I can't remember who it was."

She moved to the door. M. Caux sprang forward to open it for her, and as he did so, Poirot's voice rose gently once more.

"And the jewels? Pardon, Mademoiselle. Can you tell me anything about those?"

"The jewels? What jewels?"

"The rubies of Catherine the Great. Since you hear so much, you must have heard of them."

"I know nothing about any jewels," said Mirelle sharply.

She went out, closing the door behind her. M. Caux came back to his chair; the Examining Magistrate sighed.

"What a fury!" he said, "but *diablement chic,* I wonder if she is telling the truth? I think so."

"There is *some* truth in her story, certainly," said Poirot. "We have confirmation of it from Miss Grey. She was looking down the corridor a short time before the train reached Lyons and she saw M. Kettering go into his wife's compartment."

"The case against him seems quite clear," said the Commissary, sighing; "it is a thousand pities," he murmured.

"How do you mean?" asked Poirot.

"It has been the ambition of my life to lay the Comte de la Roche by the heels. This time, *ma foi,* I thought we had got him. This other—it is not nearly so satisfactory."

M. Carrège rubbed his nose.

"If anything goes wrong," he observed cautiously, "it will be most awkward. M. Kettering is of the aristocracy. It will get into the newspapers. If we have made a mistake——" He shrugged his shoulders forebodingly.

"The jewels now," said the Commissary, "what do you think he has done with them?"

"He took them for a plant, of course," said M. Carrège; "they must have been a great inconvenience to him and very awkward to dispose of."

Poirot smiled.

"I have an idea of my own about the jewels. Tell me, Messieurs, what do you know of a man called the Marquis?"

The Commissary leaned forward excitedly.

"The Marquis," he said, "the Marquis? Do you think he is mixed up in this affair, M. Poirot?"

"I ask you what you know of him."

The Commissary made an expressive grimace.

"Not as much as we should like to," he observed ruefully. "He works behind the scenes, you understand. He has underlings who do his dirty work for him. But he is someone high up. That we are sure of. He does not come from the criminal classes."

"A Frenchman?"

"Y—es. At least we believe so. But we are not sure. He has worked in France, in England, in America. There was a series of robberies in Switzerland last autumn which were laid at his door. By all accounts he is a *grand seigneur,* speaking French and English with equal perfection and his origin is a mystery."

Poirot nodded and rose to take his departure.

"Can you tell us nothing more, M. Poirot?" urged the Commissary.

"At present, no," said Poirot, "but I may have news awaiting me at my hotel."

M. Carrège looked uncomfortable. "If the Marquis is concerned in this——" he began, and then stopped.

"It upsets our ideas," complained M. Caux.

"It does not upset mine," said Poirot. "On the contrary, I think it agrees with them very well. *Au revoir,* Messieurs; if news of any importance comes to me I will communicate it to you immediately."

He walked back to his hotel with a grave face. In his absence a telegram had come to him. Taking a papercutter from his pocket, he slit it open. It was a long telegram, and he read it over twice before slowly putting it in his pocket. Upstairs, George was awaiting his master.

"I am fatigued, Georges, much fatigued. Will you order for me a small pot of chocolate?"

The chocolate was duly ordered and brought, and George set it at the little table at his master's elbow. As he was preparing to retire, Poirot spoke:

"I believe, Georges, that you have a good knowledge of the English aristocracy?" murmured Poirot.

George smiled apologetically.

"I think that I might say that I have, sir," he replied.

"I suppose that it is your opinion, Georges, that criminals are invariably drawn from the lower orders."

"Not always, sir. There was great trouble with one of the Duke of Devize's younger sons. He left Eton under a cloud, and after that he caused great anxiety on several occasions. The police would not accept the view that it was kleptomania. A very clever young gentleman, sir, but vicious through and through, if you take my meaning. His Grace shipped him to Australia, and I hear he was convicted out there under another name. Very odd, sir, but there it is. The young gentleman, I need hardly say, was not in want financially."

Poirot nodded his head slowly.

"Love of excitement," he murmured, "and a little kink in the brain somewhere. I wonder now——"

He drew out the telegram from his pocket and read it again.

"Then there was Lady Mary Fox's daughter," continued the valet in a mood of reminiscence. "Swindled tradespeople something shocking, she did. Very worrying to the best families, if I may say so, and there are many other queer cases I could mention."

"You have a wide experience, Georges," murmured Poirot. "I often wonder having lived so exclusively with titled families that you demean yourself by coming as a valet to me. I put it down to love of excitement on your part."

"Not exactly, sir," said George. "I happened to see in *Society Snippets* that you had been received at Buckingham Palace. That was just when I was looking for a new situation. His Majesty, so it said, had been most gracious and friendly and thought very highly of your abilities."

"Ah," said Poirot, "one always likes to know the reason for things."

He remained in thought for a few moments and then said:

"You rang up Mademoiselle Papopolous?"

"Yes, sir; she and her father will be pleased to dine with you tonight."

"Ah," said Poirot thoughtfully. He drank off his chocolate, set the cup and saucer neatly in the middle of the tray, and spoke gently, more to himself than to the valet.

"The squirrel, my good Georges, collects nuts. He stores them up in the autumn so that they may be of advantage to him later. To make a success of humanity, Georges, we must profit by the lessons of those below us in the animal kingdom. I have always done so. I have been the cat, watching at the mouse hole. I have been the good dog following up the scent, and not taking my nose from the trail. And also, my good Georges, I have been the squirrel. I have stored away the little fact here, the little fact there. I go now to my store and I take out one particular nut, a nut that I stored away—let me see, seventeen years ago. You follow me, Georges?"

"I should hardly have thought, sir," said George, "that nuts would have kept so long as that, though I know one can do wonders with preserving bottles."

Poirot looked at him and smiled.

28

Poirot Plays the Squirrel

POIROT STARTED TO keep his dinner appointment with a margin of three-quarters of an hour to spare. He had an object in this. The car took him, not straight to Monte Carlo, but to Lady Tamplin's house at Cap Martin, where he asked for Miss Grey. The ladies were dressing and Poirot was shown into a small salon to wait, and here, after a lapse of three or four minutes, Lenox Tamplin came to him.

"Katherine is not quite ready yet," she said. "Can I give her a message, or would you rather wait until she comes down?"

Poirot looked at her thoughtfully. He was a minute or two in replying, as though something of great weight hung upon his decision. Apparently the answer to such a simple question mattered.

"No," he said at last, "no, I do not think it is necessary that I should wait to see Mademoiselle Katherine. I think, perhaps, that it is better that I should not. These things are sometimes difficult."

Lenox waited politely, her eyebrows slightly raised.

"I have a piece of news," continued Poirot. "You will, perhaps, tell your friend. M. Kettering was arrested tonight for the murder of his wife."

"You want me to tell Katherine that?" asked Lenox. She breathed rather hard, as though she had been running; her face, Poirot thought, looked white and strained—rather noticeably so.

"If you please, Mademoiselle."

"Why?" said Lenox. "Do you think Katherine will be upset? Do you think she cares?"

"I don't know, Mademoiselle," said Poirot. "See, I admit it frankly. As a rule I know everything, but in this case, I—well, I do not. You, perhaps, know better than I do."

"Yes," said Lenox, "I know—but I am not going to tell you all the same." She paused for a minute or two, her dark brows drawn together in a frown.

"You believe he did it?" she said abruptly.

Poirot shrugged his shoulders.

"The police say so."

"Ah," said Lenox, "hedging, are you? So there is something to hedge about."

Again she was silent, frowning. Poirot said gently:

"You have known Derek Kettering a long time, have you not?"

"Off and on ever since I was a kid," said Lenox gruffly.

Poirot nodded his head several times without speaking.

With one of her brusque movements Lenox drew forward a chair and sat down on it, her elbows on the table and her face supported by her hands. Sitting thus, she looked directly across the table at Poirot.

"What have they got to go on?" she demanded. "Motive, I suppose. Probably came into money at her death."

"He came into two million."

"And if she had not died he would have been ruined?"

"Yes."

"But there must have been more than that," persisted Lenox. "He traveled by the same train, I know, but—that would not be enough to go on by itself."

"A cigarette case with the letter 'K' on it which did not belong to Mrs. Kettering was found in her carriage, and he was seen by two people entering and leaving the compartment just before the train got into Lyons."

"What two people?"

"Your friend Miss Grey was one of them. The other was Mademoiselle Mirelle, the dancer."

"And he, Derek, what has he got to say about it?" demanded Lenox sharply.

"He denies having entered his wife's compartment at all," said Poirot.

"Fool!" said Lenox crisply, frowning. "Just before Lyons, you say? Does nobody know when—when she died?"

"The doctors' evidence necessarily cannot be very definite," said Poirot; "they are inclined to think that death was unlikely to have occurred after leaving Lyons. And we know this much, that a few moments after leaving Lyons Mrs. Kettering was dead."

"How do you know that?"

Poirot was smiling rather oddly to himself.

"Someone else went into her compartment and found her dead."

"And they did not rouse the train?"

"No."

"Why was that?"

"Doubtless they had their reasons."

Lenox looked at him sharply.

"Do you know the reason?"

"I think so—yes."

Lenox sat still turning things over in her mind. Poirot watched her in silence. At last she looked up. A soft color had come into her cheeks and her eyes were shining.

"You think someone on the train must have killed her, but that need not be so at all. What is to stop anyone swinging themselves onto the train when it stopped at Lyons? They could go straight to her compartment, strangle her, and take the rubies and drop off the train again without anyone being the wiser. She may have been actually killed while the train was in Lyons station. Then she would have been alive when Derek went in, and dead when the other person found her."

Poirot leaned back in his chair. He drew a deep breath. He looked across at the girl and nodded his head three times, then he heaved a sigh.

"Mademoiselle," he said, "what you have said there is very just—very true. I was struggling in darkness, and you have shown me a light. There was a point that puzzled me and you have made it plain."

He got up.

"And Derek?" said Lenox.

"Who knows?" said Poirot, with a shrug of his shoulders. "But I will tell you this, Mademoiselle. I am not satisfied; no, I, Hercule Poirot, am not yet satisfied. It may be that this very night I shall learn something more. At least, I go to try."

"You are meeting someone?"

"Yes."

"Someone who knows something?"

"Someone who might know something. In these matters one must leave no stone unturned. *Au revoir,* Mademoiselle."

Lenox accompanied him to the door.

"Have I—helped?" she asked.

Poirot's face softened as he looked up at her standing on the doorstep above him.

"Yes, Mademoiselle, you have helped. If things are very dark, always remember that."

When the car had driven off he relapsed into a frowning absorption, but in his eyes was that faint green light which was always the precursor of the triumph to be.

He was a few minutes late at the rendezvous, and found that M. Papopolous and his daughter had arrived before him. His apologies were abject, and he outdid himself in politeness and small attentions. The Greek was looking particularly benign and noble this evening, a sorrowful patriarch of blameless life. Zia was looking handsome and good humored. The dinner was a pleasant one. Poirot was his best and most sparkling self. He told anecdotes, he made jokes, he paid graceful compliments to Zia Papopolous, and he told many interesting incidents of his career. The menu was a carefully selected one, and the wine was excellent.

At the close of dinner M. Papopolous inquired politely:

"And the tip I gave you? You have had your little flutter on the horse?"

"I am in communication with—er—my bookmaker," replied Poirot.

The eyes of the two men met.

"A well-known horse, eh?"

"No," said Poirot; "it is what our friends, the English, call a dark horse."

"Ah!" said M. Papopolous thoughtfully.

"Now we must step across to the Casino and have our little flutter at the roulette table," cried Poirot gaily.

At the Casino the party separated, Poirot devoting himself solely to Zia, whilst Papopolous himself drifted away.

Poirot was not fortunate, but Zia had a run of good luck, and had soon won a few thousand francs.

"It would be as well," she observed dryly to Poirot, "if I stopped now."

Poirot's eyes twinkled.

"Superb!" he exclaimed. "You are the daughter of your father, Mademoiselle Zia. To know when to stop. Ah! that is the art."

He looked around the rooms.

"I cannot see your father anywhere about," he remarked carelessly. "I will fetch your cloak for you, Mademoiselle, and we will go out in the gardens."

He did not, however, go straight to the cloakroom. His sharp eyes had seen but a little while before the departure of M. Papopolous. He was anxious to know what had become of the wily Greek. He ran him to earth unexpectedly in the big entrance hall. He was standing by one of the pillars, talking to a lady who had just arrived. The lady was Mirelle.

Poirot sidled unostentatiously around the room. He arrived at the other side of the pillar, and unnoticed by the two who were talking together in an animated fashion—or rather, that is to say, the dancer was talking, Papopolous contributing an occasional monosyllable and a good many expressive gestures.

"I tell you I must have time," the dancer was saying. "If you give me time I will get the money."

"To wait"—the Greek shrugged his shoulders—"it is awkward."

"Only a very little while," pleaded the other. "Ah! but you must! A week—ten days—that is all I ask. You can be sure of your affair. The money will be forthcoming."

Papopolous shifted a little and looked around him uneasily—to find Poirot almost at his elbow with a beaming innocent face.

"*Ah! vous voilà,* M. Papopolous. I have been looking for you. It is permitted that I take Mademoiselle Zia for a little turn in the gardens? Good evening, Mademoiselle." He bowed very low to Mirelle. "A thousand pardons that I did not see you immediately."

The dancer accepted his greetings rather impatiently. She was clearly annoyed at the interruption of her *tête-à-tête.* Poirot was quick to take the hint. Papopolous had already murmured: "Certainly—but certainly," and Poirot withdrew forthwith.

He fetched Zia's cloak, and together they strolled out into the gardens.

"This is where the suicides take place," said Zia.

Poirot shrugged his shoulders. "So it is said. Men are foolish, are they not, Mademoiselle? To eat, to drink, to breathe the good air, it is a very pleasant thing, Mademoiselle. One is foolish to leave all that simply because one has no money—or because the heart aches. *L'amour,* it causes many fatalities, does it not?"

Zia laughed.

"You should not laugh at love, Mademoiselle," said Poirot, shaking an energetic forefinger at her. "You who are young and beautiful."

"Hardly that," said Zia; "you forget that I am thirty-three, M. Poirot. I am frank with you, because it is no good being otherwise. As you told my father, it is exactly seventeen years since you aided us in Paris that time."

"When I look at you, it seems much less," said Poirot gallantly. "You were then very much as you are now, Mademoiselle, a little thinner, a little paler, a little more serious. Sixteen years old and fresh from your pension. Not quite the *petite pensionnaire,* not quite a woman. You were very delicious, very charming, Mademoiselle Zia; others thought so too, without doubt."

"At sixteen," said Zia, "one is simple and a little fool."

"That may be," said Poirot, "yes, that well may be. At sixteen one is credulous, is one not? One believes what one is told."

If he saw the quick sideways glance that the girl shot at him, he pretended not to have done so. He continued dreamily: "It was a curious affair that, altogether. Your father, Mademoiselle, has never understood the true inwardness of it."

"No?"

"When he asked me for details, for explanations, I said to him thus: 'Without scandal, I have got back for you that which was lost. You must ask no questions.' Do you know, Mademoiselle, why I said these things?"

"I have no idea," said the girl coldly.

"It was because I had a soft spot in my heart for a little pensionnaire, so pale, so thin, so serious."

"I don't understand what you are talking about," cried Zia angrily.

"Do you not, Mademoiselle? Have you forgotten Antonio Pirezzio?"

He heard the quick intake of her breath—almost a gasp.

"He came to work as an assistant in the shop, but not thus could he have got hold of what he wanted. An assistant can lift his eyes to his master's daughter, can he not? If he is young and handsome with a glib tongue. And since they cannot make love all the time, they must occasionally talk of things that interest them both—such as that very interesting thing which was temporarily in M. Papopolous' possession. And since, as you say, Mademoiselle, the young are foolish and credulous, it was easy to believe him and to give him a sight of that particular thing, to show him where it was kept. And afterwards when it is gone—when the unbelievable catastrophe has happened. Alas! The poor little pensionnaire. What a terrible position she is in. She is frightened, the poor little one. To speak or not to speak? And then there comes along that excellent fellow, Hercule Poirot. Almost a miracle it must have been, the way things arranged themselves. The priceless heirlooms are restored and there are no awkward questions."

Zia turned on him fiercely.

"You have known all the time? Who told you? Was it—was it Antonio?"

Poirot shook his head.

"No one told me," he said quietly. "I guessed. It was a good guess, was it not, Mademoiselle? You see, unless you are good at guessing, it is not much use being a detective."

The girl walked along beside him for some minutes in silence. Then she said in a hard voice:

"Well, what are you going to do about it, are you going to tell my father?"

"No," said Poirot sharply. "Certainly not."

She looked at him curiously.

"You want something from me?"

"I want your help, Mademoiselle."

"What makes you think that I can help you?"

"I do not think so. I only hope so."

"And if I do not help you, then—you will tell my father?"

"But no, but no! Debarrass yourself of that idea, Mademoiselle. I am not a blackmailer. I do not hold your secret over your head and threaten you with it."

"If I refuse to help you——" began the girl slowly.

"Then you refuse, and that is that."

"Then why——" she stopped.

"Listen, and I will tell you why. Women, Mademoiselle, are generous. If they can render a service to one who has rendered a service to them, they will do it. I was generous once to you, Mademoiselle. When I might have spoken, I held my tongue."

There was another silence; then the girl said, "My father gave you a hint the other day."

"It was very kind of him."

"I do not think," said Zia slowly, "that there is anything that I can add to that."

If Poirot was disappointed he did not show it. Not a muscle of his face changed.

"*Eh bien!*" he said cheerfully, "then we must talk of other things."

And he proceeded to chat gaily. The girl was *distraite,* however, and her answers were mechanical and not always to the point. It was when they were approaching the Casino once more that she seemed to come to a decision.

"M. Poirot?"

"Yes, Mademoiselle?"

"I—I should like to help you if I could."

"You are very amiable, Mademoiselle—very amiable."

Again there was a pause. Poirot did not press her. He was quite content to wait and let her take her own time.

"Ah bah," said Zia, "after all, why should I not tell you? My father is cautious—always cautious in everything he says. But I know that with you it is not necessary. You have told us it is only the murderer you seek, and that you are not concerned over the jewels. I believe you. You were quite right when you guessed that we were in Nice because of the rubies. They have been handed over here according to plan. My father has them now. He gave you a hint the other day as to who our mysterious client was."

"The Marquis?" murmured Poirot softly.

"Yes, the Marquis."

"Have you ever seen the Marquis, Mademoiselle Zia?"

"Once," said the girl. "But not very well," she added. "It was through a keyhole."

"That always presents difficulties," said Poirot sympathetically, "but all the same you saw him. You would know him again?"

Zia shook her head.

"He wore a mask," she explained.

"Young or old?"

"He had white hair. It may have been a wig, it may not. It fitted very well. But I do not think he was old. His walk was young, and so was his voice."

"His voice?" said Poirot thoughtfully. "Ah, his voice! Would you know it again, Mademoiselle Zia?"

"I might," said the girl.

"You were interested in him, eh? It was that that took you to the keyhole." Zia nodded.

"Yes, yes. I was curious. One had heard so much—he is not the ordinary thief—he is more like a figure of history or romance."

"Yes," said Poirot thoughtfully, "yes; perhaps so."

"But it is not this that I meant to tell you," said Zia. "It was just one other little fact that I thought might be—well—useful to you."

"Yes?" said Poirot encouragingly.

"The rubies, as I say, were handed over to my father here at Nice. I did not see the person who handed them over, but——"

"Yes?"

"I know one thing. *It was a woman.*"

29

A Letter from Home

DEAR KATHERINE—Living among grand friends as you are doing now, I don't suppose you will care to hear any of our news; but as I always thought you were a sensible girl, perhaps you are a trifle less swollen-headed than I suppose. Everything goes on much the same here. There was great trouble about the new curate, who is scandalously high. In my view, he is neither more nor less than a Roman. Everybody has spoken to the Vicar about it, but you know what the Vicar is—all Christian charity and no proper spirit. I have had a lot of trouble with maids lately. That girl Annie was no good—skirts up to her knees and wouldn't wear sensible woollen stockings. Not one of them can bear being spoken to. I have had a lot of pain with my rheumatism one way and another, and Dr. Harris persuaded me to go and see a London specialist—a waste of three guineas and a railway fare, as I told him; but by waiting until Wednesday I managed to get a cheap return. The London doctor pulled a long face and talked all round about and never straight out, until I said to him, 'I'm a plain woman, Doctor, and I like things to be plainly stated. Is it cancer, or is it not?' And then, of course, he had to say it was. They say a year with care, and not too much pain, though I am sure I can bear pain as well as any other Christian woman. Life seems rather lonely at times, with most of my friends dead or gone before. I wish you were in St. Mary Mead, my dear, and that is a fact. If you hadn't come into this money and gone off into grand society, I would have offered you double the salary poor Jane gave you to come and look after me; but there—there's no good wanting what we can't get. However, if things should go ill with you— and that is always possible. I have heard no end of tales of bogus noblemen marrying girls and getting hold of their money and then leaving them at the church door. I dare say you are too sensible for anything of the kind to happen to you, but one never knows; and never having had much attention of any kind it might easily go to your head now. So just in case, my dear, remember there is always a home for you here; and though a plain-spoken woman I am a warm-hearted one too.—Your affectionate old friend,

Amelia Viner.

P.S.—I saw a mention of you in the paper with your cousin, Viscountess Tamplin, and I cut it out and put it with my cuttings. I prayed for you on Sunday that you might be kept from pride and vainglory.

Katherine read this characteristic epistle through twice, then she laid it down and stared out of her bedroom window across the blue waters of the Mediterranean. She felt a curious lump in her throat. A sudden wave of longing for St. Mary Mead swept over her. So full of familiar, everyday, stupid little things—and yet—home. She felt very inclined to lay her head down on her arms and indulge in a real good cry.

Lenox, coming in at the moment, saved her.

"Hello, Katherine," said Lenox. "I say—what is the matter?"

"Nothing," said Katherine, grabbing up Miss Viner's letter and thrusting it into her handbag.

"You looked rather queer," said Lenox. "I say—I hope you don't mind—I rang up your detective friend, M. Poirot, and asked him to lunch with us in Nice. I said you wanted to see him, as I thought he might not come for me."

"Did you want to see him then?" asked Katherine.

"Yes," said Lenox. "I have rather lost my heart to him. I never met a man before whose eyes were really green like a cat's."

"All right," said Katherine. She spoke listlessly. The last few days had been trying. Derek Kettering's arrest had been the topic of the hour, and the Blue Train Mystery had been thrashed out from every conceivable standpoint.

"I have ordered the car," said Lenox, "and I have told Mother some lie or other—unfortunately I can't remember exactly what; but it won't matter, as she never remembers. If she knew where we were going, she would want to come too, to pump M. Poirot."

The two girls arrived at the Negresco to find Poirot waiting.

He was full of Gallic politeness, and showered so many compliments upon the two girls that they were soon helpless with laughter; yet for all that the meal was not a gay one. Katherine was dreamy and distracted, and Lenox made bursts of conversation, interspersed by silences. As they were sitting on the terrace sipping their coffee she suddenly attacked Poirot bluntly.

"How are things going? You know what I mean?"

Poirot shrugged his shoulders. "They take their course," he said.

"And you are just letting them take their course?"

He looked at Lenox a little sadly.

"You are young, Mademoiselle, but there are three things that cannot be hurried—*le bon Dieu,* Nature, and old people."

"Nonsense!" said Lenox. "You are not old."

"Ah, it is pretty what you say there."

"Here is Major Knighton," said Lenox.

Katherine looked around quickly and then turned back again.

"He is with Mr. Van Aldin," continued Lenox. "There is something I want to ask Major Knighton about. I won't be a minute."

Left alone together, Poirot bent forward and murmured to Katherine:

"You are *distraite,* Mademoiselle; your thoughts, they are far away, are they not?"

"Just as far as England, no farther."

Guided by a sudden impulse, she took the letter she had received that morning and handed it across to him to read.

"That is the first word that has come to me from my old life; somehow or other—it hurts."

He read it through and then handed it back to her. "So you are going back to St. Mary Mead?" he said slowly.

"No, I am not," said Katherine; "why should I?"

"Ah," said Poirot, "it is my mistake. You will excuse me one little minute."

He strolled across to where Lenox Tamplin was talking to Van Aldin and Knighton. The American looked old and haggard. He greeted Poirot with a curt nod but without any other sign of animation.

As he turned to reply to some observation made by Lenox, Poirot drew Knighton aside.

"M. Van Aldin looks ill," he said.

"Do you wonder?" asked Knighton. "The scandal of Derek Kettering's arrest has about put the lid on things, as far as he is concerned. He is even regretting that he asked you to find out the truth."

"He should go back to England," said Poirot.

"We are going the day after to-morrow."

"That is good news," said Poirot.

He hesitated, and looked across the terrace to where Katherine was sitting.

"I wish," he murmured, "that you could tell Miss Grey that."

"Tell her what?"

"That you—I mean that M. Van Aldin is returning to England."

Knighton looked a little puzzled, but he readily crossed the terrace and joined Katherine.

Poirot saw him go with a satisfied nod of the head, and then joined Lenox and the American. After a minute or two they joined the others. Conversation was general for a few minutes, then the millionaire and his secretary departed. Poirot also prepared to take his departure.

"A thousand thanks for your hospitality, Mesdemoiselles," he cried; "it has been a most charming luncheon. *Ma foi,* I needed it!" He swelled out his chest and thumped it. "I am now a lion—a giant. Ah, Mademoiselle Katherine, you have not seen me as I can be. You have seen the gentle, the calm Hercule Poirot; but there is another Hercule Poirot. I go now to bully, to threaten, to strike terror into the hearts of those who listen to me."

He looked at them in a self-satisfied way, and they both appeared to be duly impressed, though Lenox was biting her under lip, and the corners of Katherine's mouth had a suspicious twitch.

"And I shall do it," he said gravely. "Oh yes, I shall succeed."

He had gone but a few steps when Katherine's voice made him turn.

"M. Poirot, I—I want to tell you. I think you were right in what you said. I am going back to England almost immediately."

Poirot stared at her very hard, and under the directness of his scrutiny she blushed.

"I see," he said gravely.

"I don't believe you do," said Katherine.

"I know more than you think, Mademoiselle," he said quietly.

He left her, with an odd little smile upon his lips. Entering a waiting car, he drove to Antibes.

Hippolyte, the Comte de la Roche's wooden-faced manservant, was busy at the Villa Marina polishing his master's beautiful cut table glass. The Comte de la Roche himself had gone to Monte Carlo for the day. Chancing to look out of the window, Hippolyte espied a visitor walking briskly up to the hall door, a visitor of so uncommon a type that Hippolyte, experienced as he was, had some difficulty in placing him. Calling to his wife, Marie, who was busy in the kitchen, he drew her attention to what he called *ce type là.*

"It is not the police again?" said Marie anxiously.

"Look for yourself," said Hippolyte.

Marie looked.

"Certainly not the police," she declared. "I am glad."

"They have not really worried us much," said Hippolyte. "In fact, but for Monsieur le Comte's warning, I should never have guessed that stranger at the wineshop to be what he was."

The hall bell pealed and Hippolyte, in a grave and decorous manner, went to open the door.

"M. le Comte, I regret to say, is not at home."

The little man with the large moustaches beamed placidly.

"I know that," he replied. "You are Hippolyte Flavelle, are you not?"

"Yes, Monsieur, that is my name."

"And you have a wife, Marie Flavelle?"

"Yes, Monsieur, but——"

"I desire to see you both," said the stranger, and he stepped nimbly past Hippolyte into the hall.

"Your wife is doubtless in the kitchen," he said. "I will go there."

Before Hippolyte could recover his breath, the other had selected the right door at the back of the hall and passed along the passage and into the kitchen, where Marie paused openmouthed to stare at him.

"*Voilà,*" said the stranger, and sank into a wooden armchair; "I am Hercule Poirot."

"Yes, Monsieur?"

"You do not know the name?"

"I have never heard it," said Hippolyte.

"Permit me to say that you have been badly educated. It is the name of one of the great ones of this world."

He sighed and folded his hands across his chest.

Hippolyte and Marie were staring at him uneasily. They were at a loss what to make of this unexpected and extremely strange visitor.

"Monsieur desires——" murmured Hippolyte mechanically.

"I desire to know why you have lied to the police."

"Monsieur!" cried Hippolyte; "I—lied to the police? Never have I done such a thing."

M. Poirot shook his head.

"You are wrong," he said; "you have done it on several occasions. Let me see." He took a small notebook from his pocket and consulted it. "Ah, yes; on seven occasions at least. I will recite them to you."

In a gentle unemotional voice he proceeded to outline the seven occasions. Hippolyte was taken aback.

"But it is not of these past lapses that I wish to speak," continued Poirot, "only, my dear friend, do not get into the habit of thinking yourself too clever. I come now to the particular lie in which I am concerned—your statement that the Comte de la Roche arrived at this villa on the morning of 14th January."

"But that was no lie, Monsieur; that was the truth. Monsieur le Comte arrived here on the morning of Tuesday, the 14th. That is so, Marie, is it not?"

Marie assented eagerly.

"Ah, yes, that is quite right. I remember it perfectly."

"Ah," said Poirot, "and what did you give your good master for *déjeuner* that day?"

"I——" Marie paused, trying to collect herself.

"Odd," said Poirot, "how one remembers some things—and forgets others."

He leaned forward and struck the table a blow with his fist; his eyes flashed with anger.

"Yes, yes, it is as I say. You tell your lies and you think nobody knows. But there are two people who know. Yes—two people. One is *le bon Dieu*——"

He raised a hand to heaven, and then settling himself back in his chair and shutting his eyelids, he murmured comfortably:

"And the other is Hercule Poirot."

"I assure you, Monsieur, you are completely mistaken. Monsieur le Comte left Paris on Monday night——"

"True," said Poirot—"by the Rapide. I do not know where he broke his journey. Perhaps you do not know that. What I do know is that he arrived here on Wednesday morning, and not on Tuesday morning."

"Monsieur is mistaken," said Marie stolidly.

Poirot rose to his feet.

"Then the law must take its course," he murmured. "A pity."

"What do you mean, Monsieur?" asked Marie, with a shade of uneasiness.

"You will be arrested and held as accomplices concerned in the murder of Mrs. Kettering, the English lady who was killed."

"Murder!"

The man's face had gone chalk white, his knees knocked together. Marie dropped the rolling pin and began to weep.

"But it is impossible—impossible. I thought——"

"Since you stick to your story, there is nothing to be said. I think you are both foolish."

He was turning toward the door when an agitated voice arrested him.

"Monsieur, Monsieur, just a little moment. I—I had no idea that it was anything of this kind. I—I thought it was just a matter concerning a lady. There have been little awkwardnesses with the police over ladies before. But murder—that is very different."

"I have no patience with you," cried Poirot. He turned round on them and angrily shook his fist in Hippolyte's face. "Am I to stop here all day, arguing with a couple of imbeciles thus? It is the truth I want. If you will not give it to me, that is your look out. *For the last time, when did Monsieur le Comte arrive at the Villa Marina—Tuesday morning or Wednesday morning?"*

"Wednesday," gasped the man, and behind him Marie nodded confirmation.

Poirot regarded them for a minute or two, then inclined his head gravely.

"You are wise, my children," he said quietly. "Very nearly you were in serious trouble."

He left the Villa Marina, smiling to himself.

"One guess confirmed," he murmured to himself. "Shall I take a chance on the other?"

It was six o'clock when the card of Monsieur Hercule Poirot was brought up to Mirelle. She stared at it for a moment or two, and then nodded. When Poirot entered, he found her walking up and down the room feverishly. She turned on him furiously.

"Well?" she cried. "Well? What is it now? Have you not tortured me enough, all of you? Have you not made me betray my poor Dereek? What more do you want?"

"Just one little question, Mademoiselle. After the train left Lyons, when you entered Mrs. Kettering's compartment——"

"What is that?"

Poirot looked at her with an air of mild reproach and began again.

"I say when you entered Mrs. Kettering's compartment——"

"I never did."

"And found her——"

"I never did.

"Ah, sacré!"

He turned on her in a rage and shouted at her, so that she cowered back before him.

"Will you lie to me? I tell you I know what happened as well as though I had been there. You went into her compartment and you found her dead. I tell you I know it. To lie to me is dangerous. Be careful, Mademoiselle Mirelle."

Her eyes wavered beneath his gaze and fell.

"I—I didn't——" she began uncertainly and stopped.

"There is only one thing about which I wonder," said Poirot—"I wonder, Mademoiselle, if you found what you were looking for or whether——"

"Whether what?"

"Or whether someone else had been before you."

"I will answer no more questions," screamed the dancer. She tore herself away from Poirot's restraining hand, and flinging herself down on the floor in a frenzy, she screamed and sobbed. A frightened maid came rushing in.

Hercule Poirot shrugged his shoulders, raised his eyebrows, and quietly left the room.

But he seemed satisfied.

30

Miss Viner Gives Judgment

KATHERINE LOOKED OUT of Miss Viner's bedroom window. It was raining, not violently, but with a quiet, well-bred persistence. The window looked out on a strip of front garden with a path down to the gate and neat little flower-beds on either side, where later roses and pinks and blue hyacinths would bloom.

Miss Viner was lying in a large Victorian bedstead. A tray with the remains of breakfast had been pushed to one side and she was busy opening her correspondence and making various caustic comments upon it.

Katherine had an open letter in her hand and was reading it through for the second time. It was dated from the Ritz Hotel, Paris.

> CHÈRE MADEMOISELLE KATHERINE [it began]—I trust that you are in good health and that the return to the English winter has not proved too depressing. Me, I prosecute my inquiries with the utmost diligence. Do not think that it is the holiday that I take here. Very shortly I shall be in England, and I hope then to have the pleasure of meeting you once more. It shall be so, shall it not? On arrival in London I shall write to you. You remember that we are the colleagues in this affair? But indeed I think you know that very well.
>
> Be assured, Mademoiselle, of my most respectful and devoted sentiments.
>
> HERCULE POIROT.

Katherine frowned slightly. It was as though something in the letter puzzled and intrigued her.

"A choir boys' picnic indeed," came from Miss Viner. "Tommy Saunders and Albert Dykes ought to be left behind, and I shan't subscribe to it unless they are. What those two boys think they are doing in church on Sundays I don't know. Tommy sang, 'O God, make speed to save us,' and never opened his lips again, and if Albert Dykes wasn't sucking a mint humbug, my nose is not what it is and always has been."

"I know, they are awful," agreed Katherine.

She opened her second letter, and a sudden flush came to her cheeks. Miss Viner's voice in the room seemed to recede into the far distance.

When she came back to a sense of her surroundings Miss Viner was bringing a long speech to a triumphant termination.

"And I said to her, 'Not at all. As it happens, Miss Grey is Lady Tamplin's own cousin.' What do you think of that?"

"Were you fighting my battles for me? That was very sweet of you."

"You can put it that way if you like. There is nothing to me in a title. Vicar's wife or no vicar's wife, that woman is a cat. Hinting you had bought your way into Society."

"Perhaps she was not so very far wrong."

"And look at you," continued Miss Viner. "Have you come back a stuck-up fine lady, as well you might have done? No, there you are, as sensible as ever you were, with a pair of good Balbriggan stockings on and sensible shoes. I spoke to Ellen about it only yesterday. 'Ellen,' I said, 'you look at Miss Grey. She has been hobnobbing with some of the greatest in the land, and does she go about as you do with skirts up to her knees and silk stockings that ladder when you look at them, and the most ridiculous shoes that ever I set eyes on?' "

Katherine smiled a little to herself; it had apparently been worthwhile to conform to Miss Viner's prejudices. The old lady went on with increasing gusto.

"It has been a great relief to me that you have not had your head turned. Only the other day I was looking for my cuttings. I have several about Lady Tamplin and her War Hospital and whatnot, but I cannot lay my hand upon them. I wish you would look, my dear; your eyesight is better than mine. They are all in a box in the bureau drawer."

Katherine glanced down at the letter in her hand and was about to speak, but checked herself, and going over to the bureau found the box of cuttings and began to look over them. Since her return to St. Mary Mead her heart had gone out to Miss Viner in admiration of the old woman's stoicism and pluck. She felt that there was little she could do for her old friend, but she knew from experience how much those seemingly small trifles meant to old people.

"Here is one," she said presently. " 'Viscountess Tamplin, who is running her villa at Nice as an Officers' Hospital, has just been the victim of a sensational robbery, her jewels having been stolen. Amongst them were some very famous emeralds, heirlooms of the Tamplin family.' "

"Probably paste," said Miss Viner; "a lot of these Society women's jewels are."

"Here is another," said Katherine. "A picture of her, 'A charming camera study of Viscountess Tamplin with her little daughter Lenox.' "

"Let me look," said Miss Viner. "You can't see much of the child's face, can you? But I dare say that is just as well. Things go by contraries in this world and beautiful mothers have hideous children. I dare say the photographer realized that to take the back of the child's head was the best thing he could do for her."

Katherine laughed.

" 'One of the smartest hostesses on the Riviera this season is Viscountess Tamplin, who has a villa at Cap Martin. Her cousin, Miss Grey, who recently inherited a vast fortune in a most romantic manner, is staying with her there.' "

"That is the one I wanted," said Miss Viner. "I expect there has been a picture of you in one of the papers that I have missed; you know the kind of thing. Mrs. Somebody or other Jones-Williams, at the something or other Point-to-Point, usually carrying a shooting-stick and having one foot lifted up in the air. It must be a trial to some of them to see what they look like."

Kathcrinc did not answcr. Shc was smoothing out thc cutting with hcr finger, and her face had a puzzled, worried look. Then she drew the second letter out of its envelope and mastered its contents once more. She turned to her friend.

"Miss Viner? I wonder—there is a friend of mine, someone I met on the Riviera, who wants very much to come down and see me here?"

"A man," said Miss Viner.

"Yes."

"Who is he?"

"He is secretary to Mr. Van Aldin, the American millionaire."

"What is his name?"

"Knighton. Major Knighton."

"Hm—secretary to a millionaire. And wants to come down here. Now, Katherine, I am going to say something to you for your own good. You are a nice girl and a sensible girl, and though you have your head screwed on the right way about most things, every woman makes a fool of herself once in her life. Ten to one what this man is after is your money."

With a gesture she arrested Katherine's reply. "I have been waiting for something of this kind. What is a secretary to a millionaire? Nine times out of ten it is a young man who likes living soft. A young man with nice manners and a taste for luxury and no brains and no enterprise, and if there is anything that is a softer job than being a secretary to a millionaire it is marrying a rich woman for her money. I am not saying that you might not be some man's fancy. But you are not young, and though you have a very good complexion you are not a beauty, and what I say to you is, don't make a fool of yourself; but if you are determined to do so, do see that your money is properly tied up on yourself. There, now I have finished. What have you got to say?"

"Nothing," said Katherine; "but would you mind if he did come down to see me?"

"I wash my hands of it," said Miss Viner. "I have done my duty, and whatever happens now is on your own head. Would you like him to lunch or to dinner? I dare say Ellen could manage dinner—that is, if she didn't lose her head."

"Lunch would be very nice," said Katherine. "It is awfully kind of you, Miss Viner. He asked me to ring him up, so I will do so and say that we shall be pleased if he will lunch with us. He will motor down from town."

"Ellen does a steak with grilled tomatoes pretty fairly," said Miss Viner.

"She doesn't do it well, but she does it better than anything else. It is no good having a tart because she is heavy handed with pastry; but her little castle puddings are not bad, and I dare say you could find a nice piece of Stilton at Abbot's. I have always heard that gentlemen like a nice piece of Stilton, and there is a good deal of father's wine left, a bottle of sparkling Moselle, perhaps."

"Oh no, Miss Viner; that is really not necessary."

"Nonsense, my child. No gentleman is happy unless he drinks something with his meal. There is some good pre-war whisky if you think he would prefer that. Now do as I say and don't argue. The key of the wine-cellar is in the third drawer down in the dressing-table, in the second pair of stockings on the left-hand side."

Katherine went obediently to the spot indicated.

"The second pair, now mind," said Miss Viner. "The first pair has my diamond earrings and my filigree brooch in it."

"Oh," said Katherine, rather taken aback, "wouldn't you like them put in your jewel case?"

Miss Viner gave vent to a terrific and prolonged snort.

"No, indeed! I have much too much sense for that sort of thing, thank you. Dear, dear, I well remember how my poor father had a safe built in downstairs. Pleased as Punch he was with it, and he said to my mother, 'Now, Mary, you bring me your jewels in their case every night and I will lock them away for you.' My mother was a very tactful woman, and she knew that gentlemen like having their own way, and she brought him the jewel case locked up just as he said.

"And one night burglars broke in, and of course—naturally—the first thing they went for was the safe! It would be, with my father talking up and down the village and bragging about it until you might have thought he kept all King Solomon's diamonds there. They made a clean sweep, got the tankards, the silver cups, and the presentation gold plate that my father had had presented to him, *and* the jewel case."

She sighed reminiscently. "My father was in a great state over my mother's jewels. There was the Venetian set and some very fine cameos, and some pale pink corals, and two diamond rings with quite large stones in them. And then, of course, she had to tell him that, being a sensible woman, she had kept her jewelry rolled up in a pair of corsets, and there it was still as safe as anything."

"And the jewel case had been quite empty?"

"Oh no, dear," said Miss Viner, "it would have been too light a weight then. My mother was a very intelligent woman; she saw to that. She kept her buttons in the jewel case, and a very handy place it was. Boot buttons in the top tray, trouser buttons in the second tray, and assorted buttons below. Curiously enough, my father was quite annoyed with her. He said he didn't like deceit. But I mustn't go chattering on; you want to go and ring up your friend, and mind you choose a nice piece of steak, and tell Ellen she is not to have holes in her stockings when she waits at lunch."

"Is her name Ellen or Helen, Miss Viner? I thought——"

Miss Viner closed her eyes.

"I can sound my h's, dear, as well as anyone, but Helen is *not* a suitable name for a servant. I don't know what the mothers in the lower classes are coming to nowadays."

The rain had cleared away when Knighton arrived at the cottage. The pale fitful sunshine shone down on it and burnished Katherine's head as she stood in the doorway to welcome him. He came up to her quickly, almost boyishly.

"I say, I hope you don't mind. I simply had to see you again soon. I hope the friend you are staying with does not mind."

"Come in and make friends with her," said Katherine. "She can be most alarming, but you will soon find that she has the softest heart in the world."

Miss Viner was enthroned majestically in the drawing room, wearing a complete set of the cameos which had been so providentially preserved in the family. She greeted Knighton with dignity and an austere politeness which would have damped many men. Knighton, however, had a charm of manner which was not easily set aside, and after about ten minutes Miss Viner thawed perceptibly. Luncheon was a merry meal, and Ellen, or Helen, in a new pair of silk stockings devoid of ladders performed prodigies of waiting. Afterward, Katherine and Knighton went for a walk and they came back to have tea *tête-à-tête,* since Miss Viner had gone to lie down.

When the car had finally driven off Katherine went slowly upstairs. A voice called her and she went into Miss Viner's bedroom.

"Friend gone?"

"Yes. Thank you so much for letting me ask him down."

"No need to thank me. Do you think I am the sort of old curmudgeon who never will do anything for anybody?"

"I think you are a dear," said Katherine affectionately.

"Humph," said Miss Viner, mollified.

As Katherine was leaving the room she called her back.

"Katherine?"

"Yes."

"I was wrong about that young man of yours. A man when he is making up to anybody can be cordial and gallant and full of little attentions and altogether charming. But when a man is really in love he can't help looking like a sheep. Now, whenever that young man looked at you he looked like a sheep. I take back all I said this morning. It is genuine."

31

Mr. Aarons Lunches

"AH!" SAID MR. Joseph Aarons appreciatively.

He took a long draught from his tankard, set it down with a sigh, wiped the froth from his lips, and beamed across the table at his host, Monsieur Hercule Poirot.

"Give me," said Mr. Aarons, "a good Porterhouse steak and a tankard of something worth drinking, and anyone can have your French fallals and whatnots, your ordoovres and your omelettes and your little bits of quail. Give me," he reiterated, "a Porterhouse steak."

Poirot, who had just complied with this request, smiled sympathetically.

"Not that there is much wrong with a steak and kidney pudding," continued Mr. Aarons. "Apple tart? Yes, I will take apple tart, thank you, Miss, and a jug of cream."

The meal proceeded. Finally, with a long sigh, Mr. Aarons laid down his spoon and fork preparatory to toying with some cheese before turning his mind to other matters.

"There was a little matter of business I think you said, Monsieur Poirot," he remarked. "Anything I can do to help you I am sure I shall be most happy."

"That is very kind of you," said Poirot. "I said to myself, 'If you want to know anything about the dramatic profession there is one person who knows all that is to be known and that is my old friend, Mr. Joseph Aarons.' "

"And you don't say far wrong," said Mr. Aarons complacently; "whether it is past, present, or future, Joe Aarons is the man to come to."

"*Précisément.* Now I want to ask you, Monsieur Aarons, what you know about a young woman called Kidd."

"Kidd? Kitty Kidd?"

"Kitty Kidd."

"Pretty smart, she was. Male impersonator, song and a dance—— That one?"

"That is the one."

"*Very* smart, she was. Made a good income. Never out of an engagement. Male impersonation mostly, but, as a matter of fact, you could not touch her as a character actress."

"So I have heard," said Poirot; "but she has not been appearing lately, has she?"

"No. Dropped right out of things. Went over to France and took up with some swell nobleman there. She quitted the stage then for good and all, I guess."

"How long ago was that?"

"Let me see. Three years ago. And she has been a loss—let me tell you that."

"She was clever?"

"Clever as a cartload of monkeys."

"You don't know the name of the man she became friends with in Paris?"

"He was a swell, I know that. A Count—or was it a Marquis? Now I come to think of it, I believe it was a Marquis."

"And you know nothing about her since?"

"Nothing. Never even run across her accidentally like. I bet she is tooling it round some of these foreign resorts. Being a Marquise to the life. You couldn't put one over on Kitty. She would give as good as she got any day."

"I see," said Poirot thoughtfully.

"I am sorry I can't tell you more, Monsieur Poirot," said the other. "I would like to be of use to you if I could. You did me a good turn once."

"Ah, but we are quits on that; you, too, did me a good turn."

"One good turn deserves another. Ha, ha!" said Mr. Aarons.

"Your profession must be a very interesting one," said Poirot.

"So-so," said Mr. Aarons noncommittally. "Taking the rough with the smooth, it is all right. I don't do so badly at it, all things considered, but you have to keep your eyes skinned. Never know what the public will jump for next."

"Dancing has come very much to the fore in the last few years," murmured Poirot reflectively.

"I never saw anything in this Russian ballet, but people like it. Too high-brow for me."

"I met one dancer out on the Riviera—Mademoiselle Mirelle."

"Mirelle? She is hot stuff, by all accounts. There is always money going to back her—though, so far as that goes, the girl can dance; I have seen her, and I know what I am talking about. I never had much to do with her myself, but I hear she is a terror to deal with. Tempers and tantrums all the time."

"Yes," said Poirot thoughtfully; "yes, so I should imagine."

"Temperament!" said Mr. Aarons, "temperament! That is what they call it themselves. My missus was a dancer before she married me, but I am thankful to say she never had any temperament. You don't want temperament in the home, Monsieur Poirot."

"I agree with you, my friend; it is out of place there."

"A woman should be calm and sympathetic, and a good cook," said Mr. Aarons.

"Mirelle has not been long before the public, has she?" asked Poirot.

"About two and a half years, that is all," said Mr. Aarons. "Some French Duke started her. I hear now that she has taken up with the ex-Prime Minister of Greece. These are the chaps who manage to put money away quietly."

"That is news to me," said Poirot.

"Oh, she's not one to let the grass grow under her feet. They say that young Kettering murdered his wife on her account. I don't know, I am sure. Anyway, he is in prison, and she had to look round for herself, and pretty smart she has been about it. They say she is wearing a ruby the size of a pigeon's egg—not that I have ever seen a pigeon's egg myself, but that is what they always call it in works of fiction."

"A ruby the size of a pigeon's egg!" said Poirot. His eyes were green and catlike. "How interesting!"

"I had it from a friend of mine," said Mr. Aarons. "But, for all I know, it may be colored glass. They are all the same, these women—they never stop telling tall stories about their jewels. Mirelle goes about bragging that it has got a curse on it. 'Heart of Fire,' I think she calls it."

"But if I remember rightly," said Poirot, "the ruby that is named 'Heart of Fire' is the center stone in a necklace."

"There you are! Didn't I tell you there is no end to the lies women will tell about their jewelry? This is a single stone, hung on a platinum chain round her neck; but, as I said before, ten to one it is a bit of colored glass."

"No," said Poirot gently; "no—somehow I do not think it is colored glass."

32

Katherine and Poirot
Compare Notes

"YOU HAVE CHANGED, Mademoiselle," said Poirot suddenly. He and Katherine were seated opposite each other at a small table at the Savoy.

"Yes, you have changed," he continued.

"In what way?"

"Mademoiselle, these *nuances* are difficult to express."

"I am older."

"Yes, you are older. And by that I do not mean that the wrinkles and the crows' feet are coming. When I first saw you, Mademoiselle, you were a looker-on at life. You had the quiet, amused look of one who sits back in the stalls and watches the play."

"And now?"

"Now, you no longer watch. It is an absurd thing, perhaps, that I say here, but you have the wary look of a fighter who is playing a difficult game."

"My old lady is difficult sometimes," said Katherine, with a smile; "but I can assure you that I don't engage in deadly contests with her. You must go down and see her someday, Monsieur Poirot. I think you are one of the people who would appreciate her pluck and her spirit."

There was a silence while the waiter deftly served them with chicken *en casserole.* When he had departed, Poirot said:

"You have heard me speak of my friend Hastings?—he who said that I was a human oyster. *Eh bien,* Mademoiselle, I have met my match in you. You, far more than I, play a lone hand."

"Nonsense," said Katherine lightly.

"Never does Hercule Poirot talk nonsense. It is as I say."

Again there was a silence. Poirot broke it by inquiring:

"Have you seen any of our Riviera friends since you have been back, Mademoiselle?"

"I have seen something of Major Knighton."

"A-ha! Is that so?"

Something in Poirot's twinkling eyes made Katherine lower hers.

"So Mr. Van Aldin remains in London?"

"Yes."

"I must try to see him tomorrow or the next day."

"You have news for him?"

"What makes you think that?"

"I—wondered, that is all."

Poirot looked across at her with twinkling eyes.

"And now, Mademoiselle, there is much that you wish to ask me, I can see that. And why not? Is not the affair of the Blue Train our own 'Roman Policier'?"

"Yes, there are things I should like to ask you."

"Eh bien?"

Katherine looked up with a sudden air of resolution.

"What were you doing in Paris, Monsieur Poirot?"

Poirot smiled slightly.

"I made a call at the Russian Embassy."

"Oh."

"I see that that tells you nothing. But I will not be a human oyster. No, I will lay my cards on the table, which is assuredly a thing that oysters do not do. You suspect, do you not, that I am not satisfied with the case against Derek Kettering?"

"That is what I have been wondering. I thought, in Nice, that you had finished with the case."

"You do not say all that you mean, Mademoiselle. But I admit everything. It was I—my researches—which placed Derek Kettering where he is now. But for me the Examining Magistrate would still be vainly trying to fasten the crime on the Comte de la Roche. *Eh bien,* Mademoiselle, what I have done I do not regret. I have only one duty—to discover the truth, and that way led straight to Mr. Kettering. But did it end there? The police say yes, but I, Hercule Poirot, am not satisfied."

He broke off suddenly. "Tell me, Mademoiselle, have you heard from Mademoiselle Lenox lately?"

"One very short, scrappy letter. She is, I think, annoyed with me for coming back to England."

Poirot nodded.

"I had an interview with her the night that Monsieur Kettering was arrested. It was an interesting interview in more ways than one."

Again he fell silent, and Katherine did not interrupt his train of thought.

"Mademoiselle," he said at last, "I am now on delicate ground, yet I will say this to you. There is, I think, someone who loves Monsieur Kettering—correct me if I am wrong—and for her sake—well—for her sake I hope that I am right and the police are wrong. You know who that someone is?"

There was a pause, then Katherine said:

"Yes—I think I know."

Poirot leaned across the table toward her.

"I am not satisfied, Mademoiselle; no, I am not satisfied. The facts, the main facts, led straight to Monsieur Kettering. But there is one thing that has been left out of account."

"And what is that?"

"The disfigured face of the victim. I have asked myself, Mademoiselle, a hundred times, 'Was Derek Kettering the kind of man who would deal that smashing blow after having committed the murder?' What end would it serve? What purpose would it accomplish? Was it a likely action for one of Monsieur Kettering's temperament? And, Mademoiselle, the answer to these questions is profoundly unsatisfactory. Again and again I go back to that one point—'why?' And the only things I have to help me to a solution of the problem are these."

He whipped out his pocketbook and extracted something from it which he held between his finger and thumb.

"Do you remember, Mademoiselle? You saw me take these hairs from the rug in the railway carriage."

Katherine leaned forward, scrutinizing the hairs keenly.

Poirot nodded his head slowly several times.

"They suggest nothing to you, I see that, Mademoiselle. And yet—I think somehow that you see a good deal."

"I have had ideas," said Katherine slowly, "curious ideas. That is why I ask you what you were doing in Paris, Monsieur Poirot."

"When I wrote to you——"

"From the Ritz?"

A curious smile came over Poirot's face.

"Yes, as you say, from the Ritz. I am a luxurious person sometimes—when a millionaire pays."

"The Russian Embassy," said Katherine, frowning. "No, I don't see where that comes in."

"It does not come in directly, Mademoiselle. I went there to get certain information. I saw a particular personage and I threatened him—yes, Mademoiselle, I, Hercule Poirot, threatened him."

"With the police?"

"No," said Poirot dryly, "with the Press—a much more deadly weapon."

He looked at Katherine and she smiled at him, just shaking her head.

"Are you not just turning back into an oyster again, Monsieur Poirot?"

"No, no! I do not wish to make mysteries. See, I will tell you everything. I suspect this man of being the active party in the sale of the jewels of Monsieur Van Aldin. I tax him with it, and in the end I get the whole story out of him. I learn where the jewels were handed over, and I learn, too, of the man who paced up and down outside in the street—a man with a venerable head of white hair, but who walked with the light, springy step of a young man—and I give that man a name in my own mind—the name of 'Monsieur le Marquis.'"

"And now you have come to London to see Mr. Van Aldin?"

"Not entirely for that reason. I had other work to do. Since I have been in London I have seen two more people—a theatrical agent and a Harley Street doctor. From each of them I have got certain information. Put these things together, Mademoiselle, and see if you can make of them the same as I do."

"I?"

"Yes, you. I will tell you one thing, Mademoiselle. There has been a doubt all along in my mind as to whether the robbery and the murder were done by the same person. For a long time I was not sure——"

"And now?"

"And now I *know*."

There was a silence. Then Katherine lifted her head. Her eyes were shining.

"I am not clever like you, Monsieur Poirot. Half the things that you have been telling me don't seem to me to point anywhere at all. The ideas that came to me came from such an entirely different angle——"

"Ah, but that is always so," said Poirot quietly. "A mirror shows the truth, but everyone stands in a different place for looking into the mirror."

"My ideas may be absurd—they may be entirely different from yours, but——"

"Yes?"

"Tell me, does this help you at all?"

He took a newspaper cutting from her outstretched hand. He read it and, looking up, he nodded gravely.

"As I told you, Mademoiselle, one stands at a different angle for looking into the mirror, but it is the same mirror and the same things are reflected there."

Katherine got up. "I must rush," she said. "I have only just time to catch my train. Monsieur Poirot——"

"Yes, Mademoiselle."

"It—it mustn't be much longer, you understand. I—I can't go on much longer."

There was a break in her voice.

He patted her hand reassuringly.

"Courage, Mademoiselle, you must not fail now; the end is very near."

33

A New Theory

"Monsieur Poirot wants to see you, sir."

"Damn the fellow!" said Van Aldin.

Knighton remained sympathetically silent.

Van Aldin got up from his chair and paced up and down.

"I suppose you have seen the cursed newspapers this morning?"

"I have glanced at them, sir."

"Still at it hammer and tongs?"

"I am afraid so, sir."

The millionaire sat down again and pressed his hand to his forehead.

"If I had had an idea of this," he groaned. "I wish to God I had never got that little Belgian to ferret out the truth. Find Ruth's murderer—that was all I thought about."

"You wouldn't have liked your son-in-law to go scot free?"

Van Aldin sighed.

"I would have preferred to take the law into my own hands."

"I don't think that would have been a very wise proceeding, sir."

"All the same—are you sure the fellow wants to see me?"

"Yes, Mr. Van Aldin. He is very urgent about it."

"Then I suppose he will have to. He can come along this morning if he likes."

It was a very fresh and debonair Poirot who was ushered in. He did not seem to see any lack of cordiality in the millionaire's manner, and chatted pleasantly about various trifles. He was in London, he explained, to see his doctor. He mentioned the name of an eminent surgeon.

"No, no, *pas la guerre*—a memory of my days in the police force, a bullet of a rascally Apache."

He touched his left shoulder and winced realistically.

"I always consider you a lucky man, Monsieur Van Aldin; you are not like our popular idea of American millionaires, martyrs to the dyspepsia."

"I am pretty tough," said Van Aldin. "I lead a very simple life, you know; plain fare and not too much of it."

"You have seen something of Miss Grey, have you not?" inquired Poirot, innocently turning to the secretary.

"I—yes; once or twice," said Knighton.

He blushed slightly and Van Aldin exclaimed in surprise:

"Funny you never mentioned to me that you had seen her, Knighton?"

"I didn't think you would be interested, sir."

"I like that girl very much," said Van Aldin.

"It is a thousand pities that she should have buried herself once more in St. Mary Mead," said Poirot.

"It is very fine of her," said Knighton hotly. "There are very few people who would bury themselves down there to look after a cantankerous old woman who has no earthly claim on her."

"I am silent," said Poirot, his eyes twinkling a little; "but all the same I say it is a pity. And now, Messieurs, let us come to business."

Both the other men looked at him in some surprise.

"You must not be shocked or alarmed at what I am about to say. Supposing, Monsieur Van Aldin, that, after all, Monsieur Derek Kettering did not murder his wife?"

"What?"

Both men stared at him in blank surprise.

"Supposing, I say, that Monsieur Kettering did not murder his wife?"

"Are you mad, Monsieur Poirot?"

It was Van Aldin who spoke.

"No," said Poirot, "I am not mad. I am eccentric, perhaps—at least certain people say so; but as regards my profession, I am very much, as one says, 'all there.' I ask you, Monsieur Van Aldin, whether you would be glad or sorry if what I tell you should be the case?"

Van Aldin stared at him.

"Naturally I should be glad," he said at last. "Is this an exercise in suppositions, Monsieur Poirot, or are there any facts behind it?"

Poirot looked at the ceiling.

"There is an off chance," he said quietly, "that it might be the Comte de la Roche after all. At least I have succeeded in upsetting his alibi."

"How did you manage that?"

Poirot shrugged his shoulders modestly.

"I have my own methods. The exercise of a little tact, a little cleverness— and the thing is done."

"But the rubies," said Van Aldin, "these rubies that the Count had in his possession were false."

"And clearly he would not have committed the crime except for the rubies.

But you are overlooking one point, Monsieur Van Aldin. Where the rubies were concerned, someone might have been before him."

"But this is an entirely new theory," cried Knighton.

"Do you really believe all this rigmarole, Monsieur Poirot?" demanded the millionaire.

"The thing is not proved," said Poirot quietly. "It is as yet only a theory, but I tell you this, Monsieur Van Aldin, the facts are worth investigating. You must come out with me to the south of France and go into the case on the spot."

"You really think this is necessary—that I should go, I mean."

"I thought it would be what you yourself would wish," said Poirot.

There was a hint of reproach in his tone which was not lost upon the other.

"Yes, yes, of course," he said. "When do you wish to start, Monsieur Poirot?"

"You are very busy at present, sir," murmured Knighton.

But the millionaire had now made up his mind, and he waved the other's objections aside.

"I guess this business comes first," he said. "All right, Monsieur Poirot, tomorrow. What train?"

"We will go, I think, by the Blue Train," said Poirot, and he smiled.

34

The Blue Train Again

"THE MILLIONAIRE'S TRAIN," as it is sometimes called, swung round a curve of line at what seemed a dangerous speed. Van Aldin, Knighton, and Poirot sat together in silence. Knighton and Van Aldin had two compartments connecting with each other, as Ruth Kettering and her maid had had on the fateful journey. Poirot's own compartment was further along the coach.

The journey was a painful one for Van Aldin, recalling as it did the most agonizing memories. Poirot and Knighton conversed occasionally in low tones without disturbing him.

When, however, the train had completed its slow journey round the *ceinture* and reached the Gare de Lyon, Poirot became suddenly galvanized into activity. Van Aldin realized that part of his object in traveling by the train had been to attempt to reconstruct the crime. Poirot himself acted every part. He was in turn the maid, hurriedly shut into her own compartment, Mrs. Kettering, recognizing her husband with surprise and a trace of anxiety, and

Derek Kettering discovering that his wife was traveling on the train. He tested various possibilities, such as the best way for a person to conceal himself in the second compartment.

Then suddenly an idea seemed to strike him. He clutched at Van Aldin's arm.

"*Mon Dieu,* but that is something I have not thought of! We must break our journey in Paris. Quick, quick, let us alight at once."

Seizing suitcases he hurried from the train. Van Aldin and Knighton, bewildered but obedient, followed him. Van Aldin having once formed his opinion of Poirot's ability was slow to part from it. At the barrier they were held up. Their tickets were in charge of the conductor of the train, a fact which all three of them had forgotten.

Poirot's explanations were rapid, fluent, and impassioned, but they produced no effect upon the stolid-faced official.

"Let us get quit of this," said Van Aldin abruptly. "I gather you are in a hurry, Monsieur Poirot. For God's sake pay the fares from Calais and let us get right on with whatever you have got in your mind."

But Poirot's flood of language had suddenly stopped dead, and he had the appearance of a man turned to stone. His arm still outflung in an impassioned gesture, remained there as though stricken with paralysis.

"I have been an imbecile," he said simply. "*Ma foi,* I lose my head nowadays. Let us return and continue our journey quietly. With reasonable luck the train will not have gone."

They were only just in time, the train moving off as Knighton, the last of the three, swung himself and his suitcase on board.

The conductor remonstrated with them feelingly, and assisted them to carry their luggage back to their compartments. Van Aldin said nothing, but he was clearly disgusted at Poirot's extraordinary conduct. Alone with Knighton for a moment or two, he remarked:

"This is a wild goose chase. The man has lost his grip on things. He has got brains up to a point, but any man who loses his head and scuttles round like a frightened rabbit is no earthly darned good."

Poirot came to them in a moment or two, full of abject apologies and clearly so crestfallen that harsh words would have been superfluous. Van Aldin received his apologies gravely, but managed to restrain himself from making acid comments.

They had dinner on the train, and afterward, somewhat to the surprise of the other two, Poirot suggested that they should all three sit up in Van Aldin's compartment.

The millionaire looked at him curiously.

"Is there anything that you are keeping back from us, Monsieur Poirot?"

"I?" Poirot opened his eyes in innocent surprise. "But what an idea."

Van Aldin did not answer, but he was not satisfied. The conductor was told that he need not make up the beds. Any surprise he might have felt was obliterated by the largeness of the tip which Van Aldin handed to him. The three men sat in silence. Poirot fidgeted and seemed restless. Presently he turned to the secretary.

"Major Knighton, is the door of your compartment bolted? The door into the corridor, I mean."

"Yes; I bolted it myself just now."

"Are you sure?" said Poirot.

"I will go and make sure, if you like," said Knighton smiling.

"No, no, do not derange yourself. I will see for myself."

He passed through the connecting door and returned in a second or two, nodding his head.

"Yes, yes, it is as you said. You must pardon an old man's fussy ways."

He closed the connecting door and resumed his place in the right-hand corner.

The hours passed. The three men dozed fitfully, waking with uncomfortable starts. Probably never before had three people booked berths on the most luxurious train available, then declined to avail themselves of the accommodation they had paid for. Every now and then Poirot glanced at his watch, and then nodded his head and composed himself to slumber once more. On one occasion he rose from his seat and opened the connecting door, peered sharply into the adjoining compartment, and then returned to his seat, shaking his head.

"What is the matter?" whispered Knighton. "You are expecting something to happen, aren't you?"

"I have the nerves," confessed Poirot. "I am like the cat upon the hot tiles. Every little noise it makes me jump."

Knighton yawned.

"Of all the darned uncomfortable journeys," he murmured. "I suppose you know what you are playing at, Monsieur Poirot."

He composed himself to sleep as best he could. Both he and Van Aldin had succumbed to slumber, when Poirot, glancing for the fourteenth time at his watch, leaned across and tapped the millionaire on the shoulder."

"Eh? What is it?"

"In five or ten minutes, Monsieur, we shall arrive at Lyons."

"My God!" Van Aldin's face looked white and haggard in the dim light. "Then it must have been about this time that poor Ruth was killed."

He sat staring straight in front of him. His lips twitched a little, his mind reverting back to the terrible tragedy that had saddened his life.

There was the usual long screaming sigh of the brake, and the train slackened speed and drew into Lyons. Van Aldin let down the window and leaned out.

"If it wasn't Derek—if your new theory is correct, it is here that the man left the train?" he asked over his shoulder.

Rather to his surprise Poirot shook his head.

"No," he said thoughtfully, "no *man* left the train, but I think—yes, I think, a *woman* may have done so."

Knighton gave a gasp.

"A woman?" demanded Van Aldin sharply.

"Yes, a woman," said Poirot, nodding his head. "You may not remember, Monsieur Van Aldin, but Miss Grey in her evidence mentioned that a youth in a cap and overcoat descended on to the platform ostensibly to stretch his legs. Me, I think that that youth was most probably a woman."

"But who was she?"

Van Aldin's face expressed incredulity, but Poirot replied seriously and categorically.

"Her name—or the name under which she was known, for many years—is Kitty Kidd, but you, Monsieur Van Aldin, knew her by another name—*that of Ada Mason.*"

Knighton sprang to his feet.

"What?" he cried.

Poirot swung round to him.

"Ah!—before I forget it." He whipped something from a pocket and held it out.

"Permit me to offer you a cigarette—out of your own cigarette case. It was careless of you to drop it when you boarded the train on the *ceinture* at Paris."

Knighton stood staring at him as though stupefied. Then he made a movement, but Poirot flung up his hand in a warning gesture.

"No, don't move," he said in a silky voice; "the door into the next compartment is open, and you are being covered from there this minute. I unbolted the door into the corridor when we left Paris, and our friends the police were told to take their places there. As I expect you know, the French police want you rather urgently, Major Knighton—or shall we say—Monsieur le Marquis?"

35

Explanations

"EXPLANATIONS?"

Poirot smiled. He was sitting opposite the millionaire at a luncheon table in the latter's private suite at the Negresco. Facing him was a relieved but very puzzled man. Poirot leaned back in his chair, lit one of his tiny cigarettes, and stared reflectively at the ceiling.

"Yes, I will give you explanations. It began with the one point that puzzled me. You know what that point was? *The disfigured face.* It is not an uncommon thing to find when investigating a crime and it rouses an immediate question, the question of identity. That naturally was the first thing that occurred to me. Was the dead woman really Mrs. Kettering? But that line led me nowhere, for Miss Grey's evidence was positive and very reliable, so I put that idea aside. The dead woman *was* Ruth Kettering."

"When did you first begin to suspect the maid?"

"Not for some time, but one peculiar little point drew my attention to her. The cigarette case found in the railway carriage and which she told us was one which Mrs. Kettering had given to her husband. Now that was, on the face of it, most improbable, seeing the terms that they were on. It awakened a doubt in my mind as to the general veracity of Ada Mason's statements. There was the rather suspicious fact to be taken into consideration, that she had only been with her mistress for two months. Certainly it did not seem as if she could have had anything to do with the crime since she had been left behind in Paris and Mrs. Kettering had been seen alive by several people afterward, but——"

Poirot leaned forward. He raised an emphatic forefinger and wagged it with intense emphasis at Van Aldin.

"But I am a good detective. I suspect. There is nobody and nothing that I do not suspect. I believe nothing that I am told. I say to myself: how do we know that Ada Mason was left behind in Paris? And at first the answer to that question seemed completely satisfactory. There was the evidence of your secretary, Major Knighton, a complete outsider whose testimony might be supposed to be entirely impartial, and there was the dead woman's own words to the conductor on the train. But I put the latter point aside for the moment, because a very curious idea—an idea perhaps fantastic and impossible—was growing up in my mind. If by any outside chance it happened to be true, that particular piece of testimony was worthless.

"I concentrated on the chief stumbling-block to my theory, Major Knighton's statement that he saw Ada Mason at the Ritz after the Blue Train had left Paris. That seemed conclusive enough, but yet, on examining the facts carefully, I noted two things. First, that by a curious coincidence he, too, had been exactly two months in your service. Secondly, his initial letter was the same—'K.' Supposing—just supposing—that it was *his* cigarette case which had been found in the carriage. Then, if Ada Mason and he were working together, and she recognized it when we showed it to her, would she not act precisely as she had done? At first, taken aback, she quickly evolved a plausible theory that would agree with Mr. Kettering's guilt. *Bien entendu,* that was not the original idea. The Comte de la Roche was to be the scapegoat, though Ada Mason would not make her recognition of him too certain, in case he should be able to prove an alibi. Now, if you will cast your mind back to that time, you will remember a significant thing that happened. I suggested to Ada Mason that the man she had seen was not the Comte de la Roche, but Derek Kettering. She seemed uncertain at the time, but after I had got back to my hotel you rang me up and told me that she had come to you and said that, on thinking it over, she was now quite convinced that the man in question *was* Mr. Kettering. I had been expecting something of the kind. There could be but one explanation of this sudden certainty on her part. After my leaving your hotel, she had had time to consult with somebody, and had received instructions which she acted upon. Who had given her these instructions? Major Knighton. And there was another very small point, which might mean nothing or might mean a great deal. In casual conversation Knighton had talked of a jewel robbery in Yorkshire in a house where he was staying. Perhaps a mere coincidence—perhaps another small link in the chain."

"But there is one thing I do not understand, Monsieur Poirot. I guess I must be dense or I would have seen it before now. Who was the man in the train at Paris? Derek Kettering or the Comte de la Roche?"

"That is the simplicity of the whole thing. *There was no man.* Ah—*mille tonnerres!*—do you not see the cleverness of it all? Whose word have we for it that there ever was a man there? Only Ada Mason's. And we believe in Ada Mason because of Knighton's evidence that she was left behind in Paris."

"But Ruth herself told the conductor that she had left her maid behind there," demurred Van Aldin.

"Ah! I am coming to that. We have Mrs. Kettering's own evidence there, but, on the other hand, we have not really got her evidence, because, Monsieur Van Aldin, a dead woman cannot give evidence. It is not *her* evidence, but the evidence of the conductor of the train—a very different affair altogether."

"So you think the man was lying?"

"No, no, not at all. He spoke what he thought to be the truth. But the woman who told him that she had left her maid in Paris was not Mrs. Kettering."

Van Aldin stared at him.

"Monsieur Van Aldin, Ruth Kettering was dead before the train arrived at the Gare de Lyon. It was Ada Mason, dressed in her mistress's very distinctive clothing, who purchased a dinner basket and who made that very necessary statement to the conductor."

"Impossible!"

"No, no, Monsieur Van Aldin; not impossible. *Les femmes,* they look so much alike nowadays that one identifies them more by their clothing than by their faces. Ada Mason was the same height as your daughter. Dressed in that very sumptuous fur coat and the little red lacquer hat jammed down over her eyes, with just a bunch of auburn curls showing over each ear, it was no wonder that the conductor was deceived. He had not previously spoken to Mrs. Kettering, you remember. True, he had seen the maid just for a moment when she handed him the tickets, but his impression had been merely that of a gaunt, black-clad female. If he had been an unusually intelligent man, he might have gone so far as to say that mistress and maid were not unlike, but it is extremely unlikely that he would even think that. And remember, Ada

Mason, or Kitty Kidd, was an actress, able to change her appearance and tone of voice at a moment's notice. No, no; there was no danger of his recognizing the maid in the mistress's clothing, but there *was* the danger that when he came to discover the body he might realize it was not the woman he had talked to the night before. And now we see the reason for the disfigured face. The chief danger that Ada Mason ran was that Katherine Grey might visit her compartment after the train left Paris, and she provided against that difficulty by ordering a dinner basket and by locking herself in her compartment."

"But who killed Ruth—and when?"

"First, bear it in mind that the crime was planned and undertaken by the two of them—Knighton and Ada Mason, working together. Knighton was in Paris that day on your business. He boarded the train somewhere on its way round the *ceinture*. Mrs. Kettering would be surprised, but she would be quite unsuspicious. Perhaps he draws her attention to something out the window, and as she turns to look he slips the cord round her neck—and the whole thing is over in a second or two. The door of the compartment is locked, and he and Ada Mason set to work. They strip off the dead woman's outer clothes. Mason and Knighton roll the body up in a rug and put it on the seat in the adjoining compartment amongst the bags and suitcases. Knighton drops off the train, taking the jewel case containing the rubies with him. Since the crime is not supposed to have been committed until nearly twelve hours later he is perfectly safe, and his evidence and the supposed Mrs. Kettering's words to the conductor will provide a perfect alibi for his accomplice.

"At the Gare de Lyon Ada Mason gets a dinner basket, and shutting herself into the toilet compartment she quickly changes into her mistress's clothes, adjusts two false bunches of auburn curls, and generally makes up to resemble her as closely as possible. When the conductor comes to make up the bed, she tells him the prepared story about having left her maid behind in Paris; and whilst he is making up the berth, she stands looking out of the window, so that her back is towards the corridor and people passing along there. That was a wise precaution, because, as we know, Miss Grey was one of those passing, and she among others, was willing to swear that Mrs. Kettering was still alive at that hour."

"Go on," said Van Aldin.

"Before getting to Lyons, Ada Mason arranged her mistress's body in the bunk, folded up the dead woman's clothes neatly on the end of it, and herself changed into a man's clothes and prepared to leave the train. When Derek Kettering entered his wife's compartment, and, as he thought, saw her asleep in her berth, the scene had been set, and Ada Mason was hidden in the next compartment waiting for the moment to leave the train unobserved. As soon as the conductor had swung himself down onto the platform at Lyons, she follows, slouching along as though just taking a breath of air. At a moment when she is unobserved, she hurriedly crosses to the other platform, and takes the first train back to Paris and the Ritz Hotel. Her name has been registered there as taking a room the night before by one of Knighton's female accomplices. She has nothing to do but wait there placidly for your arrival. The jewels are not, and never have been, in her possession. No suspicion attaches to him, and, as your secretary, he brings them to Nice without the least fear of discovery. Their delivery there to Monsieur Papopolous is already arranged for and they are entrusted to Mason at the last moment to hand over to the Greek. Altogether a very neatly planned coup, as one would expect from a master of the game such as the Marquis."

"And you honestly mean that Richard Knighton is a well-known criminal, who has been at this business for years?"

Poirot nodded.

"One of the chief assets of the gentleman called the Marquis was his plausible, ingratiating manner. You fell a victim to his charm, Monsieur Van Aldin, when you engaged him as a secretary on such a slight acquaintanceship."

"I could have sworn that he never angled for the post," cried the millionaire.

"It was very astutely done—so astutely done that it deceived a man whose knowledge of other men is as great as yours is."

"I looked up his antecedents too. The fellow's record was excellent."

"Yes, yes; that was part of the game. As Richard Knighton his life was quite free from reproach. He was well born, well connected, did honorable service in the War, and seemed altogether above suspicion; but when I came to glean information about the mysterious Marquis, I found many points of similarity. Knighton spoke French like a Frenchman, he had been in America, France, and England at much the same time as the Marquis was operating. The Marquis was last heard of as engineering various jewel robberies in Switzerland, and it was in Switzerland that you had come across Major Knighton; and it was at precisely that time that the first rumors were going round of your being in treaty for the famous rubies."

"But why murder?" murmured Van Aldin brokenly. "Surely a clever thief could have stolen the jewels without running his head into a noose."

Poirot shook his head. "This is not the first murder that lies to the Marquis's charge. He is a killer by instinct; he believes, too, in leaving no evidence behind him. Dead men and women tell no tales.

"The Marquis had an intense passion for famous and historical jewels. He laid his plans far beforehand by installing himself as your secretary and getting his accomplice to obtain the situation of maid with your daughter, for whom he guessed the jewels were destined. And, though this was his matured and carefully thought-out plan, he did not scruple to attempt a shortcut by hiring a couple of Apaches to waylay you in Paris on the night you bought the jewels. That plan failed, which hardly surprised him, I think. This plan was, so he thought, completely safe. No possible suspicion could attach to Richard Knighton. But like all great men—and the Marquis was a great man —he had his weaknesses. He fell genuinely in love with Miss Grey, and suspecting her liking for Derek Kettering, he could not resist the temptation to saddle him with the crime when the opportunity presented itself. And now, Monsieur Van Aldin, I am going to tell you something very curious. Miss Grey is not a fanciful woman by any means, yet she firmly believes that she felt your daughter's presence beside her one day in the Casino Gardens at Monte Carlo, just after she had been having a long talk with Knighton. She was convinced, she says, that the dead woman was urgently trying to tell her something, and it suddenly came to her that what the dead woman was trying to say was that Knighton was her murderer! The idea seemed so fantastic at the time that Miss Grey spoke of it to no one. But she was so convinced of its truth that she acted on it—wild as it seemed. She did not discourage Knighton's advances, and she pretended to him that she was convinced of Derek Kettering's guilt."

"Extraordinary," said Van Aldin.

"Yes, it is very strange. One cannot explain these things. Oh, by the way, there is one little point that baffled me considerably. Your secretary has a decided limp—the result of a wound that he received in the War. Now the Marquis most decidedly did not limp. That was a stumbling-block. But Miss Lenox Tamplin happened to mention one day that Knighton's limp had been a surprise to the surgeons who had been in charge of the case in her mother's hospital. That suggested camouflage. When I was in London I went to the surgeon in question, and I got several technical details from him which confirmed me in that belief. I mentioned the name of that surgeon in Knighton's hearing the day before yesterday. The natural thing would have been for Knighton to mention that he had been attended by him during the War, but he said nothing—and that little point, if nothing else, gave me the last final assurance that my theory of the crime was correct. Miss Grey, too, provided me with a cutting, showing that there had been a robbery at Lady Tamplin's hospital during the time that Knighton had been there. She realized that I was on the same track as herself when I wrote to her from the Ritz in Paris.

"I had some trouble in my inquiries there, but I got what I wanted—evidence that Ada Mason arrived on the morning after the crime and not on the evening of the day before."

There was a long silence, then the millionaire stretched out a hand to Poirot across the table.

"I guess you know what this means to me, Monsieur Poirot," he said huskily. "I am sending you round a check in the morning, but no check in the world will express what I feel about what you have done for me. You are the goods, Monsieur Poirot. Every time, you are the goods."

Poirot rose to his feet; his chest swelled.

"I am only Hercule Poirot," he said modestly, "yet, as you say, in my own way I am a big man, even as you also are a big man. I am glad and happy to have been of service to you. Now I go to repair the damages caused by travel. Alas! my excellent Georges is not with me."

In the lounge of the hotel he encountered a friend—the venerable Monsieur Papopolous, his daughter Zia beside him.

"I thought you had left Nice, Monsieur Poirot," murmured the Greek as he took the detective's affectionately proffered hand.

"Business compelled me to return, my dear Monsieur Papopolous."

"Business?"

"Yes, business. And talking of business, I hope your health is better, my dear friend?"

"Much better. In fact, we are returning to Paris tomorrow."

"I am enchanted to hear such good news. You have not completely ruined the Greek ex-Minister, I hope."

"I?"

"I understand you sold him a very wonderful ruby which—strictly *entre nous*—is being worn by Mademoiselle Mirelle, the dancer?"

"Yes," murmured Monsieur Papopolous; "yes, that is so."

"A ruby not unlike the famous 'Heart of Fire.' "

"It has points of resemblance, certainly," said the Greek casually.

"You have a wonderful hand with jewels, Monsieur Papopolous. I congratulate you. Mademoiselle Zia, I am desolate that you are returning to Paris so speedily. I had hoped to see some more of you now that my business is accomplished."

"Would one be indiscreet if one asked what that business was?" asked Monsieur Papopolous.

"Not at all, not at all. I have just succeeded in laying the Marquis by the heels."

A faraway look came over Monsieur Papopolous' noble countenance.

"The Marquis?" he murmured; "now why does that seem familiar to me? No—I cannot recall it."

"You would not, I am sure," said Poirot. "I refer to a very notable criminal and jewel robber. He has just been arrested for the murder of the English lady, Madame Kettering."

"Indeed? How interesting these things are!"

A polite exchange of farewells followed, and when Poirot was out of ear-shot, Monsieur Papopolous turned to his daughter.

"Zia," he said, with feeling, "that man is the devil!"

"I like him."

"I like him myself," admitted Monsieur Papopolous. "But he is the devil, all the same."

36

By the Sea

THE MIMOSA WAS nearly over. The scent of it in the air was faintly unpleasant. There were pink geraniums twining along the balustrade of Lady Tamplin's villa, and masses of carnations below sent up a sweet, heavy perfume. The Mediterranean was at its bluest. Poirot sat on the terrace with Lenox Tamplin. He had just finished telling her the same story he had told to Van Aldin two days before. Lenox had listened to him with absorbed attention, her brows knitted and her eyes somber.

When he had finished she said simply:

"And Derek?"

"He was released yesterday."

"And he has gone—where?"

"He left Nice last night."

"For St. Mary Mead?"

"Yes, for St. Mary Mead."

There was a pause.

"I was wrong about Katherine," said Lenox. "I thought she did not care."

"She is very reserved. She trusts no one."

"She might have trusted me," said Lenox, with a shade of bitterness.

"Yes," said Poirot gravely, "she might have trusted you. But Mademoiselle Katherine has spent a great deal of her life listening, and those who have listened do not find it easy to talk; they keep their sorrows and joys to themselves and tell no one."

"I was a fool," said Lenox; "I thought she really cared for Knighton. I ought to have known better. I suppose I thought so because—well, I hoped so."

Poirot took her hand and gave it a little friendly squeeze. "Courage, Mademoiselle," he said gently.

Lenox looked very straight out across the sea, and her face, in its ugly rigidity, had for the moment a tragic beauty.

"Oh, well," she said at last, "it would not have done. I am too young for Derek; he is like a kid that has never grown up. He wants the Madonna touch."

There was a long silence, then Lenox turned to him quickly and impulsively. "But I *did* help, Monsieur Poirot—at any rate I did help."

"Yes, Mademoiselle. It was you who gave me the first inkling of the truth when you said that the person who committed the crime need not have been on the train at all. Before that, I could not see how the thing had been done."

Lenox drew a deep breath.

"I am glad," she said; "at any rate—that is something."

From far behind them there came a long-drawn-out scream of an engine's whistle.

"That is that damned Blue Train," said Lenox. "Trains are relentless things, aren't they, Monsieur Poirot? People are murdered and die, but they go on just the same. I am talking nonsense, but you know what I mean."

"Yes, yes, I know. Life is like a train, Mademoiselle. It goes on. And it is a good thing that that is so."

"Why?"

"Because the train gets to its journey's end at last, and there is a proverb about that in your language, Mademoiselle."

" 'Journeys end in lovers meeting.' " Lenox laughed. "That is not going to be true for me."

"Yes—yes, it is true. You are young, younger than you yourself know. Trust the train, Mademoiselle, for it is *le bon Dieu* who drives it."

The whistle of the engine came again.

"Trust the train, Mademoiselle," murmured Poirot again. "And trust Hercule Poirot. He knows."

MURDER
IN
MESOPOTAMIA

Dedicated to
my many archaeological friends
in Iraq and Syria

Contents

172 CONTENTS

FOREWORD

by Giles Reilly, M.D.

THE EVENTS chronicled in this narrative took place some four years ago. Circumstances have rendered it necessary, in my opinion, that a straightforward account of them should be given to the public. There have been the wildest and most ridiculous rumors suggesting that important evidence was suppressed and other nonsense of that kind. Those misconstructions have appeared more especially in the American press.

For obvious reasons it was desirable that the account should not come from the pen of one of the expedition staff, who might reasonably be supposed to be prejudiced.

I therefore suggested to Miss Amy Leatheran that she should undertake the task. She is obviously the person to do it. She has a professional character of the highest, she is not biased by having any previous connection with the University of Pittstown Expedition to Iraq and she was an observant and intelligent eyewitness.

It was not very easy to persuade Miss Leatheran to undertake this task—in fact, persuading her was one of the hardest jobs of my professional career—and even after it was completed she displayed a curious reluctance to let me see the manuscript. I discovered that this was partly due to some critical remarks she had made concerning my daughter Sheila. I soon disposed of that, assuring her that as children criticize their parents freely in print nowadays, parents are only too delighted when their offspring come in for their share of abuse! Her other objection was extreme modesty about her literary style. She hoped I would "put the grammar right and all that." I have, on the contrary, refused to alter so much as a single word. Miss Leatheran's style in my opinion is vigorous, individual and entirely apposite. If she calls Hercule Poirot "Poirot" in one paragraph and "Mr. Poirot" in the next, such a variation is both interesting and suggestive. At one moment she is, so to speak, "remembering her manners" (and hospital nurses are great sticklers for etiquette) and at the next her interest in what she is telling is that of a pure human being—cap and cuffs forgotten!

173

The only thing I have done is to take the liberty of writing a first chapter—aided by a letter kindly supplied by one of Miss Leatheran's friends. It is intended to be in the nature of a frontispiece—that is, it gives a rough sketch of the narrator.

1

Foreword

IN THE HALL of the Tigris Palace Hotel in Baghdad a hospital nurse was finishing a letter. Her fountain pen drove briskly over the paper.

> . . . Well, dear, I think that's really all my news. I must say it's been nice to see a bit of the world—though England for me every time, thank you! The *dirt* and the *mess* in Baghdad you wouldn't believe—and not romantic at all like you'd think from the Arabian Nights! Of course, it's pretty just on the river, but the town itself is just awful—and no proper shops at all. Major Kelsey took me through the bazaars, and of course there's no denying they're *quaint*—but just a lot of rubbish and hammering away at copper pans till they make your head ache —and not what I'd like to use myself unless I was sure about the cleaning. You've got to be so careful of verdigris with copper pans.
>
> I'll write and let you know if anything comes of the job that Dr. Reilly spoke about. He said this American gentleman was in Baghdad now and might come and see me this afternoon. It's for his wife—she has 'fancies,' so Dr. Reilly said. He didn't say any more than that, and of course, dear, one knows what that *usually means* (but I hope not actually D.T.s!). Of course, Dr. Reilly didn't say anything—but he had a look—if you know what I mean. This Dr. Leidner is an archaeologist and is digging up a mound out in the desert somewhere for some American museum.
>
> Well, dear, I will close now. I thought what you told me about little Stubbins was simply *killing!* Whatever did Matron say?
>
> No more now.
>
> Yours ever,
>
> Amy Leatheran.

175

Enclosing the letter in an envelope, she addressed it to Sister Curshaw, St. Christopher's Hospital, London.

As she put the cap on her fountain pen, one of the native boys approached her.

"A gentleman come see you. Dr. Leidner."

Nurse Leatheran turned. She saw a man of middle height with slightly stooping shoulders, a brown beard and gentle tired eyes.

Dr. Leidner saw a woman of thirty-five of erect, confident bearing. He saw a good-humored face with slightly prominent blue eyes and glossy brown hair. She looked, he thought, just what a hospital nurse for a nervous case ought to look. Cheerful, robust, shrewd and matter of fact.

Nurse Leatheran, he thought, would do.

2

Introducing Amy Leatheran

I DON'T PRETEND to be an author or to know anything about writing. I'm doing this simply because Dr. Reilly asked me to, and somehow when Dr. Reilly asks you to do a thing you don't like to refuse.

"Oh, but, doctor," I said, "I'm not literary—not literary at all."

"Nonsense!" he said. "Treat it as case notes, if you like."

Well, of course, you *can* look at it that way.

Dr. Reilly went on. He said that an unvarnished plain account of the Tell Yarimjah business was badly needed.

"If one of the interested parties writes it, it won't carry conviction. They'll say it's biased one way or another."

And of course that was true, too. I was in it all and yet an outsider, so to speak.

"Why don't you write it yourself, doctor?" I asked.

"I wasn't on the spot—you were. Besides," he added with a sigh, "my daughter won't let me."

The way he knuckles under to that chit of a girl of his is downright disgraceful. I had half a mind to say so, when I saw that his eyes were twinkling. That was the worst of Dr. Reilly. You never knew whether he was joking or not. He always said things in the same slow melancholy way—but half the time there was a twinkle underneath it.

"Well," I said doubtfully. "I suppose I *could.*"

"Of course you could."

"Only I don't quite know how to set about it."

"There's a good precedent for that. Begin at the beginning, go on to the end and then leave off."

"I don't even know quite where and what the beginning was," I said doubtfully.

"Believe me, nurse, the difficulty of beginning will be nothing to the difficulty of knowing how to stop. At least that's the way it is with me when I have to make a speech. Someone's got to catch hold of my coattails and pull me down by main force."

"Oh, you're joking, doctor."

"It's profoundly serious I am. Now what about it?"

Another thing was worrying me. After hesitating a moment or two I said:

"You know, doctor, I'm afraid I might tend to be—well, a little *personal* sometimes."

"God bless my soul, woman, the more personal you are the better! This is a story of human beings—not dummies! Be personal—be prejudiced—be catty —be anything you please! Write the thing your own way. We can always prune out the bits that are libelous afterwards! You go ahead. You're a sensible woman, and you'll give a sensible commonsense account of the business."

So that was that, and I promised to do my best.

And here I am beginning, but as I said to the doctor, it's difficult to know just where to start.

I suppose I ought to say a word or two about myself. I'm thirty-two and my name is Amy Leatheran. I took my training at St. Christopher's and after that did two years' maternity. I did a certain amount of private work and I was for four years at Miss Bendix's Nursing Home in Devonshire Place. I came out to Iraq with a Mrs. Kelsey. I'd attended her when her baby was born. She was coming out to Baghdad with her husband and had already got a children's nurse booked who had been for some years with friends of hers out there. Their children were coming home and going to school, and the nurse had agreed to go to Mrs. Kelsey when they left. Mrs. Kelsey was delicate and nervous about the journey out with so young a child, so Major Kelsey arranged that I should come out with her and look after her and the baby. They would pay my passage home unless we found someone needing a nurse for the return journey.

Well, there is no need to describe the Kelseys—the baby was a little love and Mrs. Kelsey quite nice, though rather the fretting kind. I enjoyed the voyage very much. I'd never been a long trip on the sea before.

Dr. Reilly was on board the boat. He was a black-haired, long-faced man who said all sorts of funny things in a low, sad voice. I think he enjoyed pulling my leg and used to make the most extraordinary statements to see if I would swallow them. He was the civil surgeon at a place called Hassanieh—a day and a half's journey from Baghdad.

I had been about a week in Baghdad when I ran across him and he asked when I was leaving the Kelseys. I said that it was funny his asking that because as a matter of fact the Wrights (the other people I mentioned) were going home earlier than they had meant to and their nurse was free to come straightaway.

He said that he had heard about the Wrights and that that was why he had asked me.

"As a matter of fact, nurse, I've got a possible job for you."

"A case?"

He screwed his face up as though considering.

"You could hardly call it a case. It's just a lady who has—shall we say—fancies?"

"Oh!" I said.

(One usually knows what *that* means—drink or drugs!)

Dr. Reilly didn't explain further. He was very discreet.

"Yes," he said. "A Mrs. Leidner. Husband's an American—an American Swede to be exact. He's the head of a large American dig."

And he explained how this expedition was excavating the site of a big Assyrian city something like Nineveh. The expedition house was not actually very far from Hassanieh, but it was a lonely spot and Dr. Leidner had been worried for some time about his wife's health.

"He's not been very explicit about it, but it seems she has these fits of recurring nervous terrors."

"Is she left alone all day amongst natives?" I asked.

"Oh, no, there's quite a crowd—seven or eight. I don't fancy she's ever alone in the house. But there seems to be no doubt that she's worked herself up into a queer state. Leidner has any amount of work on his shoulders, but he's crazy about his wife and it worries him to know she's in this state. He felt he'd be happier if he knew that some responsible person with expert knowledge was keeping an eye on her."

"And what does Mrs. Leidner herself think about it?"

Dr. Reilly answered gravely.

"Mrs. Leidner is a very lovely lady. She's seldom of the same mind about anything two days on end. But on the whole she favors the idea." He added, "She's an odd woman. A mass of affectation and, I should fancy, a champion liar—but Leidner seems honestly to believe that she is scared out of her life by something or other."

"What did she herself say to you, doctor?"

"Oh, she hasn't consulted me! She doesn't like me anyway—for several reasons. It was Leidner who came to me and propounded this plan. Well, nurse, what do you think of the idea? You'd see something of the country before you go home—they'll be digging for another two months. And excavation is quite interesting work."

After a moment's hesitation while I turned the matter over in my mind:

"Well," I said. "I really think I might try it."

"Splendid," said Dr. Reilly, rising. "Leidner's in Baghdad now. I'll tell him to come round and see if he can fix things up with you."

Dr. Leidner came to the hotel that afternoon. He was a middle-aged man with a rather nervous, hesitating manner. There was something gentle and kindly and rather helpless about him.

He sounded very devoted to his wife, but he was very vague about what was the matter with her.

"You see," he said, tugging at his beard in a rather perplexed manner that I later came to know to be characteristic of him, "my wife is really in a very nervous state. I—I'm quite worried about her."

"She is in good physical health?" I asked.

"Yes—oh, yes, I think so. No, I should not think there was anything the matter with her physically. But she—well—imagines things, you know."

"What kind of things?" I asked.

But he shied off from the point, merely murmuring perplexedly:

"She works herself up over nothing at all. . . . I really can see no foundations for these fears."

"Fears of what, Dr. Leidner?"

He said vaguely, "Oh, just—nervous terrors, you know."

Ten to one, I thought to myself, it's drugs. And he doesn't realize it! Lots of men don't. Just wonder why their wives are so jumpy and have such extraordinary changes of mood.

I asked whether Mrs. Leidner herself approved of the idea of my coming. His face lighted up.

"Yes. I was surprised. Most pleasurably surprised. She said it was a very good idea. She said she would feel very much safer."

The word struck me oddly. *Safer.* A very queer word to use. I began to surmise that Mrs. Leidner might be a mental case.

He went on with a kind of boyish eagerness.

"I'm sure you'll get on very well with her. She's really a very charming woman." He smiled disarmingly. "She feels you'll be the greatest comfort to her. I felt the same as soon as I saw you. You look, if you will allow me to say so, so splendidly healthy and full of common sense. I'm sure you're just the person for Louise."

"Well, we can but try, Dr. Leidner," I said cheerfully. "I'm sure I hope I can be of use to your wife. Perhaps she's nervous of natives and colored people?"

"Oh, dear me, no." He shook his head, amused at the idea. "My wife likes Arabs very much—she appreciates their simplicity and their sense of humor. This is only her second season—we have been married less than two years—but she already speaks quite a fair amount of Arabic."

I was silent for a moment or two, then I had one more try.

"Can't you tell me at all what it is your wife is afraid of, Dr. Leidner?" I asked.

He hesitated. Then he said slowly, "I hope—I believe—that she will tell you that herself."

And that's all I could get out of him.

3

Gossip

IT WAS ARRANGED that I should go to Tell Yarimjah the following week.

Mrs. Kelsey was settling into her house at Alwiyah, and I was glad to be able to take a few things off her shoulders.

During that time I heard one or two allusions to the Leidner expedition. A friend of Mrs. Kelsey's, a young squadron leader, pursed his lips in surprise as he exclaimed:

"Lovely Louise. So that's her latest!" He turned to me. "That's our nickname for her, nurse. She's always known as Lovely Louise."

"Is she so very handsome then?" I asked.

"It's taking her at her own valuation. *She* thinks she is!"

"Now don't be spiteful, John," said Mrs. Kelsey. "You know it's not only she who thinks so! Lots of people have been very smitten by her."

"Perhaps you're right. She's a bit long in the tooth, but she has a certain attraction."

"You were completely bowled over yourself," said Mrs. Kelsey, laughing.

The squadron leader blushed and admitted rather shamefacedly:

"Well, she has a way with her. As for Leidner himself, he worships the ground she walks on—and all the rest of the expedition has to worship too! It's expected of them!"

"How many are there altogether?" I asked.

"All sorts and nationalities, nurse," said the squadron leader cheerfully. "An English architect, a French Father from Carthage—he does the inscriptions—tablets and things, you know. And then there's Miss Johnson. She's English too—sort of general bottle-washer. And a little plump man who does the photography—he's an American. And the Mercados. Heaven knows what nationality they are—Dagos of some kind! She's quite young—a snaky-looking creature—and oh! doesn't she hate Lovely Louise! And there are a couple of youngsters, and that's the lot. A few odd fish, but nice on the whole —don't you agree, Pennyman?"

He was appealing to an elderly man who was sitting thoughtfully twirling a pair of pince-nez.

The latter started and looked up.

"Yes—yes—very nice indeed. Taken individually, that is. Of course, Mercado is rather a queer fish—"

"He has such a very *odd* beard," put in Mrs. Kelsey. "A queer limp kind."

Major Pennyman went on without noticing her interruption.

"The young 'uns are both nice. The American's rather silent, and the English boy talks a bit too much. Funny, it's usually the other way round.

Leidner himself is a delightful fellow—so modest and unassuming. Yes, individually they are all pleasant people. But somehow or other, I may have been fanciful, but the last time I went to see them I got a queer impression of something being wrong. I don't know what it was exactly. . . . Nobody seemed quite natural. There was a queer atmosphere of tension. I can explain best what I mean by saying that they all passed the butter to each other too politely."

Blushing a little, because I don't like airing my own opinions too much, I said:

"If people are too much cooped up together it's got a way of getting on their nerves. I know that myself from experience in hospital."

"That's true," said Major Kelsey, "but it's early in the season, hardly time for that particular irritation to have set in."

"An expedition is probably like our life here in miniature," said Major Pennyman. "It has its cliques and rivalries and jealousies."

"It sounds as though they'd got a good many newcomers this year," said Major Kelsey.

"Let me see." The squadron leader counted them off on his fingers. "Young Coleman is new, so is Reiter. Emmott was out last year and so were the Mercados. Father Lavigny is a newcomer. He's come in place of Dr. Byrd, who was ill this year and couldn't come out. Carey, of course, is an old hand. He's been out ever since the beginning, five years ago. Miss Johnson's been out nearly as many years as Carey."

"I always thought they got on so well together at Tell Yarimjah," remarked Major Kelsey. "They seemed like a happy family—which is really surprising when one considers what human nature is! I'm sure Nurse Leatheran agrees with me."

"Well," I said. "I don't know that you're not right! The rows I've known in hospital and starting often from nothing more than a dispute about a pot of tea."

"Yes, one tends to get petty in close communities," said Major Pennyman. "All the same I feel there must be something more to it in this case. Leidner is such a gentle, unassuming man, with really a remarkable amount of tact. He's always managed to keep his expedition happy and on good terms with each other. And yet I *did* notice that feeling of tension the other day."

Mrs. Kelsey laughed.

"And you don't see the explanation? Why, it leaps to the eye!"

"What do you mean?"

"*Mrs.* Leidner, of course."

"Oh, come, Mary," said her husband, "she's a charming woman—not at all the quarrelsome kind."

"I didn't say she was quarrelsome. She *causes* quarrels!"

"In what way? And why should she?"

"Why? Why? Because she's bored. She's not an archaeologist, only the wife of one. She's bored shut away from any excitements and so she provides her own drama. She amuses herself by setting other people by the ears."

"Mary, you don't know in the least. You're merely imagining."

"Of course I'm imagining! But you'll find I'm right. Lovely Louise doesn't look like the Mona Lisa for nothing! She mayn't mean any harm, but she likes to see what will happen."

"She's devoted to Leidner."

"Oh! I dare say. I'm not suggesting vulgar intrigues. But she's an *allumeuse,* that woman."

"Women are so sweet to each other," said Major Kelsey.

"I know. Cat, cat, cat, that's what you men say. But we're usually right about our own sex."

"All the same," said Major Pennyman thoughtfully, "assuming all Mrs. Kelsey's uncharitable surmises to be true, I don't think it would quite account for that curious sense of tension—rather like the feeling there is before a thunderstorm. I had the impression very strongly that the storm might break any minute."

"Now don't frighten nurse," said Mrs. Kelsey. "She's going there in three days' time and you'll put her right off."

"Oh, you won't frighten me," I said, laughing.

All the same I thought a good deal about what had been said. Dr. Leidner's curious use of the word "safer" recurred to me. Was it his wife's secret fear, unacknowledged or expressed perhaps, that was reacting on the rest of the party? Or was it the actual tension (or perhaps the unknown cause of it) that was reacting on *her* nerves?

I looked up the word "allumeuse" that Mrs. Kelsey had used in a dictionary, but couldn't get any sense out of it.

"Well," I thought to myself, "I must wait and see."

4

I Arrive in Hassanieh

THREE DAYS LATER I left Baghdad.

I was sorry to leave Mrs. Kelsey and the baby, who was a little love and was thriving splendidly, gaining her proper number of ounces every week. Major Kelsey took me to the station and saw me off. I should arrive at Kirkuk the following morning, and there someone was to meet me.

I slept badly. I never sleep very well in a train and I was troubled by dreams.

The next morning, however, when I looked out of the window it was a lovely day and I felt interested and curious about the people I was going to see.

As I stood on the platform hesitating and looking about me I saw a young man coming toward me. He had a round pink face, and really, in all my life, I have never seen anyone who seemed so exactly like a young man out of one of Mr. P. G. Wodehouse's books.

"Hallo, 'allo, 'allo," he said. "Are you Nurse Leatheran? Well, I mean you must be—I can see that. Ha ha! My name's Coleman. Dr. Leidner sent me along. How are you feeling? Beastly journey and all that? Don't I know these trains! Well, here we are—had any breakfast? This your kit? I say, awfully modest, aren't you? Mrs. Leidner has four suitcases and a trunk—to say nothing of a hatbox and a patent pillow, and this, that and the other. Am I talking too much? Come along to the old bus."

There was what I heard called later a station wagon waiting outside. It was a little like a wagonette, a little like a lorry and a little like a car. Mr. Coleman helped me in, explaining that I had better sit next to the driver so as to get less jolting.

Jolting! I wonder the whole contraption didn't fall to pieces! And nothing like a road—just a sort of track all ruts and holes. Glorious East indeed! When I thought of our splendid arterial roads in England it made me quite homesick.

Mr. Coleman leaned forward from his seat behind me and yelled in my ear a good deal.

"Track's in pretty good condition," he shouted just after we had all been thrown up in our seats till we nearly touched the roof.

And apparently he was speaking quite seriously.

"Very good for you—jogs the liver," he said. "You ought to know that, nurse."

"A stimulated liver won't be much good to me if my head's split open," I observed tartly.

"You should come along here after it's rained! The skids are glorious. Most of the time one's going sideways."

To this I did not respond.

Presently we had to cross the river, which we did on the craziest ferryboat you can imagine. To my mind it was a mercy we ever got across, but everyone seemed to think it was quite usual.

It took us about four hours to get to Hassanieh, which, to my surprise, was quite a big place. Very pretty it looked, too, before we got there from the other side of the river—standing up quite white and fairylike with minarets. It was a bit different, though, when one had crossed the bridge and come right into it. Such a smell, and everything ramshackle and tumbledown, and mud and mess everywhere.

Mr. Coleman took me to Dr. Reilly's house, where, he said, the doctor was expecting me to lunch.

Dr. Reilly was just as nice as ever, and his house was nice too, with a bathroom and everything spick and span. I had a nice bath, and by the time I got back into my uniform and came down I was feeling fine.

Lunch was just ready and we went in, the doctor apologizing for his daughter, whom he said was always late.

We'd just had a very good dish of eggs in sauce when she came in and Dr. Reilly said, "Nurse, this is my daughter Sheila."

She shook hands, hoped I'd had a good journey, tossed off her hat, gave a cool nod to Mr. Coleman and sat down.

"Well, Bill," she said. "How's everything?"

He began to talk to her about some party or other that was to come off at the club, and I took stock of her.

I can't say I took to her much. A thought too cool for my liking. An off-hand sort of girl, though good-looking. Black hair and blue eyes—a pale sort of face and the usual lipsticked mouth. She'd a cool, sarcastic way of talking that rather annoyed me. I had a probationer like her under me once—a girl who worked well, I'll admit, but whose manner always riled me.

It looked to me rather as though Mr. Coleman was gone on her. He stammered a bit, and his conversation became slightly more idiotic than it was before, if that was possible! He reminded me of a large stupid dog wagging its tail and trying to please.

After lunch Dr. Reilly went off to the hospital, and Mr. Coleman had some things to get in the town, and Miss Reilly asked me whether I'd like to see round the town a bit or whether I'd rather stop in the house. Mr. Coleman, she said, would be back to fetch me in about an hour.

"Is there anything to see?" I asked.

"There are some picturesque corners," said Miss Reilly. "But I don't know that you'd care for them. They're extremely dirty."

The way she said it rather nettled me. I've never been able to see that picturesqueness excuses dirt.

In the end she took me to the club, which was pleasant enough, overlooking the river, and there were English papers and magazines there.

When we got back to the house Mr. Coleman wasn't there yet, so we sat down and talked a bit. It wasn't easy somehow.

She asked me if I'd met Mrs. Leidner yet.

"No," I said. "Only her husband."

"Oh," she said. "I wonder what you'll think of her?"

I didn't say anything to that. And she went on:

"I like Dr. Leidner very much. Everybody likes him."

That's as good as saying, I thought, that you don't like his wife.

I still didn't say anything and presently she asked abruptly:

"What's the matter with her? Did Dr. Leidner tell you?"

I wasn't going to start gossiping about a patient before I got there even, so I said evasively:

"I understand she's a bit run down and wants looking after."

She laughed—a nasty sort of laugh—hard and abrupt.

"Good God," she said. "Aren't nine people looking after her already enough?"

"I suppose they've all got their work to do," I said.

"Work to do? Of course they've got work to do. But Louise comes first—she sees to that all right."

"No," I said to myself. "You *don't* like her."

"All the same," went on Miss Reilly, "I don't see what she wants with a professional hospital nurse. I should have thought amateur assistance was more in her line; not someone who'll jam a thermometer in her mouth, and count her pulse and bring everything down to hard facts."

Well, I must admit it, I was curious.

"You think there's nothing the matter with her?" I asked.

"Of course there's nothing the matter with her! The woman's as strong as an ox. 'Dear Louise hasn't slept.' 'She's got black circles under her eyes.' Yes —put there with a blue pencil! Anything to get attention, to have everybody hovering round her, making a fuss of her!"

There was something in that, of course. I had (what nurse hasn't?) come across many cases of hypochondriacs whose delight it is to keep a whole household dancing attendance. And if a doctor or a nurse were to say to them, "There's nothing on earth the matter with you!" well, to begin with they wouldn't believe it, and their indignation would be as genuine as indignation can be.

Of course it was quite possible that Mrs. Leidner might be a case of this kind. The husband, naturally, would be the first to be deceived. Husbands, I've found, are a credulous lot where illness is concerned. But all the same, it didn't quite square with what I'd heard. It didn't, for instance, fit in with that word "safer."

Funny how that word had got kind of stuck in my mind.

Reflecting on it, I asked:

"Is Mrs. Leidner a nervous woman? Is she nervous, for instance, of living out far from anywhere?"

"What is there to be nervous of? Good heavens, there are ten of them! And they've got guards too—because of the antiquities. Oh, no, she's not nervous —at least—"

She seemed struck by some thought and stopped—going on slowly after a minute or two.

"It's odd your saying that."

"Why?"

"Flight-Lieutenant Jervis and I rode over the other day. It was in the morning. Most of them were up on the dig. She was sitting writing a letter and I suppose she didn't hear us coming. The boy who brings you in wasn't about for once, and we came straight up on to the verandah. Apparently she saw Flight-Lieutenant Jervis's shadow thrown on the wall—and she fairly screamed! Apologized, of course. Said she thought it was a strange man. A bit odd, that. I mean, even if it was a strange man, why get the wind up?"

I nodded thoughtfully.

Miss Reilly was silent, then burst out suddenly.

"I don't know what's the matter with them there this year. They've all got the jumps. Johnson goes about so glum she can't open her mouth. David never speaks if he can help it. Bill, of course, never stops, and somehow his chatter seems to make the others worse. Carey goes about looking as though something would snap any minute. And they all watch each other as though —as though—Oh, I don't know, but it's *queer.*"

It was odd, I thought, that two such dissimilar people as Miss Reilly and Major Pennyman should have been struck in the same manner.

Just then Mr. Coleman came bustling in. Bustling was just the word for it. If his tongue had hung out and he had suddenly produced a tail to wag you wouldn't have been surprised.

"Hallo-allo," he said. "Absolutely the world's best shopper—that's me. Have you shown nurse all the beauties of the town?"

"She wasn't impressed," said Miss Reilly dryly.

"I don't blame her," said Mr. Coleman heartily. "Of all the one-horse tumbledown places!"

"Not a lover of the picturesque or the antique, are you, Bill? I can't think why you are an archaeologist."

"Don't blame me for that. Blame my guardian. He's a learned bird—fellow of his college—browses among books in bedroom slippers—that kind of man. Bit of a shock for him to have a ward like me."

"I think it's frightfully stupid of you to be forced into a profession you don't care for," said the girl sharply.

"Not forced, Sheila, old girl, not forced. The old man asked if I had any special profession in mind, and I said I hadn't, and so he wangled a season out here for me."

"But haven't you any idea really what you'd *like* to do? You *must* have!"

"Of course I have. My idea would be to give work a miss altogether. What I'd like to do is to have plenty of money and go in for motor racing."

"You're absurd!" said Miss Reilly.

She sounded quite angry.

"Oh, I realize that it's quite out of the question," said Mr. Coleman cheerfully. "So, if I've got to do something, I don't much care what it is so long as it isn't mugging in an office all day long. I was quite agreeable to seeing a bit of the world. Here goes, I said, and along I came."

"And a fat lot of use you must be, I expect!"

"There you're wrong. I can stand up on the dig and shout '*Y'Allah*' with anybody! And as a matter of fact I'm not so dusty at drawing. Imitating handwriting used to be my specialty at school. I'd have made a first-class forger. Oh, well, I may come to that yet. If my Rolls-Royce splashes you with mud as you're waiting for a bus, you'll know that I've taken to crime."

Miss Reilly said coldly:

"Don't you think it's about time you started instead of talking so much?"

"Hospitable, aren't we, nurse?"

"I'm sure Nurse Leatheran is anxious to get settled in."

"You're always sure of everything," retorted Mr. Coleman with a grin.

That was true enough, I thought. Cocksure little minx.

I said dryly:

"Perhaps we'd better start, Mr. Coleman."

"Right you are, nurse."

I shook hands with Miss Reilly and thanked her, and we set off.

"Damned attractive girl, Sheila," said Mr. Coleman. "But always ticking a fellow off."

We drove out of the town and presently took a kind of track between green crops. It was very bumpy and full of ruts.

After about half an hour Mr. Coleman pointed to a big mound by the riverbank ahead of us and said:

"Tell Yarimjah."

I could see little black figures moving about it like ants.

As I was looking they suddenly began to run all together down the side of the mound.

"Fidos," said Mr. Coleman. "Knocking off time. We knock off an hour before sunset."

The expedition house lay a little way back from the river.

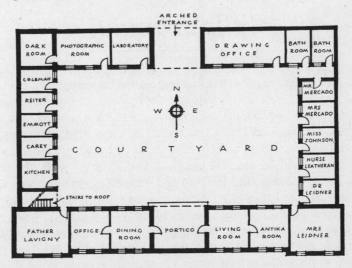

The driver rounded a corner, bumped through an extremely narrow arch and there we were.

The house was built around a courtyard. Originally it had occupied only the south side of the courtyard with a few unimportant outbuildings on the east. The expedition had continued the building on the other two sides. As the plan of the house was to prove of special interest later, I append a rough sketch of it above.

All the rooms opened onto the courtyard, and most of the windows—the exception being in the original south building where there were windows giving on the outside country as well. These windows, however, were barred on the outside. In the southwest corner a staircase ran up to a long flat roof with a parapet running the length of the south side of the building which was higher than the other three sides.

Mr. Coleman led me along the east side of the courtyard and around to where a big open veranda occupied the center of the south side. He pushed open a door at one side of it and we entered a room where several people were sitting around a tea table.

"Toodle-oodle-oo!" said Mr. Coleman. "Here's Sairey Gamp."

The lady who was sitting at the head of the table rose and came to greet me.

I had my first glimpse of Louise Leidner.

5

Tell Yarimjah

I DON'T MIND admitting that my first impression on seeing Mrs. Leidner was one of downright surprise. One gets into the way of imagining a person when one hears them talked about. I'd got it firmly into my head that Mrs. Leidner was a dark, discontented kind of woman. The nervy kind, all on edge. And then, too, I'd expected her to be—well, to put it frankly—a bit vulgar.

She wasn't a bit like what I'd imagined her! To begin with, she was very fair. She wasn't a Swede, like her husband, but she might have been as far as looks went. She had that blond Scandinavian fairness that you don't very often see. She wasn't a young woman. Midway between thirty and forty, I should say. Her face was rather haggard, and there was some gray hair mingled with the fairness. Her eyes, though, were lovely. They were the only eyes I've ever come across that you might truly describe as violet. They were very large, and there were faint shadows underneath them. She was very thin and fragile-looking, and if I say that she had an air of intense weariness and was at the same time very much alive, it sounds like nonsense—but that's the feeling I got. I felt, too, that she was a lady through and through. And that means something—even nowadays.

She put out her hand and smiled. Her voice was low and soft with an American drawl in it.

"I'm so glad you've come, nurse. Will you have some tea? Or would you like to go to your room first?"

I said I'd have tea, and she introduced me to the people sitting around the table.

"This is Miss Johnson—and Mr. Reiter. Mrs. Mercado. Mr. Emmott. Father Lavigny. My husband will be in presently. Sit down here between Father Lavigny and Miss Johnson."

I did as I was bid and Miss Johnson began talking to me, asking about my journey and so on.

I liked her. She reminded me of a matron I'd had in my probationer days whom we had all admired and worked hard for.

She was getting on for fifty, I should judge, and rather mannish in appearance, with iron-gray hair cropped short. She had an abrupt, pleasant voice, rather deep in tone. She had an ugly rugged face with an almost laughably turned-up nose which she was in the habit of rubbing irritably when anything troubled or perplexed her. She wore a tweed coat and skirt made rather like a man's. She told me presently that she was a native of Yorkshire.

Father Lavigny I found just a bit alarming. He was a tall man with a great black beard and pince-nez. I had heard Mrs. Kelsey say that there was a French monk there, and I now saw that Father Lavigny was wearing a monk's robe of some white woollen material. It surprised me rather, because I always understood that monks went into monasteries and didn't come out again.

Mrs. Leidner talked to him mostly in French, but he spoke to me in quite fair English. I noticed that he had shrewd, observant eyes which darted about from face to face.

Opposite me were the other three. Mr. Reiter was a stout, fair young man with glasses. His hair was rather long and curly, and he had very round blue eyes. I should think he must have been a lovely baby, but he wasn't much to look at now! In fact he was just a little like a pig. The other young man had very short hair cropped close to his head. He had a long, rather humorous face and very good teeth, and he looked very attractive when he smiled. He said very little, though, just nodded if spoken to or answered in monosyllables. He, like Mr. Reiter, was an American. The last person was Mrs. Mercado, and I couldn't have a good look at her because whenever I glanced in her direction I always found her staring at me with a kind of hungry stare that was a bit disconcerting to say the least of it. You might have thought a hospital nurse was a strange animal the way she was looking at me. No manners at all!

She was quite young—not more than about twenty-five—and sort of dark and slinky-looking, if you know what I mean. Quite nice-looking in a kind of way, but rather as though she might have what my mother used to call "a touch of the tar-brush." She had on a very vivid pullover and her nails matched it in color. She had a thin birdlike eager face with big eyes and rather a tight, suspicious mouth.

The tea was very good—a nice strong blend—not like the weak China stuff that Mrs. Kelsey always had and that had been a sore trial to me.

There was toast and jam and a plate of rock buns and a cutting cake. Mr. Emmott was very polite passing me things. Quiet as he was he always seemed to notice when my plate was empty.

Presently Mr. Coleman bustled in and took the place beyond Miss Johnson. There didn't seem to be anything the matter with *his* nerves. He talked away nineteen to the dozen.

Mrs. Leidner sighed once and cast a wearied look in his direction but it didn't have any effect. Nor did the fact that Mrs. Mercado, to whom he was addressing most of his conversation, was far too busy watching me to do more than make perfunctory replies.

Just as we were finishing, Dr. Leidner and Mr. Mercado came in from the dig.

Dr. Leidner greeted me in his nice kind manner. I saw his eyes go quickly and anxiously to his wife's face and he seemed to be relieved by what he saw there. Then he sat down at the other end of the table and Mr. Mercado sat down in the vacant place by Mrs. Leidner. He was a tall, thin, melancholy man, a good deal older than his wife, with a sallow complexion and a queer, soft, shapeless-looking beard. I was glad when he came in, for his wife stopped staring at me and transferred her attention to him, watching him with a kind of anxious impatience that I found rather odd. He himself stirred his tea dreamily and said nothing at all. A piece of cake lay untasted on his plate.

There was still one vacant place, and presently the door opened and a man came in.

The moment I saw Richard Carey I felt he was one of the handsomest men I'd seen for a long time—and yet I doubt if that were really so. To say a man is handsome and at the same time to say he looks like a death's head sounds a rank contradiction, and yet it was true. His head gave the effect of having the skin stretched unusually tightly over the bones—but they were beautiful bones. The lean line of jaw and temple and forehead was so sharply outlined that he reminded me of a bronze statue. Out of this lean brown face looked two of the brightest and most intensely blue eyes I have ever seen. He stood about six foot and was, I should imagine, a little under forty years of age.

Dr. Leidner said:

"This is Mr. Carey, our architect, nurse."

He murmured something in a pleasant, inaudible English voice and sat down by Mrs. Mercado.

Mrs. Leidner said:

"I'm afraid the tea is a little cold, Mr. Carey." He said:

"Oh, that's quite all right, Mrs. Leidner. My fault for being late. I wanted to finish plotting those walls."

Mrs. Mercado said, "Jam, Mr. Carey?"

Mr. Reiter pushed forward the toast.

And I remember Major Pennyman saying:

"I can explain best what I mean by saying that they all passed the butter to each other a shade too politely."

Yes, there was something a little odd about it. . . .

A shade formal. . . .

You'd have said it was a party of strangers—not people who had known each other—some of them—for quite a number of years.

6

First Evening

AFTER TEA MRS. Leidner took me to show me my room.

Perhaps here I had better give a short description of the arrangement of the rooms. This was very simple and can easily be understood by a reference to the plan.

On either side of the big open porch were doors leading into the two principal rooms. That on the right led into the dining room, where we had had tea. The one on the other side led into an exactly similar room (I have called it the living room) which was used as a sitting room and kind of informal workroom—that is, a certain amount of drawing (other than the strictly architectural) was done there, and the more delicate pieces of pottery were brought there to be pieced together. Through the living room one passed into the antiquities room where all the finds from the dig were brought in and stored on shelves and in pigeon-holes, and also laid out on big benches and tables. From the antika room there was no exit save through the living room.

Beyond the antika room, but reached through a door which gave on the courtyard, was Mrs. Leidner's bedroom. This, like the other rooms on that side of the house, had a couple of barred windows looking out over the ploughed countryside. Round the corner next to Mrs. Leidner's room, but with no actual communicating door, was Dr. Leidner's room. This was the first of the rooms on the east side of the building. Next to it was the room that was to be mine. Next to me was Miss Johnson's, with Mr. and Mrs. Mercado's beyond. After that came two so-called bathrooms.

(When I once used that last term in the hearing of Dr. Reilly he laughed at me and said a bathroom was either a bathroom or not a bathroom! All the same, when you've got used to taps and proper plumbing, it seems strange to call a couple of mud rooms with a tin hip-bath in each of them, and muddy water brought in kerosene tins, *bathrooms!*)

All this side of the building had been added by Dr. Leidner to the original Arab house. The bedrooms were all the same, each with a window and a door giving on to the courtyard.

Along the north side were the drawing office, the laboratory and the photographic rooms.

To return to the verandah, the arrangement of rooms was much the same on the other side. There was the dining room leading into the office where the files were kept and the cataloguing and typing was done. Corresponding to Mrs. Leidner's room was that of Father Lavigny, who was given the largest bedroom; he used it also for the decoding—or whatever you call it—of tablets.

In the southwest corner was the staircase running up to the roof. On the west side were first the kitchen quarters and then four small bedrooms used by the young men—Carey, Emmott, Reiter and Coleman.

At the northwest corner was the photographic-room with the darkroom leading out of it. Next to that the laboratory. Then came the only entrance—the big arched doorway through which we had entered. Outside were sleeping quarters for the native servants, the guard-house for the soldiers, and stables, etc., for the water horses. The drawing-office was to the right of the archway occupying the rest of the north side.

I have gone into the arrangements of the house rather fully here because I don't want to have to go over them again later.

As I say, Mrs. Leidner herself took me round the building and finally established me in my bedroom, hoping that I should be comfortable and have everything I wanted.

The room was nicely though plainly furnished—a bed, a chest of drawers, a washstand and a chair.

"The boys will bring you hot water before lunch and dinner—and in the morning, of course. If you want it any other time, go outside and clap your hands, and when the boy comes say, *jib mai' har.* Do you think you can remember that?"

I said I thought so and repeated it a little haltingly.

"That's right. And be sure and shout it. Arabs don't understand anything said in an ordinary 'English' voice."

"Languages are funny things," I said. "It seems odd there should be such a lot of different ones."

Mrs. Leidner smiled.

"There is a church in Palestine in which the Lord's Prayer is written up in —ninety, I think it is—different languages."

"Well!" I said, "I must write and tell my old aunt that. She *will* be interested."

Mrs. Leidner fingered the jug and basin absently and shifted the soap dish an inch or two.

"I do hope you'll be happy here," she said. "And not get too bored."

"I'm not often bored," I assured her. "Life's not long enough for that."

She did not answer. She continued to toy with the washstand as though abstractedly.

Suddenly she fixed her dark violet eyes on my face.

"What exactly did my husband tell you, nurse?"

Well, one usually says the same thing to a question of that kind.

"I gathered you were a bit run down and all that, Mrs. Leidner," I said glibly. "And that you just wanted someone to look after you and take any worries off your hands."

She bent her head slowly and thoughtfully.

"Yes," she said. "Yes—that will do very well."

That was just a little bit enigmatic, but I wasn't going to question it. Instead I said:

"I hope you'll let me help you with anything there is to do in the house. You mustn't let me be idle."

She smiled a little.

"Thank you, nurse."

Then she sat down on the bed and, rather to my surprise, began to cross-question me rather closely. I say rather to my surprise because, from the moment I set eyes on her, I felt sure that Mrs. Leidner was a lady. And a lady, in my experience, very seldom displays curiosity about one's private affairs.

But Mrs. Leidner seemed anxious to know everything there was to know about me. Where I'd trained and how long ago. What had brought me out to the East. How it had come about that Dr. Reilly had recommended me. She even asked me if I had ever been in America or had any relations in America. One or two other questions she asked me that seemed quite purposeless at the time, but of which I saw the significance later.

Then, suddenly, her manner changed. She smiled—a warm sunny smile—and she said, very sweetly, that she was very glad I had come and that she was sure I was going to be a comfort to her.

She got up from the bed and said:

"Would you like to come up to the roof and see the sunset? It's usually very lovely about this time."

I agreed willingly.

As we went out of the room she asked:

"Were there many other people on the train from Baghdad? Any men?"

I said that I hadn't noticed anybody in particular. There had been two Frenchmen in the restaurant car the night before. And a party of three men whom I gathered from their conversation had to do with the Pipe line.

She nodded and a faint sound escaped her. It sounded like a small sigh of relief.

We went up to the roof together.

Mrs. Mercado was there, sitting on the parapet, and Dr. Leidner was bending over looking at a lot of stones and broken pottery that were laid out in rows. There were big things he called querns, and pestles and celts and stone axes, and more broken bits of pottery with queer patterns on them than I've ever seen all at once.

"Come over here," called out Mrs. Mercado. "Isn't it *too,* too beautiful?"

It certainly was a beautiful sunset. Hassanieh in the distance looked quite fairylike with the setting sun behind it, and the River Tigris flowing between its wide banks looked like a dream river rather than a real one.

"Isn't it lovely, Eric?" said Mrs. Leidner.

The doctor looked up with abstracted eyes, murmured, "Lovely, lovely," perfunctorily and went on sorting potsherds.

Mrs. Leidner smiled and said:

"Archaeologists only look at what lies beneath their feet. The sky and the heavens don't exist for them."

Mrs. Mercado giggled.

"Oh, they're very queer people—you'll soon find *that* out, nurse," she said.

She paused and then added:

"We are all *so* glad you've come. We've been so very worried about our dear Mrs. Leidner, haven't we, Louise?"

"Have you?"

Her voice was not encouraging.

"Oh, yes. She really has been *very* bad, nurse. All sorts of alarms and excursions. You know when anybody says to me of someone, 'It's just nerves,' I always say: But what could be *worse?* Nerves are the core and center of one's being, aren't they?"

"Puss, puss," I thought to myself.

Mrs. Leidner said dryly:

"Well, you needn't be worried about me anymore, Marie. Nurse is going to look after me."

"Certainly I am," I said cheerfully.

"I'm sure that will make all the difference," said Mrs. Mercado. "We've all felt that she ought to see a doctor or do *something*. Her nerves have really been all to pieces, haven't they, Louise dear?"

"So much so that I seem to have got on *your* nerves with them," said Mrs. Leidner. "Shall we talk about something more interesting than my wretched ailments?"

I understood then that Mrs. Leidner was the sort of woman who could easily make enemies. There was a cool rudeness in her tone (not that I blamed her for it) which brought a flush to Mrs. Mercado's rather sallow cheeks. She stammered out something, but Mrs. Leidner had risen and had joined her husband at the other end of the roof. I doubt if he heard her coming till she laid her hand on his shoulder, then he looked up quickly. There was affection and a kind of eager questioning in his face.

Mrs. Leidner nodded her head gently. Presently, her arm through his, they wandered to the far parapet and finally down the steps together.

"He's devoted to her, isn't he?" said Mrs. Mercado.

"Yes," I said. "It's very nice to see."

She was looking at me with a queer, rather eager sidelong glance.

"What do you think is really the matter with her, nurse?" she asked, lowering her voice a little.

"Oh, I don't suppose it's much," I said cheerfully. "Just a bit run down, I expect."

Her eyes still bored into me as they had done at tea. She said abruptly:

"Are you a mental nurse?"

"Oh, dear no!" I said. "What made you think that?"

She was silent for a moment, then she said:

"Do you know how queer she's been? Did Dr. Leidner tell you?"

I don't hold with gossiping about my cases. On the other hand, it's my experience that it's often very hard to get the truth out of the relatives, and until you know the truth you're often working in the dark and doing no good. Of course, when there's a doctor in charge, it's different. He tells you what it's necessary for you to know. But in this case there wasn't a doctor in charge. Dr. Reilly had never been called in professionally. And in my own mind I wasn't at all sure that Dr. Leidner had told me all he could have done. It's often the husband's instinct to be reticent—and more honor to him, I say. But all the same, the more I knew the better I could tell which line to take. Mrs. Mercado (whom I put down in my own mind as a thoroughly spiteful little cat) was clearly dying to talk. And frankly, on the human side as well as the professional, I wanted to hear what she had to say. You can put it that I was just everyday curious if you like.

I said, "I gather Mrs. Leidner's not been quite her normal self lately?"

Mrs. Mercado laughed disagreeably.

"Normal? I should say not. Frightening us to death. One night it was fingers tapping on her window. And then it was a hand without an arm attached. But when it came to a yellow face pressed against the window—and when she rushed to the window there was nothing there—well, I ask you, it *is* a bit creepy for all of us."

"Perhaps somebody was playing a trick on her," I suggested.

"Oh, no, she fancied it all. And only three days ago at dinner they were firing off shots in the village—nearly a mile away—and she jumped up and screamed out—it scared us all to death. As for Dr. Leidner, he rushed to her and behaved in the most ridiculous way. 'It's nothing, darling, it's nothing at all,' he kept saying. I think, you know, nurse, men sometimes *encourage* women in these hysterical fancies. It's a pity because it's a bad thing. Delusions shouldn't be encouraged."

"Not if they *are* delusions," I said dryly.

"What else could they be?"

I didn't answer because I didn't know what to say. It was a funny business.

The shots and the screaming were natural enough—for anyone in a nervous condition, that is. But this queer story of a spectral face and hand was different. It looked to me like one of two things—either Mrs. Leidner had made the story up (exactly as a child shows off by telling lies about something that never happened in order to make herself the center of attraction) or else it was, as I had suggested, a deliberate practical joke. It was the sort of thing, I reflected, that an unimaginative hearty sort of young fellow like Mr. Coleman might think very funny. I decided to keep a close watch on him. Nervous patients can be scared nearly out of their minds by a silly joke.

Mrs. Mercado said with a sideways glance at me:

"She's very romantic-looking, nurse, don't you think so? The sort of woman things *happen* to."

"Have many things happened to her?" I asked.

"Well, her first husband was killed in the war when she was only twenty. I think that's very pathetic and romantic, don't you?"

"It's one way of calling a goose a swan," I said dryly.

"Oh! nurse. What an extraordinary remark!"

It was really a very true one. The amount of women you hear say, "If Donald—or Arthur—or whatever his name was—had *only* lived." And I sometimes think but if he had, he'd have been a stout, unromantic, short-tempered, middle-aged husband as likely as not.

It was getting dark and I suggested that we should go down. Mrs. Mercado agreed and asked if I would like to see the laboratory. "My husband will be there—working."

I said I would like to very much and we made our way there. The place was lighted by a lamp but it was empty. Mrs. Mercado showed me some of the apparatus and some copper ornaments that were being treated, and also some bones coated with wax.

"Where can Joseph be?" said Mrs. Mercado.

She looked into the drawing-office, where Carey was at work. He hardly looked up as we entered, and I was struck by the extraordinary look of strain on his face. It came to me suddenly: "This man is at the end of his tether. Very soon, something will snap." And I remembered somebody else had noticed that same tenseness about him.

As we went out again I turned my head for one last look at him. He was bent over his paper, his lips pressed very closely together, and that "death's head" suggestion of his bones very strongly marked. Perhaps it was fanciful, but I thought that he looked like a knight of old who was going into battle and knew he was going to be killed.

And again I felt what an extraordinary and quite unconscious power of attraction he had.

We found Mr. Mercado in the living room. He was explaining the idea of some new process to Mrs. Leidner. She was sitting on a straight wooden chair, embroidering flowers in fine silks, and I was struck anew by her strange, fragile, unearthly appearance. She looked a fairy creature more than flesh and blood.

Mrs. Mercado said, her voice high and shrill:

"Oh, *there* you are, Joseph. We thought we'd find you in the lab."

He jumped up looking startled and confused, as though her entrance had broken a spell. He said stammeringly:

"I—I must go now. I'm in the middle of—the middle of—"

He didn't complete the sentence but turned toward the door.

Mrs. Leidner said in her soft, drawling voice:

"You must finish telling me some other time. It was very interesting."

She looked up at us, smiled rather sweetly but in a faraway manner, and bent over her embroidery again.

In a minute or two she said:

"There are some books over there, nurse. We've got quite a good selection. Choose one and sit down."

I went over to the bookshelf. Mrs. Mercado stayed for a minute or two, then, turning abruptly, she went out. As she passed me I saw her face and I didn't like the look of it. She looked wild with fury.

In spite of myself I remembered some of the things Mrs. Kelsey had said and hinted about Mrs. Leidner. I didn't like to think they were true because I liked Mrs. Leidner, but I wondered, nevertheless, if there mightn't perhaps be a grain of truth behind them.

I didn't think it was all her fault, but the fact remained that dear ugly Miss Johnson, and that common little spitfire Mrs. Mercado, couldn't hold a candle to her in looks or in attraction. And after all, men are men all over the world. You soon see a lot of that in my profession.

Mercado was a poor fish, and I don't suppose Mrs. Leidner really cared two hoots for his admiration—but his wife cared. If I wasn't mistaken, she minded badly and would be quite willing to do Mrs. Leidner a bad turn if she could.

I looked at Mrs. Leidner sitting there and sewing at her pretty flowers, so remote and far away and aloof. I felt somehow I ought to warn her. I felt that perhaps she didn't know how stupid and unreasoning and violent jealousy and hate can be—and how little it takes to set them smoldering.

And then I said to myself, "Amy Leatheran, you're a fool. Mrs. Leidner's no chicken. She's close on forty if she's a day, and she must know all about life there is to know."

But I felt that all the same perhaps she didn't.

She had such a queer untouched look.

I began to wonder what her life had been. I knew she'd only married Dr. Leidner two years ago. And according to Mrs. Mercado her first husband had died nearly twenty years ago.

I came and sat down near her with a book, and presently I went and washed my hands for supper. It was a good meal—some really excellent curry. They all went to bed early and I was glad for I was tired.

Dr. Leidner came with me to my room to see I had all I wanted.

He gave me a warm handclasp and said eagerly:

"She likes you, nurse. She's taken to you at once. I'm so glad. I feel everything's going to be all right now."

His eagerness was almost boyish.

I felt, too, that Mrs. Leidner had taken a liking to me, and I was pleased it should be so.

But I didn't quite share his confidence. I felt, somehow, that there was more to it all than he himself might know.

There was *something*—something I couldn't get at. But I felt it in the air.

My bed was comfortable, but I didn't sleep well for all that. I dreamt too much.

The words of a poem by Keats, that I'd had to learn as a child, kept running through my head. I kept getting them wrong and it worried me. It was a poem I'd always hated—I suppose because I'd had to learn it whether I wanted to or not. But somehow when I woke up in the dark I saw a sort of beauty in it for the first time.

"Oh, say what ails thee, knight at arms, alone—and (what was it?)—*palely loitering . . . ?"* I saw the knight's face in my mind for the first time—and it was Mr. Carey's face—a grim, tense, bronzed face like some of those poor young men I remembered as a girl during the war . . . and I felt sorry for him—and then I fell off to sleep again and I saw that the Belle Dame sans Merci was Mrs. Leidner and she was leaning sideways on a horse with an embroidery of flowers in her hands—and then the horse stumbled and everywhere there were bones coated in wax, and I woke up all goose-flesh and shivering, and told myself that curry never *had* agreed with me at night.

7

The Man at the Window

I THINK I'D better make it clear right away that there isn't going to be any local color in this story. I don't know anything about archaeology and I don't know that I very much want to. Messing about with people and places that are buried and done with doesn't make sense to me. Mr. Carey used to tell me that I hadn't got the archaeological temperament and I've no doubt he was quite right.

The very first morning after my arrival Mr. Carey asked if I'd like to come and see the palace he was—*planning* I think he called it. Though how you can plan for a thing that's happened long ago I'm sure I don't know! Well, I said I'd like to, and to tell the truth, I was a bit excited about it. Nearly three thousand years old that palace was, it appeared. I wondered what sort of palaces they had in those days, and if it would be like the pictures I'd seen of Tutankhamen's tomb furniture. But would you believe it, there was nothing to see but *mud!* Dirty mud walls about two feet high—and that's all there was to it. Mr. Carey took me here and there telling me things—how this was the great court, and there were some chambers here and an upper storey and various other rooms that opened off the central court. And all I thought was, "But how does he *know?*" though, of course, I was too polite to say so. I can tell you it *was* a disappointment! The whole excavation looked like nothing but mud to me—no marble or gold or anything handsome—my aunt's house in Cricklewood would have made a much more imposing ruin! And those old Assyrians or whatever they were called themselves *kings.* When Mr. Carey had shown me his old "palace," he handed me over to Father Lavigny, who showed me the rest of the mound. I was a little afraid of Father Lavigny, being a monk and a foreigner and having such a deep voice and all, but he was very kind—though rather vague. Sometimes I felt it wasn't much more real to him than it was to me.

Mrs. Leidner explained that later. She said that Father Lavigny was only interested in "written documents"—as she called them. They wrote everything on clay, these people, queer heathenish-looking marks too, but quite sensible. There were even school tablets—the teacher's lesson on one side and the pupil's effort on the back of it. I confess that that did interest me rather—it seemed so human, if you know what I mean.

Father Lavigny walked round the work with me and showed me what were temples or palaces and what were private houses, and also a place which he said was an early Akkadian cemetery. He spoke in a funny jerky way, just throwing in a scrap of information and then reverting to other subjects.

He said:

"It is strange that you have come here. Is Mrs. Leidner really ill, then?"

"Not exactly ill," I said cautiously.

He said:

"She is an odd woman. A dangerous woman, I think."

"Now what do you mean by that?" I said. "Dangerous? How dangerous?"

He shook his head thoughtfully.

"I think she is ruthless," he said. "Yes, I think she could be absolutely ruthless."

"If you'll excuse me," I said, "I think you're talking nonsense."

He shook his head.

"You do not know women as I do," he said.

And that was a funny thing, I thought, for a monk to say. But of course I suppose he might have heard a lot of things in confession. But that rather puzzled me, because I wasn't sure if monks heard confessions or if it was only priests. I supposed he *was* a monk with that long woollen robe—all sweeping up the dirt—and the rosary and all!

"Yes, she could be ruthless," he said musingly. "I am quite sure of that. And yet—though she is so hard—like stone, like marble—yet she is afraid. What is she afraid of?"

That, I thought, is what we should all like to know!

At least it was possible that her husband did know, but I didn't think anyone else did.

He fixed me with a sudden bright, dark eye.

"It is odd here? You find it odd? Or quite natural?"

"Not quite natural," I said, considering. "It's comfortable enough as far as the arrangements go—but there isn't quite a comfortable feeling."

"It makes *me* uncomfortable. I have the idea"—he became suddenly a little more foreign—"that something prepares itself. Dr. Leidner, too, he is not quite himself. Something is worrying him also."

"His wife's health?"

"That perhaps. But there is more. There is—how shall I say it—an uneasiness."

And that was just it, there was an uneasiness.

We didn't say any more just then, for Dr. Leidner came toward us. He showed me a child's grave that had just been uncovered. Rather pathetic it was—the little bones—and a pot or two and some little specks that Dr. Leidner told me were a bead necklace.

It was the workmen that made me laugh. You never saw such a lot of scarecrows—all in long petticoats and rags, and their heads tied up as though they had toothache. And every now and then, as they went to and fro carrying away baskets of earth, they began to sing—at least I suppose it was meant to be singing—a queer sort of monotonous chant that went on and on over and over again. I noticed that most of their eyes were terrible—all covered with discharge, and one or two looked half blind. I was just thinking what a miserable lot they were when Dr. Leidner said, "Rather a fine-looking lot of men, aren't they?" and I thought what a queer world it was and how two different people could see the same thing each of them the other way round. I haven't put that very well, but you can guess what I mean.

After a bit Dr. Leidner said he was going back to the house for a mid-morning cup of tea. So he and I walked back together and he told me things. When *he* explained, it was all quite different. I sort of *saw* it all—how it used to be—the streets and the houses, and he showed me ovens where they baked bread and said the Arabs used much the same kind of ovens nowadays.

We got back to the house and found Mrs. Leidner had got up. She was looking better today, not so thin and worn. Tea came in almost at once and Dr. Leidner told her what had turned up during the morning on the dig. Then he went back to work and Mrs. Leidner asked me if I would like to see some of the finds they had made up to date. Of course I said "Yes," so she took me through into the antika room. There was a lot of stuff lying about—

mostly broken pots it seemed to me—or else ones that were all mended and stuck together. The whole lot might have been thrown away, I thought.

"Dear, dear," I said, "it's a pity they're all so broken, isn't it? Are they really worth keeping?"

Mrs. Leidner smiled a little and she said:

"You mustn't let Eric hear you. Pots interest him more than anything else, and some of these are the oldest things we have—perhaps as much as seven thousand years old." And she explained how some of them came from a very deep cut on the mound down toward the bottom, and how, thousands of years ago, they had been broken and mended with bitumen, showing people prized their things just as much then as they do nowadays.

"And now," she said, "we'll show you something more exciting."

And she took down a box from the shelf and showed me a beautiful gold dagger with dark-blue stones in the handle.

I exclaimed with pleasure.

Mrs. Leidner laughed.

"Yes, everybody likes gold! Except my husband."

"Why doesn't Dr. Leidner like it?"

"Well, for one thing it comes expensive. You have to pay the workmen who find it the weight of the object in gold."

"Good gracious!" I exclaimed. "But why?"

"Oh, it's a custom. For one thing it prevents them from stealing. You see, if they *did* steal it wouldn't be for the archaeological value but for the intrinsic value. They could melt it down. So we make it easy for them to be honest."

She took down another tray and showed me a really beautiful gold drinking cup with a design of rams' heads on it.

Again I exclaimed.

"Yes, it is beautiful, isn't it? These came from a prince's grave. We found other royal graves but most of them had been plundered. This cup is our best find. It is one of the most lovely ever found anywhere. Early Akkadian. Unique."

Suddenly, with a frown, Mrs. Leidner brought the cup up close to her eyes and scratched at it delicately with her nail.

"How extraordinary! There's actually wax on it. Someone must have been in here with a candle."

She detached the little flake and replaced the cup in its place.

After that she showed me some queer little terra-cotta figurines—but most of them were just rude. Nasty minds those old people had, I say.

When we went back to the porch Mrs. Mercado was sitting polishing her nails. She was holding them out in front of her admiring the effect. I thought myself that anything more hideous than that orange red could hardly have been imagined.

Mrs. Leidner had brought with her from the antika room a very delicate little saucer broken in several pieces, and this she now proceeded to join together. I watched her for a minute or two and then asked if I could help.

"Oh, yes, there are plenty more." She fetched quite a supply of broken pottery and we set to work. I soon got into the hang of it and she praised my ability. I suppose most nurses are handy with their fingers.

"How busy everybody is," said Mrs. Mercado. "It makes me feel dreadfully idle. Of course I *am* idle."

"Why shouldn't you be if you like?" said Mrs. Leidner.

Her voice was quite uninterested.

At twelve we had lunch. Afterward Dr. Leidner and Mr. Mercado cleaned some pottery, pouring a solution of hydrochloric acid over it. One pot went a lovely plum color and a pattern of bulls' horns came out on another one. It was really quite magical. All the dried mud that no washing would remove sort of foamed and boiled away.

Mr. Carey and Mr. Coleman went out on the dig and Mr. Reiter went off to the photographic room.

"What will you do, Louise?" Dr. Leidner asked his wife. "I suppose you'll rest for a bit?"

I gathered that Mrs. Leidner usually lay down every afternoon.

"I'll rest for about an hour. Then perhaps I'll go out for a short stroll."

"Good. Nurse will go with you, won't you?"

"Of course," I said.

"No, no," said Mrs. Leidner. "I like going alone. Nurse isn't to feel so much on duty that I'm not allowed out of her sight."

"Oh, but I'd like to come," I said.

"No, really, I'd rather you didn't." She was quite firm—almost peremptory. "I must be by myself every now and then. It's necessary to me."

I didn't insist, of course. But as I went off for a short sleep myself it struck me as odd that Mrs. Leidner, with her nervous terrors, should be quite content to walk by herself without any kind of protection.

When I came out of my room at half past three the courtyard was deserted save for a little boy with a large copper bath who was washing pottery, and Mr. Emmott, who was sorting and arranging it. As I went toward them Mrs. Leidner came in through the archway. She looked more alive than I had seen her yet. Her eyes shone and she looked uplifted and almost gay.

Dr. Leidner came out from the laboratory and joined her. He was showing her a big dish with bulls' horns on it.

"The prehistoric levels are being extraordinarily productive," he said. "It's been a good season so far. Finding that tomb right at the beginning was a real piece of luck. The only person who might complain is Father Lavigny. We've had hardly any tablets so far."

"He doesn't seem to have done very much with the few we have had," said Mrs. Leidner dryly. "He may be a very fine epigraphist but he's a remarkably lazy one. He spends all his afternoons sleeping."

"We miss Byrd," said Dr. Leidner. "This man strikes me as slightly unorthodox—though, of course, I'm not competent to judge. But one or two of his translations have been surprising to say the least of it. I can hardly believe, for instance, that he's right about that inscribed brick, and yet he must know."

After tea Mrs. Leidner asked me if I would like to stroll down to the river. I thought that perhaps she feared that her refusal to let me accompany her earlier in the afternoon might have hurt my feelings.

I wanted her to know that I wasn't the touchy kind, so I accepted at once.

It was a lovely evening. A path led between barley fields and then through some flowering fruit trees. Finally we came to the edge of the Tigris. Immediately on our left was the Tell with the workmen singing in their queer monotonous chant. A little to our right was a big waterwheel which made a queer groaning noise. It used to set my teeth on edge at first. But in the end I got fond of it and it had a queer soothing effect on me. Beyond the waterwheel was the village from which most of the workmen came.

"It's rather beautiful, isn't it?" said Mrs. Leidner.

"It's very peaceful," I said. "It seems funny to me to be so far away from everywhere."

"Far from everywhere," repeated Mrs. Leidner. "Yes. Here at least one might expect to be safe."

I glanced at her sharply, but I think she was speaking more to herself than to me, and I don't think she realized that her words had been revealing.

We began to walk back to the house.

Suddenly Mrs. Leidner clutched my arm so violently that I nearly cried out.

"Who's that, nurse? What's he doing?"

Some little distance ahead of us, just where the path ran near the expedition house, a man was standing. He wore European clothes and he seemed to be standing on tiptoe and trying to look in at one of the windows.

As we watched he glanced around, caught sight of us, and immediately continued on the path toward us. I felt Mrs. Leidner's clutch tighten.

"Nurse," she whispered. "Nurse . . ."

"It's all right, my dear, it's all right," I said reassuringly.

The man came along and passed us. He was an Iraqi, and as soon as she saw him near to, Mrs. Leidner relaxed with a sigh.

"He's only an Iraqi after all," she said.

We went on our way. I glanced up at the windows as I passed. Not only were they barred, but they were too high from the ground to permit of anyone seeing in, for the level of the ground was lower here than on the inside of the courtyard.

"It must have been just curiosity," I said.

Mrs. Leidner nodded.

"That's all. But just for a minute I thought—"

She broke off.

I thought to myself, "You thought *what?* That's what I'd like to know? *What* did you think?"

But I knew one thing now—that Mrs. Leidner was afraid of a definite flesh and blood person.

8

Night Alarm

IT'S A LITTLE difficult to know exactly what to note in the week that followed my arrival at Tell Yarimjah.

Looking back as I do from my present standpoint of knowledge I can see a good many little signs and indications that I was quite blind to at the time.

To tell the story properly, however, I think I ought to try and recapture the point of view that I actually held—puzzled, uneasy, and increasingly conscious of *something* wrong.

For one thing *was* certain, that curious sense of strain and constraint was *not* imagined. It was genuine. Even Bill Coleman the insensitive commented upon it.

"This place gets under my skin," I heard him say. "Are they always such a glum lot?"

It was David Emmott to whom he spoke, the other assistant. I had taken rather a fancy to Mr. Emmott; his taciturnity was not, I felt sure, unfriendly. There was something about him that seemed very steadfast and reassuring in an atmosphere where one was uncertain what anyone was feeling or thinking.

"No," he said in answer to Mr. Coleman. "It wasn't like this last year."

But he didn't enlarge on the theme, or say any more.

"What I can't make out is what it's all about," said Mr. Coleman in an aggrieved voice.

Emmott shrugged his shoulders but didn't answer.

I had a rather enlightening conversation with Miss Johnson. I liked her very much. She was capable, practical and intelligent. She had, it was quite obvious, a distinct hero worship for Dr. Leidner.

On this occasion she told me the story of his life since his young days. She knew every site he had dug, and the results of the dig. I would almost dare swear she could quote from every lecture he had ever delivered. She considered him, she told me, quite the finest field archaeologist living.

"And he's so simple. So completely unworldly. He doesn't know the meaning of the word conceit. Only a really great man could be so simple."

"That's true enough," I said. "Big people don't need to throw their weight about."

"And he's so lighthearted too. I can't tell you what fun we used to have—he and Richard Carey and I—the first years we were out here. We were such a happy party. Richard Carey worked with him in Palestine, of course. Theirs is a friendship of ten years or so. Oh, well, I've known him for seven."

"What a handsome man Mr. Carey is," I said.

"Yes—I suppose he is."

She said it rather curtly.

"But he's just a little bit quiet, don't you think?"

"He usedn't to be like that," said Miss Johnson quickly. "It's only since—" She stopped abruptly.

"Only since—?" I prompted.

"Oh, well." Miss Johnson gave a characteristic motion of her shoulders. "A good many things are changed nowadays."

I didn't answer. I hoped she would go on—and she did—prefacing her remarks with a little laugh as though to detract from their importance.

"I'm afraid I'm rather a conservative old fogy. I sometimes think that if an archaeologist's wife isn't really interested, it would be wiser for her not to accompany the expedition. It often leads to friction."

"Mrs. Mercado—" I suggested.

"Oh, her!" Miss Johnson brushed the suggestion aside. "I was really thinking of Mrs. Leidner. She's a very charming woman—and one can quite understand why Dr. Leidner 'fell for her'—to use a slang term. But I can't help feeling she's out of place here. She—it unsettles things."

So Miss Johnson agreed with Mrs. Kelsey that it was Mrs. Leidner who was responsible for the strained atmosphere. But then where did Mrs. Leidner's own nervous fears come in?

"It unsettles *him,*" said Miss Johnson earnestly. "Of course, I'm—well, I'm like a faithful but jealous old dog. I don't like to see him so worn out and worried. His whole mind ought to be on the work—not taken up with his wife and her silly fears! If she's nervous of coming to out-of-the-way places, she ought to have stayed in America. I've no patience with people who come to a place and then do nothing but grouse about it!"

And then, a little fearful of having said more than she meant to say, she went on:

"Of course I admire her very much. She's a lovely woman and she's got great charm of manner when she chooses."

And there the subject dropped.

I thought to myself that it was always the same way—wherever women are cooped up together, there's bound to be jealousy. Miss Johnson clearly didn't like her chief's wife (that was perhaps natural) and unless I was much mistaken Mrs. Mercado fairly hated her.

Another person who didn't like Mrs. Leidner was Sheila Reilly. She came out once or twice to the dig, once in a car and twice with some young man on a horse—on two horses I mean, of course. It was at the back of my mind that she had a weakness for the silent young American, Emmott. When he was on duty at the dig she used to stay talking to him, and I thought, too, that *he* admired *her*.

One day, rather injudiciously, I thought, Mrs. Leidner commented upon it at lunch.

"The Reilly girl is still hunting David down," she said with a little laugh. "Poor David, she chases you up on the dig even! How foolish girls are!"

Mr. Emmott didn't answer, but under his tan his face got rather red. He raised his eyes and looked right into hers with a very curious expression—a straight, steady glance with something of a challenge in it.

She smiled very faintly and looked away.

I heard Father Lavigny murmur something, but when I said "Pardon?" he merely shook his head and did not repeat his remark.

That afternoon Mr. Coleman said to me:

"Matter of fact I didn't like Mrs. L. any too much at first. She used to jump down my throat every time I opened my mouth. But I've begun to understand her better now. She's one of the kindest women I've ever met. You find yourself telling her all the foolish scrapes you ever got into before you know where you are. She's got her knife into Sheila Reilly, I know, but then Sheila's been damned rude to her once or twice. That's the worst of Sheila—she's got no manners. And a temper like the devil!"

That I could well believe. Dr. Reilly spoiled her.

"Of course she's bound to get a bit full of herself, being the only young woman in the place. But that doesn't excuse her talking to Mrs. Leidner as though Mrs. Leidner were her great-aunt. Mrs. L's not exactly a chicken, but she's a damned good-looking woman. Rather like those fairy women who come out of marshes with lights and lure you away." He added bitterly, "You wouldn't find Sheila luring anyone. All she does is to tick a fellow off."

I only remember two other incidents of any kind of significance.

One was when I went to the laboratory to fetch some acetone to get the stickiness off my fingers from mending the pottery. Mr. Mercado was sitting in a corner, his head was laid down on his arms and I fancied he was asleep. I took the bottle I wanted and went off with it.

That evening, to my great surprise, Mrs. Mercado tackled me.

"Did you take a bottle of acetone from the lab?"

"Yes," I said. "I did."

"You know perfectly well that there's a small bottle always kept in the antika room."

She spoke quite angrily.

"Is there? I didn't know."

"I think you did! You just wanted to come spying round. I know what hospital nurses are."

I stared at her.

"I don't know what you're talking about, Mrs. Mercado," I said with dignity. "I'm sure I don't want to spy on anyone."

"Oh, no! Of course not. Do you think I don't know what you're here for?"

Really, for a minute or two I thought she must have been drinking. I went away without saying anymore. But I thought it was very odd.

The other thing was nothing very much. I was trying to entice a pi dog pup with a piece of bread. It was very timid, however, like all Arab dogs—and was convinced I meant no good. It slunk away and I followed it—out through the archway and round the corner of the house. I came around so sharply that before I knew I had cannoned into Father Lavigny and another man who were standing together—and in a minute I realized that the second man was the same one Mrs. Leidner and I had noticed that day trying to peer through the window.

I apologized and Father Lavigny smiled, and with a word of farewell greeting to the other man he returned to the house with me.

"You know," he said, "I am very ashamed. I am a student of Oriental languages and none of the men on the work can understand me! It is humiliating, do you not think? I was trying my Arabic on that man, who is a townsman, to see if I got on better—but it still wasn't very successful. Leidner says my Arabic is too pure."

That was all. But it just passed through my head that it was odd the same man should still be hanging around the house.

That night we had a scare.

It must have been about two in the morning. I'm a light sleeper, as most nurses have to be. I was awake and sitting up in bed by the time that my door opened.

"Nurse, nurse!"

It was Mrs. Leidner's voice, low and urgent.

I struck a match and lighted the candle.

She was standing by the door in a long blue dressing gown. She was looking petrified with terror.

"There's someone—someone—in the room next to mine. . . . I heard him—scratching on the wall."

I jumped out of bed and came to her.

"It's all right," I said. "I'm here. Don't be afraid, my dear."

She whispered:

"Get Eric."

I nodded and ran out and knocked on his door. In a minute he was with us. Mrs. Leidner was sitting on my bed, her breath coming in great gasps.

"I heard him," she said. "I heard him—scratching on the wall."

"Someone in the antika room?" cried Dr. Leidner.

He ran out quickly—and it just flashed across my mind how differently these two had reacted. Mrs. Leidner's fear was entirely personal, but Dr. Leidner's mind leaped at once to his precious treasures.

"The antika room!" breathed Mrs. Leidner. "Of course! How stupid of me."

And rising and pulling her gown around her, she bade me come with her. All traces of her panic-stricken fear had vanished.

We arrived in the antika room to find Dr. Leidner and Father Lavigny. The latter had also heard a noise, had risen to investigate, and had fancied he saw a light in the antika room. He had delayed to put on slippers and snatch up a flashlight and had found no one by the time he got there. The door, moreover, was duly locked, as it was supposed to be at night.

While he was assuring himself that nothing had been taken, Dr. Leidner had joined him.

Nothing more was to be learned. The outside archway door was locked. The guard swore nobody could have got in from outside, but as they had probably been fast asleep this was not conclusive. There were no marks or traces of an intruder and nothing had been taken.

It was possible that what had alarmed Mrs. Leidner was the noise made by Father Lavigny taking down boxes from the shelves to assure himself that all was in order.

On the other hand, Father Lavigny himself was positive that he had (*a*) heard footsteps passing his window and (*b*) seen the flicker of a light, possibly a torch, in the antika room.

Nobody else had heard or seen anything.

The incident is of value in my narrative because it led to Mrs. Leidner's unburdening herself to me on the following day.

9

Mrs. Leidner's Story

WE HAD JUST finished lunch. Mrs. Leidner went to her room to rest as usual. I settled her on her bed with plenty of pillows and her book, and was leaving the room when she called me back.

"Don't go, nurse, there's something I want to say to you."

I came back into the room.

"Shut the door."

I obeyed.

She got up from the bed and began to walk up and down the room. I could see that she was making up her mind to something and I didn't like to interrupt her. She was clearly in great indecision of mind.

At last she seemed to have nerved herself to the required point. She turned to me and said abruptly:

"Sit down."

I sat down by the table very quietly. She began nervously:

"You must have wondered what all this is about?"

I just nodded without saying anything.

"I've made up my mind to tell you—everything! I must tell someone or I shall go mad."

"Well," I said. "I think really it would be just as well. It's not easy to know the best thing to do when one's kept in the dark."

She stopped in her uneasy walk and faced me.

"Do you know what I'm frightened of?"

"Some man," I said.

"Yes—but I didn't say whom—I said what."

I waited.

She said:

"I'm afraid of being killed!"

Well, it was out now. I wasn't going to show any particular concern. She was near enough hysterics as it was.

"Dear me," I said. "So that's it, is it?"

Then she began to laugh. She laughed and she laughed—and the tears ran down her face.

"The way you said that!" she gasped. "The way you said it . . ."

"Now, now," I said. "This won't do." I spoke sharply. I pushed her into a chair, went over to the washstand and got a cold sponge and bathed her forehead and wrists.

"No more nonsense," I said. "Tell me calmly and sensibly all about it."

That stopped her. She sat up and spoke in her natural voice.

"You're a treasure, nurse," she said. "You make me feel as though I'm six. I'm going to tell you."

"That's right," I said. "Take your time and don't hurry."

She began to speak, slowly and deliberately.

"When I was a girl of twenty I married. A young man in one of our state departments. It was in 1918."

"I know," I said. "Mrs. Mercado told me. He was killed in the war."

But Mrs. Leidner shook her head.

"That's what she thinks. That's what everybody thinks. The truth is something quite different. I was a queer patriotic, enthusiastic girl, nurse, full of idealism. When I'd been married a few months I discovered—by a quite unforeseeable accident—that my husband was a spy in German pay. I learned that the information supplied by him had led directly to the sinking of an American transport and the loss of hundreds of lives. I don't know what most people would have done. . . . But I'll tell you what I did. I went straight to my father, who was in the War Department, and told him the truth. Frederick *was* killed in the war—but he was killed in America—shot as a spy."

"Oh, dear, dear!" I ejaculated. "How terrible!"

"Yes," she said. "It was terrible. He was so kind, too—so gentle. . . . And all the time . . . But I never hesitated. Perhaps I was wrong."

"It's difficult to say," I said. "I'm sure I don't know what one would do."

"What I'm telling you was never generally known outside the state departments. Ostensibly my husband had gone to the front and had been killed. I had a lot of sympathy and kindness shown me as a war widow."

Her voice was bitter and I nodded comprehendingly.

"Lots of people wanted to marry me, but I always refused. I'd had too bad a shock. I didn't feel I could ever *trust* anyone again."

"Yes, I can imagine feeling like that."

"And then I became very fond of a certain young man. I wavered. An amazing thing happened! I got an anonymous letter—from Frederick—saying that if I ever married another man, he'd kill me!"

"From Frederick? From your dead husband?"

"Yes. Of course, I thought at first I was mad or dreaming. . . . At last I went to my father. He told me the truth. My husband hadn't been shot after all. He'd escaped—but his escape did him no good. He was involved in a train wreck a few weeks later and his dead body was found amongst others. My father had kept the fact of his escape from me, and since the man had died anyway he had seen no reason to tell me anything until now.

"But the letter I received opened up entirely new possibilities. Was it perhaps a fact that my husband was still alive?

"My father went into the matter as carefully as possible. And he declared that as far as one could humanly be sure the body that was buried as Frederick's *was* Frederick's. There had been a certain amount of disfiguration, so that he could not speak with absolute cast-iron certainty, but he reiterated his solemn belief that Frederick was dead and that this letter was a cruel and malicious hoax.

"The same thing happened more than once. If I seemed to be on intimate terms with any man, I would receive a threatening letter."

"In your husband's handwriting?"

She said slowly:

"That is difficult to say. I had no letters of his. I had only my memory to go by."

"There was no allusion or special form of words used that could make you sure?"

"No. There *were* certain terms—nicknames, for instance—private between us—if one of those had been used or quoted, then I should have been quite sure."

"Yes," I said thoughtfully. "That is odd. It looks as though it *wasn't* your husband. But is there anyone else it could be?"

"There is a possibility. Frederick had a younger brother—a boy of ten or twelve at the time of our marriage. He worshipped Frederick and Frederick was devoted to him. What happened to this boy, William his name was, I don't know. It seems to me possible that, adoring his brother as fanatically as he did, he may have grown up regarding me as directly responsible for his death. He had always been jealous of me and may have invented this scheme by way of punishment."

"It's possible," I said. "It's amazing the way children do remember if they've had a shock."

"I know. This boy may have dedicated his life to revenge."

"Please go on."

"There isn't very much more to tell. I met Eric three years ago. I meant never to marry. Eric made me change my mind. Right up to our wedding day I waited for another threatening letter. None came. I decided that whoever the writer might be, he was either dead, or tired of his cruel sport. *Two days after our marriage I got this.*"

Drawing a small attaché case which was on the table toward her, she unlocked it, took out a letter and handed it to me.

The ink was slightly faded. It was written in a rather womanish hand with a forward slant.

You have disobeyed. Now you cannot escape. You must be Frederick Bosner's wife only! You have got to die.

"I was frightened—but not so much as I might have been to begin with. Being with Eric made me feel safe. Then, a month later, I got a second letter."

I have not forgotten. I am making my plans. You have got to die. Why did you disobey?

"Does your husband know about this?"

Mrs. Leidner answered slowly.

"He knows that I am threatened. I showed him both letters when the second one came. He was inclined to think the whole thing a hoax. He thought also that it might be someone who wanted to blackmail me by pretending my first husband was alive."

She paused and then went on.

"A few days after I received the second letter we had a narrow escape from death by gas poisoning. Somebody entered our apartment after we were asleep and turned on the gas. Luckily I woke and smelled the gas in time. Then I lost my nerve. I told Eric how I had been persecuted for years, and I told him that I was sure this madman, whoever he might be, did really mean to kill me. I think that for the first time I really did think it *was* Frederick. There was always something a little ruthless behind his gentleness.

"Eric was still, I think, less alarmed than I was. He wanted to go to the police. Naturally I wouldn't hear of that. In the end we agreed that I should accompany him here, and that it might be wise if I didn't return to America in the summer but stayed in London and Paris.

"We carried out our plan and all went well. I felt sure that now everything would be all right. After all, we had put half the globe between ourselves and my enemy.

"And then—a little over three weeks ago—I received a letter—with an Iraq stamp on it."

She handed me a third letter.

You thought you could escape. You were wrong. You shall not be false to me and live. I have always told you so. Death is coming very soon.

"And a week ago—*this!* Just lying on the table here. It had not even gone through the post."

I took the sheet of paper from her. There was just one phrase scrawled across it.

I have arrived.

She stared at me.

"You see? You understand? He's going to kill me. It may be Frederick—it may be little William—*but he's going to kill me.*"

Her voice rose shudderingly. I caught her wrist.

"Now—now," I said warningly. "Don't give way. We'll look after you. Have you got any sal volatile?"

She nodded toward the washstand and I gave her a good dose.

"That's better," I said, as the color returned to her cheeks.

"Yes, I'm better now. But oh, nurse, do you see why I'm in this state? When I saw that man looking in through my window, I thought: *He's come.* . . . Even when *you* arrived I was suspicious. I thought you might be a man in disguise—"

"The idea!"

"Oh, I know it sounds absurd. But you might have been in league with him perhaps—not a hospital nurse at all."

"But that's nonsense!"

"Yes, perhaps. But I've got beyond sense."

Struck by a sudden idea, I said:

"You'd *recognize* your husband, I suppose?"

She answered slowly.

"I don't even know that. It's over fifteen years ago. I mightn't recognize his face."

Then she shivered.

"I saw it one night—but it was a *dead* face. There was a tap, tap, tap on the window. And then I saw a face, a dead face, ghastly and grinning against the pane. I screamed and screamed. . . . And they said there wasn't anything there!"

I remembered Mrs. Mercado's story.

"You don't think," I said hesitatingly, "that you *dreamt* that?"

"I'm sure I didn't!"

I wasn't so sure. It was the kind of nightmare that was quite likely under the circumstances and that easily might be taken for a waking occurrence. However, I never contradict a patient. I soothed Mrs. Leidner as best I could and pointed out that if any stranger arrived in the neighborhood it was pretty sure to be known.

I left her, I think, a little comforted, and I went in search of Dr. Leidner and told him of our conversation.

"I'm glad she's told you," he said simply. "It has worried me dreadfully. I feel sure that all those faces and tappings on the windowpane have been sheer imagination on her part. I haven't known what to do for the best. What do you think of the whole thing?"

I didn't quite understand the tone in his voice, but I answered promptly enough.

"It's possible," I said, "that these letters may be just a cruel and malicious hoax."

"Yes, that is quite likely. But what are we to *do?* They are driving her mad. I don't know what to think."

I didn't either. It had occurred to me that possibly a woman might be concerned. Those letters had a feminine note about them. Mrs. Mercado was at the back of my mind.

Supposing that by some chance she had learned the facts of Mrs. Leidner's first marriage. She might be indulging her spite by terrorizing the other woman.

I didn't quite like to suggest such a thing to Dr. Leidner. It's so difficult to know how people are going to take things.

"Oh, well," I said cheerfully, "we must hope for the best. I think Mrs. Leidner seems happier already from just talking about it. That's always a help, you know. It's bottling things up that makes them get on your nerves."

"I'm very glad she has told you," he repeated. "It's a good sign. It shows she likes and trusts you. I've been at my wit's end to know what to do for the best."

It was on the tip of my tongue to ask him whether he'd thought of giving a discreet hint to the local police, but afterward I was glad I hadn't done so.

What happened was this. On the following day Mr. Coleman was going in to Hassanieh to get the workmen's pay. He was also taking in all our letters to catch the air mail.

The letters, as written, were dropped into a wooden box on the dining room windowsill. Last thing that night Mr. Coleman took them out and was sorting them out into bundles and putting rubberbands around them.

Suddenly he gave a shout.

"What is it?" I asked.

He held out a letter with a grin.

"It's our Lovely Louise—she really *is* going balmy. She's addressed a letter to someone at 42nd Street, Paris, France. I don't think that can be right, do you? Do you mind taking it to her and asking what she *does* mean? She's just gone off to bed."

I took it from him and ran off to Mrs. Leidner with it and she amended the address.

It was the first time I had seen Mrs. Leidner's handwriting, and I wondered idly where I had seen it before, for it was certainly quite familiar to me.

It wasn't till the middle of the night that it suddenly came to me.

Except that it was bigger and rather more straggling, *it was extraordinarily like the writing on the anonymous letters.*

New ideas flashed through my head.

Had Mrs. Leidner conceivably written those letters *herself?*

And did Dr. Leidner half suspect the fact?

10

Saturday Afternoon

Mrs. Leidner told me her story on a Friday.

On Saturday morning there was a feeling of slight anticlimax in the air.

Mrs. Leidner, in particular, was inclined to be very off-hand with me and rather pointedly avoided any possibility of a *tête-à-tête*. Well, *that* didn't surprise me! I've had the same thing happen to me again and again. Ladies tell their nurses things in a sudden burst of confidence, and then, afterward, they feel uncomfortable about it and wish they hadn't! It's only human nature.

I was very careful not to hint or remind her in any way of what she had told me. I purposely kept my conversation as matter-of-fact as possible.

Mr. Coleman had started in to Hassanieh in the morning, driving himself in the lorry with the letters in a knapsack. He also had one or two commissions to do for the members of the expedition. It was pay-day for the men, and he would have to go to the bank and bring out the money in coins of small denominations. All this was a long business and he did not expect to be back until the afternoon. I rather suspected he might be lunching with Sheila Reilly.

Work on the dig was usually not very busy on the afternoon of pay-day as at three-thirty the paying-out began.

The little boy, Abdullah, whose business it was to wash pots, was established as usual in the center of the courtyard, and again as usual, kept up his queer nasal chant. Dr. Leidner and Mr. Emmott were going to put in some work on the pottery until Mr. Coleman returned, and Mr. Carey went up to the dig.

Mrs. Leidner went to her room to rest. I settled her as usual and then went to my own room, taking a book with me as I did not feel sleepy. It was then about a quarter to one, and a couple of hours passed quite pleasantly. I was reading *Death in a Nursing Home*—really a most exciting story—though I don't think the author knew much about the way nursing homes are run! At any rate I've never known a nursing home like that! I really felt inclined to write to the author and put him right about a few points.

When I put the book down at last (it was the red-haired parlormaid and I'd never suspected her once!) and looked at my watch I was quite surprised to find it was twenty minutes to three!

I got up, straightened my uniform, and came out into the courtyard.

Abdullah was still scrubbing and still singing his depressing chant, and David Emmott was standing by him sorting the scrubbed pots, and putting the ones that were broken into boxes to await mending. I strolled over toward them just as Dr. Leidner came down the staircase from the roof.

"Not a bad afternoon," he said cheerfully. "I've made a bit of a clearance up there. Louise will be pleased. She's complained lately that there's not room to walk about. I'll go and tell her the good news."

He went over to his wife's door, tapped on it and went in.

It must, I suppose, have been about a minute and a half later that he came out again. I happened to be looking at the door when he did so. It was like a nightmare. He had gone in a brisk, cheerful man. He came out like a drunken one—reeling a little on his feet, and with a queer dazed expression on his face.

"Nurse—" he called in a queer, hoarse voice. "Nurse—"

I saw at once something was wrong, and I ran across to him. He looked awful—his face was all gray and twitching, and I saw he might collapse any minute.

"My wife . . ." he said. "My wife . . . Oh, my God . . ."

I pushed past him into the room. Then I caught my breath.

Mrs. Leidner was lying in a dreadful huddled heap by the bed.

I bent over her. She was quite dead—must have been dead an hour at least. The cause of death was perfectly plain—a terrific blow on the front of the head just over the right temple. She must have got up from the bed and been struck down where she stood.

I didn't handle her more than I could help.

I glanced around the room to see if there was anything that might give a clue, but nothing seemed out of place or disturbed. The windows were closed and fastened, and there was no place where the murderer could have hidden. Obviously he had been and gone long ago.

I went out, closing the door behind me.

Dr. Leidner had collapsed completely now. David Emmott was with him and turned a white, inquiring face to me.

In a few low words I told him what had happened.

As I had always suspected, he was a first-class person to rely on in trouble. He was perfectly calm and self-possessed. Those blue eyes of his opened very wide, but otherwise he gave no sign at all.

He considered for a moment and then said:

"I suppose we must notify the police as soon as possible. Bill ought to be back any minute. What shall we do with Leidner?"

"Help me to get him into his room."

He nodded.

"Better lock this door first, I suppose," he said.

He turned the key in the lock of Mrs. Leidner's door, then drew it out and handed it to me.

"I guess you'd better keep this, nurse. Now then."

Together we lifted Dr. Leidner and carried him into his own room and laid him on his bed. Mr. Emmott went off in search of brandy. He returned, accompanied by Miss Johnson.

Her face was drawn and anxious, but she was calm and capable, and I felt satisfied to leave Dr. Leidner in her charge.

I hurried out into the courtyard. The station wagon was just coming in through the archway. I think it gave us all a shock to see Bill's pink, cheerful face as he jumped out with his familiar "Hallo, 'allo, 'allo! Here's the oof!" He went on gaily, "No highway robberies—"

He came to a halt suddenly. "I say, is anything up? What's the matter with you all? You look as though the cat had killed your canary."

Mr. Emmott said shortly:

"Mrs. Leidner's dead—killed."

"What?" Bill's jolly face changed ludicrously. He stared, his eyes goggling. "Mother Leidner dead! You're pulling my leg."

"Dead?" It was a sharp cry. I turned to see Mrs. Mercado behind me. "Did you say Mrs. Leidner had been *killed?"*

"Yes," I said. "Murdered."

"No!" she gasped. "Oh, no! I won't believe it. Perhaps she's committed suicide."

"Suicides don't hit themselves on the head," I said dryly. "It's murder all right, Mrs. Mercado."

She sat down suddenly on an upturned packing case.

She said, "Oh, but this is horrible—*horrible . . .*"

Naturally it was horrible. We didn't need *her* to tell us so! I wondered if perhaps she was feeling a bit remorseful for the harsh feelings she had harbored against the dead woman, and all the spiteful things she had said.

After a minute or two she asked rather breathlessly:

"What are you going to do?"

Mr. Emmott took charge in his quiet way.

"Bill, you'd better get in again to Hassanieh as quick as you can. I don't know much about the proper procedure. Better get hold of Captain Maitland, he's in charge of the police here, I think. Get Dr. Reilly first. He'll know what to do."

Mr. Coleman nodded. All the facetiousness was knocked out of him. He just looked young and frightened. Without a word he jumped into the station wagon and drove off.

Mr. Emmott said rather uncertainly, "I suppose we ought to have a hunt round." He raised his voice and called:

"Ibrahim!"

"Na'am."

The houseboy came running. Mr. Emmott spoke to him in Arabic. A vigorous colloquy passed between them. The boy seemed to be emphatically denying something.

At last Mr. Emmott said in a perplexed voice:

"He says there's not been a soul here this afternoon. No stranger of any kind. I suppose the fellow must have slipped in without their seeing him."

"Of course he did," said Mrs. Mercado. "He slunk in when the boys weren't looking."

"Yes," said Mr. Emmott.

The slight uncertainty in his voice made me look at him inquiringly.

He turned and spoke to the little potboy, Abdullah, asking him a question.

The boy replied vehemently at length.

The puzzled frown on Mr. Emmott's brow increased.

"I don't understand it," he murmured under his breath. "I don't understand it at all."

But he didn't tell me what he didn't understand.

11

An Odd Business

I'M ADHERING AS far as possible to telling only my personal part in the business. I pass over the events of the next two hours, the arrival of Captain Maitland and the police and Dr. Reilly. There was a good deal of general confusion, questioning, all the routine business, I suppose.

In my opinion we began to get down to brass tacks about five o'clock when Dr. Reilly asked me to come with him into the office.

He shut the door, sat down in Dr. Leidner's chair, motioned me to sit down opposite him, and said briskly:

"Now, then, nurse, let's get down to it. There's something damned odd here."

I settled my cuffs and looked at him inquiringly.

He drew out a notebook.

"This is for my own satisfaction. Now, what time was it exactly when Dr. Leidner found his wife's body?"

"I should say it was almost exactly a quarter to three," I said.

"And how do you know that?"

"Well, I looked at my watch when I got up. It was twenty to three then."

"Let's have a look at this watch of yours."

I slipped it off my wrist and held it out to him.

"Right to the minute. Excellent woman. Good, that's *that* fixed. Now did you form any opinion as to how long she'd been dead?"

"Oh, really, doctor," I said, "I shouldn't like to say."

"Don't be so professional. I want to see if your estimate agrees with mine."

"Well, I should say she'd been dead at least an hour."

"Quite so. I examined the body at half-past four and I'm inclined to put the time of death between 1:15 and 1:45. We'll say half-past one at a guess. That's near enough."

He stopped and drummed thoughtfully with his fingers on the table.

"Damned odd, this business," he said. "Can you tell me about it—you were resting, you say? Did you hear anything?"

"At half-past one? No, doctor. I didn't hear anything at half-past one or at any other time. I lay on my bed from a quarter to one until twenty to three and I didn't hear anything except that droning noise the Arab boy makes, and occasionally Mr. Emmott shouting up to Dr. Leidner on the roof."

"The Arab boy—yes."

He frowned.

At that moment the door opened and Dr. Leidner and Captain Maitland came in. Captain Maitland was a fussy little man with a pair of shrewd gray eyes.

Dr. Reilly rose and pushed Dr. Leidner into his chair.

"Sit down, man. I'm glad you've come. We shall want you. There's something very queer about this business."

Dr. Leidner bowed his head.

"I know." He looked at me. "My wife confided the truth to Nurse Leatheran. We mustn't keep anything back at this juncture, nurse, so please tell Captain Maitland and Dr. Reilly just what passed between you and my wife yesterday."

As nearly as possible I gave our conversation verbatim.

Captain Maitland uttered an occasional ejaculation. When I had finished he turned to Dr. Leidner.

"And this is all true, Leidner—eh?"

"Every word Nurse Leatheran has told you is correct."

"What an extraordinary story," said Dr. Reilly. "You can produce these letters?"

"I have no doubt they will be found amongst my wife's belongings."

"She took them out of the attaché case on her table," I said.

"Then they are probably still there."

He turned to Captain Maitland and his usually gentle face grew hard and stern.

"There must be no question of hushing this story up, Captain Maitland. The one thing necessary is for this man to be caught and punished."

"You believe it actually is Mrs. Leidner's former husband?" I asked.

"Don't you think so, nurse?" asked Captain Maitland.

"Well, I think it is open to doubt," I said hesitatingly.

"In any case," said Dr. Leidner, "the man is a murderer—and I should say a dangerous lunatic also. He *must* be found, Captain Maitland. He must. It should not be difficult."

Dr. Reilly said slowly:

"It may be more difficult than you think . . . eh, Maitland?"

Captain Maitland tugged at his moustache without replying.

Suddenly I gave a start.

"Excuse me," I said, "but there's something perhaps I ought to mention."

I told my story of the Iraqi we had seen trying to peer through the window, and of how I had seen him hanging about the place two days ago trying to pump Father Lavigny.

"Good," said Captain Maitland, "we'll make a note of that. It will be something for the police to go on. The man may have some connection with the case."

"Probably paid to act as a spy," I suggested. "To find out when the coast was clear."

Dr. Reilly rubbed his nose with a harassed gesture.

"That's the devil of it," he said. "Supposing the coast wasn't clear—eh?"

I stared at him in a puzzled fashion.

Captain Maitland turned to Dr. Leidner.

"I want you to listen to me very carefully, Leidner. This is a review of the evidence we've got up to date. After lunch, which was served at twelve o'clock and was over by five and twenty to one, your wife went to her room accompanied by Nurse Leatheran, who settled her comfortably. You yourself went up to the roof, where you spent the next two hours, is that right?"

"Yes."

"Did you come down from the roof at all during that time?"

"No."

"Did anyone come up to you?"

"Yes, Emmott did pretty frequently. He went to and fro between me and the boy, who was washing pottery down below."

"Did you yourself look over into the courtyard at all?"

"Once or twice—usually to call to Emmott about something."

"On each occasion the boy was sitting in the middle of the courtyard washing pots?"

"Yes."

"What was the longest period of time when Emmott was with you and absent from the courtyard?"

Dr. Leidner considered.

"It's difficult to say—perhaps ten minutes. Personally I should say two or three minutes, but I know by experience that my sense of time is not very good when I am absorbed and interested in what I am doing."

Captain Maitland looked at Dr. Reilly. The latter nodded. "We'd better get down to it," he said.

Captain Maitland took out a small notebook and opened it.

"Look here, Leidner, I'm going to read to you exactly what every member of your expedition was doing between one and two this afternoon."

"But surely—"

"Wait. You'll see what I'm driving at in a minute. First Mr. and Mrs. Mercado. Mr. Mercado says he was working in his laboratory. Mrs. Mercado says she was in her bedroom shampooing her hair. Miss Johnson says she was in the living room taking impressions of cylinder seals. Mr. Reiter says he was in the darkroom developing plates. Father Lavigny says he was working in his bedroom. As to the two remaining members of the expedition, Carey and Coleman, the former was up on the dig and Coleman was in Hassanieh. So much for the members of the expedition. Now for the servants. The cook— your Indian chap—was sitting immediately outside the archway chatting to the guard and plucking a couple of fowls. Ibrahim and Mansur, the house-boys, joined him there at about 1:15. They both remained there laughing and talking until 2:30—*by which time your wife was already dead.*"

Dr. Leidner leaned forward.

"I don't understand—you puzzle me. What are you hinting at?"

"Is there any means of access to your wife's room except by the door into the courtyard?"

"No. There are two windows, but they are heavily barred—and besides, I think they were shut."

He looked at me questioningly.

"They were closed and latched on the inside," I said promptly.

"In any case," said Captain Maitland, "even if they had been open, no one could have entered or left the room that way. My fellows and I have assured ourselves of that. It is the same with all the other windows giving on the open country. They all have iron bars and all the bars are in good condition. To have got into your wife's room, a stranger *must* have come through the arched doorway into the courtyard. But we have the united assurances of the guard, the cook and the house-boy that *nobody did so.*"

Dr. Leidner sprang up.

"What do you mean? What do you mean?"

"Pull yourself together, man," said Dr. Reilly quietly. "I know it's a shock, but it's got to be faced. *The murderer didn't come from outside*—so he must have come from *inside.* It looks as though Mrs. Leidner must have been murdered *by a member of your own expedition.*"

12

"I Didn't Believe . . ."

"No. No!"

Dr. Leidner sprang up and walked up and down in an agitated manner.

"It's impossible what you say, Reilly. Absolutely impossible. One of *us?* Why, every single member of the expedition was devoted to Louise!"

A queer little expression pulled down the corners of Dr. Reilly's mouth. Under the circumstances it was difficult for him to say anything, but if ever a man's silence was eloquent his was at that minute.

"Quite impossible," reiterated Dr. Leidner. "They were all devoted to her. Louise had such wonderful charm. Everyone felt it."

Dr. Reilly coughed.

"Excuse me, Leidner, but after all that's only your opinion. If any member of the expedition had disliked your wife they would naturally not advertise the fact to you."

Dr. Leidner looked distressed.

"True—quite true. But all the same, Reilly, I think you are wrong. I'm sure everyone was fond of Louise."

He was silent for a moment or two and then burst out:

"This idea of yours is infamous. "It's—it's frankly incredible."

"You can't get away from—er—the facts," said Captain Maitland.

"Facts? Facts? Lies told by an Indian cook and a couple of Arab houseboys. You know these fellows as well as I do, Reilly; so do you, Maitland. Truth as truth means nothing to them. They say what you want them to say as a mere matter of politeness."

"In this case," said Dr. Reilly dryly, "they are saying what we *don't* want them to say. Besides, I know the habits of your household fairly well. Just outside the gate is a kind of social club. Whenever I've been over here in the afternoon I've always found most of your staff there. It's the natural place for them to be."

"All the same I think you are assuming too much. Why shouldn't this man —this devil—have got in earlier and concealed himself somewhere?"

"I agree that that is not actually impossible," said Dr. Reilly coolly. "Let us assume that a stranger *did* somehow gain admission unseen. He would have to remain concealed until the right moment (and he certainly couldn't have done so in Mrs. Leidner's room, there is no cover there) and take the risk of being seen entering the room and leaving it—with Emmott and the boy in the courtyard most of the time."

"The boy. I'd forgotten the boy," said Dr. Leidner. "A sharp little chap.

But surely, Maitland, the boy *must* have seen the murderer go into my wife's room?"

"We've elucidated that. The boy was washing pots the whole afternoon with one exception. Somewhere around half-past one—Emmott can't put it closer than that—he went up to the roof and was with you for ten minutes—that's right, isn't it?"

"Yes. I couldn't have told you the exact time but it must have been about that."

"Very good. Well, during that ten minutes, the boy, seizing his chance to be idle, strolled out and joined the others outside the gate for a chat. When Emmott came down he found the boy absent and called him angrily, asking him what he meant by leaving his work. As far as I can see, *your wife must have been murdered during that ten minutes.*"

With a groan, Dr. Leidner sat down and hid his face in his hands.

Dr. Reilly took up the tale, his voice quiet and matter-of-fact.

"The time fits in with my evidence," he said. "She'd been dead about three hours when I examined her. The only question is—who did it?"

There was a silence. Dr. Leidner sat up in his chair and passed a hand over his forehead.

"I admit the force of your reasoning, Reilly," he said quietly. "It certainly *seems* as though it were what people call 'an inside job.' But I feel convinced that somewhere or other there is a mistake. It's plausible but there must be a flaw in it. To begin with, you are assuming that an amazing coincidence has occurred."

"Odd that you should use that word," said Dr. Reilly.

Without paying any attention Dr. Leidner went on:

"My wife receives threatening letters. She has reason to fear a certain person. Then she is—killed. And you ask me to believe that she is killed—not by that person—but by someone entirely different! I say that that is ridiculous."

"It seems so—yes," said Dr. Reilly meditatively.

He looked at Captain Maitland. "Coincidence—eh? What do you say, Maitland? Are you in favor of the idea? Shall we put it up to Leidner?"

Captain Maitland gave a nod.

"Go ahead," he said shortly.

"Have you ever heard of a man called Hercule Poirot, Leidner?"

Dr. Leidner stared at him, puzzled.

"I think I have heard the name, yes," he said vaguely. "I once heard a Mr. Van Aldin speak of him in very high terms. He is a private detective, is he not?"

"That's the man."

"But surely he lives in London, so how will that help us?"

"He lives in London, true," said Dr. Reilly, "but this is where the coincidence comes in. He is now, not in London, but in Syria, and *he will actually pass through Hassanieh on his way to Baghdad tomorrow!*"

"Who told you this?"

"Jean Berat, the French consul. He dined with us last night and was talking about him. It seems he has been disentangling some military scandal in Syria. He's coming through here to visit Baghdad, and afterwards returning through Syria to London. How's that for a coincidence?"

Dr. Leidner hesitated a moment and looked apologetically at Captain Maitland.

"What do you think, Captain Maitland?"

"Should welcome cooperation," said Captain Maitland promptly. "My fellows are good scouts at scouring the countryside and investigating Arab blood feuds, but frankly, Leidner, this business of your wife's seems to me rather out of my class. The whole thing looks confoundedly fishy. I'm more than willing to have the fellow take a look at the case."

"You suggest that I should appeal to this man Poirot to help us?" said Dr. Leidner. "And suppose he refuses?"

"He won't refuse," said Dr. Reilly.

"How do you know?"

"Because I'm a professional man myself. If a really intricate case of say—cerebrospinal meningitis comes my way and I'm invited to take a hand, I shouldn't be able to refuse. This isn't an ordinary crime, Leidner."

"No," said Dr. Leidner. His lips twitched with sudden pain.

"Will you then, Reilly, approach this Hercule Poirot on my behalf?"

"I will."

Dr. Leidner made a gesture of thanks.

"Even now," he said slowly, "I can't realize it—that Louise is really dead."

I could bear it no longer.

"Oh! Dr. Leidner," I burst out. "I—I can't tell you how badly I feel about this. I've failed so badly in my duty. It was my job to watch over Mrs. Leidner—to keep her from harm."

Dr. Leidner shook his head gravely.

"No, no, nurse, you've nothing to reproach yourself with," he said slowly. "It's *I*, God forgive me, who am to blame. . . . *I didn't believe*—all along I didn't believe . . . I didn't dream for one moment that there was any *real* danger. . . ."

He got up. His face twitched.

"*I let her go to her death*. . . . Yes, I let her go to her death—*not believing*—"

He staggered out of the room.

Dr. Reilly looked at me.

"I feel pretty culpable too," he said. "I thought the good lady was playing on his nerves."

"I didn't take it really seriously either," I confessed.

"We were all three wrong," said Dr. Reilly gravely.

"So it seems," said Captain Maitland.

13

Hercule Poirot Arrives

I DON'T THINK I shall ever forget my first sight of Hercule Poirot. Of course, I got used to him later on, but to begin with it was a shock, and I think everyone else must have felt the same!

I don't know what I'd imagined—something rather like Sherlock Holmes —long and lean with a keen, clever face. Of course, I knew he was a foreigner, but I hadn't expected him to be *quite* as foreign as he was, if you know what I mean.

When you saw him you just wanted to laugh! He was like something on the stage or at the pictures. To begin with, he wasn't above five foot five, I should think—an odd plump little man, quite old, with an enormous moustache, and a head like an egg. He looked like a hairdresser in a comic play!

And this was the man who was going to find out who killed Mrs. Leidner!

I suppose something of my disgust must have shown in my face, for almost straightaway he said to me with a queer kind of twinkle:

"You disapprove of me, *ma soeur?* Remember, the pudding proves itself only when you eat it."

The proof of the pudding's in the eating, I *suppose* he meant.

Well, that's a true enough saying, but I couldn't say I felt much confidence myself!

Dr. Reilly brought him out in his car soon after lunch on Sunday, and his first procedure was to ask us all to assemble together.

We did so in the dining room, all sitting around the table. Mr. Poirot sat at the head of it with Dr. Leidner one side and Dr. Reilly the other.

When we were all assembled, Dr. Leidner cleared his throat and spoke in his gentle, hesitating voice.

"I dare say you have all heard of M. Hercule Poirot. He was passing through Hassanieh today, and has very kindly agreed to break his journey to help us. The Iraq police and Captain Maitland are, I am sure, doing their very best, but—but there are circumstances in the case"—he floundered and shot an appealing glance at Dr. Reilly—"there may, it seems, be difficulties. . . ."

"It is not all the square and overboard—no?" said the little man at the top of the table. Why, he couldn't even speak English properly!

"Oh, he *must* be caught!" cried Mrs. Mercado. "It would be unbearable if he got away!"

I noticed the little foreigner's eyes rest on her appraisingly.

"He? Who is *he,* madame?" he asked.

"Why, the murderer, of course."

"Ah! the murderer," said Hercule Poirot.

He spoke as though the murderer was of no consequence at all!

We all stared at him. He looked from one face to another.

"It is likely, I think," he said, "that you have none of you been brought in contact with a case of murder before?"

There was a general murmur of assent.

Hercule Poirot smiled.

"It is clear, therefore, that you do not understand the A.B.C. of the position. There are unpleasantnesses! Yes, there are a lot of unpleasantnesses. To begin with, there is *suspicion.*"

"Suspicion?"

It was Miss Johnson who spoke. Mr. Poirot looked at her thoughtfully. I had an idea that he regarded her with approval. He looked as though he were thinking, "Here is a sensible, intelligent person!"

"Yes, mademoiselle," he said. "Suspicion! Let us not make the bones about it. *You are all under suspicion here in this house.* The cook, the houseboy, the scullion, the potboy—yes, and all the members of the expedition too."

Mrs. Mercado started up, her face working.

"How *dare* you? How dare you say such a thing! This is odious—unbearable! Dr. Leidner—you can't sit here and let this man—and let this man—"

Dr. Leidner said wearily:

"Please try and be calm, Marie."

Mr. Mercado stood up too. His hands were shaking and his eyes were bloodshot.

"I agree. It is an outrage—an insult—"

"No, no," said Mr. Poirot. "I do not insult you. I merely ask you all to face facts. *In a house where murder has been committed, every inmate comes in for a certain share of suspicion.* I ask you what evidence is there that the murderer came from outside at all?"

Mrs. Mercado cried:

"But of course he did! It stands to reason! Why—" She stopped and said more slowly, "Anything else would be incredible!"

"You are doubtless correct, madame," said Poirot with a bow. "I explain to you only how the matter must be approached. First I assure myself of the fact that everyone in this room is innocent. After that I seek the murderer elsewhere."

"Is it not possible that that may be a little late in the day?" asked Father Lavigny suavely.

"The tortoise, *mon père,* overtook the hare."

Father Lavigny shrugged his shoulders.

"We are in your hands," he said resignedly. "Convince yourself as soon as may be of our innocence in this terrible business."

"As rapidly as possible. It was my duty to make the position clear to you, so that you may not resent the impertinence of any questions I may have to ask. Perhaps, *mon père,* the Church will set an example?"

"Ask any questions you please of me," said Father Lavigny gravely.

"This is your first season out here?"

"Yes."

"And you arrived—when?"

"Three weeks ago almost to a day. That is, on the 27th of February."

"Coming from?"

"The Order of the *Pères Blancs* at Carthage."

"Thank you, *mon père.* Were you at any time acquainted with Mrs. Leidner before coming here?"

"No, I had never seen the lady until I met her here."

"Will you tell me what you were doing at the time of the tragedy?"

"I was working on some cuneiform tablets in my own room."

I noticed that Poirot had at his elbow a rough plan of the building.

"That is the room at the southwest corner corresponding to that of Mrs. Leidner on the opposite side?"

"Yes."

"At what time did you go to your room?"

"Immediately after lunch. I should say at about twenty minutes to one."

"And you remained there until—when?"

"Just before three o'clock. I had heard the station wagon come back—and then I heard it drive off again. I wondered why, and came out to see."

"During the time that you were there did you leave the room at all?"

"No, not once."

"And you heard or saw nothing that might have any bearing on the tragedy?"

"No."

"You have no window giving on the courtyard in your room?"

"No, both the windows give on the countryside."

"Could you hear at all what was happening in the courtyard?"

"Not very much. I heard Mr. Emmott passing my room and going up to the roof. He did so once or twice."

"Can you remember at what time?"

"No, I'm afraid I can't. I was engrossed in my work, you see."

There was a pause and then Poirot said:

"Can you say or suggest anything at all that might throw light on this business? Did you, for instance, notice anything in the days preceding the murder?"

Father Lavigny looked slightly uncomfortable.

He shot a half-questioning look at Dr. Leidner.

"That is rather a difficult question, monsieur," he said gravely. "If you ask me, I must reply frankly that in my opinion Mrs. Leidner was clearly in dread of someone or something. She was definitely nervous about strangers. I imagine she had a reason for this nervousness of hers—but I *know* nothing. She did not confide in me."

Poirot cleared his throat and consulted some notes that he held in his hand.

"Two nights ago I understand there was a scare of burglary."

Father Lavigny replied in the affirmative and retailed his story of the light seen in the antika room and the subsequent futile search.

"You believe, do you not, that some unauthorized person was on the premises at that time?"

"I don't know what to think," said Father Lavigny frankly. "Nothing was taken or disturbed in any way. It might have been one of the houseboys—"

"Or a member of the expedition?"

"Or a member of the expedition. But in that case there would be no reason for the person not admitting the fact."

"But it *might* equally have been a stranger from outside?"

"I suppose so."

"Supposing a stranger *had* been on the premises, could he have concealed himself successfully during the following day and until the afternoon of the day following that?"

He asked the question half of Father Lavigny and half of Dr. Leidner. Both men considered the question carefully.

"I hardly think it would be possible," said Dr. Leidner at last with some reluctance. "I don't see where he could possibly conceal himself, do you, Father Lavigny?"

"No—no—I don't."

Both men seemed reluctant to put the suggestion aside.

Poirot turned to Miss Johnson.

"And you, mademoiselle? Do you consider such a hypothesis feasible?"

After a moment's thought Miss Johnson shook her head.

"No," she said. "I don't. Where could anyone hide? The bedrooms are all in use and, in any case, are sparsely furnished. The darkroom, the drawing-office and the laboratory were all in use the next day—so were all these rooms. There are no cupboards or corners. Perhaps, if the servants were in collusion—"

"That is possible, but unlikely," said Poirot.

He turned once more to Father Lavigny.

"There is another point. The other day Nurse Leatheran here noticed you talking to a man outside. She had previously noticed that same man trying to peer in at one of the windows on the outside. It rather looks as though the man were hanging round the place deliberately."

"That is possible, of course," said Father Lavigny thoughtfully.

"Did you speak to this man first, or did he speak to you?"

Father Lavigny considered for a moment or two.

"I believe—yes, I am sure, that he spoke to me."

"What did he say?"

Father Lavigny made an effort of memory.

"He said, I think, something to the effect was this the American expedition house? And then something else about the Americans employing a lot of men on the work. I did not really understand him very well, but I endeavored to keep up a conversation so as to improve my Arabic. I thought, perhaps, that being a townie he would understand me better than the men on the dig do."

"Did you converse about anything else?"

"As far as I remember, I said Hassanieh was a big town—and we then agreed that Baghdad was bigger—and I think he asked whether I was an Armenian or a Syrian Catholic—something of that kind."

Poirot nodded.

"Can you describe him?"

Again Father Lavigny frowned in thought.

"He was rather a short man," he said at last, "and squarely built. He had a very noticeable squint and was of fair complexion."

Mr. Poirot turned to me.

"Does that agree with the way you would describe him?" he asked.

"Not exactly," I said hesitatingly. "I should have said he was tall rather than short, and very dark complexioned. He seemed to me of a rather slender build. I didn't notice any squint."

Mr. Poirot gave a despairing shrug of the shoulders.

"It is always so! If you were of the police how well you would know it! The description of the same man by two different people—never does it agree. Every detail is contradicted."

"I'm fairly sure about the squint," said Father Lavigny. "Nurse Leatheran may be right about the other points. By the way, when I said *fair,* I only meant fair for an *Iraqi.* I expect nurse would call that dark."

"Very dark," I said obstinately. "A dirty dark-yellow color."

I saw Dr. Reilly bite his lip and smile.

Poirot threw up his hands.

"Passons!" he said. "This stranger hanging about, he may be important— he may not. At any rate he must be found. Let us continue our inquiry."

He hesitated for a minute, studying the faces turned toward him around the table, then, with a quick nod, he singled out Mr. Reiter.

"Come, my friend," he said. "Let us have your account of yesterday afternoon."

Mr. Reiter's pink, plump face flushed scarlet.

"Me?" he said.

"Yes, you. To begin with, your name and your age?"

"Carl Reiter, twenty-eight."

"American—yes?"

"Yes, I come from Chicago."

"This is your first season?"

"Yes. I'm in charge of the photography."

"Ah, yes. And yesterday afternoon, how did you employ yourself?"

"Well—I was in the darkroom most of the time."

"Most of the time—eh?"

"Yes. I developed some plates first. Afterward I was fixing up some objects to photograph."

"Outside?"

"Oh, no, in the photographic room."

"The darkroom opens out of the photographic room?"

"Yes."

"And so you never came outside the photographic room?"

"No."

"Did you notice anything that went on in the courtyard?"

The young man shook his head.

"I wasn't noticing anything," he explained. "I was busy. I heard the car come back, and as soon as I could leave what I was doing I came out to see if there was any mail. It was then that I—heard."

"And you began your work in the photographic room—when?"

"At ten minutes to one."

"Were you acquainted with Mrs. Leidner before you joined this expedition?"

The young man shook his head.

"No, sir. I never saw her till I actually got here."

"Can you think of *anything*—any incident—however small—that might help us?"

Carl Reiter shook his head.

He said helplessly:

"I guess I don't know anything at all, sir."

"Mr. Emmott?"

David Emmott spoke clearly and concisely in his pleasant soft American voice.

"I was working with the pottery from a quarter to one till a quarter to three—overseeing the boy Abdullah, sorting it, and occasionally going up to the roof to help Dr. Leidner."

"How often did you go up to the roof?"

"Four times, I think."

"For how long?"

"Usually a couple of minutes—not more. But on one occasion after I'd been working a little over half an hour I stayed as long as ten minutes— discussing what to keep and what to fling away."

"And I understand that when you came down you found the boy had left his place?"

"Yes. I called him angrily and he reappeared from outside the archway. He had gone out to gossip with the others."

"That was the only time he left his work?"

"Well, I sent him up once or twice to the roof with pottery."

Poirot said gravely:

"It is hardly necessary to ask you, Mr. Emmott, whether you saw anyone enter or leave Mrs. Leidner's room during that time?"

Mr. Emmott replied promptly.

"I saw no one at all. Nobody even came out into the courtyard during the two hours I was working."

"And to the best of your belief it was half-past one when both you and the boy were absent and the courtyard was empty?"

"It couldn't have been far off that time. Of course, I can't say *exactly.*"

Poirot turned to Dr. Reilly.

"That agrees with your estimate of the time of death, doctor?"

"It does," said Dr. Reilly.

Mr. Poirot stroked his great curled moustaches.

"I think we can take it," he said gravely, "that Mrs. Leidner met her death during that ten minutes."

14

One of Us?

THERE WAS A little pause—and in it a wave of horror seemed to float around the room.

I think it was at that moment that I first believed Dr. Reilly's theory to be right.

I *felt* that the murderer was in the room. Sitting with us—listening. *One of us* . . .

Perhaps Mrs. Mercado felt it too. For she suddenly gave a short sharp cry.

"I can't help it," she sobbed. "I—it's so *terrible!*"

"Courage, Marie," said her husband.

He looked at us apologetically.

"She is so sensitive. She feels things so much."

"I—I was so fond of Louise," sobbed Mrs. Mercado.

I don't know whether something of what I felt showed in my face, but I suddenly found that Mr. Poirot was looking at me, and that a slight smile hovered on his lips.

I gave him a cold glance, and at once he resumed his inquiry.

"Tell me, madame," he said, "of the way you spent yesterday afternoon?"

"I was washing my hair," sobbed Mrs. Mercado. "It seems awful not to have known anything about it. I was quite happy and busy."

"You were in your room?"

"Yes."

"And you did not leave it?"

"No. Not till I heard the car. Then I came out and I heard what had happened. Oh, it was *awful!*"

"Did it surprise you?"

Mrs. Mercado stopped crying. Her eyes opened resentfully.

"What do you mean, M. Poirot? Are you suggesting—"

"What should I mean, madame? You have just told us how fond you were of Mrs. Leidner. She might, perhaps, have confided in you."

"Oh, I see. . . . No—no, dear Louise never told me anything—anything *definite*, that is. Of course, I could see she was terribly worried and nervous. And there were those strange occurrences—hands tapping on the window and all that."

"Fancies, I remember you said," I put in, unable to keep silent.

I was glad to see that she looked momentarily disconcerted.

Once again I was conscious of Mr. Poirot's amused eye glancing in my direction.

He summed up in a businesslike way.

"It comes to this, madame, you were washing your hair—you heard nothing and you saw nothing. Is there anything at all you can think of that would be a help to us in any way?"

Mrs. Mercado took no time to think.

"No, indeed there isn't. It's the deepest mystery! But I should say there is no doubt—no doubt *at all* that the murderer came from outside. Why, it stands to reason."

Poirot turned to her husband.

"And you, monsieur, what have you to say?"

Mr. Mercado started nervously. He pulled at his beard in an aimless fashion.

"Must have been. Must have been," he said. "Yet how could anyone wish to harm her? She was so gentle—so kind—" He shook his head. "Whoever killed her must have been a fiend—yes, a fiend!"

"And you yourself, monsieur, how did you pass yesterday afternoon?"

"I?" he stared vaguely.

"You were in the laboratory, Joseph," his wife prompted him.

"Ah, yes, so I was—so I was. My usual tasks."

"At what time did you go there?"

Again he looked helplessly and inquiringly at Mrs. Mercado.

"At ten minutes to one, Joseph."

"Ah, yes, at ten minutes to one."

"Did you come out in the courtyard at all?"

"No—I don't think so." He considered. "No, I am sure I didn't."

"When did you hear of the tragedy?"

"My wife came and told me. It was terrible—shocking. I could hardly believe it. Even now, I can hardly believe it is true."

Suddenly he began to tremble.

"It is horrible—horrible . . ."

Mrs. Mercado came quickly to his side.

"Yes, yes, Joseph, we all feel that. But we mustn't give way. It makes it so much more difficult for poor Dr. Leidner."

I saw a spasm of pain pass across Dr. Leidner's face, and I guessed that this emotional atmosphere was not easy for him. He gave a half glance at Poirot as though in appeal. Poirot responded quickly.

"Miss Johnson?" he said.

"I'm afraid I can tell you very little," said Miss Johnson. Her cultured well-bred voice was soothing after Mrs. Mercado's shrill treble. She went on:

"I was working in the living room—taking impressions of some cylinder seals on plasticine."

"And you saw or noticed nothing?"

"No."

Poirot gave her a quick glance. His ear had caught what mine had—a faint note of indecision.

"Are you quite sure, mademoiselle? Is there something that comes back to you vaguely?"

"No—not really—"

"Something you saw, shall we say, out of the corner of your eye hardly knowing you saw it."

"No, certainly not," she replied positively.

"Something you *heard* then. Ah, yes, something you are not quite sure whether you heard or not?"

Miss Johnson gave a short vexed laugh.

"You press me very closely, M. Poirot. I'm afraid you are encouraging me to tell you what I am, perhaps, only imagining."

"Then there *was* something you—shall we say—imagined?"

Miss Johnson said slowly, weighing her words in a detached way:

"I have imagined—since—that at some time during the afternoon I heard a very faint cry. . . . What I mean is that I dare say I *did* hear a cry. All the windows in the living room were open and one hears all sorts of sounds from people working in the barley fields. But you see—since—I've got the idea into my head that it was—that it was Mrs. Leidner I heard. And that's made me rather unhappy. Because if I'd jumped up and run along to her room—well, who knows? I might have been in time . . ."

Dr. Reilly interposed authoritatively.

"Now, don't start getting that into your head," he said. "I've no doubt but that Mrs. Leidner (forgive me, Leidner) was struck down almost as soon as the man entered the room, and it was that blow that killed her. No second blow was struck. Otherwise she would have had time to call for help and make a real outcry."

"Still, I might have caught the murderer," said Miss Johnson.

"What time was this, mademoiselle?" asked Poirot. "In the neighborhood of half-past one?"

"It must have been about that time—yes." She reflected a minute.

"That would fit in," said Poirot thoughtfully. "You heard nothing else— the opening or shutting of a door, for instance?"

Miss Johnson shook her head.

"No, I do not remember anything of that kind."

"You were sitting at a table, I presume. Which way were you facing? The courtyard? The antika room? The verandah? Or the open countryside?"

"I was facing the courtyard."

"Could you see the boy Abdullah washing pots from whcrc you were?"

"Oh, yes, if I looked up, but of course, I was very intent on what I was doing. All my attention was on that."

"If anyone had passed the courtyard window, though, you would have noticed it?"

"Oh, yes, I am almost sure of that."

"And nobody did so?"

"No."

"But if anyone had walked, say, across the middle of the courtyard, would you have noticed that?"

"I think—probably not—unless, as I said before, I had happened to look up and out of the window."

"You did not notice the boy Abdullah leave his work and go out to join the other servants?"

"No."

"Ten minutes," mused Poirot. "That fatal ten minutes."

There was a momentary silence.

Miss Johnson lifted her head suddenly and said:

"You know, M. Poirot, I think I have unintentionally misled you. On thinking it over, I do not believe that I could possibly have heard any cry uttered in Mrs. Leidner's room from where I was. The antika room lay between me and her—and I understand her windows were found closed."

"In any case, do not distress yourself, mademoiselle," said Poirot kindly. "It is not really of much importance."

"No, of course not. I understand that. But you see, it *is* of importance to me, because I feel I might have done something."

"Don't distress yourself, dear Anne," said Dr. Leidner with affection. "You must be sensible. What you heard was probably one Arab bawling to another some distance away in the fields."

Miss Johnson flushed a little at the kindliness of his tone. I even saw tears spring to her eyes. She turned her head away and spoke even more gruffly than usual.

"Probably was. Usual thing after a tragedy—start imagining things that aren't so at all."

Poirot was once more consulting his notebook.

"I do not suppose there is much more to be said. Mr. Carey?"

Richard Carey spoke slowly—in a wooden, mechanical manner.

"I'm afraid I can add nothing helpful. I was on duty at the dig. The news was brought to me there."

"And you know or can think of nothing helpful that occurred in the days immediately preceding the murder?"

"Nothing at all."

"Mr. Coleman?"

"I was right out of the whole thing," said Mr. Coleman with—was it just a shade of regret—in his tone. "I went into Hassanieh yesterday morning to get the money for the men's wages. When I came back Emmott told me what had happened and I went back in the bus to get the police and Dr. Reilly."

"And beforehand?"

"Well, sir, things were a bit jumpy—but you know that already. There was the antika room scare and one or two before that—hands and faces at the window—you remember, sir," he appealed to Dr. Leidner, who bent his head in assent. "I think, you know, that you'll find some Johnny *did* get in from outside. Must have been an artful sort of beggar."

Poirot considered him for a minute or two in silence.

"You are an Englishman, Mr. Coleman?" he asked at last.

"That's right, sir. All British. See the trademark. Guaranteed genuine."

"This is your first season?"

"Quite right."

"And you are passionately keen on archaeology?"

This description of himself seemed to cause Mr. Coleman some embarrassment. He got rather pink and shot the side look of a guilty schoolboy at Dr. Leidner.

"Of course—it's all very interesting," he stammered. "I mean—I'm not exactly a brainy chap . . ."

He broke off rather lamely. Poirot did not insist.

He tapped thoughtfully on the table with the end of his pencil and carefully straightened an inkpot that stood in front of him.

"It seems then," he said, "that that is as near as we can get for the moment. If anyone of you thinks of something that has for the time being slipped his or her memory do not hesitate to come to me with it. It will be well now, I think, for me to have a few words alone with Dr. Leidner and Dr. Reilly."

It was the signal for a breaking up of the party. We all rose and filed out of the door. When I was halfway out, however, a voice recalled me.

"Perhaps," said Mr. Poirot, "Nurse Leatheran will be so kind as to remain. I think her assistance will be valuable to us."

I came back and resumed my seat at the table.

15

Poirot Makes a Suggestion

DR. REILLY HAD risen from his seat. When everyone had gone out he carefully closed the door. Then, with an inquiring glance at Poirot, he proceeded to shut the window giving on the courtyard. The others were already shut. Then he, too, resumed his seat at the table.

"*Bien!*" said Poirot. "We are now private and undisturbed. We can speak freely. We have heard what the members of the expedition have to tell us and —But yes, *ma soeur,* what is it that you think?"

I got rather red. There was no denying that the queer little man had sharp eyes. He'd seen the thought passing through my mind—I suppose my face *had* shown a bit too clearly what I was thinking!

"Oh, it's nothing—" I said, hesitating.

"Come on, nurse," said Dr. Reilly. "Don't keep the specialist waiting."

"It's nothing really," I said hurriedly. "It only just passed through my mind, so to speak, that perhaps even if anyone did know or suspect something it wouldn't be easy to bring it out in front of everybody else—or even, perhaps, in front of Dr. Leidner."

Rather to my astonishment, M. Poirot nodded his head in vigorous agreement.

"Precisely. Precisely. It is very just what you say there. But I will explain. That little reunion we have just had—it served a purpose. In England before the races you have a parade of the horses, do you not? They go in front of the grandstand so that everyone may have an opportunity of seeing and judging them. That is the purpose of my little assembly. In the sporting phrase, I run my eye over thc possible starters."

Dr. Leidner cried out violently, "I do not believe for one minute that *any* member of my expedition is implicated in this crime!"

Then, turning to me, he said authoritatively:

"Nurse, I should be much obliged if you would tell M. Poirot here and now exactly what passed between my wife and you two days ago."

Thus urged, I plunged straightaway into my story, trying as far as possible to recall the exact words and phrases Mrs. Leidner had used.

When I had finished, M. Poirot said:

"Very good. Very good. You have the mind neat and orderly. You will be of great service to me here."

He turned to Dr. Leidner.

"You have these letters?"

"I have them here. I thought that you would want to see them first thing."

Poirot took them from him, read them, and scrutinized them carefully as he did so. I was rather disappointed that he didn't dust powder over them or examine them with a microscope or anything like that—but I realized that he wasn't a very young man and that his methods were probably not very up to date. He just read them in the way that anyone might read a letter.

Having read them he put them down and cleared his throat.

"Now," he said, "let us proceed to get our facts clear and in order. The first of these letters was received by your wife shortly after her marriage to you in America. There had been others but these she destroyed. The first letter was followed by a second. A very short time after the second arrived you both had a near escape from coal gas poisoning. You then came abroad and for nearly two years no further letters were received. They started again at the beginning of your season this year—that is to say, within the last three weeks. That is correct?"

"Absolutely."

"Your wife displayed every sign of panic and, after consulting Dr. Reilly, you engaged Nurse Leatheran here to keep your wife company and allay her fears?"

"Yes."

"Certain incidents occurred—hands tapping at the window—a spectral face—noises in the antika room. You did not witness any of these phenomena yourself?"

"No."

"In fact nobody did except Mrs. Leidner?"

"Father Lavigny saw a light in the antika room."

"Yes, I have not forgotten that."

He was silent for a minute or two, then he said:

"Had your wife made a will?"

"I do not think so."

"Why was that?"

"It did not seem worth it from her point of view."

"Is she not a wealthy woman?"

"Yes, during her lifetime. Her father left her a considerable sum of money in trust. She could not touch the principal. At her death it was to pass to any children she might have—and failing children to the Pittstown Museum."

Poirot drummed thoughtfully on the table.

"Then we can, I think," he said, "eliminate one motive from the case. It is, you comprehend, what I look for first. *Who benefits by the deceased's death?* In this case it is a museum. Had it been otherwise, had Mrs. Leidner died intestate but possessed of a considerable fortune, I should imagine that it would prove an interesting question as to who inherited the money—you—or a former husband. But there would have been this difficulty, the former husband would have had to resurrect himself in order to claim it, and I should imagine that he would then be in danger of arrest, though I hardly fancy that the death penalty would be exacted so long after the war. However, these speculations need not arise. As I say, I settle first the question of money. For the next step I proceed always to suspect the husband or wife of the deceased! In this case, in the first place, you are proved never to have gone near your wife's room yesterday afternoon, in the second place, you lose instead of gain by your wife's death, and in the third place—"

He paused.

"Yes?" said Dr. Leidner.

"In the third place," said Poirot slowly. "I can, I think, appreciate devotion when I see it. I believe, Dr. Leidner, that your love for your wife was the ruling passion of your life. It is so, is it not?"

Dr. Leidner answered quite simply:

"Yes."

Poirot nodded.

"Therefore," he said, "we can proceed."

"Hear, hear, let's get down to it," said Dr. Reilly with some impatience.

Poirot gave him a reproving glance.

"My friend, do not be impatient. In a case like this everything must be approached with order and method. In fact, that is my rule in every case. Having disposed of certain possibilities, we now approach a very important point. It is vital that, as you say—all the cards should be on the table—there must be nothing kept back."

"Quite so," said Dr. Reilly.

"That is why I demand the whole truth," went on Poirot.

Dr. Leidner looked at him in surprise.

"I assure you, M. Poirot, that I have kept nothing back. I have told you everything that I know. There have been no reserves."

"Tout de même, you have not told me *everything."*

"Yes, indeed. I cannot think of any detail that has escaped me."

He looked quite distressed.

Poirot shook his head gently.

"No," he said. *"You have not told me, for instance, why you installed Nurse Leatheran in the house."*

Dr. Leidner looked completely bewildered.

"But I have explained that. It is obvious. My wife's nervousness—her fears . . ."

Poirot leaned forward. Slowly and emphatically he wagged a finger up and down.

"No, no, no. There is something there that is not clear. Your wife is in danger, yes—she is threatened with death, yes. You send—*not for the police*—not for a private detective even—but for a *nurse!* It does not make the sense, that!"

"I—I—" Dr. Leidner stopped. The color rose in his cheeks. "I thought—" He came to a dead stop.

"Now we are coming to it," Poirot encouraged him. "You thought—what?"

Dr. Leidner remained silent. He looked harassed and unwilling.

"See you," Poirot's tone became winning and appealing, "it all rings true what you have told me, except for that. Why a *nurse?* There is an answer—yes. In fact, there can be only one answer. *You did not believe yourself in your wife's danger."*

And then with a cry Dr. Leidner broke down.

"God help me," he groaned. "I didn't. I didn't."

Poirot watched him with the kind of attention a cat gives a mouse hole—ready to pounce when the mouse shows itself.

"What *did* you think then?" he asked.

"I don't know. I don't know . . ."

"But you do know. You know perfectly. Perhaps I can help you—with a guess. *Did you, Dr. Leidner, suspect that these letters were all written by your wife herself?"*

There wasn't any need for him to answer. The truth of Poirot's guess was only too apparent. The horrified hand he held up, as though begging for mercy, told its own tale.

I drew a deep breath. So I *had* been right in my half-formed guess! I recalled the curious tone in which Dr. Leidner had asked me what I thought of it all. I nodded my head slowly and thoughtfully, and suddenly awoke to the fact that M. Poirot's eyes were on me.

"Did you think the same, nurse?"

"The idea did cross my mind," I said truthfully.

"For what reason?"

I explained the similarity of the handwriting on the letter that Mr. Coleman had shown me.

Poirot turned to Dr. Leidner.

"Had you, too, noticed that similarity?"

Dr. Leidner bowed his head.

"Yes, I did. The writing was small and cramped—not big and generous like Louise's, but several of the letters were formed the same way. I will show you."

From an inner breast pocket he took out some letters and finally selected a sheet from one which he handed to Poirot. It was part of a letter written to him by his wife. Poirot compared it carefully with the anonymous letters.

"Yes," he murmured. "Yes. There are several similarities—a curious way of forming the letter *s,* a distinctive *e.* I am not a handwriting expert—I cannot pronounce definitely (and for that matter, I have never found two handwriting experts who agree on any point whatsoever)—but one can at least say this—the similarity between the two handwritings is very marked. It seems highly probable that they were all written by the same person. But it is not *certain.* We must take all contingencies into mind.

He leaned back in his chair and said thoughtfully:

"There are three possibilities. First, the similarity of the handwriting is pure coincidence. Second, that these threatening letters were written by Mrs. Leidner herself for some obscure reason. Third, that they were written by someone *who deliberately copied her handwriting.* Why? There seems no sense in it. One of these three possibilities must be the correct one."

He reflected for a minute or two and then, turning to Dr. Leidner, he asked, with a resumal of his brisk manner.

"When the possibility that Mrs. Leidner herself was the author of these letters first struck you, what theory did you form?"

Dr. Leidner shook his head.

"I put the idea out of my head as quickly as possible. I felt it was monstrous."

"Did you search for no explanation?"

"Well," he hesitated, "I wondered if worrying and brooding over the past had perhaps affected my wife's brain slightly. I thought she might possibly have written those letters to herself without being conscious of having done so. That is possible, isn't it?" he added, turning to Dr. Reilly.

Dr. Reilly pursed up his lips.

"The human brain is capable of almost anything," he replied vaguely.

But he shot a lightning glance at Poirot, and as if in obedience to it, the latter abandoned the subject.

"The letters are an interesting point," he said. "But we must concentrate on the case as a whole. There are, as I see it, three possible solutions."

"Three?"

"Yes. Solution one: the simplest. Your wife's first husband is still alive. He first threatens her and then proceeds to carry out his threats. If we accept this solution, our problem is to discover how he got in or out without being seen.

"Solution two: Mrs. Leidner, for reasons of her own (reasons probably more easily understood by a medical man than a layman), writes herself threatening letters. The gas business is staged by her (remember, it was she who roused you by telling you she smelt gas. But, *if Mrs. Leidner wrote herself the letters, she cannot be in danger from the supposed writer.* We must, therefore, look elsewhere for the murderer. We must look, in fact, amongst the members of your staff. Yes," in answer to a murmur of protest from Dr. Leidner, "that is the only logical conclusion. To satisfy a private grudge one of them killed her. That person, I may say, was probably aware of the letters —or was at any rate aware that Mrs. Leidner feared or was pretending to fear someone. That fact, in the murderer's opinion, rendered the murder quite safe for him. He felt sure it would be put down to a mysterious outsider—the writer of the threatening letters.

"A variant of this solution is that the murderer actually wrote the letters himself, being aware of Mrs. Leidner's past history. But in that case it is not quite clear *why* the criminal should have copied Mrs. Leidner's own handwriting since, as far as we can see, it would be more to his or her advantage that they should appear to be written by an outsider.

"The third solution is the most interesting to my mind. I suggest that the letters are genuine. They are written by Mrs. Leidner's first husband (or his younger brother), *who is actually one of the expedition staff.*"

16

The Suspects

DR. LEIDNER SPRANG to his feet.

"Impossible! Absolutely impossible! The idea is absurd!"

Mr. Poirot looked at him quite calmly but said nothing.

"You mean to suggest that my wife's former husband is one of the expedition *and that she didn't recognize him?*"

"Exactly. Reflect a little on the facts. Nearly twenty years ago your wife lived with this man for a few months. Would she know him if she came across him after that lapse of time? I think not. His face will have changed, his build will have changed—his voice may not have changed so much, but that is a detail he can attend to himself. And remember, *she is not looking for him amongst her own household.* She visualizes him as somewhere *outside*—a stranger. No, I do not think she would recognize him. And there is a second possibility. The young brother—the child of those days who was so passionately devoted to his elder brother. He is now a man. Will she recognize a child of ten or twelve years old in a man nearing thirty? Yes, there is young William Bosner to be reckoned with. Remember, his brother in his eyes may not loom as a traitor but as a patriot, a martyr for his own country—Germany. In his eyes *Mrs. Leidner* is the traitor—the monster who sent his beloved brother to death! A susceptible child is capable of great hero worship, and a young mind can easily be obsessed by an idea which persists into adult life."

"Quite true," said Dr. Reilly. "The popular view that a child forgets easily is not an accurate one. Many people go right through life in the grip of an idea which has been impressed on them in very tender years."

"*Bien.* You have these two possibilities. Frederick Bosner, a man by now of fifty odd, and William Bosner, whose age would be something short of thirty. Let us examine the members of your staff from these two points of view."

"This is fantastic," murmured Dr. Leidner. "*My* staff! The members of my own expedition."

"And consequently considered above suspicion," said Poirot dryly. "A very useful point of view. *Commençons!* Who could emphatically *not* be Frederick or William?"

"The women."

"Naturally. Miss Johnson and Mrs. Mercado are crossed off. Who else?"

"Carey. He and I have worked together for years before I even met Louise—"

"And also he is the wrong age. He is, I should judge, thirty-eight or -nine, too young for Frederick, too old for William. Now for the rest. There is

Father Lavigny and Mr. Mercado. Either of them might be Frederick Bosner."

"But, my dear sir," cried Dr. Leidner in a voice of mingled irritation and amusement, "Father Lavigny is known all over the world as an epigraphist and Mercado has worked for years in a well-known museum in New York. It is *impossible* that either of them should be the man you think!"

Poirot waved an airy hand.

"Impossible—impossible—I take no account of the word! The impossible, always I examine it very closely! But we will pass on for the moment. Who else have you? Carl Reiter, a young man with a German name, David Emmott—"

"He has been with me two seasons, remember."

"He is a young man with the gift of patience. *If* he committed a crime, it would not be in a hurry. All would be very well prepared."

Dr. Leidner made a gesture of despair.

"And lastly, William Coleman," continued Poirot.

"He is an Englishman."

"*Pourquoi pas?* Did not Mrs. Leidner say that the boy left America and could not be traced? He might easily have been brought up in England."

"You have an answer to everything," said Dr. Leidner.

I was thinking hard. Right from the beginning I had thought Mr. Coleman's manner rather more like a P. G. Wodehouse book than like a real live young man. Had he really been playing a part all the time?

Poirot was writing in a little book.

"Let us proceed with order and method," he said. "On the first count we have two names. Father Lavigny and Mr. Mercado. On the second we have Coleman, Emmott and Reiter.

"Now let us pass to the opposite aspect of the matter—means and opportunity. *Who amongst the expedition had the means and the opportunity of committing the crime?* Carey was on the dig, Coleman was in Hassanieh, you yourself were on the roof. That leaves us Father Lavigny, Mr. Mercado, Mrs. Mercado, David Emmott, Carl Reiter, Miss Johnson and Nurse Leatheran."

"Oh!" I exclaimed, and I bounded in my chair.

Mr. Poirot looked at me with twinkling eyes.

"Yes, I'm afraid, *ma soeur,* that you have got to be included. It would have been quite easy for you to have gone along and killed Mrs. Leidner while the courtyard was empty. You have plenty of muscle and strength, and she would have been quite unsuspicious until the moment the blow was struck."

I was so upset that I couldn't get a word out. Dr. Reilly, I noticed, was looking highly amused.

"Interesting case of a nurse who murdered her patients one by one," he murmured.

Such a look as I gave him!

Dr. Leidner's mind had been running on a different tack.

"Not Emmott, M. Poirot," he objected. "You can't include him. He was on the roof with me, remember, during that ten minutes."

"Nevertheless we cannot exclude him. He could have come down, gone straight to Mrs. Leidner's room, killed her, and *then* called the boy back. Or he might have killed her on one of the occasions when he had *sent the boy up to you.*"

Dr. Leidner shook his head, murmuring:

"What a nightmare! It's all so—fantastic."

To my surprise Poirot agreed.

"Yes, that is true. *This is a fantastic crime.* One does not often come across them. Usually murder is very sordid—very simple. But this is unusual murder . . . I suspect, Dr. Leidner, that your wife was an unusual woman."

He had hit the nail on the head with such accuracy that I jumped.

"Is that true, nurse?" he asked.

Dr. Leidner said quietly:

"Tell him what Louise was like, nurse. You are unprejudiced."

I spoke quite frankly.

"She was very lovely," I said. "You couldn't help admiring her and wanting to do things for her. I've never met anyone like her before."

"Thank you," said Dr. Leidner and smiled at me.

"That is valuable testimony coming from an outsider," said Poirot politely. "Well, let us proceed. Under the heading of *means and opportunity* we have seven names. Nurse Leatheran, Miss Johnson, Mrs. Mercado, Mr. Mercado, Mr. Reiter, Mr. Emmott and Father Lavigny."

Once more he cleared his throat. I've always noticed that foreigners can make the oddest noises.

"Let us for the moment assume that our third theory is correct. That is, that the murderer is Frederick or William Bosner, and that Frederick or William Bosner is a member of the expedition staff. By comparing both lists we can narrow down our suspects on this count to four. Father Lavigny, Mr. Mercado, Carl Reiter and David Emmott."

"Father Lavigny is out of the question," said Dr. Leidner with decision. "He is one of the *Pères Blancs* in Carthage."

"And his beard's quite real," I put in.

"*Ma soeur,*" said Poirot, "a murderer of the first class *never* wears a false beard!"

"How do you know the murderer is of the first class?" I asked rebelliously.

"Because if he were not, the whole truth would be plain to me at this instant—and it is not."

That's pure conceit, I thought to myself.

"Anyway," I said, reverting to the beard, "it must have taken quite a time to grow."

"That is a practical observation," said Poirot. Dr. Leidner said irritably:

"But it's ridiculous—quite ridiculous. Both he and Mercado are well-known men. They've been known for years."

Poirot turned to him.

"You have not the true vision. You do not appreciate an important point. *If Frederick Bosner is not dead—what has he been doing all these years?* He must have taken a different name. He must have built himself up a career."

"As a *Père Blanc?*" asked Dr. Reilly skeptically.

"It is a little fantastic that, yes," confessed Poirot. "But we cannot put it right out of court. Besides, there are other possibilities."

"The young 'uns?" said Reilly. "If you want my opinion, on the face of it there's only one of your suspects that's even plausible."

"And that is?"

"Young Carl Reiter. There's nothing actually against him, but come down to it and you've got to admit a few things—he's the right age, he's got a German name, he's new this year and he had the opportunity all right. He'd only got to pop out of his photographic place, cross the courtyard to do his dirty work and hare back again while the coast was clear. If any one were to have dropped into the photographic room while he was out of it, he can always say later that he was in the darkroom. I don't say he's your man but if you are going to suspect someone I say he's by far and away the most likely."

M. Poirot didn't seem very receptive. He nodded gravely but doubtfully.

"Yes," he said. "He is the most plausible, but it may not be so simple as all that."

Then he said:

"Let us say no more at present. I would like now if I may to examine the room where the crime took place."

"Certainly." Dr. Leidner fumbled in his pockets then looked at Dr. Reilly.

"Captain Maitland took it," he said.

"Maitland gave it to me," said Reilly. "He had to go off on that Kurdish business."

He produced the key.

Dr. Leidner said hesitatingly:

"Do you mind—if I don't— Perhaps, nurse—"

"Of course. Of course," said Poirot. "I quite understand. Never do I wish to cause you unnecessary pain. If you will be good enough to accompany me, *ma soeur.*"

"Certainly," I said.

17

The Stain by
the Washstand

MRS. LEIDNER'S BODY had been taken to Hassanieh for the post-mortem, but otherwise her room had been left exactly as it was. There was so little in it that it had not taken the police long to go over it.

To the right of the door as you entered was the bed. Opposite the door were the two barred windows giving on the countryside. Between them was a plain oak table with two drawers that served Mrs. Leidner as a dressing table. On the east wall there was a line of hooks with dresses hung up protected by cotton bags and a deal chest of drawers. Immediately to the left of the door was the washstand. In the middle of the room was a good-sized plain oak table with a blotter and inkstand and a small attaché case. It was in the latter that Mrs. Leidner had kept the anonymous letters. The curtains were short strips of native material—white striped with orange. The floor was of stone with some goatskin rugs on it, three narrow ones of brown striped with white in front of the two windows and the washstand, and a larger better quality one of white with brown stripes lying between the bed and the writing table.

There were no cupboards or alcoves or long curtains—nowhere, in fact, where anyone could have hidden. The bed was a plain iron one with a printed cotton quilt. The only trace of luxury in the room were three pillows all made of the best soft and billowy down. Nobody but Mrs. Leidner had pillows like these.

In a few brief dry words Dr. Reilly explained where Mrs. Leidner's body had been found—in a heap on the rug beside the bed.

To illustrate his account, he beckoned me to come forward.

"If you don't mind, nurse?" he said.

I'm not squeamish. I got down on the floor and arranged myself as far as possible in the attitude in which Mrs. Leidner's body had been found.

"Leidner lifted her head when he found her," said the doctor. "But I questioned him closely and it's obvious that he didn't actually change her position."

"It seems quite straightforward," said Poirot. "She was lying on the bed, asleep or resting—someone opens the door, she looks up, rises to her feet—"

"And he struck her down," finished the doctor. "The blow would produce unconsciousness and death would follow very shortly. You see—"

He explained the injury in technical language.

"Not much blood, then?" said Poirot.

"No, the blood escaped internally into the brain."

"*Eh bien,*" said Poirot, "that seems straightforward enough—except for one thing. *If* the man who entered was a stranger, why did not Mrs. Leidner cry out at once for help? If she had screamed she would have been heard. Nurse Leatheran here would have heard her, and Emmott and the boy."

"That's easily answered," said Dr. Reilly dryly. "*Because it wasn't a stranger.*"

Poirot nodded.

"Yes," he said meditatively. "She may have been *surprised* to see the person —but she was not *afraid.* Then, as he struck, she *may* have uttered a half cry —too late."

"The cry Miss Johnson heard?"

"Yes, if she *did* hear it. But on the whole I doubt it. These mud walls are thick and the windows were closed."

He stepped up to the bed.

"You left her actually lying down?" he asked me. I explained exactly what I had done.

"Did she mean to sleep or was she going to read?"

"I gave her two books—a light one and a volume of memoirs. She usually read for a while and then sometimes dropped off for a short sleep."

"And she was—what shall I say—quite as usual?"

I considered.

"Yes. She seemed quite normal and in good spirits," I said. "Just a shade offhand, perhaps, but I put that down to her having confided in me the day before. It makes people a little uncomfortable sometimes."

Poirot's eyes twinkled.

"Ah, yes, indeed, me, I know that well."

He looked around the room.

"And when you came in here after the murder, was everything as you had seen it before?"

I looked round also.

"Yes, I think so. I don't remember anything being different."

"There was no sign of the weapon with which she was struck?"

"No."

Poirot looked at Dr. Reilly.

"What was it in your opinion?"

The doctor replied promptly.

"Something pretty powerful of a fair size and without any sharp corners or edges. The rounded base of a statue, say—something like that. Mind you, I'm not suggesting that that *was* it. But that type of thing. The blow was delivered with great force."

"Struck by a strong arm? A man's arm?"

"Yes—unless—"

"Unless—what?"

Dr. Reilly said slowly:

"It is just possible that Mrs. Leidner might have been on her knees—in which case, the blow being delivered from above with a heavy implement, the force needed would not have been so great."

"*On her knees,*" mused Poirot. "It is an idea—that."

"It's only an idea, mind," the doctor hastened to point out. "There's absolutely nothing to indicate it."

"But it's possible."

"Yes. And after all, in view of the circumstances, it's not fantastic. Her fear might have led her to kneel in supplication rather than to scream when her instinct would tell her it was too late—that nobody could get there in time."

"Yes," said Poirot thoughtfully. "It is an idea . . ."

It was a very poor one, I thought. I couldn't for one moment imagine Mrs. Leidner on her knees to anyone.

Poirot made his way slowly around the room. He opened the windows, tested the bars, passed his head through and satisfied himself that by no means could his shoulders be made to follow his head.

"The windows were shut when you found her," he said. "Were they also shut when you left her at a quarter to one?"

"Yes, they were always shut in the afternoon. There is no gauze over these windows as there is in the living room and dining room. They are kept shut to keep out the flies."

"And in any case no one could get in that way," mused Poirot. "And the walls are of the most solid—mud-brick—and there are no trapdoors and no skylights. No, there is only one way into this room—*through the door.* And there is only one way to the door—through the courtyard. And there is only one entrance to the courtyard—*through the archway.* And outside the archway there were five people and they all tell the same story, and I do not think, me, that they are lying. . . . No, they are not lying. They are not bribed to silence. The murderer was *here.* . . ."

I didn't say anything. Hadn't I felt the same thing just now when we were all cooped up around that table?

Slowly Poirot prowled around the room. He took up a photograph from the chest of drawers. It was of an elderly man with a white goatee beard. He looked inquiringly at me.

"Mrs. Leidner's father," I said. "She told me so."

He put it down again and glanced over the articles on the dressing table— all of plain tortoiseshell—simple but good. He looked up at a row of books on a shelf, repeating the titles aloud.

"*Who Were the Greeks? Introduction to Relativity. Life of Lady Hester Stanhope. Crewe Train. Back to Methuselah. Linda Condon.* Yes, they tell us something, perhaps."

"She was not a fool, your Mrs. Leidner. She had a mind."

"Oh! she was a *very* clever woman," I said eagerly. "Very well read and up in everything. She wasn't a bit ordinary."

He smiled as he looked over at me.

"No," he said. "I've already realized that."

He passed on. He stood for some moments at the washstand where there was a big array of bottles and toilet creams.

Then, suddenly, he dropped on his knees and examined the rug.

Dr. Reilly and I came quickly to join him. He was examining a small dark brown stain, almost invisible on the brown of the rug. In fact it was only just noticeable where it impinged on one of the white stripes.

"What do you say, doctor?" he said. "Is that blood?"

Dr. Reilly knelt down.

"Might be," he said. "I'll make sure if you like?"

"If you would be so amiable."

Mr. Poirot examined the jug and basin. The jug was standing on the side of the washstand. The basin was empty, but beside the washstand there was an old kerosene tin containing slop water.

He turned to me.

"Do you remember, nurse? Was this jug *out* of the basin or *in* it when you left Mrs. Leidner at a quarter to one?"

"I can't be sure," I said after a minute or two. "I rather think it was standing in the basin."

"Ah?"

"But you see," I said hastily, "I only think so because it usually was. The boys leave it like that after lunch. I just feel that if it hadn't been in I should have noticed it."

He nodded quite appreciatively.

"Yes, I understand that. It is your hospital training. If everything had not been just so in the room, you would quite unconsciously have set it to rights hardly noticing what you were doing. And after the murder? Was it like it is now?"

I shook my head.

"I didn't notice then," I said. "All I looked for was whether there was anyplace anyone could be hidden or if there were anything the murderer had left behind him."

"It's blood all right," said Dr. Reilly, rising from his knees. "Is it important?"

Poirot was frowning perplexedly. He flung out his hands with petulance.

"I cannot tell. How can I tell? It may mean nothing at all. I can say, if I like, that the murderer touched her—that there was blood on his hands—very little blood, but still blood—and so he came over here and washed them. Yes, it may have been like that. But I cannot jump to conclusions and say that it *was* so. That stain may be of no importance at all."

"There would have been very little blood," said Dr. Reilly dubiously. "None would have spurted out or anything like that. It would have just oozed a little from the wound. Of course, if he'd probed it at all . . ."

I gave a shiver. A nasty sort of picture came up in my mind. The vision of somebody—perhaps that nice pig-faced photographic boy, striking down that lovely woman and then bending over her probing the wound with his finger in an awful gloating fashion and his face, perhaps, quite different . . . all fierce and mad. . . .

Dr. Reilly noticed my shiver.

"What's the matter, nurse?" he said.

"Nothing—just goose-flesh," I said. "A goose walking over my grave."

Mr. Poirot turned round and looked at me.

"I know what you need," he said. "Presently when we have finished here and I go back with the doctor to Hassanieh we will take you with us. You will give Nurse Leatheran tea, will you not, doctor?"

"Delighted."

"Oh, no, doctor," I protested. "I couldn't think of such a thing."

M. Poirot gave me a little friendly tap on the shoulder. Quite an English tap, not a foreign one.

"You, *ma soeur,* will do as you are told," he said. "Besides, it will be of advantage to me. There is a good deal more that I want to discuss, and I cannot do it here where one must preserve the decencies. The good Dr. Leidner, he worshipped his wife and he is sure—oh, so sure—that everybody else felt the same about her! But that, in my opinion, would not be human nature! No, we want to discuss Mrs. Leidner with—how do you say—the gloves removed? That is settled then. When we have finished here, we take you with us to Hassanieh."

"I suppose," I said doubtfully, "that I ought to be leaving anyway. It's rather awkward."

"Do nothing for a day or two," said Dr. Reilly. "You can't very well go until after the funeral."

"That's all very well," I said. "And supposing I get murdered too, doctor?"

I said it half jokingly and Dr. Reilly took it in the same fashion and would, I think, have made some jocular response.

But M. Poirot, to my astonishment, stood stock still in the middle of the floor and clasped his hands to his head.

"Ah! if that were possible," he murmured. "It is a danger—yes—a great danger—and what can one do? How can one guard against it?"

"Why, M. Poirot," I said, "I was only joking! Who'd want to murder me, I should like to know?"

"You—or another," he said, and I didn't like the way he said it at all. Positively creepy.

"But why?" I persisted.

He looked at me very straight then.

"I joke, mademoiselle," he said, "and I laugh. *But there are some things that are no joke.* There are things that my profession has taught me. And one of these things, the most terrible thing, is this:

"Murder is a habit . . ."

18

Tea at Dr. Reilly's

BEFORE LEAVING, POIROT made a round of the expedition house and the outbuildings. He also asked a few questions of the servants at second hand—that is to say, Dr. Reilly translated the questions and answers from English into Arabic and vice versa.

These questions dealt mainly with the appearance of the stranger Mrs. Leidner and I had seen looking through the window and to whom Father Lavigny had been talking on the following day.

"Do you really think that fellow had anything to do with it?" asked Dr. Reilly when we were bumping along in his car on our way to Hassanieh.

"I like all the information there is," was Poirot's reply.

And really, that described his methods very well. I found later that there wasn't anything—no small scrap of insignificant gossip—in which he wasn't interested. Men aren't usually so gossipy.

I must confess I was glad of my cup of tea when we got to Dr. Reilly's house. M. Poirot, I noticed, put five lumps of sugar in his.

Stirring it carefully with his teaspoon he said:

"And now we can talk, can we not? We can make up our minds who is likely to have committed the crime."

"Lavigny, Mercado, Emmott or Reiter?" asked Dr. Reilly.

"No, no—that was theory number three. I wish to concentrate now on theory number two—leaving aside all question of a mysterious husband or brother-in-law turning up from the past. Let us discuss now quite simply which member of the expedition had the means and opportunity to kill Mrs. Leidner, and who is likely to have done so."

"I thought you didn't think much of that theory."

"Not at all. But I have some natural delicacy," said Poirot reproachfully. "Can I discuss in the presence of Dr. Leidner the motives likely to lead to the murder of his wife by a member of the expedition? That would not have been delicate at all. I had to sustain the fiction that his wife was adorable and that everyone adored her!

"But naturally it was not like that at all. Now we can be brutal and impersonal and say what we think. We have no longer to consider people's feelings. And that is where Nurse Leatheran is going to help us. She is, I am sure, a very good observer."

"Oh, I don't know about that," I said.

Dr. Reilly handed me a plate of hot scones—"to fortify yourself," he said. They were very good scones.

"Come now," said M. Poirot in a friendly, chatty way. "You shall tell me, *ma soeur,* exactly what each member of the expedition felt towards Mrs. Leidner."

"I was only there a week, M. Poirot," I said.

"Quite long enough for one of your intelligence. A nurse sums up quickly. She makes her judgments and abides by them. Come, let us make a beginning. Father Lavigny, for instance?"

"Well, there now, I really couldn't say. He and Mrs. Leidner seemed to like talking together. But they usually spoke French and I'm not very good at French myself though I learnt it as a girl at school. I've an idea they talked mainly about books."

"They were, as you might say, companionable together—yes?"

"Well, yes, you might put it that way. But, all the same, I think Father Lavigny was puzzled by her and—well—almost annoyed by being puzzled, if you know what I mean."

And I told him of the conversation I had had with him out on the dig that first day when he had called Mrs. Leidner a "dangerous woman."

"Now that is very interesting," M. Poirot said. "And she—what do you think she thought of him?"

"That's rather difficult to say, too. It wasn't easy to know what Mrs. Leidner thought of people. Sometimes, I fancy, *he* puzzled *her.* I remember her saying to Dr. Leidner that he was unlike any priest she had ever known."

"A length of hemp to be ordered for Father Lavigny," said Dr. Reilly facetiously.

"My dear friend," said Poirot. "Have you not, perhaps, some patients to attend? I would not for the world detain you from your professional duties."

"I've got a whole hospital of them," said Dr. Reilly.

And he got up and said a wink was as good as a nod to a blind horse, and went out laughing.

"That is better," said Poirot. "We will have now an interesting conversation *tête-à-tête.* But you must not forget to eat your tea."

He passed me a plate of sandwiches and suggested my having a second cup of tea. He really had very pleasant, attentive manners.

"And now," he said, "let us continue with your impressions. Who was there who in your opinion did *not* like Mrs. Leidner?"

"Well," I said, "it's only my opinion and I don't want it repeated as coming from me."

"Naturally not."

"But in my opinion little Mrs. Mercado fairly hated her!"

"Ah! And Mr. Mercado?"

"He was a bit soft on her," I said. "I shouldn't think women apart from his wife had ever taken much notice of him. And Mrs. Leidner had a nice kind way of being interested in people and the things they told her. It rather went to the poor man's head, I fancy."

"And Mrs. Mercado—she was not pleased?"

"She was just plain jealous—that's the truth of it. You've got to be very careful when there's a husband and wife about, and that's a fact. I could tell you some surprising things. You've no idea the extraordinary things women get into their heads when it's a question of their husbands."

"I do not doubt the truth of what you say. So Mrs. Mercado was jealous? And she hated Mrs. Leidner?"

"I've seen her look at her as though she'd have liked to kill her—oh, gracious!" I pulled myself up. "Indeed, M. Poirot, I didn't mean to say—I mean that is, not for one moment—"

"No, no. I quite understand. The phrase slipped out. A very convenient one. And Mrs. Leidner, was she worried by this animosity of Mrs. Mercado's?"

"Well," I said, reflecting, "I don't really think she was worried at all. In fact, I don't even know whether she noticed it. I thought once of just giving her a hint—but I didn't like to. Least said soonest mended. That's what I say."

"You are doubtless wise. Can you give me any instances of how Mrs. Mercado showed her feelings?"

I told him about our conversation on the roof.

"So she mentioned Mrs. Leidner's first marriage," said Poirot thoughtfully. "Can you remember—in mentioning it—did she look at you as though she wondered whether you had heard a different version?"

"You think she may have known the truth about it?"

"It is a possibility. She may have written those letters—and engineered a tapping hand and all the rest of it."

"I wondered something of the same kind myself. It seemed the kind of petty revengeful thing she might do."

"Yes. A cruel streak, I should say. But hardly the temperament for cold-blooded brutal murder unless, of course—"

He paused and then said:

"It is odd, that curious thing she said to you. *'I know why you are here.'* What did she mean by it?"

"I can't imagine," I said frankly.

"She thought you were there for some ulterior reason apart from the declared one. What reason? And why should she be so concerned in the matter? Odd, too, the way you tell me she stared at you all through tea the day you arrived."

"Well, she's not a lady, M. Poirot," I said primly.

"That, *ma soeur,* is an excuse but not an explanation."

I wasn't quite sure for the minute what he meant. But he went on quickly.

"And the other members of the staff?"

I considered.

"I don't think Miss Johnson liked Mrs. Leidner either very much. But she was quite open and aboveboard about it. She as good as admitted she was prejudiced. You see, she's very devoted to Dr. Leidner and had worked with him for years. And of course, marriage does change things—there's no denying it."

"Yes," said Poirot. "And from Miss Johnson's point of view it would be an unsuitable marriage. It would really have been much more suitable if Dr. Leidner had married *her.*"

"It would really," I agreed. "But there, that's a man all over. Not one in a hundred considers suitability. And one can't really blame Dr. Leidner. Miss Johnson, poor soul, isn't so much to look at. Now Mrs. Leidner was really beautiful—not young, of course—but oh! I wish you'd known her. There was something about her. . . . I remember Mr. Coleman saying she was like a thingummyjig that came to lure people into marshes. That wasn't a very good way of putting it but—oh, well—you'll laugh at me but there *was* something about her that was—well—unearthly."

"She could cast a spell—yes, I understand," said Poirot.

"Then I don't think she and Mr. Carey got on very well either," I went on. "I've an idea *he* was jealous just like Miss Johnson. He was always very stiff with her and so was she with him. You know—she passed him things and was very polite and called him Mr. Carey rather formally. He was an old friend of her husband's, of course, and some women can't stand their husband's old friends. They don't like to think that any one knew them before they did—at least that's rather a muddled way of putting it—"

"I quite understand. And the three young men? Coleman, you say, was inclined to be poetic about her."

I couldn't help laughing.

"It was funny, M. Poirot," I said. "He's such a matter-of-fact young man."

"And the other two?"

"I don't really know about Mr. Emmott. He's always so quiet and never says much. She was very nice to him always. You know—friendly—called him David and used to tease him about Miss Reilly and things like that."

"Ah, really? And did he enjoy that?"

"I don't quite know," I said doubtfully. "He'd just look at her. Rather funnily. You couldn't tell what he was thinking."

"And Mr. Reiter?"

"She wasn't always very kind to him," I said slowly. "I think he got on her nerves. She used to say quite sarcastic things to him."

"And did he mind?"

"He used to get very pink, poor boy. Of course, she didn't *mean* to be unkind."

And then suddenly, from feeling a little sorry for the boy, it came over me that he was very likely a cold-blooded murderer and had been playing a part all the time.

"Oh, M. Poirot," I exclaimed. "What do you think *really* happened?"

He shook his head slowly and thoughtfully.

"Tell me," he said. "You are not afraid to go back there tonight?"

"Oh, *no,*" I said. "Of course, I remember what you said, but who would want to murder *me?*"

"I do not think that anyone could," he said slowly. "That is partly why I have been so anxious to hear all you could tell me. No, I think—I am sure—you are quite safe."

"If anyone had told me in Baghdad—" I began and stopped.

"Did you hear any gossip about the Leidners and the expedition before you came here?" he asked.

I told him about Mrs. Leidner's nickname and just a little of what Mrs. Kelsey had said about her.

In the middle of it the door opened and Miss Reilly came in. She had been playing tennis and had her racquet in her hand.

I gathered Poirot had already met her when he arrived in Hassanieh.

She said how do you do to me in her usual offhand manner and picked up a sandwich.

"Well, M. Poirot," she said. "How are you getting on with our local mystery?"

"Not very fast, mademoiselle."

"I see you've rescued nurse from the wreck."

"Nurse Leatheran has been giving me valuable information about the various members of the expedition. Incidentally I have learnt a good deal—about the victim. And the victim, mademoiselle, is very often the clue to the mystery."

Miss Reilly said:

"That's rather clever of you, M. Poirot. It's certainly true that if ever a woman deserved to be murdered Mrs. Leidner was that woman!"

"Miss Reilly!" I cried, scandalized.

She laughed, a short, nasty laugh.

"Ah!" she said. "I thought you hadn't been hearing quite the truth. Nurse Leatheran, I'm afraid, was quite taken in, like many other people. Do you know, M. Poirot, I rather hope that this case isn't going to be one of your successes. I'd quite like the murderer of Louise Leidner to get away with it. In fact, I wouldn't much have objected to putting her out of the way myself."

I was simply disgusted with the girl. M. Poirot, I must say, didn't turn a hair. He just bowed and said quite pleasantly:

"I hope, then, that you have an alibi for yesterday afternoon?"

There was a moment's silence and Miss Reilly's racquet went clattering down onto the floor. She didn't bother to pick it up. Slack and untidy like all her sort! She said in a rather breathless voice:

"Oh, yes, I was playing tennis at the club. But, seriously, M. Poirot, I wonder if you know anything at all about Mrs. Leidner and the kind of woman she was?"

Again he made a funny little bow and said:

"You shall inform me, mademoiselle."

She hesitated a minute and then spoke with a callousness and lack of decency that really sickened me.

"There's a convention that one doesn't speak ill of the dead. That's stupid, I think. The truth's always the truth. On the whole it's better to keep your mouth shut about living people. You might conceivably injure them. The dead are past that. But the harm they've done lives after them sometimes. Not quite a quotation from Shakespeare but very nearly! Has nurse told you of the queer atmosphere there was at Tell Yarimjah? Has she told you how jumpy they all were? And how they all used to glare at each other like enemies? That was Louise Leidner's doing. When I was a kid out here three years ago they were the happiest, jolliest lot imaginable. Even last year they were pretty well all right. But this year there was a blight over them—and it was *her* doing. She was the kind of woman who won't let anybody else be happy! There *are* women like that and she was one of them! She wanted to break up things always. Just for fun—or for the sense of power—or perhaps just because she was made that way. And she was the kind of woman who had to get hold of every male creature within reach!"

"Miss Reilly," I cried, "I don't think that's true. In fact I *know* it isn't."
She went on without taking the least notice of me.

"It wasn't enough for her to have her husband adore her. She had to make a fool of that long-legged shambling idiot of a Mercado. Then she got hold of Bill. Bill's a sensible cove, but she was getting him all mazed and bewildered. Carl Reiter she just amused herself by tormenting. It was easy. He's a sensitive boy. And she had a jolly good go at David.

"David was better sport to her because he put up a fight. He felt her charm —but he wasn't having any. I think because he'd got sense enough to know that she didn't really care a damn. And that's why I hate her so. She's not sensual. She doesn't *want* affairs. It's just cold-blooded experiment on her part and the fun of stirring people up and setting them against each other. She dabbled in that too. She's the sort of woman who's never had a row with anyone in her life—but rows always happen where she is! She *makes* them happen. She's a kind of female Iago. She *must* have drama. But she doesn't want to be involved *herself.* She's always outside pulling strings—looking on —enjoying it. Oh, do you see *at all* what I mean?"

"I see, perhaps, more than you know, mademoiselle," said Poirot.

I couldn't make his voice out. He didn't sound indignant. He sounded—oh, well, I can't explain it.

Sheila Reilly seemed to understand for she flushed all over her face.

"You can think what you choose," she said. "But I'm right about her. She was a clever woman and she was bored and she experimented—with people— like other people experiment with chemicals. She enjoyed working on poor old Johnson's feelings and seeing her bite on the bullet and control herself like the old sport she is. She liked goading little Mercado into a white-hot frenzy. She liked flicking *me* on the raw—and she could do it too, every time! She liked finding out things about people and holding it over them. Oh, I don't mean crude blackmail—I mean just letting them know that she *knew*—and leaving them uncertain what she meant to do about it. My God, though, that woman was an artist! There was nothing crude about *her* methods!"

"And her husband?" asked Poirot.

"She never wanted to hurt him," said Miss Reilly slowly. "I've never known her anything but sweet to him. I suppose she was fond of him. He's a dear—wrapped up in his own world—his digging and his theories. And he worshipped her and thought her perfection. That might have annoyed some women. It didn't annoy her. In a sense he lived in a fool's paradise—and yet it wasn't a fool's paradise because to him she was what he thought her. Though it's hard to reconcile that with—"

She stopped.

"Go on, mademoiselle," said Poirot.

She turned suddenly on me.

"What have you said about Richard Carey?"

"About Mr. Carey?" I asked, astonished.

"About her and Carey?"

"Well," I said, "I've mentioned that they didn't hit it off very well—"

To my surprise she broke into a fit of laughter.

"Didn't hit it off very well! You fool! He's head over ears in love with her. And it's tearing him to pieces—because he worships Leidner too. He's been his friend for years. That would be enough for her, of course. She's made it her business to come between them. But all the same I've fancied—"

"Eh bien?"

She was frowning, absorbed in thought.

"I've fancied that she'd gone too far for once—that she was not only biter but bit! Carey's attractive. He's as attractive as hell. . . . She was a cold devil—but I believe she could have lost her coldness with him. . . ."

"I think it's just scandalous what you're saying," I cried. "Why, they hardly spoke to each other!"

"Oh, didn't they?" She turned on me. "A hell of a lot you know about it. It was 'Mr. Carey' and 'Mrs. Leidner' in the house, but they used to meet outside. She'd walk down the path to the river. And he'd leave the dig for an hour at a time. They used to meet among the fruit trees.

"I saw him once just leaving her, striding back to the dig, and she was standing looking after him. I was a female cad, I suppose. I had some glasses with me and I took them out and had a good look at her face. If you ask me I believed she cared like hell for Richard Carey. . . ."

She broke off and looked at Poirot.

"Excuse my butting in on your case," she said with a sudden rather twisted grin, "but I thought you'd like to have the local color correct."

And she marched out of the room.

"M. Poirot," I cried. "I don't believe one word of it all!"

He looked at me and he smiled, and he said (very queerly I thought):

"You can't deny, nurse, that Miss Reilly has shed a certain—illumination on the case."

19

A New Suspicion

WE COULDN'T SAY any more just then because Dr. Reilly came in, saying jokingly that he'd killed off the most tiresome of his patients.

He and M. Poirot settled down to a more or less medical discussion of the psychology and mental state of an anonymous letter-writer. The doctor cited cases that he had known professionally, and M. Poirot told various stories from his own experience.

"It is not so simple as it seems," he ended. "There is the desire for power and very often a strong inferiority complex."

Dr. Reilly nodded.

"That's why you often find that the author of anonymous letters is the last person in the place to be suspected. Some quiet inoffensive little soul who apparently can't say Boo to a goose—all sweetness and Christian meekness on the outside—and seething with all the fury of hell underneath!"

Poirot said thoughtfully:

"Should you say Mrs. Leidner had any tendency to an inferiority complex?"

Dr. Reilly scraped out his pipe with a chuckle.

"Last woman on earth I'd describe that way. No repressions about her. Life, life and more life—that's what she wanted—and got, too!"

"Do you consider it a possibility, psychologically speaking, that she wrote those letters?"

"Yes, I do. But if she did, the reason arose out of her instinct to dramatize herself. Mrs. Leidner was a bit of a film star in private life! She *had* to be the center of things—in the limelight. By the law of opposites she married Leidner who's about the most retiring and modest man I know. He adored her—but adoration by the fireside wasn't enough for her. She had to be the persecuted heroine as well."

"In fact," said Poirot, smiling, "you don't subscribe to his theory that she wrote them and retained no memory of her act?"

"No, I don't. I didn't turn down the idea in front of him. You can't very well say to a man who's just lost a dearly loved wife that that same wife was a shameless exhibitionist, and that she drove him nearly crazy with anxiety to satisfy her sense of the dramatic. As a matter of fact it wouldn't be safe to tell any man the truth about his wife! Funnily enough, I'd trust most women with the truth about their husbands. Women can accept the fact that a man is a rotter, a swindler, a drug-taker, a confirmed liar, and a general swine without batting an eyelash and without its impairing their affection for the brute in the least! Women are wonderful realists."

"Frankly, Dr. Reilly, what *was* your exact opinion of Mrs. Leidner?"

Dr. Reilly lay back in his chair and puffed slowly at his pipe.

"Frankly—it's hard to say! I didn't know her well enough. She'd got charm —any amount of it. Brains, sympathy. . . . What else? She hadn't any of the ordinary unpleasant vices. She wasn't sensual or lazy or even particularly vain. She was, I've always thought (but I've no proofs of it), a most accomplished liar. What I don't know (and what I'd like to know) is whether she lied to herself or only to other people. I'm rather partial to liars myself. A woman who doesn't lie is a woman without imagination and without sympathy. I don't think she was really a man-hunter—she just liked the sport of bringing them down 'with my bow and arrow.' If you get my daughter on the subject—"

"We have had that pleasure," said Poirot with a slight smile.

"H'm," said Dr. Reilly. "She hasn't wasted much time! Shoved her knife into her pretty thoroughly, I should imagine! The younger generation has no sentiment towards the dead. It's a pity all young people are prigs! They condemn the 'old morality' and then proceed to set up a much more hard and fast code of their own. If Mrs. Leidner had had half a dozen affairs Sheila would probably have approved of her as 'living her life fully'—or 'obeying her blood instincts.' What she doesn't see is that Mrs. Leidner was acting true to type—*her* type. The cat *is* obeying its blood instinct when it plays with the mouse! It's made that way. Men aren't little boys to be shielded and protected. They've got to meet cat women—and faithful spaniel, yours-till-death adoring women, and hen-pecking nagging bird women—and all the rest of it! Life's a battlefield—not a picnic! I'd like to see Sheila honest enough to come off her high horse and admit that she hated Mrs. Leidner for good old thoroughgoing personal reasons. Sheila's about the only young girl in this place and she naturally assumes that she ought to have it all her own way with the young things in trousers. Naturally it annoys her when a woman, who in her view is middle-aged and who has already two husbands to her credit, comes along and licks her on her own ground. Sheila's a nice child, healthy and reasonably good-looking and attractive to the other sex as she should be. But Mrs. Leidner was something out of the ordinary in that line. She'd got just that sort of calamitous magic that plays the deuce with things—a kind of Belle Dame sans Merci."

I jumped in my chair. What a coincidence his saying that!

"Your daughter—I am not indiscreet—she has perhaps a *tendresse* for one of the young men out there?"

"Oh, I don't suppose so. She's had Emmott and Coleman dancing attendance on her as a matter of course. I don't know that she cares for one more than the other. There are a couple of young Air Force chaps too. I fancy all's fish that comes to her net at present. No, I think it's age daring to defeat youth that annoys her so much! She doesn't know as much of the world as I do. It's when you get to my age that you really appreciate a schoolgirl complexion and a clear eye and a firmly knit young body. But a woman over thirty can listen with rapt attention and throw in a word here and there to show the talker what a fine fellow he is—and few young men can resist that! Sheila's a pretty girl—but Louise Leidner was beautiful. Glorious eyes and that amazing golden fairness. Yes, she was a beautiful woman."

Yes, I thought to myself, he's right. Beauty's a wonderful thing. She *had* been beautiful. It wasn't the kind of looks you were jealous of—you just sat back and admired. I felt that first day I met her that I'd do *anything* for Mrs. Leidner!

All the same, that night as I was being driven back to the Tell Yarimjah (Dr. Reilly made me stay for an early dinner) one or two things came back to my mind and made me rather uncomfortable. At the time I hadn't believed a word of all Sheila Reilly's outpouring. I'd taken it for sheer spite and malice.

But now I suddenly remembered the way Mrs. Leidner had insisted on going for a stroll by herself that afternoon and wouldn't hear of me coming with her. I couldn't help wondering if perhaps, after all, she *had* been going to meet Mr. Carey. . . . And of course, it *was* a little odd, really, the way he and she spoke to each other so formally. Most of the others she called by their Christian names.

He never seemed to look at her, I remembered. That might be because he disliked her—or it might be just the opposite. . . .

I gave myself a little shake. Here I was fancying and imagining all sorts of things—all because of a girl's spiteful outbursts! It just showed how unkind and dangerous it was to go about saying that kind of thing.

Mrs. Leidner *hadn't* been like that at all. . . .

Of course, *she* hadn't liked Sheila Reilly. She'd really been—almost catty about her that day at lunch to Mr. Emmott.

Funny, the way he'd looked at her. The sort of way that you couldn't possibly tell what he was thinking. You never could tell what Mr. Emmott was thinking. He was so quiet. But very nice. A nice dependable person.

Now Mr. Coleman was a foolish young man if there ever was one!

I'd got to that point in my meditations when we arrived. It was just on nine o'clock and the big door was closed and barred.

Ibrahim came running with his great key to let me in.

We all went to bed early at Tell Yarimjah. There weren't any lights showing in the living room. There was a light in the drawing-office and one in Dr. Leidner's office, but nearly all the other windows were dark. Everyone must have gone to bed even earlier than usual.

As I passed the drawing-office to go to my room I looked in. Mr. Carey was in his shirt sleeves working over his big plan.

Terribly ill, he looked, I thought. So strained and worn. It gave me quite a pang. I don't know what there was about Mr. Carey—it wasn't what he *said* because he hardly said anything—and that of the most ordinary nature, and it wasn't what he *did,* for that didn't amount to much either—and yet you just couldn't help noticing him, and everything about him seemed to matter more than it would have about anyone else. He just *counted,* if you know what I mean.

He turned his head and saw me. He removed his pipe from his mouth and said:

"Well, nurse, back from Hassanieh?"

"Yes, Mr. Carey. You're up working late. Everybody else seems to have gone to bed."

"I thought I might as well get on with things," he said. "I was a bit behindhand. And I shall be out on the dig all tomorrow. We're starting digging again."

"Already?" I asked, shocked.

He looked at me rather queerly.

"It's the best thing, I think. I put it up to Leidner. He'll be in Hassanieh most of tomorrow seeing to things. But the rest of us will carry on here. You know it's not too easy all sitting round and looking at each other as things are."

He was right there, of course. Especially in the nervy, jumpy state everyone was in.

"Well, of course you're right in a way," I said. "It takes one's mind off if one's got something to do."

The funeral, I knew, was to be the day after tomorrow.

He had bent over his plan again. I don't know why, but my heart just ached for him. I felt certain that he wasn't going to get any sleep.

"If you'd like a sleeping draught, Mr. Carey?" I said hesitatingly.

He shook his head with a smile.

"I'll carry on, nurse. Bad habit, sleeping draughts."

"Well, good night, Mr. Carey," I said. "If there's anything I can do—"

"Don't think so, thank you, nurse. Good night."

"I'm terribly sorry," I said, rather too impulsively I suppose.

"Sorry?" He looked surprised.

"For—for everybody. It's all so dreadful. But especially for you."

"For me? Why for me?"

"Well, you're such an old friend of them both."

"I'm an old friend of Leidner's. I wasn't a friend of hers particularly."

He spoke as though he had actually disliked her. Really, I wished Miss Reilly could have heard him!

"Well, good night," I said and hurried along to my room.

I fussed around a bit in my room before undressing. Washed out some handkerchiefs and a pair of wash-leather gloves and wrote up my diary. I just looked out of my door again before I really started to get ready for bed. The lights were still on in the drawing-office and in the south building.

I supposed Dr. Leidner was still up and working in his office. I wondered whether I ought to go and say good night to him. I hesitated about it—I didn't want to seem officious. He might be busy and not want to be disturbed. In the end, however, a sort of uneasiness drove me on. After all, it couldn't do any harm. I'd just say good night, ask if there was anything I could do and come away.

But Dr. Leidner wasn't there. The office itself was lit up but there was no one in it except Miss Johnson. She had her head down on the table and was crying as though her heart would break.

It gave me quite a turn. She was such a quiet, self-controlled woman. It was pitiful to see her.

"Whatever is it, my dear?" I cried. I put my arm around her and patted her. "Now, now, this won't do at all. . . . You mustn't sit here crying all by yourself."

She didn't answer and I felt the dreadful shuddering sobs that were racking her.

"Don't, my dear, don't," I said. "Take a hold on yourself. I'll go and make you a cup of nice hot tea."

She raised her head and said:

"No, no, it's all right, nurse. I'm being a fool."

"What's upset you, my dear?" I asked.

She didn't answer at once, then she said:

"It's all too awful. . . ."

"Now don't start thinking of it," I told her. "What's happened has happened and can't be mended. It's no use fretting."

She sat up straight and began to pat her hair.

"I'm making rather a fool of myself," she said in her gruff voice. "I've been clearing up and tidying the office. Thought it was best to *do* something. And then—it all came over me suddenly—"

"Yes, yes," I said hastily. "I know. A nice strong cup of tea and a hot-water bottle in your bed is what you want," I said.

And she had them too. I didn't listen to any protests.

"Thank you, nurse," she said when I'd settled her in bed, and she was sipping her tea and the hot-water bottle was in. "You're a nice kind sensible woman. It's not often I make such a fool of myself."

"Oh, anybody's liable to do that at a time like this," I said, "what with one thing and another. The strain and the shock and the police here, there and everywhere. Why, I'm quite jumpy myself."

She said slowly in rather a queer voice:

"What you said in there is true. What's happened has happened and can't be mended. . . ."

She was silent for a minute or two and then said—rather oddly, I thought:

"She was never a nice woman!"

Well, I didn't argue the point. I'd always felt it was quite natural for Miss Johnson and Mrs. Leidner not to hit it off.

I wondered if, perhaps, Miss Johnson had secretly had a feeling that she was pleased Mrs. Leidner was dead, and had then been ashamed of herself for the thought.

I said:

"Now you go to sleep and don't worry about anything."

I just picked up a few things and set the room to rights. Stockings over the back of the chair and coat and skirt on a hanger. There was a little ball of crumpled paper on the floor where it must have fallen out of a pocket.

I was just smoothing it out to see whether I could safely throw it away when she quite startled me.

"Give that to me!"

I did so—rather taken aback. She'd called out so peremptorily. She snatched it from me—fairly snatched it—and then held it in the candle flame till it was burnt to ashes.

As I say, I was startled—and I just stared at her.

I hadn't had time to see what the paper was—she'd snatched it so quick. But funnily enough, as it burned it curled over toward me and I just saw that there were words written in ink on the paper.

It wasn't till I was getting into bed that I realized why they'd looked sort of familiar to me.

It was the same handwriting as that of the anonymous letters.

Was *that* why Miss Johnson had given way to a fit of remorse? Had it been her all along who had written those anonymous letters?

20

Miss Johnson, Mrs. Mercado, Mr. Reiter

I DON'T MIND confessing that the idea came as a complete shock to me. I'd never thought of associating *Miss Johnson* with the letters. Mrs. Mercado, perhaps. But Miss Johnson was a real lady, and so self-controlled and sensible.

But I reflected, remembering the conversation I had listened to that evening between M. Poirot and Dr. Reilly, that that might be just *why*.

If it were Miss Johnson who had written the letters it explained a lot. Mind you, I didn't think for a minute Miss Johnson had had anything to do with the murder. But I *did* see that her dislike of Mrs. Leidner might have made her succumb to the temptation of well—putting the wind up her—to put it vulgarly.

She might have hoped to frighten away Mrs. Leidner from the dig.

But then Mrs. Leidner had been murdered and Miss Johnson had felt terrible pangs of remorse—first for her cruel trick and also, perhaps, because she realized that those letters were acting as a very good shield to the actual murderer. No wonder she had broken down so utterly. She was, I was sure, a decent soul at heart. And it explained, too, why she had caught so eagerly at my consolation of "what's happened's happened and can't be amended."

And then her cryptic remark—her vindication of herself—"She was never a nice woman!"

The question was, what was *I* to do about it?

I tossed and turned for a good while and in the end decided I'd let M. Poirot know about it at the first opportunity.

He came out next day but I didn't get a chance of speaking to him what you might call privately.

We had just a minute alone together and before I could collect myself to know how to begin, he had come close to me and was whispering instructions in my ear.

"Me, I shall talk to Miss Johnson—and others, perhaps, in the living-room. You have the key of Mrs. Leidner's room still?"

"Yes," I said.

"*Très bien.* Go there, shut the door behind you and give a cry—not a scream—a cry. You understand what I mean—it is alarm—surprise that I want you to express—not mad terror. As for the excuse if you are heard—I leave that to you—the stepped toe or what you will."

At that moment Miss Johnson came out into the courtyard and there was no time for more.

I understood well enough what M. Poirot was after. As soon as he and Miss Johnson had gone into the living-room I went across to Mrs. Leidner's room and, unlocking the door, went in and pulled the door to behind me.

I can't say I didn't feel a bit of a fool standing up in an empty room and giving a yelp all for nothing at all. Besides, it wasn't so easy to know just how loud to do it. I gave a pretty loud "Oh" and then tried it a bit higher and a bit lower.

Then I came out again and prepared my excuse of a stepped (stubbed I *suppose* he meant!) toe.

But it soon appeared that no excuse would be needed. Poirot and Miss Johnson were talking together earnestly and there had clearly been no interruption.

"Well," I thought, "that settles that. Either Miss Johnson imagined that cry she heard or else it was something quite different."

I didn't like to go in and interrupt them. There was a deck chair on the porch so I sat down there. Their voices floated out to me.

"The position is delicate, you understand," Poirot was saying. "Dr. Leidner—obviously he adored his wife—"

"He worshipped her," said Miss Johnson.

"He tells me, naturally, how fond all his staff was of her! As for them, what can they say? Naturally they say the same thing. It is politeness. It is decency. It *may* also be the truth! But also it may *not!* And I am convinced, mademoiselle, that the key to this enigma lies in a complete understanding of Mrs. Leidner's character. If I could get the opinion—the honest opinion—of every member of the staff, I might, from the whole, build up a picture. Frankly, that is why I am here today. I knew Dr. Leidner would be in Hassanieh. That makes it easy for me to have an interview with each of you here in turn, and beg your help."

"That's all very well," began Miss Johnson and stopped.

"Do not make me the British *clichés,*" Poirot begged. "Do not say it is not the cricket or the football, that to speak anything but well of the dead is not done—that—*enfin*—there is loyalty! Loyalty, it is a pestilential thing in crime. Again and again it obscures the truth."

"I've no particular loyalty to Mrs. Leidner," said Miss Johnson dryly. There was indeed a sharp and acid tone in her voice. "Dr. Leidner's a different matter. And, after all, she was his wife."

"Precisely—precisely. I understand that you would not wish to speak against your chief's wife. But this is not a question of a testimonial. It is a question of sudden and mysterious death. If I am to believe that it is a martyred angel who has been killed it does not add to the easiness of my task."

"I certainly shouldn't call her an angel," said Miss Johnson and the acid tone was even more in evidence.

"Tell me your opinion, frankly, of Mrs. Leidner—as a woman."

"H'm! To begin with, M. Poirot, I'll give you this warning. I'm prejudiced. I am—we all were—devoted to Dr. Leidner. And, I suppose, when Mrs. Leidner came along, we were jealous. We resented the demands she made on his time and attention. The devotion he showed her irritated us. I'm being truthful, M. Poirot, and it isn't very pleasant for me. I resented her presence here—yes, I did, though, of course, I tried never to show it. It made a difference to us, you see."

"Us? You say us?"

"I mean Mr. Carey and myself. We're the two old-timers, you see. And we didn't much care for the new order of things. I suppose that's natural, though perhaps it was rather petty of us. But it *did* make a difference."

"What kind of a difference?"

"Oh! to everything. We used to have such a happy time. A good deal of fun,

you know, and rather silly jokes, like people do who work together. Dr.
Leidner was quite lighthearted—just like a boy."

"And when Mrs. Leidner came she changed all that?"

"Well, I suppose it wasn't her *fault*. It wasn't so bad last year. And please
believe, M. Poirot, that it wasn't anything she *did*. She's always been charming to me—quite charming. That's why I've felt ashamed sometimes. It
wasn't her fault that little things she said and did seemed to rub me up the
wrong way. Really nobody could be nicer than she was."

"But nevertheless things were changed this season? There was a different
atmosphere."

"Oh, entirely. Really, I don't know what it was. Everything seemed to go
wrong—not with the work—I mean with us—our tempers and our nerves.
All on edge. Almost the sort of feeling you get when there is a thunderstorm
coming."

"And you put that down to Mrs. Leidner's influence?"

"Well, it was never like that before she came," said Miss Johnson dryly.
"Oh! I'm a cross-grained, complaining old dog. Conservative—liking things
always the same. You really mustn't take any notice of me, M. Poirot."

"How would you describe to me Mrs. Leidner's character and temperament?"

Miss Johnson hesitated for a moment. Then she said slowly:

"Well, of course, she was temperamental. A lot of ups and downs. Nice to
people one day and perhaps wouldn't speak to them the next. She was very
kind, I think. And very thoughtful for others. All the same you could see she
had been thoroughly spoilt all her life. She took Dr. Leidner's waiting on her
hand and foot as perfectly natural. And I don't think she ever really appreciated what a very remarkable—what a really great—man she had married.
That used to annoy me sometimes. And of course she was terribly highly
strung and nervous. The things she used to imagine and the states she used to
get into! I was thankful when Dr. Leidner brought Nurse Leatheran here. It
was too much for him having to cope both with his work and with his wife's
fears."

"What is your own opinion of these anonymous letters she received?"

I had to do it. I leaned forward in my chair till I could just catch sight of
Miss Johnson's profile turned to Poirot in answer to his question.

She was looking perfectly cool and collected.

"I think someone in America had a spite against her and was trying to
frighten or annoy her."

"*Pas plus serieux que ça?*"

"That's my opinion. She was a very handsome woman, you know, and
might easily have had enemies. I think those letters were written by some
spiteful woman. Mrs. Leidner being of a nervous temperament took them
seriously."

"She certainly did that," said Poirot. "But remember—the last of them
arrived by hand."

"Well, I suppose that *could* have been managed if anyone had given their minds to it. Women will take a lot of trouble to gratify their spite, M. Poirot."

They will indeed, I thought to myself!

"Perhaps you are right, mademoiselle. As you say, Mrs. Leidner was handsome. By the way, you know Miss Reilly, the doctor's daughter?"

"Sheila Reilly? Yes, of course."

Poirot adopted a very confidential, gossipy tone.

"I have heard a rumor (naturally I do not like to ask the doctor) that there was a *tendresse* between her and one of the members of Dr. Leidner's staff. Is that so, do you know?"

Miss Johnson appeared rather amused.

"Oh, young Coleman and David Emmott were both inclined to dance attendance. I believe there was some rivalry as to who was to be her partner in some event at the club. Both the boys went in on Saturday evenings to the club as a general rule. But I don't know that there was anything in it on her side. She's the only young creature in the place, you know, and so she's by way of being the belle of it. She's got the Air Force dancing attendance on her as well."

"So you think there is nothing in it?"

"Well—I don't know." Miss Johnson became thoughtful. "It is true that she comes out this way fairly often. Up to the dig and all that. In fact, Mrs. Leidner was chaffing David Emmott about it the other day—saying the girl was running after him. Which was rather a catty thing to say, I thought, and I don't think he liked it. . . . Yes, she was here a good deal. I saw her riding towards the dig on that awful afternoon." She nodded her head toward the open window. "But neither David Emmott nor Coleman were on duty that afternoon. Richard Carey was in charge. Yes, perhaps she *is* attracted to one of the boys—but she's such a modern unsentimental young woman that one doesn't know quite how seriously to take her. I'm sure I don't know which of them it is. Bill's a nice boy, and not nearly such a fool as he pretends to be. David Emmott is a dear—and there's a lot to him. He is the deep, quiet kind."

Then she looked quizzically at Poirot and said:

"But has this any bearing on the crime, M. Poirot?"

M. Poirot threw up his hands in a very French fashion.

"You make me blush, mademoiselle," he said. "You expose me as a mere gossip. But what will you, I am interested always in the love affairs of young people."

"Yes," said Miss Johnson with a little sigh. "It's nice when the course of true love runs smooth."

Poirot gave an answering sigh. I wondered if Miss Johnson was thinking of some love affair of her own when she was a girl. And I wondered if M. Poirot had a wife, and if he went on in the way you always hear foreigners do, with mistresses and things like that. He looks so comic I couldn't imagine it.

"Sheila Reilly has a lot of character," said Miss Johnson. "She's young and she's crude, but she's the right sort."

"I take your word for it, mademoiselle," said Poirot.

He got up and said, "Are there any other members of the staff in the house?"

"Marie Mercado is somewhere about. All the men are up on the dig today. I think they wanted to get out of the house. I don't blame them. If you'd like to go up to the dig—"

She came out on the verandah and said, smiling to me:

"Nurse Leatheran won't mind taking you, I dare say."

"Oh, certainly, Miss Johnson," I said.

"And you'll come back to lunch, won't you, M. Poirot?"

"Enchanted, mademoiselle."

Miss Johnson went back into the living room where she was engaged in cataloguing.

"Mrs. Mercado's on the roof," I said. "Do you want to see her first?"

"It would be as well, I think. Let us go up."

As we went up the stairs I said:

"I did what you told me. Did you hear anything?"

"Not a sound."

"That will be a weight off Miss Johnson's mind at any rate," I said. "She's been worrying that she might have done something about it."

Mrs. Mercado was sitting on the parapet, her head bent down, and she was so deep in thought that she never heard us till Poirot halted opposite her and bade her good-morning.

Then she looked up with a start.

She looked ill this morning, I thought, her small face pinched and wizened and great dark circles under her eyes.

"Encore moi," said Poirot. "I come today with a special object."

And he went on much in the same way as he had done to Miss Johnson, explaining how necessary it was that he should get a true picture of Mrs. Leidner.

Mrs. Mercado, however, wasn't as honest as Miss Johnson had been. She burst into fulsome praise which, I was pretty sure, was quite far removed from her real feelings.

"Dear, *dear* Louise! It's so hard to explain her to someone who didn't know her. She was such an *exotic* creature. Quite different from anyone else. You felt that, I'm sure, nurse? A martyr to nerves, of course, and full of fancies, but one put up with things in her one wouldn't from anyone else. And she was so *sweet* to us all, wasn't she, nurse? And so *humble* about herself—I mean she didn't know anything about archaeology, and she was so eager to learn. Always asking my husband about the chemical processes for treating the metal objects and helping Miss Johnson to mend pottery. Oh, we were all *devoted* to her."

"Then it is not true, madame, what I have heard, that there was a certain tenseness—an uncomfortable atmosphere—here?"

Mrs. Mercado opened her opaque black eyes very wide.

"Oh! who *can* have been telling you that? Nurse? Dr. Leidner? I'm sure *he* would never notice anything, poor man."

And she shot a thoroughly unfriendly glance at me.

Poirot smiled easily.

"I have my spies, madame," he declared gaily. And just for a minute I saw her eyelids quiver and blink.

"Don't you think," asked Mrs. Mercado with an air of great sweetness, "that after an event of this kind, everyone always pretends a lot of things that never were? You know—tension, atmosphere, a 'feeling that something was going to happen?' I think people just *make up* these things afterwards."

"There is a lot in what you say, madame," said Poirot.

"And it really *wasn't* true! We were a thoroughly happy family here."

"That woman is one of the most utter liars I've ever known," I said indignantly, when M. Poirot and I were clear of the house and walking along the path to the dig. "I'm sure she simply hated Mrs. Leidner really!"

"She is hardly the type to whom one would go for the truth," Poirot agreed.

"Waste of time talking to her," I snapped.

"Hardly that—hardly that. If a person tells you lies with her lips she is sometimes telling you truth with her eyes. What is she afraid of, little Madame Mercado? I saw fear in her eyes. Yes—decidedly she is afraid of something. It is very interesting."

"I've got something to tell you, M. Poirot," I said.

Then I told him all about my return the night before and my strong belief that Miss Johnson was the writer of the anonymous letters.

"So *she's* a liar too!" I said. "The cool way she answered you this morning about these same letters!"

"Yes," said Poirot. "It was interesting, that. *For she let out the fact that she knew all about those letters.* So far they have not been spoken of in the presence of the staff. Of course, it is quite possible that Dr. Leidner told her about them yesterday. They are old friends, he and she. But if he did not—well—then it is curious and interesting, is it not?"

My respect for him went up. It was clever the way he had tricked her into mentioning the letters.

"Are you going to tackle her about them?" I asked.

Mr. Poirot seemed quite shocked by the idea.

"No, no, indeed. Always it is unwise to parade one's knowledge. Until the last minute I keep everything here." He tapped his forehead. "At the right moment—I make the spring—like the panther—and, *mon Dieu!* the consternation!"

I couldn't help laughing to myself at little M. Poirot in the rôle of a panther.

We had just reached the dig. The first person we saw was Mr. Reiter, who was busy photographing some walling.

It's my opinion that the men who were digging just hacked out walls wherever they wanted them. That's what it looked like anyway. Mr. Carey explained to me that you could feel the difference at once with a pick, and he tried to show me—but I never saw. When the man said *"Libn"*—mud-brick —it was just ordinary dirt and mud as far as I could see.

Mr. Reiter finished his photographs and handed over the camera and the plates to his boy and told him to take them back to the house.

Poirot asked him one or two questions about exposures and film packs and so on which he answered very readily. He seemed pleased to be asked about his work.

He was just tendering his excuses for leaving us when Poirot plunged once more into his set speech. As a matter of fact it wasn't quite a set speech because he varied it a little each time to suit the person he was talking to. But I'm not going to write it all down every time. With sensible people like Miss Johnson he went straight to the point, and with some of the others he had to beat about the bush a bit more. But it came to the same in the end.

"Yes, yes, I see what you mean," said Mr. Reiter. "But indeed, I do not see that I can be much help to you. I am new here this season and I did not speak much with Mrs. Leidner. I regret, but indeed I can tell you nothing."

There was something a little stiff and foreign in the way he spoke, though, of course, he hadn't got any accent—except an American one, I mean.

"You can at least tell me whether you liked or disliked her?" said Poirot with a smile.

Mr. Reiter got quite red and stammered:

"She was a charming person—most charming. And intellectual. She had a very fine brain—yes."

"Bien! You liked her. And she liked you?"

Mr. Reiter got redder still.

"Oh, I—I don't know that she noticed me much. And I was unfortunate once or twice. I was always unlucky when I tried to do anything for her. I'm afraid I annoyed her by my clumsiness. It was quite unintentional . . . I would have done *any*thing—"

Poirot took pity on his flounderings.

"Perfectly—perfectly. Let us pass to another matter. Was it a happy atmosphere in the house?"

"Please."

"Were you all happy together? Did you laugh and talk?"

"No—no, not exactly that. There was a little—stiffness."

He paused, struggling with himself, and then said:

"You see, I am not very good in company. I am clumsy. I am shy. Dr. Leidner always he has been most kind to me. But—it is stupid—I cannot overcome my shyness. I say always the wrong thing. I upset water jugs. I am unlucky."

He really looked like a large awkward child.

"We all do these things when we are young," said Poirot, smiling. "The poise, the *savoir faire,* it comes later."

Then with a word of farewell we walked on.

He said:

"That, *ma soeur,* is either an extremely simple young man or a very remarkable actor."

I didn't answer. I was caught up once more by the fantastic notion that one of these people was a dangerous and cold-blooded murderer. Somehow, on this beautiful still sunny morning, it seemed impossible.

21

Mr. Mercado, Richard Carey

"THEY WORK IN two separate places, I see," said Poirot, halting.

Mr. Reiter had been doing his photography on an outlying portion of the main excavation. A little distance away from us a second swarm of men were coming and going with baskets.

"That's what they call the deep cut," I explained. "They don't find much there, nothing but rubbishy broken pottery, but Dr. Leidner always says it's very interesting, so I suppose it must be."

"Let us go there."

We walked together slowly for the sun was hot.

Mr. Mercado was in command. We saw him below us talking to the foreman, an old man like a tortoise who wore a tweed coat over his long striped cotton gown.

It was a little difficult to get down to them as there was only a narrow path or stair and basket boys were going up and down it constantly, and they always seemed to be as blind as bats and never to think of getting out of the way.

As I followed Poirot down he said suddenly over his shoulder:

"Is Mr. Mercado right-handed or left-handed?"

Now that was an extraordinary question if you like!

I thought a minute, then:

"Right-handed," I said decisively.

Poirot didn't condescend to explain. He just went on and I followed him.

Mr. Mercado seemed rather pleased to see us.

His long melancholy face lit up.

M. Poirot pretended to an interest in archaeology that I'm sure he couldn't have really felt, but Mr. Mercado responded at once.

He explained that they had already cut down through twelve levels of house occupation.

"We are now definitely in the fourth millennium," he said with enthusiasm.

I always thought a millennium was in the future—the time when everything comes right.

Mr. Mercado pointed out belts of ashes (how his hand did shake! I wondered if he might possibly have malaria) and he explained how the pottery changed in character, and about burials—and how they had had one level almost entirely composed of infant burials—poor little things—and about flexed position and orientation which seemed to mean the way the bones were lying.

And then suddenly, just as he was stooping down to pick up a kind of flint knife that was lying with some pots in a corner, he leaped into the air with a wild yell.

He spun round to find me and Poirot staring at him in astonishment.

He clapped his hand to his left arm.

"Something stung me—like a red-hot needle."

Immediately Poirot was galvanized into energy.

"Quick, *mon cher,* let us see. Nurse Leatheran!" I came forward.

He seized Mr. Mercado's arm and deftly rolled back the sleeve of his khaki shirt to the shoulder.

"There," said Mr. Mercado, pointing.

About three inches below the shoulder there was a minute prick from which the blood was oozing.

"Curious," said Poirot. He peered into the rolled-up sleeve. "I can see nothing. It was an ant, perhaps?"

"Better put on a little iodine," I said.

I always carry an iodine pencil with me, and I whipped it out and applied it. But I was a little absent-minded as I did so, for my attention had been caught by something quite different. Mr. Mercado's arm, all the way up the forearm to the elbow, was marked all over by tiny punctures. I knew well enough what *they* were—*the marks of a hypodermic needle.*

Mr. Mercado rolled down his sleeve again and recommenced his explanations. Mr. Poirot listened, but didn't try to bring the conversation around to the Leidners. In fact he didn't ask Mr. Mercado anything at all.

Presently we said good-bye to Mr. Mercado and climbed up the path again.

"It was neat that, did you not think so?" my companion asked.

"Neat?" I asked.

M. Poirot took something from behind the lapel of his coat and surveyed it affectionately. To my surprise I saw that it was a long sharp darning needle with a blob of sealing wax making it into a pin.

"M. Poirot," I cried, "did *you* do that?"

"I was the stinging insect—yes. And very neatly I did it, too, do you not think so? You did not see me."

That was true enough. *I* never saw him do it. And I'm sure Mr. Mercado hadn't suspected. He must have been quick as lightning.

"But, M. Poirot, why?" I asked.

He answered me by another question.

"Did you notice anything, sister?" he asked.

I nodded my head slowly.

"Hypodermic marks," I said.

"So now we know something about Mr. Mercado," said Poirot. "I suspected—but I did not *know*. It is always necessary to *know*."

"And you don't care how you set about it!" I thought, but didn't say.

Poirot suddenly clapped his hand to his pocket.

"Alas, I have dropped my handkerchief down there. I concealed the pin in it."

"I'll get it for you," I said and hurried back.

I'd got the feeling, you see, by this time, that M. Poirot and I were the doctor and nurse in charge of a case. At least, it was more like an operation and he was the surgeon. Perhaps I oughtn't to say so, but in a queer way I was beginning to enjoy myself.

I remember just after I'd finished my training, I went to a case in a private house and the need for an immediate operation arose, and the patient's husband was cranky about nursing homes. He just wouldn't hear of his wife being taken to one. Said it had to be done in the house.

Well, of course it was just splendid for me! Nobody else to have a look in! I was in charge of everything. Of course, I was terribly nervous—I thought of everything conceivable that doctor could want, but even then I was afraid I might have forgotten something. You never know with doctors. They ask for absolutely anything sometimes! But everything went splendidly! I had each thing ready as he asked for it, and he actually told me I'd done first rate after it was over—and that's a thing most doctors wouldn't bother to do! The G.P. was very nice too. And I ran the whole thing myself!

The patient recovered, too, so everybody was happy.

Well, I felt rather the same now. In a way M. Poirot reminded me of that surgeon. *He* was a little man, too. Ugly little man with a face like a monkey, but a wonderful surgeon. He knew instinctively just where to go. I've seen a lot of surgeons and I know what a lot of difference there is.

Gradually I'd been growing a kind of confidence in M. Poirot. I felt that he, too, knew exactly what he was doing. And I was getting to feel that it was my job to help him—as you might say—to have the forceps and the swabs and all handy just when he wanted them. That's why it seemed just as natural for me to run off and look for his handkerchief as it would have been to pick up a towel that a doctor had thrown on the floor.

When I'd found it and got back I couldn't see him at first. But at last I caught sight of him. He was sitting a little way from the mound talking to

Mr. Carey. Mr. Carey's boy was standing near with that great big rod thing with meters marked on it, but just at that moment he said something to the boy and the boy took it away. It seemed he had finished with it for the time being.

I'd like to get this next bit quite clear. You see, I wasn't quite sure what M. Poirot did or didn't want me to do. He might, I mean, have sent me back for that handkerchief *on purpose*. To get me out of the way.

It was just like an operation over again. You've got to be careful to hand the doctor just what he wants and not what he *doesn't* want. I mean, suppose you gave him the artery forceps at the wrong moment, and were late with them at the right moment! Thank goodness I know my work in the theater well enough. I'm not likely to make mistakes there. But in this business I was really the rawest of raw little probationers. And so I had to be particularly careful not to make any silly mistakes.

Of course, I didn't for one moment imagine that M. Poirot didn't want me to hear what he and Mr. Carey were saying. But he might have thought he'd get Mr. Carey to talk better if I wasn't there.

Now I don't want anybody to get it into their heads that I'm the kind of woman who goes about eavesdropping on private conversations. I wouldn't do such a thing. Not for a moment. Not however much I wanted to.

And what I mean is if it *had* been a private conversation I wouldn't for a moment have done what, as a matter of fact, I actually did do.

As I looked at it I was in a privileged position. After all, you hear many a thing when a patient's coming round after an anaesthetic. The patient wouldn't want you to hear it—and usually has no idea you *have* heard it—but the fact remains you *do* hear it. I just took it that Mr. Carey was the patient. He'd be none the worse for what he didn't know about. And if you think that I was just curious, well, I'll admit that I *was* curious. I didn't want to miss anything I could help.

All this is just leading up to the fact that I turned aside and went by a roundabout way up behind the big dump until I was a foot from where they were, but concealed from them by the corner of the dump. And if anyone says it was dishonorable I just beg to disagree. *Nothing* ought to be hidden from the nurse in charge of the case, though, of course, it's the doctor to say what shall be *done*.

I don't know, of course, what M. Poirot's line of approach had been, but by the time I'd got there he was aiming straight for the bull's-eye, so to speak.

"Nobody appreciates Dr. Leidner's devotion to his wife more than I do," he was saying. "But it is often the case that one learns more about a person from their enemies than from their friends."

"You suggest that their faults are more important than their virtues?" said Mr. Carey. His tone was dry and ironic.

"Undoubtedly—when it comes to murder. It seems odd that as far as I know nobody has yet been murdered for having too perfect a character! And yet perfection is undoubtedly an irritating thing."

"I'm afraid I'm hardly the right person to help you," said Mr. Carey. "To be perfectly honest, Mrs. Leidner and I didn't hit it off particularly well. I don't mean that we were in any sense of the word enemies, but we were not exactly friends. Mrs. Leidner was, perhaps, a shade jealous of my old friendship with her husband. I, for my part, although I admired her very much and thought she was an extremely attractive woman, was just a shade resentful of her influence over Leidner. As a result we were quite polite to each other, but not intimate."

"Admirably explained," said Poirot.

I could just see their heads, and I saw Mr. Carey's turn sharply as though something in M. Poirot's detached tone struck him disagreeably.

M. Poirot went on:

"Was not Dr. Leidner distressed that you and his wife did not get on together better?"

Carey hesitated a minute before saying:

"Really—I'm not sure. He never said anything. I always hoped he didn't notice it. He was very wrapped up in his work, you know."

"So the truth, according to you, is that you did not really like Mrs. Leidner?"

Carey shrugged his shoulders.

"I should probably have liked her very much if she hadn't been Leidner's wife."

He laughed as though amused by his own statement.

Poirot was arranging a little heap of broken potsherds. He said in a dreamy, far-away voice:

"I talked to Miss Johnson this morning. She admitted that she was prejudiced against Mrs. Leidner and did not like her very much, although she hastened to add that Mrs. Leidner had always been charming to her."

"All quite true, I should say," said Carey.

"So I believed. Then I had a conversation with Mrs. Mercado. She told me at great length how devoted she had been to Mrs. Leidner and how much she had admired her."

Carey made no answer to this, and after waiting a minute or two Poirot went on:

"That—I did not believe! Then I come to you and that which you tell me— well, again—*I do not believe. . . .*"

Carey stiffened. I could hear the anger—repressed anger—in his voice.

"I really cannot help your beliefs—or your disbeliefs, M. Poirot. You've heard the truth and you can take it or leave it as far as I am concerned."

Poirot did not grow angry. Instead he sounded particularly meek and depressed.

"Is it my fault what I do—or do not believe? I have a sensitive ear, you know. And then—there are always plenty of stories going about—rumors floating in the air. One listens—and perhaps—one learns something! Yes, there *are* stories. . . ."

Carey sprang to his feet. I could see clearly a little pulse that beat in his temple. He looked simply splendid! So lean and so brown—and that wonderful jaw, hard and square. I don't wonder women fell for that man.

"What stories?" he asked savagely.

Poirot looked sideways at him.

"Perhaps you can guess. The usual sort of story—about you and Mrs. Leidner."

"What foul minds people have!"

"*N'est-ce pas?* They are like dogs. However deep you bury an unpleasantness a dog will always root it up again."

"And you believe these stories?"

"I am willing to be convinced—of the truth," said Poirot gravely.

"I doubt if you'd know the truth if you heard it," Carey laughed rudely.

"Try me and see," said Poirot, watching him.

"I will then! You shall have the truth! I hated Louise Leidner—there's the truth for you! I hated her like hell!"

22

David Emmott,
Father Lavigny and a Discovery

TURNING ABRUPTLY AWAY, Carey strode off with long angry strides.

Poirot sat looking after him and presently he murmured:

"Yes—I see. . . ."

Without turning his head he said in a slightly louder voice:

"Do not come round the corner for a minute, nurse. In case he turns his head. Now it is all right. You have my handkerchief? Many thanks. You are most amiable."

He didn't say anything at all about my having been listening—and how he knew I *was* listening I can't think. He'd never once looked in that direction. I was rather relieved he didn't say anything. I mean, I felt all right with *myself* about it, but it might have been a little awkward explaining to him. So it was a good thing he didn't seem to want explanations.

"Do you think he did hate her, M. Poirot?" I asked.

Nodding his head slowly with a curious expression on his face, Poirot answered:

"Yes—I think he did."

Then he got up briskly and began to walk to where the men were working on the top of the mound. I followed him. We couldn't see anyone but Arabs at first but we finally found Mr. Emmott lying face downward blowing dust off a skeleton that had just been uncovered.

He gave his pleasant grave smile when he saw us.

"Have you come to see round?" he asked. "I'll be free in a minute."

He sat up, took his knife and began daintily cutting the earth away from around the bones, stopping every now and then to use either a bellows or his own breath. A very unsanitary proceeding the latter, I thought.

"You'll get all sorts of nasty germs in your mouth, Mr. Emmott," I protested.

"Nasty germs are my daily diet, nurse," he said gravely. "Germs can't do anything to an archaeologist—they just get naturally discouraged trying."

He scraped a little more away around the thigh bone. Then he spoke to the foreman at his side directing him exactly what he wanted done.

"There," he said, rising to his feet. "That's ready for Reiter to photograph after lunch. Rather nice stuff she had in with her."

He showed us a little verdigrisy copper bowl and some pins. And a lot of gold and blue things that had been her necklace of beads.

The bones and all the objects were brushed and cleaned with a knife and kept in position ready to be photographed.

"Who is she?" asked Poirot.

"First millennium. A lady of some consequence perhaps. Skull looks rather odd—I must get Mercado to look at it. It suggests death by foul play."

"A Mrs. Leidner of two thousand odd years ago?" said Poirot.

"Perhaps," said Mr. Emmott.

Bill Coleman was doing something with a pick to a wall face.

David Emmott called something to him which I didn't catch and then started showing M. Poirot around.

When the short explanatory tour was over Emmott looked at his watch.

"We knock off in ten minutes," he said. "Shall we walk back to the house?"

"That will suit me excellently," said Poirot.

We walked slowly along the well-worn path.

"I expect you are all glad to get back to work again," said Poirot.

Emmott replied gravely:

"Yes, it's much the best thing. It's not been any too easy loafing about the house and making conversation."

"Knowing all the time *that one of you was a murderer.*"

Emmott did not answer. He made no gesture of dissent. I knew now that he had had a suspicion of the truth from the very first when he had questioned the houseboys.

After a few minutes he asked quietly:

"Are you getting anywhere, M. Poirot?"

Poirot said gravely:

"Will you help me to get somewhere?"

"Why, naturally."

Watching him closely, Poirot said:

"The hub of the case is Mrs. Leidner. I want to know about Mrs. Leidner."

David Emmott said slowly:

"What do you mean by knowing about her?"

"I do not mean where she came from and what her maiden name was. I do not mean the shape of her face and the color of her eyes. I mean her—herself."

"You think that counts in the case?"

"I am quite sure of it."

Emmott was silent for a moment or two, then he said:

"Maybe you're right."

"And that is where you can help me. You can tell me what sort of a woman she was."

"Can I? I've often wondered about it myself."

"Didn't you make up your mind on the subject?"

"I think I did in the end."

"Eh bien?"

But Mr. Emmott was silent for some minutes, then he said:

"What did nurse think of her? Women are said to sum up other women quickly enough, and a nurse has a wide experience of types."

Poirot didn't give me any chance of speaking even if I had wanted to. He said quickly:

"What I want to know is what a *man* thought of her?"

Emmott smiled a little.

"I expect they'd all be much the same." He paused and said, "She wasn't young, but I think she was about the most beautiful woman I've ever come across."

"That's hardly an answer, Mr. Emmott."

"It's not so far off one, M. Poirot."

He was silent a minute or two and then he went on:

"There used to be a fairy story I read when I was a kid. A Northern fairy story about the Snow Queen and Little Kay. I guess Mrs. Leidner was rather like that—always taking Little Kay for a ride."

"Ah, yes, a tale of Hans Andersen, is it not? And there was a girl in it. Little Gerda, was that her name?"

"Maybe. I don't remember much of it."

"Can't you go a little further, Mr. Emmott?"

David Emmott shook his head.

"I don't even know if I've summed her up correctly. She wasn't easy to read. She'd do a devilish thing one day, and a really fine one the next. But I think you're about right when you say that she's the hub of the case. That's what she always wanted to be—*at the center of things.* And she liked to get *at* other people—I mean, she wasn't just satisfied with being passed the toast and the peanut butter, she wanted you to turn your mind and soul inside out for her to look at it."

"And if one did not give her that satisfaction?" asked Poirot.

"Then she could turn ugly!"

I saw his lips close resolutely and his jaws set.

"I suppose, Mr. Emmott, you would not care to express a plain unofficial opinion as to who murdered her?"

"I don't know," said Emmott. "I really haven't the slightest idea. I rather think that, if I'd been Carl—Carl Reiter, I mean—I would have had a shot at murdering her. She was a pretty fair devil to him. But, of course, he asks for it by being so darned sensitive. Just invites you to give him a kick in the pants."

"And did Mrs. Leidner give him—a kick in the pants?" inquired Poirot.

Emmott gave a sudden grin.

"No. Pretty little jabs with an embroidery needle—that was her method. He *was* irritating, of course. Just like some blubbering, poor-spirited kid. But a needle's a painful weapon."

I stole a glance at Poirot and thought I detected a slight quiver of his lips.

"But you don't really believe that Carl Reiter killed her?" he asked.

"No. I don't believe you'd kill a woman because she persistently made you look a fool at every meal."

Poirot shook his head thoughtfully.

Of course, Mr. Emmott made Mrs. Leidner sound quite inhuman. There was something to be said on the other side too.

There had been something terribly irritating about Mr. Reiter's attitude. He jumped when she spoke to him, and did idiotic things like passing her the marmalade again and again when he knew she never ate it. I'd have felt inclined to snap at him a bit myself.

Men don't understand how their mannerisms can get on women's nerves so that you feel you just have to snap.

I thought I'd just mention that to Mr. Poirot sometime.

We had arrived back by now and Mr. Emmott offered Poirot a wash and took him into his room.

I hurried across the courtyard to mine.

I came out again about the same time they did and we were all making for the dining room when Father Lavigny appeared in the doorway of his room and invited Poirot in.

Mr. Emmott came on around and he and I went into the dining room together. Miss Johnson and Mrs. Mercado were there already, and after a few minutes Mr. Mercado, Mr. Reiter and Bill Coleman joined us.

We were just sitting down and Mercado had told the Arab boy to tell Father Lavigny lunch was ready when we were all startled by a faint, muffled cry.

I suppose our nerves weren't very good yet, for we all jumped, and Miss Johnson got quite pale and said:

"*What was that?* What's happened?"

Mrs. Mercado stared at her and said:

"My dear, what *is* the matter with you? It's some noise outside in the fields."

But at that minute Poirot and Father Lavigny came in.

"We thought someone was hurt," Miss Johnson said.

"A thousand pardons, mademoiselle," cried Poirot. "The fault is mine. Father Lavigny, he explains to me some tablets, and I take one to the window to see better—and, *ma foi,* not looking where I was going, I steb the toe, and the pain is sharp for the moment and I cry out."

"We thought it was another murder," said Mrs. Mercado, laughing.

"Marie!" said her husband.

His tone was reproachful and she flushed and bit her lip.

Miss Johnson hastily turned the conversation to the dig and what objects of interest had turned up that morning. Conversation all through lunch was sternly archaeological.

I think we all felt it was the safest thing.

After we had had coffee we adjourned to the living room. Then the men, with the exception of Father Lavigny, went off to the dig again.

Father Lavigny took Poirot through into the antika room and I went with them. I was getting to know the things pretty well by now and I felt a thrill of pride—almost as though it were my own property—when Father Lavigny took down the gold cup and I heard Poirot's exclamation of admiration and pleasure.

"How beautiful! What a work of art!"

Father Lavigny agreed eagerly and began to point out its beauties with real enthusiasm and knowledge.

"No wax on it today," I said.

"Wax?" Poirot stared at me.

"Wax?" So did Father Lavigny.

I explained my remark.

"Ah, *je comprends,*" said Father Lavigny. "Yes, yes, candle grease."

That led direct to the subject of the midnight visitor. Forgetting my presence they both dropped into French and I left them together and went back into the living room.

Mrs. Mercado was darning her husband's socks and Miss Johnson was reading a book. Rather an unusual thing for her. She usually seemed to have something to work at.

After a while Father Lavigny and Poirot came out, and the former excused himself on the score of work. Poirot sat down with us.

"A most interesting man," he said, and asked how much work there had been for Father Lavigny to do so far.

Miss Johnson explained that tablets had been scarce and that there had been very few inscribed bricks or cylinder seals. Father Lavigny, however, had done his share of work on the dig and was picking up colloquial Arabic very fast.

That led the talk to cylinder seals, and presently Miss Johnson fetched from a cupboard a sheet of impressions made by rolling them out on plasticine.

I realized as we bent over them, admiring the spirited designs, that these must be what she had been working at on that fatal afternoon.

As we talked I noticed that Poirot was rolling and kneading a little ball of plasticine between his fingers.

"You use a lot of plasticine, mademoiselle?" he asked.

"A fair amount. We seem to have got through a lot already this year—though I can't imagine how. But half our supply seems to have gone."

"Where is it kept, mademoiselle?"

"Here—in this cupboard."

As she replaced the sheet of impressions she showed him the shelf with rolls of plasticine, Durofix, photographic paste and other stationery supplies.

Poirot stooped down.

"And this—what is this, mademoiselle?"

He had slipped his hand right to the back and had brought out a curious crumpled object.

As he straightened it out we could see that it was a kind of mask, with eyes and mouth crudely painted on in Indian ink and the whole thing roughly smeared with plasticine.

"How perfectly extraordinary," cried Miss Johnson. "I've never seen it before. How did it get there? And what is it?"

"As to how it got there, well, one hiding place is as good as another, and I presume that this cupboard would not have been turned out till the end of the season. As to what it *is*—that, too, I think, is not difficult to say. *We have here the face that Mrs. Leidner described.* The ghostly face seen in the semi-dusk outside her window—without body attached."

Mrs. Mercado gave a little shriek.

Miss Johnson was white to the lips. She murmured:

"Then it was *not* fancy. It was a trick—a wicked trick! But who played it?"

"Yes," cried Mrs. Mercado. "Who could have done such a wicked, wicked thing?"

Poirot did not attempt a reply. His face was very grim as he went into the next room, returned with an empty cardboard box in his hand and put the crumpled mask into it.

"The police must see this," he explained.

"It's horrible," said Miss Johnson in a low voice. "Horrible!"

"Do you think everything's hidden here somewhere?" cried Mrs. Mercado shrilly. "Do you think perhaps the weapon—the club she was killed with—all covered with blood still, perhaps . . . Oh! I'm frightened—I'm frightened . . ."

Miss Johnson gripped her by the shoulder.

"Be quiet," she said fiercely. "Here's Dr. Leidner. We mustn't upset him."

Indeed, at that very moment the car had driven into the courtyard. Dr.

Leidner got out of it and came straight across and in at the living room door. His face was set in lines of fatigue and he looked twice the age he had three days ago.

He said in a quiet voice:

"The funeral will be at eleven o'clock tomorrow. Major Deane will read the service."

Mrs. Mercado faltered something, then slipped out of the room.

Dr. Leidner said to Miss Johnson:

"You'll come, Anne?"

And she answered:

"Of course, my dear, we'll all come. Naturally."

She didn't say anything else, but her face must have expressed what her tongue was powerless to do, for his face lightened up with affection and a momentary ease.

"Dear Anne," he said. "You are such a wonderful comfort and help to me. My dear old friend."

He laid his hand on her arm and I saw the red color creep up in her face as she muttered, gruff as ever:

"That's all right."

But I just caught a glimpse of her expression and knew that, for one short moment, Anne Johnson was a perfectly happy woman.

And another idea flashed across my mind. Perhaps soon, in the natural course of things, turning to his old friend for sympathy, a new and happy state of things might come about.

Not that I'm really a matchmaker, and of course it was indecent to think of such a thing before the funeral even. But after all, it *would* be a happy solution. He was very fond of her, and there was no doubt she was absolutely devoted to him and would be perfectly happy devoting the rest of her life to him. That is, if she could bear to hear Louise's perfections sung all the time. But women can put up with a lot when they've got what they want.

Dr. Leidner then greeted Poirot, asking him if he had made any progress.

Miss Johnson was standing behind Dr. Leidner and she looked hard at the box in Poirot's hand and shook her head, and I realized that she was pleading with Poirot not to tell him about the mask. She felt, I was sure, that he had enough to bear for one day.

Poirot fell in with her wish.

"These things march slowly, monsieur," he said.

Then, after a few desultory words, he took his leave.

I accompanied him out to his car.

There were half a dozen things I wanted to ask him, but somehow, when he turned and looked at me, I didn't ask anything after all. I'd as soon have asked a surgeon if he thought he'd made a good job of an operation. I just stood meekly waiting for instructions.

Rather to my surprise he said:

"Take care of yourself, my child."

And then he added:

"I wonder if it is well for you to remain here?"

"I must speak to Dr. Leidner about leaving," I said. "But I thought I'd wait until after the funeral."

He nodded in approval.

"In the meantime," he said, "do not try and find out too much. You understand, I do not want you to be clever!" And he added with a smile, "It is for you to hold the swabs and for me to do the operation."

Wasn't it funny, his actually saying that?

Then he said quite irrelevantly:

"An interesting man, that Father Lavigny."

"A monk being an archaeologist seems odd to me," I said.

"Ah, yes, you are a Protestant. Me, I am a good Catholic. I know something of priests and monks."

He frowned, seemed to hesitate, then said:

"Remember, he is quite clever enough to turn you inside out if he likes."

If he was warning me against gossiping I felt that I didn't need any such warning!

It annoyed me and though I didn't like to ask him any of the things I really wanted to know, I didn't see why I shouldn't at any rate say one thing.

"You'll excuse me, M. Poirot," I said. "But it's 'stubbed your toe,' not *stepped* or *stebbed*."

"Ah? Thank you, *ma soeur*."

"Don't mention it. But it's just as well to get a phrase right."

"I will remember," he said—quite meekly for him.

And he got in the car and was driven away, and I went slowly back across the courtyard wondering about a lot of things.

About the hypodermic marks on Mr. Mercado's arm, and what drug it was he took. And about that horrid yellow smeared mask. And how odd it was that Poirot and Miss Johnson hadn't heard my cry in the living room that morning, whereas we had all heard Poirot perfectly well in the dining room at lunch time—and yet Father Lavigny's room and Mrs. Leidner's were just the same distance from the living room and the dining room respectively.

And then I felt rather pleased that I'd taught *Doctor* Poirot one English phrase correctly!

Even if he *was* a great detective he'd realize he *didn't* know *everything!*

23

I Go Psychic

THE FUNERAL WAS, I thought, a very affecting affair. As well as ourselves, all the English people in Hassanieh attended it. Even Sheila Reilly was there looking quiet and subdued in a dark coat and skirt. I hoped that she was feeling a little remorseful for all the unkind things she had said.

When we got back to the house I followed Dr. Leidner into the office and broached the subject of my departure. He was very nice about it, thanked me for what I had done (Done! I had been worse than useless) and insisted on my accepting an extra week's salary.

I protested because really I felt I'd done nothing to earn it.

"Indeed, Dr. Leidner, I'd rather not have any salary at all. If you'd just refund me my traveling expenses that's all I want."

But he wouldn't hear of that.

"You see," I said, "I don't feel I deserve it, Dr. Leidner. I mean, I've—well, I've failed. She—my coming didn't save her."

"Now don't get that idea into your head, nurse," he said earnestly. "After all, I didn't engage you as a female detective. I never dreamt my wife's life was in danger. I was convinced it was all nerves and that she'd worked herself up into a rather curious mental state. You did all anyone could do. She liked and trusted you. And I think in her last days she felt happier and safer because of your being here. There's nothing for you to reproach yourself with."

His voice quivered a little and I knew what he was thinking. *He* was the one to blame for not having taken Mrs. Leidner's fears seriously.

"Dr. Leidner," I said curiously. "Have you ever come to any conclusion about those anonymous letters?"

He said with a sigh:

"I don't know what to believe. Has M. Poirot come to any definite conclusion?"

"He hadn't yesterday," I said, steering rather neatly, I thought, between truth and fiction. After all, he hadn't until I told him about Miss Johnson.

It was on my mind that I'd like to give Dr. Leidner a hint and see if he reacted. In the pleasure of seeing him and Miss Johnson together the day before, and his affection and reliance on her, I'd forgotten all about the letters. Even now I felt it was perhaps rather mean of me to bring it up. Even if she had written them, she had had a bad time after Mrs. Leidner's death. Yet I did want to see whether that particular possibility had ever entered Dr. Leidner's head.

"Anonymous letters are usually the work of a woman," I said. I wanted to see how he'd take it.

"I suppose they are," he said with a sigh. "But you seem to forget, nurse, that these may be genuine. They may actually be written by Frederick Bosner."

"No, I haven't forgotten," I said. "But I can't believe somehow that that's the real explanation."

"I do," he said. "It's all nonsense his being one of the expedition staff. That is just an ingenious theory of M. Poirot's. I believe that the truth is much simpler. The man is a madman, of course. He's been hanging round the place —perhaps in disguise of some kind. And somehow or other he got in on that fatal afternoon. The servants may be lying—they may have been bribed."

"I suppose it's possible," I said doubtfully.

Dr. Leidner went on with a trace of irritability.

"It is all very well for M. Poirot to suspect the members of my expedition. I am perfectly certain *none* of them have anything to do with it! I have worked with them. I *know* them!"

He stopped suddenly, then he said:

"Is that your experience, nurse? That anonymous letters are usually written by women?"

"It isn't always the case," I said. "But there's a certain type of feminine spitefulness that finds relief that way."

"I suppose you are thinking of Mrs. Mercado?" he said.

Then he shook his head.

"Even if she were malicious enough to wish to hurt Louise she would hardly have the necessary knowledge," he said.

I remembered the earlier letters in the attaché case.

If Mrs. Leidner had left that unlocked and Mrs. Mercado had been alone in the house one day pottering about, she might easily have found them and read them. Men never seem to think of the simplest possibilities!

"And apart from her there is only Miss Johnson," I said, watching him.

"That would be quite ridiculous!"

The little smile with which he said it was quite conclusive. The idea of Miss Johnson being the author of the letters had never entered his head! I hesitated just for a minute—but I didn't say anything. One doesn't like giving away a fellow woman, and besides, I had been a witness of Miss Johnson's genuine and moving remorse. What was done was done. Why expose Dr. Leidner to a fresh disillusion on top of all his other troubles?

It was arranged that I should leave on the following day, and I had arranged through Dr. Reilly to stay for a day or two with the matron of the hospital whilst I made arrangements for returning to England either via Baghdad or direct via Nissibin by car and train.

Dr. Leidner was kind enough to say that he would like me to choose a memento from among his wife's things.

"Oh, no, really, Dr. Leidner," I said. "I couldn't. It's much too kind of you."

He insisted.

"But I should like you to have something. And Louise, I am sure, would have wished it."

Then he went on to suggest that I should have her tortoiseshell toilet set!

"Oh, no, Dr. Leidner! Why, that's a most *expensive* set. I couldn't, really."

"She had no sisters, you know—no one who wants these things. There is no one else to have them."

I could quite imagine that he wouldn't want them to fall into Mrs. Mercado's greedy little hands. And I didn't think he'd want to offer them to Miss Johnson.

He went on kindly:

"You just think it over. By the way, here is the key of Louise's jewel case. Perhaps you will find something there you would rather have. And I should be very grateful if you would pack up—all—all her clothes. I dare say Reilly can find a use for them amongst some of the poor Christian families in Hassanieh."

I was very glad to be able to do that for him, and I expressed my willingness.

I set about it at once.

Mrs. Leidner had only had a very simple wardrobe with her and it was soon sorted and packed up into a couple of suitcases. All her papers had been in the small attaché case. The jewel case contained a few simple trinkets—a pearl ring, a diamond brooch, a small string of pearls and one or two plain gold bar brooches of the safety pin type, and a string of large amber beads.

Naturally I wasn't going to take the pearls or the diamonds, but I hesitated a bit between the amber beads and the toilet set. In the end, however, I didn't see why I shouldn't take the latter. It was a kindly thought on Dr. Leidner's part, and I was sure there wasn't any patronage about it. I'd take it in the spirit it had been offered without any false pride. After all, I *had* been fond of her.

Well, that was all done and finished with. The suitcases packed, the jewel case locked up again and put separate to give to Dr. Leidner with the photograph of Mrs. Leidner's father and one or two other personal little odds and ends.

The room looked bare and forlorn emptied of all its accoutrements, when I'd finished. There was nothing more for me to do—and yet somehow or other I shrank from leaving the room. It seemed as though there were something still to do there—something I ought to *see*—or something I ought to have *known*.

I'm not superstitious but the idea *did* pop into my head that perhaps Mrs. Leidner's spirit was hanging about the room and trying to get in touch with me.

I remember once at the hospital some of us girls got a planchette and really it wrote some very remarkable things.

Perhaps, although I'd never thought of such a thing, I might be mediumistic.

As I say, one gets all worked up to imagine all sorts of foolishness sometimes.

I prowled around the room uneasily, touching this and that. But, of course, there wasn't anything in the room but bare furniture. There was nothing slipped behind drawers or tucked away. I couldn't hope for anything of that kind.

In the end (it sounds rather batty, but as I say, one gets worked up) I did rather a queer thing.

I went and lay down on the bed and closed my eyes.

I deliberately tried to forget who and what I was. I tried to think myself back to that fatal afternoon. I was Mrs. Leidner lying here resting, peaceful and unsuspicious.

It's extraordinary how you can work yourself up.

I'm a perfectly normal matter-of-fact individual—not the least little bit spooky, but I tell you that after I'd lain there about five minutes I began to *feel* spooky.

I didn't try to resist. I deliberately encouraged the feeling.

I said to myself:

"I'm Mrs. Leidner. I'm Mrs. Leidner. I'm lying here—half asleep. Presently—very soon now—the door's going to open."

I kept on saying that—as though I were hypnotizing myself.

"It's just about half-past one . . . it's just about the time. . . . The door is going to open . . . *the door is going to open.* . . . I shall see who comes in. . . ."

I kept my eyes glued on that door. Presently it was going to open. I should *see* it open. And I should see *the person who opened it.*

I must have been a little overwrought that afternoon to imagine I could solve the mystery that way.

But I did believe it. A sort of chill passed down my back and settled in my legs. They felt numb—paralyzed.

"You're going into a trance," I said. "And in that trance you'll see . . ."

And once again I repeated monotonously again and again:

"The door is going to open—the door is going to open. . . ."

The cold numbed feeling grew more intense.

And then, slowly, *I saw the door just beginning to open.*

It was horrible.

I've never known anything so horrible before or since.

I was paralyzed—chilled through and through. I couldn't move. For the life of me I couldn't have moved.

And I was terrified. Sick and blind and dumb with terror.

That slowly opening door.

So noiseless.

In a minute I should see . . .

Slowly—slowly—wider and wider.

Bill Coleman came quietly in.

He must have had the shock of his life!

I bounded off the bed with a scream of terror and hurled myself across the room.

He stood stock still, his blunt pink face pinker and his mouth opened wide with surprise.

"Hallo-allo-allo," he said. "What's up, nurse?"

I came back to reality with a crash.

"Goodness, Mr. Coleman," I said. "How you startled me!"

"Sorry," he said with a momentary grin.

I saw then that he was holding a little bunch of scarlet ranunculus in his hand. They were pretty little flowers and they grew wild on the sides of the Tell. Mrs. Leidner had been very fond of them.

He blushed and got rather red as he said:

"One can't get any flowers or things in Hassanieh. Seemed rather rotten not to have any flowers for the grave. I thought I'd just nip in here and put a little posy in that little pot thing she always had flowers in on her table. Sort of show she wasn't forgotten—eh? A bit asinine, I know, but—well—I mean to say—"

I thought it was very nice of him. He was all pink with embarrassment like Englishmen are when they've done anything sentimental. I thought it was a very sweet thought.

"Why, I think that's a very nice idea, Mr. Coleman," I said.

And I picked up the little pot and went and got some water in it and we put the flowers in.

I really thought much more of Mr. Coleman for this idea of his. It showed he had a heart and nice feelings about things.

He didn't ask me again what made me let out such a squeal and I'm thankful he didn't. I should have felt a fool explaining.

"Stick to common sense in future, woman," I said to myself as I settled my cuffs and smoothed my apron. "You're not cut out for this psychic stuff."

I bustled about doing my own packing and kept myself busy for the rest of the day.

Father Lavigny was kind enough to express great distress at my leaving. He said my cheerfulness and common sense had been such a help to everybody. Common sense! I'm glad he didn't know about my idiotic behavior in Mrs. Leidner's room.

"We have not seen M. Poirot today," he remarked.

I told him that Poirot had said he was going to be busy all day sending off telegrams.

Father Lavigny raised his eyebrows.

"Telegrams? To America?"

"I suppose so. He said 'All over the world!' but I think that was rather a foreign exaggeration."

And then I got rather red, remembering that Father Lavigny was a foreigner himself.

He didn't seem offended though, just laughed quite pleasantly and asked me if there were any news of the man with the squint.

I said I didn't know but I hadn't heard of any.

Father Lavigny asked me again about the time Mrs. Leidner and I had noticed the man and how he had seemed to be standing on tiptoe and peering through the window.

"It seems clear the man had some overwhelming interest in Mrs. Leidner," he said thoughtfully. "I have wondered since whether the man could possibly have been a European got up to look like an Iraqi?"

That was a new idea to me and I considered it carefully. I had taken it for granted that the man was a native, but of course, when I came to think of it, I was really going by the cut of his clothes and the yellowness of his skin.

Father Lavigny declared his intention of going round outside the house to the place where Mrs. Leidner and I had seen the man standing.

"You never know, he might have dropped something. In the detective stories the criminal always does."

"I expect in real life criminals are more careful," I said.

I fetched some socks I had just finished darning and put them on the table in the living room for the men to sort out when they came in, and then, as there was nothing much more to do, I went up on the roof.

Miss Johnson was standing there but she didn't hear me. I got right up to her before she noticed me.

But long before that I'd seen that there was something very wrong.

She was standing in the middle of the roof staring straight in front of her, and there was the most awful look on her face. As though she'd seen something she couldn't possibly believe.

It gave me quite a shock.

Mind you, I'd seen her upset the other evening, but this was quite different.

"My dear," I said, hurrying to her, "whatever's the matter?"

She turned her head at that and stood looking at me—almost as if she didn't see me.

"What is it?" I persisted.

She made a queer sort of grimace—as though she were trying to swallow but her throat were too dry. She said hoarsely:

"I've just seen something."

"What have you seen? Tell me. Whatever can it be? You look all in."

She gave an effort to pull herself together, but she still looked pretty dreadful.

She said, still in that same dreadful choked voice:

"I've seen how someone could come in from outside—and no one would ever guess."

I followed the direction of her eyes but I couldn't see anything.

Mr. Reiter was standing in the door of the photographic room and Father Lavigny was just crossing the courtyard—but there was nothing else.

I turned back puzzled and found her eyes fixed on mine with the strangest expression in them.

"Really," I said, "I don't see what you mean. Won't you explain?"

But she shook her head.

"Not now. Later. We *ought* to have seen. Oh, we ought to have seen!"

"If you'd only tell me—"

But she shook her head.

"I've got to think it out first."

And pushing past me, she went stumbling down the stairs.

I didn't follow her as she obviously didn't want me with her. Instead I sat down on the parapet and tried to puzzle things out. But I didn't get anywhere. There was only the one way into the courtyard—through the big arch. Just outside it I could see the water boy and his horse and the Indian cook talking to him. Nobody could have passed them and come in without their seeing him.

I shook my head in perplexity and went downstairs again.

24

Murder Is a Habit

WE ALL WENT to bed early that night. Miss Johnson had appeared at dinner and had behaved more or less as usual. She had, however, a sort of dazed look, and once or twice quite failed to take in what other people said to her.

It wasn't somehow a very comfortable sort of meal. You'd say, I suppose, that that was natural enough in a house where there'd been a funeral that day. But I know what I mean.

Lately our meals had been hushed and subdued, but for all that there had been a feeling of comradeship. There had been sympathy with Dr. Leidner in his grief and a fellow feeling of being all in the same boat among the others.

But tonight I was reminded of my first meal there—when Mrs. Mercado had watched me and there had been that curious feeling as though something might snap any minute.

I'd felt the same thing—only very much intensified—when we'd sat around the dining room table with Poirot at the head of it.

Tonight it was particularly strong. Everyone was on edge—jumpy—on tenterhooks. If anyone had dropped something I'm sure somebody would have screamed.

As I say, we all separated early afterward. I went to bed almost at once. The last thing I heard as I was dropping off to sleep was Mrs. Mercado's voice saying good night to Miss Johnson just outside my door.

I dropped off to sleep at once—tired by my exertions and even more by my silly experience in Mrs. Leidner's room. I slept heavily and dreamlessly for several hours.

I awoke when I did awake with a start and a feeling of impending catastrophe. Some sound had woken me, and as I sat up in bed listening I heard it again.

An awful sort of agonized choking groan.

I had lit my candle and was out of bed in a twinkling. I snatched up a torch, too, in case the candle should blow out. I came out of my door and stood listening. I knew the sound wasn't far away. It came again—from the room immediately next to mine—Miss Johnson's room.

I hurried in. Miss Johnson was lying in bed, her whole body contorted in agony. As I set down the candle and bent over her, her lips moved and she tried to speak—but only an awful hoarse whisper came. I saw that the corners of her mouth and the skin of her chin were burnt a kind of grayish white.

Her eyes went from me to a glass that lay on the floor evidently where it had dropped from her hand. The light rug was stained a bright red where it had fallen. I picked it up and ran a finger over the inside, drawing back my hand with a sharp exclamation. Then I examined the inside of the poor woman's mouth.

There wasn't the least doubt what was the matter. Somehow or other, intentionally or otherwise, she'd swallowed a quantity of corrosive acid—oxalic or hydrochloric, I suspected.

I ran out and called to Dr. Leidner and he woke the others, and we worked over her for all we were worth, but all the time I had an awful feeling it was no good. We tried a strong solution of carbonate of soda—and followed it with olive oil. To ease the pain I gave her a hypodermic of morphine sulphate.

David Emmott had gone off to Hassanieh to fetch Dr. Reilly, but before he came it was over.

I won't dwell on the details. Poisoning by a strong solution of hydrochloric acid (which is what it proved to be) is one of the most painful deaths possible.

It was when I was bending over her to give her the morphia that she made one ghastly effort to speak. It was only a horrible strangled whisper when it came.

"The window . . ." she said. *"Nurse . . . the window . . ."*

But that was all—she couldn't go on. She collapsed completely.

I shall never forget that night. The arrival of Dr. Reilly. The arrival of Captain Maitland. And finally with the dawn, Hercule Poirot.

He it was who took me gently by the arm and steered me into the dining room where he made me sit down and have a cup of good strong tea.

"There, *mon enfant,*" he said, "that is better. You are worn out."

Upon that, I burst into tears.

"It's too awful," I sobbed. "It's been like a nightmare. Such awful suffering. And her eyes . . . Oh, M. Poirot—her eyes . . ."

He patted me on the shoulder. A woman couldn't have been kinder.

"Yes, yes—do not think of it. You did all you could."

"It was one of the corrosive acids."

"It was a strong solution of hydrochloric acid."

"The stuff they use on the pots?"

"Yes. Miss Johnson probably drank it off before she was fully awake. That is—unless she took it on purpose."

"Oh, M. Poirot, what an awful idea!"

"It is a possibility, after all. What do you think?"

I considered for a moment and then shook my head decisively.

"I don't believe it. No, I don't believe it for a moment." I hesitated and then said, "I think she found out something yesterday afternoon."

"What is that you say? She found out something?"

I repeated to him the curious conversation we had had together.

Poirot gave a low soft whistle.

"La pauvre femme!" he said. "She said she wanted to think it over—eh? That is what signed her death warrant. If she had only spoken out—then—at once."

He said:

"Tell me again her exact words?"

I repeated them.

"She saw how someone could have come in from outside without any of you knowing? Come, *ma soeur,* let us go up to the roof and you shall show me just where she was standing."

We went up to the roof together and I showed Poirot the exact spot where Miss Johnson had stood.

"Like this?" said Poirot. "Now what do I see? I see half the courtyard— and the archway—and the doors of the drawing-office and the photographic room and the laboratory. Was there anyone in the courtyard?"

"Father Lavigny was just going towards the archway and Mr. Reiter was standing in the door of the photographic room."

"And still I do not see in the least how anyone could come in from outside and none of you know about it. . . . But *she* saw . . ."

He gave it up at last, shaking his head.

"Sacré nom d'un chien—va! What *did* she see?"

The sun was just rising. The whole eastern sky was a riot of rose and orange and pale, pearly gray.

"What a beautiful sunrise," said Poirot gently.

The river wound away to our left and the Tell stood up outlined in gold color. To the south were the blossoming trees and the peaceful cultivation. The waterwheel groaned in the distance—a faint unearthly sound. In the

north were the slender minarets and the clustering fairy whiteness of Hassanieh.

It was all incredibly beautiful.

And then, close at my elbow, I heard Poirot give a long deep sigh.

"Fool that I have been," he murmured. "When the truth is so clear—so
clear."

25

Suicide or Murder?

I HADN'T TIME to ask Poirot what he meant, for Captain Maitland was
calling up to us and asking us to come down.

We hurried down the stairs.

"Look here, Poirot," he said. "Here's another complication. The monk
fellow is missing."

"Father Lavigny?"

"Yes. Nobody noticed it till just now. Then it dawned on somebody that he
was the only one of the party not around, and we went to his room. His bed's
not been slept in and there's no sign of him."

The whole thing was like a bad dream. First Miss Johnson's death and then
the disappearance of Father Lavigny.

The servants were called and questioned, but they couldn't throw any light
on the mystery. He had last been seen at about eight o'clock the night before.
Then he had said he was going out for a stroll before going to bed.

Nobody had seen him come back from that stroll.

The big doors had been closed and barred at nine o'clock as usual. Nobody,
however, remembered unbarring them in the morning. The two houseboys
each thought the other one must have done the unfastening.

Had Father Lavigny ever returned the night before? Had he, in the course
of his earlier walk, discovered anything of a suspicious nature, gone out to
investigate it later, and perhaps fallen a third victim?

Captain Maitland swung round as Dr. Reilly came up with Mr. Mercado
behind him.

"Hallo, Reilly. Got anything?"

"Yes. The stuff came from the laboratory here. I've just been checking up
the quantities with Mercado. It's H.C.L. from the lab."

"The laboratory—eh? Was it locked up?"

Mr. Mercado shook his head. His hands were shaking and his face was twitching. He looked a wreck of a man.

"It's never been the custom," he stammered. "You see—just now—we're using it all the time. I—nobody ever dreamt—"

"Is the place locked up at night?"

"Yes—all the rooms are locked. The keys are hung up just inside the living room."

"So if anyone had a key to that they could get the lot."

"Yes."

"And it's a perfectly ordinary key, I suppose?"

"Oh, yes."

"Nothing to show whether she took it herself from the laboratory?" asked Captain Maitland.

"She didn't," I said loudly and positively.

I felt a warning touch on my arm. Poirot was standing close behind me.

And then something rather ghastly happened.

Not ghastly in itself—in fact it was just the incongruousness that made it seem worse than anything else.

A car drove into the courtyard and a little man jumped out. He was wearing a sun helmet and a short thick trench coat.

He came straight to Dr. Leidner, who was standing by Dr. Reilly, and shook him warmly by the hand.

"*Vous voilà, mon cher,*" he cried. "Delighted to see you. I passed this way on Saturday afternoon—en route to the Italians at Fugima. I went to the dig but there wasn't a single European about and alas! I cannot speak Arabic. I had not time to come to the house. This morning I leave Fugima at five—two hours here with you—and then I catch the convoy on. *Eh bien,* and how is the season going?"

It was ghastly.

The cheery voice, the matter-of-fact manner, all the pleasant sanity of an everyday world now left far behind. He just bustled in, knowing nothing and noticing nothing—full of cheerful bonhomie.

No wonder Dr. Leidner gave an inarticulate gasp and looked in mute appeal at Dr. Reilly.

The doctor rose to the occasion.

He took the little man (he was a French archaeologist called Verrier who dug in the Greek islands, I heard later) aside and explained to him what had occurred.

Verrier was horrified. He himself had been staying at an Italian dig right away from civilization for the last few days and had heard nothing.

He was profuse in condolences and apologies, finally striding over to Dr. Leidner and clasping him warmly by both hands.

"What a tragedy! My God, what a tragedy! I have no words. *Mon pauvre collègue.*"

And shaking his head in one last ineffectual effort to express his feelings, the little man climbed into his car and left us.

As I say, that momentary introduction of comic relief into tragedy seemed really more gruesome than anything else that had happened.

"The next thing," said Dr. Reilly firmly, "is breakfast. Yes, I insist. Come, Leidner, you must eat."

Poor Dr. Leidner was almost a complete wreck. He came with us to the dining room and there a funereal meal was served. I think the hot coffee and fried eggs did us all good, though no one actually felt they wanted to eat. Dr. Leidner drank some coffee and sat twiddling his bread. His face was gray, drawn with pain and bewilderment.

After breakfast, Captain Maitland got down to things.

I explained how I had woken up, heard a queer sound and had gone into Miss Johnson's room.

"You say there was a glass on the floor?"

"Yes. She must have dropped it after drinking."

"Was it broken?"

"No, it had fallen on the rug. (I'm afraid the acid's ruined the rug, by the way.) I picked the glass up and put it back on the table."

"I'm glad you've told us that. There are only two sets of fingerprints on it, and one set is certainly Miss Johnson's own. The other must be yours."

He was silent for a moment, then he said:

"Please go on."

I described carefully what I'd done and the methods I had tried, looking rather anxiously at Dr. Reilly for approval. He gave it with a nod.

"You tried everything that could possibly have done any good," he said. And though I was pretty sure I had done so, it was a relief to have my belief confirmed.

"Did you know exactly what she had taken?" Captain Maitland asked.

"No—but I could see, of course, that it was a corrosive acid."

Captain Maitland asked gravely:

"Is it your opinion, nurse, that Miss Johnson deliberately administered this stuff to herself?"

"Oh, no," I exclaimed. "I never thought of such a thing!"

I don't know why I was so sure. Partly, I think, because of M. Poirot's hints. His "murder is a habit" had impressed itself on my mind. And then one doesn't readily believe that anyone's going to commit suicide in such a terribly painful way.

I said as much and Captain Maitland nodded thoughtfully.

"I agree that it isn't what one would choose," he said. "But if anyone were in great distress of mind and this stuff were easily available it might be taken for that reason."

"*Was* she in great distress of mind?" I asked doubtfully.

"Mrs. Mercado says so. She says that Miss Johnson was quite unlike herself at dinner last night—that she hardly replied to anything that was said to her. Mrs. Mercado is quite sure that Miss Johnson was in terrible distress over something and that the idea of making away with herself had already occurred to her."

"Well, I don't believe it for a moment," I said bluntly.

Mrs. Mercado indeed! Nasty slinking little cat!

"Then what *do* you think?"

"I think she was murdered," I said bluntly.

He rapped out his next question sharply. I felt rather that I was in the orderly room.

"Any reasons?"

"It seems to me by far and away the most possible solution."

"That's just your private opinion. There was no reason why the lady should be murdered?"

"Excuse me," I said, "there was. She found out something."

"Found out something? What did she find out?"

I repeated our conversation on the roof word for word.

"She refused to tell you what her discovery was?"

"Yes. She said she must have time to think it over."

"But she was very excited by it?"

"Yes."

"*A way of getting in from outside.*" Captain Maitland puzzled over it, his brows knit. "Had you no idea at all of what she was driving at?"

"Not in the least. I puzzled and puzzled over it but I couldn't even get a glimmering."

Captain Maitland said:

"What do you think, M. Poirot?"

Poirot said:

"I think you have there a possible motive."

"For murder?"

"For murder."

Captain Maitland frowned.

"She wasn't able to speak before she died?"

"Yes, she just managed to get out two words."

"What were they?"

"*The window . . .*"

"The window?" repeated Captain Maitland. "Did you understand to what she was referring?"

I shook my head.

"How many windows were there in her bedroom?"

"Just the one."

"Giving on the courtyard?"

"Yes."

"Was it open or shut? Open, I seem to remember. But perhaps one of you opened it?"

"No, it was open all the time. I wondered—"

I stopped.

"Go on, nurse."

"I examined the window, of course, but I couldn't see anything unusual about it. I wondered whether, perhaps, somebody changed the glasses that way."

"Changed the glasses?"

"Yes. You see, Miss Johnson always takes a glass of water to bed with her. I think that glass must have been tampered with and a glass of acid put there in its place."

"What do you say, Reilly?"

"If it's murder, that was probably the way it was done," said Dr. Reilly promptly. "No ordinary moderately observant human being would drink a glass of acid in mistake for one of water—if they were in full possession of their waking faculties. But if anyone's accustomed to drinking off a glass of water in the middle of the night, that person might easily stretch out an arm, find the glass in the accustomed place, and still half asleep, toss off enough of the stuff to be fatal before realizing what had happened."

Captain Maitland reflected a minute.

"I'll have to go back and look at that window. How far is it from the head of the bed?"

I thought.

"With a very long stretch you could just reach the little table that stands by the head of the bed."

"The table on which the glass of water was?"

"Yes."

"Was the door locked?"

"No."

"So whoever it was could have come in that way and made the substitution?"

"Oh, yes."

"There would be more risk that way," said Dr. Reilly. "A person who is sleeping quite soundly will often wake up at the sound of a footfall. If the table could be reached from the window it would be the safer way."

"I'm not only thinking of the glass," said Captain Maitland absentmindedly.

Rousing himself, he addressed me once again.

"It's your opinion that when the poor lady felt she was dying she was anxious to let you know that somebody had substituted acid for water through the open window? Surely the person's *name* would have been more to the point?"

"She mayn't have known the name," I pointed out.

"Or it would have been more to the point if she'd managed to hint what it was that she had discovered the day before?"

Dr. Reilly said:

"When you're dying, Maitland, you haven't always got a sense of proportion. One particular fact very likely obsesses your mind. That a murderous hand had come through the window may have been the principal fact obsessing her at the minute. It may have seemed to her important that she should let people know that. In my opinion she wasn't far wrong either. It *was* important! She probably jumped to the fact that you'd think it was suicide. If she could have used her tongue freely, she'd probably have said 'It wasn't suicide. I didn't take it myself. Somebody else must have put it near my bed *through the window.*' "

Captain Maitland drummed with his fingers for a minute or two without replying. Then he said:

"There are certainly two ways of looking at it. It's either suicide or murder. Which do you think, Dr. Leidner?"

Dr. Leidner was silent for a minute or two, then he said quietly and decisively:

"Murder. Anne Johnson wasn't the sort of woman to kill herself."

"No," allowed Captain Maitland. "Not in the normal run of things. But there might be circumstances in which it would be quite a natural thing to do."

"Such as?"

Captain Maitland stooped to a bundle which I had previously noticed him place by the side of his chair. He swung it onto the table with something of an effort.

"There's something here that none of you know about," he said. "We found it under her bed."

He fumbled with the knot of the covering, then threw it back revealing a heavy great quern or grinder.

That was nothing in itself—there were a dozen or so already found in the course of the excavations.

What riveted our attention on this particular specimen was a dull, dark stain and a fragment of something that looked like hair.

"That'll be your job, Reilly," said Captain Maitland. "But I shouldn't say that there's much doubt about this being the instrument with which Mrs. Leidner was killed!"

26

Next It Will Be Me!

IT WAS RATHER horrible. Dr. Leidner looked as though he were going to faint and I felt a bit sick myself.

Dr. Reilly examined it with professional gusto.

"No fingerprints, I presume?" he threw out.

"No fingerprints."

Dr. Reilly took out a pair of forceps and investigated delicately.

"H'm—a fragment of human tissue—and hair—fair blond hair. That's the unofficial verdict. Of course, I'll have to make a proper test, blood group, etc., but there's not much doubt. Found under Miss Johnson's bed? Well, well—so *that's* the big idea. She did the murder, and then, God rest her, remorse came to her and she finished herself off. It's a theory—a pretty theory."

Dr. Leidner could only shake his head helplessly.

"Not Anne—not Anne," he murmured.

"I don't know where she hid this to begin with," said Captain Maitland. "Every room was searched after the first crime."

Something jumped into my mind and I thought, "In the stationery cupboard," but I didn't say anything.

"Wherever it was, she became dissatisfied with its hiding place and took it into her own room, which had been searched with all the rest. Or perhaps she did that after making up her mind to commit suicide."

"I don't believe it," I said aloud.

And I couldn't somehow believe that kind nice Miss Johnson had battered out Mrs. Leidner's brains. I just couldn't *see* it happening! And yet it *did* fit in with some things—her fit of weeping that night, for instance. After all, I'd said "remorse" myself—only I'd never thought it was remorse for anything but the smaller more insignificant crime.

"I don't know what to believe," said Captain Maitland. "There's the French Father's disappearance to be cleared up too. My men are out hunting around in case he's been knocked on the head and his body rolled into a convenient irrigation ditch."

"Oh! I remember now—" I began.

Everyone looked toward me inquiringly.

"It was yesterday afternoon," I said. "He'd been cross-questioning me about the man with a squint who was looking in at the window that day. He asked me just where he'd stood on the path and then he said he was going out to have a look round. He said in detective stories the criminal always dropped a convenient clue."

"Damned if any of my criminals ever do," said Captain Maitland. "So that's what he was after, was it? By jove, I wonder if he *did* find anything. A bit of a coincidence if both he and Miss Johnson discovered a clue to the identity of the murderer at practically the same time."

He added irritably, "Man with a squint? Man with a squint? There's more in this tale of that fellow with a squint than meets the eye. I don't know why the devil my fellows can't lay hold of him?"

"Probably because he hasn't got a squint," said Poirot quietly.

"Do you mean he faked it? Didn't know you could fake an actual squint."

Poirot merely said:

"A squint can be a very useful thing."

"The devil it can! I'd give a lot to know where that fellow is now, squint or no squint!"

"At a guess," said Poirot, "he has already passed the Syrian frontier."

"We've warned Tell Kotchek and Abu Kemal—all the frontier posts, in fact."

"I should imagine that he took the route through the hills. The route lorries sometimes take when running contraband."

Captain Maitland grunted.

"Then we'd better telegraph Deir ez Zor?"

"I did so yesterday—warning them to look out for a car with two men in it whose passports will be in the most impeccable order."

Captain Maitland favored him with a stare.

"*You* did, did you? Two men—eh?"

Poirot nodded.

"There are two men in this."

"It strikes me, M. Poirot, that you've been keeping quite a lot of things up your sleeve."

Poirot shook his head.

"No," he said. "Not really. The truth came to me only this morning when I was watching the sun rise. A very beautiful sunrise."

I don't think that any of us had noticed that Mrs. Mercado was in the room. She must have crept in when we were all taken aback by the production of that horrible great bloodstained stone.

But now, without the least warning, she set up a noise like a pig having its throat cut.

"Oh, my God!" she cried. "I see it all. I see it all now. *It was Father Lavigny.* He's mad—religious mania. He thinks women are sinful. *He's killing them all.* First Mrs. Leidner—then Miss Johnson. And next it will be *me. . . .*"

With a scream of frenzy she flung herself across the room and clutched at Dr. Reilly's coat.

"I won't stay here, I tell you! I won't stay here a day longer. There's danger. There's danger all round. He's hiding somewhere—waiting his time. He'll spring out on me!"

Her mouth opened and she began screaming again.

I hurried over to Dr. Reilly, who had caught her by the wrists. I gave her a sharp slap on each cheek and with Dr. Reilly's help, I sat her down in a chair.

"Nobody's going to kill you," I said. "We'll see to that. Sit down and behave yourself."

She didn't scream anymore. Her mouth closed and she sat looking at me with startled, stupid eyes.

Then there was another interruption. The door opened and Sheila Reilly came in.

Her face was pale and serious. She came straight to Poirot.

"I was at the post office early, M. Poirot," she said, "and there was a telegram there for you—so I brought it along."

"Thank you, mademoiselle."

He took it from her and tore it open while she watched his face.

It did not change, that face. He read the telegram, smoothed it out, folded it up neatly and put it in his pocket.

Mrs. Mercado was watching him. She said in a choked voice:

"Is that—from America?"

He shook his head.

"No, madame," he said. "It is from Tunis."

She stared at him for a moment as though she did not understand, then with a long sigh, she leaned back in her seat.

"Father Lavigny," she said. "I *was* right. I've always thought there was something queer about him. He said things to me once . . . I suppose he's mad. . . ." She paused and then said, "I'll be quiet. But I *must* leave this place. Joseph and I can go in and sleep at the Rest House."

"Patience, madame," said Poirot. "I will explain everything."

Captain Maitland was looking at him curiously.

"Do you consider you've definitely got the hang of this business?" he demanded.

Poirot bowed.

It was a most theatrical bow. I think it rather annoyed Captain Maitland.

"Well," he barked. "Out with it, man."

But that wasn't the way Hercule Poirot did things. I saw perfectly well that he meant to make a song and dance of it. I wondered if he really *did* know the truth, or if he was just showing off.

He turned to Dr. Reilly.

"Will you be so good, Dr. Reilly, as to summon the others?"

Dr. Reilly jumped up and went off obligingly. In a minute or two the other members of the expedition began to file into the room. First Reiter and Emmott. Then Bill Coleman. Then Richard Carey and finally Mr. Mercado.

Poor man, he really looked like death. I suppose he was mortally afraid that he'd get hauled over the coals for carelessness in leaving dangerous chemicals about.

Everyone seated themselves around the table very much as we had done on the day M. Poirot arrived. Both Bill Coleman and David Emmott hesitated before they sat down, glancing toward Sheila Reilly. She had her back to them and was standing looking out of the window.

"Chair, Sheila?" said Bill.

David Emmott said in his low pleasant drawl, "Won't you sit down?"

She turned then and stood for a minute looking at them. Each was indicating a chair, pushing it forward. I wondered whose chair she would accept.

In the end she accepted neither.

"I'll sit here," she said brusquely. And she sat down on the edge of a table quite close to the window.

"That is," she added, "if Captain Maitland doesn't mind my staying?"

I'm not quite sure what Captain Maitland would have said. Poirot forestalled him.

"Stay by all means, mademoiselle," he said. "It is, indeed, necessary that you should."

She raised her eyebrows.

"Necessary?"

"That is the word I used, mademoiselle. There are some questions I shall have to ask you."

Again her eyebrows went up but she said nothing further. She turned her face to the window as though determined to ignore what went on in the room behind her.

"And now," said Captain Maitland, "perhaps we shall get at the truth!"

He spoke rather impatiently. He was essentially a man of action. At this very moment I feel sure that he was fretting to be out and doing things—directing the search for Father Lavigny's body, or alternatively sending out parties for his capture and arrest.

He looked at Poirot with something akin to dislike.

"If the beggar's got anything to say, why doesn't he say it?"

I could see the words on the tip of his tongue.

Poirot gave a slow appraising glance at us all, then rose to his feet.

I don't know what I expected him to say—something dramatic certainly. He was that kind of person.

But I certainly didn't expect him to start off with a phrase in Arabic.

Yet that is what happened. He said the words slowly and solemnly—and really quite religiously, if you know what I mean.

"Bismillahi ar rahman ar rahim."

And then he gave the translation in English.

"In the name of Allah, the Merciful, the Compassionate."

27

Beginning of a Journey

"BISMILLAHI AR RAHMAN ar rahim. That is the Arab phrase used before starting out on a journey. *Eh bien,* we too, start on a journey. A journey into the past. A journey into the strange places of the human soul."

I don't think that up till that moment I'd ever felt any of the so-called "glamour of the East." Frankly, what had struck me was the *mess* everywhere. But suddenly, with M. Poirot's words, a queer sort of vision seemed to grow up before my eyes. I thought of words like Samarkand and Ispahan—and of merchants with long beards—and kneeling camels—and staggering porters carrying great bales on their backs held by a rope around the forehead—and women with henna-stained hair and tattooed faces kneeling by the Tigris and washing clothes, and I heard their queer, wailing chants and the far-off groaning of the waterwheel. . . .

They were mostly things I'd seen and heard and thought nothing much of. But now, somehow they seemed *different*—like a piece of fusty old stuff you take into the light and suddenly see the rich colors of an old embroidery. . . .

Then I looked around the room we were sitting in and I got a queer feeling that what M. Poirot said was true—we *were* all starting on a journey. We were here together now, but we were all going our different ways.

And I looked at everyone as though, in a sort of way, I were seeing them for the first time—*and* for the last time—which sounds stupid, but it was what I felt all the same.

Mr. Mercado was twisting his fingers nervously—his queer light eyes with their dilated pupils were staring at Poirot. Mrs. Mercado was looking at her husband. She had a strange watchful look like a tigress waiting to spring. Dr. Leidner seemed to have shrunk in some curious fashion. This last blow had just crumpled him up. You might almost say he wasn't in the room at all. He was somewhere far away in a place of his own. Mr. Coleman was looking straight at Poirot. His mouth was slightly open and his eyes protruded. He looked almost idiotic. Mr. Emmott was looking down at his feet and I couldn't see his face properly. Mr. Reiter looked bewildered. His mouth was pushed out in a pout and that made him look more like a nice clean pig than ever. Miss Reilly was looking steadily out of the window. I don't know what she was thinking or feeling. Then I looked at Mr. Carey, and somehow his face hurt me and I looked away. There we were, all of us. And somehow I felt that when M. Poirot had finished we'd all be somewhere quite different. . . .

It was a queer feeling. . . .

Poirot's voice went quietly on. It was like a river running evenly between its banks . . . running to the sea. . . .

"From the very beginning, I have felt that to understand this case one must seek not for external signs or clues, but for the truer clues of the clash of personalities and the secrets of the heart.

"And I may say that though I have now arrived at what I believe to be the true solution of the case, *I have no material proof of it.* I *know* it is so, because it *must* be so, because *in no other way* can every single fact fit into its ordered and recognized place.

"And that, to my mind, is the most satisfying solution there can be."

He paused and then went on:

"I will start my journey at the moment when I myself was brought into the case—when I had it presented to me as an accomplished happening. Now, every case, in my opinion, has a definite *shape* and *form.* The pattern of this case, to my mind, all revolved round the personality of Mrs. Leidner. Until I knew *exactly what kind of a woman Mrs. Leidner was* I should not be able to know why she was murdered and who murdered her.

"That, then, was my starting point—the personality of Mrs. Leidner.

"There was also one other psychological point of interest—the curious state of tension described as existing amongst the members of the expedition. This was attested to by several different witnesses—some of them outsiders— and I made a note that although hardly a starting point, it should neverthe- less be borne in mind during my investigations.

"The accepted idea seemed to be that it was directly the result of Mrs. Leidner's influence on the members of the expedition, but for reasons which I will outline to you later this did not seem to me entirely acceptable.

"To start with, as I say, I concentrated solely and entirely on the personal- ity of Mrs. Leidner. I had various means of assessing that personality. There were the reactions she produced in a number of people, all varying widely in character and temperament, and there was what I could glean by my own observation. The scope of the latter was naturally limited. But I *did* learn certain facts.

"Mrs. Leidner's tastes were simple and even on the austere side. She was clearly not a luxurious woman. On the other hand, some embroidery she had been doing was of an extreme fineness and beauty. That indicated a woman of fastidious and artistic taste. From the observation of the books in her bed- room I formed a further estimate. She had brains, and I also fancied that she was, essentially, an egoist.

"It had been suggested to me that Mrs. Leidner was a woman whose main preoccupation was to attract the opposite sex—that she was, in fact, a sensual woman. This I did not believe to be the case.

"In her bedroom I noticed the following books on a shelf: *Who Were the Greeks? Introduction to Relativity, Life of Lady Hester Stanhope, Back to Methuselah, Linda Condon, Crewe Train.*

"She had, to begin with, an interest in culture and in modern science—that is, a distinct intellectual side. Of the novels *Linda Condon,* and in a lesser degree *Crewe Train,* seemed to show that Mrs. Leidner had a sympathy and interest in the independent woman—unencumbered or entrapped by man. She was also obviously interested by the personality of Lady Hester Stanhope. *Linda Condon* is an exquisite study of the worship of her own beauty by a woman. *Crewe Train* is a study of a passionate individualist. *Back to Methuselah* is in sympathy with the intellectual rather than the emotional attitude to life. I felt that I was beginning to understand the dead woman.

"I next studied the reactions of those who had formed Mrs. Leidner's immediate circle—and my picture of the dead woman grew more and more complete.

"It was quite clear to me from the accounts of Dr. Reilly and others that Mrs. Leidner was one of those women who are endowed by Nature not only with beauty but with the kind of calamitous magic which sometimes accompanies beauty and can, indeed, exist independently of it. Such women usually leave a trail of violent happenings behind them. They bring disaster—sometimes on others—sometimes on themselves.

"I was convinced that Mrs. Leidner was a woman who essentially worshipped *herself* and who enjoyed more than anything else the sense of *power.* Wherever she was, she *must* be the center of the universe. And everyone round her, man or woman, had got to acknowledge her sway. With some people that was easy. Nurse Leatheran, for instance, a generous-natured woman with a romantic imagination, was captured instantly and gave in ungrudging manner full appreciation. But there was a second way in which Mrs. Leidner exercised her sway—the way of fear. Where conquest was too easy she indulged a more cruel side to her nature—but I wish to reiterate emphatically that it was not what you might call *conscious* cruelty. It was as natural and unthinking as is the conduct of a cat with a mouse. Where consciousness came in, she was essentially kind and would often go out of her way to do kind and thoughtful actions for other people.

"Now of course the first and most important problem to solve was the problem of the anonymous letters. Who had written them and why? I asked myself: Had Mrs. Leidner written them *herself?*

"To answer this problem it was necessary to go back a long way—to go back, in fact, to the date of Mrs. Leidner's first marriage. It is here we start on our journey proper. The journey of Mrs. Leidner's life.

"First of all we must realize that the Louise Leidner of all those years ago is essentially the same Louise Leidner of the present time.

"She was young then, of remarkable beauty—that same haunting beauty that affects a man's spirit and senses as no mere material beauty can—and she was already essentially an egoist.

"Such women naturally revolt from the idea of marriage. They may be attracted by men, but they prefer to belong to themselves. They are truly *La Belle Dame sans Merci* of the legend. Nevertheless Mrs. Leidner *did* marry—

and we can assume, I think, that her husband must have been a man of a certain force of character.

"Then the revelation of his traitorous activities occurs and Mrs. Leidner acts in the way she told Nurse Leatheran. She gave information to the Government.

"Now I submit that there was a psychological significance in her action. She told Nurse Leatheran that she was a very patriotic idealistic girl and that that feeling was the cause of her action. But it is a well-known fact that we all tend to deceive ourselves as to the motives for our own actions. Instinctively we select the best-sounding motive! Mrs. Leidner may have believed herself that it was patriotism that inspired her action, but I believe myself that it was really the outcome of an unacknowledged desire to get rid of her husband! She disliked domination—she disliked the feeling of belonging to someone else—in fact she disliked playing second fiddle. She took a patriotic way of regaining her freedom.

"But underneath her consciousness was a gnawing sense of guilt which was to play its part in her future destiny.

"We now come directly to the question of the letters. Mrs. Leidner was highly attractive to the male sex. On several occasions she was attracted by them—but in each case a threatening letter played its part and the affair came to nothing.

"Who wrote those letters? Frederick Bosner or his brother William or *Mrs. Leidner herself?*

"There is a perfectly good case for either theory. It seems clear to me that Mrs. Leidner was one of those women who do inspire devouring devotions in men, the type of devotion which can become an obsession. I find it quite possible to believe in a Frederick Bosner to whom Louise, his wife, mattered more than anything in the world! She had betrayed him once and he dared not approach her openly, but he was determined at least that she should be his or no one's. He preferred her death to her belonging to another man.

"On the other hand, if Mrs. Leidner had, deep down, a dislike of entering into the marriage bond, it is possible that she took this way of extricating herself from difficult positions. She was a huntress who, the prey once attained, had no further use for it! Craving drama in her life, she invented a highly satisfactory drama—a resurrected husband forbidding the banns! It satisfied her deepest instincts. It made her a romantic figure, a tragic heroine, and it enabled her not to marry again.

"This state of affairs continued over a number of years. Every time there was any likelihood of marriage—a threatening letter arrived.

"*But now we come to a really interesting point.* Dr. Leidner came upon the scene—and no forbidding letter arrived! Nothing stood in the way of her becoming Mrs. Leidner. Not until *after* her marriage did a letter arrive.

"At once we ask ourselves—why?

"Let us take each theory in turn.

"*If* Mrs. Leidner wrote the letters herself the problem is easily explained.

Mrs. Leidner really *wanted* to marry Dr. Leidner. And so she *did* marry him. But in that case, *why did she write herself a letter afterwards?* Was her craving for drama too strong to be suppressed? And why only those two letters? After that no other letter was received until a year and a half later.

"Now take the other theory, that the letters were written by her first husband, Frederick Bosner (or his brother). Why did the threatening letter arrive *after* the marriage? Presumably Frederick could not have *wanted* her to marry Leidner. Why, then, did he not stop the marriage? He had done so successfully on former occasions. And why, *having waited till the marriage had taken place,* did he then resume his threats?

"The answer, an unsatisfactory one, is that he was somehow or other unable to protest sooner. He may have been in prison or he may have been abroad.

"There is next the attempted gas poisoning to consider. It seems extremely unlikely that it was brought about by an outside agency. The likely persons to have staged it were Dr. and Mrs. Leidner themselves. There seems no conceivable reason why *Dr.* Leidner should do such a thing, so we are brought to the conclusion that *Mrs.* Leidner planned and carried it out herself.

"Why? More drama?

"After that Dr. and Mrs. Leidner go abroad and for eighteen months they lead a happy, peaceful life with no threats of death to disturb it. They put that down to having successfully covered their traces, but such an explanation is quite absurd. In these days going abroad is quite inadequate for that purpose. And especially was that so in the case of the Leidners. He was the director of a museum expedition. By inquiry at the museum, Frederick Bosner could at once have obtained his correct address. Even granting that he was in too reduced circumstances to pursue the couple himself, there would be no bar to his continuing his threatening letters. And it seems to me that a man with his obsession would certainly have done so.

"Instead nothing is heard of him until nearly two years later when the letters are resumed.

"*Why* were the letters resumed?

"A very difficult question—most easily answered by saying that Mrs. Leidner was bored and wanted more drama. But I was not quite satisfied with that. This particular form of drama seemed to me a shade too vulgar and too crude to accord well with her fastidious personality.

"The only thing to do was to keep an open mind on the question.

"There were three definite possibilities: (1) the letters were written by Mrs. Leidner herself; (2) they were written by Frederick Bosner (or young William Bosner); (3) they might have been written *originally* by either Mrs. Leidner or her first husband, but they were now *forgeries*—that is, they were being written by a *third* person who was aware of the earlier letters.

"I now come to direct consideration of Mrs. Leidner's entourage.

"I examined first the actual opportunities that each member of the staff had had for committing the murder.

"Roughly, on the face of it, *anyone* might have committed it (as far as opportunity went), with the exception of three persons.

"Dr. Leidner, by overwhelming testimony, had never left the roof. Mr. Carey was on duty at the mound. Mr. Coleman was in Hassanieh.

"But those alibis, my friends, were not *quite* as good as they looked. I except Dr. Leidner's. There is absolutely no doubt that he was on the roof all the time and did not come down until quite an hour and a quarter after the murder had happened.

"But was it *quite* certain that Mr. Carey was on the mound all the time?

"And had Mr. Coleman *actually been in Hassanieh* at the time the murder took place?"

Bill Coleman reddened, opened his mouth, shut it and looked around uneasily.

Mr. Carey's expression did not change.

Poirot went on smoothly.

"I also considered one other person who, I satisfied myself, would be perfectly capable of committing murder *if she felt strongly enough.* Miss Reilly has courage and brains and a certain quality of ruthlessness. When Miss Reilly was speaking to me on the subject of the dead woman, I said to her, jokingly, that I hoped she had an alibi. I think Miss Reilly was conscious then that she had had in her heart the desire, at least, to kill. At any rate she immediately uttered a very silly and purposeless lie. She said she had been playing tennis on that afternoon. The next day I learned from a casual conversation with Miss Johnson that far from playing tennis, Miss Reilly *had actually been near this house at the time of the murder.* It occurred to me that Miss Reilly, if not guilty of the crime, might be able to tell me something useful."

He stopped and then said quietly:

"Will you tell us, Miss Reilly, what you *did* see that afternoon?"

The girl did not answer at once. She still looked out of the window without turning her head, and when she spoke it was in a detached and measured voice.

"I rode out to the dig after lunch. It must have been about a quarter to two when I got there."

"Did you find any of your friends on the dig?"

"No, there seemed to be no one there but the Arab foreman."

"You did not see Mr. Carey?"

"No."

"Curious," said Poirot. "No more did M. Verrier when he went there that same afternoon."

He looked invitingly at Carey, but the latter neither moved nor spoke.

"Have you any explanation, Mr. Carey?"

"I went for a walk. There was nothing of interest turning up."

"In which direction did you go for a walk?"

"Down by the river."

"Not back towards the house?"

"No."

"I suppose," said Miss Reilly, "that you were waiting for someone who didn't come."

He looked at her but didn't answer.

Poirot did not press the point. He spoke once more to the girl.

"Did you see anything else, mademoiselle?"

"Yes. I was not far from the expedition house when I noticed the expedition lorry drawn up in a wadi. I thought it was rather queer. Then I saw Mr. Coleman. He was walking along with his head down as though he were searching for something."

"Look here," burst out Mr. Coleman. "I—"

Poirot stopped him with an authoritative gesture.

"Wait. Did you speak to him, Miss Reilly?"

"No, I didn't."

"Why?"

The girl said slowly:

"Because, from time to time, he started and looked round with an extraordinary furtive look. It—gave me an unpleasant feeling. I turned my horse's head and rode away. I don't think he saw me. I was not very near and he was absorbed in what he was doing."

"Look here," Mr. Coleman was not to be hushed any longer. "I've got a perfectly good explanation for what—I admit—looks a bit fishy. As a matter of fact, the day before I had slipped a jolly fine cylinder seal into my coat pocket instead of putting it in the antika room—forgot all about it. And then I discovered I'd been and lost it out of my pocket—dropped it somewhere. I didn't want to get into a row about it so I decided I'd have a jolly good search on the quiet. I was pretty sure I'd dropped it on the way to or from the dig. I rushed over my business in Hassanieh. Sent a walad to do some of the shopping and got back early. I stuck the bus where it wouldn't show and had a jolly good hunt for over an hour. And didn't find the damned thing at that! Then I got into the bus and drove on to the house. Naturally, everyone thought I'd just got back."

"And you did not undeceive them?" asked Poirot sweetly.

"Well, that was pretty natural under the circumstances, don't you think?"

"I hardly agree," said Poirot.

"Oh, come now—don't go looking for trouble—that's *my* motto! But you can't fasten anything on me. I never went into the courtyard, and you can't find anyone who'll say I did."

"That, of course, has been the difficulty," said Poirot. "The evidence of the servants that *no one entered the courtyard from outside*. But it occurred to me, upon reflection, that that was really *not* what they had said. They had sworn that *no stranger* had entered the premises. They had not been asked *if a member of the expedition* had done so."

"Well, you ask them," said Coleman. "I'll eat my hat if they saw me or Carey either."

"Ah! but that raises rather an interesting question. They would notice *a stranger* undoubtedly—but would they have even *noticed* a member of the expedition? The members of the staff are passing in and out all day. The servants would hardly notice their going and coming. It is possible, I think, that either Mr. Carey or Mr. Coleman *might* have entered and the servants' minds would have no remembrance of such an event."

"Bunkum!" said Mr. Coleman.

Poirot went on calmly:

"Of the two, I think Mr. Carey was the least likely to be noticed going or coming. Mr. Coleman had started to Hassanieh in the car that morning and he would be expected to return in it. His arrival on foot would therefore be noticeable."

"Of course it would!" said Coleman.

Richard Carey raised his head. His deep-blue eyes looked straight at Poirot.

"Are you accusing me of murder, M. Poirot?" he asked.

His manner was quite quiet but his voice had a dangerous undertone.

Poirot bowed to him.

"As yet I am only taking you all on a journey—my journey towards the truth. I had now established one fact—that all the members of the expedition staff, and also Nurse Leatheran, could in actual *fact* have committed the murder. That there was very little likelihood of some of them having committed it was a secondary matter.

"I had examined *means* and *opportunity*. I next passed to *motive*. I discovered that *one and all of you could be credited with a motive!*"

"Oh! M. Poirot," I cried. "Not *me!* Why, I was a stranger. I'd only just come."

"*Eh bien, ma soeur,* and was not that *just what Mrs. Leidner had been fearing?* A *stranger* from *outside?*"

"But—but— Why, Dr. Reilly knew all about me! He suggested my coming!"

"How much did he really know about you? *Mostly what you yourself had told him.* Impostors have passed themselves off as hospital nurses before now."

"You can write to St. Christopher's," I began.

"For the moment will you silence yourself. Impossible to proceed while you conduct this argument. I do not say I suspect you *now.* All I say is that, keeping the open mind, you might quite easily be someone other than you pretended to be. There are many successful female impersonators, you know. Young William Bosner might be something of that kind."

I was about to give him a further piece of my mind. Female impersonator indeed! But he raised his voice and hurried on with such an air of determination that I thought better of it.

"I am going now to be frank—brutally so. It is necessary. I am going to lay bare the underlying structure of this place.

"I examined and considered every single soul here. To begin with Dr. Leidner, I soon convinced myself that his love for his wife was the mainspring of his existence. He was a man torn and ravaged with grief. Nurse Leatheran I have already mentioned. If she were a female impersonator she was a most amazingly successful one, and I inclined to the belief that she was exactly what she said she was—a thoroughly competent hospital nurse."

"Thank you for nothing," I interposed.

"My attention was immediately attracted towards Mr. and Mrs. Mercado, who were both of them clearly in a state of great agitation and unrest. I considered first Mrs. Mercado. Was she capable of murder and if so for what reasons?

"Mrs. Mercado's physique was frail. At first sight it did not seem possible that she could have had the physical strength to strike down a woman like Mrs. Leidner with a heavy stone implement. If, however, Mrs. Leidner had been on her knees at the time, the thing would at least be *physically possible*. There are ways in which one woman can induce another to go down on her knees. Oh! not emotional ways! For instance, a woman might be turning up the hem of a skirt and ask another woman to put in the pins for her. The second woman would kneel on the ground quite unsuspectingly.

"But the motive? Nurse Leatheran had told me of the angry glances she had seen Mrs. Mercado direct at Mrs. Leidner. Mr. Mercado had evidently succumbed easily to Mrs. Leidner's spell. But I did not think the solution was to be found in mere jealousy. I was sure Mrs. Leidner was not in the least interested really in Mr. Mercado—and doubtless Mrs. Mercado was aware of the fact. She might be furious with her for the moment, but for *murder* there would have to be greater provocation. But Mrs. Mercado was essentially a fiercely maternal type. From the way she looked at her husband I realized, not only that she loved him, but that she would fight for him tooth and nail— and more than that—*that she envisaged the possibility of having to do so.* She was constantly on her guard and uneasy. The uneasiness was for him—not for herself. And when I studied Mr. Mercado I could make a fairly easy guess at what the trouble was. I took means to assure myself of the truth of my guess. Mr. Mercado was a drug addict—in an advanced stage of the craving.

"Now I need probably not tell you all that the taking of drugs over a long period of time has the result of considerably blunting the moral sense.

"Under the influence of drugs a man commits actions that he would not have dreamed of committing a few years earlier before he began the practice. In some cases a man has committed murder—and it has been difficult to say whether he was wholly responsible for his actions or not. The law of different countries varies slightly on that point. The chief characteristic of the drug-fiend criminal is overweening confidence in his own cleverness.

"I thought it possible that there was some discreditable incident, perhaps a criminal incident, in Mr. Mercado's past which his wife had somehow or other succeeded in hushing up. Nevertheless his career hung on a thread. If anything of this past incident were bruited about, Mr. Mercado would be ruined. His wife was always on the watch. But there was Mrs. Leidner to be reckoned with. She had a sharp intelligence and a love of power. She might even induce the wretched man to confide in her. It would just have suited her peculiar temperament to feel she knew a secret which she could reveal at any minute with disastrous effects.

"Here, then, was a possible motive for murder on the part of the Mercados. To protect her mate, Mrs. Mercado, I felt sure, would stick at nothing! Both she and her husband had had the opportunity—during that ten minutes when the courtyard was empty."

Mrs. Mercado cried out, "It's not *true!*"

Poirot paid no attention.

"I next considered Miss Johnson. Was *she* capable of murder?

"I thought she was. She was a person of strong will and iron self-control. Such people are constantly repressing themselves—and one day the dam bursts! But if Miss Johnson had committed the crime it could only be for some reason connected with Dr. Leidner. If in any way she felt convinced that Mrs. Leidner was spoiling her husband's life, then the deep unacknowledged jealousy far down in her would leap at the chance of a plausible motive and give itself full rein.

"Yes, Miss Johnson was distinctly a possibility.

"Then there were the three young men.

"First Carl Reiter. If, by any chance, one of the expedition staff was William Bosner, then Reiter was by far the most likely person. But if he *was* William Bosner, then he was certainly a most accomplished actor! If he were merely *himself,* had he any reason for murder?

"Regarded from Mrs. Leidner's point of view, Carl Reiter was far too easy a victim for good sport. He was prepared to fall on his face and worship immediately. Mrs. Leidner despised undiscriminating adoration—and the doormat attitude nearly always brings out the worst side of a woman. In her treatment of Carl Reiter Mrs. Leidner displayed really deliberate cruelty. She inserted a gibe here—a prick there. She made the poor young man's life a hell to him."

Poirot broke off suddenly and addressed the young man in a personal, highly confidential manner.

"*Mon ami,* let this be a lesson to you. You are a *man.* Behave, then, like a *man!* It is against Nature for a man to grovel. Women and Nature have almost exactly the same reactions! Remember it is better to take the largest plate within reach and fling it at a woman's head than it is to wriggle like a worm whenever she looks at you!"

He dropped his private manner and reverted to his lecture style.

"Could Carl Reiter have been goaded to such a pitch of torment that he turned on his tormentor and killed her? Suffering does queer things to a man. I could not be *sure* that it was *not* so!

"Next, William Coleman. His behavior, as reported by Miss Reilly, is certainly suspicious. If he was the criminal it could only be because his cheerful personality concealed the hidden one of William Bosner. I do not think William Coleman, as William Coleman, has the temperament of a murderer. His faults might lie in another direction. Ah! perhaps Nurse Leatheran can guess what they would be?"

How *did* the man do it? I'm sure I didn't look as though I was thinking anything at all.

"It's nothing really," I said, hesitating. "Only if it's to be all truth, Mr. Coleman *did* say once himself that he would have made a good forger."

"A good point," said Poirot. "Therefore if he had come across some of the old threatening letters, he could have copied them without difficulty."

"Oy, oy, oy!" called out Mr. Coleman. "This is what they call a frame-up."

Poirot swept on.

"As to his being or not being William Bosner such a matter is difficult of verification. But Mr. Coleman has spoken of a *guardian*—not of a father— and there is nothing definitely to veto the idea."

"Tommyrot," said Mr. Coleman. "Why all of you listen to this chap beats me."

"Of the three young men there remains Mr. Emmott," went on Poirot. "He again might be a possible shield for the identity of William Bosner. Whatever *personal* reasons he might have for the removal of Mrs. Leidner I soon realized that I should have no means of learning them from him. He could keep his own counsel remarkably well, and there was not the least chance of provoking him nor of tricking him into betraying himself on any point. Of all the expedition he seemed to be the best and most dispassionate judge of Mrs. Leidner's personality. I think that he always knew her for exactly what she was—but what impression her personality made on him I was unable to discover. I fancy that Mrs. Leidner herself must have been provoked and angered by his attitude.

"I may say that of all the expedition, *as far as character and capability were concerned,* Mr. Emmott seemed to me the most fitted to bring a clever and well-timed crime off satisfactorily."

For the first time Mr. Emmott raised his eyes from the toes of his boots.

"Thank you," he said.

There seemed to be just a trace of amusement in his voice.

"The last two people on my list were Richard Carey and Father Lavigny.

"According to the testimony of Nurse Leatheran and others, Mr. Carey and Mrs. Leidner disliked each other. They were both civil with an effort. Another person, Miss Reilly, propounded a totally different theory to account for their attitude of frigid politeness.

"I soon had very little doubt that Miss Reilly's explanation was the correct one. I acquired my certitude by the simple expedient of provoking Mr. Carey into reckless and unguarded speech. It was not difficult. As I soon saw, he was in a state of high nervous tension. In fact he was—and is—very near a complete nervous breakdown. A man who is suffering up to the limit of his capacity can seldom put up much of a fight.

"Mr. Carey's barriers came down almost immediately. He told me, with a sincerity that I did not for a moment doubt, that he hated Mrs. Leidner.

"And he was undoubtedly speaking the truth. He *did* hate Mrs. Leidner. But *why* did he hate her?

"I have spoken of women who have a calamitous magic. But men have that magic too. There are men who are able without the least effort to attract women. What they call in these days *le sex appeal!* Mr. Carey had this quality very strongly. He was to begin with devoted to his friend and employer, and indifferent to his employer's wife. That did not suit Mrs. Leidner. She *must* dominate—and she set herself out to capture Richard Carey. But here, I believe, something entirely unforeseen took place. She herself, for perhaps the first time in her life, fell a victim to an overmastering passion. She fell in love —really in love—with Richard Carey.

"And he—was unable to resist her. Here is the truth of the terrible state of nervous tension that he has been enduring. He has been a man torn by two opposing passions. He loved Louise Leidner—yes, but he also hated her. He hated her for undermining his loyalty to his friend. There is no hatred so great as that of a man who has been made to love a woman against his will.

"I had here all the motive that I needed. I was convinced that *at certain moments* the most natural thing for Richard Carey to do would have been to strike with all the force of his arm at the beautiful face that had cast a spell over him.

"All along I had felt sure that the murder of Louise Leidner was a *crime passionnel.* In Mr. Carey I had found an ideal murderer for that type of crime.

"There remains one other candidate for the title of murderer—Father Lavigny. My attention was attracted to the good Father straightaway by a certain discrepancy between his description of the strange man who had been seen peering in at the window and the one given by Nurse Leatheran. In all accounts given by different witnesses there is usually *some* discrepancy, but this was absolutely glaring. Moreover, Father Lavigny insisted on a certain characteristic—a squint—which ought to make identification much easier.

"But very soon it became apparent that *while Nurse Leatheran's description was substantially accurate,* Father Lavigny's was *nothing of the kind.* It looked almost as though Father Lavigny was deliberately misleading us—as though he did *not want the man caught.*

"But in that case *he must know something about this curious person.* He had been seen talking to the man but we had only his word for what they had been talking about.

"What had the Iraqi been doing when Nurse Leatheran and Mrs. Leidner saw him? Trying to peer through the window—Mrs. Leidner's window, so they thought, but I realized when I went and stood where they had been, that it might equally have been *the antika room window.*

"The night after that an alarm was given. Someone was in the antika room. Nothing proved to have been taken, however. The interesting point to me is that when Dr. Leidner got there he found *Father Lavigny there before him.* Father Lavigny tells his story of seeing a light. *But again we have only his word for it.*

"I begin to get curious about Father Lavigny. The other day when I make the suggestion that Father Lavigny may be Frederick Bosner Dr. Leidner pooh-poohs the suggestion. He says Father Lavigny is a well-known man. I advance the supposition that Frederick Bosner, who has had nearly twenty years to make a career for himself, under a new name, may very possibly *be* a well-known man by this time! All the same, I do not think that he has spent the intervening time in a religious community. A very much simpler solution presents itself.

"Did anyone at the expedition know Father Lavigny by sight before he came? Apparently not. Why then should not it be *someone impersonating the good Father?* I found out that a telegram had been sent to Carthage on the sudden illness of Dr. Byrd, who was to have accompanied the expedition. To intercept a telegram, what could be easier? As to the work, there was no other epigraphist attached to the expedition. With a smattering of knowledge a clever man *might* bluff his way through. There had been very few tablets and inscriptions so far, and already I gathered that Father Lavigny's pronouncements had been felt to be somewhat unusual.

"It looked very much as though Father Lavigny were an *impostor.*

"But was he Frederick Bosner?

"Somehow affairs did not seem to be shaping themselves that way. The truth seemed likely to lie in quite a different direction.

"I had a lengthy conversation with Father Lavigny. I am a practicing Catholic and I know many priests and members of religious communities. Father Lavigny struck me as not ringing quite true to his role. But he struck me, on the other hand, as familiar in quite a different capacity. I *had* met men of his type quite frequently—but they were not members of a religious community. Far from it!

"I began to send off telegrams.

"And then, unwittingly, Nurse Leatheran gave me a valuable clue. We were examining the gold ornaments in the antika room and she mentioned a trace of wax having been found adhering to a gold cup. Me, I say, 'Wax?' and Father Lavigny, he said 'Wax?' and his tone was enough! I knew in a flash exactly what he was doing here."

Poirot paused and addressed himself directly to Dr. Leidner.

"I regret to tell you, monsieur, that the gold cup in the antika room, the gold dagger, the hair ornaments and several other things *are not the genuine articles found by you.* They are very clever electrotypes. Father Lavigny, I have just learned by this last answer to my telegrams, is none other than Raoul Menier, one of the cleverest thieves known to the French police. He specializes in thefts from museums of *objets d'art* and such like. Associated with him is Ali Yusuf, a semi-Turk, who is a first-class working jeweller. Our first knowledge of Menier was when certain objects in the Louvre were found not to be genuine—in every case it was discovered that a distinguished archaeologist *not known previously by sight to the director* had recently had the handling of the spurious articles when paying a visit to the Louvre. On inquiry all these distinguished gentlemen denied having paid a visit to the Louvre at the times stated!

"I have learned that Menier was in Tunis preparing the way for a theft from the Holy Fathers when your telegram arrived. Father Lavigny, who was in ill health, was forced to refuse, but Menier managed to get hold of the telegram and substitute one of acceptance. He was quite safe in doing so. Even if the monks should read in some paper (in itself an unlikely thing) that Father Lavigny was in Iraq they would only think that the newspapers had got hold of a half truth as so often happens.

"Menier and his accomplice arrived. The latter is seen when he is reconnoitering the antika room from outside. The plan is for Father Lavigny to take wax impressions. Ali then makes clever duplicates. There are always certain collectors who are willing to pay a good price for genuine antiques and will ask no embarrassing questions. Father Lavigny will effect the substitution of the fake for the genuine article—preferably at night.

"And that is doubtless what he was doing when Mrs. Leidner heard him and gave the alarm. What can he do? He hurriedly makes up a story of having seen a light in the antika room.

"That 'went down,' as you say, very well. But Mrs. Leidner was no fool. She may have remembered the trace of wax she had noticed and then put two and two together. And if she did, what will she do then? Would it not be *dans son caractère* to do nothing at once, but to enjoy herself by letting hints slip to the discomfiture of Father Lavigny. She will let him see that she suspects— but not that she *knows.* It is, perhaps, a dangerous game, but she enjoys a dangerous game.

"And perhaps she plays that game too long. Father Lavigny sees the truth, and strikes before she realizes what he means to do.

"Father Lavigny is Raoul Menier—a thief. Is he also—a *murderer?*"

Poirot paced the room. He took out a handkerchief, wiped his forehead and went on:

"That was my position this morning. There were eight distinct possibilities and I did not know which of these possibilities was the right one. I still did not know *who was the murderer.*

"But murder is a habit. The man or woman who kills once will kill again.

"And by the second murder, the murderer was delivered into my hands.

"All along it was ever present in the back of my mind that someone of these people might have knowledge that they had kept back—knowledge incriminating the murderer.

"If so, that person would be in danger.

"My solicitude was mainly on account of Nurse Leatheran. She had an energetic personality and a brisk inquisitive mind. I was terrified of her finding out more than it was safe for her to know.

"As you all know, a second murder did take place. But the victim was not Nurse Leatheran—it was Miss Johnson.

"I like to think that I should have reached the correct solution anyway by pure reasoning, but it is certain that Miss Johnson's murder helped me to it much quicker.

"To begin with, one suspect was eliminated—Miss Johnson herself—for I did not for a moment entertain the theory of suicide.

"Let us examine now the facts of this second murder.

"Fact one: On Sunday evening Nurse Leatheran finds Miss Johnson in tears, and that same evening Miss Johnson burns a fragment of a letter which nurse believes to be in the same handwriting as that of the anonymous letters.

"Fact two: The evening before her death Miss Johnson is found by Nurse Leatheran standing on the roof in a state that nurse describes as one of incredulous horror. When nurse questions her she says, 'I've seen how someone could come in from outside—and no one would ever guess.' She won't say anymore. Father Lavigny is crossing the courtyard and Mr. Reiter is at the door of the photographic room.

"Fact three: Miss Johnson is found dying. The only words she can manage to articulate are 'the window—the window—'

"Those are the facts, and these are the problems with which we are faced:
"What is the truth of the letters?
"What did Miss Johnson see from the roof?
"What did she mean by 'the window—the window'?

"*Eh bien,* let us take the second problem first as the easiest of solution. I went up with Nurse Leatheran and I stood where Miss Johnson had stood. From there she could see the courtyard and the archway and the north side of the building and two members of the staff. Had her words anything to do with either Mr. Reiter or Father Lavigny?

"Almost at once a possible explanation leaped to my brain. If a stranger came in from *outside* he could only do so in *disguise.* And there was only *one* person whose general appearance lent itself to such an impersonation. Father Lavigny! With a sun helmet, sunglasses, black beard and a monk's long woollen robe, a stranger could pass in without the servants *realizing* that a stranger had entered.

"Was *that* Miss Johnson's meaning? Or had she gone further? Did she realize that Father Lavigny's whole *personality* was a disguise. That he was someone other than he pretended to be?

"Knowing what I did know about Father Lavigny I was inclined to call the mystery solved. Raoul Menier was the murderer. He had killed Mrs. Leidner to silence her before she could give him away. Now *another person lets him see that she has penetrated his secret.* She, too, must be removed.

"And so everything is explained! The second murder. Father Lavigny's flight—minus robe and beard. (He and his friend are doubtless careering through Syria with excellent passports as two commercial travelers.) His action in placing the blood-stained quern under Miss Johnson's bed.

"As I say, I was almost satisfied—but not quite. For the perfect solution must explain *everything*—and this does not do so.

"It does not explain, for instance, why Miss Johnson should say 'the window—the window,' as she was dying. It does not explain her fit of weeping over the letter. It does not explain her mental attitude on the roof—her incredulous horror and her refusal to tell Nurse Leatheran what it was that *she now suspected or knew.*

"It was a solution that fitted the *outer* facts, but it did not satisfy the *psychological* requirements.

"And then, as I stood on the roof, going over in my mind those three points: the letters, the roof, the window, I *saw*—just as Miss Johnson had seen!

"And this time what I saw explained everything!"

28

Journey's End

POIROT LOOKED AROUND. Every eye was now fixed upon him. There had been a certain relaxation—a slackening of tension. Now the tension suddenly returned.

There was something coming . . . something . . .

Poirot's voice, quiet and unimpassioned, went on:

"The letters, the roof, 'the window' . . . Yes, everything was explained—everything fell into place.

"I said just now that three men had alibis for the time of the crime. Two of those alibis I have shown to be worthless. I saw now my great—my amazing mistake. The third alibi was worthless too. Not only *could* Dr. Leidner have committed the murder—but I was convinced that he *had* committed it."

There was a silence, a bewildered uncomprehending silence. Dr. Leidner said nothing. He seemed lost in his faraway world still. David Emmott, however, stirred uneasily and spoke.

"I don't know what you mean to imply, M. Poirot. I told you that Dr. Leidner never left the roof until at least a quarter to three. That is the absolute truth. I swear it solemnly. I am not lying. And it would have been quite impossible for him to have done so without my seeing him."

Poirot nodded.

"Oh, I believe you. *Dr. Leidner did not leave the roof.* That is an undisputed fact. But what I saw—and what Miss Johnson had seen—was *that Dr. Leidner could murder his wife from the roof without leaving it.*"

We all stared.

"The *window,*" cried Poirot. *"Her* window! That is what I realized—just as Miss Johnson realized it. Her window was directly underneath, on the side away from the courtyard. And Dr. Leidner was alone up there with no one to witness his actions. And those heavy stone querns and grinders were up there all ready to his hand. So simple, so very simple, granted one thing—*that the murderer had the opportunity to move the body before anyone else saw it. . . .* Oh, it is beautiful—of an unbelievable simplicity!

"Listen—it went like this:

"Dr. Leidner is on the roof working with the pottery. He calls you up, Mr. Emmott, and while he holds you in talk he notices that, as usually happens, the small boy takes advantage of your absence to leave his work and go outside the courtyard. He keeps you with him ten minutes, then he lets you go and as soon as you are down below shouting to the boy he sets his plan in operation.

"He takes from his pocket the plasticine-smeared mask with which he has already scared his wife on a former occasion and dangles it over the edge of the parapet till it taps on his wife's window.

"That, remember, is the window giving on the countryside facing the opposite direction to the courtyard.

"Mrs. Leidner is lying on her bed half asleep. She is peaceful and happy. Suddenly the mask begins tapping on the window and attracts her attention. But it is not dusk now—it is broad daylight—there is nothing terrifying about it. She recognizes it for what it is—a crude form of trickery! She is not frightened but indignant. She does what any other woman would do in her place. Jumps off the bed, opens the window, passes her head through the bars and turns her face upwards to see who is playing the trick on her.

"Dr. Leidner is waiting. He has in his hands, poised and ready, a heavy quern. At the psychological moment *he drops it. . . .*

"With a faint cry (heard by Miss Johnson) Mrs. Leidner collapses on the rug underneath the window.

"Now there is a hole in this quern, and through that Dr. Leidner had previously passed a cord. He has now only to haul in the cord and bring up the quern. He replaces the latter neatly, bloodstained side down, amongst the other objects of that kind on the roof.

"Then he continues his work for an hour or more till he judges the moment has come for the second act. He descends the stairs, speaks to Mr. Emmott and Nurse Leatheran, crosses the courtyard and enters his wife's room. This is the explanation he himself gives of his movements there.

" *'I saw my wife's body in a heap by the bed. For a moment or two I felt paralyzed as though I couldn't move. Then at last I went and knelt down by her and lifted up her head. I saw she was dead. . . . At last I got up. I felt dazed and as though I were drunk. I managed to get to the door and call out.'*

"A perfectly possible account of the actions of a grief-dazed man. Now listen to what I believe to be the truth. Dr. Leidner enters the room, hurries to the window, and having pulled on a pair of gloves, closes and fastens it, then picks up his wife's body and transports it to a position between the bed and the door. Then he notices a slight stain on the window-side rug. He cannot change it with the other rug, they are a different size, but he does the next best thing. He puts the stained rug in front of the washstand and the rug from the washstand under the window. *If* the stain is noticed, it will be connected with the *washstand*—not with the *window*—a very important point. There must be no suggestion that the window played any part in the business. Then he comes to the door and acts the part of the overcome husband, and that, I imagine, is not difficult. For he *did* love his wife."

"My good man," cried Dr. Reilly impatiently, "if he loved her, why did he kill her? Where's the motive? Can't you speak, Leidner? Tell him he's mad."

Dr. Leidner neither spoke nor moved.

Poirot said:

"Did I not tell you all along that this was a *crime passionnel?* Why did her first husband, Frederick Bosner, threaten to kill her? Because he loved her. . . . And in the end, you see, he made his boast good. . . .

"Mais oui—mais oui—once I realize that it is Dr. Leidner who did the killing everything falls into place. . . .

"For the second time I recommence my journey from the beginning—Mrs. Leidner's first marriage—the threatening letters—her second marriage. The letters prevented her marrying any other man—but they did not prevent her marrying Dr. Leidner. How simple that is—*if Dr. Leidner is actually Frederick Bosner.*

"Once more let us start our journey—from the point of view this time of young Frederick Bosner.

"To begin with he loves his wife Louise with an overpowering passion such as only a woman of her kind can evoke. She betrays him. He is sentenced to death. He escapes. He is involved in a railway accident but he manages to emerge with a second personality—*that of a young Swedish archaeologist, Eric Leidner,* whose body is badly disfigured and who will be conveniently buried as Frederick Bosner.

"What is the new Eric Leidner's attitude to the woman who was willing to send him to his death? First and most important, *he still loves her.* He sets to work to build up his new life. He is a man of great ability, his profession is congenial to him and he makes a success of it. *But he never forgets the ruling passion of his life.* He keeps himself informed of his wife's movements. Of one thing he is coldbloodedly determined (remember Mrs. Leidner's own description of him to Nurse Leatheran—gentle and kind but ruthless), *she shall belong to no other man.* Whenever he judges it necessary he despatches a letter. He imitates some of the peculiarities of her handwriting in case she should think of taking his letters to the police. Women who write sensational anonymous letters to themselves are such a common phenomenon that the police will be sure to jump to that solution given the likeness of the handwriting. At the same time he leaves her in doubt as to whether he is really alive or not.

"At last, after many years, he judges that the time has arrived; he reenters her life. All goes well. His wife never dreams of his real identity. He is a well-known man. The upstanding, good-looking young fellow is now a middle-aged man with a beard and stooping shoulders. And so we see history repeating itself. As before, Frederick is able to dominate Louise. For the second time she consents to marry him. *And no letter comes to forbid the banns.*

"But *afterwards* a letter *does* come. Why?

"I think that Dr. Leidner was taking no chances. The intimacy of marriage *might* awaken a memory. He wishes to impress on his wife, once and for all, *that Eric Leidner and Frederick Bosner are two* different people. So much so that a threatening letter comes from the former on account of the latter. The rather puerile gas poisoning business follows—arranged by Dr. Leidner, of course. Still with the same object in view.

"After that he is satisfied. No more letters need come. They can settle down to happy married life together.

"And then, after nearly two years, *the letters recommence.*

"*Why? Eh bien,* I think I know. *Because the threat underlying the letters was always a genuine threat.* (That is why Mrs. Leidner has always been frightened. She *knew* her Frederick's gentle but ruthless nature.) *If she belongs to any other man but him he would kill her. And she has given herself to Richard Carey.*

"And so, having discovered this, cold-bloodedly, calmly, Dr. Leidner prepares the scene for murder.

"You see now the important part played by Nurse Leatheran? Dr. Leidner's rather curious conduct (it puzzled me at the very first) in securing her services for his wife is explained. It was vital that a reliable professional witness should be able to state incontrovertibly that Mrs. Leidner had been dead *over an hour* when her body was found—that is, that she had been killed at a time when *everybody could swear her husband was on the roof.* A suspicion *might* have arisen that he had killed her when he entered the room and found the body—but that was out of the question when a trained hospital nurse would assert positively that she had already been dead an hour.

"Another thing that is explained is the curious state of tension and strain that had come over the expedition this year. I never from the first thought that that could be attributed solely to *Mrs.* Leidner's influence. For several years this particular expedition had had a reputation for happy good-fellowship. In my opinion the state of mind of a community is always directly due to the influence of the man at the top. Dr. Leidner, quiet though he was, was a man of great personality. It was due to his tact, to his judgment, to his sympathetic manipulation of human beings that the atmosphere had always been such a happy one.

"If there was a change, therefore, the change must be due to the man at the top—in other words, to Dr. Leidner. It was *Dr.* Leidner, not Mrs. Leidner, who was responsible for the tension and uneasiness. No wonder the staff felt the change without understanding it. The kindly genial Dr. Leidner, outwardly the same, was only playing the part of himself. The real man was an obsessed fanatic plotting to kill.

"And now we will pass on to the second murder—that of Miss Johnson. In tidying up Dr. Leidner's papers in the office (a job she took on herself unasked, craving for something to do) she must have come on some unfinished draft of one of the anonymous letters.

"It must have been both incomprehensible and extremely upsetting to her! Dr. Leidner has been deliberately terrorizing his wife! She cannot understand it—but it upsets her badly. It is in this mood that Nurse Leatheran discovers her crying.

"I do not think at the moment that she suspected Dr. Leidner of being the murderer, but my experiments with sounds in Mrs. Leidner's and Father Lavigny's rooms are not lost upon her. She realizes that if it *was* Mrs. Leidner's cry she heard, *the window in her room must have been open, not shut.* At the moment that conveys nothing vital to her, *but she remembers it.*

"Her mind goes on working—ferreting its way towards the truth. Perhaps she makes some reference to the letters which Dr. Leidner understands and his manner changes. She may see that he is, suddenly, afraid.

"But Dr. Leidner *cannot* have killed his wife! He was on the *roof* all the time.

"And then, one evening, as she herself is on the roof puzzling about it, the truth comes to her in a flash. Mrs. Leidner has been killed from up *here,* through the open window.

"It was at that minute that Nurse Leatheran found her.

"And immediately, her old affection reasserting itself, she puts up a quick camouflage. Nurse Leatheran must not guess the horrifying discovery she has just made.

"She looks deliberately in the opposite direction (towards the courtyard) and makes a remark suggested to her by Father Lavigny's appearance as he crosses the courtyard.

"She refuses to say more. She has got to 'think things out.'

"And Dr. Leidner, who has been watching her anxiously, *realizes that she knows the truth.* She is not the kind of woman to conceal her horror and distress from him.

"It is true that as yet she has not given him away—but how long can he depend upon her?

"Murder is a habit. That night he substitutes a glass of acid for her glass of water. There is just a chance she may be believed to have deliberately poisoned herself. There is even a chance she may be considered to have done the first murder and has now been overcome with remorse. To strengthen the latter idea he takes the quern from the roof and puts it under her bed.

"No wonder that poor Miss Johnson, in her death agony, could only try desperately to impart her hard-won information. Through 'the window,' *that* is how Mrs. Leidner was killed, *not* through the door—through the *window.* . . .

"And so thus, everything is explained, everything falls into place. . . . Psychologically perfect.

"But there is no proof. No proof at all. . . ."

None of us spoke. We were lost in a sea of horror. . . . Yes, and not only horror. Pity, too.

Dr. Leidner had neither moved nor spoken. He sat just as he had done all along. A tired, worn, elderly man.

At last he stirred slightly and looked at Poirot with gentle tired eyes.

"No," he said, "there is no proof. But that does not matter. You knew that I would not deny truth. . . . I have never denied truth . . . I think—really—I am rather glad . . . I'm so tired . . ."

Then he said simply:

"I'm sorry about Anne. That was bad—senseless—it wasn't *me!* And she suffered, too, poor soul. Yes, that wasn't me. It was fear. . . ."

A little smile just hovered on his pain-twisted lips.

"You would have made a good archaeologist, M. Poirot. You have the gift of re-creating the past.

"It was all very much as you said.

"I loved Louise and I killed her . . . If you'd known Louise you'd have understood. . . . No, I think you understand anyway. . . ."

29

L'Envoi

THERE ISN'T REALLY any more to say about things.

They got "Father" Lavigny and the other man just as they were going on board a steamer at Beyrouth.

Sheila Reilly married young Emmott. I think that will be good for her. He's no doormat—he'll keep her in her place. She'd have ridden roughshod over poor Bill Coleman.

I nursed him, by the way, when he had appendicitis a year ago. I got quite fond of him. His people were sending him out to farm in South Africa.

I've never been out East again. It's funny—sometimes I wish I could. I think of the noise the waterwheel made and the women washing, and that queer haughty look that camels give you—and I get quite a homesick feeling. After all, perhaps dirt isn't really so unhealthy as one is brought up to believe!

Dr. Reilly usually looks me up when he's in England, and as I said, it's he who's got me into this. "Take it or leave it," I said to him. "I know the grammar's all wrong and it's not properly written or anything like that—but there it is."

And he took it. Made no bones about it. It will give me a queer feeling if it's ever printed.

M. Poirot went back to Syria and about a week later he went home on the Orient Express and got himself mixed up in another murder. He was clever, I don't deny it, but I shan't forgive him in a hurry for pulling my leg the way he did. Pretending to think I might be mixed up in the crime and not a real hospital nurse at all!

Doctors are like that sometimes. Will have their joke, some of them will, and never think of *your* feelings!

I've thought and thought about Mrs. Leidner and what she was really like. . . . Sometimes it seems to me she was just a terrible woman—and other times I remember how nice she was to me and how soft her voice was—and her lovely fair hair and everything—and I feel that perhaps, after all, she was more to be pitied than blamed. . . .

And I can't help but pity Dr. Leidner. I know he was a murderer twice over, but it doesn't seem to make any difference. He was so dreadfully fond of her. It's awful to be fond of anyone like that.

Somehow, the more I get older, and the more I see of people and sadness and illness and everything, the sorrier I get for everyone. Sometimes, I declare, I don't know what's become of the good strict principles my aunt brought me up with. A very religious woman she was, and most particular. There wasn't one of our neighbors whose faults she didn't know backward and forward. . . .

Oh, dear, it's quite true what Dr. Reilly said. How does one stop writing? If I could find a really good telling phrase.

I must ask Dr. Reilly for some Arab one.

Like the one M. Poirot used.

In the name of Allah, the Merciful, the Compassionate . . .

Something like that.

THEY
CAME
TO
BAGHDAD

1

CAPTAIN CROSBIE CAME out of the bank with the pleased air of one who has cashed a check and has discovered that there is just a little more in his account than he thought there was.

Captain Crosbie often looked pleased with himself. He was that kind of man. In figure he was short and stocky, with rather a red face and a bristling military moustache. He strutted a little when he walked. His clothes were, perhaps, just a trifle loud, and he was fond of a good story. He was popular among other men. A cheerful man, commonplace but kindly, unmarried. Nothing remarkable about him. There are heaps of Crosbies in the East.

The street into which Captain Crosbie emerged was called Bank Street for the excellent reason that most of the banks in the city were situated in it. Inside the bank it was cool and dark and rather musty. The predominant sound was of large quantities of typewriters clicking in the background.

Outside in Bank Street it was sunny and full of swirling dust, and the noises were terrific and varied. There were the persistent honking of motor horns, the cries of vendors of various wares. There were hot disputes between small groups of people who seemed ready to murder each other but were really fast friends; men, boys and children were selling every type of tree, sweetmeats, oranges and bananas, bath towels, combs, razor blades and other assorted merchandise carried rapidly through the streets on trays. There was also a perpetual and ever renewed sound of throat clearing and spitting, and above it the thin melancholy wail of men conducting donkeys and horses among the stream of motors and pedestrians shouting *"Balek-Balek!"*

It was eleven o'clock in the morning in the city of Baghdad.

Captain Crosbie stopped a rapidly running boy with an armful of newspapers and bought one. He turned the corner of Bank Street and came into Rashid Street which is the main street of Baghdad, running through it for about four miles, parallel with the river Tigris.

Captain Crosbie glanced at the headlines in the paper, tucked it under his arm, walked for about two hundred yards and then turned down a small alleyway and into a large Khan or Court. At the further side of this he pushed open a door with a brass plate and found himself in an office.

A neat young Iraqi clerk left his typewriter and came forward smiling a welcome.

"Good morning, Captain Crosbie. What can I do for you?"

"Mr. Dakin in his room? Good, I'll go through."

He passed through a door, up some very steep stairs and along a rather dirty passage. He knocked at the end door and a voice said "Come in."

It was a high rather bare room. There were an oil stove with a saucer of water on top of it, a long low cushioned seat with a little coffee table in front of it and a large rather shabby desk. The electric light was on and the daylight was carefully excluded. Behind the shabby desk was a rather shabby man, with a tired and indecisive face—the face of one who has not got on in the world and knows it and has ceased to care.

The two men, the cheerful self-confident Crosbie, and the melancholy fatigued Dakin, looked at each other.

Dakin said, "Hullo, Crosbie. Just in from Kirkuk?"

The other nodded. He shut the door carefully behind him. It was a shabby looking door, badly painted, but it had one rather unexpected quality; it fitted well, with no crevices and no space at the bottom.

It was, in fact, soundproof.

With the closing of the door, the personalities of both men changed ever so slightly. Captain Crosbie became less aggressive and cocksure. Mr. Dakin's shoulders drooped less, his manner was less hesitating. If anyone had been in the room listening they would have been surprised to find that Dakin was the man in authority.

"Any news, sir?" asked Crosbie.

"Yes." Dakin sighed. He had before him a paper which he had just been busy decoding. He dotted down two more letters and said:

"It's to be held in Baghdad."

Then he struck a match, set light to the paper and watched it burn. When it had smoldered to ashes, he blew gently. The ashes flew up and scattered.

"Yes," he said. "They've settled on Baghdad. Twentieth of next month. We're to 'preserve all secrecy.' "

"They've been talking about it in the Suq—for three days," said Crosbie dryly.

The tall man smiled his weary smile.

"Top secret! No top secrets in the East, are there, Crosbie?"

"No, sir. If you ask me, there aren't any top secrets anywhere. During the war I often noticed a barber in London knew more than the High Command."

"It doesn't matter much in this case. If the meeting is arranged for Baghdad it will soon have to be made public. And then the fun—our particular fun —starts."

"Do you think it ever will take place, sir?" asked Crosbie skeptically.

"Does the great Dictator" (thus disrespectfully did Captain Crosbie refer to the head of a Great European Power) "really mean to come?"

"I think he does this time, Crosbie," said Dakin thoughtfully. "Yes, I think so. And if the meeting comes off—comes off without a hitch—well, it might be the saving of—everything. If some kind of understanding could only be reached—" he broke off.

Crosbie still looked slightly skeptical. "Is—forgive me, sir—is understanding of any kind possible?"

"In the sense you mean, Crosbie, probably not! If it were just a bringing together of two men representing totally different idcologies, probably the whole thing would end as usual—in increased suspicion and misunderstanding. But there's the third element. If that fantastic story of Carmichael's is true—"

He broke off.

"But surely, sir, it can't be true. It's too fantastic!"

The other was silent for a few moments. He was seeing, very vividly, an earnest troubled face, hearing a quiet nondescript voice saying fantastic and unbelievable things. He was saying to himself, as he had said then, "Either my best, my most reliable man has gone mad; or else—this thing is true. . . ."

He said in the same thin melancholy voice:

"Carmichael believed it. Everything he could find out confirmed his hypothesis. He wanted to go there to find out more—to get proof . . . Whether I was wise to let him or not, I don't know. If he doesn't get back, it's only my story of what Carmichael told me, which again is a story of what someone told him. Is that enough? I don't think so. It is, as you say, such a fantastic story . . . But if the man himself is here, in Baghdad, on the twentieth, to tell his own story, the story of an eyewitness and to produce proof—"

"Proof?" said Crosbie sharply.

The other nodded.

"Yes, he's got proof."

"How do you know?"

"The agreed formula. The message came through Salah Hassan." He quoted carefully: *"A white camel with a load of oats is coming over the Pass."*

He paused and then went on:

"So Carmichael has got what he went to get, but he didn't get away unsuspected. They're on his trail. Whatever route he takes will be watched, and what is far more dangerous, they'll be waiting for him—here. First on the frontier. And if he succeeds in passing the frontier, there will be a cordon drawn round the Embassies and the Consulates. Look at this."

He shuffled among the papers on his desk and read out:

"An Englishman traveling in his car from Persia to Iraq shot dead—Supposedly by bandits. A Kurdish merchant traveling down from the hills ambushed and killed. Another Kurd, Abdul Hassan, suspected of being a cigarette smuggler, shot by the police. Body of a man, afterwards identified as an

Armenian lorry driver, found on the Rowanduz road. All of them, mark you, of roughly the same description. Height, weight, hair, build, it corresponds with a description of Carmichael. They're taking no chances. They're out to get him. Once he's in Iraq the danger will be greater still. A gardener at the Embassy, a servant at the Consulate, an official at the Airport, in the Customs, at the Railway Stations . . . all hotels watched . . . A cordon, stretched tight."

Crosbie raised his eyebrows.

"You think it's as widespread as all that, sir?"

"I've no doubt of it. Even in our show there have been leakages. That's the worst of all. How am I to be sure that the measures we're adopting to get Carmichael safely into Baghdad aren't known already to the other side? It's one of the elementary moves of the game, as you know, to have someone in the pay of the other camp."

"Is there anyone you—suspect?"

Slowly Dakin shook his head.

Crosbie sighed.

"In the meantime," he said, "we carry on?"

"Yes."

"What about Crofton Lee?"

"He's agreed to come to Baghdad."

"Everyone's coming to Baghdad," said Crosbie. "Even the great Dictator, according to you, sir. But if anything should happen to the President—while he's here—the balloon will go up with a vengeance."

"Nothing must happen," said Dakin. "That's our business. To see it doesn't."

When Crosbie had gone Dakin sat bent over his desk. He murmured under his breath,

"They came to Baghdad. . . ."

On the blotting pad he drew a circle and wrote under it *Baghdad*— Then, dotted round it, he sketched a camel, an airplane, a steamer, a small puffing train—all converging on the circle. Then on the corner of the pad he drew a spider's web. In the middle of the spider's web he wrote a name: *Anna Scheele.* Underneath that he put a big query mark.

Then he took his hat, and left the office. As he walked along Rashid Street some man asked another who that was.

"That? Oh, that's Dakin. In one of the oil companies. Nice fellow, but never gets on. Too lethargic. They say he drinks. He'll never get anywhere. You've got to have drive to get on in this part of the world."

"Have you got the reports on the Krugenhorf property, Miss Scheele?"

"Yes, Mr. Morganthal."

Miss Scheele, cool and efficient, slipped the papers in front of her employer. He grunted as he read.

"Satisfactory, I think."

"I certainly think so, Mr. Morganthal."

"Is Schwartz here?"

"He's waiting in the outer office."

"Have him sent right in now."

Miss Scheele pressed a buzzer—one of six.

"Will you require me, Mr. Morganthal?"

"No, I don't think so, Miss Scheele."

Anna Scheele glided noiselessly from the room.

She was a platinum blonde—but not a glamorous blonde. Her pale flaxen hair was pulled straight back from her forehead into a neat roll at the neck. Her pale blue intelligent eyes looked out on the world from behind strong glasses. Her face had neat small features, but was quite expressionless. She had made her way in the world not by her charm but by sheer efficiency. She could memorize anything, however complicated, and produce names, dates and times without having to refer to notes. She could organize the staff of a big office in such a way that it ran as by well oiled machinery. She was discretion itself and her energy, though controlled and disciplined, never flagged.

Otto Morganthal, head of the New York firm of Morganthal, Brown and Shipperke, international bankers, was well aware that to Anna Scheele he owed more than mere money could repay. He trusted her completely. Her memory, her experience, her judgment, her cool level head were invaluable. He paid her a large salary and would have made it a larger one, had she asked for it.

She knew not only the details of his business but the details of his private life. When he had consulted her in the matter of the second Mrs. Morganthal, she had advised divorce and suggested the exact amount of alimony. She had not expressed sympathy or curiosity. She was not, he would have said, that kind of woman. He didn't think she had any feelings, and it had never occurred to him to wonder what she thought about. He would indeed have been astonished if he had been told that she had any thoughts—other that is, than thoughts connected with Morganthal, Brown and Shipperke, and with the problems of Otto Morganthal.

So it was with complete surprise that he heard her say as she prepared to leave his office,

"I should like three weeks' absence from New York if I might have it, Mr. Morganthal. Starting from Tuesday next."

Staring at her, he said uneasily: "It will be awkward—very awkward."

"I don't think it will be too difficult, Mr. Morganthal. Miss Wygate is fully competent to deal with things. I shall leave her my notes and full instructions. Mr. Cornwall can attend to the Ascher Merger."

Still uneasily he asked:

"You're not ill, or anything?"

He couldn't imagine Miss Scheele being ill. Even germs respected Anna Scheele and kept out of her way.

"Oh no, Mr. Morganthal. I want to go to London to see my sister there."

"Your sister?" He didn't know she had a sister. He had never conceived of Miss Scheele as having any family or relations. She had never mentioned having any. And here she was, casually referring to a sister in London. She had been over in London with him last fall but she had never mentioned having a sister then.

With a sense of injury he said,

"I never knew you had a sister in England?"

Miss Scheele smiled very faintly.

"Oh yes, Mr. Morganthal. She is married to an Englishman connected with the British Museum. It is necessary for her to undergo a very serious operation. She wants me to be with her. I should like to go."

In other words, Otto Morganthal saw, she had made up her mind to go.

He said grumblingly, "All right, all right . . . Get back as soon as you can. I've never seen the market so jumpy. All this damned communism. War may break out at any moment. It's the only solution, I sometimes think. The whole country's riddled with it—riddled with it. And now the President's determined to go to this fool conference at Baghdad. It's a put-up job in my opinion. They're out to get him. Baghdad! Of all the outlandish places!"

"Oh I'm sure he'll be very well guarded," Miss Scheele said soothingly.

"They got the Shah of Persia last year, didn't they? They got Bernadotte in Palestine. It's madness—that's what it is—madness."

"But then," added Mr. Morganthal heavily, "all the world is mad."

2

VICTORIA JONES WAS sitting moodily on a seat in FitzJames Gardens. She was wholly given up to reflections—or one might almost say moralizations— on the disadvantages inherent in employing one's particular talents at the wrong moment.

Victoria was, like most of us, a girl with both qualities and defects. On the credit side she was generous, warm-hearted and courageous. Her natural leaning toward adventure may be regarded as either meritorious or the reverse in this modern age which places the value of security high. Her principal defect was a tendency to tell lies at both opportune and inopportune moments. The superior fascination of fiction to fact was always irresistible to Victoria. She lied with fluency, ease and artistic fervor. If Victoria was late for an appointment (which was often the case) it was not sufficient for her to murmur an excuse of her watch having stopped (which actually was quite often the case) or of an unaccountably delayed bus. It would appear preferable to Victoria to tender the mendacious explanation that she had been hindered by an escaped elephant lying across a main bus route, or by a thrilling smash and grab raid in which she herself had played a part to aid the police. To Victoria an agreeable world would be one where tigers lurked in the Strand and dangerous bandits infested Tooting.

A slender girl, with an agreeable figure and first-class legs, Victoria's features might actually have been described as plain. They were small and neat. But there was a piquancy about her, for "little indiarubber face," as one of her admirers had named her, could twist those immobile features into a startling mimicry of almost anybody.

It was this last named talent that had led to her present predicament. Employed as a typist by Mr. Greenholtz of Greenholtz, Simmon and Lederbetter, of Graysholme Street, London, W.C.2, Victoria had been whiling away a dull morning by entertaining the three other typists and the office boy with a vivid performance of Mrs. Greenholtz paying a visit to her husband's office. Secure in the knowledge that Mr. Greenholtz had gone round to his solicitors, Victoria let herself go.

"Why do you say we not have that Knole settee, dad-dee?" she demanded in a high whining voice. "Mrs. Dievtakis she have one in electric blue satin. You say it is money that is tight? But then why you take that blond girl out dining and dancing—Ah! you think I do not know—and if you take that girl —then I have a settee and all done plum colored and gold cushions. And when you say it is a business dinner you are a damn fool—yes—and come back with lipstick on your shirt. So I have the Knole settee and I order a fur cape—very nice—all like mink but not really and I get him very cheap and it is good business—"

The sudden failure of her audience—at first entranced, but now suddenly resuming work with spontaneous agreement caused Victoria to break off and swing round to where Mr. Greenholtz was standing in the doorway, observing her.

Victoria, unable to think of anything relevant to say, merely said "Oh!"

Mr. Greenholtz grunted.

Flinging off his overcoat Mr. Greenholtz proceeded to his private office and banged the door. Almost immediately his buzzer sounded, two shorts and a long. That was a summons for Victoria.

"It's for you, Jonesey," a colleague remarked unnecessarily, her eyes alight with the pleasure occasioned by the misfortunes of others. The other typists collaborated in this sentiment by ejaculating: "You're for it, Jones" and "On the mat, Jonesey." The office boy, an unpleasant child, contented himself with drawing a forefinger across his throat and uttering a sinister noise.

Victoria picked up her notebook and pencil and sailed into Mr. Greenholtz's office with such assurance as she could muster.

"You want me, Mr. Greenholtz?" she murmured, fixing a limpid gaze on him.

Mr. Greenholtz was rustling three pound notes and searching his pockets for coin of the realm.

"So there you are," he observed. "I've had about enough of you, young lady. Do you see any particular reason why I shouldn't pay you a week's salary in lieu of notice and pack you off here and now?"

Victoria (an orphan) had just opened her mouth to explain how the plight of a mother at this moment suffering a major operation had so demoralized her that she had become completely light headed, and how her small salary was all the aforesaid mother had to depend upon, when, taking an opening glance at Mr. Greenholtz's unwholesome face, she shut her mouth and changed her mind.

"I couldn't agree with you more," she said heartily and pleasantly. "I think you're absolutely right, if you know what I mean."

Mr. Greenholtz appeared slightly taken aback. He was not used to having his dismissals treated in this approving and congratulatory spirit. To conceal a slight discomfiture he sorted through the pile of coins on the desk in front of him. He then sought once more in his pockets.

"Ninepence short," he murmured gloomily.

"Never mind," said Victoria kindly. "Take yourself to the pictures or spend it on sweets."

"Don't seem to have any stamps, either."

"It doesn't matter. I never write letters."

"I could send it after you," said Mr. Greenholtz but without much conviction.

"Don't bother. What about a reference?" said Victoria.

Mr. Greenholtz's choler returned.

"Why the hell should I give you a reference?" he demanded wrathfully.

"It's usual," said Victoria.

Mr. Greenholtz drew a piece of paper toward him and scrawled a few lines. He shoved it toward her.

"That do for you?"

Miss Jones has been with me two months as a shorthand typist. Her shorthand is inaccurate and she cannot spell. She is leaving owing to wasting time in office hours.

Victoria made a grimace.

"Hardly a recommendation," she observed.

"It wasn't meant to be," said Mr. Greenholtz.

"I think," said Victoria, "that you ought at least to say I'm honest, sober and respectable. I am, you know. And perhaps you might add that I'm discreet."

"Discreet?" barked Mr. Greenholtz.

Victoria met his gaze with an innocent stare.

"Discreet," she said gently.

Remembering sundry letters taken down and typed by Victoria, Mr. Greenholtz decided that prudence was the better part of rancor.

He snatched back the paper, tore it up and indited a fresh one.

"Miss Jones has been with me for two months as a shorthand typist. She is leaving owing to redundancy of office staff."

"How about that?"

"It could be better," said Victoria, "but it will do."

So it was that with a week's salary (less ninepence) in her bag Victoria was sitting in meditation upon a bench in FitzJames Gardens, which are a triangular plantation of rather sad shrubs flanking a church and overlooked by a tall warehouse.

It was Victoria's habit on any day when it was not actually raining to purchase one cheese, and one lettuce and tomato sandwich at a Milk Bar and eat this simple lunch in these pseudorural surroundings.

Today, as she munched meditatively, she was telling herself, not for the first time, that there was a time and place for everything—and that the office was definitely not the place for imitations of the boss's wife. She must, in future, curb the natural exuberance that led her to brighten up the performance of a dull job. In the meantime, she was free of Greenholtz, Simmon and Lederbetter, and the prospect of obtaining a situation elsewhere filled her with pleasurable anticipation. Victoria was always delighted when she was about to take up a new job. One never knew, she always felt, what might happen.

She had just distributed the last crumb of bread to three attentive sparrows who immediately fought each other with fury for it, when she became aware of a young man sitting at the other end of the seat. Victoria had noticed him vaguely already, but her mind full of good resolutions for the future, she had not observed him closely until now. What she now saw (out of the corner of her eye) she liked very much. He was a good-looking young man, cherubically fair, but with a firm chin and extremely blue eyes which had been, she rather imagined, examining her with covert admiration for some time.

Victoria had no inhibitions about making friends with strange young men in public places. She considered herself an excellent judge of character and well able to check any manifestations of freshness on the part of unattached males.

She proceeded to smile frankly at him and the young man responded like a marionette when you pull the string.

"Hullo," said the young man. "Nice place, this. Do you often come here?"

"Nearly every day."

"Just my luck that I never came here before. Was that your lunch you were eating?"

"Yes."

"I don't think you eat enough. I'd be starving if I only had two sandwiches. What about coming along and having a sausage at the S.P.O. in Tottenham Court Road?"

"No, thanks. I'm quite all right. I couldn't eat any more now."

She rather expected that he would say: "Another day" but he did not. He merely sighed—then he said:

"My name's Edward. What's yours?"

"Victoria."

"Why did your people want to call you after a railway station?"

"Victoria isn't only a railway station," Miss Jones pointed out. "There's Queen Victoria as well."

"Mm, yes. What's your other name?"

"Jones."

"Victoria Jones," said Edward trying it over on his tongue. He shook his head. "They don't go together."

"You're quite right," said Victoria with feeling. "If I were Jenny it would be rather nice—Jenny Jones. But Victoria needs something with a bit more class to it. Victoria Sackville-West for instance. That's the kind of thing one needs. Something to roll round the mouth."

"You could tack something on to the Jones," said Edward with sympathetic interest.

"Bedford Jones."

"Carisbrooke Jones."

"St. Clair Jones."

"Lonsdale Jones."

This agreeable game was interrupted by Edward's glancing at his watch and uttering a horrified ejaculation.

"I must tear back to my blinking boss—er—what about you?"

"I'm out of a job. I was sacked this morning."

"Oh I say, I am sorry," said Edward with real concern.

"Well, don't waste sympathy, because I'm not sorry at all. For one thing, I'll easily get another job, and besides that, it was really rather fun."

And delaying Edward's return to duty still further, she gave him a spirited rendering of this morning's scene, reenacting her impersonation of Mrs. Greenholtz to Edward's immense enjoyment.

"You really are marvelous, Victoria," he said. "You ought to be on the stage."

Victoria accepted this tribute with a gratified smile and remarked that Edward had better be running along if he didn't want to get the sack himself.

"Yes—and I shouldn't get another job as easily as you will. It must be wonderful to be a good shorthand typist," said Edward with envy in his voice.

"Well actually I'm not a good shorthand typist," Victoria admitted frankly, "but fortunately even the lousiest of shorthand typists can get some sort of a job nowadays—at any rate an educational or charitable one—they can't afford to pay much and so they get people like me. I prefer the learned type of job best. These scientific names and places and terms are so frightful anyway that if you can't spell them properly it doesn't really shame you because nobody could. What's your job? I suppose you're out of one of the services. R.A.F.?"

"Good guess."

"Fighter pilot?"

"Right again. They're awfully decent about getting us jobs and all that, but you see, the trouble is, that we're not particularly brainy. I mean one didn't need to be brainy in the R.A.F. They put me in an office with a lot of files and figures and some thinking to do and I just folded up. The whole thing seemed utterly purposeless anyway. But there it is. It gets you down a bit to know that you're absolutely no good."

Victoria nodded sympathetically—Edward went on bitterly:

"Out of touch. Not in the picture any more. It was all right during the war —one could keep one's end up all right—I got the D.F.C. for instance—but now—well, I might as well write myself off the map."

"But there ought to be—"

Victoria broke off. She felt unable to put into words her conviction that those qualities that brought a D.F.C. to their owner should somewhere have their appointed place in the world of 1950.

"It's got me down, rather," said Edward. "Being no good at anything, I mean. Well—I'd better be pushing off—I say—would you mind—would it be most awful cheek—if I only could—"

As Victoria opened surprised eyes, stammering and blushing, Edward produced a small camera.

"I would like so awfully to have a snapshot of you. You see, I'm going to Baghdad tomorrow."

"To Baghdad?" exclaimed Victoria with lively disappointment.

"Yes. I mean I wish I wasn't—now. Earlier this morning I was quite bucked about it—it's why I took this job really—to get out of this country."

"What sort of job is it?"

"Pretty awful. Culture—poetry, all that sort of thing. A Dr. Rathbone's my boss. Strings of letters after his name, peers at you soulfully through pince-nez. He's terrifically keen on uplift and spreading it far and wide. He opens bookshops in remote places—he's starting one in Baghdad. He gets Shakespeare's and Milton's works translated into Arabic and Kurdish and Persian and Armenian and has them all on tap. Silly, I think, because you've got the British Council doing much the same thing all over the place. Still, there it is. It gives me a job so I oughtn't to complain."

"What do you actually do?" asked Victoria.

"Well, really it boils down to being the old boy's personal Yes-man and

Dogsbody. Buy the tickets, make the reservations, fill up the passport forms, check the packing of all the horrid little poetic manuals, run round here, there, and everywhere. Then, when we get out there I'm supposed to fraternize—kind of glorified youth movement—all nations together in a united drive for uplift." Edward's tone became more and more melancholy. "Frankly, it's pretty ghastly, isn't it?"

Victoria was unable to administer much comfort.

"So you see," said Edward, "if you wouldn't mind awfully—one sideways and one looking right at me—oh I say, that's wonderful—"

The camera clicked twice and Victoria showed that purring complacence displayed by young women who know they have made an impression on an attractive member of the opposite sex.

"But it's pretty foul really, having to go off just when I've met you," said Edward. "I've half a mind to chuck it—but I suppose I couldn't do that at the last moment—not after all those ghastly forms and visas and everything. Wouldn't be a very good show, what?"

"It mayn't turn out as bad as you think," said Victoria consolingly.

"N-no," said Edward doubtfully. "The funny thing is," he added, "that I've got a feeling there's something fishy somewhere."

"Fishy?"

"Yes. Bogus. Don't ask me why. I haven't any reason. Sort of feeling one gets sometimes. Had it once about my port oil. Began fussing about the damned thing and sure enough there was a washer wedged in the spur-gear pump."

The technical terms in which this was couched made it quite unintelligible to Victoria, but she got the main idea.

"You think he's bogus—Rathbone?"

"Don't see how he can be. I mean he's frightfully respectable and learned and belongs to all these societies—and sort of hobnobs with Archbishops and Principals of Colleges. No, it's just a feeling— Well, time will show. So long. I wish you were coming, too."

"So do I," said Victoria.

"What are you going to do?"

"Go round to St. Guildric's Agency in Gower Street and look for another job," said Victoria gloomily.

"Goodbye, Victoria. Partir, say mourir un peu," added Edward with a very British accent. "These French johnnies know their stuff. Our English chaps just maunder on about parting being a sweet sorrow—silly asses."

"Goodbye, Edward, good luck."

"I don't suppose you'll ever think about me again."

"Yes, I shall."

"You're absolutely different from any girl I've ever seen before—I only wish—" The clock chimed a quarter, and Edward said, "Oh hell—I must fly—"

Retreating rapidly, he was swallowed up by the great maw of London.

Victoria, remaining behind on her seat absorbed in meditation, was conscious of two distinct streams of thought.

One dealt with the theme of Romeo and Juliet. She and Edward, she felt, were somewhat in the position of that unhappy couple, although perhaps Romeo and Juliet had expressed their feelings in rather more high class language. But the position, Victoria thought, was the same. Meeting, instant attraction—frustration—two fond hearts thrust asunder. A remembrance of a rhyme once frequently recited by her old nurse came to mind.

> *Jumbo said to Alice, "I love you."*
> *Alice said to Jumbo, "I don't believe you do;*
> *If you really loved me, as you say you do,*
> *You wouldn't go to America and leave me in the Zoo."*

Substitute Baghdad for America and there you were!

Victoria rose at last, dusting crumbs from her lap, and walked briskly out of FitzJames Gardens in the direction of Gower Street. Victoria had come to two decisions: the first was that (like Juliet) she loved this young man, and meant to have him.

The second decision that Victoria had come to was that as Edward would shortly be in Baghdad, the only thing to do was for her to go to Baghdad also. What was now occupying her mind was how this could be accomplished. That it could be accomplished somehow or other, Victoria did not doubt. She was a young woman of optimism and force of character.

Parting is such sweet sorrow appealed to her as a sentiment no more than it did to Edward.

"Somehow," said Victoria to herself, "I've got to get to Baghdad!"

3

THE SAVOY HOTEL welcomed Miss Anna Scheele with the empressment due to an old and valued client—they inquired after the health of Mr. Morganthal —and assured her that if her suite was not to her liking she had only to say so —for Anna Scheele represented *Dollars.*

Miss Scheele bathed, dressed, made a telephone call to a Kensington number and then went down in the lift. She passed through the revolving doors and asked for a taxi. It drew up and she got in and directed it to Cartier's in Bond Street.

As the taxi turned out of the Savoy approach into the Strand a little dark man who had been standing looking into a shop window suddenly glanced at his watch and hailed a taxi that was conveniently cruising past and which had been singularly blind to the hails of an agitated woman with parcels a moment or two previously.

The taxi followed along the Strand keeping the first taxi in sight. As they were both held up by the lights in going round Trafalgar Square, the man in the second taxi looked out of the left hand window and made a slight gesture with his hand. A private car, which had been standing in the side street by the Admiralty Arch started its engine and swung into the stream of traffic behind the second taxi.

The traffic had started on again. As Anna Scheele's taxi followed the stream of traffic going to the left into Pall Mall, the taxi containing the little dark man swung away to the right continuing round Trafalgar Square. The private car, a gray Standard, was now close behind Anna Scheele. It contained two passengers, a fair, rather vacant-looking young man at the wheel and a smartly dressed young woman beside him. The Standard followed Anna Scheele's taxi along Piccadilly and up Bond Street. Here for a moment it paused by the curb and the young woman got out.

She called brightly and conventionally,

"Thanks so much."

The car went on. The young woman walked along glancing every now and again into a window. A block held up the traffic. The young woman passed both the Standard and Anna Scheele's taxi. She arrived at Cartier's and went inside.

Anna Scheele paid off her taxi and went into the jeweler's. She spent some time looking at various pieces of jewelry. In the end she selected a sapphire and diamond ring. She wrote a check for it on a London bank. At the sight of the name on it, a little extra empressment came into the assistant's manner.

"Glad to see you in London again, Miss Scheele. Is Mr. Morganthal over?"

"No."

"I wondered. We have a very fine star sapphire here—I know he is interested in star sapphires. If you would care to see it?"

Miss Scheele expressed her willingness to see it, duly admired it, and promised to mention it to Mr. Morganthal.

She went out again into Bond Street, and the young woman who had been looking at clip earrings expressed herself as unable to make up her mind and emerged also.

The gray Standard car, having turned to the left in Grafton Street and gone down to Piccadilly, was just coming up Bond Street again. The young woman showed no signs of recognition.

Anna Scheele had turned into the Arcade. She entered a florist's. She ordered three dozen long stemmed roses, a bowl full of sweet big purple violets, a dozen sprays of white lilac, and a jar full of mimosa. She gave an address for them to be sent.

"That will be twelve pounds, eighteen shillings, madam."

Anna Scheele paid and went out. The young woman who had just come in asked the price of a bunch of primroses but did not buy them.

Anna Scheele crossed Bond Street and went along Burlington Street and turned into Savile Row. Here she entered the establishment of one of those tailors who, while catering essentially for men, occasionally condescend to cut a suit for certain favored members of the feminine sex.

Mr. Bolford received Miss Scheele with the greeting accorded to a valued client, and the materials for a suit were considered.

"Fortunately, I can give you our export quality. When will you be returning to New York, Miss Scheele?"

"On the twenty-third."

"We can manage that nicely. By the clipper, I presume?"

"Yes."

"And how are things in America? They are very sadly here—very sadly indeed." Mr. Bolford shook his head like a doctor describing a patient. "No heart in things, if you know what I mean. And no one coming along who takes any pride in a good job of work. D'you know who will cut your suit, Miss Scheele? Mr. Lantwick—seventy-two years of age he is, and he's the only man I've got I can really trust to cut for our best people. All the others—"

Mr. Bolford's plump hands waved them away.

"Quality," he said. "That's what this country used to be renowned for. Quality! Nothing cheap, nothing flashy. When we try mass production we're no good at it, and that's a fact. That's your country's specialty, Miss Scheele. What we ought to stand for, and I say it again, is quality. Take time over things, and trouble, and turn out an article that no one in the world can beat. Now what day shall we say for the first fitting? This day week? At 11:30? Thank you very much."

Making her way through the archaic gloom around bales of material, Anna Scheele emerged into daylight again. She hailed a taxi and returned to the Savoy. A taxi that was drawn up on the opposite side of the street and which contained a little dark man, took the same route but did not turn into the Savoy. It drove round to the Embankment and there picked up a short plump woman who had recently emerged from the service entrance of the Savoy.

"What about it, Louisa? Been through her room?"

"Yes. Nothing."

Anna Scheele had lunch in the restaurant. A table had been kept for her by the window. The maitre d'hôtel inquired affectionately after the health of Otto Morganthal.

After lunch Anna Scheele took her key and went up to her suite. The bed had been made, fresh towels were in the bathroom and everything was spick and span. Anna crossed to the two light air cases that constituted her luggage, one was open, the other locked. She cast an eye over the contents of the unlocked one, then taking her keys from her purse she unlocked the other. All was neat, folded, as she had folded things, nothing had apparently been touched or disturbed. A briefcase of leather lay on top. A small Leica camera and two rolls of film were in one corner. The films were still sealed and unopened. Anna ran her nail across the flap and pulled it up. Then she smiled, very gently. The single almost invisible blond hair that had been there was there no longer. Deftly she scattered a little powder over the shiny leather of the briefcase and blew it off. The briefcase remained clear and shiny. There were no fingerprints. But that morning after patting a little brilliantine onto the smooth flaxen cap of her hair, she had handled the briefcase. There should have been fingerprints on it, her own.

She smiled again.

"Good work," she said to herself. "But not quite good enough. . . ."

Deftly, she packed a small overnight case and went downstairs again. A taxi was called and she directed the driver to 17 Elmsleigh Gardens.

Elmsleigh Gardens was a quiet, rather dingy Kensington Square. Anna paid off the taxi and ran up the steps to the peeling front door. She pressed the bell. After a few minutes an elderly woman opened the door with a suspicious face which immediately changed to a beam of welcome.

"Won't Miss Elsie be pleased to see you! She's in the study at the back. It's only the thought of your coming that's been keeping her spirits up."

Anna went quickly along the dark hallway and opened the door at the far end. It was a small shabby, comfortable room with large worn leather armchairs. The woman sitting in one of them, jumped up.

"Anna, darling."

"Elsie."

The two women kissed each other affectionately.

"It's all arranged," said Elsie. "I go in tonight. I do hope—"

"Cheer up," said Anna. "Everything is going to be quite all right."

ii

The small dark man in the raincoat entered a public call box at High Street Kensington Station, and dialed a number.

"Valhalla Gramophone Company?"

"Yes."

"Sanders here."

"Sanders of the River? What river?"

"River Tigris. Reporting on A.S. arrived this morning from New York. Went to Cartier's. Bought sapphire and diamond ring costing one hundred and twenty pounds. Went to florist's, Jane Kent—twelve pounds eighteen shillings' worth of flowers to be delivered at a nursing home in Portland Place. Ordered coat and skirt at Bolford and Avory's. None of these firms known to have any suspicious contacts, but particular attention will be paid to them in future. A.S.'s room at Savoy gone through. Nothing suspicious found. Briefcase in suitcase containing papers relating to Paper Merger with

Wolfensteins. All aboveboard. Camera and two rolls of apparently unexposed films. Possibility of films being photostatic records, substituted other films for them, but original films reported upon as being straightforward unexposed films. A.S. took small overnight case and went to sister at 17 Elmsleigh Gardens. Sister entering nursing home in Portland Place this evening for internal operation. This confirmed from nursing home and also appointment book of surgeon. Visit of A.S. seems perfectly aboveboard. Showed no uneasiness or consciousness of being followed. Understand she is spending tonight at nursing home. Has kept on her room at the Savoy. Return passage to New York by clipper booked for twenty-third."

The man who called himself Sanders of the River paused and added a postscript off the record as it were.

"And if you ask what I think, it's all a mare's nest! Throwing money about, that's all she's doing. Twelve pounds eighteen on flowers! I ask you!"

4

IT SAYS A good deal for the buoyancy of Victoria's temperament that the possibility of failing to attain her objective did not for a moment occur to her. Not for her the lines about ships that pass in the night. It was certainly unfortunate, when she had—well—frankly—fallen for an attractive young man, that that young man should prove to be just on the verge of departure to a place distant some three thousand miles. He might so easily have been going to Aberdeen or Brussels or even Birmingham.

That it should be Baghdad, thought Victoria, was just her luck! Nevertheless, difficult though it might be, she intended to get to Baghdad somehow or other. Victoria walked purposefully along Tottenham Court Road, revolving ways and means. Baghdad. What went on in Baghdad? According to Edward: "Culture." Could she, in some way, play up culture? Unesco? Unesco was always sending people here, there and everywhere, sometimes to the most delectable places. But these were usually, Victoria reflected, superior young women with university degrees who had got into the racket early on.

Victoria, deciding that first things came first, finally bent her steps to a travel agency, and there made her inquiries. There was no difficulty, it seemed, in traveling to Baghdad. You could go by air, by long sea to Basrah, by train to Marseilles and by boat to Beirut and across the desert by car. You could go via Egypt. You could go all the way by train if you were determined to do so, but visas were at present difficult and uncertain and were apt to have actually expired by the time you received them. Baghdad was in the sterling area and money therefore presented no difficulties. Not, that is to say, in the clerk's meaning of the word. What it all boiled down to was that there was no difficulty whatsoever in getting to Baghdad, so long as you had between sixty and a hundred pounds in cash.

As Victoria had at this moment three pounds ten (less ninepence), an extra twelve shillings, and five pounds in the P.O. Savings Bank, the simple and straightforward way was out of the question.

She made tentative queries as to a job as Air Hostess or stewardess, but these, she gathered, were highly coveted posts for which there was a waiting list.

Victoria next visited St. Guildric's Agency where Miss Spenser, sitting behind her efficient desk, welcomed her as one of those who were destined to pass through the office with reasonable frequency.

"Dear me, Miss Jones, not out of a post again. I really hoped this last one—"

"Quite impossible," said Victoria firmly. "I really couldn't begin to tell you what I had to put up with."

A pleasurable flush rose in Miss Spenser's pallid cheek.

"Not—" she began—"I do hope not— He didn't seem to me really that sort of a man—but of course he is a trifle gross—I do hope—"

"It's quite all right," said Victoria. She conjured up a pale brave smile. "I can take care of myself."

"Oh, of course, but it's the unpleasantness."

"Yes," said Victoria. "It is unpleasant. However—" she smiled bravely again.

Miss Spenser consulted her books.

"The St. Leonard's Assistance to Unmarried Mothers want a typist," said Miss Spenser. "Of course, they don't pay very much—"

"Is there any chance," asked Victoria brusquely, "of a post in Baghdad?"

"In Baghdad?" said Miss Spenser in lively astonishment.

Victoria saw she might as well have said in Kamskatka or at the South Pole.

"I should very much like to get to Baghdad," said Victoria.

"I hardly think—in a secretary's post you mean?"

"Anyhow," said Victoria. "As a nurse or a cook, or looking after a lunatic. Anyway at all."

Miss Spenser shook her head.

"I'm afraid I can't hold out much hope. There was a lady in yesterday with two little girls who was offering a passage to Australia."

Victoria waved away Australia.

She rose. "If you did hear of anything. Just the fare out—that's all I need." She met the curiosity in the other woman's eye by explaining—"I've got—er —relations out there. And I understand there are plenty of well paid jobs. But of course, one has to get there first."

"Yes," repeated Victoria to herself as she walked away from St. Guildric's Bureau. "One has to get there."

It was an added annoyance to Victoria that, as is customary, when one has had one's attention suddenly focused on a particular name or subject, everything seemed to have suddenly conspired to force the thought of Baghdad on to her attention.

A brief paragraph in the evening paper she bought stated that Dr. Pauncefoot Jones, the well known archaeologist, had started excavation on the ancient city of Murik, situated a hundred and twenty miles from Baghdad. An advertisement mentioned Shipping Lines to Basrah (and thence by train to Baghdad, Mosul etc.). In the newspaper that lined her stocking drawer, a few lines of print about students in Baghdad leaped to her eyes. *The Thief of Baghdad* was on at the local cinema, and in the high class highbrow bookshop into whose window she always gazed, a New Biography of Haroun al Rashid, Caliph of Baghdad, was prominently displayed.

The whole world, it seemed to her, had suddenly become Baghdad conscious. And until that afternoon at approximately 1:45 she had, for all intents and purposes, never heard of Baghdad, and certainly never thought about it.

The prospects of getting there were unsatisfactory, but Victoria had no idea of giving up. She had a fertile brain and the optimistic outlook that if you want to do a thing there is always some way of doing it.

She employed the evening in drawing up a list of possible approaches. It ran:

Insert advertisement?

Try Foreign Office?

Try Iraq Legation?

What about Date firms?

Ditto Shipping firms?

British Council?

Selfridge's Information Bureau?

Citizen's Advice Bureau?

None of them, she was forced to admit, seemed very promising. She added to the list:

Somehow or other, get hold of a hundred pounds?

ii

The intense mental efforts of concentration that Victoria had made overnight, and possibly the subconscious satisfaction at no longer having to be punctually in the office at nine A.M., made Victoria oversleep herself.

She awoke at five minutes past ten, and immediately jumped out of bed and began to dress. She was just passing a final comb through her rebellious dark hair when the telephone rang.

Victoria reached for the receiver.

A positively agitated Miss Spenser was at the other end.

"So glad to have caught you, my dear. Really the most amazing coincidence."

"Yes?" cried Victoria.

"As I say, really a startling coincidence. A Mrs. Hamilton Clipp—traveling to Baghdad in three days' time—has broken her arm—needs someone to assist her on journey—I rang you up at once. Of course I don't know if she has also applied to any other agencies—"

"I'm on my way," said Victoria. "Where is she?"

"The Savoy."

"And what's her silly name? Tripp?"

"Clipp, dear. Like a paper clip, but with two P's—I can't think why, but she's an American," ended Miss Spenser as if that explained everything.

"Mrs. Clipp at the Savoy."

"Mr. and Mrs. Hamilton Clipp. It was actually the husband who rang up."

"You're an angel," said Victoria. "Goodbye."

She hurriedly brushed her suit and wished it were slightly less shabby, recombed her hair so as to make it seem less exuberant and more in keeping with the role of ministering angel and experienced traveler. Then she took out Mr. Greenholtz's recommendation and shook her head over it.

We must do better than that, said Victoria.

From a 19 bus, Victoria alighted at Green Park, and entered the Ritz Hotel. A quick glance over the shoulder of a woman reading in the bus had proved rewarding. Entering the writing room Victoria wrote herself some generous lines of praise from Lady Cynthia Bradbury who had been announced as having just left England for East Africa . . . *"excellent in illness,"* wrote Victoria, *"and most capable in every way. . . ."*

Leaving the Ritz she crossed the road and walked a short way up Albemarle Street until she came to Balderton's Hotel, renowned as the haunt of the higher clergy and of old-fashioned dowagers up from the country.

In less dashing handwriting, and making neat small Greek e's she wrote a recommendation from the Bishop of Llangow.

Thus equipped, Victoria caught a No. 9 bus and proceeded to the Savoy.

At the reception desk she asked for Mrs. Hamilton Clipp and gave her name as coming from St. Guildric's Agency. The clerk was just about to pull the telephone toward him when he paused, looked across, and said,

"That is Mr. Hamilton Clipp now."

Mr. Hamilton Clipp was an immensely tall and very thin gray-haired American of kindly aspect and slow deliberate speech.

Victoria told him her name and mentioned the Agency.

"Why now, Miss Jones, you'd better come right up and see Mrs. Clipp. She's still in our suite. I fancy she's interviewing some other young lady, but she may have gone by now."

Cold panic clutched at Victoria's heart.

Was it to be so near and yet so far?

They went up in the lift to the third floor.

As they walked along the deep carpeted corridor, a young woman came out of a door at the far end and came toward them. Victoria had a kind of hallucination that it was herself who was approaching. Possibly, she thought, because the young woman's tailormade suit was so exactly what she would have liked to be wearing herself. "And it would fit me too. I'm just her size. How I'd like to tear it off her," thought Victoria with a reversion to primitive female savagery.

The young woman passed them. A small velvet hat perched on the side of her fair hair partially hid her face, but Mr. Hamilton Clipp turned to look after her with an air of surprise.

"Well now," he said to himself. "Who'd have thought of that? Anna Scheele."

He added in an explanatory way,

"Excuse me, Miss Jones. I was surprised to recognize a young lady whom I saw in New York only a week ago, secretary to one of our big International bankers—"

He stopped as he spoke at a door in the corridor. The key was hanging in the lock and with a brief tap, Mr. Hamilton Clipp opened the door and stood aside for Victoria to precede him into the room.

Mrs. Hamilton Clipp was sitting on a high backed chair near the window and jumped up as they came in. She was a short birdlike sharp-eyed woman. Her right arm was encased in plaster.

Her husband introduced Victoria.

"Why, it's all been most unfortunate," exclaimed Mrs. Clipp breathlessly. "Here we were, with a full itinerary, and enjoying London and all our plans made and my passage booked. I'm going out to pay a visit to my married daughter in Iraq, Miss Jones. I've not seen her for nearly two years. And then what do I do but take a crash—as a matter of fact, it was actually in Westminster Abbey—down some stone steps—and there I was. They rushed me to Hospital and they've set it, and all things considered it's not too uncomfortable—but there it is, I'm kind of helpless, and however I'd manage traveling, I don't know. And George here, is just tied up with business, and simply can't get away for at least another three weeks. He suggested that I should take a nurse along with me—but after all, once I'm out there I don't need a nurse hanging around, Sadie can do all that's necessary—and it means paying her fare back as well, and so I thought I'd ring up the Agencies and see if I couldn't find someone who'd be willing to come along just for the fare out."

"I'm not exactly a nurse," said Victoria managing to imply that that was practically what she was. "But I've had a good deal of experience of nursing." She produced the first testimonial. "I was with Lady Cynthia Bradbury for over a year. And if you should want any correspondence or secretarial work done, I acted as my uncle's secretary for some months. My uncle," said Victoria modestly, "is the Bishop of Llangow."

"So your uncle's a Bishop. Dear me, how interesting."

Both the Hamilton Clipps were, Victoria thought, decidedly impressed. And so they should be after the trouble she had taken!

Mrs. Hamilton Clipp handed the two testimonials to her husband.

"It really seems quite wonderful," she said reverently. "Quite Providential. It's an answer to prayer."

Which, indeed, was exactly what it was, thought Victoria.

"You're taking up a position of some kind out there? Or joining a relative?" asked Mrs. Hamilton Clipp.

In the flurry of manufacturing testimonials, Victoria had quite forgotten that she might have to account for her reasons for traveling to Baghdad. Caught unprepared, she had to improvise rapidly. The paragraph she had read yesterday came to her mind.

"I'm joining my uncle out there. Dr. Pauncefoot Jones," she explained.

"Indeed? The archaeologist?"

"Yes." For one moment Victoria wondered whether she were perhaps endowing herself with too many distinguished uncles. "I'm terribly interested in his work, but of course I've no special qualifications so it was out of the question for the Expedition to pay my fare out. They're not too well off for funds. But if I can get out on my own, I can join them and make myself useful."

"It must be very very interesting work," said Mr. Hamilton Clipp, "and Mesopotamia is certainly a great field for archaeology."

"I'm afraid," said Victoria turning to Mrs. Clipp, "that my uncle the Bishop is up in Scotland this moment. But I can give you his secretary's telephone number. She is staying in London at the moment. Pimlico 87693— one of the Fulham Palace extensions. She'll be there any time from (Victoria's eyes slid to the clock on the mantelpiece) 11:30 onwards if you would like to ring her up and ask about me."

"Why, I'm sure—" Mrs. Clipp began, but her husband interrupted.

"Time's very short, you know. This plane leaves day after tomorrow. Now have you got a passport, Miss Jones?"

"Yes." Victoria felt thankful that owing to a short holiday trip to France last year, her passport was up to date. "I brought it with me in case," she added.

"Now that's what I call businesslike," said Mr. Clipp approvingly. If any other candidate had been in the running, she had obviously dropped out now. Victoria with her good recommendations, and her uncles, and her passport on the spot had successfully made the grade.

"You'll want the necessary visas," said Mr. Clipp, taking the passport. "I'll run round to our friend Mr. Burgeon in American Express, and he'll get everything fixed up. Perhaps you'd better call round this afternoon, so you can sign whatever's necessary."

This Victoria agreed to do.

As the door of the apartment closed behind her, she heard Mrs. Hamilton Clipp say to Mr. Hamilton Clipp—

"Such a nice straightforward girl. We really are in luck."

Victoria had the grace to blush.

She hurried back to her flat and sat glued to the telephone prepared to assume the gracious refined accents of a Bishop's secretary in case Mrs. Clipp should seek confirmation of her capability. But Mrs. Clipp had obviously been so impressed by Victoria's straightforward personality that she was not going to bother with these technicalities. After all, the engagement was only for a few days as a traveling companion.

In due course, papers were filled up and signed, the necessary visas were obtained and Victoria was bidden to spend the final night at the Savoy so as to be on hand to help Mrs. Clipp get off at 7 A.M. on the following morning for Airways House and Heathrow Airport.

5

THE BOAT THAT had left the marshes two days before paddled gently along the Shatt el Arab. The stream was swift and the old man who was propelling the boat needed to do very little. His movements were gentle and rhythmic. His eyes were half closed. Almost under his breath he sang very softly, a sad unending Arab chant

ASRI BI LEL YA YAMALI
HADHI ALEK YA IBN ALI

Thus, on innumerable other occasions, had Abdul Suleiman of the Marsh Arabs come down the river to Basrah. There was another man in the boat, a figure often seen nowadays, with a pathetic mingling of West and East in his clothing. Over his long robe of striped cotton he wore a discarded khaki tunic, old and stained and torn. A faded red knitted scarf was tucked into the ragged coat. His head showed again the dignity of the Arab dress, the inevitable keffiyah of black and white held in place by the black silk *agal*. His eyes, unfocused in a wide stare, looked out blearily over the river bund. Presently he, too, began to hum in the same key and tone. He was a figure like thousands of other figures in the Mesopotamia landscape. There was nothing to show that he was an Englishman, and that he carried with him a secret that influential men in almost every country in the world were striving to intercept and to destroy, along with the man who carried it.

His mind went hazily back over the last weeks. The ambush in the mountains. The ice cold of the snow coming over the Pass. The caravan of camels. The four days spent trudging on foot over bare desert in company with two men carrying a portable "cinema." The days in the black tent and the journeying with the Aneizeh tribe, old friends of his. All difficult, all fraught with danger—slipping again and again through the cordon spread out to look for him and intercept him.

"Henry Carmichael. British agent. Age about thirty. Brown hair, dark eyes, five foot ten. Speaks Arabic, Kurdish, Persian, Armenian, Hindustani, Turkish and many mountain dialects. Befriended by the tribesmen. Dangerous."

Carmichael had been born in Kashgar where his father was a Government official. His childish tongue had lisped various dialects and patois—his nurses, and later his bearers, had been natives of many different races. In nearly all the wild places of the Middle East he had friends.

Only in the cities and the towns did his contacts fail him. Now, approaching Basrah, he knew that the critical moment of his mission had come. Sooner or later, he had got to reenter the civilized zone. Though Baghdad was his ultimate destination, he had judged it wise not to approach it direct. In every town in Iraq facilities were awaiting him, carefully discussed and arranged many months beforehand. It had had to be left to his own judgment where he should, so to speak, make his landing ground. He had sent no word to his superiors, even through the indirect channels where he could have done so. It was safer thus. The easy plan, the aeroplane waiting at the appointed rendezvous—had failed, as he had suspected it would fail. That rendezvous had been known to his enemies. Leakage! Always that deadly, that incomprehensible, leakage.

And so it was that his apprehensions of danger were heightened. Here in Basrah, in sight of safety, he felt instinctively sure that the danger would be greater than during the wild hazards of his journey. And to fail at the last lap —that would hardly bear thinking about.

Rhythmically pulling at his oars, the old Arab murmured without turning his head.

"The moment approaches, my son. May Allah prosper you."

"Do not tarry long in the city, my father. Return to the marshes. I would not have harm befall you."

"That is as Allah decrees. It is in his hands."

"In shâ Allâh," the other repeated.

For a moment he longed intensely to be a man of Eastern and not of Western blood. Not to worry over the chances of success or failure, not to calculate again and again the hazards, repeatedly asking himself if he had planned wisely and with forethought. To throw responsibility on the All Merciful, the All Wise. In shâ Allâh, I shall succeed!

Even saying the words over to himself he felt the calmness and the fatalism of the country overwhelming him and he welcomed it. Now, in a few moments, he must step from the haven of the boat, walk the streets of the city, run the gauntlet of keen eyes. Only by feeling as well as looking like an Arab could he succeed.

The boat turned gently into the waterway that ran at right angles to the river. Here all kinds of river craft were tied up, and other boats were coming in before and after them. It was a lovely, almost Venetian scene; the boats with their high scrolled prows and the soft faded colors of their paintwork. There were hundreds of them tied up close alongside each other.

The old man asked softly,

"The moment has come. There are preparations made for you?"

"Yes, indeed, my plans are set. The hour has come for me to leave."

"May God make your path straight, and may He lengthen the years of your life."

Carmichael gathered his striped skirts about him and went up the slippery stone steps to the wharf above.

All about him were the usual waterside figures. Small boys, orange sellers squatting down by their trays of merchandise. Sticky squares of cakes and sweetmeats, trays of bootlaces and cheap combs and pieces of elastic. Contemplative strollers, spitting raucously from time to time, wandering along with their beads clicking in their hands. On the opposite side of the street where the shops were and the banks, busy young *effendis* walked briskly in European suits of a slightly purplish tinge. There were Europeans, too, English and foreigners. And nowhere was there interest shown, or curiosity, because one among fifty or so Arabs had just climbed onto the wharf from a boat.

Carmichael strolled along very quietly, his eyes taking in the scene with just the right touch of childlike pleasure in his surroundings. Every now and then he hawked and spat, not too violently, just to be in the picture. Twice he blew his nose with his fingers.

And so, the stranger come to town, he reached the bridge at the top of the canal, and turned over it and passed into the Suq.

Here all was noise and movement. Energetic tribesmen strode along, pushing others out of their way—laden donkeys made their way along, their drivers calling out raucously, *Balek-balek* . . . Children quarreled and squealed and ran after Europeans calling hopefully, Baksheesh, madame. Baksheesh. Meskin-meskin . . .

Here the produce of the West and the East were equally for sale, side by side. Aluminum saucepans, cups and saucers and teapots, hammered copperware, silverwork from Amara, cheap watches, enamel mugs, embroideries and gay patterned rugs from Persia. Brass bound chests from Kuwait, secondhand coats and trousers and children's woolly cardigans. Local quilted bedcovers, painted glass lamps, stacks of clay water jars and pots. All the cheap merchandise of civilization together with the native products.

All as normal and as usual. After his long sojourn in the wilder spaces, the bustle and confusion seemed strange to Carmichael, but it was all as it should be, he could detect no jarring note, no sign of interest in his presence. And yet, with the instinct of one who has for long years known what it is to be a hunted man, he felt a growing uneasiness—a vague sense of menace. He could detect nothing amiss. No one had looked at him. No one, he was almost sure, was following him or keeping him under observation. Yet he had that indefinable certainty of danger.

He moved up a narrow dark turning, again to the right, then to the left. Here, among the small booths, he came to the opening of a khan, and stepped through the doorway into the court. Various shops were all around it. Carmichael went to one where *ferwahs* were hanging—the sheepskin coats of the North. He stood there handling them tentatively. The owner of the store was offering coffee to a customer, a tall bearded man of fine presence, who wore green round his fez, showing him to be a Hajji who had been to Mecca.

Carmichael stood there fingering the *ferwah*.

"Besh hadha?" he asked.

"Seven dinars."

"Too much."

The Hajji said, "You will deliver the carpets at my Khan?"

"Without fail," said the merchant. "You start tomorrow?"

"At dawn for Kerbela."

"It is my city, Kerbela," said Carmichael. "It is fifteen years now since I have seen the Tomb of the Hussein."

"It is a holy city," said the Hajji.

The shopkeeper said over his shoulder to Carmichael,

"There are cheaper *ferwahs* in the inner room."

"A white *ferwah* from the north is what I need."

"I have such a one in the farther room."

The merchant indicated the door set back in the inner wall.

The ritual had gone according to pattern—a conversation such as might be heard any day in any Suq—but the sequence was exact—the keywords all there—Kerbela—white *ferwah*.

Only, as Carmichael passed to cross the room and enter the inner enclosure, he raised his eyes to the merchant's face—and knew instantly that the face was not the one he expected to see. Though he had seen this particular man only once before, his keen memory was not at fault. There was a resemblance, a very close resemblance, but it was not the same man.

He stopped. He said, his tone one of mild surprise,

"Where, then, is Salah Hassan?"

"He was my brother. He died three days ago. His affairs are in my hands."

Yes, this was probably a brother. The resemblance was very close. And it was possible that the brother was also employed by the department. Certainly the responses had been correct. Yet it was with an increased awareness that Carmichael passed through into the dim inner chamber. Here again was merchandise piled on shelves, coffee pots and sugar hammers of brass and copper, old Persian silver, heaps of embroideries, folded abas, enameled Damascus trays and coffee sets.

A white *ferwah* lay carefully folded by itself on a small coffee table. Carmichael went to it and picked it up. Underneath it was a set of European clothes, a worn, slightly flashy business suit. The pocketbook with money and credentials was already in the breast pocket. An unknown Arab had entered the store; Mr. Walter Williams of Messrs. Cross and Co. Importers and Shipping agents would emerge and would keep certain appointments made for him in advance. There was, of course, a real Mr. Walter Williams—it was as careful as that—a man with a respectable open business past. All according to plan. With a sigh of relief Carmichael started to unbutton his ragged Army jacket. All was well.

If a revolver had been chosen as the weapon, Carmichael's mission would have failed then and there. But there are advantages in a knife—noticeably noiselessness.

On the shelf in front of Carmichael was a big copper coffee pot and that coffee pot had been recently polished to the order of an American tourist who was coming in to collect it. The gleam of the knife was reflected in that shining rounded surface—a whole picture, distorted but apparent, was reflected there. The man slipping through the hangings behind Carmichael, the long curved knife he had just pulled from beneath his garments. In another moment that knife would have been buried in Carmichael's back.

Like a flash Carmichael wheeled round. With a low flying tackle he brought the other to the ground. The knife flew across the room. Carmichael disentangled himself quickly, leaped over the other's body, rushed through the outer room where he caught a glimpse of the merchant's startled malevolent face and the placid surprise of the fat Hajji. Then he was out, across the Khan, back into the crowded Suq, turning first one way, then another, strolling again now, showing no signs of haste in a country where to hurry is to appear unusual.

And walking thus, almost aimlessly, stopping to examine a piece of stuff, to feel a texture, his brain was working with furious activity. The machinery had broken down! Once more, he was on his own, in hostile country. And he was disagreeably aware of the significance of what had just happened.

It was not only the enemies on his trail he had to fear. Nor was it the enemies guarding the approaches to civilization. There were enemies to fear within the system. For the passwords had been known, the responses had come pat and correct. The attack had been timed for exactly the moment when he had been lulled into security. Not surprising, perhaps, that there was treachery from within. It must have always been the aim of the enemy to introduce one or more of their own number into the system. Or, perhaps, to buy the man that they needed. Buying a man was easier than one might think —one could buy with other things than money.

Well, no matter how it had come about, there it was. He was on the run— back on his own resources. Without money, without the help of a new personality, and his appearance known. Perhaps at this very moment he was being quietly followed.

He did not turn his head. Of what use would that be? Those who followed were not novices at the game.

Quietly, aimlessly, he continued to stroll. Behind his listless manner he was reviewing various possibilities. He came out of the Suq at last and crossed the little bridge over the canal. He walked on until he saw the big painted hatchment over the doorway and the legend: British Consulate.

He looked up the street and down. No one seemed to be paying the least attention to him. Nothing, it appeared, was easier than just to step into the British Consulate.

He thought, for a moment, of a mousetrap, an open mousetrap with its enticing piece of cheese. That, too, was easy and simple for the mouse . . .

Well, the risk had to be taken. He didn't see what else he could do.

He went through the doorway.

6

RICHARD BAKER SAT in the outer office of the British Consulate waiting until the Consul was disengaged.

He had come ashore from the *Indian Queen* that morning and seen his baggage through the customs. It consisted almost entirely of books. Pyjamas and shirts were strewn among them, rather as an afterthought.

The *Indian Queen* had arrived on time and Richard, who had allowed a margin of two days, since small cargo boats such as the *Indian Queen* were frequently delayed, had now two days in hand before he need proceed, via Baghdad, to his ultimate destination, Tell Aswad, the site of the ancient city of Murik.

His plans were already made as to what to do with these two days. A certain reputed mound containing ancient remains at a spot near the seashore in Kuwait had long excited his curiosity. This was a heaven-sent opportunity to investigate same.

He drove to the Airport Hotel and inquired as to the methods of getting to Kuwait. A plane left at ten o'clock the following morning, he was told, and he could return the next day. Everything therefore was plain sailing. There were, of course, the inevitable formalities, exit visa and visa for Kuwait. For these he would have to repair to the British Consulate. The Consul General at Basrah, Mr. Clayton, Richard had met some years previously in Persia. It would be pleasant, Richard thought, to meet him again.

The Consulate had several entrances. A main gate for cars. Another small gate leading out from the garden to the road that lay alongside the Shatt el Arab. The business entrance to the Consulate was in the main street. Richard went in, gave his card to the man on duty, was told the Consul General was engaged at the moment but would soon be free, and was shown into a small waiting room to the left of the passage which ran straight through from the entrance to the garden beyond.

There were several people already in the waiting room. Richard hardly glanced at them. He was, in any case, seldom interested by members of the human race. A fragment of antique pottery was always more exciting to him than a mere human being born somewhere in the twentieth century A.D.

He allowed his thoughts to dwell pleasantly on some aspects of the Mari letters and the movements of the Benjaminite tribes in 1750 B.C.

It would be hard to say exactly what awoke him to a vivid sense of the present and of his fellow human beings. It was, first, an uneasiness, a sense of tension. It came to him, he thought, though he could not be sure, through his nose. Nothing you could diagnose in concrete terms—but it was there, unmistakable, taking him back to days in the late war. One occasion in particular when he, and two others, had been parachuted from a plane, and had waited in the small cold hours of dawn for the moment to do their stuff. A moment when morale was low, when the full hazards of the undertaking were clearly perceived, a moment of dread lest one might not be adequate, a shrinking of the flesh. The same acrid, almost imperceptible tang in the air.

The smell of fear . . .

For some moments, this registered only subconsciously. Half of his mind still obstinately strove to focus itself B.C. But the pull of the present was too strong.

Someone in this small room was in deadly fear . . .

He looked around. An Arab in a ragged khaki tunic, his fingers idly slipping over the amber beads he held. A stoutish Englishman with a gray moustache—the commercial traveler type—who was jotting down figures in a small notebook and looking absorbed and important. A tired looking man, very dark skinned, who was leaning back in a reposeful attitude, his face placid and uninterested. A man who looked like an Iraqi clerk. An elderly Persian in flowing snowy robes. They all seemed quite unconcerned.

The clicking of the amber beads fell into a definite rhythm. It seemed, in an odd way, familiar. Richard jerked himself to attention. He had been nearly asleep. Short long—long—short—that was Morse—definite Morse signaling. He was familiar with Morse; part of his job during the war had dealt with signaling. He could read it easily enough. *OWL*. F.L.O.R.E.A.T.E.T.O.N.A. What the devil! Yes, that was it. It was being repeated *Floreat Etona*. Tapped out (or rather clicked out) by a ragged Arab. Hullo, what was this? "Owl. Eton. Owl."

His own nickname at Eton—where he had been sent with an unusually large and solid pair of spectacles.

He looked across the room at the Arab, noting every detail of his appearance—the striped robe—the old khaki tunic—the ragged hand-knitted red scarf full of dropped stitches. A figure such as you saw hundreds of on the waterfront. The eyes met his vacantly with no sign of recognition. But the beads continued to click.

Fakir here. Stand by. Trouble.

Fakir? *Fakir?* Of course! Fakir Carmichael! A boy who had been born or who had lived in some outlandish part of the world—Turkestan, Afghanistan?—

Richard took out his pipe. He took an exploratory pull at it—peered into the bowl and then tapped it on an adjacent ashtray: *Message received.*

After that, things happened very fast. Later, Richard was at pains to sort them out.

The Arab in the torn army jacket got up and crossed toward the door. He stumbled as he was passing Richard, his hand went out and clutched Richard to steady himself. Then he righted himself, apologized and moved toward the door.

It was so surprising and happened so quickly that it seemed to Richard like a cinema scene rather than real life. The stout commercial traveler dropped his notebook and tugged at something in his coat pocket. Because of his plumpness and the tight fit of the coat, he was a second or two in getting it out and in that second or two Richard acted. As the man brought the revolver up, Richard struck it out of his hand. It went off and a bullet buried itself in the floor.

The Arab had passed through the doorway and had turned toward the Consul's office, but he paused suddenly, and turning he ran swiftly the other way to the door by which he had entered and into the busy street.

The kavass ran to Richard's side where he stood holding the stout man's arm. Of the other occupants of the room, the Iraqi clerk was dancing excitedly on his feet, the dark thin man was staring and the elderly Persian gazed into space unmoved.

Richard said:

"What the devil are you doing, brandishing a revolver like that?"

There was just a moment's pause, and then the stout man said in a plaintive cockney voice,

"Sorry, old man. Absolute accident. Just clumsy."

"Nonsense. You were going to shoot at that Arab fellow who's just run out."

"No, no, old man, not shoot him. Just give him a fright. Recognized him suddenly as a fellow who swindled me over some antikas. Just a bit of fun."

Richard Baker was a fastidious soul who disliked publicity of any kind. His instincts were to accept the explanation at its face value. After all, what could he prove? And would old Fakir Carmichael thank him for making a song and dance about the matter? Presumably if he were on some hush-hush, cloak and dagger business he would not.

Richard relaxed his grasp on the man's arm. The fellow was sweating, he noticed.

The kavass was talking excitedly. It was very wrong, he was saying, to bring firearms into the British Consulate. It was not allowed. The Consul would be very angry.

"I apologize," said the fat man. "Little accident—that's all." He thrust some money into the kavass's hand who pushed it back again indignantly.

"I'd better get out of this," said the stout man. "I won't wait to see the Consul." He thrust a card suddenly on Richard. "That's me and I'm at the Airport Hotel if there's any fuss, but actually it was a pure accident. Just a joke if you know what I mean."

Reluctantly, Richard watched him walk with an uneasy swagger out of the room and turn toward the street.

He hoped he had done right, but it was a difficult thing to know what to do when one was as much in the dark as he was.

"Mr. Clayton, he is disengaged now," said the kavass.

Richard followed the man along the corridor. The open circle of sunlight at the end grew larger. The Consul's room was on the right at the extreme end of the passage.

Mr. Clayton was sitting behind his desk. He was a quiet gray haired man with a thoughtful face.

"I don't know whether you remember me?" said Richard. "I met you in Teheran two years ago."

"Of course. You were with Dr. Pauncefoot Jones, weren't you? Are you joining him again this year?"

"Yes. I'm on my way there now, but I've got a few days to spare, and I rather wanted to run down to Kuwait. There's no difficulty, I suppose?"

"Oh, no. There's a plane tomorrow morning. It's only about an hour and a half. I'll wire to Archie Gaunt—he's the President there. He'll put you up. And we can put you up here for the night."

Richard protested slightly.

"Really—I don't want to bother you and Mrs. Clayton. I can go to the hotel."

"The Airport Hotel's very full. We'd be delighted to have you here. I know my wife would like to meet you again. At the moment—let me see—we've got Crosbie of the Oil Company and some young sprig of Dr. Rathbone's who's down here clearing some cases of books through the customs. Come upstairs and see Rosa—"

He got up and escorted Richard out through the door and into the sunlit garden. A flight of steps led up to the living quarters of the Consulate.

Gerald Clayton pushed open the wire door at the top of the steps and ushered his guest into a long dim hallway with attractive rugs on the floor and choice examples of furniture on either side. It was pleasant coming into the cold dimness after the glare outside.

Clayton called, "Rosa, Rosa," and Mrs. Clayton whom Richard remembered as a buoyant personality with abounding vitality came out of an end room.

"You remember Richard Baker, dear? He came to see us with Dr. Pauncefoot Jones in Teheran."

"Of course," said Mrs. Clayton shaking hands. "We went to the bazaars together and you bought some lovely rugs."

It was Mrs. Clayton's delight when not buying things herself to urge on her friends and acquaintances to seek for bargains in the local Suqs. She always had a wonderful knowledge of values and was an excellent bargainer.

"One of the best purchases I've ever made," said Richard. "And entirely owing to your good offices."

"Baker wants to fly to Kuwait tomorrow," said Gerald Clayton. "I've said that we can put him up here for tonight."

"But if it's any trouble," began Richard.

"Of course, it's no trouble," said Mrs. Clayton. "You can't have the best spare room, because Captain Crosbie has got it, but we can make you quite comfortable. You don't want to buy a nice Kuwait chest, do you? Because they've got some lovely ones in the Suq just now. Gerald won't let me buy another one for here, though it would be quite useful to keep extra blankets in."

"You've got three already, dear," said Clayton mildly. "Now, if you'll excuse me, Baker. I must get back to the office. There seems to have been a spot of trouble in the outer office. Somebody let off a revolver, I understand."

"One of the local sheikhs, I suppose," said Mrs. Clayton. "They are so excitable and they do so love firearms."

"On the contrary," said Richard. "It was an Englishman. His intention seemed to be to take a pot shot at an Arab." He added gently, "I knocked his arm up."

"So you were in it all," said Clayton. "I didn't realize that." He fished a card out of his pocket. "Robert Hall. Achilles Works, Enfield seems to be his name. I don't know what he wanted to see me about. He wasn't drunk, was he?"

"He said it was a joke," said Richard dryly, "and that the gun went off by accident."

Clayton raised his eyebrows.

"Commercial travelers don't usually carry loaded guns in their pockets," he said.

Clayton, Richard thought, was no fool.

"Perhaps I ought to have stopped him going away."

"It's difficult to know what one should do when these things happen. The man he fired at wasn't hurt."

"No."

"Probably was better to let the thing slide, then."

"I wonder what was behind it?"

"Yes, yes . . . I wonder too."

Clayton looked a little distraught.

"Well, I must be getting back," he said and hurried away.

Mrs. Clayton took Richard into the drawing room, a large inside room, with green cushions and curtains, and offered him a choice of coffee or beer. He chose beer and it came deliciously iced.

She asked him why he was going to Kuwait and he told her.

She asked him why he hadn't got married yet, and Richard said he didn't think he was the marrying kind, to which Mrs. Clayton said briskly: "Nonsense." Archaeologists, she said, made splendid husbands—and were there any young women coming out to the Dig this season? One or two, Richard said, and Mrs. Pauncefoot Jones of course.

Mrs. Clayton asked hopefully if they were nice girls who were coming out, and Richard said he didn't know because he hadn't met them yet. They were very inexperienced, he said.

For some reason this made Mrs. Clayton laugh.

Then a short stocky man with an abrupt manner came in and was introduced as Captain Crosbie. Mr. Baker, said Mrs. Clayton, was an archaeologist and dug up the most wildly interesting things thousands of years old. Captain Crosbie said he never could understand how archaeologists were able to say so definitely how old these things were. Always used to think they must be the most awful liars, ha ha, said Captain Crosbie. Richard looked at him in a rather tired kind of way. No, said Captain Crosbie, but how did an archaeologist know how old a thing was? Richard said that that would take a long time to explain, and Mrs. Clayton quickly took him away to see his room.

"He's very nice," said Mrs. Clayton, "but not quite quite, you know. Hasn't got any idea of culture."

Richard found his room exceedingly comfortable, and his appreciation of Mrs. Clayton as a hostess rose still higher.

Feeling in the pocket of his coat, he drew out a folded up piece of dirty paper. He looked at it with surprise, for he knew quite well that it had not been there earlier in the morning.

He remembered how the Arab had clutched him when he stumbled. A man with deft fingers might have slipped this into his pocket without his being aware of it.

He unfolded the paper. It was dirty and seemed to have been folded and refolded many times.

In six lines of rather crabbed handwriting Major John Wilberforce recommended one Ahmed Mohammed as an industrious and willing worker, able to drive a lorry and do minor repairs and strictly honest— It was, in fact, the usual type of "chit" or recommendation given in the East. It was dated eighteen months back, which again is not unusual, as these chits are hoarded carefully by their possessors.

Frowning to himself, Richard went over the events of the morning in his precise orderly fashion.

Fakir Carmichael, he was now well assured, had been in fear of his life. He was a hunted man and he had bolted into the Consulate. Why? To find security? But instead of that he had found a more instant menace. The enemy, or a representative of the enemy, had been waiting for him. This commercial traveler chap must have had very definite orders—to be willing to risk shooting Carmichael in the Consulate in the presence of witnesses. It must, therefore, have been very urgent. And Carmichael had appealed to his old school friend for help, and had managed to pass this seemingly innocent document into his possession. It must, therefore, be very important, and if Carmichael's enemies caught up with him, and found that he no longer possessed this document, they would doubtless put two and two together and look for any person or persons to whom Carmichael might conceivably have passed it on.

What then was Richard Baker to do with it?

He could pass it on to Clayton, as His Britannic Majesty's representative.

Or he could keep it in his own possession until such time as Carmichael claimed it?

After a few minutes' reflection he decided to do the latter.

But first he took certain precautions.

Tearing a blank half sheet of paper off an old letter, he sat down to compose a reference for a lorry driver in much the same terms, but using different wording—if this message was a code that took care of that—though it was possible, of course, that there was a message written in some kind of invisible ink.

Then he smeared his own composition with dust from his shoes—rubbed it in his hands, folded and refolded it—until it gave a reasonable appearance of age and dirt.

Then he crumpled it up and put it into his pocket. The original he stared at for some time while he considered and rejected various possibilities.

Finally, with a slight smile, he folded and refolded it until he had a small oblong. Taking a stick of plasticine (without which he never traveled) out of his bag, he first wrapped his packet in oilsilk cut from his spongebag, then encased it in plasticine. This done he rolled and patted out the plasticine till he had a smooth surface. On this he rolled out an impression from a cylinder seal that he had with him.

He studied the result with grim appreciation.

It showed a beautifully carved design of the Sun God Shamash, armed with the Sword of Justice.

"Let's hope that's a good omen," he said to himself.

That evening, when he looked in the pocket of the coat he had worn in the morning, the screwed up paper had gone.

7

LIFE, THOUGHT VICTORIA, life at last! Sitting in her seat at Airways Terminal there had come the magic moment when the words "Passengers for Cairo, Baghdad and Teheran, take your places in the bus, please," had been uttered.

Magic names, magic words. Devoid of glamour to Mrs. Hamilton Clipp who, as far as Victoria could make out, had spent a large portion of her life jumping from boats into airplanes and from airplanes into trains, with brief intervals at expensive hotels in between. But to Victoria they were a marvellous change from the oft repeated phrases "Take this down, please, Miss Jones." "The kettle's boiling, ducks, just make the tea, will you." "I know where you can get the most marvellous perm." Trivial boring everyday happenings! And now: Cairo, Baghdad, Teheran—all the romance of the glorious East (and Edward at the end of it).

Victoria returned to earth to hear her employer, whom she had already diagnosed as a nonstop talker, concluding a series of remarks by saying:

"—and nothing really clean if you know what I mean. I'm always very very careful what I eat. The filth of the streets and the bazaars you wouldn't believe. And the unhygienic rags the people wear. And some of the toilets— why, you just couldn't call them toilets at all!"

Victoria listened dutifully to these depressing remarks, but her own sense of glamour remained undimmed. Dirt and germs meant nothing in her young life. They arrived at Heathrow and she assisted Mrs. Clipp to alight from the bus. She was already in charge of passports, tickets, money, etc.

"My," said that lady, "it certainly is a comfort to have you with me, Miss Jones. I just don't know what I'd have done if I'd had to travel alone."

Traveling by air, Victoria thought, was rather like being taken on a school treat. Brisk teachers, kind but firm, were at hand to shepherd you at every turn. Air hostesses, in trim uniform with the authority of nursery governesses dealing with feebleminded children, explained kindly just what you were to do. Victoria almost expected them to preface their remarks with: "Now, children."

Tired looking young gentlemen behind desks extended weary hands to check passports, to inquire intimately of money and jewelry. They managed to induce a sense of guilt in those questioned. Victoria, suggestible by nature, knew a sudden longing to describe her one meager brooch as a diamond tiara value ten thousand pounds, just to see the expression on the bored young man's face. Thoughts of Edward restrained her.

The various barriers passed, they sat down to wait once more in a large room giving directly on the airfield. Outside the roar of a plane being revved up gave the proper background. Mrs. Hamilton Clipp was now happily engaged in making a running commentary on their fellow travelers.

"Aren't those two little children just too cute for words? But what an ordeal to travel alone with a couple of children. British, I guess they are. That's a well-cut suit the mother has on. She looks kind of tired, though. That's a good-looking man—rather Latin-looking, I'd say. What a loud check that man has on—I'd call it very bad taste. Business, I guess. That man over there's a Dutchman; he was just ahead of us at the controls. That family over there is either Turkish or Persian, I should say. There don't seem to be any Americans. I guess they go mostly Pan American. I'd say those three men talking together are Oil, wouldn't you? I just love looking at people and wondering about them. Mr. Clipp says to me I've got a real yen for human nature. It seems to me just natural to take an interest in your fellow creatures. Wouldn't you say that mink coat over there cost every bit of three thousand dollars?"

Mrs. Clipp sighed. Having duly appraised her fellow travelers, she became restless.

"I'd like to know what we are waiting for like this. That plane's revved up four times. We're all here. Why can't they get on with things? They're certainly not keeping to schedule."

"Would you like a cup of coffee, Mrs. Clipp? I see there is a buffet at the end of the room?"

"Why, no, thank you, Miss Jones. I had coffee before I started, and my stomach feels too unsettled right now to take anything more. What are we waiting for, I'd like to know?"

Her question seemed to be answered almost before the words were out of her mouth.

The door leading from the corridor out of the Customs and Passport department swung open with a rush and a tall man came through with the effect of a gust of wind. Air officials of the line hovered around him. Two large canvas sacks sealed were carried by an officer of B.O.A.C.

Mrs. Clipp sat up with alacrity.

"He's certainly some big noise," she remarked.

"And knows it," thought Victoria.

There was something of calculated sensationalism about the late traveler. He wore a kind of dark gray traveling cloak with a capacious hood at the back. On his head was what was in essence a wide sombrero, but in light gray. He had silver gray curling hair, worn rather long, and a beautiful silver gray moustache curling up at the ends. The effect was that of a handsome stage bandit. Victoria, who disliked theatrical men who posed, looked at him with disapproval.

The Air Officials were, she noted with displeasure, all over him.

"Yes, Sir Rupert." "Of course, Sir Rupert." "The plane is leaving immediately, Sir Rupert."

With a swirl of his voluminous cloak, Sir Rupert passed out through the door leading to the airfield. The door swung to behind him with vehemence.

"Sir Rupert," murmured Mrs. Clipp. "Now who would he be, I wonder?"

Victoria shook her head, though she had a vague feeling that the face and general appearance were not unknown to her.

"Somebody important in your Government," suggested Mrs. Clipp.

"I shouldn't think so," said Victoria.

The few members of the Government she had ever seen had impressed her as men anxious to apologize for being alive. Only on platforms did they spring into pompous and didactic life.

"Now then, please," said the smart Nursery Governess Air Hostess. "Take your seats in the plane. This way. As quickly as you can, please."

Her attitude implied that a lot of dawdling children had been keeping the patient grown-ups waiting.

Everybody filed out onto the airfield.

The great plane was waiting, its engine ticking over like the satisfied purring of a gigantic lion.

Victoria and a steward helped Mrs. Clipp on board and settled her in her seat. Victoria sat next to her on the aisle. Not until Mrs. Clipp was comfortably ensconced, and Victoria had fastened her safety belt, did the girl have leisure to observe that in front of them was sitting the great man.

The doors closed. A few seconds later, the plane began to move slowly along the ground.

"We're really going," thought Victoria in ecstasy. "Oh, isn't it frightening. Suppose it never gets up off the ground? Really I don't see how it can!"

During what seemed an age the plane taxied along the airfield, then it turned slowly around and stopped. The engines rose to a ferocious roar. Chewing gum, barley sugar and cotton wool were handed round.

Louder and louder, fiercer and fiercer. Then, once more, the airplane moved forward. Mincingly at first, then faster—faster still—they were rushing along the ground.

"It will never go up," thought Victoria, "we'll be killed."

Faster—more smoothly—no jars—no bumps—they were off the ground skimming along, up, around, back over the car park and the main road, up, higher—a silly little train puffing below—dolls' houses—toy cars on roads . . . Higher still—and suddenly the earth below lost interest, was no longer human or alive—just a large flat map with lines and circles and dots.

Inside the plane people undid their safety belts, lit cigarettes, opened magazines. Victoria was in a new world—a world so many feet long and a very few feet wide, inhabited by twenty to thirty people. Nothing else existed.

She peered out of the small window again. Below her were clouds, a fluffy pavement of clouds. The plane was in the sun. Below the clouds somewhere was the world she had known heretofore.

Victoria pulled herself together. Mrs. Hamilton Clipp was talking. Victoria removed cotton wool from her ear and bent attentively toward her.

In the seat in front of her, Sir Rupert rose, tossed his wide brimmed gray felt hat to the rack, drew up his hood over his head and relaxed into his seat.

"Pompous ass," thought Victoria, unreasonably prejudiced.

Mrs. Clipp was established with a magazine open in front of her. At intervals, she nudged Victoria when on trying to turn the page with one hand, the magazine slipped.

Victoria looked around her. She decided that air travel was really rather boring. She opened a magazine, found herself faced with an advertisement that said "Do you want to increase your efficiency as a shorthand typist?" shuddered, shut the magazine, leaned back, and began to think of Edward.

They came down at Castel Benito Airport in a storm of rain. Victoria was by now feeling slightly sick, and it took all her energies to accomplish her duties *vis-à-vis* with her employer. They were driven through scurrying rain to the rest house. The magnificent Sir Rupert, Victoria noted, had been met by an officer in uniform with red tabs, and hurried off in a staff car to some dwelling of the mighty in Tripolitania.

They were allotted rooms; Victoria helped Mrs. Clipp with her toilet and left her to rest on her bed in a dressing gown until it was time for the evening meal. Victoria retired to her own room, lay down and closed her eyes, grateful to be spared the sight of the heaving and sinking floor.

She awakened an hour later in good health and spirits and went to help Mrs. Clipp. Presently a rather more peremptory air hostess instructed them that cars were ready to convey them to the evening meal. After dinner, Mrs. Clipp got into conversation with some of her fellow travelers. The man in the loud check coat seemed to have taken a fancy to Victoria and told her at some length all about the manufacture of lead pencils.

Later, they were conveyed back to their sleeping quarters and told curtly that they must be ready to depart at 5:30 A.M. the following morning.

"We haven't seen much of Tripolitania, have we," said Victoria rather sadly. "Is air travel always like this?"

"Why, yes, I'd say so. It's just positively sadistic the way they get you up in the mornings. After that, often they keep you hanging round the airport for an hour or two. Why, in Rome, I remember they called us at 3:30. Breakfast in the restaurant at 4 o'clock. And then actually at the airport we didn't leave until eight. Still the great thing is they get you to your destination right away with no fooling about on the way."

Victoria sighed. She could have done with a good deal of fooling about. She wanted to see the world.

"And what do you know, my dear," continued Mrs. Clipp excitedly, "you know that interesting-looking man? The Britisher? The one that there's all the fuss about. I've found out who he is. That's Sir Rupert Crofton Lee, the great traveler. You've heard of him, of course."

Yes, Victoria remembered now. She had seen several pictures in the press about six months ago. Sir Rupert was a great authority upon the interior of China. He was one of the few people who had been to Tibet and visited Lhasa. He had traveled through the unknown parts of Kurdistan and Asia Minor. His books had had a wide sale, for they had been racily and wittily written. If Sir Rupert was just noticeably a self-advertiser, it was with good reason. He made no claims that were not fully justified. The cloak with the hood and the wide brimmed hat were, Victoria remembered now, a deliberate fashion of his own choosing.

"Isn't that thrilling, now?" demanded Mrs. Clipp with all a lion hunter's enthusiasm as Victoria adjusted the bedclothes over her recumbent form.

Victoria agreed that it was very thrilling, but she said to herself that she preferred Sir Rupert's books to his personality. He was, she considered, what children call "a show off!"

A start was made in good order the next morning. The weather had cleared and the sun was shining. Victoria still felt disappointed to have seen so little of Tripolitania. Still the plane was due to arrive at Cairo by lunch time and the departure to Baghdad did not take place until the following morning, so she would at least be able to see a little of Egypt in the afternoon.

They were flying over the sea, but clouds soon blocked out the blue water below them and Victoria settled back in her seat with a yawn. In front of her Sir Rupert was already asleep. The hood had fallen back from his head which was hanging forward, nodding at intervals. Victoria observed with a faint malicious pleasure that he had a small boil starting on the back of his neck. Why she should have been pleased at this fact was hard to say—perhaps it made the great man seem more human and vulnerable. He was as other men, after all—prone to the small annoyances of the flesh. It may be said that Sir Rupert had kept up his Olympian manner and had taken no notice whatever of his fellow travelers.

"Who does he think he is, I wonder?" thought Victoria to herself. The answer was obvious. He was Sir Rupert Crofton Lee, a celebrity, and she was Victoria Jones, an indifferent shorthand typist, and of no account whatever.

On arrival at Cairo, Victoria and Mrs. Hamilton Clipp had lunch together. The latter then announced that she was going to nap until six o'clock, and suggested that Victoria might like to go and see the Pyramids.

"I've arranged for a car for you, Miss Jones, because I know that owing to your Treasury regulations, you won't be able to cash any money here."

Victoria who had in any case no money to cash, was duly grateful, and said so with some effusion.

"Why, that's nothing at all. You've been very very kind to me. And, traveling with dollars, everything is easy for us. Mrs. Kitchin—the lady with the two cute children—is very anxious to go, also, so I suggested you'd join up with her—if that suits you?"

So long as she saw the world, anything suited Victoria.

"That's fine. Then you'd better get off right now."

The afternoon at the Pyramids was duly enjoyed. Victoria, though reasonably fond of children, might have enjoyed it more without Mrs. Kitchin's offspring. Children when sight seeing is in progress are apt to be somewhat of a handicap. The youngest child became so fretful that the two women returned earlier from the expedition than they had meant to do.

Victoria threw herself on her bed with a yawn. She wished very much that she could stay a week in Cairo—perhaps go up the Nile. "And what would you use for money, my girl?" she asked herself witheringly. It was already a miracle that she was being transported to Baghdad free of charge.

And what, inquired a cold inward voice, are you going to do, once you are landed in Baghdad with only a few pounds in your pocket?

Victoria waved that query aside. Edward must find her a job. Or failing that, she would find herself a job. Why worry?

Her eyes, dazzled with strong sunlight, closed gently.

A knock on the door, as she thought, roused her. She called "Come in"; then as there was no response, she got off the bed, crossed to the door and opened it.

But the knock had not been at her door, but at the next door down the passage. Another of the inevitable air hostesses, dark haired and trim in her uniform, was knocking at Sir Rupert Crofton Lee's door. He opened it just as Victoria looked out.

"What's the matter now?"

He sounded annoyed and sleepy.

"I'm so sorry to disturb you, Sir Rupert," cooed the air hostess, "but would you mind coming to the B.O.A.C. office. It's just three doors down the passage here. Just a small detail about the flight to Baghdad tomorrow."

"Oh, very well."

Victoria withdrew into her room. She was less sleepy now. She glanced at her watch. Only half past four. An hour and a half until Mrs. Clipp would be requiring her. She decided to go out and walk about Heliopolis. Walking, at least, required no money.

She powdered her nose and resumed her shoes. They felt rather full of feet. The visit to the Pyramids had been hard on feet.

She came out of her room and walked along the corridor toward the main hall of the hotel. Three doors down she passed the B.O.A.C. office. It had a card announcing the fact nailed to the door. Just as she passed it, the door opened and Sir Rupert came out. He was walking fast and he overtook her in a couple of strides. He went on ahead of her, his cloak swinging, and Victoria fancied that he was annoyed about something.

Mrs. Clipp was in a somewhat petulant mood when Victoria reported for duty at six o'clock.

"I'm worried about the excess on my baggage, Miss Jones. I took it that I'd paid for that right through, but it seems that it's only paid until Cairo. We go on tomorrow by Iraqi Airways. My ticket is a through ticket, but not the excess baggage. Perhaps you'd go and find out if that is really so? Because maybe I ought to change another traveler's check."

Victoria agreed to make inquiries. She could not find the B.O.A.C. office at first, and finally located it in the far corridor—the other side of the hall—quite a big office. The other, she supposed, had been a small office only used during the afternoon siesta hours. Mrs. Clipp's fears about the excess baggage were found to be justified which annoyed that lady very much.

8

ON THE FIFTH floor of a block of offices in the city of London are situated the offices of the Valhalla Gramophone Company. The man who sat behind the desk in that office was reading a book on economics. The telephone rang and he picked up the receiver. He said in a quiet unemotional voice:

"Valhalla Gramophone Company."

"Sanders here."

"Sanders of the River? What River?"

"River Tigris. Reporting as to A.S. We've lost her."

There was a moment's silence. Then the quiet voice spoke again, with a steely note in it.

"Did I hear what you said correctly?"

"We've lost Anna Scheele."

"No names. This is a very serious error on your part. How did it come about?"

"She went into that nursing home. I told you before. Her sister was having an operation."

"Well?"

"The operation went off all right. We expected A.S. to return to the Savoy. She had kept on her suite. She didn't return. Watch had been kept on the nursing home and we were quite sure she hadn't left it. We assumed she was still there."

"And she isn't?"

"We've just found out. She left there, in an ambulance, the day after the operation."

"She deliberately fooled you?"

"Looks like it. I'd swear she didn't know she was being followed. We took every precaution. There were three of us and—"

"Never mind the excuses. Where did the ambulance take her?"

"To University College Hospital."

"What have you learned from the hospital?"

"That a patient was brought in accompanied by a hospital nurse. The hospital nurse must have been Anna Scheele. They've no idea where she went after she brought the patient in."

"And the patient?"

"The patient knows nothing. She was under morphia."

"So Anna Scheele walked out of University College Hospital dressed as a nurse and may now be anywhere?"

"Yes. If she goes back to the Savoy—"

The other interrupted.

"She won't go back to the Savoy."

"Shall we check up on other hotels?"

"Yes, but I doubt if you'll get any result. That's what she'd expect you to do."

"What instructions otherwise?"

"Check on the ports—Dover, Folkestone, etc. Check with Air Lines. In particular check all bookings to Baghdad by plane for the next fortnight. The passage won't be booked in her own name. Check up on all passengers of suitable age."

"Her baggage is still at the Savoy. Perhaps she'll claim."

"She won't do anything of the sort. You may be a fool—she isn't! Does the sister know anything?"

"We're in contact with her special nurse at the Home. Apparently the sister thinks A.S. is in Paris doing business for Morgánthal and staying at Ritz Hotel. She believes A.S. is flying home to States on 23rd."

"In other words A.S. has told her nothing. She wouldn't. Check up on those air passages. It's the only hope. She's got to get to Baghdad—and Air is the only way she can do it in time, and, Sanders—"

"Yes?"

"No more failures. This is your last chance."

9

YOUNG MR. SHRIVENHAM of the British Embassy shifted from one foot to the other and gazed upward as the plane zoomed over Baghdad airport. There was a considerable duststorm in progress. Palm trees, houses, human beings were all shrouded in a thick brown haze. It had come on quite suddenly.

Lionel Shrivenham observed in a tone of deep distress:

"Ten to one they can't come down here."

"What will they do?" asked his friend Harold.

"Go on to Basrah, I imagine. It's clear there, I hear."

"You're meeting some kind of a V.I.P., aren't you?"

Young Mr. Shrivenham groaned again.

"Just my luck. The new Ambassador has been delayed coming out. Lansdowne, the Counselor, is in England. Rice, the Oriental Counselor, is ill in bed with gastric flu, dangerously high temperature. Best is in Teheran, and here am I, left with the whole bag of tricks. No end of a flap about this fellow. I don't know why. Even the hush hush boys are in a flap. He's one of these world travelers, always off somewhere inaccessible on a camel. Don't see why he's so important, but apparently he's absolutely the cat's whiskers, and I'm to conform to his slightest wish. If he gets carried on to Basrah he'll probably be wild. Don't know what arrangements I'd better lay on. Train up tonight? Or get the R.A.F. to fly him up tomorrow?"

Mr. Shrivenham sighed again, as his sense of injury and responsibility deepened. Since his arrival three months ago in Baghdad he had been consistently unlucky. One more raspberry, he felt, would finally blight what might have been a promising career.

The plane swooped overhead once more.

"Evidently thinks he can't make it," said Shrivenham, then added excitedly: "Hullo—I believe he's coming down."

A few moments later and the plane had taxied sedately to its place and Shrivenham stood ready to greet the V.I.P.

His unprofessional eye noted "rather a pretty girl . . ." before he sprang forward to greet the buccaneerlike figure in the swirling cloak.

"Practically fancy dress," he thought to himself disapprovingly as he said aloud:

"Sir Rupert Crofton Lee? I'm Shrivenham of the Embassy."

Sir Rupert, he thought, was slightly curt in manner—perhaps understandable after the strain of circling round the city uncertain whether a landing could be effected or not.

"Nasty day," continued Shrivenham. "Had a lot of this sort of thing this year. Ah, you've got the bags. Then, if you'll follow me, sir, it's all laid on . . ."

As they left the airport in the car, Shrivenham said:

"I thought for a bit that you were going to be carried on to some other airport, sir. Didn't look as though the pilot could make a landing. Came up suddenly, this duststorm."

Sir Rupert blew out his cheeks importantly as he remarked:

"That would have been disastrous—quite disastrous. Had my schedule been jeopardized, young man, I can tell you that the results would have been grave and far-reaching in the extreme."

"Lot of cock," thought Shrivenham disrespectfully. "These V.I.P.'s think their potty affairs are what makes the world go round."

Aloud he said respectfully:

"I expect that's so, sir."

"Have you any idea when the Ambassador will reach Baghdad?"

"Nothing definite as yet, sir."

"I shall be sorry to miss him. Haven't seen him since—let me see, yes, India in 1938."

Shrivenham preserved a respectful silence.

"Let me see, Rice is here, isn't he?"

"Yes, sir, he's Oriental Counselor."

"Capable fellow. Knows a lot. I'll be glad to meet him again."

Shrivenham coughed.

"As a matter of fact, sir, Rice is on the sick list. They've taken him to hospital for observation. Violent type of gastroenteritis. Something a bit worse than the usual Baghdad tummy, apparently."

"What's that?" Sir Rupert turned his head sharply. "Bad gastroenteritis—hm. Came on suddenly, did it?"

"Day before yesterday, sir."

Sir Rupert was frowning. The rather affected grandiloquence of manner had dropped from him. He was a simpler man—and somewhat of a worried one.

"I wonder," he said. "Yes, I wonder."

Shrivenham looked politely enquiring.

"I'm wondering," said Sir Rupert, "if it might be a case of Scheele's Green. . . ."

Baffled, Shrivenham remained silent.

They were just approaching the Feisal Bridge, and the car swung off to the left toward the British Embassy.

Suddenly Sir Rupert leaned forward.

"Just stop a minute, will you?" he said sharply. "Yes, right hand side. Where all those pots are."

The car glided in to the right hand curb and stopped. It was a small native shop piled high with crude white clay pots and water jars.

A short stocky European who had been standing talking to the proprietor moved away toward the bridge as the car drew up. Shrivenham thought it was Crosbie of the I and P whom he had met once or twice.

Sir Rupert sprang from the car and strode up to the small booth. Picking up one of the pots, he started a rapid conversation in Arabic with the proprietor. The flow of speech was too fast for Shrivenham whose Arabic was as yet slow and painstaking and distinctly limited in vocabulary.

The proprietor was beaming, his hands flew wide, he gesticulated, he explained at length. Sir Rupert handled different pots, apparently asking questions about them. Finally he selected a narrow-mouthed water jar, tossed the man some coins and went back to the car.

"Interesting technique," said Sir Rupert. "Been making them like this for thousands of years, same shape as in one of the hill districts in Armenia."

His finger slipped down through the narrow aperture, twisting round and round.

"It's very crude stuff," said Shrivenham unimpressed.

"Oh, no artistic merit! But interesting historically. See these indications of lugs here? You pick up many a historical tip from observation of the simple things in daily use. I've got a collection of them."

The car turned in through the gates of the British Embassy.

Sir Rupert demanded to be taken straight to his room. Shrivenham was amused to note that, his lecture on the clay pot ended, Sir Rupert had left it nonchalantly in the car. Shrivenham made a point of carrying it upstairs and placing it meticulously upon Sir Rupert's bedside table.

"Your pot, sir."

"Eh? Oh, thank you, my boy."

Sir Rupert appeared distraught. Shrivenham left him after repeating that luncheon would be ready shortly and drinks awaited his choice.

When the young man had left the room, Sir Rupert went to the window and unfolded the small slip of paper that had been tucked into the mouth of the pot. He smoothed it out. There were two lines of writing on it. He read them over carefully, then set light to the paper with a match.

Then he summoned a servant.

"Yes, sir? I unpack for you, sir?"

"Not yet. I want to see Mr. Shrivenham—up here."

Shrivenham arrived with a slight apprehensive expression.

"Anything I can do, sir? Anything wrong?"

"Mr. Shrivenham, a drastic change has occurred in my plans. I can count upon your discretion, of course?"

"Oh absolutely, sir."

"It is some time since I was in Baghdad; actually I have not been here since the war. The hotels lie mainly on the other bank, do they not?"

"Yes, sir. In Rashid Street."

"Backing on the Tigris?"

"Yes. Babylonian Palace is the biggest of them. That's the more or less official hotel."

"What do you know about a hotel called the Tio?"

"Oh, a lot of people go there. Food's rather good and it's run by a terrific character called Marcus Tio. He's quite an institution in Baghdad."

"I want you to book me a room there, Mr. Shrivenham."

"You mean—you're not going to stay at the Embassy?" Shrivenham looked nervously apprehensive. "But—but—it's all laid on, sir."

"What is laid on can be laid off," barked Sir Rupert.

"Of-of course, sir. I didn't mean . . ."

Shrivenham broke off. He had a feeling that in the future someone was going to blame him.

"I have certain somewhat delicate negotiations to carry out. I learn that they cannot be carried out from the Embassy. I want you to book me a room tonight at the Tio Hotel and I wish to leave the Embassy in a reasonably unobtrusive manner. That is to say I do not want to drive up to the Tio in an Embassy car. I also require a seat booked on the plane leaving for Cairo the day after tomorrow."

Shrivenham looked more dismayed still.

"But I understood you were staying five days—"

"That is no longer the case. It is imperative that I reach Cairo as soon as my business here is terminated. It would not be safe for me to remain longer."

"Safe?"

A sudden grim smile transformed Sir Rupert's face. The manner which Shrivenham had been likening to that of a Prussian drill sergeant was laid aside. The man's charm became suddenly apparent.

"Safety hasn't usually been one of my preoccupations, I agree," he said. "But in this case it isn't only my own safety I have to consider—my safety includes the safety of a lot of other people as well. So make those arrangements for me. If the air passage is difficult, apply for priority. Until I leave here tonight, I shall remain in my room." He added, as Shrivenham's mouth opened in surprise, "Officially, I'm sick. Touch of malaria." The other nodded. "So I shan't need food."

"But surely we can send you up—"

"Twenty-four hours' fast is nothing to me. I've gone hungrier longer than that on some of my journeys. You just do as I tell you."

Downstairs, Shrivenham was greeted by his colleagues and groaned in answer to their inquiries.

"Cloak and dagger stuff in a big way," he said. "Can't quite make his grandiloquence Sir Rupert Crofton Lee out. Whether it's genuine or playacting. That swirling cloak and bandit's hat and all the rest of it. Fellow who'd read one of his books told me that although he's a bit of a self-advertiser, he really has done all these things and been to these places—but I don't know . . . Wish Thomas Rice was up and about to cope. That reminds me, what's Scheele's Green?"

"Scheele's Green?" said his friend, frowning. "Something to do with wallpaper, isn't it? Poisonous. It's a form of arsenic, I think."

"Cripes!" said Shrivenham, staring, "I thought it was a disease. Something like amebic dysentery."

"Oh, no, it's something in the chemical line. What wives do their husbands in with, or vice versa."

Shrivenham had relapsed into startled silence. Certain disagreeable facts were becoming clear to him. Crofton Lee had suggested, in effect, that Thomas Rice, Oriental Counselor to the Embassy was suffering, not from gastroenteritis, but from arsenical poisoning. Added to that Sir Rupert had suggested that his own life was in danger, and his decision not to eat food and drink prepared in the kitchens of the British Embassy shook Shrivenham's decorous British soul to the core. He couldn't imagine what to make of it all.

10

VICTORIA, BREATHING IN hot choking yellow dust, was unfavorably impressed by Baghdad. From the Airport to the Tio Hotel, her ears had been assailed by continuous and incessant noise. Horns of cars blaring with maddening persistence, voices shouting, whistles blowing, then more deafening senseless blaring of motor horns. Added to the loud incessant noises of the street was a small thin trickle of continuous sound which was Mrs. Hamilton Clipp talking.

Victoria arrived at the Tio Hotel in a dazed condition.

A small alleyway led back from the fanfare of Rashid Street toward the Tigris. A short flight of steps to go up and there at the entrance of the Hotel, they were greeted by a very stout young man with a beaming smile who, metaphorically at least, gathered them to his heart. This, Victoria gathered was Marcus—or more correctly Mr. Tio, the owner of the Tio Hotel.

His words of welcome were interrupted by shouted orders to various underlings regarding the disposal of their baggage.

"And here you are, once more, Mrs. Clipp—but your arm—why is it in that funny stuff?—(You fools, do not carry that with the strap! Imbeciles! Don't trail that coat!)—But, my dear—what a day to arrive—never, I thought, would the plane land. It went round and round and round. Marcus, I said to myself—it is not you that will travel by planes—all this hurry, what does it matter?—And you have brought a young lady with you—it is nice always to see a new young lady in Baghdad—why did not Mr. Harrison come down to meet you—I expected him yesterday—but my dear, you must have a drink at once—"

Now, somewhat dazed, Victoria, her head reeling slightly under the effect of a double whiskey authoritatively pressed upon her by Marcus, was standing in a high whitewashed room containing a large brass bedstead, a very sophisticated dressing table of newest French design, an aged Victorian wardrobe, and two vivid plush chairs. Her modest baggage reposed at her feet and a very old man with a yellow face and white whiskers had grinned and nodded at her as he placed towels in the bathroom and asked her if she would like the water made hot for a bath.

"How long would it take?"

"Twenty minutes, half an hour. I go and do it now."

With a fatherly smile he withdrew. Victoria sat down on the bed and passed an experimental hand over her hair. It felt clogged with dust and her face was sore and gritty. She looked at herself in the glass. The dust had changed her hair from black to a strange reddish brown. She pulled aside a corner of the curtain and looked out onto a wide balcony which gave on the river. But there was nothing to be seen of the Tigris except a thick yellow haze. A prey to deep depression, Victoria said to herself: "What a hateful place."

Then rousing herself, she stepped across the landing and tapped on Mrs. Clipp's door. Prolonged and active ministrations would be required of her here before she could attend to her own cleansing and rehabilitation.

After a bath, lunch and a prolonged nap, Victoria stepped out from her bedroom onto the balcony and gazed with approval across the Tigris. The duststorm had subsided. Instead of a yellow haze, a pale clear light was appearing. Across the river was a delicate silhouette of palm trees and irregularly placed houses.

Voices came up to Victoria from the garden below. She stepped to the edge of the balcony and looked over.

Mrs. Hamilton Clipp, that indefatigable talker and friendly soul, had struck up an acquaintanceship with an Englishwoman—one of those weatherbeaten Englishwomen of indeterminate age who can always be found in any foreign city.

"—and whatever I'd have done without her, I really don't know," Mrs. Clipp was saying. "She's just the sweetest girl you can imagine. And very well connected. A niece of the Bishop of Llangow."

"Bishop of who?"

"Why, Llangow, I think it was."

"Nonsense, there's no such person," said the other.

Victoria frowned. She recognized the type of County Englishwoman who is unlikely to be taken in by the mention of spurious Bishops.

"Why, then, perhaps I got the name wrong," Mrs. Clipp said doubtfully.

"But," she resumed, "she certainly is a very charming and competent girl."

The other said "Ha!" in a noncommittal manner.

Victoria resolved to give this lady as wide a berth as possible. Something told her that inventing stories to satisfy that kind of woman was no easy job.

Victoria went back into her room, sat on the bed, and gave herself up to speculation on her present position.

She was staying at the Tio Hotel which was, she was fairly sure, not at all inexpensive. She had four pounds seventeen shillings in her possession. She had eaten a hearty lunch for which she had not yet paid and for which Mrs. Hamilton Clipp was under no obligation to pay. Traveling expenses to Baghdad were what Mrs. Clipp had offered. The bargain was completed. Victoria had got to Baghdad. Mrs. Clipp had received the skilled attention of a Bishop's niece, an ex-hospital nurse and competent secretary. All that was over, to the mutual satisfaction of both parties. Mrs. Hamilton Clipp would depart on the evening train to Kirkuk—and that was that. Victoria toyed hopefully with the idea that Mrs. Clipp might press upon her a parting present in the form of hard cash, but abandoned it reluctantly as unlikely. Mrs. Clipp could have no idea that Victoria was in really dire financial straits.

What then must Victoria do? The answer came immediately. Find Edward, of course.

With a sense of annoyance she realized that she was quite unaware of Edward's last name. Edward—Baghdad. Very much, Victoria reflected, like the Saracen maid who arrived in England knowing only the name of her lover "Gilbert" and "England." A romantic story—but certainly inconvenient. True that in England at the time of the Crusades, nobody, Victoria thought, had had any surname at all. On the other hand England was larger than Baghdad. Still, England was sparsely populated then—

Victoria wrenched her thoughts away from these interesting speculations and returned to hard facts. She must find Edward immediately and Edward must find her a job. Also immediately.

She did not know Edward's last name, but he had come to Baghdad as the secretary of a Dr. Rathbone and presumably Dr. Rathbone was a man of importance.

Victoria powdered her nose, patted her hair and started downstairs in search of information.

The beaming Marcus, passing through the hall of his establishment, hailed her with delight.

"Ah, it is Miss Jones, you will come with me and have a drink, will you not, my dear? I like very much English ladies. All the English ladies in Baghdad, they are my friends. Everyone is very happy in my hotel. Come, we will go into the bar."

Victoria, not at all averse to free hospitality, consented gladly.

Sitting on a stool and drinking gin, she began her search for information.

"Do you know a Dr. Rathbone who has just come to Baghdad?" she asked.

"I know everyone in Baghdad," said Marcus Tio joyfully. "And everybody knows Marcus. That is true, what I am telling you. Oh! I have many many friends."

"I'm sure you have," said Victoria. "Do you know Dr. Rathbone?"

"Last week I have the Air Marshal commanding all Middle East passing through. He says to me, 'Marcus, you villain, I haven't seen you since '46. You haven't grown any thinner.' Oh, he is very nice man. I like him very much."

"What about Dr. Rathbone? Is he a nice man?"

"I like, you know, people who can enjoy themselves. I do not like sour faces. I like people to be gay and young and charming—like you. He says to me, that Air Marshal, 'Marcus you like too much the women.' But I say to him: 'No, my trouble is I like too much Marcus . . .'" Marcus roared with laughter, breaking off to call out, "Jesus—Jesus!"

Victoria looked startled, but it appeared that Jesus was the barman's Christian name. Victoria felt again that the East was an odd place.

"Another gin and orange, and whiskey," Marcus commanded.

"I don't think I—"

"Yes, yes, you will—they are very very weak."

"About Dr. Rathbone," persisted Victoria.

"That Mrs. Hamilton Clipp—what an odd name—with whom you arrive, she is American—is she not? I like also American people but I like English best. American peoples, they look always very worried. But sometimes, yes, they are good sports. Mr. Summers—you know him?—he drink so much when he come to Baghdad, he go to sleep for three days and not wake up. It is too much, that. It is not nice."

"Please, do help me," said Victoria.

Marcus looked surprised.

"But of course I help you. I always help my friends. You tell me what you want—and at once it shall be done. Special steak—or turkey cooked very nice with rice and raisins and herbs—or little baby chickens.''

"I don't want baby chickens," said Victoria. "At least not now," she added prudently. "I want to find this Dr. Rathbone. Dr. Rathbone. He's just arrived in Baghdad. With a—with a—secretary.''

"I do not know," said Marcus. "He does not stay at the Tio.''

The implication was clearly that anyone who did not stay at the Tio did not exist for Marcus.

"But there are other hotels," persisted Victoria, "or perhaps he has a house?''

"Oh, yes, there are other hotels. Babylonian Palace, Senacherib, Zobeide Hotel. They are good hotels, yes, but they are not like the Tio.''

"I'm sure they're not," Victoria assured him. "But you don't know if Dr. Rathbone is staying at one of them? There is some kind of society he runs—something to do with culture—and books.''

Marcus became quite serious at the mention of culture.

"It is what we need," he said. "There must be much culture. Art and music, it is very nice, very nice indeed. I like violin sonatas myself if it is not very long.''

While thoroughly agreeing with him, especially in regard to the end of the speech, Victoria realized that she was not getting any nearer to her objective. Conversation with Marcus was, she thought, most entertaining, and Marcus was a charming person in his childlike enthusiasm for life, but conversation with him reminded her of Alice in Wonderland's endeavors to find a path that led to the hill. Every topic found them returning to the point of departure—Marcus!

She refused another drink and rose sadly to her feet. She felt slightly giddy. The cocktails had been anything but weak. She went out from the bar onto the terrace outside and stood by the railing looking across the river, when somebody spoke from behind her.

"Excuse me, but you'd better go and put a coat on. Daresay it seems like summer to you coming out from England, but it gets very cold about sundown.''

It was the Englishwoman who had been talking to Mrs. Clipp earlier. She had the hoarse voice of one who is in the habit of training and calling to sporting dogs. She wore a fur coat, had a rug over her knees and was sipping a whiskey and soda.

"Oh, thank you," said Victoria and was about to escape hurriedly when her intentions were defeated.

"I must introduce myself. I'm Mrs. Cardew Trench." (The implication was clearly: one of the Cardew Trenches.) "I believe you arrived with Mrs.—what's her name—Hamilton Clipp.''

"Yes," said Victoria, "I did.''

"She told me you were the niece of the Bishop of Llangow.''

Victoria rallied.

"Did she really?" she inquired with the correct trace of light amusement.

"Got it wrong, I suppose?"

Victoria smiled.

"Americans are bound to get some of our names wrong. It does sound a little like Llangow. My uncle," said Victoria improvising rapidly, "is the Bishop of Languao."

"Languao?"

"Yes—in the Pacific Archipelago. He's a Colonial bishop, of course."

"Oh, a Colonial bishop," said Mrs. Cardew Trench, her voice falling at least three semitones.

As Victoria had anticipated: Mrs. Cardew Trench was magnificently unaware of Colonial bishops.

"That explains it," she added.

Victoria thought with pride that it explained it very well for a spur-of-the-moment plunge!

"And what are you doing out here?" asked Mrs. Cardew Trench with that inexorable geniality that conceals natural curiosity of disposition.

"Looking for a young man I talked to for a few moments in a public square in London," was hardly an answer that Victoria could give. She said, remembering the newspaper paragraph she had read, and her statement to Mrs. Clipp, "I'm joining my uncle, Dr. Pauncefoot Jones."

"Oh, so that's who you are." Mrs. Cardew Trench was clearly delighted at having "placed" Victoria. "He's a charming little man, though a bit absent-minded—still I suppose that's only to be expected. Heard him lecture last year in London—excellent delivery—couldn't understand a word of what it was all about, though. Yes, he passed through Baghdad about a fortnight ago. I think he mentioned some girls were coming out later in the season."

Hurriedly, having established her status, Victoria chipped in with a question.

"Do you know if Dr. Rathbone's out here?" she asked.

"Just come out," said Mrs. Cardew Trench. "I believe they've asked him to give a lecture at the Institute next Thursday. On World Relationships and Brotherhood—or something like that. All nonsense if you ask me. The more you try to get people together, the more suspicious they get of each other. All this poetry and music and translating Shakespeare and Wordsworth into Arabic and Chinese and Hindustani. 'A primrose by the river's brim, etc.' . . . what's the good of that to people who've never seen a primrose?"

"Where is he staying, do you know?"

"At the Babylonian Palace Hotel, I believe. But his headquarters are up near the Museum. The Olive Branch—ridiculous name. Full of young women in slacks with unwashed necks and spectacles."

"I know his secretary slightly," said Victoria.

"Oh yes, whatshisname Edward Thingummy—nice boy—too good for that long-haired racket—did well in the war, I hear. Still a job's a job, I suppose.

Nice-looking boy—those earnest young women are quite fluttered by him, I fancy."

A pang of devastating jealousy pierced Victoria.

"The Olive Branch," she said. "Where did you say it was?"

"Up past the turning to the second bridge. One of the turnings off Rashid Street—tucked away rather. Not far from the copper bazaar.

"And how's Mrs. Pauncefoot Jones?" continued Mrs. Cardew Trench. "Coming out soon? I hear she's been in poor health?"

But having got the information she wanted, Victoria was taking no more risks in invention. She glanced at her wristwatch and uttered an exclamation.

"Oh dear—I promised to wake Mrs. Clipp at half past six and help her to prepare for the journey. I must fly."

The excuse was true enough, though Victoria had substituted half past six for seven o'clock. She hurried upstairs feeling quite exhilarated. Tomorrow she would get in touch with Edward at the Olive Branch. Earnest young women with unwashed necks, indeed! They sounded most unattractive . . . Still, Victoria reflected uneasily that men are less critical of dingy necks than middle-aged hygienic Englishwomen are—especially if the owners of the said necks are gazing with large eyes of admiration and adoration at the male subject in question.

The evening passed rapidly. Victoria had an early meal in the dining room with Mrs. Hamilton Clipp, the latter talking nineteen to the dozen on every subject under the sun. She urged Victoria to come and pay a visit later—and Victoria noted down the address carefully, because, after all, one never knew . . . She accompanied Mrs. Clipp to Baghdad North station, saw her safely ensconced in her compartment and was introduced to an acquaintance also traveling to Kirkuk who would assist Mrs. Clipp with her toilet on the following morning.

The engine uttered loud melancholy screams, like a soul in distress. Mrs. Clipp thrust a thick envelope into Victoria's hand, said: "Just a little remembrance, Miss Jones, of our very pleasant companionship which I hope you will accept with my most grateful thanks." Victoria said: "But it's really too kind of you, Mrs. Clipp," in a delighted voice, the engine gave forth a final supreme banshee wail of anguish, and the train pulled slowly out of the station.

Victoria took a taxi from the station back to the hotel since she had not the faintest idea how to get back to it any other way and there did not seem anyone about whom she could ask.

On her return to the Tio, she ran up to her room and eagerly opened the envelope. Inside were a couple of pairs of nylon stockings.

Victoria at any other moment would have been enchanted—nylon stockings having been usually beyond the reach of her purse. At the moment, however, hard cash was what she had been hoping for. Mrs. Clipp, however, had been far too delicate to think of giving her a five dinar note. Victoria wished heartily that she had not been quite so delicate.

However, tomorrow there would be Edward. Victoria undressed, got into bed and in five minutes was fast asleep, dreaming that she was waiting at an airfield for Edward, but that he was held back from joining her by a spectacled girl who clasped him firmly round the neck while the airplane began slowly to move away . . .

11

VICTORIA AWOKE TO a morning of vivid sunshine. Having dressed, she went out onto the wide balcony outside her window. Sitting in a chair a little way along with his back to her was a man with curling gray hair growing down onto a muscular red brown neck. When the man turned his head sideways Victoria recognized, with a distinct feeling of surprise, Sir Rupert Crofton Lee. Why she should be so surprised she could hardly have said. Perhaps because she had assumed as a matter of course that a V.I.P. such as Sir Rupert would have been staying at the Embassy and not at a hotel. Nevertheless, there he was, staring at the Tigris with a kind of concentrated intensity. She noticed, even, that he had a pair of field glasses slung over the side of his chair. Possibly, she thought, he studied birds.

A young man whom Victoria had at one time thought attractive, had been a bird enthusiast, and she had accompanied him on several weekend tramps, to be made to stand as though paralyzed in wet weeds and icy winds, for what seemed like hours, to be at last told in tones of ecstasy to look through the glasses at some drab-looking bird on a remote twig which in appearance, as far as Victoria could see, compared unfavorably in bird appeal with a common robin or chaffinch.

Victoria made her way downstairs, encountering Marcus Tio on the terrace between the two buildings of the hotel.

"I see you've got Sir Rupert Crofton Lee staying here," she said.

"Oh, yes," said Marcus, beaming, "he's a nice man—a very nice man."

"Do you know him well?"

"No, this is the first time I see him. Mr. Shrivenham of the British Embassy bring him here last night. Mr. Shrivenham, he is very nice man, too. I know him very well."

Proceeding into breakfast, Victoria wondered if there was anyone whom Marcus would not consider a very nice man. He appeared to exercise a wide charity.

After breakfast, Victoria started forth in search of the Olive Branch.

A London-bred Cockney, she had no idea of the difficulties involved in finding any particular place in a city such as Baghdad, until she had started on her quest.

Coming across Marcus again on her way out, she asked him to direct her to the Museum.

"It is a very nice Museum," said Marcus, beaming. "Yes. Full of interesting, very very old things. Not that I have been there myself. But I have friends, archaeological friends, who stay here always when they come through Baghdad. Mr. Baker—Mr. Richard Baker, you know him? And Professor Kalzman? And Dr. Pauncefoot Jones—and Mr. and Mrs. McIntyre—they all come to the Tio. They are my friends. And they tell me about what is in the Museum. Very very interesting."

"Where is it, and how do I get there?"

"You go straight along Rashid Street—a long way—past the turn to the Feisal Bridge and past Bank Street—you know Bank Street?"

"I don't know anything," said Victoria.

"And then there is another street—also going down to a bridge and it is along there on the right. You ask for Mr. Betoun Evans, he is English Adviser there—very nice man. And his wife, she is very nice, too, she came here as Transport Sergeant during the war. Oh, she is very very nice."

"I don't really want to go actually to the Museum," said Victoria. "I want to find a place—a Society—a kind of club called the Olive Branch."

"If you want olives," said Marcus, "I give you beautiful olives—very fine quality. They keep them especially for me—for the Tio Hotel. You see, I send you some to your table tonight."

"That's very kind of you," said Victoria and escaped toward Rashid Street.

"To the left," Marcus shouted after her, "not to the right. But it is a long way to the Museum. You had better take a taxi."

"Would a taxi know where the Olive Branch was?"

"No, they do not know where anything is! You say to the driver left, right, stop, straight on—just where you want to go."

"In that case, I might as well walk," said Victoria.

She reached Rashid Street and turned to the left.

Baghdad was entirely unlike her idea of it. A crowded main thoroughfare thronged with people, cars hooting violently, people shouting, European goods for sale in the shop windows, hearty spitting all around her with prodigious throat clearing as a preliminary. No mysterious Eastern figures, most of the people wore tattered or shabby Western clothes, old army and air force tunics, the occasional shuffling black-robed and veiled figures were almost inconspicuous among the hybrid European styles of dress. Whining beggars came up to her—women with dirty babies in their arms. The pavement under her feet was uneven with occasional gaping holes.

She pursued her way, feeling suddenly strange and lost and far from home. Here was no glamour of travel, only confusion.

She came at last to the Feisal Bridge, passed it and went on. In spite of herself she was intrigued by the curious mixtures of things in the shop windows. Here were babies' shoes and woollies, toothpaste and cosmetics, electric torches and china cups and saucers—all shown together. Slowly a kind of fascination came over her, the fascination of assorted merchandise coming from all over the world to meet the strange assorted and varied wants of a mixed population.

She found the Museum, but not the Olive Branch. To one accustomed to finding her way about London it seemed incredible that here was no one she could ask. She knew no Arabic. Those shopkeepers who spoke to her in English as she passed, pressing their wares, presented blank faces when she asked for direction to the Olive Branch.

If one could only "ask a policeman," but gazing at the policeman actively waving their arms, and blowing their whistles, she realized that here that would be no solution.

She went into a bookshop with English books in the window, but a mention of the Olive Branch drew only a courteous shrug and shake of the head. Regrettably they had no idea at all.

And then, as she walked along the street, a prodigious hammering and clanging came to her ears and peering down a long dim alley, she remembered that Mrs. Cardew Trench had said the Olive Branch was near the Copper Bazaar. Here, at least, was the Copper Bazaar.

Victoria plunged in, and for the next three quarters of an hour she forgot the Olive Branch completely. The Copper Bazaar fascinated her. The blowlamps, the melting metal, the whole business of craftsmanship came like a revelation to the little Cockney used only to finished products stacked up for sale. She wandered at random through the Suq, passed out of the Copper Bazaar, came to the gay striped horse blankets, and the cotton quilted bed covers. Here European merchandise took on a totally different guise, in the arched cool darkness it had the exotic quality of something from overseas, something strange and rare. Bales of cheap printed cottons in gay colors made a feast for the eyes.

Occasionally with a shout of *Balek, Balek,* a donkey or laden mule pushed past her, or men bearing great loads balanced on their backs. Little boys rushed up to her with trays slung around their necks.

"See, lady, elastic, good elastic, English elastic. Comb, English comb?"

The wares were thrust at her, close to her nose, with vehement urgings to buy. Victoria walked in a happy dream. This was really seeing the world. At every turn of the vast arched cool world of alleyways you came to something totally unexpected—an alley of tailors, sitting stitching, with smart pictures of European men's tailoring, a line of watches and cheap jewelry. Bales of velvets and rich metal embroidered brocades, then a chance turn and you were walking down an alley of cheap and shoddy second-hand European clothes, quaint pathetic little faded jumpers and long straggly vests.

Then every now and then there were glimpses into vast quiet courtyards open to the sky.

She came to a vast vista of men's trouserings, with crosslegged dignified merchants in turbans sitting in the middle of their little square recesses.

"Balek!"

A heavily laden donkey coming up behind her made Victoria turn aside into a narrow alleyway open to the sky that twisted through tall houses. Walking along it she came, quite by chance, to the object of her search. Through an opening she looked into a small square courtyard and at the farther side of it an open doorway with THE OLIVE BRANCH on a huge sign and a rather impossible-looking plaster bird holding an unrecognizable twig in its beak.

Joyously Victoria sped across the courtyard and in at the open door. She found herself in a dimly lit room with tables covered with books and periodicals and more books ranged round on shelves. It looked a little like a bookshop, except that there were little groups of chairs arranged together here and there.

Out of the dimness a young woman came up to Victoria and said in careful English,

"What can I do for you, yes, please?"

Victoria looked at her. She wore corduroy trousers and an orange flannel shirt and had black dank hair cut in a kind of depressed bob. So far she would have looked more suited to Bloomsbury, but her face was not Bloomsbury. It was a melancholy face with great sad dark eyes and a heavy nose.

"This is—is this—is—is Dr. Rathbone here?"

Maddening still not to know Edward's surname! Even Mrs. Cardew Trench had called him Edward Thingummy.

"Yes. Dr. Rathbone. The Olive Branch. You wish to join us? Yes? That will be very nice."

"Well, perhaps. I'd—can I see Dr. Rathbone, please?"

The young woman smiled in a tired way.

"We do not disturb. I have a form. I tell you all about everything. Then you sign your name. It is two dinars, please."

"I'm not sure yet that I want to join," said Victoria, alarmed at the mention of two dinars. "I'd like to see Dr. Rathbone—or his secretary. His secretary would do."

"I explain. I explain to you everything. We are all friends here, friends together, friends for the future—reading very fine educational books—reciting poems each to other."

"Dr. Rathbone's secretary," said Victoria loudly and clearly. "He particularly told me to ask for him."

A kind of mulish sullenness came into the young woman's face.

"Not today," she said. "I explain—"

"Why not today? Isn't he here? Isn't Dr. Rathbone here?"

"Yais, Dr. Rathbone is here. He is upstairs. We do not disturb."

A kind of Anglo-Saxon intolerance of foreigners swept over Victoria. Regrettably, instead of the Olive Branch creating friendly international feelings, it seemed to be having the opposite effect as far as she was concerned.

"I have just arrived from England," she said—and her accents were almost those of Mrs. Cardew Trench herself—"and I have a very important message for Dr. Rathbone which I must deliver to him personally. Please take me to him at once! I am sorry to disturb him, but I have got to see him.

"At once!" she added, to clinch matters.

Before an imperious Briton who means to get his or her own way, barriers nearly always fall. The young woman turned at once and led the way to the back of the room and up a staircase and along a gallery overlooking the courtyard. Here she stopped before a door and knocked. A man's voice said, Come in.

Victoria's guide opened the door and motioned to Victoria to pass in.

"It is a lady from England for you."

Victoria walked in.

From behind a large desk covered with papers, a man got up to greet her.

He was an imposing-looking elderly man of about sixty with a high domed forehead and white hair. Benevolence, kindliness and charm were the most apparent qualities of his personality. A producer of plays would have cast him without hesitation for the role of the great philanthropist.

He greeted Victoria with a warm smile and an outstretched hand.

"So you've just come out of England," he said. "First visit East, eh?"

"Yes."

"I wonder what you think of it all . . . You must tell me sometime. Now, let me see, have I met you before or not? I'm so short-sighted and you didn't give your name."

"You don't know me," said Victoria, "but I'm a friend of Edward's."

"A friend of Edward's," said Dr. Rathbone. "Why, that's splendid. Does Edward know you're in Baghdad?"

"Not yet," said Victoria.

"Well, that will be a pleasant surprise for him when he gets back."

"Back?" said Victoria, her voice falling.

"Yes, Edward's in Basrah at the moment. I had to send him down there to see about some crates of books that have come out for us. There have been most vexatious delays in the Customs—we simply have not been able to get them cleared. The personal touch is the only thing, and Edward's good at that sort of thing. He knows just when to charm and when to bully, and he won't rest till he's got the thing through. He's a sticker. A very fine quality in a young man. I think a lot of Edward."

His eyes twinkled.

"But I don't suppose I need to sing Edward's praises to you, young lady."

"When—when will Edward be back from Basrah?" asked Victoria faintly.

"Well—now that I couldn't say. He won't come back till he's finished the job—and you can't hurry things too much in this country. Tell me where you are staying and I'll make sure he gets in touch with you as soon as he gets back."

"I was wondering—" Victoria spoke desperately, aware of her financial plight. "I was wondering if—if I could do some work here?"

"Now that I do appreciate," said Dr. Rathbone warmly. "Yes, of course you can. We need all the workers, all the help we can get. And especially English girls. Our work is going splendidly—quite splendidly—but there's lot more to be done. Still people are keen. I've got thirty voluntary helpers already—thirty—all of 'em keen as mustard! If you're really in earnest, you can be most valuable."

The word voluntary struck unpleasantly on Victoria's ear.

"I really wanted a paid position," she said.

"Oh dear!" Dr. Rathbone's face fell. "That's rather more difficult. Our paid staff is very small—and for the moment, with the voluntary help, it's quite adequate."

"I can't afford not to take a job," explained Victoria. "I'm a competent shorthand typist," she added without a blush.

"I'm sure you're competent, my dear young lady, you radiate competence, if I may say so. But with us it's a question of L.S.D. But even if you take a job elsewhere, I hope you'll help us in your spare time. Most of our workers have their own regular jobs. I'm sure you'll find helping us really inspiring. There must be an end of all the savagery in the world, the wars, the misunderstandings, the suspicions. A common meeting ground, that's what we all need. Drama, art, poetry—the great things of the spirit—no room there for petty jealousies or hatreds."

"N-no," said Victoria doubtfully, recalling friends of hers who were actresses and artists and whose lives seemed to be obsessed by jealousy of the most trivial kind, and by hatreds of a peculiarly virulent intensity.

"I've had the 'Midsummer Night's Dream' translated into forty different languages," said Dr. Rathbone. "Forty different sets of young people all reacting to the same wonderful piece of literature. Young people—that's the secret. I've no use for anybody but the young. Once the mind and spirit are musclebound, it's too late. No, it's the young who must get together. Take that girl downstairs, Catherine, the one who showed you up here. She's a Syrian from Damascus. You and she are probably about the same age. Normally you'd never come together, you'd have nothing in common. But at the Olive Branch you and she and many many others, Russians, Jewesses, Iraqis, Turkish girls, Armenians, Egyptians, Persians, all meet and like each other and read the same books and discuss pictures and music (we have excellent lecturers who come out) all of you finding out and being excited by encountering a different point of view—why, that's what the world is meant to be."

Victoria could not help thinking that Dr. Rathbone was slightly overoptimistic in assuming that all those divergent elements who were coming together would necessarily like each other. She and Catherine, for instance, had not liked each other at all. And Victoria strongly suspected that the more they saw of each other the greater their dislike would grow.

"Edward's splendid," said Dr. Rathbone. "Gets on with everybody. Better, perhaps, with the girls than with the young men. The men students out here are apt to be difficult at first—suspicious—almost hostile. But the girls adore Edward, they'll do anything for him. He and Catherine get on particularly well."

"Indeed," said Victoria coldly. Her dislike of Catherine grew even more intense.

"Well," said Dr. Rathbone, smiling, "come and help us if you can."

It was a dismissal. He pressed her hand warmly. Victoria went out of the room and down the stairs. Catherine was standing near the door talking to a girl who had just come in with a small suitcase in her hand. She was a good-looking dark girl, and just for a moment Victoria fancied that she had seen her before somewhere. But the girl looked at her without any sign of recognition. The two young women had been talking eagerly together in some language Victoria did not know. They stopped when she appeared and remained silent, staring at her. She walked past them to the door, forcing herself to say "Goodbye" politely to Catherine as she went out.

She found her way out from the winding alley into Rashid Street and slowly back to the Hotel, her eyes unseeing of the throngs around her. She tried to keep her mind from dwelling on her own predicament (penniless in Baghdad) by fixing her mind on Dr. Rathbone and the general setup of the Olive Branch. Edward had had an idea in London that there was something "fishy" about his job. What was fishy? Dr. Rathbone? Or the Olive Branch itself?

Victoria could hardly believe that there was anything fishy about Dr. Rathbone. He appeared to her to be one of those misguided enthusiasts who insist on seeing the world in their own idealistic manner, regardless of realities.

What had Edward meant by fishy? He'd been very vague. Perhaps he didn't really know himself.

Could Dr. Rathbone be some kind of colossal fraud?

Victoria, fresh from the soothing charm of his manner, shook her head. His manner had certainly changed, ever so slightly, at the idea of paying her a salary. He clearly preferred people to work for nothing.

But that, thought Victoria, was a sign of common sense.

Mr. Greenholtz, for instance, would have felt just the same.

12

VICTORIA ARRIVED BACK at the Tio, rather footsore, to be hailed enthusiastically by Marcus who was sitting out on the grass terrace overlooking the river and talking to a thin rather shabby middle-aged man.

"Come and have a drink with us, Miss Jones. Martini—sidecar? This is Mr. Dakin. Miss Jones from England. Now then, my dear, what will you have?"

Victoria said she would have a sidecar "and some of those lovely nuts?" she suggested hopefully, remembering that nuts were nutritious.

"You like nuts. Jesus!" He gave the other in rapid Arabic. Mr. Dakin said in a sad voice that he would have a lemonade.

"Ah," cried Marcus, "but that is ridiculous. Ah, here is Mrs. Cardew Trench. You know Mr. Dakin? What will you have?"

"Gin and lime," said Mrs. Cardew Trench, nodding to Dakin in an offhand manner. "You look hot," she added to Victoria.

"I've been walking round seeing the sights."

When the drinks came, Victoria ate a large plateful of pistachio nuts and also some potato chips.

Presently, a short thickset man came up the steps and the hospitable Marcus hailed him in his turn. He was introduced to Victoria as Captain Crosbie; and by the way his slightly protuberant eyes goggled at her, Victoria gathered that he was susceptible to feminine charm.

"Just come out?" he asked her.

"Yesterday."

"Thought I hadn't seen you around."

"She is very nice and beautiful, is she not?" said Marcus joyfully. "Oh, yes, it is very nice to have Miss Victoria. I will give a party for her—a very nice party."

"With baby chickens?" said Victoria hopefully.

"Yes, yes—and foie gras—Strasburg foie gras—and perhaps caviar—and then we have a dish with fish—very nice—a fish from the Tigris, but all with sauce and mushrooms. And then there is a turkey stuffed in the way we have it at my home—with rice and raisins and spice—and all cooked so! Oh, it is very good—but you must eat very much of it—not just a tiny spoonful. Or if you like it better you shall have a steak—a really big steak and tender—I see to it. We will have a long dinner that goes on for hours. It will be very nice. I do not eat myself—I only drink."

"That will be lovely," said Victoria in a faint voice. The description of these viands made her feel quite giddy with hunger. She wondered if Marcus really meant to give this party and if so, how soon it could possibly happen.

"Thought you'd gone to Basrah," said Mrs. Cardew Trench to Crosbie.

"Got back yesterday," said Crosbie.

He looked up at the balcony.

"Who's the bandit?" he asked. "Feller in fancy dress in the big hat."

"That, my dear, is Sir Rupert Crofton Lee," said Marcus. "Mr. Shrivenham brought him here from the Embassy last night. He is very nice man, very distinguished traveler. He rides on camels over the Sahara, and climbs up mountains. It is very uncomfortable and dangerous, that kind of life. I should not like it myself."

"Oh, he's that chap, is he?" said Crosbic. "I've read his book."

"I came over on the plane with him," said Victoria.

Both men, or so it seemed to her, looked at her with interest.

"He's frightfully stuck up and pleased with himself," said Victoria with disparagement.

"Knew his aunt in Simla," said Mrs. Cardew Trench. "The whole family is like that. Clever as they make them, but can't help boasting of it."

"He's been sitting out there doing nothing all the morning," said Victoria with slight disapproval.

"It is his stomach," explained Marcus. "Today he cannot eat anything. It is sad."

"I can't think," said Mrs. Cardew Trench, "why you're the size you are, Marcus, when you never eat anything."

"It is the drink," said Marcus. He sighed deeply. "I drink far too much. Tonight my sister and her husband come. I will drink and drink almost until morning." He sighed again, then uttered his usual sudden roar. "Jesus! Jesus! Bring the same again."

"Not for me," said Victoria hastily, and Mr. Dakin refused also, finishing up his lemonade, and ambling gently away while Crosbie went up to his room.

Mrs. Cardew Trench flicked Dakin's glass with her fingernail. "Lemonade as usual?" she said. "Bad sign, that."

Victoria asked why it was a bad sign.

"When a man only drinks when he's alone."

"Yes, my dear," said Marcus. "That is so."

"Does he really drink, then?" asked Victoria.

"That's why he's never got on," said Mrs. Cardew Trench. "Just manages to keep his job and that's all."

"But he is a very nice man," said the charitable Marcus.

"Pah," said Mrs. Cardew Trench. "He's a wet fish. Potters and dilly dallies about—no stamina—no grip on life. Just one more Englishman who's come out East and gone to seed."

Thanking Marcus for the drink and refusing a second, Victoria went up to her room, removed her shoes, and lay down on her bed to do some serious thinking. The three pounds odd to which her capital had dwindled was, she fancied, already due to Marcus for board and lodging. Owing to his generous disposition, and if she could sustain life mainly on alcoholic liquor assisted by nuts, olives and chip potatoes, she might solve the purely alimentary problem of the next few days. How long would it be before Marcus presented her with her bill, and how long would he allow it to run unpaid? She had no idea. He was not really, she thought, careless in business matters. She ought, of course, to find somewhere cheaper to live. But how would she find out where to go? She ought to find herself a job—quickly. But where did one apply for jobs? What kind of a job? Who could she ask about looking for one? How terribly handicapping to one's style it was to be dumped down practically penniless in a foreign city where one didn't know the ropes. With just a little knowledge of the terrain, Victoria felt confident (as always) that she could hold her own. When would Edward get back from Basrah? Perhaps (horror) Edward would have forgotten all about her. Why on earth had she come rushing out to Baghdad in this asinine way? Who and what was Edward after all? Just another young man with an engaging grin and an attractive way of saying things. And what—what—what was his surname? If she knew that, she might wire him—no good, she didn't even know where he was staying. She didn't know anything—that was the trouble—that was what was cramping her style.

And there was no one to whom she could go for advice. Not Marcus who was kind but never listened. Not Mrs. Cardew Trench (who had had suspicions from the first). Not Mrs. Hamilton Clipp who had vanished to Kirkuk. Not Dr. Rathbone—

She must get some money—or get a job—any job. Look after children, stick stamps on in an office, serve in a restaurant . . . Otherwise they would send her to a Consul and she would be repatriated to England and never see Edward again . . .

At this point, worn out with emotion, Victoria fell asleep.

She woke some hours later and deciding that she might as well be hanged for a sheep as a lamb, went down to the restaurant and worked her way solidly through the entire menu—a generous one. When she had finished, she felt slightly like a boa constrictor, but definitely heartened.

"It's no good worrying any more," thought Victoria. "I'll leave it all till tomorrow. Something may turn up, or I may think of something, or Edward may come back."

Before going to bed she strolled out onto the terrace by the river. Since in the feelings of those living in Baghdad it was arctic winter, nobody else was out there except one of the waiters who was leaning over a railing staring down into the water, and he sprang away guiltily when Victoria appeared and hurried back into the hotel by the service door.

Victoria to whom, coming from England, it appeared to be an ordinary summer night with a slight nip in the air, was enchanted by the Tigris seen in the moonlight with the further bank looking mysterious and Eastern with its fringes of palms.

"Well, anyway, I've got here," said Victoria, cheering up a good deal, "and I'll manage somehow. Something is bound to turn up."

With this Micawber-like pronouncement, she went up to bed, and the waiter slipped quietly out again and resumed his task of attaching a knotted rope so that it hung down to the river's edge.

Presently another figure came out of the shadows and joined him. Mr. Dakin said in a low voice,

"All in order?"

"Yes, sir, nothing suspicious to report."

Having completed the task to his satisfaction, Mr. Dakin retreated into the shadows, exchanged his waiter's white coat for his own nondescript blue pinstripe and ambled gently along the terrace until he stood outlined against the water's edge, just where the steps led up from the street below.

"Getting pretty chilly in the evenings now," said Crosbie strolling out from the bar and down to join him. "Suppose you don't feel it so much, coming from Teheran."

They stood there for a moment or two smoking. Unless they raised their voices, nobody could overhear them. Crosbie said quietly,

"Who's the girl?"

"Niece apparently of the archaeologist, Pauncefoot Jones."

"Oh well—that should be all right. But coming on the same plane as Crofton Lee—"

"It's certainly as well," said Dakin, "to take nothing for granted."

The men smoked in silence for a few moments.

Crosbie said: "You really think it's advisable to shift the thing from the Embassy to here?"

"I think so, yes."

"In spite of the whole thing being taped down to the smallest detail."

"It was taped down to the smallest detail in Basrah—and that went wrong."

"Oh, I know. Mohammed Salah Hassan was poisoned, by the way."

"Yes—he would be. Was there any signs of an approach to the Consulate?"

"I suspect there may have been. Bit of a shindy there. Chap drew a revolver." He paused and added, "Richard Baker grabbed him and disarmed him."

"Richard Baker," said Dakin thoughtfully.

"Know him? He's—"

"Yes, I know him."

There was a pause and then Dakin said,

"Improvisation. That's what I'm banking on. If we have, as you say, got everything taped—and our plans are known, then it's easy for the other side to have got us taped, too. I very much doubt if Carmichael would even so much as get near the Embassy—and even if he reached it—" He shook his head.

"Here, only you and I and Crofton Lee are wise to what's going on."

"They'll know Crofton Lee moved here from the Embassy."

"Oh, of course. That was inevitable. But don't you see, Crosbie, that whatever show they put up against our improvisation has got to be improvised, too. It's got to be hastily thought of and hastily arranged. It's got to come, so to speak, from the outside. There's no question here of someone established in the Tio six months ago waiting. The Tio's never been in the picture until now. There's never been any idea or suggestion of using the Tio as the rendezvous."

He looked at his watch. "I'll go up now and see Crofton Lee."

Dakin's raised hand had no need to tap on Sir Rupert's door. It opened silently to let him in.

The traveler had only one small reading lamp alight and had placed his chair beside it. As he sat down again, he gently slipped a small automatic pistol onto the table within reach of his hand.

He said: "What about it, Dakin? Do you think he'll come?"

"I think so, yes, Sir Rupert." Then he said, "You've never met him, have you?"

The other shook his head.

"No. I'm looking forward to meeting him tonight. That young man, Dakin, must have got guts."

"Oh yes," said Mr. Dakin in his flat voice. "He's got guts."

He sounded a little surprised at the fact needing to be stated.

"I don't mean only courage," said the other. "Lots of courage in the war—magnificent. I mean—"

"Imagination?" suggested Dakin.

"Yes. To have the guts to believe something that isn't in the least degree probable. To risk your life finding out that a ridiculous story isn't ridiculous at all. That takes something that the modern young man usually hasn't got. I hope he'll come."

"I think he'll come," said Mr. Dakin.

Sir Rupert glanced at him sharply.

"You've got it all sewn up?"

"Crosbie's on the balcony, and I shall be watching the stairs. When Carmichael reaches you, tap on the wall and I'll come in."

Crofton Lee nodded.

Dakin went softly out of the room. He went to the left and onto the balcony and walked to the extreme corner. Here, too, a knotted rope dropped over the edge and came to earth in the shade of a eucalyptus tree and some Judas bushes.

Mr. Dakin went back past Crofton Lee's door and into his own room beyond. His room had a second door in it, leading onto the passage behind the rooms, and it opened within a few feet of the head of the stairs. With this door unobtrusively ajar, Mr. Dakin settled down to his vigil.

It was about four hours later that a *gufa*, that primitive craft of the Tigris, dropped gently downstream and came to shore on the mud flat beneath the Tio Hotel. A few moments later a slim figure swarmed up the rope and crouched among the Judas trees.

13

IT HAD BEEN Victoria's intention to go to bed and to sleep and to leave all problems until the morning; but having already slept most of the afternoon, she found herself devastatingly wide awake.

In the end she switched on the light, finished a magazine story she had been reading in the plane, darned her stockings, tried on her new nylons, wrote out several different advertisements requiring employment—(she could ask tomorrow where these should be inserted) wrote three or four tentative letters to Mrs. Hamilton Clipp, each setting out a different and more ingenious set of unforeseen circumstances which had resulted in her being "stranded" in Baghdad, sketched out one or two telegrams appealing for help to her sole surviving relative, a very old, crusty, and unpleasant gentleman in the North of England who had never helped anybody in his life, tried out a new style of hairdo, and finally with a sudden yawn decided that at last she really was desperately sleepy and ready for bed and repose.

It was at this moment that without any warning her bedroom door swung open, a man slipped in, turned the key in the lock behind him and said to her urgently,

"For God's sake hide me somewhere—quickly . . ."

Victoria's reactions were never slow. In the twinkling of an eye she had noted the labored breathing, the fading voice, the way the man held an old red knitted scarf bunched on his breast with a desperate clutching hand. And she rose immediately in response to the adventure.

The room did not lend itself to many hiding places. There was the wardrobe, a chest of drawers, a table and the rather pretentious dressing table. The bed was a large one—almost a double bed and memories of childish hide-and-seek made Victoria's reaction prompt.

"Quick," she said. She swept off pillows, and raised sheet and blanket. The man lay across the top of the bed. Victoria pulled sheet and blanket over him, dumped the pillows on top and sat down herself on the side of the bed.

Almost immediately there came a low insistent knocking on the door.

Victoria called out, "Who is it?" in a faint alarmed voice.

"Please," said a man's voice outside. "Open, please. It is the police."

Victoria crossed the room, pulling her dressing gown around her. As she did so, she noticed the man's red knitted scarf was lying on the floor and she caught it up and swept it into a drawer, then she turned the key and opened the door of her room a small way, peering out with an expression of alarm.

A dark-haired young man in a mauve pinstripe suit was standing outside and behind him was a man in police officer's uniform.

"What's the matter?" Victoria asked, letting a quaver creep into her voice.

The young man smiled brilliantly and spoke in very passable English.

"I am so sorry, miss, to disturb you at this hour," he said, "but we have a criminal escaped. He has run into this hotel. We must look in every room. He is a very dangerous man."

"Oh dear!" Victoria fell back, opening the door wide. "Do come in, please, and look. How very frightening. Look in the bathroom, please. Oh! and the wardrobe—and, I wonder, would you mind looking under the bed? He might have been there all the evening."

The search was very rapid.

"No, he is not here."

"You're sure he's not under the bed? No, how silly of me. He couldn't be in here at all. I locked the door when I went to bed."

"Thank you, miss, and good evening."

The young man bowed and withdrew with his uniformed assistant.

Victoria, following him to the door, said,

"I'd better lock it again, hadn't I? To be safe."

"Yes, that will be best, certainly. Thank you."

Victoria relocked the door and stood by it for some few minutes. She heard the police officers knock in the same way on the door the other side of the passage, heard the door open, an exchange of remarks and the indignant hoarse voice of Mrs. Cardew Trench, and then the door closing. It reopened a few minutes later, and the sound of their footsteps moved down the passage. The next knock came from much further away.

Victoria turned and walked across the room to the bed. It was born in upon her that she had probably been excessively foolish. Led away by the romantic spirit, and by the sound of her own language, she had impulsively lent aid to what was probably an extremely dangerous criminal. A disposition to be on the side of the hunted against the hunter sometimes brings unpleasant consequences. Oh, well, thought Victoria, I'm in for it now, anyway!

Standing beside the bed she said curtly,

"Get up."

There was no movement, and Victoria said sharply, though without raising her voice,

"They've gone. You can get up now."

But still there was no sign of movement from under the slightly raised hump of pillows. Impatiently, Victoria threw them all off.

The young man lay just as she had left him. But now his face was a queer grayish color and his eyes were closed.

Then, with a sharp catch in her breath, Victoria noticed something else—a bright red stain seeping through onto the blanket.

"Oh no," said Victoria, almost as though pleading with someone. "Oh, no —no!"

And as though in recognition of that plea the wounded man opened his eyes. He stared at her, stared as though from very far away at some object he was not quite certain of seeing.

His lips parted—the sound was so faint that Victoria scarcely heard.

She bent down.

"What?"

She heard this time. With difficulty, great difficulty, the young man said two words. Whether she heard them correctly or not Victoria did not know. They seemed to her quite nonsensical and without meaning. What he said was, *"Lucifer—Basrah . . ."*

The eyelids drooped and flickered over the wide anxious eyes. He said one word more—a name. Then his head jerked back a little and he lay still.

Victoria stood quite still, her heart beating violently. She was filled now with an intense pity and anger. What to do next she had no idea. She must call someone—get someone to come— She was alone here with a dead man and sooner or later the police would want an explanation.

While her brain worked rapidly on the situation, a small sound made her turn her head. The key had fallen out of her bedroom door, and as she stared at it, she heard the sound of the lock turning. The door opened and Mr. Dakin came in, carefully closing the door behind him.

He walked across to her, saying quietly,

"Nice work, my dear. You think quickly. How is he?"

With a catch in her voice Victoria said:

"I think he's—he's dead."

She saw the other's face alter, caught just a flash of intense anger, then his face was just as she had seen it the day before—only now it seemed to her that the indecision and flabbiness of the man had vanished, giving place to something quite different.

He bent down—and gently loosened the ragged tunic.

"Very neatly stabbed through the heart," said Dakin as he straightened up. "He was a brave lad—and a clever one."

Victoria found her voice.

"The police came. They said he was a criminal. Was he a criminal?"

"No. He wasn't a criminal."

"Were they—were they the police?"

"I don't know," said Dakin. "They may have been. It's all the same."

Then he asked her:

"Did he say anything—before he died?"

"Yes."

"What was it?"

"He said Lucifer—and then Basrah. And then after a pause he said a name —a French name it sounded like—but I mayn't have got it right."

"What did it sound like to you?"

"I think it was Lefarge."

"Lefarge," said Dakin thoughtfully.

"What does it all mean?" said Victoria, and added with some dismay, "And what am I to do?"

"We must get you out of it as far as we can," said Dakin. "As for what it's all about, I'll come back and talk to you later. The first thing to do is to get hold of Marcus. It's his hotel and Marcus has a great deal of sense, though one doesn't always realize it in talking to him. I'll get hold of him. He won't have gone to bed. It's only half past one. He seldom goes to bed before two o'clock. Just attend to your appearance before I bring him in. Marcus is very susceptible to beauty in distress."

He left the room. As though in a dream she moved over to the dressing table, combed back her hair, made up her face to a becoming pallor and collapsed onto a chair as she heard footsteps approaching. Dakin came in without knocking. Behind him loomed the bulk of Marcus Tio. This time Marcus was serious. There was not the usual smile on his face.

"Now, Marcus," said Mr. Dakin, "you must do what you can about this. It's been a terrible shock to this poor girl. The fellow burst in, collapsed—she's got a very kind heart and she hid him from the police. And now he's dead. She oughtn't to have done it, perhaps, but girls are softhearted."

"Of course she did not like the police," said Marcus. "Nobody likes the police. I do not like the police. But I have to stand well with them because of my hotel. You want me to square them with money?"

"We just want to get the body away quietly."

"That is very nice, my dear. And I, too, I do not want a body in my hotel. But it is, as you say, not so easy to do?"

"I think it could be managed," said Dakin. "You've got a doctor in your family, haven't you?"

"Yes, Paul, my sister's husband, is a doctor. He is a very nice boy. But I do not want him to get into trouble."

"He won't," said Dakin. "Listen, Marcus. We move the body from Miss Jones' room across into my room. That lets her out of it. Then I use your telephone. In ten minutes' time a young man reels into the hotel from the street. He is very drunk, he clutches his side. He demands me at the top of his voice. He staggers into my room and collapses. I come out and call you and ask for a doctor. You produce your brother-in-law. He sends for an ambulance and he goes in it with this drunken friend of mine. Before they get to the hospital my friend is dead. He has been stabbed. That is all right for you. He has been stabbed in the street before coming into your hotel."

"My brother-in-law takes away the body—and the young man who plays the part of the drunkard, he goes away quietly in the morning perhaps?"

"That's the idea."

"And there is no body found in my hotel? And Miss Jones she does not get any worry or annoyance? I think, my dear, that that is all a very good idea."

"Good, then if you'll make sure the coast is clear, I'll get the body across to my room. Those servants of yours potter round the corridors half the night. Go along to your room and raise a shindy. Get them all running to fetch you things."

Marcus nodded and left the room.

"You're a strong girl," said Dakin. "Can you manage to help me to carry him across the corridor to my room?"

Victoria nodded. Between them they lifted the limp body, carried it across the deserted corridor (in the distance Marcus' voice could be heard upraised in furious anger) and laid it on Dakin's bed.

Dakin said:

"Got a pair of scissors? Then cut off the top of your underblanket where it's stained. I don't think the stain's gone through to the mattress. The tunic soaked up most of it. I'll come along to you in about an hour. Here, wait a minute, take a pull from this flask of mine."

Victoria obeyed.

"Good girl," said Dakin. "Now go back to your room. Turn out the light. As I said, I'll be along in about an hour."

"And you'll tell me what it all means?"

He gave her a long rather peculiar stare but did not answer her question.

14

VICTORIA LAY IN bed with her light out, listening through the darkness. She heard sounds of loud drunken altercation. Heard a voice declaring: "Felt I got to look you up, ole man. Had a row with a fellow outside." She heard bells ring. Heard other voices. Heard a good deal of commotion. Then came a stretch of comparative silence—except for the far off playing of Arab music on a gramophone in somebody's room. When it seemed to her as though hours had passed, she heard the gentle opening of her door, sat up in bed and switched on the bedside lamp.

"That's right," said Dakin approvingly.

He brought a chair up to the bedside and sat down in it. He sat there, staring at her in the considering manner of a physician making a diagnosis.

"Tell me what it's all about?" demanded Victoria.

"Suppose," said Dakin, "that you tell me all about yourself first. What are you doing here? Why did you come to Baghdad?"

Whether it was the events of the night, or whether it was something in Dakin's personality (Victoria thought afterward that it was the latter) Victoria for once did not launch out on an inspired and meretricious account of her presence in Baghdad. Quite simply and straightforwardly she told him everything. Her meeting with Edward, her determination to get to Baghdad, the miracle of Mrs. Hamilton Clipp, and her own financial destitution.

"I see," said Dakin when she'd finished.

He was silent for a moment before he spoke.

"Perhaps I'd like to keep you out of this. I'm not sure. But the point is you can't be kept out of it! You're in it, whether I like it or not. And as you're in it, you might as well work for me."

"You've got a job for me?" Victoria sat up in bed, her cheeks bright with anticipation.

"Perhaps. But not the kind of job you're thinking of. This is a serious job, Victoria. And it's dangerous."

"Oh, that's all right," said Victoria cheerfully. She added doubtfully, "It's not dishonest, is it? Because though I know I tell an awful lot of lies, I wouldn't really like to do anything that was dishonest."

Dakin smiled a little.

"Strangely enough, your capacity to think up a convincing lie quickly is one of your qualifications for the job. No, it's not dishonest. On the contrary, you are enlisted in the cause of law and order. I'm going to put you in the picture—only in a general kind of way, but so that you can understand fully what it is you are doing and exactly what the dangers are. You seem to be a sensible young woman and I don't suppose you've thought much about world politics which is just as well, because as Hamlet very wisely remarked, 'There is nothing either good or bad, but thinking makes it so.' "

"I know everybody says there's going to be another war sooner or later," said Victoria.

"Exactly," said Mr. Dakin. "Why does everybody say so, Victoria?"

She frowned. "Why, because Russia—the Communists—America—" she stopped.

"You see," said Dakin. "Those aren't your own opinions or words. They're picked up from newspapers, and casual talk, and the wireless. There are two divergent points of view dominating different parts of the world; that is true enough. And they are represented loosely in the public mind as 'Russia and the Communists' and 'America.' Now the only hope for the future, Victoria, lies in peace, in production, in constructive activities and not destructive ones. Therefore, everything depends on those who hold those two divergent viewpoints, either agreeing to differ and each contenting themselves with their respective spheres of activity, or else finding a mutual basis for agreement or at least toleration. Instead of that, the opposite is happening, a wedge is being driven in the whole time to force two mutually suspicious groups further and further apart. Certain things led one or two people to believe that this activity comes from a third party or group working undercover and so far absolutely unsuspected by the world at large. Whenever there is a chance of agreement being reached or any sign of dispersal of suspicion, some incident occurs to plunge one side back in distrust, or the other side into definite hysterical fear. These things are not accidents, Victoria, they are deliberately produced for a calculated effect."

"But why do you think so and who's doing it?"

"One of the reasons we think so is because of money. The money, you see, is coming from the wrong sources. Money, Victoria, is always the great clue to what is happening in the world. As a physician feels your pulse, to get a clue to your state of health, so money is the life blood that feeds any great movement or cause. Without it, the movement can't make headway. Now here, there are very large sums of money involved and although very cleverly and artfully camouflaged, there is definitely something wrong about where the money comes from and where it is going. A great many unofficial strikes, various threats to governments in Europe who show signs of recovery, are staged and brought into being by Communists, zealots for their cause—but the funds for these measures do not come from Communist sources, and traced back, they come from very strange and unlikely quarters. It is not Capitalist money, though it naturally passes through Capitalist hands. Another point, enormous sums of money seem to be going completely out of circulation. As much as though—to put it simply—you spent your salary every week on things—bracelets or tables or chairs—and those things then disappeared or passed out of ordinary circulation and sight. All over the world a great demand for diamonds and other precious stones has arisen. They change hands a dozen or more times until finally they disappear and cannot be traced.

"This, of course, is only a vague sketch. The upshot is that somewhere a third group of people whose aim is as yet obscure, are fomenting strife and misunderstanding and are engaging in cleverly camouflaged money and jewel transactions for their own ends. We have reason to believe that in every country there are agents of this group, some established there many years ago. Some are in very high and responsible positions, others are playing humble parts, but all are working with one unknown end in view. In substance, it is exactly like the Fifth Column activities at the beginning of the last war, only this time it is on a worldwide scale."

"But who are these people?" Victoria demanded.

"They are not, we think, of any special nationality. What they want is, I fear, the betterment of the world! The delusion that by force you can impose the Millennium on the human race is one of the most dangerous delusions in existence. Those who are out only to line their own pockets can do little harm —mere greed defeats its own ends. But the belief in a superstratum of human beings—in Supermen to rule the rest of the decadent world—that, Victoria, is the most evil of all beliefs. For when you say, 'I am not as other men'—you have lost the two most valuable qualities we have ever tried to attain:— humility and brotherhood."

He coughed. "Well, I mustn't preach a sermon. Let me just explain to you what we do know. There are various centers of activity. One in the Argentine, one in Canada—certainly one or more in the United States of America, and I should imagine, though we can't tell, one in Russia. And now we come to a very interesting phenomenon.

"In the past two years, twenty-eight promising young scientists of various nationalities have quietly faded out of their background. The same thing has happened with constructional engineers, with aviators, with electricians and many other skilled trades. These disappearances have this in common: those concerned are all young, all ambitious, and all without close ties. Besides those we know of, there must be many many more, and we are beginning to guess at something of what they may be accomplishing."

Victoria listened, her brows drawn together.

"You might say it was impossible in these days for anything to go on in any country, unknown to the rest of the world. I do not, of course, mean under-cover activities; those may go on anywhere. But anything on a large scale of up-to-date production. And yet there are still obscure parts of the world, remote from trade routes, cut off by mountains and deserts, in the midst of peoples who still have the power to bar out strangers and which are never known or visited except by a solitary and exceptional traveler. Things could go on there the news of which would never penetrate to the outside world, or only as a dim and ridiculous rumor.

"I won't particularize the spot. It can be reached from China—and nobody knows what goes on in the interior of China. It can be reached from the Himalayas, but the journey there, save to the initiated, is hard and long to travel. Machinery and personnel dispatched from all over the globe reaches it, after being diverted from its ostensible destination. The mechanics of it all need not be gone into.

"But one man got interested in following up a certain trail. He was an unusual man, a man who has friends and contacts throughout the East. He was born in Kashgar and he knows a score of local dialects and languages. He suspected and he followed up the trail. What he heard was so incredible that when he got back to civilization and reported it, he was not believed. He admitted that he had had fever and he was treated as a man who had had delirium.

"Only two people believed his story. One was myself. I never object to believing impossible things—they're so often true. The other—" he hesitated.

"Yes?" said Victoria.

"The other was Sir Rupert Crofton Lee, a great traveler, and a man who had himself traveled through these remote regions and who knew something about their possibilities.

"The upshot of it all was that Carmichael, that's my man, decided to go and find out for himself. It was a desperate and hazardous journey, but he was as well equipped as any man to carry it through. That was nine months back. We heard nothing until a few weeks ago and then news came through. He was alive and he'd got what he went to get. Definite proof.

"But the other side were on to him. It was vital to them that he should never get back with his proofs. And we've had ample evidence of how the whole system is penetrated and infiltrated with their agents. Even in my own department there are leaks. And some of those leaks, Heaven help us, are at a very high level.

"Every frontier has been watched for him. Innocent lives have been sacrificed in mistake for his—they don't set much store by human life. But somehow or other he got through unscathed—until tonight."

"Then that was who—he was?"

"Yes, my dear. A very brave and indomitable young man."

"But what about the proofs? Did they get those?"

A very slow smile showed on Dakin's tired face.

"I don't think they did. No, knowing Carmichael, I'm pretty sure they didn't. But he died without being able to tell us where those proofs are and how to get hold of them. I think he probably tried to say something when he was dying that should give us the clue." He repeated slowly, "Lucifer—Basrah—Lefarge. He'd been in Basrah—tried to report at the Consulate and narrowly missed being shot. It's possible that he left the proofs somewhere in Basrah. What I want you to do, Victoria, is to go there and try to find out."

"Me?"

"Yes. You've no experience. You don't know what you're looking for. But you heard Carmichael's last words and they may suggest something to you when you get there. Who knows—you may have beginner's luck?"

"I'd love to go to Basrah," said Victoria eagerly.

Dakin smiled.

"Suits you because your man is there, eh? That's all right. Good camouflage, too. Nothing like a genuine love affair for camouflage. You go to Basrah, keep your eyes and ears open and look about you. I can't give you any instructions on how to set about things—in fact, I'd much rather not. You seem a young woman with plenty of ingenuity of your own. What the words Lucifer and Lefarge mean—assuming that you heard correctly—I don't know. I'm inclined to agree with you that Lefarge must be a name. Look out for that name."

"How do I get to Basrah?" said Victoria in a businesslike way. "And what do I use for money?"

Dakin took out his pocketbook and handed her a wad of paper money.

"That's what you use for money. As for how you get to Basrah, fall into conversation with that old trout Mrs. Cardew Trench tomorrow morning, say you're anxious to visit Basrah before you go off to this dig you're pretending to work at. Ask her about a hotel. She'll tell you at once you must stay at the Consulate and will send a telegram to Mrs. Clayton. You'll probably find your Edward there. The Claytons keep open house—everyone who passes through stays with them. Beyond that, I can't give you any tips except one. If —er—anything unpleasant happens, if you're asked what you know and who put you up to what you're doing—don't try and be heroic. Spill the beans at once."

"Thank you very much," said Victoria gratefully. "I'm an awful coward about pain, and if anyone were to torture me I'm afraid I shouldn't hold out."

"They won't bother to torture you," said Mr. Dakin. "Unless some sadistic element enters in. Torture's very old-fashioned. A little prick with a needle and you answer every question truthfully without realizing you're doing it. We live in a scientific age. That's why I didn't want you to get grand ideas of secrecy. You won't be telling them anything they don't know already. They'll be wise to me after this evening—bound to be. And to Rupert Crofton Lee."

"What about Edward? Do I tell him?"

"That I must leave to you. Theoretically, you're to hold your tongue about what you're doing to everybody. Practically!" His eyebrows went up quizzically. "You put him in danger, too. There's that aspect of it. Still, I gather he had a good record in the Air Force. I don't suppose danger will worry him. Two heads are often better than one. So he thinks there's something fishy about this 'Olive Branch' he's working for? That's interesting—very interesting."

"Why?"

"Because we think so, too," said Dakin.

Then he added:

"Just two parting tips. First, if you don't mind my saying so, don't tell too many different kinds of lies. It's harder to remember and live up to. I know you're a bit of a virtuoso, but keep it simple, is my advice."

"I'll remember," said Victoria with becoming humility. "And the other tip?"

"Just keep your ears strained for any mention of a young woman called Anna Scheele."

"Who is she?"

"We don't know much about her. We could do with knowing a little more."

15

"OF COURSE YOU must stay at the Consulate," said Mrs. Cardew Trench. "Nonsense, my dear—you can't stay at the Airport Hotel. The Claytons will be delighted. I've known them for years. We'll send a wire and you can go down on tonight's train. They know Dr. Pauncefoot Jones quite well."

Victoria had the grace to blush. The Bishop of Llangow, alias the Bishop of Languao was one thing; a real flesh and blood Dr. Pauncefoot Jones was quite another.

"I suppose," thought Victoria guiltily, "I could be sent to prison for that—false pretenses or something."

Then she cheered herself up by reflecting that it was only if you attempted to obtain money by false statements that the rigors of the law were set in motion. Whether this was really so or not, Victoria did not know, being as ignorant of the law as most average people, but it had a cheering sound.

The train journey had all the fascination of novelty—to Victoria's idea the train was hardly an express—but she had begun to feel conscious of her Western impatience.

A Consular car met her at the station and she was driven to the Consulate.

The car drove in through big gates into a delightful garden and drew up before a flight of steps leading up to a balcony surrounding the house. Mrs. Clayton, a smiling energetic woman, came through the swinging wire mesh door to meet her.

"We're so pleased to see you," she said. "Basrah's really delightful this time of year, and you oughtn't to leave Iraq without seeing it. Luckily there's no one much here just at the moment—sometimes we just don't know where to turn so as to fit people in, but there's no one here now except Dr. Rathbone's young man who's quite charming. You've just missed Richard Baker, by the way. He left before I got Mrs. Cardew Trench's telegram."

Victoria had no idea who Richard Baker was—but it seemed fortunate that he had left when he did.

"He had been down to Kuwait for a couple of days," continued Mrs. Clayton. "Now that's a place you ought to see—before it's spoilt. I daresay it soon will be. Every place gets ruined sooner or later. What would you like first—a bath or some coffee?"

"A bath, please," said Victoria gratefully.

"How's Mrs. Cardew Trench? This is your room and the bathroom's along here. Is she an old friend of yours?"

"Oh no," said Victoria truthfully. "I've only just met her."

"And I suppose she turned you inside out in the first quarter of an hour? She's a terrific gossip as I expect you've gathered. Got quite a mania for knowing all about everybody. But she's quite good company and a really first-class bridge player. Now are you sure you wouldn't like some coffee or something first?"

"No, really."

"Good—then I'll see you later. Have you got everything you want?"

Mrs. Clayton buzzed away like a cheerful bee, and Victoria took a bath, and attended to her face and her hair with the meticulous care of a young woman who is shortly going to be reunited to a young man who has taken her fancy.

If possible, Victoria hoped to meet Edward alone. She did not think that he would make any tactless remarks—fortunately he knew her as Jones and the additional Pauncefoot would probably cause him no surprise. The surprise would be that she was in Iraq at all, and for that Victoria hoped that she could catch him alone even for a bare second or two.

With this end in view, when she had put on a summer frock (for to her the climate of Basrah recalled a June day in London) she slipped out quietly through the wire door and took up her position on the balcony where she could intercept Edward when he arrived back from whatever he was doing—wrestling with the Customs officials, she presumed.

The first arrival was a tall thin man with a thoughtful face, and as he came up the steps, Victoria slipped around the corner of the balcony. As she did so, she actually saw Edward entering through a garden door that gave on to the river bend.

Faithful to the tradition of Juliet, Victoria leaned over the balcony and gave a prolonged hiss.

Edward (who was looking, Victoria thought, more attractive than ever) turned his head sharply, looking about him.

"Hist! Up here," called Victoria in a low voice.

Edward raised his head, and an expression of utter astonishment appeared on his face.

"Good Lord," he exclaimed. "It's Charing Cross!"

"Hush. Wait for me. I'm coming down."

Victoria sped round the balcony, down the steps and along round the corner of the house to where Edward had remained obediently standing, the expression of bewilderment still on his face.

"I can't be drunk so early in the day," said Edward. "It is you?"

"Yes, it's me," said Victoria happily and ungrammatically.

"But what are you doing here? How did you get here? I thought I was never going to see you again."

"I thought so too."

"It's really just like a miracle. How did you get here?"

"I flew."

"Naturally you flew. You couldn't have got here in the time, otherwise. But I mean what blessed and wonderful chance brought you to Basrah?"

"The train," said Victoria.

"You're doing it on purpose, you little brute. God, I'm pleased to see you. But how did you get here—really?"

"I came out with a woman who'd broken her arm—a Mrs. Clipp. An American. I was offered the job the day after I met you, and you'd talked about Baghdad, and I was a bit fed up with London, so I thought, well, why not see the world?"

"You really are awfully sporting, Victoria. Where's this Clipp woman, here?"

"No, she's gone to a daughter near Kirkuk. It was only a journey out job."

"Then what are you doing now?"

"I'm still seeing the world," said Victoria. "But it has required a few subterfuges. That's why I wanted to get at you before we met in public, I mean, I don't want any tactless references to my being a shorthand typist out of a job when you last saw me."

"As far as I'm concerned, you're anything you say you are. I'm ready for briefing."

"The idea is," said Victoria, "that I am Miss Pauncefoot Jones. My uncle is an eminent archaeologist who is excavating in some more or less inaccessible place out here, and I am joining him there shortly."

"And none of that is true?"

"Naturally not. But it makes quite a good story."

"Oh, yes, excellent. But suppose you and old Pussyfoot Jones come face to face?"

"Pauncefoot. I don't think that is likely. As far as I can make out once archaeologists start to dig, they go on digging like mad, and don't stop."

"Rather like terriers. I say, there's a lot in what you say. Has he got a real niece?"

"How should I know?" said Victoria.

"Oh, then you're not impersonating anybody in particular. That makes it easier."

"Yes, after all, a man can have lots of nieces. Or, at a pinch, I could say I'm only a cousin but that I always call him uncle."

"You think of everything," said Edward admiringly. "You really are an amazing girl, Victoria. I've never met anyone like you. I thought I wouldn't see you again for years, and when I did see you, you'd have forgotten all about me. And now here you are."

The admiring and humble glance which Edward cast on her caused Victoria intense satisfaction. If she had been a cat she would have purred.

"But you'll want a job, won't you?" said Edward. "I mean, you haven't come into a fortune or anything?"

"Far from it! Yes," said Victoria slowly, "I shall want a job. I went into your Olive Branch place, as a matter of fact, and saw Dr. Rathbone and asked him for a job, but he wasn't very responsive—not to a salaried job, that is."

"The old beggar's fairly tight with his money," said Edward. "His idea is that everybody comes and works for the love of the thing."

"Do you think he's a phoney, Edward?"

"N-o. I don't know exactly what I do think. I don't see how he can be anything but on the square—he doesn't make any money out of the show. So far as I can see all that terrific enthusiasm must be genuine. And yet, you know, I don't really feel he's a fool."

"We'd better go in," said Victoria. "We can talk later."

"I'd no idea you and Edward knew each other," exclaimed Mrs. Clayton.

"Oh, we're old friends," laughed Victoria. "Only, as a matter of fact, we'd lost sight of each other. I'd no idea Edward was in this country."

Mr. Clayton, who was the quiet thoughtful-looking man Victoria had seen coming up the steps, asked:

"How did you get on this morning, Edward? Any progress?"

"It seems very uphill work, sir. The cases of books are there, all present and correct, but the formalities needed to clear them seem unending."

Clayton smiled.

"You're new to the delaying tactics of the East."

"The particular official who's wanted always seems to be away that day," complained Edward. "Everyone is very pleasant and willing—only nothing seems to happen."

Everyone laughed and Mrs. Clayton said consolingly:

"You'll get them through in the end. Very wise of Dr. Rathbone to send someone down personally. Otherwise they'd probably stay here for months."

"They are very suspicious about bombs. Also subversive literature. They suspect everything."

"Dr. Rathbone isn't shipping out bombs here disguised as books, I hope," said Mrs. Clayton laughing.

Victoria thought she caught a sudden flicker in Edward's eye, as though Mrs. Clayton's remark had opened up a new line of thought.

Clayton said, with a hint of reproof: "Dr. Rathbone's a very learned and well-known man, my dear. He's a Fellow of various important Societies and is known and respected all over Europe."

"That would make it all the easier for him to smuggle in bombs," Mrs. Clayton pointed out with irrepressible spirits.

Victoria could see that Gerald Clayton did not quite like this lighthearted suggestion.

He frowned at his wife.

Business being at a standstill during the midday hours, Edward and Victoria went out together after lunch to stroll about and see the sights. Victoria was delighted with the river, the Shatt el Arab, with its bordering of date palm groves. She adored the Venetian look of the high-powered Arab boats tied up in the canal in the town. Then they wandered into the Suq and looked at Kuwait bride chests studded with patterned brass and other attractive merchandise.

It was not until they turned toward the Consulate and Edward was preparing himself to assail the Customs department once more that Victoria said suddenly,

"Edward, what's your name?"

Edward stared at her.

"What on earth do you mean, Victoria?"

"Your last name. Don't you realize that I don't know it."

"Don't you? No, I suppose you don't. It's Goring."

"Edward Goring. You've no idea what a fool I felt going into that Olive Branch place and wanting to ask for you and not knowing anything but Edward."

"Was there a dark girl there? Rather long bobbed hair?"

"Yes."

"That's Catherine. She's awfully nice. If you'd said Edward she'd have known at once."

"I daresay she would," said Victoria with reserve.

"She's a frightfully nice girl. Didn't you think so?"

"Oh quite . . ."

"Not actually good-looking—in fact nothing much to look at, but she's frightfully sympathetic."

"Is she?" Victoria's voice was now quite glacial—but Edward apparently noticed nothing.

"I don't really know what I should have done without her. She put me in the picture and helped me out when I might have made a fool of myself. I'm sure you and she will be great friends."

"I don't suppose we shall have the opportunity."

"Oh yes, you will. I'm going to get you a job in the show."

"How are you going to manage that?"

"I don't know but I shall manage it somehow. Tell old Rattlebones what a wonderful typist et cetera you are."

"He'll soon find out I'm not," said Victoria.

"Anyway, I shall get you into the Olive Branch somehow. I'm not going to have you beetling round on your own. Next thing I know, you'd be heading for Burma or darkest Africa. No, young Victoria, I'm going to have you right under my eye. I'm not going to take any chances on your running out on me. I don't trust you an inch. You're too fond of seeing the world."

"You sweet idiot," thought Victoria, "don't you know wild horses wouldn't drive me away from Baghdad!"

Aloud she said: "Well, it would be quite fun to have a job at the Olive Branch."

"I wouldn't describe it as fun. It's all terribly earnest. As well as being absolutely goofy."

"And you still think there's something wrong about it?"

"Oh, that was only a wild idea of mine."

"No," said Victoria thoughtfully. "I don't think it was only a wild idea. I think it's true."

Edward turned on her sharply.

"What makes you say that?"

"Something I heard—from a friend of mine."

"Who was it?"

"Just a friend."

"Girls like you have too many friends," grumbled Edward. "You are a devil, Victoria. I love you madly and you don't care a bit."

"Oh, yes, I do," said Victoria. "Just a little bit."

Then, concealing her delighted satisfaction, she asked:

"Edward, is there anyone called Lefarge connected with the Olive Branch or with anything else?"

"Lefarge?" Edward looked puzzled. "No, I don't think so. Who is he?"

Victoria pursued her inquiries.

"Or anyone called Anna Scheele?"

This time Edward's reaction was very different. He turned on her abruptly, caught her by the arm and said:

"What do you know about Anna Scheele?"

"Ow! Edward, let go! I don't know anything about her. I just wanted to know if you did."

"Where did you hear about her? Mrs. Clipp?"

"No—not Mrs. Clipp—at least I don't think so, but actually she talked so fast and so unendingly about everyone and everything that I probably wouldn't remember if she had mentioned her."

"But what made you think this Anna Scheele had anything to do with the Olive Branch?"

"Has she?"

Edward said slowly, "I don't know . . . It's all so—so vague."

They were standing outside the garden door to the Consulate. Edward glanced at his watch. "I must go and do my stuff," he said. "Wish I knew some Arabic. But we've got to get together, Victoria. There's a lot I want to know."

"There's a lot I want to tell you," said Victoria.

Some tender heroine of a more sentimental age might have sought to keep her man out of danger. Not so, Victoria. Men, in Victoria's opinion were born to danger as the sparks fly upward. Edward wouldn't thank her for keeping him out of things. And, on reflection, she was quite certain that Mr. Dakin hadn't intended her to keep him out of things.

ii

At sunset that evening Edward and Victoria walked together in the Consulate garden. In deference to Mrs. Clayton's insistence that the weather was wintry Victoria wore a woollen coat over her summer frock. The sunset was magnificent but neither of the young people noticed it. They were discussing more important things.

"It began quite simply," said Victoria, "with a man coming into my room at the Tio Hotel and getting stabbed."

It was not, perhaps, most people's idea of a simple beginning. Edward stared at her and said: "Getting what?"

"Stabbed," said Victoria. "At least I think it was stabbed, but it might have been shot, only I don't think so because then I would have heard the noise of the shot. Anyway," she added, "he was dead."

"How could he come into your room if he was dead?"

"Oh, Edward, don't be stupid."

Alternately baldly and vaguely, Victoria told her story. For some mysterious reason Victoria could never tell of truthful occurrences in a dramatic fashion. Her narrative was halting and incomplete and she told it with the air of one offering a palpable fabrication.

When she had come to the end, Edward looked at her doubtfully and said, "You do feel all right, Victoria, don't you? I mean you haven't had a touch of the sun or—a dream, or anything?"

"Of course not."

"Because, I mean, it seems such an absolutely impossible thing to have happened."

"Well, it did happen," said Victoria touchily.

"And all that melodramatic stuff about world forces and mysterious secret installations in the heart of Tibet or Baluchistan. I mean, all that simply couldn't be true. Things like that don't happen."

"That's what people always say before they've happened."

"Honest to God, Charing Cross—are you making all this up?"

"No!" cried Victoria exasperated.

"And you've come down here looking for someone called Lefarge and someone called Anna Scheele—"

"Whom you've heard of yourself," Victoria put in. "You had heard of her, hadn't you?"

"I'd heard the name—yes."

"How? Where? At the Olive Branch?"

Edward was silent for some moments, then he said:

"I don't know if it means anything. It was just—odd—"

"Go on. Tell me."

"You see, Victoria, I'm so different from you; I'm not as sharp as you are. I just feel, in a queer kind of way, that things are wrong somehow—I don't know why I think so. You spot things as they go along and deduce things from them. I'm not clever enough for that. I just feel vaguely that things are —well—wrong—but I don't know why."

"I feel like that sometimes, too," said Victoria. "Like Sir Rupert on the balcony of the Tio."

"Who's Sir Rupert?"

"Sir Rupert Crofton Lee. He was on the plane coming out. Very haughty and showing off. A V.I.P. You know. And when I saw him sitting out on the balcony at the Tio in the sun, I had that queer feeling you've just said of something being wrong, but not knowing what it was."

"Rathbone asked him to lecture to the Olive Branch, I believe, but he couldn't make it. Flew back to Cairo or Damascus or somewhere yesterday morning."

"Well, go on about Anna Scheele."

"Oh, Anna Scheele. It was nothing really. It was just one of the girls."

"Catherine?" said Victoria instantly.

"I believe it was Catherine now I think of it."

"Of course, it was Catherine. That's why you don't want to tell me about it."

"Nonsense, that's quite absurd."

"Well, what was it?"

"Catherine said to one of the other girls, 'When Anna Scheele comes, we can go forward. Then we take our orders from her—and from her alone.'"

"That's frightfully important, Edward."

"Remember, I'm not even sure that that was the name," Edward warned her.

"Didn't you think it queer at the time?"

"No, of course I didn't. I thought it was just some female who was coming out to boss things. A kind of Queen Bee. Are you sure you're not imagining all this, Victoria?"

Immediately he quailed slightly before the glance his young friend gave him.

"All right, all right," he said hastily. "Only you'll admit the whole story does sound queer. So like a thriller—a young man coming in and gasping out one word that doesn't mean anything—and then dying— It just doesn't seem real."

"You didn't see the blood," said Victoria and shivered slightly.

"It must have given you a terrible shock," said Edward sympathetically.

"It did," said Victoria. "And then on top of it, you come along and ask me if I'm making it all up."

"I'm sorry. But you are rather good at making things up. The Bishop of Llangow and all that!"

"Oh, that was just girlish *joie de vivre,*" said Victoria. "This is serious, Edward, really serious."

"This man, Dakin—is that his name?—impressed you as knowing what he was talking about?"

"Yes, he was very convincing. But, look here, Edward, how do you know—"

A hail from the balcony interrupted her.

"Come in—you two—drinks waiting."

"Coming," called Victoria.

Mrs. Clayton, watching them coming toward the steps, said to her husband:

"There's something in the wind here! Nice couple of children—probably haven't got a bean between them. Shall I tell you what I think, Gerald?"

"Certainly, dear. I'm always interested to hear your ideas."

"I think that girl has come out here to join her uncle on his Dig simply and solely because of that young man."

"I hardly think so, Rosa. They were quite astonished to see each other."

"Poosh!" said Mrs. Clayton. "That's nothing. He was astonished, I daresay."

Gerald Clayton shook his head at her and smiled.

"She's not an archaeological type," said Mrs. Clayton. "They're usually earnest girls with spectacles—and very often damp hands."

"My dear, you can't generalize in that way."

"—And intellectual and all that. This girl is an amiable nitwit with a lot of common sense. Quite different. He's a nice boy. A pity he's tied up with all this silly Olive Branch stuff—but I suppose jobs are hard to get. They should find jobs for these boys."

"It's not so easy, dear, they do try. But you see, they've no training, no experience and usually not much habit of concentration."

Victoria went to bed that night in a turmoil of mixed feelings.

The object of her quest was attained, Edward was found! She suffered from the inevitable reaction. Do what she might a feeling of anticlimax persisted.

It was partly Edward's disbelief that made everything that had happened seem stagey and unreal. She, Victoria Jones, a little London typist, had arrived in Baghdad, had seen a man murdered almost before her eyes, had become a secret agent or something equally melodramatic, and had finally met the man she loved in a tropical garden with palms waving overhead, and in all probability not far from the spot where the original Garden of Eden was said to be situated.

A fragment of a nursery rhyme floated through her head.

> *How many miles to Babylon?*
> *Threescore and ten:*
> *Can I get there by candlelight?*
> *Yes, and back again.*

But she wasn't back again—she was still in Babylon.

Perhaps she would never get back—she and Edward in Babylon.

Something she had meant to ask Edward—there in the garden. Garden of Eden—she and Edward— Ask Edward—but Mrs. Clayton had called—and it had gone out of her head— But she must remember—because it was important— It didn't make sense—Palms—garden—Edward—Saracen Maiden—Anna Scheele—Rupert Crofton Lee— All wrong somehow— And if only she could remember—

A woman coming toward her along a hotel corridor—a woman in a tailored suit—it was herself—but when the woman got near she saw the face was Catherine's. Edward and Catherine—absurd! "Come with me," she said to Edward, "we will find M. Lefarge—" And suddenly there he was, wearing lemon yellow kid gloves and a little pointed black beard.

Edward was gone now and she was alone. She must get back from Babylon before the candles went out.

And we are for the dark.

Who had said that? Violence, terror—evil—blood on a ragged khaki tunic. She was running—running—down a hotel corridor. And they were coming after her.

Victoria woke up with a gasp.

iii

"Coffee?" said Mrs. Clayton. "How do you like your eggs? Scrambled?"

"Lovely."

"You look rather washed out. Not feeling ill?"

"No, I didn't sleep very well last night. I don't know why. It's a very comfortable bed."

"Turn the wireless on, will you, Gerald? It's time for the news."

Edward came in just as the pips were sounding.

"In the House of Commons last night, the Prime Minister gave fresh details of the cuts in dollar imports.

"A report from Cairo announces that the body of Sir Rupert Crofton Lee has been taken from the Nile." Victoria put down her coffee cup sharply and Mrs. Clayton uttered an ejaculation. *"Sir Rupert left his hotel yesterday afternoon, after arriving by plane from Baghdad, and did not return to it that night. He had been missing for twenty-four hours when his body was recovered. Death was due to a stab wound in the heart and not to drowning. Sir Rupert was a renowned traveler, was famous for his travels through China and Baluchistan and was the author of several books."*

"Murdered!" exclaimed Mrs. Clayton. "I think Cairo is worse than any-place now. Did you know anything about all this, Gerry?"

"I knew he was missing," said Mr. Clayton. "It appears he got a note, brought by hand, and left the hotel in a great hurry on foot without saying where he was going."

"You see," said Victoria to Edward after breakfast when they were alone together. "It is all true. First this man Carmichael and now Sir Rupert Crofton Lee. I feel sorry now I called him a show off. It seems unkind. All the people who know or guess about this queer business are being got out of the way. Edward, do you think it will be me next?"

"For Heaven's sake don't look so pleased by the idea, Victoria! Your sense of drama is much too strong. I don't see why anyone should eliminate you because you don't really know anything—but do, please, do, be awfully careful."

"We'll both be careful. I've dragged you into it."

"Ah. That's all right. Relieves the monotony."

"Yes, but take care of yourself."

She gave a sudden shiver.

"It's rather awful. He was so very much alive—Crofton Lee, I mean—and now he's dead too. It's frightening, really frightening."

16

"FIND YOUR YOUNG man?" asked Mr. Dakin.

Victoria nodded.

"Find anything else?"

Rather mournfully, Victoria shook her head.

"Well, cheer up," said Mr. Dakin. "Remember in this game, results are few and far between. You might have picked up something there—one never knows, but I wasn't in any way counting on it."

"Can I still go on trying?" asked Victoria.

"Do you want to?"

"Yes, I do. Edward thinks he can get me a job at the Olive Branch. If I keep my ears and eyes open, I might find out something, mightn't I? They know something about Anna Scheele there."

"Now that's very interesting, Victoria. How did you learn that?"

Victoria repeated what Edward had told her—about Catherine's remarks that when "Anna Scheele came" they would take their orders from her.

"Very interesting," said Mr. Dakin.

"Who is Anna Scheele?" asked Victoria. "I mean, you must know something about her—or is she just a name?"

"She's more than a name. She's confidential secretary to an American banker—head of an international banking firm. She left New York and came to London about ten days ago. Since then she's disappeared."

"Disappeared? She's not dead?"

"If so, her dead body hasn't been found."

"But she may be dead?"

"Oh yes, she may be dead."

"Was she—coming to Baghdad?"

"I've no idea. It would seem from the remarks of this young woman Catherine, that she was. Or shall we say—is—since as yet there's no reason to believe she isn't still alive."

"Perhaps I can find out more at the Olive Branch."

"Perhaps you can—but I must warn you once more to be very careful, Victoria. The organization you are up against are quite ruthless. I would much rather not have your dead body found floating down the Tigris."

Victoria gave a little shiver and murmured:

"Like Sir Rupert Crofton Lee. You know that morning he was at the hotel here there was something odd about him—something that surprised me. I wish I could remember what it was . . ."

"In what way—odd?"

"Well—different." Then in response to the inquiring look, she shook her head vexedly. "It will come back to me, perhaps. Anyway I don't suppose it really matters."

"Anything might matter."

"If Edward gets me a job, he thinks I ought to get a room like the other girls in a sort of boarding house or paying guest place, not stay on here."

"It would create less surmise. Baghdad hotels are very expensive. Your young man seems to have his head screwed on the right way."

"Do you want to see him?"

Dakin shook his head emphatically.

"No, tell him to keep right away from me. You, unfortunately, owing to the circumstances on the night of Carmichael's death, are bound to be suspect.

But Edward is not linked with that occurrence or with me in any way—and that's valuable."

"I've been meaning to ask you," said Victoria. "Who actually did stab Carmichael? Was it someone who followed him here?"

"No," said Dakin slowly. "That couldn't have been so."

"Couldn't?"

"He came in a *gufa*—one of those native boats—and he wasn't followed. We know that because I had someone watching the river."

"Then it was someone—in the hotel?"

"Yes, Victoria. And what is more someone in one particular wing of the hotel—for I myself was watching the stairs and no one came up them."

He watched her rather puzzled face and said quietly:

"That doesn't really give us very many names. You and I and Mrs. Cardew Trench, and Marcus and his sisters. A couple of elderly servants who have been here for years. A man called Harrison from Kirkuk against whom nothing is known. A nurse who works at the Jewish Hospital . . . It might be any of them—yet all of them are unlikely for one very good reason."

"What is that?"

"Carmichael was on his guard. He knew that the peak moment of his mission was approaching. He was a man with a very keen instinct for danger. How did that instinct let him down?"

"Those police that came—" began Victoria.

"Ah, they came after—up from the street. They'd had a signal, I suppose. But they didn't do the stabbing. That must have been done by someone Carmichael knew well, whom he trusted . . . or alternately whom he judged negligible. If I only knew . . ."

ii

Achievement brings with it its own anticlimax. To get to Baghdad, to find Edward, to penetrate the secrets of the Olive Branch: all this had appeared as an entrancing program. Now, her objective attained, Victoria, in a rare moment of self-questioning, sometimes wondered what on earth she was doing! The rapture of reunion with Edward had come and gone. She loved Edward, Edward loved her. They were, on most days, working under the same roof—but thinking about it dispassionately, what on earth were they doing?

By some means or other, sheer force of determination, or ingenious persuasion, Edward had been instrumental in Victoria's being offered a meagerly paid job at the Olive Branch. She spent most of her time in a small dark room with the electric light on, typing on a very faulty machine various notices and letters and manifestos of the milk and water program of the Olive Branch activities. Edward had had a hunch there was something wrong about the Olive Branch. Mr. Dakin had seemed to agree with that view. She, Victoria, was here to find out what she could, but as far as she could see, there was nothing to find out! The Olive Branch activities dripped with the honey of international peace. Various gatherings were held with orangeade to drink and depressing edibles to go with it, and at these Victoria was supposed to act as quasi hostess; to mix, to introduce, to promote general good feeling among various foreign nationals, who were inclined to stare with animosity at one another, and wolf refreshments hungrily.

As far as Victoria could see, there were no undercurrents, no conspiracies, no inner rings. All was aboveboard, mild as milk and water, and desperately dull. Various dark-skinned young men made tentative love to her, others lent her books to read which she skimmed through and found tedious. She had, by now, left the Tio Hotel and had taken up her quarters with some other young women workers of various nationalities in a house on the West Bank of the river. Among these young women was Catherine, and it seemed to Victoria that Catherine watched her with a suspicious eye; but whether this was because Catherine suspected her of being a spy on the activities of the Olive Branch or whether it was the more delicate matter of Edward's affections, Victoria was unable to make up her mind. She rather fancied the latter. It was known that Edward had secured Victoria her job and several pairs of jealous dark eyes looked at her without undue affection.

The fact was, Victoria thought moodily, that Edward was far too attractive. All these girls had fallen for him, and Edward's engaging friendly manner to one and all did nothing to help. By agreement between them, Victoria and Edward were to show no signs of special intimacy. If they were to find out anything worth finding out, they must not be suspected of working together. Edward's manner to her was the same as to any of the other young women, with an added shade of coldness.

Though the Olive Branch itself seemed so innocuous, Victoria had a distinct feeling that its head and founder was in a different category. Once or twice she was aware of Dr. Rathbone's dark thoughtful gaze resting upon her, and though she countered it with her most innocent and kittenlike expression, she felt a sudden throb of something like fear.

Once, when she had been summoned to his presence (for explanation of a typing error), the matter went further than a glance.

"You are happy working with us, I hope?" he asked.

"Oh, yes, indeed, sir," said Victoria, and added: "I'm sorry I make so many mistakes."

"We don't mind mistakes. A soulless machine would be no use to us. We need youth, generosity of spirit, broadness of outlook."

Victoria endeavored to look eager and generous.

"You must love the work . . . love the object for which you are working . . . look forward to the glorious future. Are you truly feeling all that, dear child?"

"It's all so new to me," said Victoria. "I really don't feel I have taken it all in yet."

"Get together—get together—young people everywhere must get together.

That is the main thing. You enjoy our evenings of free discussion and comradeship?"

"Oh! yes," said Victoria who loathed them.

"Agreement, not dissension—brotherhood, not hatred. Slowly and surely it
is growing—you do feel that, don't you?"

Victoria thought of the endless petty jealousies, the violent dislikes, the
endless quarrels, hurt feelings, apologies demanded; and hardly knew what
she was expected to say.

"Sometimes," she said cautiously, "people are difficult."

"I know . . . I know . . ." Dr. Rathbone sighed. His noble domed forehead furrowed itself in perplexity. "What is this I hear of Michael Rakounian
striking Isaac Nahoum and cutting his lip open?"

"They were just having a little argument," said Victoria.

Dr. Rathbone brooded mournfully.

"Patience and faith," he murmured. "Patience and faith."

Victoria murmured a dutiful assent and turned to leave. Then, remembering she had left her typescript, she came back again. The glance she caught in
Dr. Rathbone's eye startled her a little. It was a keen suspicious glance, and
she wondered uneasily just how closely she was being watched, and what Dr.
Rathbone really thought about her.

Her instructions from Mr. Dakin were very precise. She was to obey certain rules for communicating with him if she had anything to report. He had
given her an old faded pink handkerchief. If she had anything to report she
was to walk, as she often did when the sun was setting, along the riverbank,
near her hostel. There was a narrow path in front of the houses there for
perhaps a quarter of a mile. In one place a big flight of steps led down to the
water's edge and boats were constantly being tied up there. There was a rusty
nail in one of the wooden posts at the top. Here she was to affix a small piece
of the pink handkerchief if she wanted to get into communication with
Dakin. So far, Victoria reflected bitterly, there had been no need for anything
of the sort. She was merely doing an ill-paid job in a slovenly fashion. Edward
she saw at rare intervals, since he was always being sent to faroff places by
Dr. Rathbone. At the moment, he had just come back from Persia. During
his absence, she had had one short and somewhat unsatisfactory interview
with Dakin. Her instructions had been to go to the Tio Hotel and ask if she
had left a cardigan behind. The answer having been in the negative, Marcus
appeared and immediately swept her out onto the riverbank for a drink.
During the process Dakin had shambled in from the street and had been
hailed by Marcus to join them and presently, as Dakin supped lemonade,
Marcus had been called away and the two of them sat there on opposite sides
of the small painted table.

Rather apprehensively Victoria confessed her utter lack of success, but
Dakin was indulgently reassuring.

"My dear child, you don't even know what you are looking for or even if there is anything to find. Taken by and large, what is your considered opinion of the Olive Branch?"

"It's a thoroughly dim show," said Victoria slowly.

"Dim, yes. But not bogus?"

"I don't know," said Victoria slowly. "People are so sold on the idea of culture if you know what I mean?"

"You mean that where anything cultured is concerned, nobody examines *bona fides* in the way they would if it were a charitable or a financial proposition? That's true. And you'll find genuine enthusiasts there, I've no doubt. But is the organization being used?"

"I think there's a lot of Communist activity going on," said Victoria doubtfully. "Edward thinks so, too—he's making me read Karl Marx and leave it about just to see what reactions there will be."

Dakin nodded.

"Interesting. Any response so far?"

"No, not yet."

"What about Rathbone? Is he genuine?"

"I think really that he is—" Victoria sounded doubtful.

"He's the one I worry about, you see," said Dakin. "Because he's a big noise. Suppose there is Communist plotting going on—students and young revolutionaries have very little chance of coming in contact with the President. Police measures will look after bombs thrown from the street. But Rathbone's different. He's one of the high-ups, a distinguished man with a fine record of public beneficence. He could come in close contact with the distinguished visitors. He probably will. I'd like to know about Rathbone."

Yes, Victoria thought to herself, it all revolved around Rathbone. On that first meeting in London, weeks ago, Edward's vague remarks about the "fishiness" of the show had had their origin in his employer. And there must, Victoria decided suddenly, have been some incident, some word, that had awakened Edward's uneasiness. For that, in Victoria's belief, was how minds worked. Your vague doubt or distrust was never just a hunch—it was really always due to a cause. If Edward, now, could be made to think back, to remember; between them they might hit upon the fact or incident that had aroused his suspicions. In the same way, Victoria thought, she herself must try to think back to what it was that had so surprised her when she came out upon the balcony at the Tio and found Sir Rupert Crofton Lee sitting there in the sun. It was true that she had expected him to be at the Embassy and not at the Tio Hotel but that was not enough to account for the strong feeling she had had that his sitting there was quite impossible! She would go over and over the events of that morning, and Edward must be urged to go over and over his early association with Dr. Rathbone. She would tell him so when next she got him alone. But to get Edward alone was not easy. To begin with, he had been away in Persia and now that he was back, private communications at the Olive Branch were out of the question where the slogan of the last war *(Les oreilles enemis nous écoutent)* might have been written up all over the walls. In the Armenian household where she was a paying guest, privacy was equally impossible. Really, thought Victoria to herself, for all I see of Edward, I might as well have stayed in England!

That this was not quite true, was proved very shortly afterward.

Edward came to her with some sheets of manuscript and said:

"Dr. Rathbone would like this typed out at once, please, Victoria. Be especially careful of the second page, there are some rather tricky Arab names on it."

Victoria, with a sigh, inserted a sheet of paper in her typewriter and started off in her usual dashing style. Dr. Rathbone's handwriting was not particularly difficult to read and Victoria was just congratulating herself that she had made fewer mistakes than usual. She laid the top sheet aside and proceeded to the next—and at once realized the meaning of Edward's injunction to be careful of the second page. A tiny note in Edward's handwriting was pinned to the top of it.

Go for a walk along the Tigris bank past the Beit Melik Ali tomorrow morning about eleven.

The following day was Friday, the weekly holiday. Victoria's spirits rose mercurially. She would wear her jade green pullover. She ought really to get her hair shampooed. The amenities of the house where she lived made it difficult to wash it herself. "And it really needs it," she murmured aloud.

"What did you say?" Catherine, at work on a pile of circulars and envelopes, raised her head suspiciously from the next table.

Victoria quickly crumpled up Edward's note in her hand as she said lightly:

"My hair wants washing. Most of these hairdressing places look so frightfully dirty, I don't know where to go."

"Yes, they are dirty and expensive, too. But I know a girl who washes hair very well and the towels are clean. I will take you there."

"That's very kind of you, Catherine," said Victoria.

"We will go tomorrow. It is holiday."

"Not tomorrow," said Victoria.

"Why not tomorrow?"

A suspicious stare was bent upon her. Victoria felt her usual annoyance and dislike of Catherine rising.

"I'd rather go for a walk—get some air. One is so cooped up here."

"Where can you walk? There is nowhere to walk in Baghdad."

"I shall find somewhere," said Victoria.

"It would be better to go to the Cinema. Or there is an interesting lecture."

"No, I want to get out. In England we like going for walks."

"Because you are English, you are so proud and stuck up. What does it mean to be English? Next than nothing. Here we spit upon the English."

"If you start spitting on me you may get a surprise," said Victoria, wondering as usual at the ease with which angry passions seemed to rise at the Olive Branch.

"What would you do?"

"Try and see."

"Why do you read Karl Marx? You cannot understand it. You are much too stupid. Do you think they would ever accept you as a member of the Communist party? You are not well enough educated politically."

"Why shouldn't I read it? It was meant for people like me—workers."

"You are not a worker. You are bourgeoise. You cannot even type properly. Look at the mistakes you make."

"Some of the cleverest people can't spell," said Victoria with dignity. "And how can I work when you keep talking to me?"

She rattled off a line at breakneck speed—and was then somewhat chagrined to find that as a result of unwittingly depressing the shift key, she had written a line of exclamation points, figures and brackets. Removing the sheet from the machine she replaced it with another and applied herself diligently until, her task finished, she took the result in to Dr. Rathbone.

Glancing over it and murmuring, "Shiraz is in Iran not Iraq—and anyway you don't spell Iraq with a K . . . Wasit—not Wuzle—er—thank you, Victoria."

Then, as she was leaving the room, he called her back.

"Victoria, are you happy here?"

"Oh yes, Dr. Rathbone."

The dark eyes under the massive brows were very searching. She felt uneasiness rising.

"I'm afraid we do not pay you very much."

"That doesn't matter," said Victoria. "I like the work."

"Do you really?"

"Oh, yes," said Victoria. "One feels," she added, "that this sort of thing is really worthwhile."

Her limpid gaze met the dark searching eyes and did not falter.

"And you manage—to live?"

"Oh yes—I've found quite a good cheap place—with some Armenians. I'm quite all right."

"There is a shortage at present of shorthand typists in Baghdad," said Dr. Rathbone. "I think, you know, that I could get you a better position than the one you have here."

"But I don't want any other position."

"You might be wise to take one."

"Wise?" Victoria faltered a little.

"That is what I said. Just a word of warning—of advice."

There was something faintly menacing now in his tone.

Victoria opened her eyes still wider.

"I really don't understand, Dr. Rathbone," she said.

"Sometimes it is wiser not to mix oneself up in things one does not understand."

She felt quite sure of the menace this time, but she continued to stare in kitten-eyed innocence.

"Why did you come and work here, Victoria? Because of Edward?"

Victoria flushed angrily.

"Of course not," she said indignantly. She was much annoyed.

Dr. Rathbone nodded his head.

"Edward has his way to make. It will be many many years before he is in a position to be of any use to you. I should give up thinking of Edward if I were you. And, as I say, there are good positions to be obtained at present, with a good salary and prospects—and which will bring you among your own kind."

He was still watching her, Victoria thought, very closely. Was this a test? She said with an affectation of eagerness,

"But I really am very keen on the Olive Branch, Dr. Rathbone."

He shrugged his shoulders then and she left him, but she could feel his eyes in the center of her spine as she left the room.

She was somewhat disturbed by the interview. Had something occurred to arouse his suspicions? Did he guess that she might be a spy placed in the Olive Branch to find out its secrets? His voice and manner had made her feel unpleasantly afraid. His suggestion that she had come there to be near Edward had made her angry at the time and she had vigorously denied it, but she realized now that it was infinitely safer that Dr. Rathbone should suppose her to have come to the Olive Branch for Edward's sake, than to have even an inkling that Mr. Dakin had been instrumental in the matter. Anyway, owing to her idiotic blush, Rathbone probably did think that it was Edward—so that all had really turned out for the best.

Nevertheless, she went to sleep that night with an unpleasant little clutch of fear at her heart.

17

IT PROVED FAIRLY simple on the following morning for Victoria to go out by herself with few explanations. She had inquired about the Beit Melek Ali and had learned it was a big house built right out on the river some way down the west bank.

So far, Victoria had had very little time to explore her surroundings and she was agreeably surprised when she came to the end of the narrow street and found herself actually on the riverbank. She turned to her right and made her way slowly along the edge of the high bank. Sometimes the going was precarious—the bank had been eaten away and had not always been repaired or built up again. One house had steps in front of it which, if you took one more, would land you in the river on a dark night. Victoria looked down at the water below and edged her way around. Then, for a while, the way was wide and paved. The houses on her right hand had an agreeable air of secrecy. They offered no hint as to their occupancy. Occasionally the central door stood open, and peering inside Victoria was fascinated by the contrasts. On one such occasion she looked into a courtyard with a fountain playing and cushioned seats and deck chairs around it, with tall palms growing up and a garden beyond, that looked like the backcloth of a stage set. The next house, looking much the same outside, opened on a litter of confusion and dark passages, with five or six dirty children playing in rags. Then she came to palm gardens in thick groves. On her left she had passed uneven steps leading down to the river and an Arab boatman seated in a primitive rowing boat gesticulated and called, asking evidently if she wanted to be taken across to the other side. She must by now, Victoria judged, be just about opposite the Tio Hotel, though it was hard to distinguish difference in the architecture viewed from this side, and the hotel buildings looked more or less alike. She came now to a road leading down through the palms and then to two tall houses with balconies. Beyond was a big house built right out onto the river with a garden and balustrade. The path on the bank passed on the inside of what must be the Beit Melek Ali or the House of King Ali.

In a few minutes more Victoria had passed its entrance and had come to a more squalid part; the river was hidden from her by palm plantations fenced off with rusty barbed wire. On the right were tumbledown houses inside rough mudbrick walls, and small shanties with children playing in the dirt and clouds of flies hanging over garbage heaps. A road led away from the river and a car was standing there—a somewhat battered and archaic car. By the car, Edward was standing.

"Good," said Edward, "you've got here. Get in."

"Where are we going?" asked Victoria, entering the battered automobile with delight. The driver, who appeared to be an animate bundle of rags, turned round and grinned happily at her.

"We're going to Babylon," said Edward. "It's about time we had a day out."

The car started with a terrific jerk and bumped madly over the rude paving stones.

"To Babylon?" cried Victoria. "How lovely it sounds. Really to Babylon?"

The car swerved to the left and they were bowling upon a well paved road of imposing width.

"Yes, but don't expect too much. Babylon—if you know what I mean—isn't quite what it was."

Victoria hummed:

"How many miles to Babylon?
Three score and ten:

Can I get there by candlelight?
Yes, and back again.

I used to sing that when I was a small child. It always fascinated me. And
now we're really going there!"

"And we'll get back by candlelight. Or we should. Actually you never
know in this country."

"This car looks very much as though it might break down."

"It probably will. There's sure to be simply everything wrong with it. But
these Iraqis are frightfully good at tying it up with string and saying Inshallah, and then it goes again."

"It's always Inshallah, isn't it?"

"Yes, nothing like laying the responsibility upon the Almighty."

"The road isn't very good, is it?" gasped Victoria, bouncing in her seat.
The deceptively well-paved and wide road had not lived up to its promise.
The road was still wide but was now corrugated with ruts.

"It gets worse later on," shouted Edward.

They bounced and bumped happily. The dust rose in clouds around them.
Large lorries covered with Arabs tore along in the middle of the track and
were deaf to all intimations of the horn.

They passed walled-in gardens, and parties of women and children and
donkeys, and to Victoria it was all new and part of the enchantment of going
to Babylon with Edward beside her.

They reached Babylon bruised and shaken in a couple of hours. The meaningless pile of ruined mud and burned brick was somewhat of a disappointment to Victoria who expected something in the way of columns and arches,
looking like pictures she had seen on Baalbek.

But little by little her disappointment ebbed as they scrambled over
mounds and lumps of burned brick, led by the guide. She listened with only
half an ear to his profuse explanations, but as they went along the Proces-
sional Way to the Ishtar Gate, with the faint reliefs of unbelievable animals
high on the walls, a sudden sense of the grandeur of the past came to her and
a wish to know something about this vast proud city that now lay dead and
abandoned. Presently, their duty to antiquity accomplished, they sat down by
the Babylonian Lion to eat the picnic lunch that Edward had brought with
him. The guide moved away, smiling indulgently and telling them firmly that
they must see the Museum later.

"Must we?" said Victoria dreamily. "Things all labeled and put into cases
don't seem a bit real somehow. I went to the British Museum once. It was
awful, and dreadfully tiring on the feet."

"The past is always boring," said Edward. "The future's much more important."

"This isn't boring," said Victoria waving a sandwich toward the panorama
of tumbled brick. "There's a feeling of—of greatness here. What's the poem

When you were a King in Babylon
And I was a Christian Slave?

Perhaps we were. You and I, I mean."

"I don't think there were any Kings in Babylon by the time there were Christians," said Edward. "I think Babylon stopped functioning somewhere about five or six hundred B.C. Some archeologist or other is always turning up to give lectures about these things—but I really never grasp any of the dates—I mean not until proper Greek and Roman ones."

"Would you have liked being a King in Babylon, Edward?"

Edward drew a deep breath.

"Yes, I should."

"Then we'll say you were. You're in a new incarnation now."

"They understood how to be Kings in those days!" said Edward. "That's why they could rule the world and bring it into shape."

"I don't know that I should have liked being a slave much," said Victoria meditatively, "Christian or otherwise."

"Milton was quite right," said Edward. "Better to reign in Hell than serve in Heaven. I always admired Milton's Satan."

"I never quite got around to Milton," said Victoria apologetically. "But I did go and see Comus at Sadler's Wells and it was lovely, and Margot Fonteyn danced like a kind of frozen angel."

"If you were a slave, Victoria," said Edward, "I should free you and take you into my harem—over there," he added gesticulating vaguely at a pile of debris.

A glint came into Victoria's eye.

"Talking of harems—" she began.

"How are you getting on with Catherine?" asked Edward hastily.

"How did you know I was thinking about Catherine?"

"Well, you were, weren't you? Honestly, Viccy, I do want you to become friends with Catherine."

"Don't call me Viccy."

"All right, Charing Cross. I want you to become friends with Catherine."

"How fatuous men are! Always wanting their girlfriends to like each other."

Edward sat up energetically. He had been reclining with his hands behind his head.

"You've got it all wrong, Charing Cross. Anyway, your references to harems are simply silly—"

"No, they're not. The way all those girls glower intensely at you and yearn at you! It makes me mad."

"Splendid," said Edward. "I love you to be mad. But to return to Catherine. The reason I want you to be friends with Catherine is that I'm fairly sure she's the best way of approach to all the things we want to find out. She knows something."

"You really think so?"

"Remember what I heard her say about Anna Scheele."

"I'd forgotten that."

"How have you been getting on with Karl Marx? Any results?"

"Nobody's made a beeline at me and invited me into the fold. In fact, Catherine told me yesterday the Party wouldn't accept me, because I'm not sufficiently politically educated. And to have to read all that dreary stuff—honestly, Edward, I haven't the brains for it."

"You're not politically aware, are you?" Edward laughed. "Poor Charing Cross. Well, well, Catherine may be frantic with brains and intensity and political awareness, my fancy is still a little cockney typist who can't spell any words of three syllables."

Victoria frowned suddenly. Edward's words brought back to her mind the curious interview she had had with Dr. Rathbone. She told Edward about it. He seemed much more upset than she would have expected him to be.

"This is serious, Victoria, really serious. Try and tell me exactly what he said."

Victoria tried her best to recall the exact words Rathbone had used.

"But I don't see," she said, "why it upsets you so."

"Eh?" Edward seemed abstracted. "You don't see— But my dear girl, don't you realize that this shows that they've got wise to you. They're warning you off. I don't like it, Victoria—I don't like it at all."

He paused and then said gravely,

"Communists, you know, are very ruthless. It's part of their creed to stick at nothing. I don't want you knocked on the head and thrown into the Tigris, darling."

How odd, thought Victoria, to be sitting amid the ruins of Babylon debating whether or not she was likely in the near future to be knocked on the head and thrown into the Tigris. Half closing her eyes, she thought dreamily, "I shall wake up soon and find I'm in London dreaming a wonderful melodramatic dream about dangerous Babylon. Perhaps," she thought, closing her eyes altogether, "I am in London . . . and the alarm clock will go off very soon, and I shall get up and go to Mr. Greenholtz's office—and there won't be any Edward—"

And at that last thought she opened her eyes again hastily to make sure that Edward was indeed really there (and what was it I was going to ask him at Basrah and they interrupted us and I forgot?) and it was not a dream. The sun was glaring down in a dazzling and most un-Londonlike way, and the ruins of Babylon were pale and shimmering with a background of dark palms, and sitting up with his back a little toward her was Edward. How extraordinarily nicely his hair grew down with a little twirl into his neck—and what a nice neck—bronzed red brown from the sun—with no blemishes on it—so many men had necks with cysts or pimples where their collars had rubbed—a neck like Sir Rupert's, for instance, with a boil just starting—

Suddenly with a stifled exclamation Victoria sat bolt upright and her daydreams were a thing of the past. She was wildly excited.

Edward turned an inquiring head.

"What's the matter, Charing Cross?"

"I've just remembered," said Victoria, "about Sir Rupert Crofton Lee—"

As Edward still turned a blank inquiring look upon her Victoria proceeded to elucidate her meaning which, truth to tell, she did not do very clearly.

"It was a boil," she said, "on his neck."

"A boil on his neck?" Edward was puzzled.

"Yes, in the airplane. He sat in front of me, you know, and that hood thing he wore fell back and I saw it—the boil."

"Why shouldn't he have a boil? Painful, but lots of people get them."

"Yes, yes, of course they do. But the point is that that morning on the balcony he hadn't."

"Hadn't what?"

"Hadn't got a boil. Oh Edward, do try and take it in. In the airplane he had a boil and on the balcony at the Tio he hadn't got a boil. His neck was quite smooth and unscarred—like yours now."

"Well, I suppose it had gone away."

"Oh no, Edward, it couldn't have. It was only a day later, and it was just coming up. It couldn't have gone away—not completely without a trace. So you see it means—yes, it must mean—the man at the Tio wasn't Sir Rupert at all."

She nodded her head with vehemence. Edward stared at her.

"You're crazy, Victoria. It must have been Sir Rupert. You didn't see any other difference in him."

"But don't you see, Edward, I'd never really looked at him properly—only at his—well, you might call it general effect. The hat—and the cape—and the swashbuckling attitude. He'd be a very easy man to impersonate."

"But they'd have known at the Embassy—"

"He didn't stay at the Embassy, did he? He came to the Tio. It was one of the minor secretaries of people who met him. The Ambassador's in England. Besides, he's traveled and been away from England so much."

"But why—"

"Because of Carmichael, of course. Carmichael was coming to Baghdad to meet him—to tell him what he'd found out. Only they'd never met before. So Carmichael wouldn't know he wasn't the right man—and he wouldn't be on his guard. Of course—it was Rupert Crofton Lee (the false one) who stabbed Carmichael! Oh, Edward, it all fits in."

"I don't believe a word of it. It's crazy. Don't forget Sir Rupert was killed afterwards in Cairo."

"That's where it all happened. I know now. Oh Edward, how awful. I saw it happen."

"You saw it happen—Victoria, are you quite mad?"

"No, I'm not in the least mad. Just listen, Edward. There was a knock on my door—in the hotel in Heliopolis—at least I thought it was on my door and I looked out, but it wasn't—it was one door down, Sir Rupert Crofton Lee's. It was one of the stewardesses or air hostesses or whatever they call them. She asked him if he would mind coming to B.O.A.C. office—just along the corridor. I came out of my room just afterwards. I passed a door which had a notice with B.O.A.C. on it, and the door opened and he came out. I thought then that he had had some news that made him walk quite differently. Do you see, Edward? It was a trap, the substitute was waiting, all ready, and as soon as he came in, they just conked him on the head and the other one came out and took up the part. I think they probably kept him somewhere in Cairo, perhaps in the hotel as an invalid, kept him drugged and then killed him just at the right moment when the wrong one had come back to Cairo."

"It's a magnificent story," said Edward. "But you know, Victoria, quite frankly you are making the whole thing up. There's no corroboration of it."

"There's the boil—"

"Oh, damn the boil!"

"And there are one or two other things."

"What?"

"That B.O.A.C. notice on the door. It wasn't there later. I remember being puzzled when I found the B.O.A.C. office was the other side of the entrance hall. That's one thing. And there's another. That air stewardess, the one who knocked at his door. I've seen her since—here in Baghdad—and what's more, at the Olive Branch. The first day I went there. She came in and spoke to Catherine. I thought then I'd seen her before."

After a moment's silence, Victoria said:

"So you must admit, Edward, that it isn't all my fancy."

Edward said slowly:

"It all comes back to the Olive Branch—and to Catherine. Victoria, all ragging apart, you've got to get closer to Catherine. Flatter her, butter her up, talk Bolshie ideas to her. Somehow or other get sufficiently intimate with her to know who her friends are and where she goes and who she's in touch with outside the Olive Branch."

"It won't be easy," said Victoria, "but I'll try. What about Mr. Dakin? Ought I to tell him about this?"

"Yes, of course. But wait a day or two. We may have more to go on." Edward sighed. "I shall take Catherine to Le Select to hear the Cabaret one night."

And this time Victoria felt no pang of jealousy. Edward had spoken with a grim determination that ruled out any anticipation of pleasure in the commission he had undertaken.

ii

Exhilarated by her discoveries, Victoria found it no effort to greet Catherine on the following day with an effusion of friendliness. It was so kind of Catherine, she said, to have told her of a place to have her hair washed. It needed washing terribly badly. (This was undeniable; Victoria had returned from Babylon with her dark hair the color of red rust from the clogging sand.)

"It is looking terrible, yes," said Catherine, eyeing it with a certain malicious satisfaction. "You went out then in that dust storm yesterday afternoon?"

"I hired a car and went to see Babylon," said Victoria. "It was very interesting, but on the way back, the duststorm got up and I was nearly choked and blinded."

"It is interesting, Babylon," said Catherine, "but you should go with someone who understands it and can tell you about it properly. As for your hair, I will take you to this Armenian girl tonight. She will give you a cream shampoo. It is the best."

"I don't know how you keep your hair looking so wonderful," said Victoria, looking with what appeared to be admiring eyes at Catherine's heavy erections of greasy sausagelike curls.

A smile appeared on Catherine's usually sour face, and Victoria thought how right Edward had been about flattery.

When they left the Olive Branch that evening, the two girls were on the friendliest of terms. Catherine wove in and out of narrow passages and alleys and finally tapped on an unpromising door which gave no sign of hairdressing operations being conducted on the other side of it. They were, however, received by a plain but competent-looking young woman who spoke careful slow English and who led Victoria to a spotlessly clean basin with shining taps and various bottles and lotions ranged round it. Catherine departed and Victoria surrendered her mop of hair into Miss Ankoumian's deft hands. Soon her hair was a mass of creamy lather.

"And now if you please—"

Victoria bent forward over the basin. Water streamed over her hair and gurgled down the waste pipe.

Suddenly her nose was assailed by a sweet rather sickly smell that she associated vaguely with hospitals. A wet saturated pad was clasped firmly over her nose and mouth. She struggled wildly, twisting and turning, but an iron grip kept the pad in place. She began to suffocate, her head reeled dizzily, a roaring sound came in her ears . . .

And after that, blackness, deep and profound.

18

WHEN VICTORIA REGAINED consciousness, it was with a sense of an immense passage of time. Confused memories stirred in her—jolting in a car—high jabbering and quarreling in Arabic—lights that flashed into her eyes—a horrible attack of nausea—then vaguely she remembered lying on a bed and someone lifting her arm—the sharp agonizing prick of a needle—then more confused dreams and darkness and behind it a mounting sense of urgency . . .

Now at last, dimly, she was herself—Victoria Jones . . . And something had happened to Victoria Jones—a long time ago—months—perhaps years . . . after all, perhaps only days.

Babylon—sunshine—dust—hair—Catherine—Catherine, of course, smiling, her eyes sly under the sausage curls—Catherine had taken her to have her hair shampooed and then—what had happened? That horrible smell—she could still smell it—nauseating—chloroform, of course. They had chloroformed her and taken her—where?

Cautiously Victoria tried to sit up. She seemed to be lying on a bed—a very hard bed—her head ached and felt dizzy—she was still drowsy, horribly drowsy . . . that prick, the prick of a hypodermic, they had been drugging her . . . she was still half drugged.

Well, anyway, they hadn't killed her (why not?). So that was all right. The best thing, thought the still half-drugged Victoria, is to go to sleep. And promptly did so.

When next she awakened she felt much more clearheaded. It was daylight now and she could see more clearly where she was.

She was in a small but very high room, distempered a depressing pale bluish gray. The floor was of beaten earth. The only furniture in the room seemed to be the bed on which she was lying, with a dirty rug thrown over her, and a rickety table with a cracked enamel basin on it and a zinc bucket underneath it. There was a window with a kind of wooden latticework outside it. Victoria got gingerly off the bed, feeling distinctly headachy and queer, and approached the window. She could see through the latticework quite plainly, and what she saw was a garden with palm trees beyond it. The garden was quite a pleasant one by Eastern standards, though it would have been looked down on by an English suburban householder. It had a lot of bright orange marigolds in it, and some dusty eucalyptus trees and some rather wispy tamarisks.

A small child with a face tattooed in blue and a lot of bangles on, was tumbling about with a ball and singing in a high nasal whine rather like distant bagpipes.

Victoria next turned her attention to the door which was large and massive. Without much hope she went to it and tried it. The door was locked. Victoria went back and sat on the side of the bed.

Where was she? Not in Baghdad, that was certain. And what was she going to do next?

It struck her after a minute or two that the last question did not really apply. What was more to the point was what was someone else going to do to her? With an uneasy feeling in the pit of her stomach she remembered Mr. Dakin's admonition to tell all she knew. But perhaps they had already got all that out of her while she was under the drug.

Still—Victoria returned to this one point with determined cheerfulness— she was alive. If she could manage to keep alive until Edward found her— what would Edward do when he found she had vanished? Would he go to Mr. Dakin? Would he play a lone hand? Would he put the fear of the Lord into Catherine and force her to tell— Would he suspect Catherine at all? The more Victoria tried to conjure up a reassuring picture of Edward in action, the more the image of Edward faded and became a kind of faceless abstraction. How clever was Edward? That was really what it amounted to. Edward was adorable. Edward had glamour. But had Edward got brains? Because clearly, in her present predicament, brains were going to be needed.

Mr. Dakin, now, would have the necessary brains. But would he have the impetus? Or would he merely cross off her name from a mental ledger, scoring it through, and writing after it a neat R.I.P. After all, to Mr. Dakin she was merely one of a crowd. They took their chance, and if luck failed, it was just too bad. No, she didn't see Mr. Dakin staging a rescue. After all, he had warned her.

And Dr. Rathbone had warned her. (Warned her or threatened her?) And on her refusing to be threatened, there had not been much delay in carrying out the threat . . .

But I'm still alive, repeated Victoria, determined to look upon the bright side of things.

Footsteps approached outside and there was the grinding of a key in a rusty lock. The door staggered on its hinges and flew open. In the aperture appeared an Arab. He carried an old tin tray on which were dishes.

He appeared to be in good spirits, grinned broadly, uttered some incomprehensible remarks in Arabic, deposited the tray, opened his mouth and pointed down his throat and departed, re-locking the door behind him.

Victoria approached the tray with interest. There was a large bowl of rice, something that looked like rolled up cabbage leaves and a large flap of Arab bread. Also a jug of water and a glass.

Victoria started by drinking a large glass of water and then fell to on the rice, the bread, and the cabbage leaves which were full of rather peculiar-tasting chopped meat. When she had finished everything on the tray she felt a good deal better.

She tried her best to think things out clearly. She had been chloroformed and kidnapped. How long ago? As to that, she had only the foggiest idea.

From drowsy memories of sleeping and waking she judged that it was some days ago. She had been taken out of Baghdad—where? There again, she had no means of knowing. Owing to her ignorance of Arabic, it was not even possible to ask questions. She could not find out a place, or a name, or a date.

Several hours of acute boredom followed.

That evening her jailer reappeared with another tray of food. With him this time came a couple of women. They were in rusty black with their faces hidden. They did not come into the room but stood just outside the door. One had a baby in her arms. They stood there and giggled. Through the thinness of the veil their eyes, she felt, were appraising her. It was exciting to them and highly humorous to have a European woman imprisoned here.

Victoria spoke to them in English and in French, but got only giggles in reply. It was queer, she thought, to be unable to communicate with her own sex. She said slowly and with difficulty one of the few phrases she had picked up.

"El hamdu lillah."

Its utterance was rewarded by a delighted spate of Arabic. They nodded their heads vigorously. Victoria moved toward them, but quickly the Arab servant or whatever he was, stepped back and barred her way. He motioned the two women back and went out himself, closing and locking the door again. Before he did so, he uttered one word several times over.

"Bukra—Bukra . . ."

It was a word Victoria had heard before. It meant tomorrow.

Victoria sat down on her bed to think things over. Tomorrow? Tomorrow, someone was coming or something was going to happen. Tomorrow her imprisonment would end (or wouldn't it?)—or if it did end, she herself might end too! Taking all things together, Victoria didn't much care for the idea of tomorrow. She felt instinctively that it would be much better if by tomorrow she was somewhere else.

But was that possible? For the first time, she gave this problem full attention. She went first to the door and examined it. Certainly nothing doing there. This wasn't the kind of lock you picked with a hairpin—if indeed she would have been capable of picking any lock with a hairpin, which she very much doubted.

There remained the window. The window, she soon found, was a much more hopeful proposition. The wooden latticework that screened it was in the final stages of decrepitude. Granted she could break away sufficient of the rotten woodwork to force herself through, she could hardly do so without a good deal of noise which could not fail to attract attention. Moreover since the room in which she was confined was on an upper floor, it meant either fashioning a rope of some kind or else jumping with every likelihood of a sprained ankle or other injury. In books, thought Victoria, you make a rope of strips of bedclothes. She looked doubtfully at the thick cotton quilt and ragged blanket. Neither of them seemed at all suited to her purpose. She had nothing with which to cut the quilt in strips, and though she could probably tear the blanket, its condition of rottenness would preclude any possibility of trusting her weight to it.

"Damn," said Victoria aloud.

She was more and more enamored of the idea of escape. As far as she could judge, her jailers were people of very simple mentality to whom the mere fact that she was locked in a room spelled finality. They would not be expecting her to escape for the simple reason that she was a prisoner and could not. Whoever had used the hypodermic on her and presumably brought her here was not now on the premises—of that she was sure. He or she or they were expected "bukra." They had left her in some remote spot in the guardianship of simple folk who would obey instructions but who would not appreciate subtleties, and who were not, presumably, alive to the inventive faculties of a European young woman in imminent fear of extinction.

"I'm getting out of here somehow," said Victoria to herself.

She approached the table and helped herself to the new supply of food. She might as well keep her strength up. There was rice again and some oranges, and some bits of meat in a bright orange sauce.

Victoria ate everything and then had a drink of water. As she replaced the jug on the table, the table tilted slightly and some of the water went on the floor. The floor in that particular spot at once became a small puddle of liquid mud. Looking at it, an idea stirred in Miss Victoria Jones' always fertile brain.

The question was, had the key been left in the lock on the outside of the door?

The sun was setting now. Very soon it would be dark. Victoria went over to the door, knelt down and peered into the immense keyhole. She could see no light. Now what she needed was something to prod with—a pencil or the end of a fountain pen. How tiresome that her handbag had been taken away. She looked around the room frowning. The only article of cutlery on the table was a large spoon. That was no good for her immediate need, though it might come in handy later. Victoria sat down to puzzle and contrive. Presently she uttered an exclamation, took off her shoe and managed to pull out the inner leather sole. She rolled this up tightly. It was reasonably stiff. She went back to the door, squatted down and poked vigorously through the keyhole. Fortunately the immense key fitted loosely into the lock. After three or four minutes it responded to the efforts and fell out of the door on the outside. It made little noise falling on the earthen floor.

Now, Victoria thought, I must hurry, before the light goes altogether. She fetched the jug of water and poured a little carefully on a spot at the bottom of the door frame as near as possible to where she judged the key had fallen. Then, with the spoon and her fingers she scooped and scrabbled in the muddy patch that resulted. Little by little, with fresh applications of water from the jug, she scooped out a low trough under the door. Lying down she tried to peer through it but it wasn't easy to see anything. Rolling up her sleeves, she found she could get her hand and part of her arm under the door. She felt about with exploratory fingers and finally the tip of one finger touched something metallic. She had located the key, but she was unable to get her arm far enough to claw it nearer. Her next procedure was to secure the safety pin which was holding up a torn shoulder strap. Bending it into a hook, she embedded it in a wodge of Arab bread and lay down again to fish. Just as she was ready to cry with vexation the hooked safety pin caught in the key and she was able to draw it within reach of her fingers and then to pull it through the muddy trough to her side of the door.

Victoria sat back on her heels full of admiration for her own ingenuity. Grasping the key in her muddy hand, she got up and fitted it into the lock. She waited for a moment when there was a good chorus of pi-dogs barking in the near neighborhood and turned it. The door yielded to her push and swung open a little way. Victoria peered cautiously through the aperture. The door gave onto another small room with an open door at the end of it. Victoria waited a moment, then tiptoed out and across. This outside room had large gaping holes in the roof and one or two in the floor. The door at the end gave on the top of a flight of rough mudbrick stairs affixed to the side of the house, and which led down to the garden.

That was all Victoria wanted to see. She tiptoed back to her own place of imprisonment. There was little likelihood that anyone would come near her again tonight. She would wait until it was dark and the village or town more or less settled down to sleep and then she would go.

One other thing she had noted. A torn shapeless bit of black material lay in a heap near the outside door. It was, she thought, an old *Aba* and would come in useful to cover her Western clothes.

How long she waited Victoria did not know. It seemed to her interminable hours. Yet at last the various noises of local humankind died down. The far-off blasting of a gramophone or phonograph stopped its Arab songs, the raucous voices and the spitting ceased, and there was no more far-off women's high-pitched squealing laughter; no children's crying.

At last she heard only a far-off howling noise which she took to be jackals, and the intermittent bursts of dog barking, which she knew would continue all through the night.

"Well, here goes!" said Victoria and stood up.

After a moment's cogitation she locked the door of her prison on the outside and left the key in the lock. Then she felt her way across the outer room, picked up the black heap of material and came out at the top of the mud stairs. There was a moon, but it was still low in the sky. It gave sufficient light for Victoria to see her way. She crept down the stairs, then paused about four stairs from the bottom. She was level here with the mudwall that enclosed the garden. If she continued down the stairs she would have to pass along the side of the house. She could hear snoring from the downstairs rooms. If she went along the top of the wall it might be better. The wall was sufficiently thick to walk along.

She chose the latter course and went swiftly and somewhat precariously to where the wall turned at right angles. Here, outside, was what seemed to be a palm garden, and at one point the wall was crumbling away. Victoria found her way there, partly jumped and partly slithered down and a few moments later was threading her way through palm trees toward a gap in the far wall. She came out upon a narrow street of a primitive nature, too small for the passage of a car, but suitable for donkeys. It ran between mudbrick walls. Victoria sped along it as fast as she could.

Now dogs began to bark furiously. Two fawn-colored pi-dogs came snarlingly out of a doorway at her. Victoria picked up a handful of rubble and brick and shied a piece at them. They yelped and ran away. Victoria sped on. She rounded a corner and came into what was evidently the main street. Narrow and heavily rutted, it ran through a village of mudbrick houses, uniformly pale in the moonlight. Palms peeped over walls, dogs snarled and barked. Victoria took a deep breath and ran. Dogs continued to bark, but no human being took any interest in this possible night marauder. Soon she came out on a wide space with a muddy stream and a decrepit humpbacked bridge over it. Beyond the road or track lay heading toward what seemed infinite space. Victoria continued to run until she was out of breath.

The village was well behind her now. The moon was high in the sky. To the left and the right and in front of her was bare stony ground, uncultivated and without a sign of human habitation. It looked flat but was really faintly contoured. It had, as far as Victoria could see, no landmarks, and she had no idea in what direction the track led. She was not learned enough in the stars to know even toward what point of the compass she was heading. There was something subtly terrifying in this large empty waste, but it was impossible to turn back. She could only go on.

Pausing a few moments to get her breath back, and assuring herself by looking back over her shoulder, that her flight had not been discovered, she set forth, walking a steady three and a half miles an hour toward the unknown.

Dawn came at last to find Victoria weary, footsore and almost on the verge of hysteria. By noting the light in the sky she ascertained that she was heading roughly southwest, but since she did not know where she was, that knowledge was of little use to her.

A little to the side of the road ahead of her was a kind of small compact hill or knob. Victoria left the track and made her way to the knob, the sides of which were quite steep, and climbed up to the top of it.

Here she was able to take a survey of the country all around and her feeling of meaningless panic returned. For everywhere there was nothing . . . The scene was beautiful in the early morning light. The ground and horizon shimmered with faint pastel shades of apricot and cream and pink on which were patterns of shadows. It was beautiful but frightening. "I know what it means now," thought Victoria, "when anyone says they are alone in the world . . ."

There was a little faint scrubby grass in dark patches here and there and some dry thorn. But otherwise there was no cultivation, and no signs of life. There was only Victoria Jones.

Of the village from which she had fled there were no signs either. The road along which she had come stretched back apparently into an infinity of waste. It seemed incredible to Victoria that she could have walked so far as to have lost the village altogether from view. For a moment she had a panic-stricken yearning to go back. Somehow or other to regain touch with humankind . . .

Then she took herself in hand. She had meant to escape, and had escaped, but her troubles were not likely to be at an end simply because she had placed several miles between her and her jailers. A car, however old and rickety, would make short work of those miles. As soon as her escape was discovered, someone would come in search of her. And how on earth was she going to take cover or hide? There simply wasn't anywhere to hide. She still carried the ragged black *Aba* she had snatched up. Now tentatively she wrapped herself in its folds, pulling it down over her face. She had no idea what she looked like because she had no mirror with her. If she took off her European shoes and stockings and shuffled along with bare feet, she might possibly evade detection. A virtuously veiled Arab woman, however ragged and poor, had, she knew, all possible immunity. It would be the height of bad manners for any man to address her. But would that disguise fool Western eyes who might be out in a car looking for her? At any rate, it was the only chance.

She was much too tired to go on at present. She was terribly thirsty, too, but it was impossible to do anything about that. The best thing, she decided, was to lie down on the side of this hillock. She could hear a car coming and if she kept herself flattened into a little ravine which had eroded down the side of the hillock, she could get some idea of who was in the car.

She could take cover by moving round the back of the hillock so as to keep out of sight of the road.

On the other hand, what she badly needed was to get back to civilization, and the only means, as far as she could see, was to stop a car with Europeans in it and ask for a lift.

But she must be sure that the Europeans were the right Europeans. And how on earth was she to make sure of that?

Worrying over this point, Victoria quite unexpectedly fell asleep, worn out by her long trudge and her general exhaustion.

When she awoke the sun was directly overhead. She felt hot and stiff and dizzy, and her thirst was now a raging torment. Victoria gave a groan, but as the groan issued from her dry sore lips, she suddenly stiffened and listened. She heard faintly but distinctly the sound of a car. Very cautiously she raised her head. The car was not coming from the direction of the village but toward it. That meant that it was not in pursuit. It was as yet a small black dot far off on the track. Still lying as much concealed as she could, Victoria watched it come nearer. How she wished she had field glasses with her.

It disappeared for a few minutes in a depression of the landscape, then reappeared surmounting a rise not very far away. There was an Arab driver and beside him was a man in European dress.

"Now," thought Victoria, "I've got to decide." Was this her chance? Should she run down to the road and hail the car to stop?

Just as she was getting ready to do so, a sudden qualm stopped her. Suppose, just suppose, that this was the Enemy?

After all, how could she tell? The track was certainly a very deserted one. No other car had passed. No lorry. Not even a train of donkeys. This car was making, perhaps, for the village she had left last night . . .

What should she do? It was a horrible decision to have to make at a moment's notice. If it was the Enemy, it was the end. But if it wasn't the Enemy, it might be her only hope of survival. Because if she went on wandering about, she would probably die of thirst and exposure. What should she do?

And as she crouched paralyzed with indecision, the note of the approaching car changed. It slackened speed, then, swerving, it came off the road and across the stony ground toward the mound on which she squatted.

It had seen her! It was looking for her!

Victoria slithered down the gully and crawled round the back of the mound away from the approaching car. She heard it come to a stop and the bang of the door as someone got out.

Then somebody said something in Arabic. After that, nothing happened. Suddenly, without any warning, a man came into view. He was walking around the mound, about halfway up it. His eyes were bent on the ground and from time to time he stooped and picked something up. Whatever he was looking for, it did not seem to be a girl called Victoria Jones. Moreover, he was unmistakably an Englishman.

With an exclamation of relief Victoria struggled to her feet and came toward him. He lifted his head and stared in surprise.

"Oh please," said Victoria. "I'm so glad you've come."

He still stared.

"Who on earth," he began. "Are you English? But—"

With a spurt of laughter, Victoria cast away the enveloping *Aba*.

"Of course I'm English," she said. "And please, can you take me back to Baghdad?"

"I'm not going to Baghdad. I've just come from it. But what on earth are you doing all alone out here in the middle of the desert?"

"I was kidnapped," said Victoria breathlessly. "I went to have my hair shampooed and they gave me chloroform. And when I woke up I was in an Arab house in a village over there."

She gesticulated toward the horizon.

"In Mandali?"

"I don't know its name. I escaped last night. I walked all through the night and then I hid behind this hill in case you were an Enemy."

Her rescuer was staring at her with a very odd expression on his face. He was a man of about thirty-five, fair-haired, with a somewhat supercilious expression. His speech was academic and precise. He now put on a pair of pince-nez and stared at her through them with an expression of distaste. Victoria realized this man did not believe a word of what she was saying.

She was immediately moved to furious indignation.

"It's perfectly true," she said. "Every word of it!"

The stranger looked more disbelieving than ever.

"Very remarkable," he said in a cold tone.

Despair seized Victoria. How unfair it was that while she could always make a lie sound plausible, in recitals of stark truth she lacked the power to make herself believed. Actual facts she told badly and without conviction.

"And if you haven't got anything to drink with you, I shall die of thirst," she said. "I shall die of thirst anyway, if you leave me here and go on without me."

"Naturally I shouldn't dream of doing that," said the stranger stiffly. "It is most unsuitable for an Englishwoman to be wandering about alone in the wilds. Dear me, your lips are quite cracked . . . Abdul."

"Sahib?"

The driver appeared around the side of the mound.

On receiving instructions in Arabic he ran off toward the car, to return shortly with a large thermos flask and a Bakelite cup.

Victoria drank water avidly.

"Oo!" she said. "That's better."

"My name's Richard Baker," said the Englishman.

Victoria responded.

"I'm Victoria Jones," she said. And then, in an effort to recover lost ground and to replace the disbelief she saw by a respectful attention, she added:

"Pauncefoot Jones. I'm joining my uncle, Dr. Pauncefoot Jones, on his excavation."

"What an extraordinary coincidence," said Baker, staring at her surprisedly. "I'm on my way to the dig myself. It's only about fifteen miles from here. I'm just the right person to have rescued you, aren't I?"

To say that Victoria was taken aback is to put it mildly. She was completely flabbergasted. So much so, that she was quite incapable of saying a word of any kind. Meekly and in silence she followed Richard to the car and got in.

"I suppose you're the anthropologist," said Richard, as he settled her in the back seat and removed various impedimenta. "I heard you were coming out, but I didn't expect you so early in the season."

He stood for a moment sorting through various potsherds which he removed from his pockets and which, Victoria now realized, were what he had been picking up from the surface of the mound.

"Likely looking little *tell,*" he said, gesturing toward the mound. "But nothing out of the way on it, so far as I can see. Late Assyrian ware mostly—

a little Parthian, some quite good ring bases of the Kassite period." He smiled as he added, "I'm glad to see that in spite of your troubles your archaeological instincts led you to examine a *tell.*"

Victoria opened her mouth and then shut it again. The driver let in the clutch and they started off.

What, after all, could he say? True, she would be unmasked as soon as they reached the Expedition House—but it would be infinitely better to be unmasked there and confess penitence for her inventions, than it would be to confess all to Mr. Richard Baker in the middle of nowhere. The worst they could do to her would be to send her into Baghdad. And anyway, thought Victoria, incorrigible as ever, perhaps before I get there I shall have thought of something. Her busy imagination got to work forthwith. A lapse of memory? She had traveled out with a girl who had asked her to—no really, as far as she could see, she would have to make a complete breast of it. But she infinitely preferred making a clean breast of it to Dr. Pauncefoot Jones, whatever kind of man he was, than to Mr. Richard Baker, with his supercilious way of lifting his eyebrows and his obvious disbelief of the exact and true story she had told him.

"We don't go right into Mandali," said Mr. Baker, turning in the front seat. "We branch off from the road into the desert about a mile further on. A bit difficult to hit the exact spot sometimes with no particular landmarks."

Presently he said something to Abdul and the car turned sharply off the track and made straight for the desert. With no particular landmarks to guide him, as far as Victoria could see, Richard Baker directed Abdul with gestures —he bent now to the right—now to the left. Presently Richard gave an exclamation of satisfaction.

"On the right track now," he said.

Victoria could not see any track at all. But presently she did catch sight every now and again of faintly marked tire marks.

Once they crossed a slightly more clearly marked track and when they did so, Richard made an exclamation and ordered Abdul to stop.

"Here's an interesting sight for you," he said to Victoria. "Since you're new to this country you won't have seen it before."

Two men were advancing toward the car along the cross track. One man carried a short wooden bench on his back, the other a big wooden object about the size of an upright piano.

Richard hailed them; they greeted him with every sign of pleasure. Richard produced cigarettes and a thoroughly party spirit seemed to be developing.

Then Richard turned to her.

"Fond of the cinema? Then you shall see a performance."

He spoke to the two men and they smiled with pleasure. They set up the bench and motioned to Victoria and Richard to sit on it. Then they set up the round contrivance on a stand of some kind. It had two eyeholes in it and as she looked at it, Victoria cried,

"It's like things on piers. *What the butler saw.*"

"That's it," said Richard. "It's a primitive form of same."

Victoria applied her eyes to the glass-fronted peephole, one man began slowly to turn a crank or handle, and the other began a monotonous kind of chant.

"What is he saying?" Victoria asked.

Richard translated as the singsong chant continued,

"Draw near and prepare yourself for much wonder and delight. Prepare to behold the wonders of antiquity."

A crudely colored picture of negroes reaping wheat swam into Victoria's gaze.

"Fellahin in America," announced Richard, translating.

Then came:

"The wife of the great Shah of the Western world," and the Empress Eugenie simpered and fingered a long ringlet. A picture of the King's Palace in Montenegro, another of the Great Exhibition.

An odd and varied collection of pictures followed each other, all completely unrelated and sometimes announced in the strangest terms.

The Prince Consort, Disraeli, Norwegian Fjords and Skaters in Switzerland completed this strange glimpse of olden far-off days.

The showman ended his exposition with the following words,

"And so we bring to you the wonders and marvels of antiquity in other lands and far-off places. Let your donation be generous to match the marvels you have seen, for all these things are true."

It was over. Victoria beamed with delight.

"That really was marvelous!" she said. "I wouldn't have believed it."

The proprietors of the traveling cinema were smiling proudly. Victoria got up from the bench and Richard who was sitting on the other end of it was thrown to the ground in a somewhat undignified posture. Victoria apologized but was not ill-pleased. Richard rewarded the cinema men and with courteous farewells and expressions of concern for each other's welfare, and invoking the blessing of God on each other, they parted company. Richard and Victoria got into the car again and the men trudged away into the desert.

"Where are they going?" asked Victoria.

"They travel all over the country. I met them first in Transjordan coming up the road from the Dead Sea to Amman. Actually they're bound now for Kerbela, going of course by unfrequented routes so as to give shows in remote villages."

"Perhaps someone will give them a lift?"

Richard laughed.

"They probably wouldn't take it. I offered an old man a lift once who was walking from Basrah to Baghdad. I asked him how long he expected to be and he said a couple of months. I told him to get in and he would be there late that evening, but he thanked me and said no. Two months ahead would suit him just as well. Time doesn't mean anything out here. Once one gets that into one's head, one finds a curious satisfaction in it."

"Yes, I can imagine that."

"Arabs find our Western impatience for doing things quickly extraordinarily hard to understand, and our habit of coming straight to the point in conversation strikes them as extremely ill-mannered. You should always sit around and offer general observations for about an hour—or if you prefer, you need not speak at all."

"Rather odd if we did that in offices in London. One would waste a lot of time."

"Yes, but we're back again at the question: What is time? And what is waste?"

Victoria meditated on these points. The car still appeared to be proceeding to nowhere with the utmost confidence.

"Where is this place?" she said at last.

"Tell Aswad? Well out in the middle of the desert. You'll see the Ziggurat very shortly now. In the meantime, look over to your left. There—where I'm pointing."

"Are they clouds?" asked Victoria. "They can't be mountains."

"Yes, they are. The snow-capped mountains of Kurdistan. You can only see them when it's very clear."

A dreamlike feeling of contentment came over Victoria. If only she could drive on like this forever. If only she wasn't such a miserable liar. She shrank like a child at the thought of the unpleasant denouement ahead of her. What would Dr. Pauncefoot Jones be like? Tall, with a long gray beard, and a fierce frown. Never mind, however annoyed Dr. Pauncefoot Jones might be, she had circumvented Catherine and the Olive Branch and Dr. Rathbone.

"There you are," said Richard.

He pointed ahead. Victoria made out a kind of pimple on the far horizon.

"It looks miles away."

"Oh no, it's only a few miles now. You'll see."

And, indeed, the pimple developed with astonishing rapidity into first a blob and then a hill and finally into a large and impressive *tell*. On one side of it was a long sprawling building of mudbrick.

"The Expedition House," said Richard.

They drew up with a flourish amid the barking of dogs. White-robed servants rushed out to greet them, beaming with smiles.

After an interchange of greetings, Richard said:

"Apparently they weren't expecting you so soon. But they'll get your bed made. And they'll take you in hot water at once. I expect you'd like to have a wash and a rest? Dr. Pauncefoot Jones is up on the *tell*. I'm going up to him. Ibrahim will look after you."

He strode away and Victoria followed the smiling Ibrahim into the house. It seemed dark inside at first after coming in out of the sun. They passed through a living room with some big tables and a few battered armchairs and she was then led round a courtyard and into a small room with one tiny window. It held a bed, a rough chest of drawers, a chair and a table with a jug and basin on it. Ibrahim smiled and nodded and brought her a large jug of rather muddy-looking hot water and a rough towel. Then, with an apologetic smile, he returned with a small mirror which he carefully affixed upon a nail on the wall.

Victoria was thankful to have the chance of a wash. She was just beginning to realize how utterly weary and worn out she was and how very much encrusted with grime.

"I suppose I look simply frightful," she said to herself and approached the mirror.

For some moments she stared at her reflection uncomprehendingly.

This wasn't her—this wasn't Victoria Jones.

And then she realized that, though the features were the small neat features of Victoria Jones, her hair was now platinum blond!

19

RICHARD FOUND DR. Pauncefoot Jones in the excavations, squatting by the side of his foreman and tapping gently with a small pick at a section of wall.

Dr. Pauncefoot Jones greeted his colleague in a matter-of-fact manner.

"Hullo, Richard my boy, so you've turned up. I had an idea you were arriving on Tuesday, I don't know why."

"This is Tuesday," said Richard.

"Is it really now?" said Dr. Pauncefoot Jones without interest. "Just come down here and see what you think of this. Perfectly good walls coming out already and we're only down three feet. Seems to me there are a few traces of paint here. Come and see what you think. It looks very promising to me."

Richard leaped down into the trench and the two archaeologists enjoyed themselves in a highly technical manner for about a quarter of an hour.

"By the way," said Richard. "I've brought a girl."

"Oh, have you? What sort of girl?"

"She says she's your niece."

"My niece?" Dr. Pauncefoot Jones brought his mind back with a struggle from his contemplation of mudbrick walls. "I don't think I have a niece," he said doubtfully, as though he might have had one and forgotten about her.

"She's coming to work with you here, I gathered."

"Oh." Dr. Pauncefoot Jones' face cleared. "Of course. That will be Veronica."

"Victoria, I think she said."

"Yes, yes, Victoria. Emerson wrote to me about her from Cambridge. A very able girl, I understand. An anthropologist. Can't think why anyone wants to be an anthropologist, can you?"

"I heard you had some anthropologist girl coming out."

"There's nothing in her line so far. Of course we're only just beginning. Actually I understood she wasn't coming out for another fortnight or so, but I didn't read her letter very carefully, and then I mislaid it, so I didn't really remember what she said. My wife arrives next week—or the week after—now what have I done with her letter?—and I rather thought Venetia was coming out with her—but of course I may have got it all wrong. Well, well, I daresay we can make her useful. There's a lot of pottery coming up."

"There's nothing odd about her, is there?"

"Odd?" Dr. Pauncefoot Jones peered at him. "In what way?"

"Well, she hasn't had a nervous breakdown or anything?"

"Emerson did say, I remember, that she had been working very hard. Diploma or degree or something, but I don't think he said anything about a breakdown. Why?"

"Well, I picked her up at the side of the road, wandering about all by herself. It was on that little *tell,* as a matter of fact, that you come to about a mile before you turn off the road—"

"I remember," said Dr. Pauncefoot Jones. "You know, I once picked up a bit of Nuzu ware on that *tell.* Extraordinary really, to find it so far south."

Richard refused to be diverted to archaeological topics and went on firmly.

"She told me the most extraordinary story. Said she'd gone to have her hair shampooed, and they chloroformed her and kidnapped her and carried her off to Mandali and imprisoned her in a house, and she'd escaped in the middle of the night—the most preposterous rigmarole you ever heard."

Dr. Pauncefoot Jones shook his head.

"Doesn't sound at all probable," he said. "Country's perfectly quiet and well policed. It's never been safer."

"Exactly. She'd obviously made the whole thing up. That's why I asked if she'd had a breakdown. She must be one of those hysterical girls who say curates are in love with them, or that doctors assault them. She may give us a lot of trouble."

"Oh I expect she'll calm down," said Dr. Pauncefoot Jones optimistically. "Where is she now?"

"I left her to have a wash and brush up." He hesitated. "She hasn't got any luggage of any kind with her."

"Hasn't she? That really is awkward. You don't think she'll expect me to lend her pajamas? I've only got two pairs and one of them is badly torn."

"She'll have to do the best she can until the lorry goes in next week. I must say I wonder what she can have been up to—all alone and out in the blue."

"Girls are amazing nowadays," said Dr. Pauncefoot Jones vaguely. "Turn up all over the place. Great nuisance when you want to get on with things. This place is far enough out, you'd think, to be free of visitors, but you'd be surprised how cars and people turn up when you can least do with them. Dear me, the men have stopped work. It must be lunch time. We'd better go back to the house."

ii

Victoria, waiting in some trepidation, found Dr. Pauncefoot Jones wildly far from her imaginings. He was a small rotund man with a semibald head and a twinkling eye. To her utter amazement he came toward her with outstretched hands.

"Well, well, Venetia—I mean Victoria," he said. "This is quite a surprise. Got it into my head you weren't arriving until next month. But I'm delighted to see you. Delighted! How's Emerson? Not troubled too much by asthma, I hope?"

Victoria rallied her scattered senses and said cautiously that the asthma hadn't been too bad.

"Wraps his throat up too much," said Dr. Pauncefoot Jones. "Great mistake. I told him so. All these academic fellows who stick around universities get far too absorbed in their health. Shouldn't think about it—that's the way to keep fit. Well, I hope you'll settle down—my wife will be out next week— or the week after—she's been seedy, you know. I really must find her letter. Richard tells me your luggage has gone astray. How are you going to manage? Can't very well send the lorry in before next week?"

"I expect I can manage until then," said Victoria. "In fact, I shall have to."

Dr. Pauncefoot Jones chuckled.

"Richard and I can't lend you much. Toothbrush will be all right. There are a dozen of them in our stores—and cotton wool if that's any good to you and—let me see—talcum powder—and some spare socks and handkerchiefs. Not much else, I'm afraid."

"I shall be all right," said Victoria and smiled happily.

"No signs of a cemetery for you," Dr. Pauncefoot Jones warned her. "Some nice walls coming up—and quantities of potsherds from the far trenches. Might get some joins. We'll keep you busy somehow or other. I forget if you do photography?"

"I know something about it," said Victoria cautiously, relieved by a mention of something that she did actually have a working knowledge of.

"Good, good. You can develop negatives? I'm old-fashioned—use plates still. The darkroom is rather primitive. You young people who are used to all the gadgets, often find these primitive conditions rather upsetting."

"I shan't mind," said Victoria.

From the Expedition's stores, she selected a toothbrush, toothpaste, a sponge and some talcum powder.

Her head was still in a whirl as she tried to understand exactly what her position was. Clearly she was being mistaken for a girl called Venetia Something who was coming out to join the expedition and who was an anthropologist. Victoria didn't even know what an anthropologist was. If there was a dictionary somewhere about, she must look it up. The other girl was presumably not arriving for at least another week. Very well then, for a week—or until such time as the car or the lorry went into Baghdad, Victoria would be Venetia Thingummy, keeping her end up as best she could. She had no fears for Dr. Pauncefoot Jones who seemed delightfully vague, but she was nervous of Richard Baker. She disliked the speculative way he looked at her, and she had an idea that unless she was careful he would soon see through her pretenses. Fortunately she had been, for a brief period, a secretary typist at the Archaeological Institute in London, and she had a smattering of phrases and odds and ends that would be useful now. But she would have to be very careful not to make any real slip. Luckily, thought Victoria, men were always so superior about women that any slip she did make would be treated less as a suspicious circumstance than as a proof of how ridiculously addlepated all women were!

This interval would give her a respite which, she felt, she badly needed. For, from the point of view of the Olive Branch, her complete disappearance would be very disconcerting. She had escaped from her prison, but what had happened to her afterward would be very hard to trace. Richard's car had not passed through Mandali so that nobody could guess she was now at Tell Aswad. No, from their point of view, Victoria would seem to have vanished into thin air. They might conclude, very possibly they would conclude, that she was dead. That she had strayed into the desert and died of exhaustion.

Well, let them think so. Regrettably, of course, Edward would think so, too! Very well, Edward must lump it. In any case he would not have to lump it long. Just when he was torturing himself with remorse for having told her to cultivate Catherine's society—there she would be—suddenly restored to him—back from the dead—only a blonde instead of a brunette.

That brought her back to the mystery of why They (whoever they were) had dyed her hair. There must, Victoria thought, be some reason—but she could not for the life of her understand what the reason could be. As it was, she was soon going to look very peculiar when her hair started growing out black at the roots. A phoney platinum blonde, with no face powder and no lipstick! Could any girl be more unfortunately placed? Never mind, thought Victoria, I'm alive, aren't I? And I don't see at all why I shouldn't enjoy myself a good deal—at any rate for a week. It was really great fun to be on an Archaeological Expedition and see what it was like. If only she could keep her end up and not give herself away.

She did not find her role altogether easy. Reference to people, to publications, to styles of architecture and categories of pottery had to be dealt with cautiously. Fortunately a good listener is always appreciated. Victoria was an excellent listener to the two men, and warily feeling her way, she began to pick up the jargon fairly easily.

Surreptitiously, she read furiously when she was alone in the house. There

was a good library of archaeological publications. Victoria was quick to pick
up a smattering of the subject. Unexpectedly, she found the life quite enchanting. Tea brought to her in the early morning, then out on the dig. Helping
Richard with camera work. Piecing together and sticking up pottery. Watching the men at work, appreciating the skill and delicacy of the pickmen—
enjoying the songs and laughter of the little boys who ran to empty their
baskets of earth on the dump. She mastered the periods, realized the various
levels where digging was going on, and familiarized herself with the work of
the previous season. The only thing she dreaded was that burials might turn
up. Nothing that she read gave her any idea of what would be expected of her
as a working anthropologist! "If we do get bones or a grave," said Victoria to
herself, "I shall have to have a frightful cold—no, a severe bilious attack—
and take to my bed."

But no graves did appear. Instead, the walls of a palace were slowly exca-
vated. Victoria was fascinated and had no occasion to show any aptitude or
special skill.

Richard Baker still looked at her quizzically sometimes and she sensed his
unspoken criticism, but his manner was pleasant and friendly, and he was
genuinely amused by her enthusiasm.

"It's all new to you coming out from England," he said one day. "I remember how thrilled I was my first season."

"How long ago was that?"

He smiled.

"Rather a long time. Fifteen—no, sixteen years ago."

"You must know this country very well."

"Oh, it's not only been here. Syria—and Persia as well."

"You talk Arabic very well, don't you. If you were dressed as one could
you pass as an Arab?"

He shook his head.

"Oh no—that takes some doing. I doubt if any Englishman has ever been
able to pass as an Arab—for any length of time, that is."

"Lawrence?"

"I don't think Lawrence ever passed as an Arab. No, the only man I know
who is practically indistinguishable from the native product is a fellow who
was actually born out in these parts. His father was Consul at Kashgar and
other wild spots. He talked all kinds of outlandish dialects as a child and, I
believe, kept them up later."

"What happened to him?"

"I lost sight of him after we left school. We were at school together. Fakir,
we used to call him, because he could sit perfectly still and go into a queer
sort of trance. I don't know what he's doing now—though actually I could
make a pretty good guess."

"You never saw him after school?"

"Strangely enough, I ran into him only the other day—at Basrah, it was.
Rather a queer business altogether."

"Queer?"

"Yes. I didn't recognize him. He was got up as an Arab, keffiyah and striped robe and an old Army coat. He had a string of those amber beads they carry sometimes and he was clicking it through his fingers in the orthodox way—only, you see, he was actually using Army code. Morse. He was clicking out a message—to me!"

"What did it say?"

"My name—or nickname, rather—and his, and then a signal to stand by, expecting trouble."

"And was there trouble?"

"Yes. As he got up and started out the door, a quiet inconspicuous commercial traveler sort of fellow tugged out a revolver. I knocked his arm up—and Carmichael got away."

"Carmichael?"

He switched his head round quickly at her tone.

"That was his real name. Why—do you know him?"

Victoria thought to herself: How odd it would sound if I said, "He died in my bed."

"Yes," she said slowly. "I knew him."

"Knew him? Why—is he—"

Victoria nodded.

"Yes," she said. "He's dead."

"When did he die?"

"In Baghdad. In the Tio Hotel." She added quickly, "It was—hushed up. Nobody knows."

He nodded his head slowly.

"I see. It was that kind of business. But you—" He looked at her. "How do you know?"

"I got mixed up in it—by accident."

He gave her a long considering look.

Victoria asked suddenly,

"Your nickname at school wasn't Lucifer, was it?"

He looked surprised.

"Lucifer? no. I was called Owl—because I always had to wear shiny glasses."

"You don't know anyone who is called Lucifer—in Basrah?"

Richard shook his head.

"Lucifer, Son of the Morning—the fallen Angel."

He added, "Or an old-fashioned wax match. Its merit, if I remember rightly, was that it didn't go out in a wind."

He watched her closely as he spoke, but Victoria was frowning abstractedly.

"I wish you'd tell me," she said presently, "exactly what happened at Basrah."

"I have told you."

"No. I mean where were you when all this occurred?"

"Oh I see. Actually it was in the waiting room of the Consulate. I was waiting to see Clayton, the Consul."

"And who else was there? This commercial traveler person, and Carmichael? Anyone else?"

"There were a couple of others, a thin dark Frenchman or Syrian, and an old man—a Persian, I should say."

"And the commercial traveler got the revolver out and you stopped him, and Carmichael got out—how—?"

"He turned first toward the Consul's office. It's at the other end of a passage with a garden—"

She interrupted.

"I know. I stayed there for a day or two. As a matter of fact, it was just after you left."

"It was, was it?" Once again he watched her narrowly—but Victoria was unaware of it. She was seeing the long passage at the Consulate, but with the door open at the other end—opening onto green trees and sunlight.

"Well, as I was saying, Carmichael headed that way first. Then he wheeled round and dashed the other way into the street. That's the last I saw of him."

"What about the commercial traveler?"

Richard shrugged his shoulders.

"I understand he told some garbled story about having been attacked and robbed by a man the night before and fancying he had recognized his assailant in the Arab in the Consulate. I didn't hear much more about it because I flew on to Kuwait."

"Who was staying at the Consulate just then?" Victoria asked.

"A fellow called Crosbie—one of the oil people. Nobody else. Oh yes, I believe there was someone else down from Baghdad, but I didn't meet him. Can't remember his name."

"Crosbie," thought Victoria. She remembered Captain Crosbie, his short stocky figure, his staccato conversation. A very ordinary person. A decent soul without much finesse about him. And Crosbie had been back in Baghdad the night when Carmichael came to the Tio. Could it be because he had seen Crosbie at the other end of the passage, silhouetted against the sunlight, that Carmichael had turned so suddenly and made for the street instead of attempting to reach the Consul General's office?

She had been thinking this out in some absorption. She started rather guiltily when she looked up to find Richard Baker watching her with close attention.

"Why do you want to know all this?" he asked.

"I'm just interested."

"Any more questions?"

Victoria asked:

"Do you know anybody called Lefarge?"

"No—can't say I do. Man or woman?"

"I don't know."

She was wondering again about Crosbie. Crosbie? Lucifer?

Did Lucifer equal Crosbie?

That evening, when Victoria had said good night to the two men and gone to bed, Richard said to Dr. Pauncefoot Jones,

"I wonder if I might have a look at that letter from Emerson. I'd like to see just exactly what he said about this girl."

"Of course, my dear fellow, of course. It's somewhere lying around. I made some notes on the back of it, I remember. He spoke very highly of Veronica, if I remember rightly—said she was terrifically keen. She seems to me a charming girl—quite charming. Very plucky the way she's made so little fuss about the loss of her luggage. Most girls would have insisted on being motored into Baghdad the very next day to buy a new outfit. She's what I call a sporting girl. By the way, how was it that she came to lose her luggage?"

"She was chloroformed, kidnapped, and imprisoned in a native house," said Richard impassively.

"Dear, dear, yes, so you told me. I remember now. All most improbable. Reminds me—now what does it remind me of?—ah! yes, Elizabeth Canning, of course. You remember she turned up with the most impossible story after being missing a fortnight. Very interesting conflict of evidence—about some gypsies, if it's the right case I'm thinking of. And she was such a plain girl, it didn't seem likely there could be a man in the case. Now little Victoria—Veronica—I never *can* get her name right—she's a remarkably pretty little thing. Quite likely there is a man in her case."

"She'd be better looking if she didn't dye her hair," said Richard dryly.

"Does she dye it? In-deed. How knowledgeable you are in these matters."

"About Emerson's letter, sir—"

"Of course—of course—I've no idea where I put it. But look anywhere you choose—I'm anxious to find it anyway because of those notes I made on the back—and a sketch of that coiled wire bead."

20

ON THE FOLLOWING afternoon Dr. Pauncefoot Jones uttered a disgusted exclamation as the sound of a car came faintly to his ears. Presently he located it, winding across the desert toward the *tell.*

"Visitors," he said with venom. "At the worst possible moment, too. I want to superintend the cellulosing of that painted rosette on the northeast corner. Sure to be some idiots come out from Baghdad with a lot of social chatter and expecting to get shown all over the excavations."

"This is where Victoria comes in useful," said Richard. "You hear, Victoria? It's up to you to do a personally conducted tour."

"I shall probably say all the wrong things," said Victoria. "I'm really very inexperienced, you know."

"I think you're doing very well indeed," said Richard pleasantly. "Those remarks you made this morning about plano convex bricks might have come straight out of Delougaz's book."

Victoria changed color slightly, and resolved to paraphrase her erudition more carefully. Sometimes the quizzical glance through the thick lenses made her uncomfortable.

"I'll do my best," she said meekly.

"We push all the odd jobs on to you," said Richard.

Victoria smiled.

Indeed, her activities during the last five days surprised her not a little. She had developed plates with water filtered through cotton wool and by the light of a primitive dark lantern containing a candle which always went out at the most crucial moment. The darkroom table was a packing case and to work she had to crouch or kneel—the darkroom itself being, as Richard remarked, a modern model of the famous medieval Little Ease. There would be more amenities in the seasons to come, Dr. Pauncefoot Jones assured her—but at the moment every penny was needed to pay workmen and get results.

The baskets of broken potsherds had at first excited her astonished derision (though this she had been careful not to display). All these broken bits of coarse stuff—what was the good of them?

Then as she found joins, stuck them and propped them up in boxes of sand, she began to take an interest. She learned to recognize shapes and even periods. And she came finally to try and reconstruct in her own mind just how and for what these vessels had been used some three thousand odd years ago. In the small area where some poor quality private houses had been dug, she pictured the houses as they had originally stood and the people who had lived in them with their wants and possessions and occupations, their hopes and their fears. Since Victoria had a lively imagination, a picture rose up easily enough in her mind. On a day when a small clay pot was found encased in a wall with a half dozen gold earrings in it, she was enthralled. Probably dowry of a daughter, Richard Baker had said smiling.

Dishes filled with grain, gold earrings saved up for a dowry, bone needles, querns and mortars, little figurines and amulets. All the everyday life and fears and hopes of a community of unimportant simple people.

"That's what I find so fascinating," said Victoria to Richard. "You see I always used to think that archaeology was just Royal Graves and Palaces."

"Kings in Babylon," she added, with a strange little smile. "But what I like so much about all this is that it's the ordinary everyday people—people like me. My St. Anthony who finds things for me when I lose them—and a lucky china pig I've got—and an awfully nice mixing bowl, blue inside and white out, that I used to make cakes in. It got broken and the new one I bought wasn't a bit the same. I can understand why these people mended up their favorite bowls or dishes so carefully with bitumen. Life's all the same really, isn't it—then or now?"

She was thinking of these things as she watched the visitors ascending the side of the *tell*. Richard went to greet them, Victoria following behind him.

They were two Frenchmen, interested in Archaeology, who were making a tour through Syria and Iraq. After civil greetings, Victoria took them round the excavations, reciting parrotwise what was going on, but being unable to resist, being Victoria, adding sundry embellishments of her own, just, as she put it to herself, to make it more exciting.

She noticed that the second man was a very bad color, and that he dragged himself along without much interest. Presently he said, if Mademoiselle would excuse him, he would retire to the house. He had not felt well since early that morning—and the sun was making him worse.

He departed in the direction of the Expedition House, and the other, in suitably lowered tones explained that, unfortunately, it was his estomac. The Baghdad Tummy they called it, did they not? He should not really have come out today.

The tour was completed, the Frenchman remained talking to Victoria, finally Fidos was called and Dr. Pauncefoot Jones, with a determined air of hospitality, suggested the guests should have tea before departing.

To this, however, the Frenchman demurred. They must not delay their departure until it was dark or they would never find the way. Richard Baker said immediately that this was quite right. The sick friend was retrieved from the house and the car rushed off at top speed.

"I suppose that's just the beginning," grunted Dr. Pauncefoot Jones. "We shall have visitors every day now."

He took a large flap of Arab bread and covered it thickly with apricot jam.

Richard went to his room after tea. He had letters to answer, and others to write in preparation for going into Baghdad on the following day.

Suddenly he frowned. Not a man of particular neatness to the outward view, he yet had a way of arranging his clothes and his papers that never varied. Now he saw at once that every drawer had been disturbed. It was not the servants, of that he was sure. It must be, then, that the sick visitor who had made a pretext to go down to the house, had coolly ransacked through his belongings. Nothing was missing, he assured himself of that. His money was untouched. What, then, had they been looking for? His face grew grave as he considered the implications.

He went into the antika room and looked into the drawer which held the seals and seal impressions. He gave a grim smile—nothing had been touched or removed. He went into the living room. Dr. Pauncefoot Jones was out in the courtyard with the foremen. Only Victoria was there, curled up with a book.

Richard said, without preamble, "Somebody's been searching my room."

Victoria looked up, astonished.

"But why? And who?"

"It wasn't you?"

"Me?" Victoria was indignant. "Of course not. Why should I want to pry among your things?"

He gave her a hard stare. Then he said,

"It must have been that damned stranger—the one who shammed sick and came down to the house."

"Did he steal something?"

"No," said Richard. "Nothing was taken."

"But why on earth should someone—"

Richard cut in to say,

"I thought you might know that."

"Me?"

"Well, by your own account, rather odd things have happened to you."

"Oh that—yes." Victoria looked rather startled. She said slowly, "But I don't see why they should search your room. You've nothing to do with—"

"With what?"

Victoria did not answer for a moment or two. She seemed lost in thought.

"I'm sorry," she said at last. "What did you say? I wasn't listening."

Richard did not repeat his question. Instead he asked:

"What are you reading?"

Victoria made a slight grimace.

"You don't have much choice of light fiction here. 'Tale of Two Cities,' 'Pride and Prejudice' and 'The Mill on the Floss.' I'm reading the 'Tale of Two Cities.' "

"Never read it before?"

"Never. I always thought Dickens would be stuffy."

"What an idea!"

"I'm finding it most exciting."

"Where have you got to?" He looked over her shoulder and read out, " 'And the knitting women count One.' "

"I think she's awfully frightening," said Victoria.

"Madame Defarge? Yes, a good character. Though whether you could keep a register of names in knitting has always seemed to me rather doubtful. But then, of course, I'm not a knitter."

"Oh I think you could," said Victoria, considering the point. "Plain and purl—and fancy stitches—and the wrong stitch at intervals and dropped stitches. Yes—it could be done . . . Camouflaged, of course, so that it just looked like someone who was rather bad at knitting and made mistakes . . ."

Suddenly, with a vividness like a flash of lightning, two things came together in her mind and affected her with the force of an explosion. A name—and a visual memory. The man with the ragged handknitted red scarf clasped in his hands—the scarf she had hurriedly picked up later and flung into a drawer. And together with that a name. *Defarge*—not Lefarge—*Defarge*, Madame Defarge.

She was recalled to herself by Richard saying to her courteously, "Is anything the matter?"

"No—no, that is, I just thought of something."

"I see." Richard raised his eyebrows in his most supercilious way.

Tomorrow, thought Victoria, they would all go into Baghdad. Tomorrow her respite would be over. For over a week she had had safety, peace, time to pull herself together. And she had enjoyed that time—enjoyed it enormously. Perhaps I'm a coward, thought Victoria, perhaps that's it. She had talked gaily about adventure, but she hadn't liked it very much when it really came. She had hated that struggle against chloroform and the slow suffocation, and she had been frightened, horribly frightened, in that upper room when the ragged Arab had said "Bukra."

And now she'd got to go back to it all. Because she was employed by Mr. Dakin and paid by Mr. Dakin and she had to earn her pay and show a brave front! She might even have to go back to the Olive Branch. She shivered a little when she remembered Dr. Rathbone and that searching dark glance of his. He'd warned her . . .

But perhaps she wouldn't have to go back. Perhaps Mr. Dakin would say it was better not—now that they knew about her. But she would have to go back to her lodgings and get her things because thrust carelessly into her suitcase was the red knitted scarf . . . She had bundled everything into suitcases when she left for Basrah. Once she had put that scarf into Mr. Dakin's hands, perhaps her task would be done. He would say to her, perhaps, like on the pictures, "Oh! Good show, Victoria."

She looked up to find Richard Baker watching her.

"By the way," he said, "will you be able to get hold of your passport tomorrow?"

"My passport?"

Victoria considered the position. It was characteristic of her that she had not as yet defined her plan of action as regarded the Expedition. Since the real Veronica (or Venetia) would shortly be arriving from England, a retreat in good order was necessary. But whether she would merely fade away, or confess her deception with suitable penitence, or indeed what she intended to do, had not yet presented itself as a problem to be solved. Victoria was always prone to adopt the Micawber-like attitude that Something Would Turn Up.

"Well," she said temporizing, "I'm not sure."

"It's needed, you see, for the police of this district," explained Richard. "They enter its number and your name and age and special distinguishing marks, etc., all the whole caboodle. As we haven't got the passport, I think we ought at any rate to send your name and description to them. By the way, what is your last name? I've always called you 'Victoria.'"

Victoria rallied gallantly.

"Come now," she said. "You know my last name as well as I do."

"That's not quite true," said Richard. His smile curved upward with a hint of cruelty. "I do know your last name. It's you, I think, who don't know it."

Through the glasses the eyes watched her.

"Of course I know my own name," snapped Victoria.

"Then I'll challenge you to tell it to me—now."

His voice was suddenly hard and curt.

"It's no good lying," he said. "The game's up. You've been very clever about it all. You've read up your subject, you've brought out very telling bits of knowledge—but it's the kind of imposture you can't keep up all the time. I've laid traps for you and you've fallen into them. I've quoted bits of sheer rubbish to you and you've accepted them." He paused. "You're not Venetia Savile. Who are you?"

"I told you who I was the first time I met you," said Victoria. "I'm Victoria Jones."

"Dr. Pauncefoot Jones' niece?"

"I'm not his niece—but my name is Jones."

"You told me a lot of other things."

"Yes, I did. And they were all true! But I could see you didn't believe me. And that made me mad, because though I do tell lies sometimes—in fact quite often—what I'd just told you wasn't a lie. And so, just to make myself more convincing, I said my name was Pauncefoot Jones—I've said that before out here, and it's always gone down frightfully well. How could I tell you were actually coming to this place?"

"It must have been a slight shock to you," said Richard grimly. "You carried it off very well—cool as a cucumber."

"Not inside," said Victoria. "I was absolutely shaking. But I felt that if I waited to explain until I got here—well at any rate I should be safe."

"Safe?" he considered the word. "Look here, Victoria, was that incredible rigmarole you told about you being chloroformed really true?"

"Of course it was true! Don't you see, if I wanted to make up a story I could make up a much better one than that, and tell it better!"

"Knowing you a little more closely now, I can see the force of that! But you must admit that, on first hearing, the story was wildly improbable."

"But you are willing to think it's possible now. Why?"

Richard said slowly,

"Because if, as you say, you were mixed up in Carmichael's death—well, then it might be true."

"That's what it all began with," said Victoria.

"You'd better tell me about it."

Victoria stared at him very hard.

"I'm wondering," she said, "if I can trust you."

"The boot is on the other leg! Do you realize that I've had grave suspicions that you'd planted yourself here under a false name in order to get information out of me? And perhaps that is what you are doing."

"Meaning that you know something about Carmichael that They would like to know?"

"Who exactly are They?"

"I shall have to tell you all about it," said Victoria. "There isn't any other way—and if you are one of Them you know it already, so it doesn't matter."

She told him of the night of Carmichael's death, of her interview with Mr. Dakin, of her journey to Basrah, her employment in the Olive Branch, of Catherine's hostility, of Dr. Rathbone and his warning and of the final denouement, including this time the enigma of the dyed hair. The only things she left out were the red scarf and Madame Defarge.

"Dr. Rathbone?" Richard seized on that point. "You think he's mixed up in this? Behind it? But my dear girl, he's a very important man. He's known all over the world. Subscriptions pour in from all over the globe for his schemes."

"Wouldn't he have to be all those things?" asked Victoria.

"I've always regarded him as a pompous ass," said Richard meditatively.

"And that's a very good camouflage, too."

"Yes—yes, I suppose it is. Who was Lefarge that you asked me about?"

"Just another name," said Victoria. "There's Anna Scheele, too," she said.

"Anna Scheele? No, I've never heard of her."

"She's important," said Victoria. "But I don't know exactly how or why. It's all so mixed up."

"Just tell me again," said Richard. "Who's the man who started you on to all this?"

"Edwar— Oh, you mean Mr. Dakin. He's in Oil, I think."

"Is he a tired, stooping, rather vacant-looking chap?"

"Yes—but he's not really. Vacant, I mean."

"Doesn't he drink?"

"People say so, but I don't think he does."

Richard sat back and looked at her.

"Phillips Oppenheim, William Le Queux and several distinguished imitators since? Is this real? Are you real? And are you the persecuted heroine, or the wicked adventuress?"

Victoria said in a practical manner,

"The real point is, what are you going to say to Dr. Pauncefoot Jones about me?"

"Nothing," said Richard. "It really won't be necessary."

21

THEY STARTED IN to Baghdad early. Victoria's spirits felt curiously low. She had almost a lump in her throat as she looked back on the Expedition House. However, the acute discomfort entailed in the mad bumping of the lorry effectively distracted her mind from anything but the torture of the moment. It seemed strange to be driving along a so-called road again, passing donkeys and meeting dusty lorries. It took nearly three hours to reach the outskirts of Baghdad. The lorry decanted them at the Tio Hotel and then went off with the cook and the driver to do all necessary shopping. A large bundle of mail was awaiting Dr. Pauncefoot Jones and Richard. Marcus appeared suddenly, massive and beaming, and welcomed Victoria with his usual friendly radiance.

"Ah," he said, "it is a long time since I have seen you. You do not come to my hotel. Not for a week—two weeks. Why is that? You lunch here today, you have everything you want? The baby chickens? The big steak? Only not the turkey stuffed very special with flavoring and rice, because for that you must let me know the day before."

It seemed clear that as far as the Tio Hotel was concerned, the kidnapping of Victoria had not been noticed. Possibly Edward, on the advice of Mr. Dakin, had not been to the police.

"Is Mr. Dakin in Baghdad, do you know, Marcus?" she asked.

"Mr. Dakin—ah yes, very nice man—of course, he is friend of yours. He was here yesterday—no, day before. And Captain Crosbie, you know him? A friend of Mr. Dakin's. He arrives today from Kermanshah."

"You know where Mr. Dakin's office is?"

"Sure I know. Everybody knows the Iraqi Iranian Oil Co."

"Well, I want to go there now. In a taxi. But I want to be sure the taxi knows where to take me."

"I tell him myself," said Marcus obligingly.

He escorted her to the head of the alleyway and yelled in his usual violent fashion. A startled minion arrived at a run. Marcus commanded him to procure a taxi. Then Victoria was escorted to the taxi and Marcus addressed the driver. Then he stepped back and waved a hand.

"And I want a room," said Victoria. "Can I have one?"

"Yes, yes. I give you a beautiful room and I order you the big steak and tonight I have—very special—some caviar. And before that we have a little drink."

"Lovely," said Victoria. "Oh Marcus, can you lend me some money?"

"Of course, my dear. Here you are. Take all you want."

The taxi started off with a violent honk and Victoria fell back onto the seat clutching an assortment of coins and notes.

Five minutes later Victoria entered the offices of the Iraqi Iranian Oil Co. and asked for Mr. Dakin.

Mr. Dakin looked up from the desk where he was writing when Victoria was shown in. He rose and shook hands with her in a formal manner.

"Miss—er—Miss Jones, isn't it? Bring coffee, Abdullah."

As the soundproof door closed behind the clerk, he said quietly,

"You shouldn't really come here, you know."

"I had to this time," said Victoria. "There's something I've got to tell you at once—before anything more happens to me."

"Happens to you? Has anything happened to you?"

"Don't you know?" asked Victoria. "Hasn't Edward told you?"

"As far as I know, you are still working at the Olive Branch. Nobody had told me anything."

"Catherine," exclaimed Victoria.

"I beg your pardon."

"That cat Catherine! I bet she's stuffed Edward up with some tale or other and the goop has believed her."

"Well, let's hear about it," said Mr. Dakin. "Er—if I may say so," his eye went discreetly to Victoria's blond head, "I prefer you as a brunette."

"That's only part of it," said Victoria.

There was a tap at the door and the messenger entered with two little cups of sweet coffee. When he had gone, Dakin said,

"Now take your time and tell me all about it. We can't be overheard here."

Victoria plunged into the story of her adventures. As always when she was talking to Dakin, she managed to be both coherent and concise. She finished her story with an account of the red scarf Carmichael had dropped and her association of it with Madame Defarge.

Then she looked anxiously at Dakin.

He had seemed to her when she came in, to be even more bowed and tired looking. Now she saw a new glint come into his eye.

"I should read my Dickens more often," he said.

"Then you do think I'm right? You think it was Defarge he said—and you think some message is knitted into the scarf?"

"I think," said Dakin, "that this is the first real break we've had—and we've got you to thank for it. But the important thing is the scarf. Where is it?"

"With all the rest of my things. I shoved it into a drawer that night—and when I packed I remember bundling everything in without sorting or anything."

"And you've never happened to mention to anyone—to anyone *at all*— that that scarf belonged to Carmichael?"

"No, because I'd forgotten all about it. I bundled it into a suitcase with some other things when I went to Basrah and I've never even opened the case since."

"Then it ought to be all right. Even if they've been through your things, they won't have attached any importance to an old dirty woollen scarf—unless they were tipped off to it which as far as I can see, is impossible. All we've got to do now is to have all your things collected and sent to you at—have you got anywhere to stay, by the way?"

"I've booked a room at the Tio."

Dakin nodded.

"Best place for you."

"Have I—do you want me—to go back to the Olive Branch?"

Dakin looked at her keenly.

"Scared?"

Victoria stuck her chin out.

"No," she said with defiance. "I'll go if you like."

"I don't think it's necessary—or even wise. However they learned it, I presume that someone there got wise to your activities. That being so, you wouldn't be able to find out anything more, so you'd better stay clear."

He smiled.

"Otherwise you may be a redhead next time I see you."

"That's what I want to know most of all," cried Victoria. "Why did they dye my hair? I've thought and I've thought and I can't see any point in it. Can you?"

"Only the somewhat unpleasant one that your dead body might be less easy to identify."

"But if they wanted me to be a dead body, why didn't they kill me straight-away?"

"That's a very interesting question, Victoria. It's the question I want answered most of all."

"And you haven't any idea?"

"I haven't got a clue," said Mr. Dakin with a faint smile.

"Talking of clues," said Victoria, "do you remember my saying that there was something about Sir Rupert Crofton Lee that didn't seem right, that morning at the Tio?"

"Yes."

"You didn't know him personally, did you?"

"I hadn't met him before, no."

"I thought not. Because, you see, he wasn't Sir Rupert Crofton Lee."

And she plunged once more into animated narrative, starting with the incipient boil on the back of Sir Rupert's neck.

"So that was how it was done," said Dakin. "I didn't see how Carmichael could have been sufficiently off his guard to be killed that night. He got safely to Crofton Lee—and Crofton Lee stabbed him, but he managed to get away and burst into your room before he collapsed. And he hung on to the scarf—literally like grim death."

"Do you think it was because I was coming to tell you this that they kidnapped me? But nobody knew except Edward."

"I think they felt they had to get you out of the picture quickly. You were tumbling to too much that was going on at the Olive Branch."

"Dr. Rathbone warned me," said Victoria. "It was—more of a threat than a warning. I think he realized that I wasn't what I pretended to be."

"Rathbone," said Dakin dryly, "is no fool."

"I'm glad I haven't got to go back there," said Victoria. "I pretended to be brave just now—but really I'm scared stiff. Only if I don't go to the Olive Branch, how can I get hold of Edward?"

Dakin smiled.

"If Mohammed won't come to the mountain, the mountain must come to Mohammed. Write him a note now. Just say you're at the Tio and ask him to get your clothes and luggage and bring them along there. I'm going to consult Dr. Rathbone this morning about one of his Club Soirées. It will be easy for me to slip a note to his secretary—so there will be no danger of your enemy Catherine causing it to go astray. As for you, go back to the Tio and stay there—and, Victoria—"

"Yes?"

"If you're in a jam—of any kind—do the best you can for yourself. As far as possible you'll be watched over, but your adversaries are rather formidable, and unfortunately you know rather a lot. Once your luggage is in the Tio Hotel, your obligations to me are over. Understand that."

"I'll go straight back to the Tio now," said Victoria. "At least I shall just buy some face powder and lipstick and vanishing cream on the way. After all—"

"After all," said Mr. Dakin, "one cannot meet one's young man completely unarmored."

"It didn't matter so much with Richard Baker, though I'd like him to know I can look quite nice if I try," said Victoria. "But Edward—"

22

HER BLOND HAIR carefully arranged, her nose powdered and her lips freshly painted, Victoria sat upon the balcony of the Tio, once more in the role of a modern Juliet, waiting for Romeo.

And in due course Romeo came. He appeared on the grass sward, looking this way and that.

"Edward," said Victoria.

Edward looked up.

"Oh, there you are. Victoria—"

"Come up here."

"Right."

A moment later he came out upon the balcony which was deserted.

"It's more peaceful up here," said Victoria. "We'll go down and let Marcus give us drinks presently."

Edward was staring at her in perplexity.

"I say, Victoria, haven't you done something to your hair?"

Victoria gave an exasperated sigh.

"If anybody mentions hair to me, I really think I shall bat them over the head."

"I think I liked it better as it was," said Edward.

"Tell Catherine so!"

"Catherine? What has she got to do with it?"

"Everything," said Victoria. "You told me to chum up to her, and I did, and I don't suppose you've any idea what it let me in for!"

"Where've you been all this time, Victoria? I've been getting quite worried."

"Oh you have, have you? Where did you think I'd been?"

"Well, Catherine gave me your message. Said you'd told her to tell me that you'd had to go off to Mosul suddenly. It was something very important and good news, and I'd hear from you in due course."

"And you believed that?" asked Victoria in an almost pitying voice.

"I thought you'd got on the track of something. Naturally, you couldn't say much to Catherine—"

"It didn't occur to you that Catherine was lying, and that I'd been knocked on the head."

"What?" Edward stared.

"Drugged, chloroformed—starved . . ."

Edward cast a sharp glance round.

"Good Lord! I never dreamed—look here, I don't like talking out here. All these windows. Can't we go to your room?"

"All right. Did you bring my luggage?"

"Yes, I dumped it all with the porter."

"Because when one hasn't had a change of clothes for a fortnight—"

"Victoria, what has been happening? I know—I've got the car here. Let's go out to Devonshire. You've never been there, have you?"

"Devonshire?" Victoria stared in surprise.

"Oh, it's just a name for a place not far out of Baghdad. It's rather lovely this time of year. Come on. I haven't had you to myself for years."

"Not since Babylon. But what will Dr. Rathbone and the Olive Branch say?"

"Blast Dr. Rathbone. I'm fed up with the old ass anyway."

They ran down the stairs and out to where Edward's car was parked. Edward drove southward through Baghdad, along a wide avenue. Then he turned off from there; they jolted and twisted through palm groves and over irrigation bridges. Finally, with a strange unexpectedness they came to a small wooded copse surrounded and pierced by irrigation streams. The trees of the copse, mostly almond and apricot, were just coming into blossom. It was an idyllic spot. Beyond the copse, at a little distance, was the Tigris.

They got out of the car and walked together through the blossoming trees.

"This is lovely," said Victoria, sighing deeply. "It's like being back in England in Spring."

The air was soft and warm. Presently they sat down on a fallen tree trunk with pink blossom hanging down over their heads.

"Now, darling," said Edward. "Tell me what's been happening to you. I've been so dreadfully miserable."

"Have you?" she smiled dreamily.

Then she told him. Of the girl hairdresser. Of the smell of chloroform and her struggle. Of waking up drugged and sick. Of how she had escaped and of her fortuitous meeting with Richard Baker, and of how she had claimed to be Victoria Pauncefoot Jones on her way to the Excavations, and of how she had almost miraculously sustained the part of an archaeological student arriving from England.

At this point Edward shouted with laughter.

"You are marvelous, Victoria! The things you think of—and invent."

"I know," said Victoria. "My uncles. Dr. Pauncefoot Jones and before him —the Bishop."

And at that she suddenly remembered what it was she had been going to ask Edward at Basrah when Mrs. Clayton had interrupted by calling them in for drinks.

"I meant to ask you before," she said. "How did you know about the Bishop?"

She felt the hand that held hers stiffen suddenly. He said quickly, too quickly:

"Why, you told me, didn't you?"

Victoria looked at him. It was odd, she thought afterward, that that one silly childish slip should have accomplished what it did.

For he was taken completely by surprise. He had no story ready—his face was suddenly defenseless and unmasked.

And as she looked at him, everything shifted and settled itself into a pattern, exactly as a kaleidoscope does, and she saw the truth. Perhaps it was not really sudden. Perhaps in her subconscious mind that question: How did Edward know about the Bishop? had been teasing and worrying, and she had been slowly arriving at the one, the inevitable, answer . . . Edward had not learned about the Bishop of Llangow from her, and the only other persons he could have learned it from, would have been Mr. or Mrs. Hamilton Clipp. But they could not possibly have seen Edward since her arrival in Baghdad, for Edward had been in Basrah then, so he must have learned it from them before he himself left England. He must have known all along, then, that Victoria was coming out with them—and the whole wonderful coincidence was not, after all, a coincidence. It was planned and intended . . .

And as she stared at Edward's unmasked face, she knew, suddenly, what Carmichael had meant by Lucifer. She knew what he had seen that day as he looked along the passage to the Consulate Garden. He had seen that young beautiful face that she was looking at now—for it was a beautiful face—

Lucifer, Son of the Morning, how art thou fallen?

Not Dr. Rathbone—Edward! Edward, playing a minor part, the part of the secretary, but controlling and planning and directing, using Rathbone as a figurehead—and Rathbone, warning her to go while she could . . .

As she looked at that beautiful evil face, all her silly adolescent calf love faded away, and she knew that what she felt for Edward had never been love. It had been the same feeling that she had experienced some years earlier for Humphrey Bogart, and later for the Duke of Edinburgh. It had been glamour. And Edward had never loved her. He had exerted his charm and his glamour deliberately. He had picked her up that day, using his charm so easily, so naturally, that she had fallen for it without a struggle. She'd been a sucker.

It was extraordinary how much could flash through your mind in just a few seconds. You didn't have to think it out. It just came. Full and instant knowledge. Perhaps because really, underneath, you'd known it all along. . . .

And at the same time some instinct of self-preservation, quick as all Victoria's mental processes were quick, kept her face in an expression of foolish unthinking wonder. For she knew, instinctively, that she was in great danger. There was only one thing that could save her, only one card she could play. She made haste to play it.

"You knew all along!" she said. "You knew I was coming out here. You must have arranged it. Oh Edward, you are wonderful!"

Her face, that plastic impressionable face, showed one emotion only—an almost cloying adoration. And she saw the response—the faintly scornful smile, the relief. She could almost feel Edward saying to himself, "The little fool! She'll swallow anything! I can do what I like with her."

"But how did you arrange it?" she said. "You must be very powerful. You must be quite different from what you pretend to be. You're—it's like what you said the other day—you're a King in Babylon."

She saw the pride that lit up his face. She saw the power and strength and beauty and cruelty that had been disguised behind the façade of a modest likeable young man.

"And I'm only a Christian slave," thought Victoria. She said quickly and anxiously, as a final artistic touch (and what its cost was to her pride no one will ever know), "But you do love me, don't you?"

His scorn was hardly to be hidden now. This little fool—all these fools of women! So easy to make them think you loved them and that was all they cared about! They'd no conception of greatness of construction, of a new world, they just whined for love! They were slaves and you used them as slaves to further your ends.

"Of course I love you," he said.

"But what is it all about? Tell me, Edward. Make me understand."

"It's a new world, Victoria. A new world that will rise out of the muck and ashes of the old."

"Tell me."

He told her, and in spite of herself she was almost carried away, carried into the dream. The old bad things must destroy each other. There must be total war—total destruction. And then—the new Heaven and the new Earth. The small chosen band of higher beings, the scientists, the agricultural experts, the administrators— The young men like Edward—the young Siegfrieds of the New World. All young, all believing in their destiny as Supermen. When destruction had run its course, they would step in and take over.

It was madness—but it was constructive madness. It was the sort of thing that in a world, shattered and disintegrating, could happen.

"But think," said Victoria, "of all the people who will be killed first."

"You don't understand," said Edward. "That doesn't matter."

It doesn't matter—that was Edward's creed. And suddenly, for no reason, a remembrance of that three thousand years' old coarse pottery bowl mended with bitumen flashed across Victoria's mind. Surely those were the things that mattered—the little everyday things, the family to be cooked for, the four walls that enclosed the home, the one or two cherished possessions. All the thousands of ordinary people on the earth, minding their own business, and tilling that earth, and making pots and bringing up families and laughing and crying, and getting up in the morning and going to bed at night. They were the people who mattered, not these Angels with wicked faces who wanted to make a new world and who didn't care who they hurt to do it.

And carefully, feeling her way, for here in Devonshire she knew that death might be very near, she said:

"You are wonderful, Edward. But what about me? What can I do?"

"You want to—help? You believe in it?"

But she was prudent. Not sudden conversion. That would be too much.

"I think I just believe in you!" she said. "Anything you tell me to do, Edward, I'll do."

"Good girl," he said.

"Why did you arrange for me to come out here to begin with? There must have been some reason?"

"Of course there was. Do you remember I took a snap of you that day?"

"I remember," said Victoria.

(You fool, how flattered you were, how you simpered! she thought to herself.)

"I'd been struck by your profile—by your resemblance to someone. I took that snap to make sure."

"Who do I resemble?"

"A woman who's been causing us a good deal of trouble—Anna Scheele."

"Anna Scheele," Victoria stared at him in blank surprise. Whatever she had expected, it was not this. "You mean—she looks like me?"

"Quite remarkably so, side-view. The features in profile, are almost exactly the same. And there's one most extraordinary thing, you've got a tiny mark of a scar on your upper lip, left side—"

"I know. It's where I fell on a tin horse when I was a child. It had a sharp ear sticking up and it cut quite deep in. It doesn't show much—not with powder on."

"Anna Scheele has a mark in just the same place. That was a most valuable point. You're alike in height and build—she's about four or five years older than you. The real difference is the hair, you're a brunette and she's a blonde. And your style of hairdressing is quite different. Your eyes are a darker blue, but that wouldn't matter with tinted glasses."

"And that's why you wanted me to come to Baghdad? Because I looked like her."

"Yes, I thought the resemblance might—come in useful."

"So you arranged the whole thing . . . The Clipps—who are the Clipps?"

"They're not important—they just do as they're told."

Something in Edward's tone sent a faint shiver down Victoria's spine. It was as though he had said with inhuman detachment, "They are under Obedience."

There was a religious flavor about this mad project. "Edward," she thought, "is his own God. That's what's so frightening."

Aloud she said:

"You told me that Anna Scheele was the boss, the Queen Bee, in your show?"

"I had to tell you something to put you off the scent. You had already learned too much."

"And if I hadn't happened to look like Anna Scheele that would have been the end of me," thought Victoria.

She said:

"Who is she really?"

"She's confidential secretary to Otto Morganthal, the American and international banker. But that isn't all she is. She has the most remarkable financial brain. We've reason to believe she's traced out a lot of our financial operations. Three people have been dangerous to us—Rupert Crofton Lee, Carmichael—well, they're both wiped out. There remains Anna Scheele. She's due in Baghdad in three days' time. In the meantime, she's disappeared."

"Disappeared? Where?"

"In London. Vanished, apparently, off the face of the earth."

"And does no one know where she is?"

"Dakin may know."

But Dakin didn't know. Victoria knew that, though Edward didn't—so where was Anna Scheele?

She asked:

"You really haven't the least idea?"

"We've an idea," said Edward slowly.

"Well?"

"It's vital that Anna Scheele should be here in Baghdad for the Conference. That, as you know, is in five days' time."

"As soon as that? I'd no idea."

"We've got every entry into this country taped. She's certainly not coming here under her own name. And she's not coming in on a Government service plane. We've our means of checking that. So we've investigated all the private bookings. There's a passage booked by B.O.A.C. in the name of Grete Harden. We've traced Grete Harden back and there's no such person. It's an assumed name. The address given is a phoney one. It's our idea that Grete Harden is Anna Scheele."

He added:

"Her plane will touch down at Damascus the day after tomorrow."

"And then?"

Edward's eyes looked suddenly into hers.

"That's up to you, Victoria."

"To me?"

"You'll take her place."

Victoria said slowly:

"Like Rupert Crofton Lee?"

It was almost a whisper. In the course of that substitution Rupert Crofton Lee had died. And when Victoria took her place, presumably Anna Scheele, or Grete Harden, would die . . . But even if she didn't agree, Anna Scheele would still die.

And Edward was waiting—and if for one moment Edward doubted her loyalty, then she, Victoria, would die—and die without the possibility of warning anyone.

No, she must agree and seize a chance to report to Mr. Dakin.

She drew a deep breath and said:

"I—I—oh, but Edward, I couldn't do it. I'd be found out. I can't do an American voice."

"Anna Scheele has practically no accent. In any case, you will be suffering from laryngitis. One of the best doctors in this part of the world will say so."

"They've got people everywhere," thought Victoria.

"What would I have to do?" she asked.

"Fly from Damascus to Baghdad as Grete Harden. Take to your bed immediately. Be allowed up by our reputable doctor just in time to go to the Conference. There you will lay before them the documents which you have brought with you."

Victoria asked: "The real documents?"

"Of course not. We shall substitute our version."

"What will the documents show?"

Edward smiled.

"Convincing details of the most stupendous plot in America."

Victoria thought: "How well they've got it planned."

Aloud she said:

"Do you really think I can get away with it, Edward?"

Now that she was playing a part, it was quite easy for Victoria to ask it with every appearance of anxious sincerity.

"I'm sure you can. I've noticed that your playing of a part affords you such enjoyment that it's practically impossible to disbelieve you."

Victoria said meditatively:

"I still feel an awful fool when I think of the Hamilton Clipps."

He laughed in a superior way.

Victoria, her face still a mask of adoration, thought to herself viciously, "But you were an awful fool, too, to let slip that about the Bishop at Basrah. If you hadn't I'd never have seen through you."

She said suddenly: "What about Dr. Rathbone?"

"What do you mean 'What about him?' "

"Is he just a figurehead?"

Edward's lips curved in cruel amusement.

"Rathbone has got to toe the line. Do you know what he's been doing all these years? Cleverly appropriating about three quarters of the subscriptions which pour in from all over the world to his own use. It's the cleverest swindle since the time of Horatio Bottomley. Oh yes, Rathbone's completely in our hands—we can expose him at any time and he knows it."

Victoria felt a sudden gratitude to the old man with the noble domed head, and the mean acquisitive soul. He might be a swindler—but he had known pity—he had tried to get her to escape in time.

"All things work towards our new order," said Edward.

She thought to herself, "Edward, who looks so sane, is really mad! You get mad, perhaps, if you try and act the part of God. They always say humility is a Christian virtue—now I see why. Humility is what keeps you sane and a human being. . . ."

Edward got up.

"Time to be moving," he said. "We've got to get you to Damascus and our plans there worked out by the day after tomorrow."

Victoria rose with alacrity. Once she was away from Devonshire, back in Baghdad with its crowds, in the Tio Hotel with Marcus shouting and beaming and offering her a drink, the near persistent menace of Edward would be removed. Her part was to play a double game—continue to fool Edward by a sickly doglike devotion, and counter his plans secretly.

She said: "You think that Mr. Dakin knows where Anna Scheele is? Perhaps I could find that out. He might drop some hint."

"Unlikely—and in any case, you won't be seeing Dakin."

"He told me to come and see him this evening," said Victoria mendaciously, a slightly chilly feeling attacking her spine. "He'll think it odd if I don't turn up."

"It doesn't matter at this stage what he thinks," said Edward. "Our plans are made." He added, "You won't be seen in Baghdad again."

"But Edward, all my things are at the Tio! I've booked a room."

The scarf. The precious scarf.

"You won't need your things for some time to come. I've got a rig-out waiting for you. Come on."

They got in the car again. Victoria thought, "I ought to have known that Edward would never be such a fool as to let me get in touch with Mr. Dakin after I'd found him out. He believes I'm besotted about him—yes, I think he's sure of that—but all the same he isn't going to take any chances."

She said: "Won't there be a search for me if I—don't turn up?"

"We'll attend to that. Officially you'll say goodbye to me at the bridge and go off to see some friends on the West Bank."

"And actually?"

"Wait and see."

Victoria sat silent as they bumped over the rough track and twisted round palm gardens and over the little irrigation bridges.

"Lefarge," murmured Edward. "I wish we knew what Carmichael meant by that."

Victoria's heart gave a leap of anxiety.

"Oh," she said. "I forgot to tell you. I don't know if it means anything. A M. Lefarge came to the excavations one day at Tell Aswad."

"What?" Edward almost stalled the car in his excitement. "When was this?"

"Oh! About a week ago. He said he came from some dig in Syria. M. Parrot's, would it be?"

"Did two men called André and Juvet come while you were there?"

"Oh yes," said Victoria. "One of them had a sick stomach. He went to the house and lay down."

"They were two of our people," said Edward.

"Why did they come there? To look for me?"

"No—I'd no idea where you were. But Richard Baker was in Basrah at the same time as Carmichael. We had an idea Carmichael might have passed something on to Baker."

"He said his things had been searched. Did they find anything?"

"No—now think carefully, Victoria. Did this man Lefarge come before the other two or afterwards?"

Victoria reflected in a convincing manner, as she decided what movements to impute to the mythical M. Lefarge.

"It was—yes, the day before the other two came," she said.

"What did he do?"

"Well," said Victoria, "he went over the dig—with Dr. Pauncefoot Jones. And then Richard Baker took him down to the house to see some of the things in the antika room there."

"He went to the house with Richard Baker. They talked together?"

"I suppose so," said Victoria. "I mean, you wouldn't look at things in absolute silence, would you?"

"Lefarge," murmured Edward. "Who is Lefarge? Why have we got no line on him?"

Victoria longed to say, "He's brother to Mrs. Harris," but refrained. She was pleased with her invention of M. Lefarge. She could see him quite clearly now in her mind's eye—a thin rather consumptive-looking young man with dark hair and a little moustache. Presently, when Edward asked her, she described him carefully and accurately.

They were driving now through the suburbs of Baghdad. Edward turned off down a side street of modern villas built in a pseudo European style, with balconies and gardens around them. In front of one house a big touring car was standing. Edward drew up behind it and he and Victoria got out, and went up the steps to the front door.

A thin dark woman came out to meet them and Edward spoke to her rapidly in French. Victoria's French was not sufficiently good to understand fully what was said, but it seemed to be to the effect that this was the young lady and that the change must be effected at once.

The woman turned to her and said politely in French:

"Come with me, please."

She led Victoria into a bedroom where, spread out on a bed, was the habit of a nun. The woman motioned to her, and Victoria undressed and put on the stiff wool undergarment and the voluminous medieval folds of dark stuff. The Frenchwoman adjusted the headdress. Victoria caught a glimpse of herself in the glass. Her small pale face under the gigantic (was it wimple?) with the white folds under her chin, looked strangely pure and unearthly. The Frenchwoman threw a Rosary of wooden beads over her head. Then, shuffling in the overlarge coarse shoes, Victoria was led out to rejoin Edward.

"You look all right," he said approvingly. "Keep your eyes down, particularly when there are men about."

The Frenchwoman rejoined them a moment or two later similarly appareled. The two nuns went out of the house and got into the touring car which now had a tall dark man in European dress in the driver's seat.

"It's up to you now, Victoria," said Edward. "Do exactly as you are told."

There was a slight steely menace behind the words.

"Aren't you coming, Edward?" Victoria sounded plaintive.

He smiled at her.

"You'll see me in three days' time," he said. And then, with a resumption of his persuasive manner, he murmured, "Don't fail me, darling. Only you could do this—I love you, Victoria. I daren't be seen kissing a nun—but I'd like to."

Victoria dropped her eyes in approved nunlike fashion, but actually to conceal the fury that showed for a moment.

"Horrible Judas," she thought.

Instead she said with an assumption of her usual manner:

"Well, I seem to be a Christian slave all right."

"That's the girl!" said Edward. He added, "Don't worry. Your papers are in perfect order—you'll have no difficulty at the Syrian frontier. Your name in religion, by the way, is Sister Marie des Anges. Sister Thérèse who accompanies you has all the documents and is in full charge, and for God's sake obey orders—or I warn you frankly, you're for it."

He stepped back, waved his hand cheerfully, and the touring car started off.

Victoria leaned back against the upholstery and gave herself up to contemplation of possible alternatives. She could, as they were passing through Baghdad, or when they got to the frontier control, make an agitation, scream for help, explain that she was being carried off against her will—in fact, adopt one or other variants of immediate protest.

What would that accomplish? In all probability it would mean the end of Victoria Jones. She had noticed that Sister Thérèse had slipped into her sleeve a small and businesslike automatic pistol. She would be given no chance of talking.

Or she could wait until she got to Damascus? Make her protest there? Possibly, the same fate would be meted out, or her statements might be overborne by the evidence of the driver and her fellow nun. They might be able to produce papers saying that she was mentally afflicted.

The best alternative was to go through with things—to acquiesce in the plan. To come to Baghdad as Anna Scheele and to play Anna Scheele's part. For, after all, if she did so, there would come a moment, at the final climax, when Edward could no longer control her tongue or her actions. If she could continue to convince Edward that she would do anything he told her, then the moment would come when she was standing with her forged documents before the Conference—and Edward would not be there.

And no one could stop her then from saying, "I am not Anna Scheele and these papers are forged and untrue."

She wondered that Edward did not fear her doing just that. But she reflected that vanity was a strangely blinding quality. Vanity was the Achilles heel. And there was also the fact to be considered that Edward and his crowd had more or less got to have an Anna Scheele if their scheme was to succeed. To find a girl who sufficiently resembled Anna Scheele—even to the point of having a scar in the right place was extremely difficult. In the Lyons Mail, Victoria remembered, Dubosc and Lesurque had the extraordinary coincidence of both having a scar above one eyebrow and also of having a distortion, one by birth and one by accident, of the little finger of one hand. These coincidences must be very rare. No, the Supermen needed Victoria Jones, typist—and to that extent Victoria Jones had them in her power—not the other way around.

The car sped across the bridge. Victoria watched the Tigris with a nostalgic longing. Then they were speeding along a wide dusty highway. Victoria let the beads of her Rosary pass through her fingers. Their click was comforting.

"After all," thought Victoria with sudden comfort. "I am a Christian. And if you're a Christian, I suppose it's a hundred times better to be a Christian martyr than a King in Babylon—and I must say, there seems to me a great possibility that I am going to be a martyr. Oh! well, anyway, it won't be lions. I should have hated lions!"

23

THE BIG SKYMASTER swooped down from the air and made a perfect landing. It taxied gently along the runway and presently came to a stop at the appointed place. The passengers were invited to descend. Those going on to Basrah were separated from those who were catching a connecting plane to Baghdad.

Of the latter there were four. A prosperous-looking Iraqi businessman, a young English doctor and two women. They all passed through the various controls and questioning.

A dark woman with untidy hair imperfectly bound in a scarf and a tired face came first.

"Mrs. Pauncefoot Jones? British. Yes. To join your husband. Your address in Baghdad, please? What money have you? . . ."

It went on. Then the second woman took the first one's place.

"Grete Harden. Yes. Nationality? Danish. From London. Purpose of visit? Masseuse at hospital? Address in Baghdad? What money have you?"

Grete Harden was a thin fair-haired young woman wearing dark glasses. She wore neat but slightly shabby clothes.

Her French was halting—occasionally she had to have the question repeated.

Then the four passengers were told that the Baghdad plane took off that afternoon. They would be driven now to the Abbassid Hotel for a rest and lunch.

Grete Harden was sitting on her bed when a tap came on the door. She opened it and found a tall dark young woman wearing B.O.A.C. uniform.

"I'm so sorry, Miss Harden. Would you come with me to the B.O.A.C. office? A little difficulty has arisen about your ticket. This way, please."

Grete Harden followed her guide down the passage. On a door was a large board lettered in gold B.O.A.C. Office.

The air hostess opened the door and motioned the other inside. Then, as Grete Harden passed through, she closed the door from outside and quickly unhooked the board.

As Grete Harden came through the door, two men who had been standing behind it passed a cloth over her head. They stuffed a gag into her mouth. One of them rolled her sleeve up, and bringing out a hypodermic syringe gave her an injection.

In a few minutes her body sagged and went limp.

The young doctor said cheerfully, "That ought to take care of her for about six hours, anyway. Now then, you two, get on with it."

He nodded toward two other occupants of the room. They were nuns who were sitting immobile by the window. The men went out of the room. The elder of the two nuns went to Grete Harden and began to take the clothes off her inert body. The younger nun, trembling a little, started taking off her habit. Presently Grete Harden, dressed in a nun's habit, lay reposefully on the bed. The younger nun was now dressed in Grete Harden's clothes.

The older nun turned her attention to her companion's flaxen hair. Looking at a photograph which she propped up against the mirror, she combed and dressed the hair, bringing it back from the forehead and coiling it low on the neck.

She stepped back and said in French:

"Astonishing how it changes you. Put on the dark spectacles. Your eyes are too deep a blue. Yes—that is admirable."

There was a slight tap on the door and the two men came in again. They were grinning.

"Grete Harden is Anna Scheele all right," one said. "She'd got the papers in her luggage, carefully camouflaged between the leaves of a Danish publication on Hospital Massage. Now then, Miss Harden," he bowed with mock ceremony to Victoria, "you will do me the honor to have lunch with me."

Victoria followed him out of the room and along to the hall. The other woman passenger was trying to send off a telegram at the desk.

"No," she was saying, "P.A.U.N.C.E. foot. Dr. Pauncefoot Jones. Arriving today Tio Hotel. Good journey—"

Victoria looked at her with sudden interest. This must be Dr. Pauncefoot Jones' wife, coming out to join him. That she was a week earlier than expected did not seem to Victoria at all extraordinary since Dr. Pauncefoot Jones had several times lamented that he had lost her letter giving the date of arrival but that he was almost certain it was the 26th!

If only she could somehow or other send a message through Mrs. Pauncefoot Jones to Richard Baker. . . .

Almost as though he read her thoughts, the man accompanying her steered her by the elbow away from the desk.

"No conversations with fellow travelers, Miss Harden," he said. "We don't want that good woman to notice that you're a different person from the one she came out from England with."

He took her out of the hotel to a restaurant for lunch. As they came back, Mrs. Pauncefoot Jones was coming down the steps of the hotel. She nodded without suspicion at Victoria.

"Been sightseeing?" she called. "I'm just going to the bazaars."

"If I could slip something into her luggage—" thought Victoria.

But she was not left alone for a moment.

The Baghdad plane left at three o'clock.

Mrs. Pauncefoot Jones' seat was right up in front. Victoria's was in the tail, near the door, and across the aisle sat the fair young man who was her jailer. Victoria had no chance of reaching the other woman or of introducing a message into any of her belongings.

The flight was not a long one. For a second time, Victoria looked down from the air and saw the city outlined below her, the Tigris dividing it like a streak of gold.

So she had seen it less than a month ago. How much had happened since then.

In two days' time the men who represented the two predominant ideologies of the world would meet here to discuss the future—

And she, Victoria Jones, would have a part to play.

ii

"You know," said Richard Baker, "I'm worried about that girl."

Dr. Pauncefoot Jones said vaguely,

"What girl?"

"Victoria."

"Victoria?" Dr. Pauncefoot Jones peered about. "Where is—why, God bless me, we came back without her yesterday."

"I wondered if you'd noticed it," said Richard.

"Very remiss of me. I was so interested by that report of the Excavations at Tell Yameni. Completely unsound stratification. Didn't she know where to find the lorry?"

"There was no question of her coming back here," said Richard. "As a matter of fact, she isn't Venetia Savile."

"Not Venetia Savile? How very odd. But I thought you said her Christian name was Victoria."

"It is. But she's not an anthropologist. And she doesn't know Emerson. As a matter of fact, the whole thing has been a—well—a misunderstanding."

"Dear me. That seems very odd." Dr. Pauncefoot Jones reflected for some moments. "Very odd. I do hope—am I to blame? I know I am somewhat absentminded. The wrong letter, perhaps?"

"I can't understand it," said Richard Baker frowning and paying no attention to Dr. Pauncefoot Jones' speculations. "She went off in a car with a young man, it seems, and she didn't come back. What's more, her baggage was there and she hadn't bothered to open it. That seems to me very strange —considering the mess she was in. I'd have thought she'd be sure to doll herself up. And we agreed to meet for lunch . . . No, I can't understand it. I hope nothing's happened to her."

"Oh, I shouldn't think so for a moment," said Dr. Pauncefoot Jones comfortably. "I shall start going down in H. tomorrow. From the general plan I should say that would be the best chance of getting a record office. That fragment of tablet was very promising."

"They've kidnapped her once," said Richard. "What's to prevent their having kidnapped her again?"

"Very improbable—very improbable," said Dr. Pauncefoot Jones. "The country's really very settled nowadays. You said so yourself."

"If I could only remember the name of that man in some oil company. Was it Deacon? Deacon, Dakin? Something like that."

"Never heard of him," said Dr. Pauncefoot Jones. "I think I shall change over Mustafa and his gang to the northeast corner. Then we might extend Trench J—"

"Would you mind awfully, sir, if I went in to Baghdad again tomorrow?"

Dr. Pauncefoot Jones, suddenly giving his colleague his full attention, stared at him.

"Tomorrow? But we were there yesterday."

"I'm worried about that girl. I really am."

"Dear me, Richard, I had no idea there was anything of that kind."

"What kind?"

"That you'd formed an attachment. That's the worst of having women on a dig—especially good-looking ones. I really did think we were safe with Sybil Muirfield the year before last, a really distressingly plain girl—and see what came of it! I ought to have listened to Claude in London—these Frenchmen always hit the nail on the head. He commented on her legs at the time—was most enthusiastic about them. Of course this girl, Victoria Venetia, whatever her name is—most attractive and such a nice little thing. You've got good taste, Richard, I will admit that. Funny thing, she's the first girl I've ever known you take any interest in."

"There's nothing of that kind," said Richard, blushing and looking even more supercilious than usual. "I'm just—er—worried about her. I must go to Baghdad."

"Well, if you are going tomorrow," said Dr. Pauncefoot Jones, "you might bring back those extra picks. That fool of a driver forgot them."

Richard started into Baghdad at early dawn and went straight to the Tio Hotel. Here he learned that Victoria had not returned.

"And it was all arranged that she was to have special dinner with me," said Marcus. "And I kept her a very nice room. It is odd, is it not?"

"Have you been to the police?"

"Ah no, my dear, it would not be nice, that. She might not like it. And I certainly would not like it."

After a little inquiry, Richard tracked down Mr. Dakin and called upon him in his office.

His memory of the man had not played him false. He looked at the stooping figure, the indecisive face and the slight tremor of the hands. This man was no good! He apologized to Mr. Dakin if he was wasting his time, but had he seen Miss Victoria Jones.

"She called on me the day before yesterday."

"Can you give me her present address?"

"She's at the Tio Hotel, I believe."

"Her luggage is there, but she isn't."

Mr. Dakin raised his eyebrows slightly.

"She has been working with us on the Excavations at Tell Aswad," explained Richard.

"Oh I see. Well—I'm afraid I don't know anything that can help you. She has several friends in Baghdad, I believe—but I don't know her well enough to say who they are."

"Would she be at this Olive Branch?"

"I don't think so. You could ask."

Richard said: "Look here. I'm not leaving Baghdad until I find her."

He frowned angrily at Mr. Dakin and strode out of the room.

Mr. Dakin, as the door closed behind Richard, smiled and shook his head.

"Oh Victoria," he murmured reproachfully.

Fuming into the Tio Hotel, Richard was met by a beaming Marcus.

"She's come back," cried Richard eagerly.

"No, no, it is Mrs. Pauncefoot Jones. She has just arrived by plane. Dr. Pauncefoot Jones, he told me she was coming next week."

"He always gets dates wrong. What about Victoria Jones?"

Marcus's face went grave again.

"No, I have heard nothing of her. And I do not like it, Mr. Baker. It is not nice. She is so young a girl. And so pretty. And so gay and charming."

"Yes, yes," said Richard flinching. "I'd better go up and see Mrs. Pauncefoot Jones. What's her number?"

"She is in 19."

With a heavy tread, Richard went up the stairs.

iii

"You!" said Victoria with undisguised hostility.

Ushered up to her room in the Babylonian Palace Hotel, the first person she saw was Catherine.

Catherine nodded her head with equal venom.

"Yes," she said. "It is I. And now please go to bed. The doctor will soon arrive."

Catherine was dressed as a hospital nurse and she took her duties seriously, being obviously quite determined never to leave Victoria's side. Victoria, lying disconsolately in bed, murmured:

"If I could get hold of Edward—"

"Edward—Edward!" said Catherine scornfully. "Edward has never cared for you, you stupid English girl. It is me whom Edward loves!"

Victoria looked at Catherine's stubborn fanatical face without enthusiasm.

Catherine went on:

"Always I have hated you from that first morning you came in and demanded to see Dr. Rathbone with such rudeness."

Searching about for an irritant, Victoria said:

"At any rate I'm much more indispensable than you are. Anybody could do your hospital nurse act. But the whole thing depends on me doing mine."

Catherine said with prim smugness:

"Nobody is indispensable. We are taught that."

"Well, I am. For goodness' sake order up a substantial meal. If I don't get something to eat, how do you expect me to give a good performance of an American banker's secretary when the time comes?"

"I suppose you might as well eat while you can," said Catherine grudgingly.

Victoria took no notice of the sinister implication.

iv

Captain Crosbie said:

"I understand you've got a Miss Harden just arrived."

The suave gentleman in the office of the Babylonian Palace inclined his head.

"Yes, sir. From England."

"She's a friend of my sister's. Will you take my card up to her?"

He penciled a few words on the card and sent it up in an envelope.

Presently the boy who had taken it returned.

"The lady is not well, sir. Very bad throat. Doctor coming soon. She has hospital nurse with her."

Crosbie turned away. He went along to the Tio where he was accosted by Marcus.

"Ah, my dear, let us have a drink. This evening my hotel is quite full. It is for the Conference. But what a pity. Dr. Pauncefoot Jones went back to his Expedition the day before yesterday and now here is his wife who arrives and expects that he will be here to meet her. And she is not pleased, no! She says she told him she was coming on this plane. But you know what he is like, that one. Every date, every time—he always gets it wrong. But he is a very nice man," finished Marcus with his usual charity. "And I have had to squeeze her in somehow—I turn out a very important man from UNO—"

"Baghdad seems quite mad."

"All the police they have drafted in—they are taking great precautions—

they say—have you heard?—there is a plot to assassinate the President! They have arrested sixty-five students! They are very suspicious of everybody. But all this is very good for trade—very good indeed."

v

The telephone bell rang and was promptly answered.

"American Embassy."

"This is the Babylonian Palace Hotel. Miss Anna Scheele is staying here."

Anna Scheele? Presently one of the Attachés was speaking. Could Miss Scheele come to the phone?

"Miss Scheele is ill in bed with laryngitis. This is Dr. Smallbrook. I am attending Miss Scheele. She has some important papers with her and would like some responsible person from the Embassy to come and fetch them. Immediately? Thank you. I will be waiting for you."

vi

Victoria turned from the mirror. She was wearing a well-cut tailored suit. Every blond hair was in place. She felt nervous but exhilarated.

As she turned, she caught the exultant gleam in Catherine's eye and was suddenly on her guard. Why was Catherine exultant?

What was going on?

"What are you so pleased about?" she asked.

"Soon you will see."

The malice was quite unconcealed now.

"You think you are so clever," said Catherine scornfully. "You think everything depends on you. Pah, you are just a fool."

With a bound Victoria was upon her! She caught her by the shoulder and dug her fingers in.

"Tell me what you mean, you horrible girl."

"Ach—you hurt me."

"Tell me—"

A knock came on the door. A knock twice repeated and then, after a pause, a single one.

"Now you will see!" cried Catherine.

The door opened and a man slipped in. He was a tall man, dressed in the uniform of the International Police. He locked the door behind him and removed the key. Then he advanced to Catherine.

"Quickly," he said.

He took a length of thin cord from his pocket and, with Catherine's full cooperation, bound her swiftly to a chair. Then he produced a scarf and tied it over her mouth. He stood back and nodded appreciatively.

"So—that will do nicely."

Then he turned toward Victoria. She saw the heavy truncheon he was brandishing and in a moment it flashed across her brain what the real plan was. They had never intended that she should play the part of Anna Scheele at the Conference. How could they risk such a thing? Victoria was too well known in Baghdad. No, the plan was, had always been, that Anna Scheele should be attacked and killed at the last moment—killed in such a way that her features would not be too recognizable . . . Only the papers she had brought with her—those carefully forged papers—would remain.

Victoria turned away to the window—she screamed. And with a smile the man came at her—

Then several things happened—there was a crash of broken glass—a heavy hand sent her headlong down—she saw stars—and blackness . . . Then out of the blackness a voice spoke, a reassuring English voice.

"Are you all right, Miss?" it asked.

Victoria murmured something.

"What did she say?" asked a second voice.

The first man scratched his head.

"Said it was better to serve in Heaven than reign in Hell," he said doubtfully.

"That's a quotation," said the other. "But she's got it wrong," he added.

"No, I haven't," said Victoria and fainted.

vii

The telephone rang and Dakin picked up the receiver. A voice said:

"Operation Victoria successfully concluded."

"Good," said Dakin.

"We've got Catherine Serakis and the medico. The other fellow threw himself off the balcony. He's fatally injured."

"The girl's not hurt?"

"She fainted—but she's O.K."

"No news still of the real A.S.?"

"No news whatever."

Dakin laid down the receiver.

At any rate Victoria was all right—Anna herself, he thought, must be dead . . . She had insisted on playing a lone hand, had reiterated that she would be in Baghdad without fail on the 19th. Today was the 19th and there was no Anna Scheele. Perhaps she had been right not to trust the official setup—he didn't know. Certainly there had been leakages—betrayals. But apparently her own native wits had served her no better. . . .

And without Anna Scheele, the evidence was incomplete.

A messenger came in with a piece of paper on which was written Mr. Richard Baker and Mrs. Pauncefoot Jones.

"I can't see anybody now," said Dakin. "Tell them I am very sorry. I am engaged."

The messenger withdrew, but presently returned. He handed Dakin a note. Dakin tore open the envelope and read:

"I want to see you about Henry Carmichael. R.B."

"Show him in," said Dakin.

Presently Richard Baker and Mrs. Pauncefoot Jones came in. Richard Baker said:

"I don't want to take up your time, but I was at school with a man called Henry Carmichael. We lost sight of each other for many years, but when I was at Basrah a few weeks ago I encountered him in the Consulate waiting room. He was dressed as an Arab, and without giving any overt sign of recognition, he managed to communicate with me. Does this interest you?"

"It interests me very much," said Dakin.

"I formed the idea that Carmichael believed himself to be in danger. This was very soon verified. He was attacked by a man with a revolver which I managed to knock up. Carmichael took to his heels but before he went, he slipped something into my pocket which I found later—It didn't appear to be important—it seems to be just a 'chit'—a reference for one Ahmed Moham-med. But I acted on the assumption that to Carmichael it was important.

"Since he gave me no instructions, I kept it carefully, believing that he would one day reclaim it. The other day I learned from Victoria Jones that he was dead. From other things that she told me, I have come to the conclusion that the right person to deliver this object to is you."

He got up and placed a dirty sheet of paper with writing on it on Dakin's desk.

"Does this mean anything to you?"

Dakin drew a deep sigh.

"Yes," he said. "It means more than you can possibly imagine."

He got up.

"I'm deeply obliged to you, Baker," he said. "Forgive my cutting this interview short, but there is a lot that I have to see to without wasting a minute." He shook hands with Mrs. Pauncefoot Jones, saying, "I suppose you are joining your husband on his dig. I hope you have a good season."

"It's a good thing Pauncefoot Jones didn't come into Baghdad with me this morning," said Richard. "Dear old John Pauncefoot Jones doesn't notice much that goes on, but he'd probably notice the difference between his wife and his wife's sister."

Dakin looked with slight surprise at Mrs. Pauncefoot Jones. She said in a low pleasant voice,

"My sister Elsie is still in England. I dyed my hair black and came out on her passport. My sister's maiden name was Elsia Scheele. *My name, Mr. Dakin, is Anna Scheele.*"

BAGHDAD WAS TRANSFORMED. Police lined the streets—police drafted in from outside, the International Police. At last the historic Conference had begun.

In a small anteroom certain events were taking place which might well alter the course of history. Like most momentous happenings, the proceedings were not at all dramatic.

Doctor Alan Breck of the Harwell Atomic Institute contributed his quota of information in a small precise voice.

Certain specimens had been left with him for analysis by the late Sir Rupert Crofton Lee. They had been acquired in the course of one of Sir Rupert's journeys through China and Turkestan through Kurdistan to Iraq. Dr. Breck's evidence then became severely technical. Metallic ores . . . high uranium content . . . Source of deposit not known exactly, since Sir Rupert's notes and diaries had been destroyed during the war by enemy action.

Then Mr. Dakin took up the tale. In a gentle tired voice he told the saga of Henry Carmichael, of his belief in certain rumors and wild tales of vast installations and underground laboratories functioning in a remote valley beyond the bounds of civilization. Of his search—and of the success of his search. Of how that great traveler, Sir Rupert Crofton Lee, the man who had believed Carmichael because of his own knowledge of those regions, had agreed to come to Baghdad, and of how he had died. And of how Carmichael had met his own death at the hands of Sir Rupert's impersonator.

"Sir Rupert is dead, and Henry Carmichael is dead. But there is a third witness who is alive and who is here today. I will call upon Miss Anna Scheele to give us her testimony."

Anna Scheele, as calm and composed as if she were in Mr. Morganthal's office, gave lists of names and figures. From the depths of that remarkable financial brain of hers, she outlined the vast financial network that had drained money from circulation, and poured it into the financing of activities that should tend to split the civilized world into two opposing factions. It was no mere assertion. She produced facts and figures to support her contention. To those who listened she carried a conviction that was not as yet fully accorded to Carmichael's wild tale.

Dakin spoke again.

"Henry Carmichael is dead," he said. "But he brought back with him from that hazardous journey tangible and definite proofs. He did not dare to keep those proofs on him—his enemies were too close on his track. But he was a man of many friends. By the hands of two of those friends, he sent the proofs to the safekeeping of another friend—a man whom all Iraq reveres and respects. He has courteously consented to come here today. I refer to Sheikh Hussein el Ziyara of Kerbela."

Sheikh Hussein el Ziyara was renowned, as Dakin had said, throughout the Moslem world, both as a holy man and a poet. He was considered by many to be a saint. He stood up now, an imposing figure with his deep brown hennaed beard. His gray jacket edged with gold braid was covered by a flowing brown cloak of gossamer fineness. Round his head he wore a green cloth headdress which was bound with many strands of heavy gold *agal* and which gave him a patriarchal appearance. He spoke in a deep sonorous voice.

"Henry Carmichael was my friend," he said. "I knew him as a boy and he studied with me the verses of our great poets. Two men came to Kerbela, men who travel the country with a picture show. They are simple men, but good followers of the Prophet. They brought me a packet which they said they had been told to deliver into my hands from my friend the Englishman Carmichael. I was to keep this in secrecy and security and to deliver it only to Carmichael himself, or to a messenger who should repeat certain words."

Dakin said, "Sayyid, the Arabic poet Mutanabbi, called sometimes the Pretender to Prophecy, who lived just one thousand years ago, wrote an Ode to Prince Sayfu 'l-Dawla at Aleppo in which these words occur: *Zid hashshi bashshi tafaddal adni surra sili.*"*

With a smile Sheikh Hussein el Ziyara held out a packet to Dakin.

"I say, as Prince Sayfu 'l-Dawla said: 'You shall have your desire' . . ."

"Gentlemen," said Dakin. "These are the microfilms brought back by Henry Carmichael in proof of his story . . ."

One more witness spoke—a tragic broken figure: an old man with a fine domed head who had once been universally admired and respected.

He spoke with a tragic dignity.

"Gentlemen," he said. "I shall shortly be arraigned as a common swindler. But there are some things that even I cannot countenance. There is a band of men, mostly young men, so evil in their hearts and aims that the truth would hardly be believed."

He lifted up his head and roared out:

"Antichrist! I say this thing must be stopped! We have got to have peace—peace to lick our wounds and make a new world—and to do that we must try to understand each other. I started a racket to make money—but, by God, I've ended in believing in what I preach—though I don't advocate the methods I've used. For God's sake, gentlemen, let's start again and try to pull together . . ."

There was a moment's silence, and then a thin official voice, with the bloodless impersonality of bureaucracy, said:

"These facts will be put forthwith before the Powers Assembled. . . ."

* Add, laugh, rejoice, bring nigh, gladden, show favor, give!

25

"WHAT BOTHERS ME," said Victoria, "is that poor Danish woman who got killed by mistake in Damascus."

"Oh! she's all right," said Mr. Dakin cheerfully. "As soon as your plane had taken off, we arrested the French woman and took Grete Harden to hospital. She came round all right. They were going to keep her drugged for a bit until they were sure the Baghdad business went off all right. She was one of our people, of course."

"Was she?"

"Yes, when Anna Scheele disappeared, we thought it might be as well to give the other side something to think about. So we booked a passage for Grete Harden and carefully didn't give her a background. They fell for it—jumped to the conclusion that Grete Harden must be Anna Scheele. We gave her a nice little set of faked papers to prove it."

"While the real Anna Scheele remained quietly in the nursing home till it was time for Mrs. Pauncefoot Jones to join her husband out here."

"Yes. Simple—but effective. Acting on the assumption that in times of stress the only people you can really trust are your own family. She's an exceedingly clever young woman."

"I really thought I was for it," said Victoria. "Were your people really keeping tabs on me?"

"All the time. Your Edward wasn't really quite so clever as he thought himself, you know. Actually we'd been investigating the activities of young Edward Goring for some time. When you told me your story, the night Carmichael was killed, I was frankly very worried about you.

"The best thing I could think of was to send you deliberately into the setup as a spy. If your Edward knew that you were in touch with me, you'd be reasonably safe, because he'd learn through you what we were up to. You'd be too valuable to kill. And he could also pass on false information to us through you. You were a link. But then you spotted the Rupert Crofton Lee impersonation, and Edward decided you'd better be kept out of it until you were needed (if you should be needed) for the impersonation of Anna Scheele. Yes, Victoria, you're very lucky to be sitting where you are now, eating all those pistachio nuts."

"I know I am."

Mr. Dakin said:

"How much do you mind—about Edward?"

Victoria looked at him steadily.

"Not at all. I was just a silly little fool. I let Edward pick me up and do his glamour act. I just had a thoroughly schoolgirl crush on him—fancying myself Juliet and all sorts of silly things."

"You needn't blame yourself too much. Edward had a wonderful natural gift for attracting women."

"Yes, and he used it."

"He certainly used it."

"Next time I fall in love," said Victoria, "it won't be looks that attract me, or glamour. I'd like a real man—not one who says pretty things to you. I shan't mind if he's bald or wears spectacles or anything like that. I'd like him to be interesting—and know about interesting things."

"About thirty-five or fifty-five?" asked Mr. Dakin.

Victoria stared.

"Oh thirty-five," she said.

"I am relieved. I thought for a moment you were proposing to me."

Victoria laughed.

"And—I know I mustn't ask questions—but was there really a message knitted into the scarf?"

"There was a name. The *tricoteuses* of whom Madame Defarge was one, knitted a register of names. The scarf and the 'chit' were the two halves of the clue. One gave us the name of Sheikh Hussein el Ziyara of Kerbela. The other when treated with iodine vapor gave us the words to induce the Sheikh to part with his trust. There couldn't have been a safer place to hide the thing, you know, than in the sacred City of Kerbela."

"And it was carried through the country by those two wandering cinema men—the ones we actually met?"

"Yes. Simple well-known figures. Nothing political about them. Just Carmichael's personal friends. He had a lot of friends."

"He must have been very nice. I'm sorry he's dead."

"We've all got to die sometime," said Mr. Dakin. "And if there's another life after this which I myself fully believe, he'll have the satisfaction of knowing that his faith and his courage have done more to save this sorry old world from a fresh attack of bloodletting and misery than almost anyone that one can think of."

"It's odd, isn't it," said Victoria meditatively, "that Richard should have had one half of the secret and I should have had the other. It almost seems as though—"

"As though it were meant to be," finished Mr. Dakin with a twinkle. "And what are you going to do next, may I ask?"

"I shall have to find a job," said Victoria. "I must start looking about."

"Don't look too hard," said Mr. Dakin. "I rather think a job is coming towards you."

He ambled gently away to give place to Richard Baker.

"Look here, Victoria," said Richard. "Venetia Savile can't come out after all. Apparently she's got mumps. You were quite useful on the dig. Would you like to come back? Only your keep, I'm afraid. And probably your passage back to England—but we'll talk about that later. Mrs. Pauncefoot Jones is coming out next week. Well, what do you say?"

"Oh, do you really want me?" cried Victoria.

For some reason Richard Baker became very pink in the face. He coughed and polished his pince-nez.

"I think," he said, "we could find you—er—quite useful."

"I'd love it," said Victoria.

"In that case," said Richard, "you'd better collect your luggage and come along back to the dig now. You don't want to hang about Baghdad, do you?"

"Not in the least," said Victoria.

"So there you are, my dear Veronica," said Dr. Pauncefoot Jones. "Richard went off in a great state about you. Well, well—I hope you'll both be very happy."

"What does he mean?" asked Victoria bewildered, as Dr. Pauncefoot Jones pottered away.

"Nothing," said Richard. "You know what he's like. He's being—just a little—premature."

SO MANY
STEPS
TO
DEATH

To
ANTHONY
who likes foreign travel
as much as I do

1

THE MAN BEHIND the desk moved a heavy glass paperweight four inches to the right. His face was not so much thoughtful or abstracted as expressionless. He had the pale complexion that comes from living most of the day in artificial light. This man, you felt, was an indoor man. A man of desks and files. The fact that to reach his office you had to walk through long twisting underground corridors was somehow strangely appropriate. It would have been difficult to guess his age. He looked neither old nor young. His face was smooth and unwrinkled, and in his eyes was a great tiredness.

The other man in the room was older. He was dark with a small military moustache. There was about him an alert nervous energy. Even now, unable to sit still, he was pacing up and down, from time to time throwing off a remark in a jerky manner.

"Reports!" he said explosively. "Reports, reports and more reports, and none of them any damn good!"

The man at the desk looked down at the papers in front of him. On top was an official card headed, "Betterton, Thomas Charles." After the name was an interrogation mark. The man at the desk nodded thoughtfully. He said,

"You've followed up these reports and none of them any good?"

The other shrugged his shoulders.

"How can one tell?" he asked.

The man behind the desk sighed.

"Yes," he said, "there is that. One can't tell really."

The older man went on with a kind of machine gun volley abruptness,

"Reports from Rome; reports from Touraine; seen on the Riviera; noticed in Antwerp; definitely identified in Oslo; positively seen in Biarritz; observed behaving suspiciously in Strasburg; seen on the beach at Ostend with a glamorous blonde; noticed walking in the streets in Brussels with a grayhound! Hasn't been seen yet in the Zoo with his arm round a zebra, but I daresay that will come!"

"You've no particular fancy yourself, Wharton? Personally I had hopes of

481

the Antwerp report, but it hasn't led to anything. Of course by now . . ." the young man stopped speaking and seemed to go into a coma. Presently he came out of it again and said cryptically, "Yes, probably . . . and yet—I wonder?"

Colonel Wharton sat down abruptly on the arm of a chair.

"But we've got to find out," he said insistently. "We've got to break the back of all this *how* and *why* and *where?* You can't lose a tame scientist every month or so and have no idea *how* they go or *why* they go or *where!* Is it where we think—or isn't it? We've always taken it for granted that it is, but now I'm not so sure. You've read all the last dope on Betterton from America?"

The man behind the desk nodded.

"Usual Left Wing tendencies at the period when everyone had them. Nothing of a lasting or permanent nature as far as can be found out. Did sound work before the war though nothing spectacular. When Mannheim escaped from Germany Betterton was assigned as Assistant to him, and ended by marrying Mannheim's daughter. After Mannheim's death he carried on, on his own, and did brilliant work. He leaped into fame with the startling discovery of ZE Fission. ZE Fission was a brilliant and absolutely revolutionary discovery. It put Betterton absolutely tops. He was all set for a brilliant career over there, but his wife had died soon after their marriage and he was all broken up over it. He came to England. He has been at Harwell for the last eighteen months. Just six months ago he married again."

"Anything there?" asked Wharton sharply.

The other shook his head.

Not that we can find out. She's the daughter of a local solicitor. Worked in an insurance office before her marriage. No violent political affinities so far as we've been able to discover."

"ZE Fission," said Colonel Wharton gloomily, with distaste. "What they mean by all these terms beats me. I'm old-fashioned. I never really even visualized a molecule, but here they are nowadays splitting up the universe! Atom bombs, Nuclear fission, ZE fission, and all the rest of it. And Betterton was one of the splitters in chief! What do they say of him at Harwell?"

"Quite a pleasant personality. As to his work, nothing outstanding or spectacular. Just variations on the practical applications of ZEF."

Both men were silent for a moment. Their conversation had been desultory, almost automatic. The security reports lay in a pile on the desk and the security reports had had nothing of value to tell.

"He was thoroughly screened on arrival here, of course," said Wharton.

"Yes, everything was quite satisfactory."

"Eighteen months ago," said Wharton thoughtfully. "It gets 'em down, you know. Security precautions. The feeling of being perpetually under the microscope, the cloistered life. They get nervy, queer. I've seen it often enough. They begin to dream of an ideal world. Freedom and brotherhood, and pool-all-secrets and work for the good of humanity! That's exactly the moment when someone who's more or less the dregs of humanity, sees his chance and takes it!" He rubbed his nose. "Nobody's so gullible as the scientist," he said. "All the phony mediums say so. Can't quite see why."

The other smiled, a very tired smile.

"Oh, yes," he said, "it would be so. They think they *know,* you see. That's always dangerous. Now, our kind are different. We're humble-minded men. We don't expect to save the world, only pick up one or two broken pieces and remove a monkey wrench or two when it's jamming up the works." He tapped thoughtfully on the table with his finger. "If I only knew a little more about Betterton," he said. "Not his life and actions, but the revealing, everyday things. What sort of jokes he laughed at. What made him swear. Who were the people he admired and who made him mad."

Wharton looked at him curiously.

"What about the wife—you've tried her?"

"Several times."

"Can't she help?"

The other shrugged his shoulders.

"She hasn't so far."

"You think she knows something?"

"She doesn't admit, of course, that she knows anything. All the established reactions: worry, grief, desperate anxiety, no cue or suspicion beforehand, husband's life perfectly normal, no stress of any kind—and so on and so on. Her own theory is that he's been kidnapped."

"And you don't believe her?"

"I'm handicapped," said the man behind the desk bitterly. "I never believe anybody."

"Well," said Wharton slowly, "I suppose one has to keep an open mind. What's she like?"

"Ordinary sort of woman you'd meet any day playing bridge."

Wharton nodded comprehendingly.

"That makes it more difficult," he said.

"She's here to see me now. We shall go over all the same ground again."

"It's the only way," said Wharton. "*I* couldn't do it, though. Haven't got the patience." He got up. "Well, I won't keep you. We've not got much further, have we?"

"Unfortunately, no. You might do a special checkup on that Oslo report. It's a likely spot."

Wharton nodded and went out. The other man raised the receiver by his elbow and said:

"I'll see Mrs. Betterton now. Send her in."

He sat staring into space until there was a tap on the door and Mrs. Betterton was shown in. She was a tall woman, about twenty-seven years of age. The most noticeable thing about her was a most magnificent head of auburn red hair. Beneath the splendor of this, her face seemed almost insignificant. She had the blue eyes and light eyelashes that so often go with red hair. She was wearing no makeup, he noticed. He considered the significance of that while he was greeting her, settling her comfortably in a chair near the desk. It inclined him very slightly to the belief that Mrs. Betterton knew more than she had said she knew.

In his experience, women suffering from violent grief and anxiety did not neglect their makeup. Aware of the ravages grief made in their appearance, they did their best to repair those ravages. He wondered if Mrs. Betterton calculatingly abstained from makeup, the better to sustain the part of the distracted wife. She said now, rather breathlessly,

"Oh, Mr. Jessop, I do hope—is there any news?"

He shook his head and said gently,

"I'm so sorry to ask you to come up like this, Mrs. Betterton. I'm afraid we haven't got any definite news for you."

Olive Betterton said quickly,

"I know. You said so in your letter. But I wondered if—since then—oh! I was glad to come up. Just sitting at home wondering and brooding—that's the worst of it all. Because there's nothing one *can* do!"

The man called Jessop said soothingly:

"You mustn't mind, Mrs. Betterton, if I go over the same ground again and again, ask you the same questions, stress the same points. You see it's always possible that some small point *might* arise. Something that you hadn't thought of before, or perhaps hadn't thought worth mentioning."

"Yes. Yes, I understand. Ask me all over again about everything."

"The last time you saw your husband was on the 23rd of August?"

"Yes."

"That was when he left England to go to Paris to a Conference there."

"Yes."

Jessop went on rapidly,

"He attended the first two days of the Conference. The third day he did not turn up. Apparently he had mentioned to one of his colleagues that he was going instead for a trip on a *bateau mouche* that day."

"A *bateau mouche?* What's a *bateau mouche?*"

Jessop smiled.

"One of those small boats that go along the Seine." He looked at her sharply. "Does that strike you as unlike your husband?"

She said doubtfully,

"It does, rather. I should have thought he'd be so keen on what was going on at the Conference."

"Possibly. Still the subject for discussion on this particular day was not one in which he had any special interest, so he might reasonably have given himself a day off. But it doesn't strike you as being quite like your husband?"

She shook her head.

"He did not return that evening to his hotel," went on Jessop. "As far as can be ascertained he did not pass any frontier, certainly not on his own passport. Do you think he could have had a second passport, in another name perhaps?"

"Oh, no, why should he?"

He watched her.

"You never saw such a thing in his possession?"

She shook her head with vehemence.

"No, and I don't believe it. I don't believe it for a moment. I don't believe he went away deliberately as you all try to make out. Something's happened to him, or else—or else perhaps he's lost his memory."

"His health had been quite normal?"

"Yes. He was working rather hard and sometimes felt a little tired, nothing more than that."

"He'd not seemed worried in any way or depressed?"

"He wasn't worried or depressed about *anything!*" With shaking fingers she opened her bag and took out her handkerchief. "It's all so awful." Her voice shook. "I can't believe it. He'd never have gone off without a word to me. Something's happened to him. He's been kidnapped or he's been attacked perhaps. I try not to think it but sometimes I feel that that must be the solution. He must be dead."

"Now please, Mrs. Betterton, please—there's no need to entertain that supposition yet. If he's dead, his body would have been discovered by now."

"It might not. Awful things happen. He might have been drowned or pushed down a sewer. I'm sure anything could happen in Paris."

"Paris, I can assure you, Mrs. Betterton, is a very well policed city."

She took the handkerchief away from her eyes and stared at him with sharp anger.

"I know what you think, but it isn't so! Tom wouldn't sell secrets or betray secrets. He wasn't a communist. His whole life is an open book."

"What were his political beliefs, Mrs. Betterton?"

"In America he was a Democrat, I believe. Here he voted Labour. He wasn't interested in politics. He was a scientist, first and last." She added defiantly, "He was a brilliant scientist."

"Yes," said Jessop, "he was a brilliant scientist. That's really the crux of the whole matter. He might have been offered, you know, very considerable inducements to leave this country and go elsewhere."

"It's not true." Anger leaped out again. "That's what the papers try to make out. That's what you all think when you come questioning me. It's not true. He'd never go without telling me, without giving me some idea."

"And he told you—nothing?"

Again he was watching her keenly.

"Nothing. I don't know where he is. I think he was kidnapped, or else, as I say, dead. But if he's dead, I must know. I must know soon. I can't go on like this, waiting and wondering. I can't eat or sleep. I'm sick and ill with worry. Can't you help me? Can't you help me *at all?*"

He got up then and moved around his desk. He murmured,

"I'm so very sorry, Mrs. Betterton, so very sorry. Let me assure you that we are trying our very best to find out what has happened to your husband. We get reports in every day from various places."

"Reports from where?" she asked sharply. "What do they say?"

He shook his head.

"They all have to be followed up, sifted and tested. But as a rule, I am afraid, they're vague in the extreme."

"I must *know*," she murmured brokenly again. "I can't go on like this."

"Do you care for your husband very much, Mrs. Betterton?"

"Of course I care for him. Why, we've only been married six months. Only six months."

"Yes, I know. There was—forgive me for asking—no quarrel of any kind between you?"

"Oh, *no!*"

"No trouble over any other woman?"

"Of course not. I've told you. We were only married last April."

"Please believe that I'm not suggesting such a thing is likely, but one has to take every possibility into account that might allow for his going off in this way. You say he had not been upset lately, or worried—not on edge—not nervy in any way?"

"No, no, *no!*"

"People do get nervy, you know, Mrs. Betterton, in such a job as your husband had. Living under exacting security conditions. In fact—" he smiled, "—it's almost normal to be nervy."

She did not smile back.

"He was just as usual," she said stolidly.

"Happy about his work? Did he discuss it at all with you?"

"No, it was all so technical."

"You don't think he had any qualms over its—destructive possibilities, shall I say? Scientists do feel that sometimes."

"He never said anything of the kind."

"You see, Mrs. Betterton," he leaned forward over the desk, dropping some of his impassiveness, "what I am trying to do is to get a picture of your husband. The sort of man he was. And somehow you're not helping me."

"But what more can I say or do? I've answered all your questions."

"Yes, you've answered my questions, mostly in the negative. I want something positive, something constructive. Do you see what I mean? You can look for a man so much better when you know what kind of a man he is."

She reflected for a moment. "I see. At least, I suppose I see. Well, Tom was cheerful and good-tempered. And clever, of course."

Jessop smiled.

"That's a list of qualities. Let's try and get more personal. Did he read much?"

"Yes, a fair amount."

"What sort of books?"

"Oh, biographies. Book Society recommendations, crime stories if he was tired."

"Rather a conventional reader, in fact. No special preferences? Did he play cards or chess?"

"He played bridge. We used to play with Dr. Evans and his wife once or twice a week."

"Did your husband have many friends?"

"Oh, yes, he was a good mixer."

"I didn't mean just that. I mean was he a man who—cared very much for his friends?"

"He played golf with one or two of our neighbors."

"No special friends or cronies of his own?"

"No. You see, he'd been in the U.S.A. for so long, and he was born in Canada. He didn't know many people over here."

Jessop consulted a scrap of paper at his elbow.

"Three people visited him recently from the States, I understand. I have their names here. As far as we can discover, these three were the only people with whom he recently made contact from *outside,* so to speak. That's why we've given them special attention. Now first, Walter Griffiths. He came to see you at Harwell."

"Yes, he was over in England on a visit and he came to look up Tom."

"And your husband's reactions?"

"Tom was surprised to see him, but very pleased. They'd known each other quite well in the States."

"What did this Griffiths seem like to you? Just describe him in your own way."

"But surely you know all about him?"

"Yes, we know all about him. But I want to hear what you thought of him."

She reflected for a moment.

"Well, he was solemn and rather long-winded. Very polite to me and seemed very fond of Tom and anxious to tell him about things that had happened after Tom had come to England. All local gossip I suppose. It wasn't very interesting to me because I didn't know any of the people. Anyway, I was getting dinner ready while they were reminiscing."

"No question of politics came up?"

"You're trying to hint that he was a communist." Olive Betterton's face flushed. "I'm sure he was nothing of the sort. He had some government job— in the District Attorney's office, I think. And anyway when Tom said something laughing about witch hunts in America, he said solemnly that we didn't understand over here. They were *necessary.* So that shows he *wasn't* a communist!"

"Please, please, Mrs. Betterton, now don't get upset."

"Tom wasn't a communist! I keep telling you so and you don't believe me."

"Yes, I do, but the point is bound to come up. Now for the second contact from abroad, Dr. Mark Lucas. You ran across him in London in the Dorset."

"Yes. We'd gone up to do a show and we were having supper at the Dorset afterwards. Suddenly this man, Luke or Lucas, came along and greeted Tom. He was a research chemist of some kind and the last time he had seen Tom was in the States. He was a German refugee who'd taken American nationality. But surely you . . ."

"But surely I know that? Yes, I do, Mrs. Betterton. Was your husband surprised to see him?"

"Yes, very surprised."

"Pleased?"

"Yes, yes—I think so—"

"But you're not sure?" He pressed her.

"Well, he was a man Tom didn't much care about, or so he told me afterwards, that's all."

"It was just a casual meeting? There was no arrangement made to meet at some future date?"

"No, it was just a casual encounter."

"I see. The third contact from abroad was a woman, Mrs. Carol Speeder, also from the States. How did that come about?"

"She was something to do with UNO, I believe. She'd known Tom in America, and she rang him up from London to say she was over here, and asked if we could come up and lunch one day."

"And did you?"

"No."

"*You* didn't, but your husband did!"

"What!" She stared.

"He didn't tell you?"

"No."

Olive Betterton looked bewildered and uneasy. The man questioning her felt a little sorry for her, but he did not relent. For the first time he thought he might be getting somewhere.

"I don't understand it," she said uncertainly. "It seems very odd he shouldn't have said anything about it to me."

"They lunched together at the Dorset where Mrs. Speeder was staying, on Wednesday August 12th."

"August 12th?"

"Yes."

"Yes, he did go to London about then. . . . He never said anything—" she broke off again, and then shot out a question. "What is she like?"

He answered quickly and reassuringly.

"Not at all a glamorous type, Mrs. Betterton. A competent young career woman of thirty-odd, not particularly good-looking. There's absolutely no suggestion of her ever having been on intimate terms with your husband. That is just why it's odd that he didn't tell you about the meeting."

"Yes, yes, I see that."

"Now think carefully, Mrs. Betterton. Did you notice any change in your husband about that time? About the middle of August, shall we say? That would be about a week before the conference."

"No—No, I noticed nothing. There was nothing to notice."

Jessop sighed.

The instrument on his desk buzzed discreetly. He picked up the receiver.

"Yes," he said.

The voice at the other end said,

"There's a man who's asking to see someone in authority about the Betterton case, sir."

"What's his name?"

The voice at the other end coughed discreetly.

"Well, I'm not exactly sure how you pronounce it, Mr. Jessop. Perhaps I'd better spell it."

"Right. Go ahead."

He jotted down on his blotter the letters as they came over the wire.

"Polish?" he said interrogatively, at the end.

"He didn't say, sir. He speaks English quite well, but with a bit of an accent."

"Ask him to wait."

"Very good, sir."

Jessop replaced the telephone. Then he looked across at Olive Betterton. She sat there quite quietly with a disarming, hopeless placidity. He tore off the leaf on his desk pad with the name he had just written on it, and shoved it across to her.

"Know anybody of that name?" he asked.

Her eyes widened as she looked at it. For a moment he thought she looked frightened.

"Yes," she said. "Yes, I do. He wrote to me."

"When?"

"Yesterday. He's a cousin of Tom's first wife. He's just arrived in this country. He was very concerned about Tom's disappearance. He wrote to ask if I had had any news and—and to give me his most profound sympathy."

"You'd never heard of him before that?"

She shook her head.

"Ever hear your husband speak of him?"

"No."

"So really he mightn't be your husband's cousin at all?"

"Well, no, I suppose not. I never thought of that." She looked startled. "But Tom's first wife was a foreigner. She was Professor Mannheim's daughter. This man seemed to know all about her and Tom in his letter. It was very correct and formal and—and foreign, you know. It seemed quite genuine. And anyway, what would be the point—if he weren't genuine, I mean?"

"Ah, that's what one always asks oneself." Jessop smiled faintly. "We do it so much here that we begin to see the smallest thing quite out of proportion!"

"Yes, I should think you might." She shivered suddenly. "It's like this room of yours, in the middle of a labyrinth of corridors, just like a dream when you think you will never get out. . . ."

"Yes, yes, I can see it might have a claustrophobic effect," said Jessop pleasantly.

Olive Betterton put a hand up and pushed back her hair from her forehead.

"I can't stand it much longer, you know," she said. "Just sitting and waiting. I want to get away somewhere for a change. Abroad for choice. Somewhere where reporters won't ring me up all the time, and people stare at me. I'm always meeting friends and they keep asking if I have had any news?" She paused, then went on, "I think—I think I'm going to break down. I've tried to be brave, but it's too much for me. My doctor agrees. He says I ought to go right away somewhere for three or four weeks. He wrote me a letter. I'll show you."

She fumbled in her bag, took out an envelope and pushed it across the desk to Jessop.

"You'll see what he says."

Jessop took the letter out of the envelope and read it.

"Yes," he said. "Yes, I see."

He put the letter back in the envelope.

"So—so it would be all right for me to go?" Her eyes watched him nervously.

"But of course, Mrs. Betterton," he replied. He raised surprised eyebrows. "Why not?"

"I thought you might object."

"Object—why? It's entirely your own business. You'll arrange it so that I can get in touch with you while you're away in case any news should come through."

"Oh, of course."

"Where were you thinking of going?"

"Somewhere where there is sun and not too many English people. Spain or Morocco."

"Very nice. Do you a lot of good, I'm sure."

"Oh, thank you. Thank you very much."

She rose, excited, elated—her nervousness still apparent.

Jessop rose, shook hands with her, pressed the buzzer for a messenger to see her out. He went back to his chair and sat down. For a few moments his face remained as expressionless as before, then very slowly he smiled. He lifted the phone.

"I'll see Major Glydr now," he said.

2

"MAJOR GLYDR?" JESSOP hesitated a little over the name.

"It is difficult, yes." The visitor spoke with humorous appreciation. "Your compatriots, they have called me Glider in the war. And now, in the States, I shall change my name to Glyn, which is more convenient for all."

"You come from the States now?"

"Yes, I arrive a week ago. You are—excuse me—Mr. Jessop?"

"I'm Jessop."

The other looked at him with interest.

"So," he said. "I have heard of you."

"Indeed? From whom?"

The other smiled.

"Perhaps we go too fast. Before you permit that I should ask you some questions, I present you first this letter from the U.S. Embassy."

He passed it with a bow. Jessop took it, read the few lines of polite introduction, put it down. He looked appraisingly at his visitor. A tall man, carrying himself rather stiffly, aged thirty or thereabouts. The fair hair was close cropped in the continental fashion. The stranger's speech was slow and careful with a very definite foreign intonation, though grammatically correct. He was, Jessop noticed, not at all nervous or unsure of himself. That in itself was unusual. Most of the people who came into this office were nervous or excited or apprehensive. Sometimes they were shifty, sometimes vehement.

This was a man who had complete command of himself, a man with a poker face who knew what he was doing and why, and who would not be easily tricked or betrayed into saying more than he meant to say. Jessop said pleasantly,

"And what can we do for you?"

"I came to ask if you had any further news of Thomas Betterton, who disappeared recently in what seems a somewhat sensational manner. One cannot, I know, believe exactly what one reads in the press, so I ask where I can go for reliable information. They tell me—*you.*"

"I'm sorry we've no definite information about Betterton."

"I thought perhaps he might have been sent abroad on some mission." He paused and added, rather quaintly, "You know, hush-hush."

"My dear sir." Jessop looked pained. "Betterton was a scientist, not a diplomat or a secret agent."

"I am rebuked. But labels are not always correct. You will want to inquire my interest in the matter. Thomas Betterton was a relation of mine by marriage."

"Yes. You are the nephew, I believe, of the late Professor Mannheim."

"Ah, that you knew already. You are well informed here."

491

"People come along and tell us things," murmured Jessop. "Betterton's wife was here. She told me. You had written to her."

"Yes, to express my condolences and to ask if she had had any further news."

"That was very correct."

"My mother was Professor Mannheim's only sister. They were much attached. In Warsaw when I was a child I was much at my uncle's house, and his daughter, Elsa, was to me like a sister. When my father and mother died my home was with my uncle and cousin. They were happy days. Then came the war, the tragedies, the horrors. . . . Of all that we will not speak. My uncle and Elsa escaped to America. I myself remained in the underground Resistance, and after the war ended I had certain assignments. One visit I paid to America to see my uncle and cousin, that was all. But there came a time when my commitments in Europe are ended. I intend to reside in the States permanently. I shall be, I hope, near my uncle and my cousin and her husband. But alas—" he spread out his hands, "—I get there and my uncle, he is dead, my cousin, too, and her husband he has come to this country and has married again. So once more I have no family. And then I read of the disappearance of the well-known scientist Thomas Betterton, and I come over to see what can be done." He paused and looked enquiringly at Jessop.

Jessop looked expressionlessly back at him.

"Why did he disappear, Mr. Jessop?"

"That," said Jessop pleasantly, "is just what we'd like to know."

"Perhaps you do know?"

Jessop appreciated with some interest how easily their roles might become reversed. In this room he was accustomed to ask questions of people. This stranger was not the inquisitor. Still smiling pleasantly, Jessop replied,

"I assure you we do not."

"But you suspect?"

"It is possible," said Jessop cautiously, "that the thing follows a certain pattern. . . . There have been occurrences of this kind before."

"I know." Rapidly the visitor cited a half dozen cases. "All scientists," he said, with significance.

"Yes."

"They have gone beyond the Iron Curtain?"

"It is a possibility, but we do not know."

"But they have gone of their own free will?"

"Even that," said Jessop, "is difficult to say."

"It is not my business you think?"

"Oh, please."

"But you are right. It is of interest to me only because of Betterton."

"You'll forgive me," said Jessop, "if I don't quite understand your interest. After all, Betterton is only a relation by marriage. You didn't even know him."

"That is true. But for us Poles, the family is very important. There are obligations." He stood up and bowed stiffly. "I regret that I have trespassed upon your time, and I thank you for your courtesy."

Jessop rose also.

"I'm sorry we cannot help you," he said, "but I assure you we are completely in the dark. If I do hear of anything can I reach you?"

"Care of the U.S. Embassy will find me. I thank you." Again he bowed formally.

Jessop touched the buzzer. Major Glydr went out. Jessop lifted the receiver.

"Ask Colonel Wharton to come to my room."

When Wharton entered the room Jessop said:

"Things are moving—at last."

"How?"

"Mrs. Betterton wants to go abroad."

Wharton whistled.

"Going to join hubby?"

"I'm hopeful. She came provided with a convenient letter from her medical adviser. Complete need of rest and change of scene."

"Looks good!"

"Though, of course, it may be true," Jessop warned him. "A simple statement of fact."

"We never take that view here," said Wharton.

"No. I must say she does her stuff very convincingly. Never slips up for a moment."

"You got nothing further from her, I suppose?"

"One faint lead. The Speeder woman with whom Betterton lunched at the Dorset."

"Yes?"

"He didn't tell his wife about the lunch."

"Oh." Wharton considered. "You think that's relevant?"

"It might be. Carol Speeder was had up before the Committee for the investigation of un-American Activities. She cleared herself, but all the same . . . yes, all the same she was, or they thought she was, tarred with that brush. It *may* be a possible contact. The only one we've found for Betterton so far."

"What about Mrs. Betterton's contacts—any possible contact lately who could have instigated the going abroad business?"

"No personal contact. She had a letter yesterday from a Pole. A cousin of Betterton's first wife. I had him here just now asking for details, etc."

"What's he like?"

"Not real," said Jessop. "All very foreign and correct, got all the 'gen,' curiously unreal as a personality."

"Think he's been the contact to tip her off?"

"It could be. I don't know. He puzzles me."

"Going to keep tabs on him?"

Jessop smiled.

"Yes. I pressed the buzzer twice."

"You old spider—with your tricks." Wharton became businesslike again. "Well, what's the form?"

"Janet, I think, and the usual. Spain, or Morocco."

"Not Switzerland?"

"Not this time."

"I should have thought Spain or Morocco would have been difficult for them."

"We mustn't underestimate our adversaries."

Wharton flipped the security files disgustedly with his nail.

"About the only two countries where Betterton *hasn't* been seen," he said with chagrin. "Well, we'll lay it all on. My God, if we fall down on the job this time—"

Jessop leaned back in his chair.

"It's a long time since I've had a holiday," he said. "I'm rather sick of this office. I *might* take a little trip abroad. . . ."

3

"FLIGHT 108 TO Paris. Air France. This way please."

The persons in the lounge at Heathrow Airport rose to their feet. Hilary Craven picked up her small, lizardskin traveling case and moved in the wake of the others, out onto the tarmac. The wind blew sharply cold after the heated air of the lounge.

Hilary shivered and drew her furs a little closer round her. She followed the other passengers across to where the aircraft was waiting. This was it! She was off—escaping! Out of the grayness, the coldness, the dead numb misery. Escaping to sunshine and blue skies and a new life. She would leave all this weight behind, this dead weight of misery and frustration. She went up the gangway of her plane, bending her head as she passed inside and was shown by the steward to her seat. For the first time in months she savored relief from a pain that had been so sharply acute as almost to be physical. "I shall get away," she said to herself, hopefully. "I *shall* get away."

The roaring and the revolutions of the plane excited her. There seemed a kind of elemental savagery in it. Civilized misery, she thought, is the worst misery. Gray and hopeless. "But now," she thought, "I shall escape."

The plane taxied gently along the runway. The air hostess said:

"Fasten your belts, please."

The plane made a half turn and stood waiting its signal to depart. Hilary thought, "Perhaps the plane will crash. . . . Perhaps it will never rise off the ground. Then that will be the end, that will be the solution to everything." They seemed to wait for ages out on the airfield. Waiting for the signal to start off to freedom, Hilary thought, absurdly; "I shall never get away, never. I shall be kept here—a prisoner. . . ."

Ah, at last.

A final roar of engines, then the plane started forward. Quicker, quicker, racing along. Hilary thought, "It won't rise. It can't. . . . This is the end." Ah, they were above the ground now, it seemed. Not so much that the plane rose as that the earth was falling away, dropping down, thrusting its problems and its disappointments and its frustrations beneath the soaring creature rising up so proudly into the clouds. Up they went, circling round, the airport looking like a ridiculous child's toy beneath. Funny little roads, strange little railways with toy trains on them. A ridiculous childish world where people loved and hated and broke their hearts. None of it mattered because they were all so ridiculous and so pettily small and unimportant. Now there were clouds below them, a dense, grayish-white mass. They must be over the Channel now. Hilary leaned back, closing her eyes. Escape. Escape. She had left England, left Nigel, left the sad little mound that was Brenda's grave. All left behind. She opened her eyes, closed them again with a long sigh. She slept. . . .

ii

When Hilary awoke, the plane was coming down. "Paris," thought Hilary, as she sat up in her seat and reached for her handbag. But it was not Paris. The air hostess came down the car saying, with that nursery governess brightness that some travelers found so annoying:

"We are landing you at Beauvais as the fog is very thick in Paris."

The suggestion in her manner was: "Won't that be nice, children?" Hilary peered down through the small space of window at her side. She could see little. Beauvais also appeared to be wreathed in fog. The plane was circling round slowly. It was some time before it finally made its landing. Then the passengers were marshaled through cold, damp mist into a rough wooden building with a few chairs and a long wooden counter.

Depression settled down on Hilary but she tried to fight it off. A man near her murmured:

"An old war airport. No heating or comforts here. Still, fortunately being the French, they'll serve us out some drinks."

True enough, almost immediately a man came along with some keys and presently passengers were being served with various forms of alcoholic refreshment to boost their morale. It helped to buoy the passengers up for the long and irritating wait.

Some hours passed before anything happened. Other planes appeared out of the fog and landed, also diverted from Paris. Soon the small room was crowded with cold, irritable people grumbling about the delay.

To Hilary it all had an unreal quality. It was as though she was still in a dream, mercifully protected from contact with reality. This was only a delay, only a matter of waiting. She was still on her journey—her journey of escape. She was still getting away from it all, still going toward that spot where her life would start again. Her mood held. Held through the long, fatiguing delay, held through the moments of chaos when it was announced, long after dark, that buses had come to convey the travelers to Paris.

There was then a wild confusion, of coming and going, passengers, officials, porters all carrying baggage, hurrying and colliding in the darkness. In the end Hilary found herself, her feet and legs icy cold, in a bus slowly rumbling its way through the fog toward Paris.

It was a long weary drive taking four hours. It was midnight when they arrived at the Invalides and Hilary was thankful to collect her baggage and drive to the hotel where accommodation was reserved for her. She was too tired to eat—just had a hot bath and tumbled into bed.

The plane to Casablanca was due to leave Orly Airport at ten-thirty the following morning, but when they arrived at Orly everything was confusion. Planes had been grounded in many parts of Europe, arrivals had been delayed as well as departures.

A harassed clerk at the departure desk shrugged his shoulders and said:

"Impossible for Madame to go on the flight where she had reservations! The schedules have all had to be changed. If Madame will take a seat for a little minute, presumably all will arrange itself." In the end she was summoned and told that there was a place on a plane going to Dakar which normally did not touch down at Casablanca but would do so on this occasion.

"You will arrive three hours later, that is all, Madame, on this later service."

Hilary acquiesced without protest and the official seemed surprised and positively delighted by her attitude.

"Madame has no conceptions of the difficulties that have been made to me this morning," he said. *"Enfin,* they are unreasonable, Messieurs the travelers. It is not I who made the fog! Naturally it has caused the disruptions. One must accommodate oneself with the good humor—that is what I say, however displeasing it is to have one's plans altered. *Après tout,* Madame, a little delay of an hour or two hours or three hours, what does it matter? How can it matter by what plane one arrives at Casablanca?"

Yet on that particular day it mattered more than the little Frenchman knew when he spoke those words. For when Hilary finally arrived and stepped out into the sunshine onto the tarmac, the porter who was moving beside her with his piled-up trolley of luggage observed:

"You have the lucky chance, Madame, not to have been on the plane before this, the regular plane for Casablanca."

Hilary said: "Why, what happened?"

The man looked uneasily to and fro, but after all, the news could not be kept secret. He lowered his voice confidentially and leaned toward her.

"Mauvaise affaire!" he muttered. "It crashed—landing. The pilot and the navigator are dead and most of the passengers. Four or five were alive and have been taken to hospital. Some of those are badly hurt."

Hilary's first reaction was a kind of blinding anger. Almost unprompted there leaped into her mind the thought, "Why wasn't *I* in that plane? If I had been, it would have been all over now—I should be dead, out of it all. No more heartaches, no more misery. The people in that plane wanted to live. And I—I don't care. Why shouldn't it have been me?"

She passed through the Customs, a perfunctory affair, and drove with her baggage to the hotel. It was a glorious, sunlit afternoon, with the sun just sinking to rest. The clear air and golden light—it was all as she had pictured it. She had arrived! She had left the fog, the cold, the darkness of London; she had left behind her misery and indecision and suffering. Here there was pulsating life and color and sunshine.

She crossed her bedroom and threw open the shutters, looking out into the street. Yes, it was all as she had pictured it would be. Hilary turned slowly away from the window and sat down on the side of the bed. Escape, escape! That was the refrain that had hummed incessantly in her mind ever since she left England. Escape. Escape. And now she knew—knew with a horrible, stricken coldness, *that there was no escape.*

Everything was just the same here as it had been in London. She herself, Hilary Craven, was the same. It was from Hilary Craven that she was trying to escape, and Hilary Craven was Hilary Craven in Morocco just as much as she had been Hilary Craven in London. She said very softly to herself:

"What a fool I've been—what a fool I *am.* Why did I think that I'd feel differently if I got away from England?"

Brenda's grave, that small pathetic mound, was in England and Nigel would shortly be marrying his new wife, in England. Why had she imagined that those two things would matter less to her here? Wishful thinking, that was all. Well, that was all over now. She was up against reality. The reality of herself and what she could bear, and what she could *not* bear. One could bear things, Hilary thought, so long as there was a *reason* for bearing them. She had borne her own long illness, she had borne Nigel's defection and the cruel and brutal circumstances in which it had operated. She had borne these things because there was Brenda. Then had come the long, slow, losing fight for Brenda's life—the final defeat. . . . Now there was nothing to live for any longer. It had taken the journey to Morocco to prove that to her. In London she had had a queer, confused feeling that if only she could get somewhere else she could forget what lay behind her and start again. And so she had booked her journey to this place which had no associations with the past, a place quite new to her which had the qualities she loved so much: sunlight, pure air and the strangeness of new people and things. Here, she had thought, things will be different. But they were not different. They were the same. The facts were quite simple and unescapable. She, Hilary Craven, had no longer any wish to go on living. It was as simple as that.

If the fog had not intervened, if she had traveled on the plane on which her reservations had been made, then her problem might have been solved by now. She might be lying now in some French official mortuary, a body broken and battered with her spirit at peace, freed from suffering. Well, the same end could be achieved, but she would have to take a little trouble.

It would have been so easy if she had had sleeping stuff with her. She remembered how she had asked Dr. Grey and the rather queer look on his face as he had answered:

"Better not. Much better to learn to sleep naturally. May be hard at first, but it will come."

A queer look on his face. Had he known then or suspected that it would come to this? Oh well, it should not be difficult. She rose to her feet with decision. She would go out now to a chemist's shop.

iii

Hilary had always imagined that drugs were easy to buy in foreign cities. Rather to her surprise, she found that this was not so. The chemist she went to first supplied her with only two doses. For more than that amount, he said, a doctor's prescription would be advisable. She thanked him smilingly and nonchalantly and went rather quickly out of the shop, colliding as she did so with a tall, rather solemn-faced young man, who apologized in English. She heard him asking for toothpaste as she left the shop.

Somehow that amused her. Toothpaste. It seemed so ridiculous, so normal, so everyday. Then a sharp pang pierced her, for the toothpaste he had asked for was the brand that Nigel had always preferred. She crossed the street and went into a shop opposite. She had been to four chemists' shops by the time she returned to the hotel. It had amused her a little that in the third shop the owlish young man had again appeared, once more asking obstinately for his particular brand of toothpaste which evidently was not one commonly stocked by French chemists in Casablanca.

Hilary felt almost lighthearted as she changed her frock and made up her face before going down for dinner. She purposely went down as late as possible since she was anxious not to encounter any of her fellow travelers or the personnel of the airplane. That was hardly likely in any case, since the plane had gone on to Dakar, she thought that she had been the only person put off at Casablanca.

The restaurant was almost empty by the time she came into it, though she noticed that the young Englishman with the owllike face was just finishing his meal at the table by the wall. He was reading a French newspaper and seemed quite absorbed in it.

Hilary ordered herself a good meal with a half bottle of wine. She was feeling a heady kind of excitement. She thought to herself, "What is this after all, but the last adventure?" Then she ordered a bottle of Vichy water to be sent up to her room and went straight up after leaving the dining room.

The waiter brought the Vichy, uncapped it, placed it on the table, and wishing her goodnight, left the room. Hilary drew a sigh of relief. As he closed the door after him, she went to it and turned the key in the lock. She took from the drawer of the dressing table the four little packets she had obtained from the chemists, and unwrapped them. She laid the tablets out on the table and poured herself out a glass of Vichy water. Since the drugs were in tablet form, she had only to swallow them, and wash them down with the Vichy water.

She undressed, wrapped her dressing gown round her and came back to sit by the table. Her heart beat faster. She felt something like fear now, but the fear was half fascination and not the kind of flinching that would have tempted her to abandon her plan. She was quite calm and clear about that. This was escape at last—real escape. She looked at the writing table, debating whether she would leave a note. She decided against it. She had no relations, no close or dear friends, there was nobody to whom she wished to say good-bye. As for Nigel, she had no wish to burden him with useless remorse even if a note from her would have achieved that object. Nigel would read presumably in the paper that a Mrs. Hilary Craven had died of an overdose of sleeping tablets in Casablanca. It would probably be quite a small paragraph. He would accept it at its face value. "Poor old Hilary," he would say, "bad luck"—and it might be that, secretly, he would be rather relieved. Because she guessed that she was, slightly, on Nigel's conscience, and he was a man who wished to feel comfortable with himself.

Already Nigel seemed very far away and curiously unimportant. There was nothing more to be done. She would swallow the pills and lie down on her bed and sleep. From that sleep she would not wake. She had not, or thought she had not, any religious feeling. Brenda's death had shut down on all that. So there was nothing more to consider. She was once again a traveler as she had been at Heathrow Airport, a traveler waiting to depart for an unknown destination, unencumbered by baggage, unaffected by farewells. For the first time in her life she was free, entirely free, to act as she wished to act. Already the past was cut away from her. The long aching misery that had dragged her down in her waking hours was gone. Yes. Light, free, unencumbered! Ready to start on her journey.

She stretched out her hand toward the first tablet. As she did so there came a soft, discreet tap on the door. Hilary frowned. She sat there, her hand arrested in midair. Who was it—a chambermaid? No, the bed had already been turned down. Somebody, perhaps, about papers or passport? She shrugged her shoulders. She would not answer the door. Why should she bother? Presently whoever it was would go away and come back at some further opportunity.

The knock came again, a little louder this time. But Hilary did not move. There could be no real urgency, and whoever it was would soon go away.

Her eyes were on the door, and suddenly they widened with astonishment. The key was slowly turning backward round the lock. It jerked forward and fell on the floor with a metallic clang. Then the handle turned, the door opened and a man came in. She recognized him as the solemn, owlish young man who had been buying toothpaste. Hilary stared at him. She was too startled for the moment to say or do anything. The young man turned round, shut the door, picked the key up from the floor, put it into the lock and turned it. Then he came across toward her and sat down in a chair the other side of the table. He said, and it seemed to her a most incongruous remark:

"My name's Jessop."

The color rose sharply in Hilary's face. She leaned forward. She said with cold anger,

"What do you think you're doing here, may I ask?"

He looked at her solemnly—and blinked.

"Funny," he said. "I came to ask you that." He gave a quick sideways nod toward the preparations on the table. Hilary said sharply:

"I don't know what you mean."

"Oh yes, you do."

Hilary paused, struggling for words. There were so many things she wanted to say. To express indignation. To order him out of the room. But strangely enough, it was curiosity that won the day. The question rose to her lips so naturally that she was almost unaware of asking it.

"That key," she said, "it turned, of itself, in the lock?"

"Oh, that!" The young man gave a sudden boyish grin that transformed his face. He put his hand into his pocket, and taking out a metal instrument, he handed it to her to examine.

"There you are," he said, "very handy little tool. Insert it into the lock the other side, it grips the key and turns it." He took it back from her and put it in his pocket. "Burglars use them," he said.

"So you're a burglar?"

"No, no, Mrs. Craven, do me justice. I did knock, you know. Burglars don't knock. Then, when it seemed you weren't going to let me in, I used this."

"But why?"

Again her visitor's eyes strayed to the preparations on the table.

"I shouldn't do it if I were you," he said. "It isn't a bit what you think, you know. You think you just go to sleep and you don't wake up. But it's not quite like that. All sorts of unpleasant effects. Convulsions sometimes, gangrene of the skin. If you're resistant to the drug, it takes a long time to work, and someone gets to you in time and then all sorts of unpleasant things happen. Stomach pump. Castor oil, hot coffee, slapping and pushing. All very undignified, I assure you."

Hilary leaned back in her chair, her eyelids narrowed. She clenched her hands slightly. She forced herself to smile.

"What a ridiculous person you are," she said. "Do you imagine that I was committing suicide, or something like that?"

"Not only imagine it," said the young man called Jessop, "I'm quite sure of it. I was in that chemist, you know, when you came in. Buying toothpaste, as a matter of fact. Well, they hadn't got the sort I like, so I went to another shop. And there you were, asking for sleeping pills again. Well, I thought that was a bit odd, you know, so I followed you. All those sleeping pills at different places. It could only add up to one thing."

His tone was friendly, offhand, but quite assured. Looking at him Hilary Craven abandoned pretense.

"Then don't you think it is unwarrantable impertinence on your part to try and stop me?"

He considered the point for a moment or two. Then he shook his head.

"No. It's one of those things that you can't *not* do—if you understand."

Hilary spoke with energy. "You can stop me for the moment. I mean you can take the pills away—thrown them out of the window or something like that—but you can't stop me from buying more another day or throwing myself down from the top floor of the building, or jumping in front of a train."

The young man considered this.

"No," he said. "I agree I can't stop you doing any of those things. But it's a question, you know, whether you will do them. Tomorrow, that is."

"You think I shall feel differently tomorrow?" asked Hilary, faint bitterness in her tone.

"People do," said Jessop, almost apologetically.

"Yes, perhaps," she considered. "If you're doing things in a mood of hot despair. But when it's cold despair, it's different. I've nothing to live for, you see."

Jessop put his rather owlish head on one side, and blinked.

"Interesting," he remarked.

"Not really. Not interesting at all. I'm not a very interesting woman. My husband, whom I loved, left me, my only child died very painfully of meningitis. I've no near friends or relations. I've no vocation, no art or craft or work that I love doing."

"Tough," said Jessop appreciatively. He added, rather hesitantly: "You don't think of it as—wrong?"

Hilary said heatedly: "Why should it be wrong? It's *my* life."

"Oh yes, yes," Jessop repeated hastily. "I'm not taking a high moral line myself, but there *are* people, you know, who think it's wrong."

Hilary said,

"I'm not one of them."

Mr. Jessop said, rather inadequately,

"Quite."

He sat there looking at her, blinking his eyes thoughtfully. Hilary said:

"So perhaps now, Mr.—er—"

"Jessop," said the young man.

"So perhaps now, Mr. Jessop, you will leave me alone."

But Jessop shook his head.

"Not just yet," he said. "I wanted to know, you see, just what was behind it all. I've got it clear now, have I? You're not interested in life, you don't want to live any longer, you more or less welcome the idea of death?"

"Yes."

"Good," said Jessop, cheerfully. "So now we know where we are. Let's go on to the next step. Has it *got* to be sleeping pills?"

"What do you mean?"

"Well, I've already told you that they're not as romantic as they sound. Throwing yourself off a building isn't too nice, either. You don't always die at once. And the same applies to falling under a train. What I'm getting at is that there *are* other ways."

"I don't understand what you mean."

"I'm suggesting another method. Rather a sporting method, really. There's some excitement in it, too. I'll be fair with you. There's just a hundred to one chance that you mightn't die. But I don't believe under the circumstances, that you'd really object by that time."

"I haven't the faintest idea what you're talking about."

"Of course you haven't," said Jessop. "I've not begun to tell you about it yet. I'm afraid I'll have to make rather a thing about it—tell you a story, I mean. Shall I go ahead?"

"I suppose so."

Jessop paid no attention to the grudgingness of the assent. He started off in his most owllike manner.

"You're the sort of woman who reads the papers and keeps up with things generally, I expect," he said. "You'll have read about the disappearance of various scientists from time to time. There was that Italian chap about a year ago, and about two months ago a young scientist called Thomas Betterton disappeared."

Hilary nodded. "Yes, I read about that in the papers."

"Well, there's been a good deal more than has appeared in the papers. More people, I mean, have disappeared. They haven't always been scientists. Some of them have been young men who were engaged in important medical research. Some of them have been research chemists, some of them have been physicists, there was one barrister. Oh, quite a lot here and there and everywhere. Well, ours is a so-called free country. You can leave it if you like. But in these peculiar circumstances we've got to know why these people left it and where they went, and, also important, *how* they went. Did they go of their own free will? Were they kidnapped? Were they blackmailed into going? What route did they take—what kind of organization is it that sets this in motion and what is its ultimate aim? Lots of questions. We want the answers to them. You might be able to help get us that answer."

Hilary stared at him.

"Me? How? Why?"

"I'm coming down to the particular case of Thomas Betterton. He disappeared from Paris just over two months ago. He left a wife in England. She was distracted—or said she was distracted. She swore that she had no idea why he'd gone or where or how. That may be true, or it may not. Some people—and I'm one of them—think it wasn't true."

Hilary leaned forward in her chair. In spite of herself she was becoming interested. Jessop went on.

"We prepared to keep a nice, unobtrusive eye on Mrs. Betterton. About a fortnight ago she came to me and told me she had been ordered by her doctor to go abroad, take a thorough rest and get some distraction. She was doing no good in England, and people were continually bothering her—newspaper reporters, relations, kind friends."

Hilary said dryly: "I can imagine it."

"Yes, tough. Quite natural she would want to get away for a bit."

"Quite natural, I should think."

"But we've got nasty, suspicious minds in our department, you know. We arranged to keep tabs on Mrs. Betterton. Yesterday she left England as arranged, for Casablanca."

"Casablanca?"

"Yes—*en route* to other places in Morocco, of course. All quite open and aboveboard, plans made, bookings ahead. But it may be that this trip to Morocco is where Mrs. Betterton steps off into the unknown."

Hilary shrugged her shoulders.

"I don't see where I come into all this."

Jessop smiled.

"You come into it because you've got a very magnificent head of red hair, Mrs. Craven."

"Hair?"

"Yes. It's the most noticeable thing about Mrs. Betterton—her hair. You've heard, perhaps, that the plane before yours today crashed on landing."

"I know. I should have been on that plane. I actually had reservations for it."

"Interesting," said Jessop. "Well, Mrs. Betterton *was* on that plane. She wasn't killed. She was taken out of the wreckage still alive, and she is in hospital now. But according to the doctor, she won't be alive tomorrow morning."

A faint glimmer of light came to Hilary. She looked at him inquiringly.

"Yes," said Jessop, "perhaps now you see the form of suicide I'm offering you. I'm suggesting that Mrs. Betterton goes on with her journey. I'm suggesting that you should become Mrs. Betterton."

"But surely," said Hilary, "that would be quite impossible. I mean, they'd know at once she wasn't me."

Jessop put his head on one side.

"That, of course, depends entirely on who you mean by 'they.' It's a very vague term. Who is or are 'they?' Is there such a thing, are there such persons as 'they?' We don't know. But I can tell you this. If the most popular explanation of 'they' is accepted, then these people work in very close, self-contained cells. They do that for their own security. If Mrs. Betterton's journey had a purpose and is planned, then the people who were in charge of it here will know nothing about the English side of it. At the appointed moment they will contact a certain woman at a certain place, and carry on from there. Mrs. Betterton's passport description is five-feet-seven, red hair, blue eyes, mouth medium, no distinguishing marks. Good enough."

"But the authorities here. Surely they—"

Jessop smiled. "That part of it will be quite all right. The French have lost a few valuable young scientists and chemists of their own. They'll cooperate. The facts will be as follows. Mrs. Betterton, suffering from concussion, is taken to hospital. Mrs. Craven, another passenger in the crashed plane will also be admitted to hospital. Within a day or two *Mrs. Craven will die in hospital,* and Mrs. Betterton will be discharged, suffering slightly from concussion, but able to proceed on her tour. The crash was genuine, the concussion is genuine, and concussion makes a very good cover for you. It excuses a lot of things like lapses of memory and various unpredictable behavior."

Hilary said:

"It would be madness!"

"Oh, yes," said Jessop, "it's madness, all right. It's a very tough assignment and if our suspicions are realized, you'll probably cop it. You see, I'm being quite frank, but according to you, you're prepared and anxious to cop it. As an alternative to throwing yourself in front of a train or something like that. I should think you'd find it far more amusing."

Suddenly and unexpectedly Hilary laughed.

"I do believe," she said, "that you're quite right."

"You'll do it?"

"Yes. Why not."

"In that case," said Jessop, rising in his seat with sudden energy, "there's absolutely no time to be lost."

4

It was not really cold in the hospital but it felt cold. There was a smell of antiseptics in the air. Occasionally in the corridor outside could be heard the rattle of glasses and instruments as a trolley was pushed by. Hilary Craven sat in a hard iron chair by a bedside.

In the bed, lying flat under a shaded light with her head bandaged, Olive Betterton lay unconscious. There was a nurse standing on one side of the bed and the doctor on the other. Jessop sat in a chair in the far corner of the room. The doctor turned to him and spoke in French.

"It will not be very long now," he said. "The pulse is very much weaker."

"And she will not recover consciousness?"

The Frenchman shrugged his shoulders.

"That I cannot say. It may be, yes, at the very end."

"There is nothing you can do—no stimulant?"

The doctor shook his head. He went out. The nurse followed him. She was replaced by a nun who moved to the head of the bed, and stood there, fingering her rosary. Hilary looked at Jessop and in obedience to a glance from him came to join him.

"You heard what the doctor said?" he asked in a low voice.

"Yes. What is it you want to say to her?"

"If she regains consciousness I want any information you can possibly get, any password, any sign, any message, *anything*. Do you understand? She is more likely to speak to you than to me."

Hilary said with sudden emotion:

"You want me to betray someone who is dying?"

Jessop put his head on one side in the birdlike manner which he sometimes adopted.

"So it seems like that to you, does it?" he said, considering.

"Yes, it does."

He looked at her thoughtfully.

"Very well then, you shall say and do what you please. For myself I can have no scruples! You understand that?"

"Of course. It's your duty. You'll do whatever questioning you please, but don't ask *me* to do it."

"You're a free agent."

"There is one question we shall have to decide. Are we to tell her that she is dying?"

"I don't know. I shall have to think it out."

She nodded and went back to her place by the bed. She was filled now with a deep compassion for the woman who lay there dying. The woman who was on her way to join the man she loved. Or were they all wrong? Had she come to Morocco simply to seek solace, to pass the time until perhaps some definite news could come to her as to whether her husband were alive or dead? Hilary wondered.

Time went on. It was nearly two hours later when the click of the nun's beads stopped. She spoke in a soft impersonal voice.

"There is a change," she said. "I think, Madame, it is the end that comes. I will fetch the doctor."

She left the room. Jessop moved to the opposite side of the bed, standing back against the wall so that he was out of the woman's range of vision. The eyelids flickered and opened. Pale incurious blue eyes looked into Hilary's. They closed, then opened again. A faint air of perplexity seemed to come into them.

"Where . . . ?"

The word fluttered between the almost breathless lips, just as the doctor entered the room. He took her hand in his, his finger on the pulse, standing by the bed looking down on her.

"You are in hospital, Madame," he said. "There was an accident to the plane."

"To the plane?"

The words were repeated dreamily in that faint breathless voice.

"Is there anyone you want to see in Casablanca, Madame? Any message we can take?"

Her eyes were raised painfully to the doctor's face. She said:
"No."

She looked back again at Hilary.

"Who—who—"

Hilary bent forward and spoke clearly and distinctly.

"I came out from England on a plane, too—if there is anything I can do to help you, please tell me."

"No—nothing—nothing—unless—"

"Yes?"

"Nothing."

The eyes flickered again and half closed—Hilary raised her head and looked across to meet Jessop's imperious commanding glance. Firmly, she shook her head.

Jessop moved forward. He stood close beside the doctor. The dying woman's eyes opened again. Sudden recognition came into them. She said:

"I know *you.*"

"Yes, Mrs. Betterton, you know me. Will you tell me anything you can about your husband?"

"No."

Her eyelids fell again. Jessop turned quietly and left the room. The doctor looked across at Hilary. He said very softly,

"*C'est la fin!*"

The dying woman's eyes opened again. They traveled painfully round the room, then they remained fixed on Hilary. Olive Betterton made a very faint motion with her hand, and Hilary instinctively took the white cold hand between her own. The doctor, with a shrug of his shoulders and a little bow, left the room. The two women were alone together. Olive Betterton was trying to speak:

"Tell me—tell me—"

Hilary knew what she was asking, and suddenly her own course of action opened clearly before her. She leaned down over the recumbent form.

"Yes," she said, her words clear and emphatic. "You are dying. That's what you want to know, isn't it? Now listen to me. I am going to try and reach your husband. Is there any message you want me to give him if I succeed?"

"Tell him—tell him—to be careful. Boris—Boris—dangerous. . . ."

The breath fluttered off again with a sigh. Hilary bent closer.

"Is there anything you can tell me to help me—help me in my journey, I mean? Help me to get in contact with your husband?"

"Snow."

The word came so faintly that Hilary was puzzled. Snow? *Snow?* She repeated it uncomprehendingly. A faint, ghostlike little giggle came from Olive Betterton. Faint words came tumbling out:

> "Snow, snow, beautiful snow!
> You slip on a lump, and over you go!"

She repeated the last word. "Go . . . Go? Go and tell him about Boris. I didn't believe it. I *wouldn't* believe it. But perhaps it's true. . . . If so, if so . . ." A kind of agonized question came into her eyes which stared up into Hilary's. ". . . take care. . . ."

A queer little rattle came to her throat. Her lips jerked.

Olive Betterton died.

ii

The next five days were strenuous mentally, though inactive physically. Immured in a private room in the hospital, Hilary was set to work. Every evening she had to pass an examination on what she had studied that day. All the details of Olive Betterton's life, as far as they could be ascertained, were set down on paper and she had to memorize and learn them by heart. The house she had lived in, the daily women she had employed, her relations, the names of her pet dog and her canary, every detail of the six months of her married life with Thomas Betterton. Her wedding, the names of her bridesmaids, their dresses, the patterns of curtains, carpets and chintzes. Olive Betterton's tastes, predilections and day by day activities. Her preferences in food and drink. Hilary was forced to marvel at the amount of seemingly meaningless information that had been massed together. Once she said to Jessop,

"Can any of this possibly *matter?*"

And to that he had replied quietly:

"Probably not. But you've got to make yourself into the authentic article. Think of it this way, Hilary. You're a writer. You're writing a book about a woman. The woman is Olive. You describe scenes of her childhood, her girlhood; you describe her marriage, the house she lived in. All the time that you do it she becomes more and more of a real person to you. Then you go over it a second time. You write it this time as an autobiography. You write it *in the first person.* Do you see what I mean?"

She nodded slowly, impressed in spite of herself.

"You can't think of yourself as Olive Betterton until you *are* Olive Betterton. It would be better if you had time to learn it up, but *we can't afford time.* So I've got to cram you. Cram you like a schoolboy—like a student who is going in for an important examination." He added, "You've got a quick brain and a good memory, thank the Lord."

He looked at her in cool appraisement.

The passport descriptions of Olive Betterton and Hilary Craven were almost identical, but actually the two faces were entirely different. Olive Betterton had had a quality of rather commonplace and insignificant prettiness. She had looked obstinate but not intelligent. Hilary's face had power and an intriguing quality. The deep set bluish-green eyes under dark level brows had fire and intelligence in their depths. Her mouth curved upward in a wide and generous line. The plane of the jaw was unusual—a sculptor would have found the angles of the face interesting.

Jessop thought: "There's passion there—and guts—and somewhere, damped but not quenched, there's a gay spirit that's tough—and that enjoys life and searches out for adventure."

"You'll do," he said to her. "You're an apt pupil."

This challenge to her intellect and her memory had stimulated Hilary. She was becoming interested now, keen to achieve success. Once or twice objections occurred to her. She voiced them to Jessop.

"You say that I shan't be rejected as Olive Betterton. You say that they won't know what she looks like, except in general detail. But how sure can you be of that?"

Jessop shrugged his shoulders.

"One can't be sure—of anything. But we do know a certain amount about the setup of these shows, and it does seem that internationally there is very little communication from one country to another. Actually, that's a great advantage to *them.* If we come upon a weak link in England (and, mind you, in every organization there always will be a weak link), that weak link in the chain knows nothing about what's going on in France, or Italy, or Germany, or wherever you like, we are brought up short by a blank wall. They know their own little part of the whole—no more. The same applies the opposite way round. I dare swear that all the cell operating here knows is that Olive Betterton will arrive on such and such a plane and is to be given such and such instructions. You see, it's not as though she were important in *herself.* If they're bringing her to her husband, it's because her husband wants her brought to him and because they think they'll get better work out of him if she joins him. She herself is a mere pawn in the game. You must remember too, that the idea of substituting a false Olive Betterton is definitely a spur of the moment improvisation—occasioned by the plane accident and the color of your hair. Our plan of operation was to keep tabs on Olive Betterton and find out where she went, *how* she went, whom she met—and so on. That's what the other side will be on the lookout for."

Hilary asked:

"Haven't you tried all that before?"

"Yes. It was tried in Switzerland. Very unobtrusively. And it failed as far as our main objective was concerned. *If* anyone contacted her there we didn't know about it. So the contact must have been very brief. Naturally they'll expect that someone will be keeping tabs on Olive Betterton. They'll be prepared for that. It's up to us to do our job more thoroughly than last time. We've got to try and be rather more cunning than our adversaries."

"So you'll be keeping tabs on me?"

"Of course."

"How?"

He shook his head.

"I shan't tell you that. Much better for you not to know. What you don't know you can't give away."

"Do you think I would give it away?"

Jessop put on his owllike expression again.

"I don't know how good an actress you are—how good a liar. It's not easy, you know. It's not a question of *saying* anything indiscreet. It can be anything, a sudden intake of the breath, the momentary pause in some action— lighting a cigarette, for instance. Recognition of a name or a friend. You could cover it up quickly, but just a flash might be enough!"

"I see. It means—being on your guard for every single split second."

"Exactly. In the meantime, on with the lessons! Quite like going back to school, isn't it? You're pretty well word-perfect on Olive Betterton, now. Let's go on to the other."

Codes, responses, various properties. The lesson went on, the questioning, the repetition, the endeavor to confuse her, to trip her up; then hypothetical schemes and her own reactions to them. In the end, Jessop nodded his head and declared himself satisfied.

"You'll do," he said. He patted her on the shoulder in an avuncular manner. "You're an apt pupil. And remember this, however much you may feel at times that you're all alone in this, you're probably not. I say *probably*—I won't put it higher than that. These are clever devils."

"What happens," said Hilary, "if I reach journey's end?"

"You mean?"

"I mean when at last I come face to face with Tom Betterton."

Jessop nodded grimly.

"Yes," he said. "That's the danger moment. I can only say that at that moment, *if all has gone well,* you *should* have protection. If, that is to say, things have gone as we *hope;* but the very basis of this operation, as you may remember, was that there wasn't a very high chance of survival."

"Didn't you say one in a hundred?" said Hilary dryly.

"I think we can shorten the odds a little. I didn't know what you were like."

"No, I suppose not." She was thoughtful. "To you, I suppose, I was just . . ."

He finished the sentence for her:

"A woman with a noticeable head of red hair and who hadn't the pluck to go on living."

She flushed.

"That's a harsh judgment."

"It's a true one, isn't it? I don't go in for being sorry for people. For one thing it's insulting. One is only sorry for people when they're sorry for themselves. Self-pity is one of the biggest stumbling blocks in the world today."

Hilary said thoughtfully:

"I think perhaps you're right. Will you permit yourself to be sorry for me when I've been liquidated or whatever the term is, in fulfilling this mission?"

"Sorry for you? No. I shall curse like hell because we've lost someone who's worthwhile taking a bit of trouble over."

"A compliment at last." In spite of herself she was pleased.

She went on in a practical tone:

"There's just one other thing that occurred to me. You say nobody's likely to know what Olive Betterton looks like, but what about being recognized as *myself?* I don't know anyone in Casablanca, but there are the people who traveled here with me in the plane. Or one may of course run across somebody one knows among the tourists here."

"You needn't worry about the passengers in the plane. The people who flew with you from Paris were businessmen who went on to Dakar and a man who got off here who has since flown back to Paris. You will go to a different hotel when you leave here, the hotel for which Mrs. Betterton had reservations. You will be wearing her clothes and her style of hairdressing and one or two strips of plaster at the sides of your face will make you look very different in feature. We've got a doctor coming to work upon you, by the way. Local anaesthetic, so it won't hurt, but you will have to have a few genuine marks of the accident."

"You're very thorough," said Hilary.

"Have to be."

"You've never asked me," said Hilary, "whether Olive Betterton told me anything before she died."

"I understood you had scruples."

"I'm sorry."

"Not at all. I respect you for them. I'd like to indulge in them myself—but they're not in the schedule."

"She did say something that perhaps I ought to tell you. She said 'Tell him' —Betterton, that is—'tell him to be careful—Boris—dangerous—' "

"Boris." Jessop repeated the name with interest. "Ah! Our correct foreign Major Boris Glydr."

"You know him? Who is he?"

"A Pole. He came to see me in London. He's supposed to be a cousin of Tom Betterton by marriage."

"Supposed?"

"Let us say, more correctly, that if he is who he says he is, he is a cousin of the late Mrs. Betterton. But we've only his word for it."

"She was frightened," said Hilary, frowning. "Can you describe him? I'd like to be able to recognize him."

"Yes. It might be as well. Six foot. Weight roughly 160 pounds. Fair— rather wooden poker face—light eyes—foreign stilted manner—English very correct, but a pronounced accent, military bearing."

He added:

"I had him tailed when he left my office. Nothing doing. He went straight to the U.S. Embassy—quite correctly—he'd brought me an introductory letter from there. The usual kind they send out when they want to be polite but noncommittal. I presume he left the Embassy either in somebody's car or by the back entrance disguised as a footman or something. Anyway he evaded us. Yes—I should say that Olive Betterton was perhaps right when she said that Boris Glydr was dangerous."

5

IN THE SMALL formal salon of the Hotel St. Louis, three ladies were sitting, each engaged in her particular occupation. Mrs. Calvin Baker, short, plump, with well blued hair, was writing letters with the same driving energy she applied to all forms of activity. No one could have mistaken Mrs. Calvin Baker for anything but a traveling American, comfortably off, with an inexhaustible thirst for precise information on every subject under the sun.

In an uncomfortable Empire type chair, Miss Hetherington who again could not have been mistaken for anything but traveling English, was knitting one of those melancholy shapeless-looking garments that English ladies of middle age always seem to be knitting. Miss Hetherington was tall and thin with a scraggy neck, badly arranged hair, and a general expression of moral disapprovement of the Universe.

Mademoiselle Jeanne Maricot was sitting gracefully in an upright chair, looking out of the window and yawning. Mademoiselle Maricot was a brunette dyed blond, with a plain but excitingly made-up face. She was wearing chic clothes and had no interest whatsoever in the other occupants of the room whom she dismissed contemptuously in her mind as being exactly what they were! She was contemplating an important change in her sex life and had no interest to spare for these animals of tourists!

Miss Hetherington and Mrs. Calvin Baker, having both spent a couple of nights under the roof of the St. Louis, had become acquainted. Mrs. Calvin Baker, with American friendliness, talked to everybody. Miss Hetherington, though just as eager for companionship, talked only to English and Americans of what she considered a certain social standing. The French she had no truck with unless guaranteed of respectable family life as evidenced by little ones who shared the parental table in the dining room.

A Frenchman looking like a prosperous businessman glanced into the salon, was intimidated by its air of female solidarity and went out again with a look of lingering regret at Mademoiselle Jeanne Maricot.

Miss Hetherington began to count stitches *sotto voce*.

"Twenty-eight, twenty-nine—now what can I have— Oh, I see."

A tall woman with red hair looked into the room and hesitated a moment before going on down the passage toward the dining room.

Mrs. Calvin Baker and Miss Hetherington were immediately alert. Mrs. Baker slewed herself round from the writing table and spoke in a thrilled whisper.

"Did you happen to notice that woman with red hair who looked in, Miss Hetherington? They say she's the only survivor of that terrible plane crash last week."

"I saw her arrive this afternoon," said Miss Hetherington, dropping another stitch in her excitement. *"In an ambulance."*

"Straight from the hospital, so the Manager said. I wonder now if it was wise—to leave hospital so soon. She's had concussion, I believe."

"She's got strapping on her face, too—cut, perhaps, by the glass. What a mercy she wasn't burnt. Terrible injuries from burning in these air accidents, I believe."

"It just doesn't bear thinking about. Poor young thing. I wonder if she had a husband with her and if he was killed?"

"I don't think so." Miss Hetherington shook her yellow gray head. "It said in the paper, one woman passenger."

"That's right. It gave her name, too. A Mrs. Beverly—no, Betterton, that was it."

"Betterton," said Miss Hetherington reflectively. "Now what does that remind me of? Betterton. In the papers. Oh, dear, I'm sure that was the name."

"*Tant pis pour Pierre,*" Mademoiselle Maricot said to herself. "*Il est vraiment insupportable! Mais le petit Jules, lui il est bien gentil. Et son père est très bien placé dans les affaires. Enfin, je me decide!*"

And with long graceful steps Mademoiselle Maricot walked out of the small salon and out of the story.

ii

Mrs. Thomas Betterton had left the hospital that afternoon five days after the accident. An ambulance had driven her to the Hotel St. Louis.

Looking pale and ill, her face strapped and bandaged, Mrs. Betterton was shown at once to the room reserved for her, a sympathetic manager hovering in attendance.

"What emotions you must have experienced, Madame!" he said, after inquiring tenderly as to whether the room reserved suited her, and turning on all the electric lights quite unnecessarily. "But what an escape! What a miracle! What good fortune. Only three survivors, I understand, and one of them in a critical condition still."

Hilary sank down on a chair wearily.

"Yes, indeed," she murmured. "I can hardly believe it myself. Even now I can remember so little. The last twenty-four hours before the crash are still quite vague to me."

The manager nodded sympathetically.

"Ah, yes. That is the result of the concussion. That happens once to a sister of mine. She was in London in the war. A bomb came, she was knocked unconscious. But presently she gets up, she walks about London and she takes a train from the station of Euston and, *figurez-vous,* she wakes up at Liverpool and she cannot remember anything of the bomb, of going across London, of the train or of getting there! The last thing she remembers is hanging up her skirt in the wardrobe in London. Very curious these things, are they not?"

Hilary agreed that they were, indeed. The manager bowed and departed. Hilary got up and looked at herself in the mirror. So imbued was she now with her new personality that she positively felt the weakness in her limbs which would be natural to one who had just come out of hospital after a severe ordeal.

She had already inquired at the desk, but there had been no messages or letters for her there. The first steps in her new role had to be taken very much in the dark. Olive Betterton might perhaps have been told to ring a certain number or to contact a certain person at Casablanca. As to that there was no clue. All the knowledge she had to go on was Olive Betterton's passport, her letter of credit, and her book of Cook's tickets and reservations. These provided for two days in Casablanca, six days in Fez and five days in Marrakesh. These reservations were now, of course, out of date, and would have to be dealt with accordingly. The passport, the Letter of Credit and the accompanying Letter of Identification had been suitably dealt with. The photograph on the passport was now that of Hilary, the signature on the Letter of Credit was *Olive Betterton* in Hilary's handwriting. Her credentials were all in order. Her task was to play her part adequately and to wait. Her master card must be the plane accident, and its resultant loss of memory and general haziness.

It had been a genuine accident and Olive Betterton had been genuinely on board the plane. The fact of concussion would adequately cover her failure to adopt any measures in which she might have been instructed. Bewildered, dazed, weak, Olive Betterton would await orders.

The natural thing to do would be to rest. Accordingly she lay down on the bed. For two hours she went over in her mind all that she had been taught. Olive's luggage had been destroyed in the plane. Hilary had a few things with her supplied at the hospital. She passed a comb through her hair, touched her lips with a lipstick and went down to the hotel dining room for dinner.

She was looked at, she noticed, with a certain amount of interest. There were several tables occupied by businessmen and these hardly vouchsafed a glance at her. But at other tables, clearly occupied by tourists, she was conscious of a murmur and a whisper going on.

"That woman over there—the one with the red hair—she's a survivor of the plane crash, my dear. Yes, came from hospital in an ambulance. I saw her arrive. She looks terribly ill still. I wonder if they ought to have let her out so soon. What a frightful experience. What a merciful escape!"

After dinner Hilary sat for a short while in the small formal salon. She wondered if anyone would approach her in any way. There were one or two other women scattered about the room, and presently a small, plump, middle-aged woman with well-blued white hair, moved to a chair near hers. She opened proceedings in a brisk, pleasant American voice.

"I do hope you'll excuse me, but I just felt I had to say a word. It's you, isn't it, who had the *wonderful* escape from that air crash the other day?"

Hilary put down the magazine she was reading.

"Yes," she said.

"My! Isn't that terrible? The crash I mean. Only three survivors, they say. Is that right?"

"Only two," said Hilary. "One of the three died in hospital."

"My! You don't say! Now, if you don't mind my asking, Miss—Mrs. . . ."

"Betterton."

"Well, if you don't mind my asking, just where were you sitting in that plane? Were you up at the front or near the tail?"

Hilary knew the answer to that one and gave it promptly.

"Near the tail."

"They always say, don't they, that's the safest place. I just insist now on always having a place near the rear doors. Did you hear that, Miss Hetherington?" She turned her head to include another middle-aged lady. This one was uncompromisingly British with a long, sad, horselike face. "It's just as I was saying the other day. Whenever you go into an airplane, don't you let those air hostesses take you right up to the front."

"I suppose someone has to sit at the front," said Hilary.

"Well, it won't be me," said her new American friend promptly. "My name's Baker, by the way, Mrs. Calvin Baker."

Hilary acknowledged the introduction and Mrs. Baker plunged on, monopolizing the conversation easily.

"I've just come here from Mogador and Miss Hetherington has come from Tangier. We became acquainted here. Are you going to visit Marrakesh, Mrs. Betterton?"

"I'd arranged to do so," said Hilary. "Of course, this accident has thrown out all my time schedule."

"Why, naturally, I can see that. But you really mustn't miss Marrakesh, wouldn't you say so, Miss Hetherington?"

"Marrakesh is terribly expensive," said Miss Hetherington. "This miserable travel allowance makes everything so difficult."

"There's a wonderful hotel, the Mamounia," continued Mrs. Baker.

"Wickedly expensive," said Miss Hetherington. "Out of the question for *me*. Of course, it's different for you, Mrs. Baker—dollars, I mean. But someone gave me the name of a small hotel there, really very nice and clean, and the food, they say, is not at all bad."

"Where else do you plan to go, Mrs. Betterton?" asked Mrs. Calvin Baker.

"I would like to see Fez," said Hilary, cautiously. "I shall have to get fresh reservations, of course."

"Oh, yes, you certainly oughtn't to miss Fez or Rabat."

"You've been there?"

"Not yet. I'm planning to go there shortly, and so is Miss Hetherington."

"I believe the old city is quite unspoilt," said Miss Hetherington.

The conversation continued in desultory fashion for some time further. Then Hilary pleaded fatigue from her first day out of the hospital and went up to her bedroom.

The evening so far had been quite indecisive. The two women who had talked to her had been such well-known traveling types that she could hardly believe that they were other than they seemed. Tomorrow, she decided, if she had received no word or communication of any kind, she would go to Cook's and raise the question of fresh reservations at Fez and Marrakesh.

There were no letters, messages or telephone calls the following morning and about eleven o'clock she made her way to the travel agency. There was somewhat of a queue, but when she at last reached the counter and began talking to the clerk, an interruption occurred. A somewhat more senior clerk with glasses elbowed the young man aside. He beamed at Hilary through his glasses.

"It is Madame Betterton, is it not? I have all your reservations made."

"I am afraid," said Hilary, "that they will be out of date. I have been in hospital and . . ."

"Ah, *mais oui,* I know all that. Let me congratulate you on your escape, Madame. But I got your telephone message about fresh reservations, and we have them here ready for you."

Hilary felt a faint quickening of her pulse. As far as she knew no one had phoned the travel agency. Here then were definite signs that Olive Betterton's traveling arrangements were being supervised. She said,

"I wasn't sure if they had telephoned or not."

"But yes, Madame. Here, I will show you."

He produced railway tickets, and vouchers for hotel accommodation, and a few minutes later the transactions were completed. Hilary was to leave for Fez on the following day.

Mrs. Calvin Baker was not in the restaurant either for lunch or dinner. Miss Hetherington was. She acknowledged Hilary's bow as the latter passed to her table, but made no attempt to get into conversation with her. On the following day, after making some necessary purchases of clothes and under-clothing, Hilary left by train for Fez.

iii

It was on the day of Hilary's departure that Mrs. Calvin Baker coming into the hotel in her usual brisk fashion, was accosted by Miss Hetherington whose long thin nose was quivering with excitement.

"I've remembered about the name *Betterton*—the disappearing scientist. It was in all the papers. About two months ago."

"Why, now I do remember something. A British scientist—yes—he'd been at some conference in Paris."

"Yes—that's it. Now I wonder, do you think—this could possibly be his *wife.* I looked in the register and I see her address is Harwell—Harwell, you know, is the Atom Station. I do think all these atom bombs are very wrong. And Cobalt. Such a lovely color in one's paintbox and I used it a lot as a child; the worst of all, I understand *nobody* can survive. We weren't meant to do these experiments. Somebody told me the other day that her cousin who is a very shrewd man, said the whole world might go *radioactive.*"

"My, my," said Mrs. Calvin Baker.

6

CASABLANCA HAD VAGUELY disappointed Hilary by being such a prosperous-looking French town with no hint of the orient or mystery about it, except for the crowds in the streets.

The weather was still perfect, sunny and clear, and she enjoyed looking out of the train at the passing landscape as they journeyed northward. A small Frenchman who looked like a commercial traveler sat opposite to her, in the far corner was a somewhat disapproving-looking nun telling her beads, and two Moorish ladies with a great many packages who conversed gaily with one another, completed the complement of the carriage. Offering a light for her cigarette, the little Frenchman opposite soon entered into conversation. He pointed out things of interest as they passed, and gave her various information about the country. She found him interesting and intelligent.

"You should go to Rabat, Madame. It is a great mistake not to go to Rabat."

"I shall try to do so. But I have not very much time. Besides," she smiled. "Money is short. We can only take so much with us abroad, you know."

"But that is simple. One arranges with a friend here."

"I'm afraid I haven't got a convenient friend in Morocco."

"Next time you travel, Madame, send me a little word. I will give you my card. And I arrange everything. I travel often in England on business and you repay me there. It is all quite simple."

"That's very kind of you, and I hope I shall pay a second visit to Morocco."

"It must be a change for you, Madame, to come here from England. So cold, so foggy, so disagreeable."

"Yes, it's a great change."

"I, too, I traveled from Paris three weeks ago. It was then fog, rain and all of the most disgusting. I arrive here and all is sunshine. Though, mind you, the air is cold. But it is pure. Good pure air. How was the weather in England when you left?"

"Much as you say," said Hilary. "Fog."

"Ah yes, it is the foggy season. Snow—you have had snow this year?"

"No," said Hilary, "there has been no snow." She wondered to herself, amusedly, if this much-traveled little Frenchman was following what he considered to be the correct trend of English conversation, dealing principally with the weather. She asked him a question or two about the political situation in Morocco and in Algiers, and he responded willingly, showing himself to be well informed.

Glancing across at the far corner, Hilary observed the nun's eyes fixed disapprovingly on her. The Moroccan ladies got out and other travelers got in. It was evening when they arrived at Fez.

"Permit me to assist you, Madame."

Hilary was standing, rather bewildered at the bustle and noise of the station. Arab porters were seizing her luggage from her hands, shouting, yelling, calling, recommending different hotels. She turned gratefully to her new French acquaintance.

"You are going to the Palais Jamail, *n'est-ce pas,* Madame?"

"Yes."

"That is right. It is eight kilometers from here, you understand."

"Eight kilometers?" Hilary was dismayed. "It's not in the town, then."

"It is by the old town," the Frenchman explained. "Me, I stay here at the hotel in the commercial new city. But for the holiday, the rest, the enjoyment, naturally you go to the Palais Jamail. It was a former residence, you understand, of the Moroccan nobility. It has beautiful gardens, and you go straight from it into the old city of Fez which is untouched. It does not seem as though the hotel had sent to meet this train. If you permit, I will arrange for a taxi for you."

"You're very kind, but . . ."

The Frenchman spoke in rapid Arabic to the porters and shortly afterward Hilary took her place in a taxi, her baggage was pushed in, and the Frenchman told her exactly what to give the rapacious porters. He also dismissed them with a few sharp words of Arabic when they protested that the remuneration was inadequate. He whipped a card from his pocket and handed it to her.

"My card, Madame, and if I can be of assistance to you at any time, tell me. I shall be at the Grand Hotel here for the next four days."

He raised his hat and went away. Hilary looked down at the card which she could just see before they moved out of the lighted station.

Monsieur Henri Laurier

The taxi drove briskly out of the town, through the country, up a hill. Hilary tried to see, looking out of the windows, where she was going, but darkness had set in now. Except when they passed a lighted building nothing much could be seen. Was this, perhaps, where her journey diverged from the normal and entered the unknown? Was Monsieur Laurier an emissary from the organization that had persuaded Thomas Betterton to leave his work, his home and his wife? She sat in the corner of the taxi, nervously apprehensive, wondering where it was taking her.

It took her, however, in the most exemplary manner to the Palais Jamail. She dismounted there, passed through an arched gateway and found herself, with a thrill of pleasure, in an oriental interior. There were long divans, coffee tables, and native rugs. From the reception desk she was taken through several rooms which led out of each other, out onto a terrace, passing by orange trees and scented flowers, and then up a winding staircase and into a pleasant bedroom, still oriental in style but equipped with all the *conforts modernes* so necessary to twentieth-century travelers.

Dinner, the porter informed her, took place from seven-thirty. She unpacked a little, washed, combed her hair and went downstairs through the long oriental smoking room, out on the terrace and across and up some steps to a lighted dining room running at right angles to it.

The dinner was excellent, and as Hilary ate, various people came and went from the restaurant. She was too tired to size them up and classify them this particular evening, but one or two outstanding personalities took her eye. An elderly man, very yellow of face, with a little goatee beard. She noticed him because of the extreme deference paid to him by the staff. Plates were whisked away and placed for him at the mere raising of his head. The slightest turn of an eyebrow brought a waiter rushing to his table. She wondered who he was. The majority of diners were clearly touring on pleasure trips. There was a German at a big table in the center, there was a middle-aged man with a fair, very beautiful girl whom she thought might be Swedes, or possibly Danes. There was an English family with two children, and various groups of traveling Americans. There were three French families.

After dinner she had coffee on the terrace. It was slightly cold but not unduly so and she enjoyed the smell of scented blossoms. She went to bed early.

Sitting on the terrace the following morning in the sunshine under the red striped umbrella that protected her from the sun, Hilary felt how fantastic the whole thing was. Here she sat, pretending to be a dead woman, expecting something melodramatic and out of the common to occur. After all, wasn't it only too likely that poor Olive Betterton had come abroad merely to distract her mind and heart from sad thoughts and feelings? Probably the poor woman had been just as much in the dark as everybody else.

Certainly the words she had said before she died admitted of a perfectly ordinary explanation. She had wanted Thomas Betterton warned against somebody called Boris. Her mind had wandered—she had quoted a strange little jingle—she had gone on to say that she couldn't believe it at first. Couldn't believe what? Possibly only that Thomas Betterton had been spirited away the way he had been.

There had been no sinister undertones, no helpful clues. Hilary stared down at the terrace garden below her. It was beautiful here. Beautiful and peaceful. Children chattered and ran up and down the terrace, French mammas called to them or scolded them. The blond Swedish girl came and sat down by a table and yawned. She took out a pale pink lipstick and touched up her already exquisitely painted lips. She appraised her face seriously, frowning a little.

Presently her companion—husband, Hilary wondered, or it might possibly be her father—joined her. She greeted him without a smile. She leaned forward and talked to him, apparently expostulating about something. He protested and apologized.

The old man with the yellow face and the little goatee came up the terrace from the gardens below. He went and sat at a table against the extreme wall, and immediately a waiter darted forth. He gave an order and the waiter bowed before him and went away, in all haste to execute it. The fair girl caught her companion excitedly by the arm and looked toward the elderly man.

Hilary ordered a Martini, and when it came she asked the waiter in a low voice,

"Who is the old man there against the wall?"

"Ah!" The waiter leaned forward dramatically, "That is Monsieur Aristides. He is enormously—but yes, enormously—rich."

He sighed in ecstasy at the contemplation of so much wealth and Hilary looked over at the shriveled up, bent figure at the far table. Such a wrinkled, dried up, mummified old morsel of humanity. And yet, because of his enormous wealth, waiters darted and sprang and spoke with awe in their voices. Old Monsieur Aristides shifted his position. Just for a moment his eyes met hers. He looked at her for a moment, then looked away.

"Not so insignificant after all," Hilary thought to herself. Those eyes, even at that distance, had been wonderfully intelligent and alive.

The blond girl and her escort got up from their table and went into the dining room. The waiter who now seemed to consider himself as Hilary's guide and mentor, stopped at her table as he collected glasses and gave her further information.

"*Ce Monsieur là,* he is a big business magnate from Sweden. Very rich, very important. And the lady with him she is a film star—another Garbo, they say. Very chic—very beautiful—but does she make him the scenes, the histories! Nothing pleases her. She is, as you say, 'fed up' to be here, in Fez, where there are no jewelers' shops—and no other expensive women to admire and envy her toilettes. She demands that he should take her somewhere more amusing tomorrow. Ah, it is not always the rich who can enjoy the tranquillity and peace of mind."

Having uttered this last in a somewhat sententious fashion, he saw a beckoning forefinger and sprang across the terrace as though galvanized.

"Monsieur?"

Most people had gone in to lunch, but Hilary had had breakfast late and was in no hurry for her midday meal. She ordered herself another drink. A good-looking young Frenchman came out of the bar and across the terrace, cast a swift, discreet glance at Hilary which, thinly disguised, meant: "Is there anything doing here, I wonder?" and then went down the steps to the terrace below. As he did so he half sang, half hummed a snatch of French opera,

"*Le long des lauriers roses,*
Revant de douces choses."

The words formed a little pattern on Hilary's brain. *Le long des lauriers roses.* Laurier. *Laurier?* That was the name of the Frenchman in the train. Was there a connection here or was it coincidence? She opened her bag and hunted in it for the card he had given her. *Mons. Henri Laurier, 3 Rue des Croissants, Casablanca.* She turned the card over and there seemed to be faint pencil marks on the back of it. It was as though something has been written on it and then rubbed out. She tried to decipher what the marks were. *"Où sont,"* the message began, then something which she could not decipher, and finally she made out the words *"D'antan."* For a moment she had thought that it might be a message, but now she shook her head and put the card back in her bag. It must have been some quotation that he had once written on it and then rubbed out.

A shadow fell on her and she looked up, startled. Mr. Aristides was standing there between her and the sun. His eyes were not on her. He was looking across over the gardens below toward the silhouette of hills in the distance. She heard him sigh and then he turned abruptly toward the dining room and as he did so, the sleeve of his coat caught the glass on her table and sent it flying to the terrace where it broke. He wheeled round quickly and politely.

"Ah. *Mille pardons, Madame."*

Hilary assured him smilingly in French that it did not matter in the least. With the swift flick of a finger he summoned a waiter. The waiter as usual came running. He ordered a replacement of Madame's drink and then, once more apologizing, he made his way into the restaurant.

The young Frenchman, still humming, came up the steps again. He lingered noticeably as he passed Hilary, but as she gave no sign, he went on into lunch with a slight philosophic shrug of the shoulders.

A French family passed across the terrace, the parents calling to their young.

"Mais viens, donc, Bobo. Qu'est-ce que tu fais? Dépêches toi!"

"Laisse ta balle, chérie, on va dejeuner."

They passed up the steps and into the restaurant, a happy contented little nucleus of family life. Hilary felt suddenly alone and frightened.

The waiter brought her drink. She asked him if M. Aristides was all alone here.

"Oh, Madame, naturally, anyone so rich as M. Aristides would never travel *alone.* He has here his valet and two secretaries and a chauffeur."

The waiter was quite shocked at the idea of M. Aristides traveling unaccompanied.

Hilary noted, however, when she at last went into the dining room that the old man sat at a table by himself as he had done on the previous evening. At a table nearby sat two young men whom she thought were probably the secretaries since she noticed that one or the other of them was always on the alert and looked constantly toward the table where M. Aristides, shriveled and monkeylike, ate his lunch and did not seem to notice their existence. Evidently to M. Aristides, secretaries were not human!

The afternoon passed in a vague dreamlike manner. Hilary strolled through the gardens, descending from terrace to terrace. The peace and the beauty seemed quite astounding. There was the splash of water, the gleam of the golden oranges, and innumerable scents and fragrances. It was the Oriental atmosphere of seclusion about it that Hilary found so satisfying. *As a garden enclosed is my sister, my spouse* . . . This was what a garden was meant to be, a place shut away from the world—full of green and gold—

If I could stay here, thought Hilary. If I could stay here always . . .

It was not the actual garden of the Palais Jamail that was in her thoughts, it was the state of mind it typified. When she no longer looked for peace, she had found it. And peace of mind had come to her at a moment when she was committed to adventure and danger.

But perhaps there was no danger and no adventure . . . Perhaps she could stay here awhile and nothing would happen . . . and then . . .

And then—what?

A little cold breeze sprang up and Hilary gave a quick shiver. You strayed into the garden of peaceful living, but in the end you would be betrayed from within. The turmoil of the world, the harshness of living, the regrets and despairs, all these she carried within her.

And it was late afternoon, and the sun had lost its power. Hilary went up the various terraces and into the hotel.

In the gloom of the Oriental Lounge, something voluble and cheerful resolved itself, as Hilary's eyes got attuned to the dimness, into Mrs. Calvin Baker, her hair newly blued, and her appearance immaculate as ever.

"I've just got here by air," she explained. "I simply can't stand these trains —the time they take! And the people in them, as often as not, quite unsanitary! They've no idea at all of hygiene in these countries. My dear, you should see the meat in the *souks*—all smothered in flies. They just seem to think it's *natural* to have flies settling on everything."

"I suppose it is really," said Hilary.

Mrs. Calvin Baker was not going to allow such a heretical statement to pass.

"I'm a great believer in the Clean Food movement. At home everything perishable is wrapped in cellophane—but even in London your bread and cakes just stand about unwrapped. Now tell me, have you been getting around? You've been doing the old city today, I expect?"

"I'm afraid I haven't 'done' anything," said Hilary, smiling. "I've just been sitting about in the sun."

"Ah, of course—you're just out of hospital. I forgot." Clearly only recent illness was accepted by Mrs. Calvin Baker as an excuse for failure to sight-see. "How could I be so stupid? Why, it's perfectly true, after concussion you ought to lie down and rest in a dark room most of the day. By and by we can make some expeditions together. I'm one of those people who likes a real packed day—everything planned and arranged. Every minute filled."

In Hilary's present mood, this sounded like a foretaste of hell, but she congratulated Mrs. Calvin Baker on her energy.

"Well, I will say that for a woman of my age I get around pretty well. I hardly ever feel fatigue. Do you remember Miss Hetherington at Casablanca? An Englishwoman with a long face. She'll be arriving this evening. She prefers train to flying. Who's staying in the hotel? Mostly French, I suppose. And honeymoon couples. I must run along now and see about my room. I didn't like the one they gave me and they promised to change it."

A miniature whirlwind of energy, Mrs. Calvin Baker departed.

When Hilary entered the dining room that evening, the first thing she saw was Miss Hetherington at a small table against the wall eating her dinner with a Penguin book propped up in front of her.

The three ladies had coffee together after dinner and Miss Hetherington displayed a pleasurable excitement over the Swedish magnate and the blond film star.

"Not married, I understand," she breathed, disguising her pleasure with a correct disapproval. "One sees so much of that sort of thing abroad. That seemed a nice French family at the table by the window. The children seemed so fond of their papa. Of course, French children are allowed to sit up far too late. Ten o'clock sometimes before they go to bed, and they go through every course on the menu instead of just having milk and biscuits as children should."

"They seem to look quite healthy on it," said Hilary laughing.

Miss Hetherington shook her head and uttered a cluck of disapproval.

"They'll pay for it later," she said with grim foreboding. "Their parents even let them drink *wine.*"

Horror could go no further.

Mrs. Calvin Baker began making plans for the next day.

"I don't think I shall go to the old city," she said. "I did that very thoroughly last time. Most interesting and quite a labyrinth, if you know what I mean. So quaint and old world. If I hadn't had the guide with me, I don't think I should have found my way back to the hotel. You just kind of lose your sense of direction. But the guide was a very nice man and told me quite a lot of interesting things. He has a brother in the States—in Chicago, I think he said. Then when we'd finished with the town, he took me up to a kind of eating house or tea room, right up on the hillsides looking down over the old city—a marvelous view. I had to drink that dreadful mint tea, of course, which is really very nasty. And they wanted me to buy various things, some quite nice, but some just rubbish. One has to be very firm, I find."

"Yes, indeed," said Miss Hetherington.

She added rather wistfully, "And, of course, one can't really spare the money for souvenirs. These money restrictions are so worrying."

7

Hilary hoped to avoid having to see the old city of Fez in the depressing company of Miss Hetherington. Fortunately the latter was invited by Mrs. Baker to come with her on an expedition by car. Since Mrs. Baker made it clear that she was going to pay for the car, Miss Hetherington, whose traveling allowance was dwindling in an alarming manner, accepted with avidity. Hilary, after inquiry at the desk, was supplied with a guide, and set forth to see the city of Fez.

They started from the terrace, going down through the succession of terraced gardens until they reached an enormous door in the wall at the bottom. The guide produced a key of mammoth proportions, unlocked the door which swung slowly open, and motioned Hilary to pass through.

It was like stepping into another world. All about her were the walls of Old Fez. Narrow winding streets, high walls, and occasionally, through a doorway, a glimpse of an interior or a courtyard, and moving all around her were laden donkeys, men with their burdens, boys, women veiled and unveiled, the whole busy secret life of this Moorish city. Wandering through the narrow streets she forgot everything else, her mission, the past tragedy of her life, even herself. She was all eyes and ears, living and walking in a dream world. The only annoyance was the guide who talked unceasingly, and urged her into various establishments into which she had no particular wish to go.

"You look, lady. This man have very nice things, very cheap, really old, really Moorish. He have gowns and silks. You like very nice beads?"

The eternal commerce of East selling to West went on, but it hardly disturbed the charm for Hilary. She soon lost all sense of place or direction. Here within this walled city she had little idea of whether she was walking north or south or whether she were retracing her steps over the same streets through which she had already passed. She was quite exhausted when the guide made his final suggestion, which was evidently part of the routine.

"I take you very nice house, now, very superior. Friends of mine. You have mint tea there and they show you plenty lovely things."

Hilary recognized the well-known gambit which Mrs. Calvin Baker had described. However, she was willing to see, or be taken to see, anything that was suggested. Tomorrow, she promised herself, she would come into the Old City alone and wander around without a guide chattering by her elbow. So she allowed herself to be guided through a gateway and up a winding path climbing up more or less outside the city walls. They arrived at last as a garden surrounding an attractive house built in native style.

Here in a big room with a fine view out over the city, she was urged to sit down at a small coffee table. In due course glasses of mint tea were brought. To Hilary who did not like sugar with her tea, it was somewhat of an ordeal to drink it. But by banishing the idea of tea from her mind, and merely

524

thinking of it as a new kind of lemonade, she managed almost to enjoy it. She enjoyed, too, being shown rugs and beads and draperies, embroideries and various other things. She made one or two small purchases more out of good manners than for any other reason. The indefatigable guide then said,

"I have car ready now and take you very nice short drive. One hour, not more, see very beautiful scenery and country. And then back to hotel." He added, assuming a suitably discreet expression, "This girl here, she take you first to very nice ladies' toilet."

The girl who had served the tea was standing by them smiling, and said at once in careful English,

"Yes, yes, Madame. You come with me. We have very fine toilet, oh very fine. Just like the Ritz Hotel. Same as in New York or Chicago. You see!"

Smiling a little, Hilary followed the girl. The toilet hardly rose to the heights claimed for it, but it did at least have running water. There was a washbasin and a small cracked mirror which had such distorting proportions that Hilary almost shrank back in alarm at the sight of her own face. When she had washed and dried her hands, which she did on her own handkerchief, not much caring for the appearance of the towel, she turned to leave.

In some way, however, the door of the toilet appeared to have stuck. She turned and rattled the handle unavailingly. It would not move. Hilary wondered whether it had been bolted or locked from the outside. She grew angry. What was the idea of shutting her in there? Then she noticed that there was another door in a corner of the room. Going to it she turned the handle. This time the door opened easily enough. She passed through.

She found herself in a small eastern-looking room with light that came only from slits high in the wall. Sitting there on a low divan, smoking, was the little Frenchman she had met in the train, M. Henri Laurier.

ii

He did not rise to greet her. He merely said, and the timbre of his voice was slightly changed,

"Good afternoon, Mrs. Betterton."

For a moment Hilary stood motionless. Astonishment held her in its grip. So this—was *it!* She pulled herself together. "This is what you've been expecting. Act as you think *she* would act." She came forward and said eagerly,

"You have news for me? You can help me?"

He nodded, then said reproachfully:

"I found you, Madame, somewhat obtuse upon the train. Perhaps you are too well accustomed to talk of the weather."

"The weather?" She stared at him, bewildered.

What had he said about weather on the train? Cold? Fog? Snow?

Snow. That was what Olive Betterton had whispered as she lay dying. And she had quoted a silly little jingle—what was it?

Snow, snow, beautiful snow,
You slip on a lump and over you go.

Hilary repeated it falteringly now.

"Exactly—why did you not respond with that immediately as ordered?"

"You don't understand. I have been ill. I was in a plane crash and afterwards in hospital with concussion. It's affected my memory in all sorts of ways. Everything long ago is clear enough, but there are terrible blanks—great gaps." She let her hands rise to her head. She found it easy enough to go on with a real tremor in her voice. "You can't understand how frightening that is. I keep feeling that I've forgotten important things—really important things. The more I try to get them back, the less they will come."

"Yes," said Laurier, "the airplane crash was unfortunate." He spoke in a cold businesslike way. "It is going to be a question of whether you have the necessary stamina and courage to continue your journey."

"Of course I'm going to continue my journey," cried Hilary. "My husband—" her voice broke.

He smiled, but not a very pleasant smile. Faintly catlike.

"Your husband," he said, "is, I understand, awaiting you with eagerness."

Hilary's voice broke.

"You have no idea," she said, "no idea what it's been like these months since he went away."

"Do you think the British authorities came to a definite conclusion as to what you did or did not know?"

Hilary stretched out her hands with a wide gesture.

"How do I know—how can I tell? They *seemed* satisfied."

"All the same . . ." he stopped.

"I think it quite possible," said Hilary slowly, "that I have been followed here. I can't pick out any one particular person but I have had the feeling ever since I left England that I am under observation."

"Naturally," said Laurier, coldly. "We expected no less."

"I thought I ought to warn you."

"My dear Mrs. Betterton, we are not children. We understand what we are doing."

"I'm sorry," said Hilary, humbly. "I'm afraid I'm very ignorant."

"It does not matter if you are ignorant so long as you are obedient."

"I shall be obedient," said Hilary in a low voice.

"You were closely watched in England, I have no doubt, ever since the day of your husband's departure. Nevertheless, the message came to you, did it not?"

"Yes," said Hilary.

"Now," said Laurier in a businesslike manner, "I will give you your instructions, Madame."

"Please do."

"From here you will proceed to Marrakesh the day after tomorrow. That is as you planned and in accordance with your reservations."

"Yes."

"The day after you arrive there you will receive a telegram from England. What it will say I do not know, but it will be sufficient for you to make plans immediately to return to England."

"I am to *return to England?*"

"Please listen. I have not finished. You will book a seat on a plane leaving Casablanca the following day."

"Supposing I cannot get reservations—supposing the seats are all booked?"

"They will not be all booked. Everything is arranged for. Now, you understand your instructions?"

"I understand."

"Then please return to where your guide is waiting. You have been long enough in this ladies' toilet. By the way, you have become friendly with an American woman and an English woman who are now staying at the Palais Jamail?"

"Yes. Has that been a mistake? It has been difficult to avoid."

"Not at all. It suits our plans admirably. If you can persuade one or other of them to accompany you to Marrakesh, so much the better. Goodbye, Madame."

"*Au revoir,* Monsieur."

"It is unlikely," Monsieur Laurier told her with a complete lack of interest, "that I shall meet you again."

Hilary retraced her steps to the ladies' toilet. This time she found the other door unfastened. A few minutes later she had rejoined the guide in the tea room.

"I got very nice car waiting," said the guide. "I take you now for very pleasant instructive drive."

The expedition proceeded according to plan.

iii

"So you're leaving for Marrakesh tomorrow," said Miss Hetherington. "You haven't made a very long stay in Fez, have you? Wouldn't it have been much easier to go to Marrakesh first and then to Fez, returning to Casablanca afterwards?"

"I suppose it would really," said Hilary, "but reservations are rather difficult to obtain. It's pretty crowded here."

"Not with English people," said Miss Hetherington, rather disconsolately. "It really seems dreadful nowadays the way one meets hardly *any* of one's fellow countrymen." She looked around her disparagingly and said, "It's all the French."

Hilary smiled faintly. The fact that Morocco was a French colonial possession did not seem to count much with Miss Hetherington. Hotels anywhere abroad she regarded as the prerogative of the English traveling public.

"The French and the Germans *and* the Greeks," said Mrs. Calvin Baker, with a little cackle of laughter. "That scruffy little old man is a Greek, I believe."

"I was told he was Greek," said Hilary.

"Looks like a person of importance," said Mrs. Baker. "You see how the waiters fly about for him."

"They give the English hardly any attention nowadays," said Miss Hetherington, gloomily. "They always give them the most terrible back bedrooms—the ones maids and valets used to have in the old days."

"Well, I can't say I've found any fault with the accommodation I've had since I came to Morocco," said Mrs. Calvin Baker. "I've managed to get a most comfortable room and bath every time."

"You're an American," said Miss Hetherington, sharply, and with some venom in her voice. She clicked her knitting needles furiously.

"I wish I could persuade you two to come to Marrakesh with me," said Hilary. "It's been so pleasant meeting you and talking to you here. Really, it's very lonely traveling all by oneself."

"I've *been* to Marrakesh," said Miss Hetherington in a shocked voice.

Mrs. Calvin Baker, however, appeared to be somewhat sold on the idea.

"Well, it certainly is an idea," she said. "It's over a month since I was in Marrakesh. I'd be glad to go there again for a spell, and I could show you around, too, Mrs. Betterton and prevent you being imposed upon. It's not until you've been to a place and looked around it that you learn the ropes. I wonder now. I'll go to the office and see what I can fix up."

Miss Hetherington said acidly, when she had departed;

"That's exactly like these American women. Rushing from place to place, never settling down anywhere. Egypt one day, Palestine the next. Sometimes I really don't think they know what country they're in."

She shut her lips with a snap and rising and gathering up her knitting carefully, she left the Turkish room with a little nod to Hilary as she went. Hilary glanced down at her watch. She felt inclined not to change this evening for dinner, as she usually did. She sat on there alone in the low, rather dark room with its Oriental hangings. A waiter looked in, then went away after turning on two lamps. They did not give out very much light and the room seemed pleasantly dim. It had an Eastern sort of serenity. Hilary sat back on the low divan, thinking of the future.

Only yesterday she had been wondering if the whole business upon which she had been engaged was a mare's nest. And now—now she was on the point of starting on her real journey. She must be careful, very careful. She must make no slip. She must be Olive Betterton, moderately well educated, inartistic, conventional but with definite Left Wing sympathies, and a woman who was devoted to her husband.

"I must make no mistake," said Hilary to herself, under her breath.

How strange it felt to be sitting here alone in Morocco. She felt as though she had got into a land of mystery and enchantment. That dim lamp beside her! If she were to take the carved brass between her hands and rub, would a Djin of the Lamp appear? As the thought came to her, she started. Materializing quite suddenly from beyond the lamp, she saw the small wrinkled face and pointed beard of M. Aristides. He bowed politely before sitting down beside her, saying;

"You permit, Madame?"

Hilary responded politely.

Taking out his cigarette case he offered her a cigarette. She accepted and he lit one himself also.

"It pleases you, this country, Madame?" he asked after a moment or two.

"I have been here only a very short time," said Hilary. "I find it so far quite enchanting."

"Ah. And you have been into the old city? You liked it?"

"I think it is wonderful."

"Yes, it is wonderful. It is the past there—the past of commerce, of intrigue, of whispering voices, shuttered activities, all the mystery and passion of a city enclosed in its narrow streets and walls. Do you know what I think of, Madame, when I walk through the streets of Fez?"

"No."

"I think of your Great West Road in London. I think of your great factory buildings on each side of the road. I think of those buildings lit throughout with their neon lighting and the people inside, that you see so clearly from the road as you drive along in your car. There is nothing hidden, there is nothing mysterious. There are not even curtains to the windows. No, they do their work there with the whole world observing them if it wants to do so. It is like slicing off the top of an anthill."

"You mean," said Hilary, interested, "that it is the contrast that interests you?"

Mr. Aristides nodded his elderly, tortoiselike head.

"Yes," he said. "There everything is in the open and in the old streets of Fez nothing is *à jour*. Everything is hidden, dark. . . . *But—*" he leaned forward and tapped a finger on the little brass coffee table "—but the same things go on. The same cruelties, the same oppressions, the same wish for power, the same bargaining and haggling."

"You think that human nature is the same everywhere?" Hilary asked.

"In every country. In the past as in the present there are always the two things that rule. Cruelty and benevolence! One or the other. Sometimes both." He continued with hardly a change of manner, "They have told me, Madame, that you were in a very bad airplane accident the other day at Casablanca?"

"Yes, that is true."

"I envy you," Mr. Aristides said unexpectedly.

Hilary looked at him in an astonished manner. Again he waggled his head in vehement assertion.

"Yes," he added, "you are to be envied. You have had an experience. I should like the experience of having come so near to death. To have that, yet survive—do you not feel yourself different since then, Madame?"

"In a rather unfortunate way," said Hilary. "I had concussion and that gives me very bad headaches, and it also affects my memory."

"Those are mere inconveniences," said Mr. Aristides with a wave of the hand, "but it is an adventure of the spirit you have passed through, is it not?"

"It is true," said Hilary slowly, "that I have passed through an adventure of the spirit."

She was thinking of a bottle of Vichy water and a little heap of sleeping pills.

"I have never had that experience," said Mr. Aristides in his dissatisfied voice. "So many other things, but not that."

He rose, bowed, said, *"Mes homages, Madame,"* and left her.

8

How ALIKE, HILARY thought to herself, all airports were! They had a strange anonymity about them. They were all at some distance from the town or city they served, and in consequence you had a queer, stateless feeling of existing nowhere. You could fly from London to Madrid, to Rome, to Istanbul, to Cairo, to anywhere you liked and if your journey was a through one by air, you would never have the faintest idea of what any of these cities looked like! If you caught a glimpse of them from the air, they were only a kind of glorified map, something built with a child's box of bricks.

And why, she thought vexedly, looking round her, does one always have to be at these places so much too early?

They had spent nearly half an hour in the waiting room. Mrs. Calvin Baker, who had decided to accompany Hilary to Marrakesh had been talking nonstop ever since their arrival. Hilary had answered almost mechanically. But now she realized that the flow had been diverted. Mrs. Baker had now switched her attention to two other travelers who were sitting near her. They were both tall, fair young men. One an American with a broad, friendly grin, the other a rather solemn looking Dane or Norwegian. The Dane talked heavily, slowly, and rather pedantically in careful English. The American was clearly delighted to find another American traveler. Presently, in conscientious fashion, Mrs. Calvin Baker turned to Hilary.

"Mr.—? I'd like to have you know my friend, Mrs. Betterton."

"Andrew Peters—Andy to my friends."

The other young man rose to his feet, bowed rather stiffly and said, "Torquil Ericsson."

"So now we're all acquainted," said Mrs. Baker happily. "Are we all going to Marrakesh? It's my friend's first visit there—"

"I, too," said Ericsson. "I, too, for the first time go."

"That goes for me too," said Peters.

The loudspeaker was suddenly switched on and a hoarse announcement in French was made. The words were barely distinguishable but it appeared to be their summons to the plane.

There were four passengers besides Mrs. Baker and Hilary. Besides Peters and Ericsson, there was a thin, tall Frenchman, and a severe-looking nun.

It was a clear, sunny day and flying conditions were good. Leaning back in her seat with half closed eyes, Hilary studied her fellow passengers, seeking to distract herself that way from the anxious questionings which were going on in her mind.

One seat ahead of her, on the other side of the aisle, Mrs. Calvin Baker in her gray traveling costume looked like a plump and contented duck. A small hat with wings was perched on her blue hair and she was turning the pages of a glossy magazine. Occasionally she leaned forward to tap the shoulder of the man sitting in front of her, who was the cheerful-looking fair young American, Peters. When she did so he turned around, displaying his good-humored grin, and responding energetically to her remarks. How very good-natured and friendly Americans were, Hilary thought to herself. So different from the stiff traveling English. She could not imagine Miss Hetherington, for instance, falling into easy conversation with a young man even of her own nation, on a plane, and she doubted if the latter would have responded as good-naturedly as this young American was doing.

Across the aisle from her was the Norwegian, Ericsson.

As she caught his eye, he made her a stiff little bow and leaning across offered her his magazine, which he was just closing. She thanked him and took it. In the seat behind him was the thin, dark Frenchman. His legs were stretched out and he seemed to be asleep.

Hilary turned her head over her shoulder. The severe-faced nun was sitting behind her, and the nun's eyes, impersonal, incurious, met Hilary's with no expression in them. She sat immovable, her hands clasped. It seemed to Hilary an odd trick of Time that a woman in traditional medieval costume should be traveling by air in the twentieth century.

Six people, thought Hilary, traveling together for a few hours, traveling to different places with different aims, scattering perhaps at the end of that few hours and never meeting again. She had read a novel which had hinged on a similar theme and where the lives of those six people were followed up. The Frenchman, she thought, must be on a holiday. He seemed so tired. The young American was perhaps a student of some kind. Ericsson was perhaps going to take up a job. The nun was doubtless bound for her convent.

Hilary closed her eyes and forgot her fellow travelers. She puzzled, as she had done all last night, over the instructions that had been given her. She was to return to England! It seemed crazy! Or could it be that in some way she had been found wanting, was not trusted: had failed to supply certain words or credentials that the real Olive would have supplied. She sighed and moved restlessly. "Well," she thought, "I can do no more than I am doing. If I've failed—I've failed. At any rate, I've done my best."

Then another thought struck her. Henri Laurier had accepted it as natural and inevitable that a close watch was being kept upon her in Morocco—was this a means of disarming suspicion? With the abrupt return of Mrs. Betterton to England it would surely be assumed that she had *not* come to Morocco in order to "disappear" like her husband. Suspicion would relax—she would be regarded as a *bona fide* traveler.

She would leave for England, going by Air France via Paris—and perhaps in Paris—

Yes, of course—in Paris. In Paris where Tom Betterton had disappeared. How much easier to stage a disappearance there. Perhaps Tom Betterton had never left Paris. Perhaps—tired of profitless speculation Hilary went to sleep. She woke—dozed again, occasionally glancing without interest, at the magazine she held. Awakening suddenly from a deeper sleep, she noticed that the plane was rapidly losing height and circling round. She glanced at her watch, but it was still some time earlier than the estimated time of arrival. Moreover, looking down through the window, she could not see any signs of an airfield beneath.

For a moment a faint qualm of apprehension struck her. The thin, dark Frenchman rose, yawned, stretched his arms and looked out and said something in French which she did not catch. But Ericsson leaned across the aisle and said,

"We are coming down here, it seems—but why?"

Mrs. Calvin Baker, leaning out of her seat, turned her head and nodded brightly as Hilary said,

"We seem to be landing."

The plane swooped round in ever lower circles. The country beneath them seemed to be practically desert. There were no signs of houses or villages. The wheels touched with a decided bump, bouncing along and taxiing until they finally stopped. It had been a somewhat rough landing, but it was a landing in the middle of nowhere.

Had something gone wrong with the engine, Hilary wondered, or had they run out of petrol? The pilot, a dark-skinned, handsome young man, came through the forward door and along the plane.

"If you please," he said, "you will all get out."

He opened the rear door, let down a short ladder and stood there waiting for them all to pass out. They stood in a little group on the ground, shivering a little. It was chilly here, with the wind blowing sharply from the mountains in the distance. The mountains, Hilary noticed, were covered with snow and singularly beautiful. The air was crisply cold and intoxicating. The pilot descended too, and addressed them, speaking French:

"You are all here? Yes? Excuse, please, you will have to wait a little minute, perhaps. Ah, no, I see it is arriving."

He pointed to where a small dot on the horizon was gradually growing nearer. Hilary said in a slightly bewildered voice:

"But why have we come down here? What is the matter? How long shall we have to be here?"

The French traveler said,

"There is, I understand, a station wagon arriving. We shall go on in that."

"Did the engine fail?" asked Hilary.

Andy Peters smiled cheerfully.

"Why no, I shouldn't say so," he said, "the engine sounded all right to me. However, they'll fix up something of that kind, no doubt."

She stared, puzzled. Mrs. Calvin Baker murmured,

"My, but it's chilly, standing about here. That's the worst of this climate. It seems so sunny but it's cold the moment you get near sunset."

The pilot was murmuring under his breath, swearing, Hilary thought. He was saying something like:

"Toujours des retards insupportables."

The station wagon came toward them at a breakneck pace. The Berber driver drew up with a grinding of brakes. He sprang down and was immediately engaged by the pilot in angry conversation. Rather to Hilary's surprise, Mrs. Baker intervened in the dispute—speaking in French.

"Don't waste time," she said peremptorily. "What's the good of arguing? We want to get out of here."

The driver shrugged his shoulders, and going to the station wagon, he unhitched the back part of it which let down. Inside was a large packing case. Together with the pilot and with help from Ericsson and Peters, they got it down onto the ground. From the effort it took, it seemed to be heavy. Mrs. Calvin Baker put her hand on Hilary's arm and said, as the man began to raise the lid of the case,

"I shouldn't watch, my dear. It's never a pretty sight."

She led Hilary a little way away, on the other side of the wagon. The Frenchman and Peters came with them. The Frenchman said in his own language,

"What is it then, this maneuver there that they do?"

Mrs. Baker said,

"You are Dr. Barron?"

The Frenchman bowed.

"Pleased to meet you," said Mrs. Baker. She stretched out her hand, rather like a hostess welcoming him to a party. Hilary said in a bewildered tone,

"But I don't understand. What is in that case? Why is it better not to look?"

Andy Peters looked down on her consideringly. He had a nice face, Hilary thought. Something square and dependable about it. He said,

"I know what it is. The pilot told me. It's not very pretty perhaps, but I guess it's necessary." He added quietly, "There are bodies in there."

"Bodies!" She stared at him.

"Oh, they haven't been murdered or anything," he grinned reassuringly. "They were obtained in a perfectly legitimate way for research—medical research, you know."

But Hilary still stared.

"I don't understand."

"Ah. You see, Mrs. Betterton, this is where the journey ends. One journey, that is."

"Ends?"

"Yes. They'll arrange the bodies in that plane and then the pilot will fix things and presently, as we're driving away from here, we shall see in the distance the flames going up in the air. Another plane that has crashed and come down in flames, *and no survivors!*"

"But why? How fantastic!"

"But surely—" It was Dr. Barron now who spoke to her. "But surely you know where we are going?"

Mrs. Baker, drawing near, said cheerfully,

"Of course she knows. But maybe she didn't expect it quite so soon."

Hilary said, after a short bewildered pause,

"But you mean—all of us?" She looked round.

"We're fellow travelers," said Peters gently.

The young Norwegian, nodding his head, said with an almost fanatical enthusiasm,

"Yes, we are all fellow travelers."

9

THE PILOT CAME up to them.

"You will start now, please," he said. "As soon as possible. There is much to be done, and we are late on schedule."

Hilary recoiled for a moment. She put her hand nervously to her throat. The pearl choker she was wearing broke under the strain of her fingers. She picked up the loose pearls and crammed them into her pocket.

They all got into the station wagon. Hilary was on a long bench crowded up with Peters one side of her and Mrs. Baker the other. Turning her head toward the American woman, Hilary said,

"So you—so you—are what you might call the liaison officer, Mrs. Baker?"

"That hits it off exactly. And though I say it myself, I'm well qualified. Nobody is surprised to find an American woman getting around and traveling a lot."

She was still plump and smiling, but Hilary sensed, or thought she sensed, a difference. The slight fatuity and surface conventionality had gone. This was an efficient, probably ruthless woman.

"It will make a fine sensation in the headlines," said Mrs. Baker. She laughed with some enjoyment. "*You,* I mean, my dear. Persistently dogged by ill luck, they'll say. First nearly losing your life in the crash at Casablanca, then being killed in this further disaster."

Hilary realized suddenly the cleverness of the plan.

"These others?" she murmured. "Are they who they say they are?"

"Why yes. Dr. Barron is a bacteriologist, I believe. Mr. Ericsson a very brilliant young physicist, Mr. Peters is a research chemist, Miss Needheim, of course, isn't a nun, she's an endocrinologist. Me, as I say, I'm only the liaison officer. I don't belong in this scientific bunch." She laughed again as she said, "That Hetherington woman never had a chance."

"Miss Hetherington—was she—was she—"

Mrs. Baker nodded emphatically.

"If you ask me, she's been tailing you. Took over in Casablanca from whoever followed you out."

"But she didn't come with us today although I urged her to?"

"That wouldn't have been in character," said Mrs. Baker. "It would have looked a little too obvious to go back again to Marrakesh after having been there already. No, she'll have sent a telegram or a phone message through and there'll be someone waiting at Marrakesh to pick you up when you arrive. When you arrive! That's a good laugh, isn't it? Look! Look there now! Up she goes."

They had been driving rapidly away across the desert, and now as Hilary craned forward to look through the little window, she saw a great glow behind them. A faint sound of an explosion came to her ears. Peters threw his head back and laughed. He said:

"Six people die when plane to Marrakesh crashes!"

Hilary said almost under her breath:

"It's—it's rather frightening."

"Stepping off into the unknown?" It was Peters who spoke. He was serious enough now. "Yes, but it's the only way. We're leaving the Past and stepping out toward the Future." His face lit up with sudden enthusiasm. "We've got to get quit of all the bad, mad old stuff. Corrupt governments and the warmongers. We've got to go into the new world—the world of science, clean away from the scum and the driftwood."

Hilary drew a deep breath.

"That's like the things my husband used to say," she said, deliberately.

"Your husband?" He shot her a quick glance. "Why, was he *Tom* Better-ton?"

Hilary nodded.

"Well that's great. I never knew him out in the States, though I nearly met him more than once. ZE Fission is one of the most brilliant discoveries of this age—yes, I certainly take my hat off to him. Worked with old Mannheim, didn't he?"

"Yes," said Hilary.

"Didn't they tell me he'd married Mannheim's daughter. But surely *you're* not—"

"I'm his second wife," said Hilary, flushing a little. "He—his—Elsa died in America."

"I remember. Then he went to Britain to work there. Then he riled them by disappearing." He laughed suddenly. "Walked slap out of some Paris Conference into nowhere." He added, as though in further appreciation, "Lord, you can't say they don't organize well."

Hilary agreed with him. The excellence of their organization was sending a cold pang of apprehension through her. All the plans, codes, signs that had been so elaborately arranged were going to be useless now, for now there would be no trail to pick up. Things had been so arranged that everyone on the fatal plane had been fellow travelers bound for the Unknown Destination where Thomas Betterton had gone before them. There would be no trace left. Nothing. Nothing but a burnt-out plane. Could they—was it possible that Jessop and his organization could guess that she, Hilary, was *not* one of those charred bodies? She doubted it. The accident had been so convincing, so clever—there would even be charred bodies in the plane.

Peters spoke again. His voice was boyish with enthusiasm. For him there were no qualms, no looking back, only eagerness to go forward.

"I wonder," he said, "where do we go from here?"

Hilary, too, wondered, because again much depended on that. Sooner or later there *must* be contacts with humanity. Sooner or later, if investigation was made, the fact that a station wagon with six people in it resembling the description of those who had left that morning by plane, might possibly be noted by someone. She turned to Mrs. Baker, and asked, trying to make her tone the counterpart of the childish eagerness of the young American beside her,

"Where are we going—what happens next?"

"You'll see," said Mrs. Baker, and for all the pleasantness of her voice, there was something somehow ominous in those words.

They drove on. Behind them the flare of the plane still showed in the sky, showed all the more clearly because the sun was now dropping below the horizon. Night fell. Still they drove. The going was bad since they were obviously not on any main road. Sometimes they seemed to be on field tracks, at other times they drove over open country.

For a long time Hilary remained awake, thoughts and apprehensions turning round in her head excitedly. But at last, shaken and tossed from side to side, exhaustion had its way and she fell asleep. It was a broken sleep. Various ruts and jars in the road awoke her. For a moment or two she would wonder confusedly where she was, then reality would come back to her. She would remain awake for a few moments, her thoughts racing round in confused apprehension, then once more her head would drop forward and nod, and once again she would sleep.

She was awakened suddenly by the car coming to an abrupt stop. Very gently Peters shook her by the arm.

"Wake up," he said, "we seem to have arrived somewhere."

Everyone got out of the station wagon. They were all cramped and weary. It was still dark and they seemed to have drawn up outside a house surrounded by palm trees. Some distance away they could see a few dim lights as though there were a village there. Guided by a lantern they were ushered into the house. It was a native house with a couple of giggling Berber women who stared curiously at Hilary and Mrs. Calvin Baker. They took no interest in the nun.

The three women were taken to a small upstairs room. There were three mattresses on the floor and some heaps of coverings, but no other furniture.

"I'll say I'm stiff," said Mrs. Baker. "Gets you kind of cramped, riding along the way we've been doing."

"Discomfort does not matter," said the nun.

She spoke with a harsh, guttural assurance. Her English, Hilary found, was good and fluent, though her accent was bad.

"You're living up to your part, Miss Needheim," said the American woman. "I can just see you in the convent, kneeling on the hard stones at four in the morning."

Miss Needheim smiled contemptuously.

"Christianity has made fools of women," she said. "Such a worship of weakness, such sniveling humiliation! Pagan women had strength. They rejoiced and conquered! And in order to conquer, no discomfort is unbearable. Nothing is too much to suffer."

"Right now," said Mrs. Baker, yawning, "I wish I was in my bed at the Palais Jamail at Fez. What about you, Mrs. Betterton? That shaking hasn't done your concussion any good, I'll bet."

"No, it hasn't," Hilary said.

"They'll bring us something to eat presently, and then I'll fix you up with some aspirin and you'd better get to sleep as fast as you can."

Steps were heard coming up the stairs outside and giggling female voices. Presently the two Berber women came into the room. They carried a tray with a big dish of semolina and meat stew. They put it down on the floor, came back again with a metal basin with water in it and a towel. One of them felt Hilary's coat, passing the stuff between her fingers and speaking to the

other woman who nodded her head in rapid agreement, and did the same to
Mrs. Baker. Neither of them paid any attention to the nun.

"Shoo," said Mrs. Baker, waving them away. "Shoo, shoo."

It was exactly like shooing chickens. The women retreated, still laughing,
and left the room.

"Silly creatures," said Mrs. Baker, "it's hard to have patience with them. I
suppose babies and clothes are their only interest in life."

"It is all they are fit for," said Fraulein Needheim, "they belong to a slave
race. They are useful to serve their betters, but no more."

"Aren't you a little harsh?" said Hilary, irritated by the woman's attitude.

"I have no patience with sentimentality. There are those that rule, the few;
and there are the many that serve."

"But surely . . ."

Mrs. Baker broke in in an authoritative manner.

"We've all got our own ideas on these subjects, I guess," she said, "and
very interesting they are. But this is hardly the time for them. We'll want to
get what rest we can."

Mint tea arrived. Hilary swallowed some aspirin willingly enough, since
her headache was quite a genuine one. Then the three women lay down on
the mattresses and fell asleep.

They slept late into the following day. They were not to go on again until
the evening, so Mrs. Baker informed them. From the room in which they had
slept, there was an outside staircase leading onto a flat roof where they had a
certain amount of view over the surrounding country. A little distance away
was a village, but here where they were, the house was isolated in a large
palm garden. On awakening, Mrs. Baker had indicated three heaps of clothing which had been brought and laid down just inside the door.

"We're going native for the next lap," she explained, "we leave our other
clothes here."

So the smart little American woman's neat suiting and Hilary's tweed coat
and skirt and the nun's habit were all laid aside and three native Moroccan
women sat on the roof of the house and chatted together. The whole thing
had a curiously unreal feeling.

Hilary studied Miss Needheim more closely now that she had left the
anonymity of her nun's habit. She was a younger woman than Hilary had
thought her, not more, perhaps, than thirty-three or thirty-four. There was a
neat spruceness in her appearance. The pale skin, the short stubby fingers,
and the cold eyes in which burned from time to time the gleam of the fanatic,
repelled rather than attracted. Her speech was brusque and uncompromising.
Toward both Mrs. Baker and Hilary she displayed a certain amount of contempt as toward people unworthy to associate with her. This arrogance Hilary found very irritating. Mrs. Baker, on the other hand, seemed hardly to
notice it. In a queer way Hilary felt far nearer and more in sympathy with the
two giggling Berber women who brought them food, than with her two companions of the Western world. The young German woman was obviously

indifferent to the impression she created. There was a certain concealed impatience in her manner, and it was obvious that she was longing to get on with her journey and that she had no interest in her two companions.

Appraising Mrs. Baker's attitude, Hilary found more difficult. At first Mrs. Baker seemed a natural and normal person after the inhumanity of the German woman specialist. But as the sun sank lower in the sky she felt almost more intrigued and repelled by Mrs. Baker than by Helga Needheim. Mrs. Baker's social manner was almost robotlike in its perfection. All her comments and remarks were natural, normal, everyday currency, but one had a suspicion that the whole thing was like an actor playing a part for perhaps the seven hundredth time. It was an automatic performance, completely divorced from what Mrs. Baker might really have been thinking or feeling. Who was Mrs. Calvin Baker, Hilary wondered? Why had she come to play her part with such machinelike perfection? Was she, too, a fanatic? Had she dreams of a brave new world—was she in violent revolt against the capitalist system? Had she given up all normal life because of her political beliefs and aspirations? Impossible to tell.

They resumed their journey that evening. It was no longer the station wagon. This time it was an open touring car. Everyone was in native dress, the men with white djellabos round them, the women with their faces hidden. Packed tightly in, they started off once more, driving all through the night.

"How are you feeling, Mrs. Betterton?"

Hilary smiled up at Andy Peters. The sun had just risen and they had stopped for breakfast. Native bread, eggs, and tea made over a primus.

"I feel as though I were taking part in a dream," said Hilary.

"Yes, it has rather that quality."

"Where are we?"

He shrugged his shoulders.

"Who knows? Our Mrs. Calvin Baker, no doubt, but no other."

"It's a very lonely country."

"Yes, practically desert. But then it would have to be, wouldn't it."

"You mean so as to leave no trace?"

"Yes. One realizes, doesn't one, that the whole thing must be very carefully thought out. Each stage of our journey is, as it were, quite independent of the other. A plane goes up in flames. An old station wagon drives through the night. If anyone notices it, it has on it a plate stating that it belongs to a certain archaeological expedition that is excavating in these parts. The following day there is a touring car full of Berbers, one of the commonest sights on the road to be seen. For the next stage—" he shrugged his shoulders "—who knows?"

"But where are we going?"

Andy Peters shook his head.

"No use to ask. We shall find out."

The Frenchman, Dr. Barron, had joined them.

"Yes," he said, "we shall find out. But how true it is that we cannot but ask? That is our western blood. We can never say 'sufficient for the day.' It is always tomorrow, tomorrow with us. To leave yesterday behind, to proceed to tomorrow. That is what we demand."

"You want to hurry the world on, Doctor, is that it?" asked Peters.

"There is so much to achieve," said Dr. Barron, "life is too short. One must have more time. More time, more time." He flung out his hands in a passionate gesture.

Peters turned to Hilary.

"What are the four freedoms you talk about in your country? Freedom from want, freedom from fear . . ."

The Frenchman interrupted. "Freedom from fools," he said bitterly. "That is what *I* want! That is what my work needs. Freedom from incessant, pettifogging economies! Freedom from all the nagging restrictions that hamper one's work!"

"You are a bacteriologist, are you not, Dr. Barron?"

"Yes, I am a bacteriologist. Ah, you have no idea, my friend, what a fascinating study that is! But it needs patience, infinite patience, repeated experiment—and *money*—much money! One must have equipment, assistants, raw materials! Given that you have all you ask for, what can one not achieve?"

"Happiness?" asked Hilary.

He flashed her a quick smile, suddenly human again.

"Ah, you are a woman, Madame. It is women who ask always for happiness."

"And seldom get it?" asked Hilary.

He shrugged his shoulders.

"That may be."

"Individual happiness does not matter," said Peters seriously, "there must be the happiness of *all*, the brotherhood of the spirit! The workers, free and united, owning the means of production, free of the warmongers, of the greedy, insatiable men who keep everything in their own hands. Science is for *all*, and must not be held jealously by one power or the other."

"So!" said Ericsson appreciatively, "you are right. The scientists must be masters. They must control and rule. They and they alone are the Supermen. It is only the Supermen who matter. The slaves must be well treated, but they *are* slaves."

Hilary walked a little way away from the group. After a minute or two Peters followed her.

"You look just a little scared," he said humorously.

"I think I am." She gave a short, breathless laugh. "Of course what Dr. Barron said was quite true. I'm only a woman. I'm not a scientist, I don't do research or surgery, or bacteriology. I haven't, I suppose, much mental ability. I'm looking, as Dr. Barron said, for happiness—just like any other fool of a woman."

"And what's wrong with that?" said Peters.

"Well, maybe I feel a little out of my depth in this company. You see, I'm just a woman who's going to join her husband."

"Good enough," said Peters. "You represent the fundamental."

"It's nice of you to put it that way."

"Well, it's true." He added in a lower voice, "You care for your husband very much?"

"Would I be here if I didn't?"

"I suppose not. You share his views? I take it that he's a Communist?"

Hilary avoided giving a direct answer.

"Talking of being a Communist," she said, "has something about our little group struck you as curious?"

"What's that?"

"Well, that although we're all bound for the same destination, the views of our fellow travelers don't seem really alike."

Peters said thoughtfully,

"Why, no. You've got something there. I hadn't thought of it quite that way—but I believe you're right."

"I don't think," said Hilary, "that Dr. Barron is politically minded at all! He wants money for his experiments. Helga Needheim talks like a Fascist, not a Communist. And Ericsson—"

"What about Ericsson?"

"I find him frightening—he's got a dangerous kind of single-mindedness. He's like a mad scientist in a film!"

"And I believe in the Brotherhood of men, and you're a loving wife, and our Mrs. Calvin Baker—where would you place her?"

"I don't know. I find her more hard to place than anyone."

"Oh, I wouldn't say that. I'd say she was easy enough."

"How do you mean?"

"I'd say it was money all the way with her. She's just a well-paid cog in the wheel."

"She frightens me, too," said Hilary.

"Why? Why on earth does *she* frighten you? No touch of the mad scientist about her."

"She frightens me because she's so ordinary. You know, just like anybody else. And yet she's mixed up in all this."

Peters said grimly,

"The Party is realistic, you know. It employs the best man or woman for the job."

"But is someone who only wants money the best person for the job? Mightn't they desert to the other side?"

"That would be a very big risk to take," said Peters, quietly. "Mrs. Calvin Baker's a shrewd woman. I don't think she'd take that risk."

Hilary shivered suddenly.

"Cold?"

"Yes. It is a bit cold."

"Let's move around a little."

They walked up and down. As they did so Peter stooped and picked up something.

"Here. You're dropping things."

Hilary took it from him.

"Oh, yes, it's a pearl from my choker. I broke it the other day—no, yesterday. What ages ago that seems already."

"Not real pearls, I hope."

Hilary smiled.

"No, of course not. Costume jewelry."

Peters took a cigarette case from his pocket.

"Costume jewelry," he said, "what a term!"

He offered her a cigarette.

"It does sound foolish—here." She took a cigarette. "What an odd case. How heavy it is."

"Made of lead, that's why. It's a war souvenir—made out of a bit of a bomb that just failed to blow me up."

"You were—in the war then?"

"I was one of the backroom boys who tickled things to see if they'd go bang! Don't let's talk about wars. Let's concentrate on tomorrow."

"Where are we going?" asked Hilary. "Nobody's told me anything. Are we—"

He stopped her.

"Speculations," he said, "are not encouraged. You go where you're told and do what you're told."

With sudden passion Hilary said,

"Do you like being dragooned, being ordered about, having no say of your own?"

"I'm prepared to accept it if it's necessary. And it is necessary. We've got to have World Peace, World Discipline, World Order."

"Is it possible? Can it be got?"

"Anything's better than the muddle we live in. Don't you agree to that?"

For a moment, carried away by fatigue, by the loneliness of her surroundings and the strange beauty of the early morning light, Hilary nearly burst out into a passionate denial.

She wanted to say,

"Why do you decry the world we live in? There are good people in it. Isn't muddle a better breeding ground for kindliness and individuality than a world order that's imposed, a world order that may be right today and wrong tomorrow? I would rather have a world of kindly, faulty, human beings, than a world of superior robots who've said goodbye to pity and understanding and sympathy."

But she restrained herself in time. She said instead, with a deliberate subdued enthusiasm,

"How right you are. I was tired. We must obey and go forward."

He grinned.

"That's better."

10

A DREAM JOURNEY. So it seemed; more so every day. It was as though, Hilary felt, she had been traveling all her life with these five strangely assorted companions. They had stepped off from the beaten track into the void. In one sense this journey of theirs could not be called a flight. They were all, she supposed, free agents; free, that is, to go where they chose. As far as she knew they had committed no crime, they were not wanted by the police. Yet great pains had been taken to hide their tracks. Sometimes she wondered why this was, since they were not fugitives. It was as though they were in process of becoming not themselves but someone else.

That indeed was literally true in her case. She who had left England as Hilary Craven had become Olive Betterton, and perhaps her strange feeling of unreality had something to do with that. Every day the glib political slogans seemed to come more easily to her lips. She felt herself becoming earnest and intense, and that again she put down to the influence of her companions.

She knew now that she was afraid of them. She had never before spent any time in close intimacy with people of genius. This was genius at close quarters, and genius had that something above normal in it that was a great strain upon the ordinary mind and feeling. All five were different from each other, yet each had that curious quality of burning intensity, the single-mindedness of purpose that made such a terrifying impression. She did not know whether it were a quality of brain or rather a quality of outlook, of intensity. But each of them, she thought, was in his or her way a passionate idealist. To Dr. Barron life was a passionate desire to be once more in his laboratory, to be able to calculate and experiment and work with unlimited money and unlimited resources. To work for what? She doubted if he ever put that question to himself. He spoke to her once of the powers of destruction that he could let loose on a vast continent, which could be contained in one little phial. She had said to him,

"But could you ever *do* that? Actually really do it?"

And he replied, looking at her with faint surprise,

"Yes. Yes, of course, if it became necessary."

He had said it in a merely perfunctory fashion. He had gone on,

"It would be amazingly interesting to see the exact course, the exact progress." And he had added with a deep half sigh, "You see, there's so much more to know, so much more to find out."

For a moment Hilary understood. For a moment she stood where he stood, impregnated with that single hearted desire for knowledge which swept aside life and death for millions of human beings as essentially unimportant. It was a point of view and in a way a not ignoble one. Toward Helga Needheim she felt more antagonistic. The young woman's superb arrogance revolted her. Peters she liked but was from time to time repulsed and frightened by the sudden fanatical gleam in his eye. She said to him once,

"It is not a new world you want to create. It is destroying the old one that you will enjoy."

"You're wrong, Olive. What a thing to say."

"No, I'm not wrong. There's hate in you. I can feel it. Hate. The wish to destroy."

Ericsson she found the most puzzling of all. Ericsson, she thought, was a dreamer, less practical than the Frenchman, further removed from destructive passion than the American. He had the strange, fanatical idealism of the Norseman.

"We must conquer," he said, "we must conquer the world. Then we can rule."

"We?" she asked.

He nodded, his face strange and gentle with a deceptive mildness about the eyes.

"Yes," he said, "we few who count. The brains. That is all that matters."

Hilary thought, where are we going? Where is all this leading. These people are mad, but they're not mad in the same way as each other. It's as though they were all going toward different goals, different mirages. Yes, that was the word. *Mirages.* And from them she turned to a contemplation of Mrs. Calvin Baker. Here there was no fanaticism, no hate, no dream, no arrogance, no aspiration. There was nothing here that Hilary could find or take notice of. She was a woman, Hilary thought, without either heart or conscience. She was the efficient instrument in the hands of a big unknown force.

It was the end of the third day. They had come to a small town and alighted at a small native hotel. Here, Hilary found, they were to resume European clothing. She slept that night in a small, bare, whitewashed room, rather like a cell. At early dawn Mrs. Baker woke her.

"We're going off right now," said Mrs. Baker. "The plane's waiting."

"The plane?"

"Why yes, my dear. We're returning to civilized traveling, thank the Lord."

They came to the airfield and the plane after about an hour's drive. It looked like a disused army airfield. The pilot was a Frenchman. They flew for some hours, their flight taking them over mountains. Looking down from the plane Hilary thought what a curious sameness the world has, seen from above. Mountains, valleys, roads, houses. Unless one was really an aerial expert all places looked alike. That in some the population was denser than in others, was about all that one could say. And half of the time one saw nothing owing to traveling over clouds.

In the early afternoon they began to lose height and circle down. They were in mountainous country still but coming down in a flat plain. There was a well-marked airfield here and a white building beside it. They made a perfect landing.

Mrs. Baker led the way toward the building. Beside it were two powerful cars with chauffeurs standing by them. It was clearly a private airfield of some kind, since there appeared to be no official reception.

"Journey's end," said Mrs. Baker cheerfully. "We all go in and have a good wash and brush up. And then the cars will be ready."

"Journey's end?" Hilary stared at her. "But we've not—we haven't crossed the sea at all."

"Did you expect to?" Mrs. Baker seemed amused. Hilary said confusedly, "Well, yes. Yes, I did. I thought . . ." She stopped.

Mrs. Baker nodded her head.

"Why, so do a lot of people. There's a lot of nonsense talked about the iron curtain, but what I say is an iron curtain can be anywhere. People don't think of that."

Two Berber servants received them. After a wash and freshening up they sat down to coffee and sandwiches and biscuits. Then Mrs. Baker glanced at her watch.

"Well, so long, folks," she said. "This is where I leave you."

"Are you going back to Morocco?" asked Hilary, surprised.

"That wouldn't quite do," said Mrs. Calvin Baker, "with me being supposed to be burnt up in a plane accident! No, I shall be on a different run this time."

"But someone might still recognize you," said Hilary. "Someone, I mean, who'd met you in hotels in Casablanca or Fez."

"Ah," said Mrs. Baker, "but they'd be making a mistake. I've got a different passport now, though it's true enough that a sister of mine, a Mrs. Calvin Baker, lost her life that way. My sister and I are supposed to be very alike." She added, "And to the casual people one comes across in hotels one traveling American woman is very like another."

Yes, Hilary thought, that was true enough. All the outer, unimportant characteristics were present in Mrs. Baker. The neatness, the trimness, the carefully arranged blue hair, the highly monotonous, prattling voice. Inner characteristics, she realized, were carefully masked or, indeed, absent. Mrs. Calvin Baker presented to the world and to her companions a façade, but what was behind the façade was not easy to fathom. It was as though she had deliberately extinguished those tokens of individuality by which one personality is distinguishable from another.

Hilary felt moved to say so. She and Mrs. Baker were standing a little apart from the rest.

"One doesn't know," said Hilary, "in the least what you're really like?"

"Why should you?"

"Yes. Why should I? And yet, you know, I feel I ought to. We've traveled together in rather intimate circumstances and it seems odd to me that I know nothing about you. Nothing, I mean, of the essential you, of what you feel and think, of what you like and dislike, of what's important to you and what isn't."

"You've such a probing mind, my dear," said Mrs. Baker. "If you'll take my advice, you'll curb that tendency."

"I don't even know what part of the United States you come from."

"That doesn't matter either. I've finished with my own country. There are reasons why I can never go back there. If I can pay off a grudge against that country, I'll enjoy doing it."

For just a second or two malevolence showed both in her expression and in the tone of her voice. Then it relaxed once more into cheerful tourist tones.

"Well, so long, Mrs. Betterton, I hope you have a very agreeable reunion with your husband."

Hilary said helplessly,

"I don't even know where I am, what part of the world, I mean."

"Oh, that's easy. There needs to be no concealment about that now. A remote spot in the High Atlas my dear. That's near enough—"

Mrs. Baker moved away and started saying goodbye to the others. With a final gay wave of her hand she walked out across the tarmac. The plane had been refueled and the pilot was standing waiting for her. A faint cold chill went over Hilary. Here, she felt, was her last link with the outside world. Peters, standing near her, seemed to sense her reaction.

"The place of no return," he said softly. "That's us, I guess."

Dr. Barron said softly,

"Have you still courage, Madame, or do you at this moment want to run after your American friend and climb with her into the plane and go back— back to the world you have left?"

"Could I go if I wanted to?" asked Hilary.

The Frenchman shrugged his shoulders.

"One wonders."

"Shall I call to her?" asked Andy Peters.

"Of course not," said Hilary sharply.

Helga Needheim said scornfully,

"There is no room here for women who are weaklings."

"She is not a weakling," said Dr. Barron softly, "but she asks herself questions as any intelligent woman would do." He stressed the word "intelligent" as though it were a reflection upon the German woman. She, however, was unaffected by his tone. She despised all Frenchmen and was happily assured of her own worth. Ericsson said, in his high nervous voice,

"When one has at last reached freedom, can one even contemplate going back?"

Hilary said,

"But if it is not possible to go back, or to choose to go back, then it is not freedom!"

One of the servants came to them and said,

"If you please, the cars are ready now to start."

They went out through the opposite door of the building. Two Cadillac cars were standing there with uniformed chauffeurs. Hilary indicated a preference for sitting in front with the chauffeur. She explained the swinging motion of a large car occasionally made her feel car sick. This explanation seemed to be accepted easily enough. As they drove along Hilary made a little desultory conversation from time to time. The weather, the excellence of the car. She spoke French quite easily and well, and the chauffeur responded agreeably. His manner was entirely natural and matter of fact.

"How long will it take us?" she asked presently.

"From the airport to the hospital? It is a drive of perhaps two hours, Madame."

The words struck Hilary with faintly disagreeable surprise. She had noted, without thinking much about it, that Helga Needheim had changed at the rest house and was now wearing a hospital nurse's kit. This fitted in.

"Tell me something about the hospital," she said to the chauffeur.

His reply was enthusiastic.

"Ah, Madame, it is magnificent. The equipment, it is the most up-to-date in the world. Many doctors come and visit it, and all of them go away full of praise. It is a great thing that is being done there for humanity."

"It must be," said Hilary, "yes, yes, indeed it must."

"These miserable ones," said the chauffeur, "they have been sent in the past to perish miserably on a lonely island. But here this new treatment of Dr. Kolini's cures a very high percentage. Even those who are far gone."

"It seems a lonely place to have a hospital," said Hilary.

"Ah, Madame, but you would have to be lonely in the circumstances. The authorities would insist upon it. But it is good air here, wonderful air. See, Madame, you can see now where we are going." He pointed.

They were approaching the first spurs of a mountain range, and on the side of it, set flat against the hillside, was a long gleaming white building.

"What an achievement," said the chauffeur, "to raise such a building out here. The money spent must have been fantastic. We owe much, Madame, to the rich philanthropists of this world. They are not like governments who do things always in a cheap way. Here money has been spent like water. Our patron, he is one of the richest men in the world, they say. Here truly he has built a magnificent achievement for the relief of human suffering."

He drove up a winding track. Finally they came to rest outside great barred iron gates.

"You must dismount here, Madame," said the chauffeur. "It is not permitted that I take the car through these gates. The garages are a kilometer away."

The travelers got out of the car. There was a big bellpull at the gate, but before they could touch it the gates swung slowly open. A white-robed figure with a black, smiling face bowed to them and bade them enter. They passed through the gate; at one side screened by a high fence of wire, there was a big courtyard where men were walking up and down. As these men turned to look at the arrivals, Hilary uttered a gasp of horror.

"But they're lepers!" she exclaimed. "Lepers!"

A shiver of horror shook her entire frame.

11

THE GATES OF the Leper Colony closed behind the travelers with a metallic clang. The noise struck on Hilary's startled consciousness with a horrible note of finality. *Abandon hope,* it seemed to say, *all ye who enter here . . .* This, she thought, was the end . . . really the end. Any way of retreat there might have been was now cut off.

She was alone now among enemies, and in, at most, a very few minutes, she would be confronted with discovery and failure. Subconsciously, she supposed, she had known that all day, but some undefeatable optimism of the human spirit, some persistence in the belief that that entity oneself could not possibly cease to exist, had been masking that fact from her. She had said to Jessop in Casablanca "And when do I reach Tom Betterton?" and he had said then gravely that that was when the danger would become acute. He had added that he hoped that by then he might be in a position to give her protection, but that hope, Hilary could not but realize, had failed to materialize.

If "Miss Hetherington" had been the agent on whom Jessop was relying, "Miss Hetherington" had been outmaneuvered and left to confess failure at Marrakesh. But in any case, what could Miss Hetherington have done?

The party of travelers had arrived at the place of no return. Hilary had gambled with death and lost. And she knew now that Jessop's diagnosis had been correct. She no longer wanted to die. She wanted to live. The zest of living had come back to her in full strength. She could think of Nigel, of the little mound that was Brenda's grave, with a sad wondering pity, but no longer with the cold lifeless despair that had urged her on to seek oblivion in death. She thought: "I'm alive again, sane, whole . . . and now I'm like a rat in a trap. If only there were some way out. . . ."

It was not that she had given no thought to the problem. She had. But it seemed to her, reluctantly, that once confronted with Betterton, there could be no way out. . . .

Betterton would say: "But that's not my wife—" And that would be that! Eyes turning toward her . . . realization . . . a spy in their midst. . . .

Because what other solution could there be? Supposing she were to get in first? Supposing she were to cry out, before Tom Betterton could get in a word— "Who are you? You're not my husband!" If she could simulate indignation, shock, horror, sufficiently well—might it, just credibly, raise a doubt? A doubt whether Betterton was Betterton—or some other scientist sent to impersonate him. A spy, in other words. But if they believed that, then it might be rather hard on Betterton! But, she thought, her mind turning in tired circles, if Betterton was a traitor, a man willing to sell his country's secrets, could anything be "hard on him"? How difficult it was, she thought, to make any appraisement of loyalties—or indeed any judgments of people or things. . . . At any rate it might be worth trying. To create a doubt—

With a giddy feeling, she returned to her immediate surroundings. Her thoughts had been running underground with the frenzied violence of a rat caught in a trap. But during that time her surface stream of consciousness had been playing its appointed part.

The little party from the outside world had been welcomed by a big handsome man—a linguist, it would seem, since he had said a word or two to each person in his or her own language.

"Enchanté de faire votre connaissance, mon cher docteur," he was murmuring to Dr. Barron, and then turning to her:

"Ah, Mrs. Betterton, we're very pleased to welcome you here. A long confusing journey, I'm afraid. Your husband's very well and, naturally, awaiting you with impatience."

He gave her a discreet smile; it was a smile, she noticed, that did not touch his cold pale eyes.

"You must," he added, "be longing to see him."

The giddiness increased—she felt the group around her approaching and receding like the waves of the sea. Beside her, Andy Peters put out an arm and steadied her.

"I guess you haven't heard," he said to their welcoming host. "Mrs. Betterton had a bad crash at Casablanca—concussion. This journey's done her no good. Nor the excitement of looking forward to meeting her husband. I'd say she ought to lie down right now in a darkened room."

Hilary felt the kindness of his voice, of the supporting arm. She swayed a little more. It would be easy, incredibly easy, to crumple at the knees, to drop flaccidly down . . . to feign unconsciousness—or at any rate near unconsciousness. To be laid on a bed in a darkened room—to put off the moment of discovery just a little longer. . . . But Betterton would come to her there— any husband would. He would come there and lean over the bed in the dim gloom and at the first murmur of her voice, the first dim outline of her face as his eye became accustomed to the twilight he would realize that she was not Olive Betterton.

Courage came back to Hilary. She straightened up. Color came into her cheeks. She flung up her head.

If this were to be the end, let it be a gallant end! She would go to Betterton and when he repudiated her, she would try out the last lie, come out with it confidently, fearlessly:

"No, of course I'm not your wife. Your wife—I'm terribly sorry, it's awful —she's dead. I was in hospital with her when she died. I promised her I'd get to you somehow and give you her last messages. I wanted to. You see, I'm in sympathy with what you did—with what all of you are doing. I agree with you politically. I want to help. . . ."

Thin, thin, all very thin . . . And such awkward trifles to explain—the faked passport—the forged letter of credit. Yes, but people did get by sometimes with the most audacious lies—if one lied with sufficient confidence—if you had the personality to put a thing over. One could at any rate go down fighting.

She drew herself up, gently freeing herself from Peters' support.

"Oh, no. I must see Tom," she said. "I must go to him—now—at once—please."

The big man was hearty about it. Sympathetic. (Though the cold eyes were still pale and watchful.)

"Of course, of course, Mrs. Betterton. I quite understand how you are feeling. Ah, here's Miss Jennsen."

A thin spectacled girl had joined them.

"Miss Jennsen, meet Mrs. Betterton, Fraulein Needheim, Dr. Barron, Mr. Peters, Dr. Ericsson. Show them into the Registry, will you? Give them a drink. I'll be with you in a few minutes. Just take Mrs. Betterton along to her husband. I'll be with you again shortly."

He turned to Hilary again, saying:

"Follow me, Mrs. Betterton."

He strode forward, she followed. At a bend in the passage, she gave a last look over her shoulder. Andy Peters was still watching her. He had a faintly puzzled unhappy look—she thought for a moment he was going to come with her. He must have realized, she thought, that there's something wrong, realized it from *me,* but he doesn't know what it is.

And she thought, with a slight shiver: "It's the last time, perhaps, that I'll ever see him. . . ."

And so, as she turned the corner after her guide, she raised a hand and waved a goodbye. . . .

The big man was talking cheerfully.

"This way, Mrs. Betterton. I'm afraid you'll find our buildings rather confusing at first, so many corridors, and all rather alike."

Like a dream, Hilary thought, a dream of hygienic white corridors along which you pass forever, turning, going on, never finding your way out. . . .

She said:

"I didn't realize it would be a—a hospital."

"No, no, of course. You couldn't realize anything, could you?"

There was a faint sadistic note of amusement in his voice.

"You've had, as they say, to 'fly blind.' My name's Van Heidem, by the way. Paul Van Heidem."

"It's all a little strange—and rather terrifying," said Hilary. "The lepers . . ."

"Yes, yes, of course. Picturesque—and usually so very unexpected. It does upset newcomers. But you'll get used to them—oh yes, you'll get used to them in time."

He gave a slight chuckle.

"A very good joke, I always think myself."

He paused suddenly.

"Up one flight of stairs—now don't hurry. Take it easy. Nearly there now."

Nearly there—nearly there . . . so many steps to death . . . up—up—deep steps, deeper than European steps. And now another of the hygienic passages and Van Heidem was stopping by a door. He tapped, waited, and then opened it.

"Ah, Betterton—here we are at last. Your wife!"

He stood aside with a slight flourish.

Hilary walked into the room. No holding back. No shrinking. Chin up. Forward to doom.

A man stood half turned from the window, an almost startlingly good-looking man. She noted that, recognizing his fair handsomeness with a feeling almost of surprise. He wasn't, somehow, her idea of Tom Betterton. Surely, the photograph of him that she had been shown wasn't in the least—

It was that confused feeling of surprise that decided her. She would go all out for her first desperate expedient.

She made a quick movement forward, then drew back. Her voice rang out, startled, dismayed . . .

"But—that isn't Tom. That isn't my husband. . . ."

It was well done, she felt it herself. Dramatic, but not overdramatic. Her eyes met Van Heidem's in bewildered questioning.

And then Tom Betterton laughed. A quiet, amused, almost triumphant laugh.

"Pretty good, eh, Van Heidem?" he said, "if even my own wife doesn't know me!"

With four quick steps he had crossed to her and gathered her tightly into his arms.

"Olive, darling. Of course you know me. I'm Tom all right even if I haven't got quite the same face as I used to have."

His face pressed against hers, his lips by her ear, she caught the faint whispered addition,

"Play up. For God's sake. Danger."

He released her for a moment, caught her to him again.

"Darling! It's seemed years—years and years. But you're here at last!"

She could feel the warning pressure of his fingers below her shoulder blades, admonishing her, giving their urgent message.

Only after a moment or two did he release her, push her a little from him and look into her face.

"I still can't quite believe it," he said with an excited little laugh. "Still, you know it's me now, don't you?"

His eyes, burning into hers, still held that message of warning.

She didn't understand it—couldn't understand it. But it was a miracle from heaven and she rallied to play her part.

"Tom!" she said, and there was a catch in her voice that her listening ears approved. "Oh, Tom—but what—"

"Plastic surgery! Hertz of Vienna is here. And he's a living marvel. Don't say you regret my old crushed nose."

He kissed her again, lightly, easily, this time, then turned to the watching Van Heidem with a slight apologetic laugh.

"Forgive the transports, Van," he said.

"But naturally, naturally—" the Dutchman smiled benevolently.

"It's been so long," said Hilary, "and I—" she swayed a little, "I—please, can I sit down."

Hurriedly Tom Betterton eased her into a chair.

"Of course, darling. You're all in. That frightful journey. And the plane accident. My God, what an escape!"

(So there was full communication. They knew all about the plane crash.)

"It's left me terribly woolly-headed," said Hilary, with an apologetic little laugh. "I forget things and get muddled up, and have awful headaches. And then, finding you looking like a total stranger, I'm a bit of a mess, darling. I hope I won't be a bother to you!"

"You a bother? Never. You'll just have to take it easy for a bit, that's all. There's all the—time in the world here."

Van Heidem moved gently toward the door.

"I will leave you now," he said. "After a little you will bring your wife to the Registry, Betterton? For the moment you will like to be alone."

He went out, shutting the door behind him.

Immediately Betterton dropped on his knees by Hilary and buried his face on her shoulder.

"Darling, darling," he said.

And once again she felt that warning pressure of the fingers. The whisper, so faint as hardly to be heard, was urgent and insistent.

"Keep it up. There might be a microphone—one never knows."

That was it, of course. One never knew. . . . Fear—uneasiness—uncertainty—danger—always danger—she could feel it in the atmosphere.

Tom Betterton sat back on his haunches.

"It's so wonderful to see you," he said softly. "And yet, you know, it's like a dream—not quite real. Do you feel like that, too?"

"Yes, that's just it—a dream—being here—with you—at last. It doesn't seem real, Tom."

She had placed both hands on his shoulders. She was looking at him, a faint smile on her lips. (There might be a spy hole as well as a microphone.)

Coolly and calmly she appraised what she saw. A nervous good-looking man of thirty-odd who was badly frightened—a man nearly at the end of his tether—a man who had, presumably, come here full of high hopes and had been reduced—to this.

Now that she had surmounted her first hurdle, Hilary felt a curious exhilaration in the playing of her part. She must *be* Olive Betterton. Act as Olive would have acted, feel as Olive would have felt. And life was so unreal that that seemed quite natural. Somebody called Hilary Craven had died in an airplane accident. From now on she wouldn't even remember her.

Instead, she rallied her memories of the lessons she had studied so assiduously.

"It seems such ages since Firbank," she said. "Whiskers—you remember Whiskers? She had kittens—just after you went away. There are so many things, silly everyday little things, you don't even know about. That's what seems so odd."

"I know. It's breaking with an old life and beginning a new one."

"And—it's all right here? You're happy?"

A necessary wifely question that any wife would ask.

"It's wonderful." Tom Betterton squared his shoulders, threw his head back. Unhappy, frightened eyes looked out of a smiling confident face. "Every facility. No expense spared. Perfect conditions to get on with the job. And the organization! It's unbelievable."

"Oh, I'm sure it is. My journey—did you come the same way?"

"One doesn't talk about that. Oh, I'm not snubbing you, darling. But—you see, you've got to learn about everything."

"But the lepers? Is it really a Leper Colony?"

"Oh yes. Perfectly genuine. There's a team of medicos doing very fine work in research on the subject. But it's quite self-contained. It needn't worry you. It's just—clever camouflage."

"I see." Hilary looked round her. "Are these our quarters?"

"Yes. Sitting room, bathroom there, bedroom beyond. Come, I'll show you."

She got up and followed him through a well-appointed bathroom into a good-sized bedroom with twin beds, big built-in cupboards, a dressing table, and a bookshelf near the beds. Hilary looked into the cupboard space with some amusement.

"I hardly know what I'm going to put in here," she remarked. "All I've got is what I stand up in."

"Oh that. You can fit yourself out with all you want. There's a fashion model department and all accessories, cosmetics, everything. All first class.

The Unit is quite self-contained—all you want on the premises. No need to go outside ever again."

He said the words lightly, but it seemed to Hilary's sensitive ear that there was despair concealed behind the words.

No need to go outside ever again. No chance of ever going outside again. *Abandon hope all ye who enter here* . . . The well-appointed cage! Was it for this, she thought, that all these varying personalities had abandoned their countries, their loyalties, their everyday lives? Dr. Barron, Andy Peters, young Ericsson with his dreaming face, the overbearing Helga Needheim? Did they know what they were coming to find? Would they be content? Was this what they had wanted?

She thought: "I'd better not ask too many questions . . . If someone is listening."

Was someone listening? Were they being spied upon? Tom Betterton evidently thought it might be so. But was he right? Or was it nerves—hysteria? Tom Betterton, she thought, was very near to a breakdown.

"Yes," she thought grimly, "and so may you be, my girl, in six months' time . . ."

What did it do to people, she wondered, living like this?

Tom Betterton said to her:

"Would you like to lie down—to rest?"

"No—" she hesitated. "No, I don't think so."

"Then perhaps you'd better come with me to the Registry."

"What's the Registry?"

"Everyone who clocks in goes through the Registry. They record everything about you. Health, teeth, blood pressure, blood group, psychological reactions, tastes, dislikes, allergies, aptitudes, preferences."

"It sounds very military—or do I mean medical?"

"Both," said Tom Betterton. "Both. This organization—it's really formidable."

"One's always heard so," said Hilary. "I mean that everything behind the Iron Curtain is really properly planned."

She tried to put a proper enthusiasm into her voice. After all, Olive Betterton had presumably been a sympathizer with the Party, although, perhaps by order, she had not been known to be a Party member.

Betterton said evasively,

"There's a lot for you to—understand." He added quickly: "Better not try to take in too much at once."

He kissed her again, a curious, apparently tender and even passionate kiss, that was actually cold as ice, murmured very low in her ear, "Keep it up," and said aloud, "And now, come down to the Registry."

12

THE REGISTRY WAS presided over by a woman who looked like a strict nursery governess. Her hair was rolled into a rather hideous bun and she wore some very efficient-looking pince-nez. She nodded approval as the Bettertons entered the severe officelike room.

"Ah," she said, "you've brought Mrs. Betterton. That's right."

Her English was perfectly idiomatic but it was spoken with a stilted precision which made Hilary believe that she was probably a foreigner. Actually, her nationality was Swiss. She motioned Hilary to a chair, opened a drawer beside her and took out a sheaf of forms upon which she commenced to write rapidly. Tom Betterton said rather awkwardly:

"Well then, Olive, I'll leave you."

"Yes, please, Dr. Betterton. It's much better to get through all the formalities straightaway."

Betterton went out, shutting the door behind him. The Robot, for as such Hilary thought of her, continued to write.

"Now then," she said, in a businesslike way. "Full name, please. Age. Where born. Father's and mother's names. Any serious illnesses. Tastes. Hobbies. List of any jobs held. Degrees at any university. Preferences in food and drink."

It went on, a seemingly endless catalogue. Hilary responded vaguely, almost mechanically. She was glad now of the careful priming she had received from Jessop. She had mastered it all so well that the responses came automatically, without having to pause or think. The Robot said finally, as she made the last entry,

"Well, that seems to be all for this department. Now we'll hand you over to Doctor Schwartz for medical examination."

"Really!" said Hilary. "Is all this necessary? It seems most absurd."

"Oh, we believe in being thorough, Mrs. Betterton. We like to have everything down in the records. You'll like Dr. Schwartz very much. Then from her you go on to Doctor Rubec."

Dr. Schwartz was fair and amiable and female. She gave Hilary a meticulous physical examination and then said,

"So! That is finished. Now you go to Dr. Rubec."

"Who is Dr. Rubec?" Hilary asked. "Another doctor?"

"Dr. Rubec is a psychologist."

"I don't want a psychologist. I don't like psychologists."

"Now please don't get upset, Mrs. Betterton. You're not going to have treatment of any kind. It's simply a question of an intelligence test and of your type-group personality."

Dr. Rubec was a tall, melancholy Swiss of about forty years of age. He greeted Hilary, glanced at the card that had been passed on to him by Dr. Schwartz and nodded his head approvingly.

"Your health is good, I am glad to see," he said. "You have had an airplane crash recently, I understand?"

"Yes," said Hilary. "I was four or five days in hospital at Casablanca."

"Four or five days are not enough," said Dr. Rubec reprovingly. "You should have been there longer."

"I didn't want to be there longer. I wanted to get on with my journey."

"That, of course, is understandable, but it is important with concussion that plenty of rest should be had. You may appear quite well and normal after it but it may have serious effects. Yes, I see your nerve reflexes are not quite what they should be. Partly the excitement of the journey and partly, no doubt, due to concussion. Do you get headaches?"

"Yes. Very bad headaches. And I get muddled up every now and then and can't remember things."

Hilary felt it well to continually stress this particular point. Dr. Rubec nodded soothingly.

"Yes, yes, yes. But do not trouble yourself. All that will pass. Now we will have a few association tests, so as to decide what type of mentality you are."

Hilary felt faintly nervous but all appeared to pass off well. The test seemed to be of a merely routine nature. Dr. Rubec made various entries on a long form.

"It is a pleasure," he said at last, "to deal with someone (if you will excuse me, Madame, and not to take amiss what I am going to say), to deal with someone who is not in any way a genius!"

Hilary laughed.

"Oh, I'm certainly not a genius," she said.

"Fortunately for you," said Dr. Rubec. "I can assure you your existence will be far more tranquil." He sighed. "Here, as you probably understand, I deal mostly with keen intellects, but with the type of sensitive intellect that is apt to become easily unbalanced, and where the emotional stress is strong. The man of science, Madame, is not the cool, calm individual he is made out to be in fiction. In fact," said Dr. Rubec, thoughtfully, "between a first-class tennis player, an operatic prima donna and a nuclear physicist there is really very little difference as far as emotional instability goes."

"Perhaps you are right," said Hilary, remembering that she was supposed to have lived for some years in close proximity to scientists. "Yes, they *are* rather temperamental sometimes."

Dr. Rubec threw up a pair of expressive hands.

"You would not believe," he said, "the emotions that arise here! The quarrels, the jealousies, the *touchiness!* We have to take steps to deal with all that. But you, Madame," he smiled. "You are in a class that is in a small minority here. A fortunate class, if I may so express myself."

"I don't quite understand you. What kind of a minority?"

"Wives," said Dr. Rubec. "We have not many wives here. Very few are permitted. One finds them, on the whole, refreshingly free from the brain-storms of their husbands and their husbands' colleagues."

"What do wives do here?" asked Hilary. She added apologetically, "You see it's all so new to me. I don't understand anything yet."

"Naturally not. Naturally. That is bound to be the case. There are hobbies, recreations, amusements, instructional courses. A wide field. You will find it, I hope, an agreeable life."

"As you do?"

It was a question, and rather an audacious one and Hilary wondered a moment or two later whether she had been wise to ask it. But Dr. Rubec merely seemed amused.

"You are quite right, Madame," he said. "I find life here peaceful and interesting in the extreme."

"You don't ever regret—Switzerland?"

"I am not homesick. No. That is partly because, in my case, my home conditions were bad. I had a wife and several children. I was not cut out, Madame, to be a family man. Here conditions are infinitely more pleasant. I have ample opportunity of studying certain aspects of the human mind which interest me and on which I am writing a book. I have no domestic cares, no distractions, no interruptions. It all suits me admirably."

"And where do I go next?" asked Hilary, as he rose and shook her courteously and formally by the hand.

"Mademoiselle La Roche will take you to the dress department. The result, I am sure—" he bowed "—will be admirable."

After the severe Robotlike females she had met so far, Hilary was agreeably surprised by Mademoiselle La Roche. Mademoiselle La Roche had been a *vendeuse* in one of the Paris houses of *haute couture* and her manner was thrillingly feminine.

"I am delighted, Madame, to make your acquaintance. I hope that I can be of assistance to you. Since you have just arrived and since you are, no doubt, tired, I would suggest that you select now just a few essentials. Tomorrow and indeed during the course of next week, you can examine what we have in stock at your leisure. It is tiresome I always think, to have to select things rapidly. It destroys all the pleasure of *la toilette*. So I would suggest, if you agree, just a set of underclothing, a dinner dress, and perhaps a *tailleur."*

"How delightful it sounds," said Hilary. "I cannot tell you how odd it feels to own nothing but a toothbrush and a sponge."

Mademoiselle La Roche laughed cheeringly. She took a few rapid measures and led Hilary into a big apartment with built-in cupboards. There were clothes here of every description, made of good material and excellent cut and in a large variety of sizes. When Hilary had selected the essentials of *la toilette,* they passed on to the cosmetics department where Hilary made a selection of powders, creams and various other toilet accessories. These were handed to one of the assistants, a native girl with a shining dark face, dressed in spotless white, and she was instructed to see that they were delivered to Hilary's apartment.

All these proceedings had seemed to Hilary more and more like a dream.

"And we shall have the pleasure of seeing you again shortly, I hope," said Mademoiselle La Roche, gracefully. "It will be a great pleasure, Madame, to assist you to select from our models. *Entre nous* my work is sometimes disappointing. These scientific ladies often take very little interest in *la toilette*. In fact, not half an hour ago I had a fellow traveler of yours."

"Helga Needheim?"

"Ah yes, that was the name. She is, of course, a *Boche,* and the *Boches* are not sympathetic to us. She is not actually bad looking if she took a little care of her figure; if she chose a flattering line she could look very well. But no! She has no interest in clothes. She is a doctor, I understand. A specialist of some kind. Let us hope she takes more interest in her patients than she does in her *toilette*— Ah, that one, what man will look at her twice?"

Miss Jennsen, the thin, dark, spectacled girl who had met the party on arrival, now entered the fashion salon.

"Have you finished here, Mrs. Betterton?" she asked.

"Yes, thank you," said Hilary.

"Then perhaps you will come and see the Deputy Director."

Hilary said *"au revoir"* to Mademoiselle La Roche and followed the earnest Miss Jennsen.

"Who is the Deputy Director?" she asked.

"Doctor Nielson."

Everybody, Hilary reflected, in this place was doctor of something.

"Who exactly is Doctor Nielson?" she asked. "Medical, scientific, what?"

"Oh, he's not medical, Mrs. Betterton. He's in charge of Administration. All complaints have to go to him. He's the administrative head of the Unit. He always has an interview with everyone when they arrive. After that I don't suppose you'll ever see him again unless something very important should arise."

"I see," said Hilary, meekly. She had an amused feeling of having been put severely in her place.

Admission to Dr. Nielson was through two antechambers where stenographers were working. She and her guide were finally admitted into the inner sanctum where Dr. Nielson rose from behind a large executive's desk. He was a big florid man with an urbane manner. Of trans-Atlantic origin, Hilary thought, though he had very little American accent.

"Ah!" he said, rising and coming forward to shake Hilary by the hand. "This is—yes—let me see—yes, Mrs. Betterton. Delighted to welcome you here, Mrs. Betterton. We hope you'll be very happy with us. Sorry to hear of the unfortunate accident during the course of your journey, but I'm glad it was no worse. Yes, you were lucky there. Very lucky indeed. Well, your husband's been awaiting you impatiently and I hope now you've got here you will settle down and be very happy amongst us."

"Thank you, Dr. Nielson."

Hilary sat down in the chair he drew forward for her.

"Any questions you want to ask me?" Dr. Nielson leaned forward over his desk in an encouraging manner. Hilary laughed a little.

"That's a most difficult thing to answer," she said. "The real answer is, of course, that I've got so many questions to ask that I don't know where to begin."

"Quite, quite. I understand that. If you'll take my advice—this is just advice, you know, nothing more—I shouldn't ask anything. Just adapt yourself and see what comes. That's the best way, believe me."

"I feel I know so little," said Hilary. "It's all so—so very unexpected."

"Yes. Most people think that. The general idea seems to have been that one was going to arrive in Moscow." He laughed cheerfully. "Our desert home is quite a surprise to most people."

"It was certainly a surprise to me."

"Well, we don't tell people too much beforehand. They mightn't be discreet, you know, and discretion's rather important. But you'll be comfortable here, you'll find. Anything you don't like—or particularly would like to have . . . just put in a request for it and we'll see what can be managed. Any artistic requirement, for instance. Painting, sculpture, music, we have a department for all that sort of thing."

"I'm afraid I'm not talented that way."

"Well, there's plenty of social life too, of a kind. Games, you know. We have tennis courts, squash courts. It takes a week or two, we often find, for people to find their feet, especially the wives, if I may say so. Your husband's got his job and he's busy with it and it takes a little time, sometimes, for the wives to find—well—other wives who are congenial. All that sort of thing. You understand me."

"But does one—does one—stay here?"

"Stay here? I don't quite understand you, Mrs. Betterton."

"I mean, does one stay here or go on somewhere else?"

Dr. Nielson became rather vague.

"Ah," he said. "That depends on your husband. Ah, yes, yes, that depends very much on him. There are possibilities. Various possibilities. But it's better not to go into all that just now. I'd suggest, you know, that you—well—come and see me again perhaps in three weeks' time. Tell me how you've settled down. All that kind of thing."

"Does one—go out at all?"

"Go out, Mrs. Betterton?"

"I mean outside the walls. The gates."

"A very natural question," said Dr. Nielson. His manner was now rather heavily beneficent. "Yes, very natural. Most people ask it when they come here. But the point of our Unit is that it's a world in itself. There is nothing, if I may so express myself, to go out *to*. Outside us there is only desert. Now I'm not blaming you, Mrs. Betterton. Most people feel like that when they first get here. Slight claustrophobia. That's how Dr. Rubec puts it. But I assure you that it passes off. It's a hangover, if I may so express it, from the world that you have left. Have you ever observed an ant hill, Mrs. Betterton? An interesting sight. Very interesting and very instructive. Hundreds of little black insects hurrying to and fro, so earnest, so eager, so purposeful. And yet the whole thing's such a muddle. That's the bad old world you have left. Here there is leisure, purpose, infinite time. I assure you," he smiled, "an earthly paradise."

13

"IT'S LIKE A school," said Hilary.

She was back once more in her own suite. The clothes and accessories she had chosen were awaiting her in the bedroom. She hung the clothes in the cupboard and arranged the other things to her liking.

"I know," said Betterton, "I felt like that at first."

Their conversation was wary and slightly stilted. The shadow of a possible microphone still hung over them. He said in an oblique manner,

"I think it's all right, you know. I think I was probably imagining things. But all the same . . ."

He left it at that, and Hilary realized that what he had left unsaid was, "but all the same, we had better be careful."

The whole business was, Hilary thought, like some fantastic nightmare. Here she was, sharing a bedroom with a strange man, and yet so strong was the feeling of uncertainty, and danger, that to neither of them did the intimacy appear embarrassing. It was like, she thought, climbing a Swiss mountain where you share a hut in close proximity with guides and other climbers as a matter of course. After a minute or two Betterton said,

"It all takes a bit of getting used to, you know. Let's just be very natural. Very ordinary. More or less as if we were at home still."

She realized the wisdom of that. The feeling of unreality persisted and would persist, she supposed, some little time. The reasons for Betterton leaving England, his hopes, his disillusionment could not be touched upon between them at this moment. They were two people playing a part with an undefined menace hanging over them, as it were. She said presently,

"I was taken through a lot of formalities. Medical, psychological and all that."

"Yes. That's always done. It's natural I suppose."

"Did the same happen to you?"

"More or less."

"Then I went in to see the—Deputy Director I think they called him?"

"That's right. He runs this place. Very capable and a thoroughly good administrator."

"But he's not really the head of it all?"

"Oh no, there's the Director himself."

"Does one—do I—shall I see the Director?"

"Sooner or later I expect. But he doesn't often appear. He gives us an address from time to time—he's got a wonderfully stimulating personality."

There was a faint frown between Betterton's brows and Hilary thought it wise to abandon the subject. Betterton said, glancing at a watch,

"Dinner is at eight. Eight to eight-thirty, that is. We'd better be getting down, if you're ready?"

He spoke exactly as though they were staying in a hotel.

Hilary had changed into the dress she had selected. A soft shade of gray-green that made a good background for her red hair. She clasped a necklace of rather attractive costume jewelry around her neck and said she was ready. They went down the stairs and along corridors and finally into a large dining room. Miss Jennsen came forward and met them.

"I have arranged a slightly larger table for you, Tom," she said to Betterton. "A couple of your wife's fellow travelers will sit with you—and the Murchisons, of course."

They went along to the table indicated. The room contained mostly small tables seating four, eight or ten persons. Andy Peters and Ericsson were already sitting at the table and rose as Hilary and Tom approached. Hilary introduced her "husband" to the two men. They sat down, and presently they were joined by another couple. These Betterton introduced as Dr. and Mrs. Murchison.

"Simon and I work in the same lab," he said, in an explanatory fashion.

Simon Murchison was a thin, anemic-looking young man of about twenty-six. His wife was dark and stocky. She spoke with a strong foreign accent and was, Hilary gathered, an Italian. Her Christian name was Bianca. She greeted Hilary politely but, or so it seemed to Hilary, with a certain reserve.

"Tomorrow," she said, "I will show you around the place. You are not a scientist, no?"

"I'm afraid," said Hilary, "that I have had no scientific training." She added, "I worked as a secretary before my marriage."

"Bianca has had legal training," said her husband. "She has studied economics and commercial law. Sometimes she gives lectures here but it is difficult to find enough to do to occupy one's time."

Bianca shrugged her shoulders.

"I shall manage," she said. "After all, Simon, I came here to be with you and I think that there is much here that could be better organized. I am studying conditions. Perhaps Mrs. Betterton, since she will not be engaged on scientific work, can help me with these things."

Hilary hastened to agree to this plan. Andy Peters made them all laugh by saying ruefully,

"I guess I feel rather like a homesick little boy who's just gone to boarding school. I'll be glad to get down to doing some work."

"It's a wonderful place for working," said Simon Murchison with enthusiasm. "No interruptions and all the apparatus you want."

"What's your line?" asked Andy Peters.

Presently the three men were talking a jargon of their own which Hilary found difficult to follow. She turned to Ericsson who was leaning back in his chair, his eyes abstracted.

"And you?" she asked. "Do you feel like a homesick little boy too?"

He looked at her as though from a long way away.

"I do not need a home," he said. "All these things; home, ties of affection, parents, children; all these are a great hindrance. To work one should be quite free."

"And you feel that you will be free here?"

"One cannot tell yet. One hopes so."

Bianca spoke to Hilary.

"After dinner," she said, "there is a choice of many things to do. There is a card room and you can play bridge; or there is a cinema or three nights a week theatrical performances are given and occasionally there is dancing."

Ericsson frowned disapprovingly.

"All these things are unnecessary," he said. "They dissipate energy."

"Not for us women," said Bianca. "For us women they are necessary."

He looked at her with an almost cold and impersonal dislike.

Hilary thought: "To him women are unnecessary, too."

"I shall go to bed early," said Hilary. She yawned deliberately. "I don't think I want to see a film or play bridge this evening."

"No, dear," said Tom Betterton hastily. "Much better to go to bed really early and have a good night's rest. You've had a very tiring journey, remember."

As they rose from the table, Betterton said:

"The air here is wonderful at night. We usually take a turn or two on the roof garden after dinner, before dispersing to recreations or study. We'll go up there for a little and then you'd better go to bed."

They went up in a lift manned by a magnificent-looking native in white robes. The attendants were darker-skinned and of a more massive build than the slighter Berbers—a desert type, Hilary thought. She was startled by the unexpected beauty of the roof garden, and also by the lavish expenditure that must have gone to create it. Tons of earth must have been brought and carried up here. The result was like an Arabian Nights fairy tale. There was the plash of water, tall palms, the tropical leaves of bananas and other plants and paths of beautiful colored tiles with designs of Persian flowers.

"It's unbelievable," said Hilary. "Here in the middle of the desert." She spoke out what she had felt: "It's an Arabian Nights fairy tale."

"I agree with you, Mrs. Betterton," said Murchison. "It looks exactly as though it has come into being by conjuring up a Djin! Ah well—I suppose even in the desert there's nothing you can't do, given water and money—plenty of both of them."

"Where does the water come from?"

"Spring tapped deep in the mountain. That's the *raison d'être* of the Unit."

A fair sprinkling of people was on the roof garden, but little by little they dwindled away. The Murchisons excused themselves. They were going to watch some ballet.

There were few people left now. Betterton guided Hilary with his hand on her arm to a clear space near the parapet. The stars showed above them and the air was cold now, crisp and exhilarating. They were alone here. Hilary sat down on the low concrete, and Betterton stood in front of her.

"Now then," he said in a low nervous voice, *"Who the hell are you?"*

She looked up at him for a moment or two without answering. Before she replied to his question there was something that she herself had got to know.

"Why did you recognize me as your wife?" she asked.

They looked at each other. Neither of them wished to be the first to answer the other's question. It was a duel of wills between them, but Hilary knew that whatever Tom Betterton had been like when he left England, his will was now inferior to her own. She had arrived here fresh in the self-confidence of organizing her own life—Tom Betterton had been living a planned existence. She was the stronger.

He looked away from her at last, and muttered sullenly:

"It was—just an impulse. I was probably a damned fool. I fancied that you might have been sent—to get me out of here."

"You want to get out of here, then?"

"My God, can you ask?"

"How did you get here from Paris?"

Tom Betterton gave a short unhappy laugh.

"I wasn't kidnapped or anything like that, if that's what you mean. I came of my own free will, under my own steam. I came keenly and enthusiastically."

"You knew that you were coming here?"

"I'd no idea I was coming to Africa, if that's what you mean. I was caught by the usual lure. Peace on earth, free sharing of scientific secrets amongst the scientists of the world; suppression of capitalists and warmongers—all the usual jargon! That fellow Peters who came with you is the same, he's swallowed the same bait."

"And when you got here—it wasn't like that?"

Again he gave that short bitter laugh.

"You'll see for yourself. Oh, perhaps it *is* that, more or less! But it's not the way you thought it would be. It's not—*freedom.*"

He sat down beside her frowning to himself.

"That's what got me down at home, you know. The feeling of being watched and spied upon. All the security precautions. Having to account for one's actions, for one's friends . . . All necessary, I daresay, but it gets you down in the end . . . And so when someone comes along with a proposition —well, you listen . . . It all sounds fine . . ." He gave a short laugh. "And one ends up—here!"

Hilary said slowly:

"You mean you've come to exactly the same circumstances as those from which you tried to escape? You're being watched and spied upon in just the same way—or worse?"

Betterton pushed his hair back nervously from his forehead.

"I don't know," he said. "Honestly. I don't know. I can't be sure. It may be all going on in my own mind. I don't know that I'm being watched at all. Why should I be? Why should they bother? They've got me here—in prison."

"It isn't in the least as you imagined it?"

"That's the odd thing. I suppose it *is* in a way. The working conditions are perfect. You've every facility, every kind of apparatus. You can work for as long a time as you like or as short a time. You've got every comfort and accessory. Food, clothes, living quarters, but you're conscious all the time that you're in prison."

"I know. When the gates clanged behind us today as we came in it was a horrible feeling." Hilary shuddered.

"Well," Betterton seemed to pull himself together. "I've answered your question. Now answer mine. What are you doing here pretending to be Olive?"

"Olive—" she stopped, feeling for words.

"Yes? What about Olive? What's happened to her? What are you trying to say?"

She looked with pity at his haggard nervous face.

"I've been dreading having to tell you."

"You mean—something's happened to her?"

"Yes. I'm sorry, terribly sorry. . . . Your wife's dead. . . . She was coming to join you and the plane crashed. She was taken to hospital and died two days later."

He stared straight ahead of him. It was as though he was determined to show no emotion of any kind. He said quietly:

"So Olive's dead? I see . . ."

There was a long silence. Then he turned to her.

"All right. I can go on from there. You took her place and came here, why?"

This time Hilary was ready with her response. Tom Betterton had believed that she had been sent "to get him out of here" as he had put it. That was not the case. Hilary's position was that of a spy. She had been sent to gain information not to plan the escape of a man who had placed himself willingly in the position he now was. Moreover she could command no means of deliverance, she was a prisoner as much as he was.

To confide in him fully would, she felt, be dangerous. Betterton was very near a breakdown. At any moment he might go completely to pieces. In those circumstances it would be madness to expect him to keep a secret.

She said,

"I was in the hospital with your wife when she died. I offered to take her place and try and reach you. She wanted to get a message to you very badly."

He frowned.

"But surely—"

She hurried on—before he could realize the weakness of the tale.

"It's not so incredible as it sounds. You see I had a lot of sympathy with all these ideas—the ideas you've just been talking about. Scientific secrets shared with all nations—a new World Order. I was enthusiastic about it all. And then my hair—if what they expected was a red-haired woman of the right age, I thought I'd get through. It seemed worth trying anyway."

"Yes," he said. His eyes swept over her head. "You hair's exactly like Olive's."

"And then, you see, your wife was so insistent—about the message she wanted me to give to you."

"Oh yes, the message. What message?"

"To tell you to be careful—very careful—that you were in danger—from someone called Boris?"

"Boris? Boris Glydr, do you mean?"

"Yes, do you know him?"

He shook his head.

"I've never met him. But I know him by name. He's a relation of my first wife's. I know about him."

"Why should he be dangerous?"

"What?"

He spoke absently.

Hilary repeated her question.

"Oh, that." He seemed to come back from far away. "I don't know why he should be dangerous to *me,* but it's true that by all accounts he's a dangerous sort of chap."

"In what way?"

"Well, he's one of those half balmy idealists who would quite happily kill off half humanity if they thought for some reason it would be a good thing."

"I know the sort of person you mean."

She felt she did know—vividly. (But why?)

"Had Olive seen him? What did he say to her?"

"I can't tell you. That's all she said. About danger—oh yes, she said she couldn't believe it."

"Believe what?"

"I don't know." She hesitated a minute and then said, "You see—she was dying . . ."

A spasm of pain convulsed his face.

"I know . . . I know . . . I shall get used to it in time. At the moment I can't realize it. But I'm puzzled about Boris. How could he be dangerous to me *here?* If he'd seen Olive he was in London, I suppose?"

"He was in London, yes."

"Then I simply don't get it. . . . Oh well, what does it matter? What the hell does anything matter? Here we are, stuck in this bloody Unit surrounded by a lot of inhuman Robots . . ."

"That's just how they felt to me."

"And we can't get out." He pounded with his fist on the concrete. *"We can't get out."*

"Oh yes, we can," said Hilary.

He turned to stare at her in surprise.

"What on earth do you mean?"

"We'll find a way," said Hilary.

"My dear girl," his laugh was scornful. "You haven't the faintest idea what you're up against in this place."

"People escaped from the most impossible places during the war," said Hilary stubbornly. She was not going to give in to despair. "They tunneled, or something."

"How can you tunnel through sheer rock? And where to? It's desert all round."

"Then it will have to be 'or something.' "

He looked at her. She smiled with a confidence that was dogged rather than genuine.

"What an extraordinary girl you are. You sound quite sure of yourself."

"There's always a way. I daresay it will take time, and a lot of planning." His face clouded over again.

"Time," he said. "Time . . . That's what I can't afford."

"Why?"

"I don't know whether you'll be able to understand . . . It's like this. I can't really—do my stuff here."

She frowned.

"How do you mean?"

"How shall I put it? I can't work. I can't *think.* In my stuff one has to have a high degree of concentration. A lot of it is—well—*creative.* Since coming here I've just lost the urge. All I can do is good sound hack work. The sort of thing any twopenny-halfpenny scientific chap can do. But that's not what they brought me here for. They want original stuff and I can't *do* original stuff. And the more nervous and afraid I get, the less I'm fit to turn out anything worth turning out. And it's driving me off my rocker, do you see?"

Yes, she saw now. She recalled Dr. Rubec's remarks about prima donnas and scientists.

"If I can't deliver the goods, what is an outfit like this going to do about it? They'll liquidate me."

"Oh no."

"Oh yes they will. They're not sentimentalists here. What's saved me so far is this plastic surgery business. They do it a little at a time, you know. And naturally a fellow who's having constant minor operations can't be expected to concentrate. But they've finished the business now."

"But why was it done at all? What's the point?"

"Oh, that! For safety. My safety, I mean. It's done if—if you're a 'wanted' man."

"Are you a 'wanted' man, then?"

"Yes, didn't you know? Oh, I suppose they wouldn't advertise the fact in the papers. Perhaps even Olive didn't know. But I'm wanted right enough."

"You mean for—*treason* is the word, isn't it? You mean you've sold them atom secrets?"

He avoided her eyes.

"I didn't sell anything. I gave them what I knew of our processes—gave it freely. If you can believe me, I *wanted* to give it to them. It was part of the whole setup—the pooling of scientific knowledge. Oh, can't you understand?"

She could understand. She could understand Andy Peters doing just that. She could see Ericsson with his fanatical dreamer's eyes betraying his country with a high-souled enthusiasm.

Yet it was hard for her to visualize Tom Betterton doing it—and she realized with a shock that all that showed was the difference between Betterton a few months ago, arriving in all the zeal of enthusiasm, and Betterton now, nervous, defeated, down-to-earth—an ordinary badly frightened man.

Even as she accepted the logic of that, Betterton looked round him nervously and said:

"Everyone's gone down. We'd better—"

She rose.

"Yes. But it's all right, you know. They'll think it quite natural—under the circumstances."

He said awkwardly:

"We'll have to go on with this now, you know. I mean—you'll have to go on being—my wife."

"Of course."

"And we'll have to share a room and all that. But it will be quite all right. I mean, you needn't be afraid that—"

He swallowed in an embarrassed manner.

"How handsome he is," thought Hilary, looking at his profile, "and how little it moves me . . ."

"I don't think we need worry about that," she said cheerfully. "The important thing is to get out of here alive."

14

In a room at the Hotel Mamounia, Marrakesh, the man called Jessop was talking to Miss Hetherington. A different Miss Hetherington this, from the one that Hilary had known at Casablanca and at Fez. The same appearance, the same twin set, the same depressing hair-do. But the manner had changed. It was a woman now both brisk, competent, and seeming years younger than her appearance.

The third person in the room was a dark stocky man with intelligent eyes. He was tapping gently on the table with his fingers and humming a little French song under his breath.

". . . and as far as you know," Jessop was saying, "those are the only people she talked to at Fez?"

Janet Hetherington nodded.

"There was the Calvin Baker woman, whom we'd already met at Casablanca. I'll say frankly I still can't make up my mind about her. She went out of her way to be friendly with Olive Betterton, and with me for that matter. But Americans are friendly, they do enter into conversation with people in hotels, and they like joining them on trips."

"Yes," said Jessop, "it's all a little too overt for what we're looking for."

"And besides," went on Janet Hetherington, "*she* was on this plane, too."

"You're assuming," said Jessop, "that the crash was planned." He looked sideways toward the dark, stocky man. "What about it, Leblanc?"

Leblanc stopped humming his tune, and stopped his little tattoo on the table for a moment or two.

"*Ça ce peut,*" he said. "There may have been sabotage to the machine and that is why it crashed. We shall never know. The plane crashed and went up in flames and everyone on board was killed."

"What do you know of the pilot?"

"Alcadi? Young, reasonably competent. No more. Badly paid." He added the two last words with a slight pause in front of them.

Jessop said:

"Open therefore to other employment, but presumably not a candidate for suicide?"

"There were seven bodies," said Leblanc. "Badly charred, unrecognizable, but seven bodies. One cannot get away from that."

Jessop turned back to Janet Hetherington.

"You were saying?" he said.

"There was a French family at Fez that Mrs. Betterton exchanged a few words with. There was a rich Swedish businessman with a glamour girl. And the rich oil magnate, Mr. Aristides."

"Ah," said Leblanc, "that fabulous figure himself. What must it feel like, I have often asked myself, to have all the money in the world? For me," he added frankly, "I would keep race horses and women, and all the world has to offer. But old Aristides shuts himself up in his castle in Spain—literally his castle in Spain, *mon cher*—and collects, so they say, Chinese potteries of the Sung period. But one must remember," he added, "that he is at least seventy. It is possible at that age that Chinese potteries are all that interest one."

"According to the Chinese themselves," said Jessop, "the years between sixty and seventy are the most rich in living and one is then most appreciative of the beauty and delight of life."

"*Pas moi!*" said Leblanc.

"There were some Germans at Fez, too," continued Janet Hetherington, "but as far as I know they didn't exchange any remarks with Olive Betterton."

"A waiter or a servant, perhaps," said Jessop.

"That's always possible."

"And she went out into the old town alone, you say?"

"She went with one of the regular guides. Someone may have contacted her on that tour."

"At any rate she decided quite suddenly to go to Marrakesh."

"Not suddenly," she corrected him. "She already had her reservations."

"Ah, I'm wrong," said Jessop. "What I mean is that Mrs. Calvin Baker decided rather suddenly to accompany her." He got up and paced up and down. "She flew to Marrakesh," he said, "and the plane crashed and came down in flames. It seems ill-omened, does it not, for anyone called Olive Betterton to travel by air. First the crash near Casablanca, and then this one. Was it an accident or was it contrived? If there were people who wished to get rid of Olive Betterton, there would be easier ways to do it than by wrecking a plane, I should say."

"One never knows," said Leblanc. "Understand me, *mon cher*. Once you have got into that state of mind where the taking of human lives no longer counts, then if it is simpler to put a little explosive package under a seat in a plane, than to wait about at the corner on a dark night and stick a knife into someone, then the package will be left and the fact that six other people will die also is not even considered."

"Of course," said Jessop, "I know I'm in a minority of one, but I still think there's a third solution—that they faked the crash."

Leblanc looked at him with interest.

"That could be done, yes. The plane could be brought down and it could be set on fire. But you cannot get away from the fact, *mon cher* Jessop, that there were *people* in the plane. The charred bodies were actually *there.*"

"I know," said Jessop. "That's the stumbling block. Oh, I've no doubt my ideas are fantastic, but it's such a neat ending to our hunt. Too neat. That's what I feel. It says finish to us. We write down R.I.P. in the margin of our report and it's ended. There's no further trail to take up." He turned again to Leblanc. "You are having that search instituted?"

"For two days now," said Leblanc. "Good men, too. It's a particularly lonely spot, of course, where the plane crashed. It was off its course, by the way."

"Which is significant," Jessop put in.

"The nearest villages, the nearest habitations, the nearest traces of a car, all those are being investigated fully. In this country as well as in yours, we fully realize the importance of the investigation. In France, too, we have lost some of our best young scientists. In my opinion, *mon cher,* it is easier to control temperamental opera singers than it is to control a scientist. They are brilliant, these young men, erratic, rebellious; and finally and dangerously, they are most completely credulous. What do they imagine goes on *là-bas?* Sweetness and light and desire for truth and the millennium? Alas, poor children, what disillusionment awaits them."

"Let's go over the passenger list once more," said Jessop.

The Frenchman reached out a hand, picked it out of a wire basket and set it before his colleague. The two men pored over it together.

"Mrs. Calvin Baker, American. Mrs. Betterton, English. Torquil Ericsson, Norwegian—what do you know of him, by the way?"

"Nothing that I can recall," said Leblanc. "He was young, not more than twenty-seven or twenty-eight."

"I know his name," said Jessop, frowning. "I think—I am almost sure—that he read a paper before the Royal Society."

"Then there is the *religieuse,*" Leblanc said, turning back to the list. "Sister Marie something or other. Andrew Peters, also American. Dr. Barron. That is a celebrated name, *le docteur Barron.* A man of great brilliance. An expert on virus diseases."

"Biological warfare," said Jessop. "It fits. It all fits."

"A man poorly paid and discontented," said Leblanc.

"How many going to St. Ives?" murmured Jessop.

The Frenchman shot him a quick look and he smiled apologetically.

"Just an old nursery rhyme," he said. "For St. Ives read question mark. Journey to nowhere."

The telephone on the table buzzed and Leblanc picked up the receiver.

"Allo?" he said. *"Qu'est-ce qu'il y a?* Ah, yes, send them up." He turned his head toward Jessop. His face was suddenly alive, vigorous. "One of my men reporting," he said. "They have found something. *Mon cher collègue,* it is possible—I say no more—possible that your optimism is justified."

A few moments later two men entered the room. The first bore a rough resemblance to Leblanc, the same type, stocky, dark, intelligent. His manner was respectful but exhilarated. He wore European clothes badly stained and marked, covered with dust. He had obviously just arrived from a journey. With him was a native wearing the white local dress. He had the dignified composure of the dweller in remote places. His manner was courteous but not subservient. He looked with a faint wonder round the room while the other man explained things in rapid French.

"The reward was offered and circulated," the man explained, "and this fellow and his family and a great many of his friends have been searching diligently. I let him bring you the find himself as there may be questions you want to ask him."

Leblanc turned to the Berber—

"You have done good work," he said, speaking now in the man's own language. "You have the eyes of the hawk, my father. Show us then what you have discovered."

From a fold in his white robe the man took out a small object, and stepping forward laid it on the table before the Frenchman. It was rather a large sized pinkish gray synthetic pearl.

"It is like the one shown to me and shown to others," he said. "It is of value and I have found it."

Jessop stretched out a hand and took the pearl. From his pocket he drew out another exactly like it and examined both. Then he walked across the room to the window, and examined them both through a powerful lens.

"Yes," he said, "the mark is there." There was jubilation now in his voice and he came back to the table. "Good girl," he said, "good girl, good girl! She managed it!"

Leblanc was questioning the Berber in a rapid exchange of Arabic. Finally he turned to Jessop.

"I make my apologies, *mon cher collègue,*" he said. "This pearl was found at a distance of nearly *half a mile* from the flaming plane."

"Which shows," said Jessop, "that Olive Betterton was a survivor, and that though seven people left Fez in the plane and seven charred bodies were found, one of those charred bodies was definitely not hers."

"We extend the search now," said Leblanc. He spoke again to the Berber and the man smiled back happily. He left the room with the man who had brought him in. "He will be handsomely rewarded as promised," said Leblanc, "and there will be a hunt now all over the countryside for these pearls. They have hawk eyes, these people, and the knowledge that these are worth good money in reward will pass round like a grapevine. I think—I think, *mon cher collègue,* that we shall get results! If only they have not tumbled to what she was doing."

Jessop shook his head.

"It would be such a natural occurrence," he said. "The sudden breaking of a necklace of costume jewelery such as most women wear, the picking up apparently of what loose pearls she can find and stuffing them into her pocket, then a little hole in the pocket. Besides, why should they suspect her? She is Olive Betterton, anxious to join her husband."

"We must review this matter in a new light," said Leblanc. He drew the passenger list toward him. "Olive Betterton. Dr. Barron," he said, ticking off the two names. "Two at least who are going—wherever they are going. The American woman, Mrs. Calvin Baker. As to her we keep an open mind. Torquil Ericsson you say has read papers before the Royal Society. The American, Peters, was described on his passport as a Research Chemist. The *religieuse*—well, it would make a good disguise. In fact, a whole cargo of people cleverly shepherded from different points to travel in that one plane on that particular day. And then the plane is discovered in flames and inside it the requisite number of charred bodies. How did they manage that, I wonder? *Enfin, c'est colossal!"*

"Yes," said Jessop. "It was the final convincing touch. But we know now that six or seven people have started off on a fresh journey, and we know where their point of departure is. What do we do next—visit the spot?"

"But precisely," said Leblanc. "We take up advanced headquarters. If I mistake not, now that we are on the track, other evidence will come to light."

"If our calculations are exact," Leblanc said, "there should be results."

The calculations were many and devious. The rate of progress of a car, the likely distance where it would refuel, possible villages where travelers might have stayed the night. The tracks were many and confusing, disappointments were continual, but every now and then there came a positive result.

"Voilà, mon capitaine! A search of the latrines, as you ordered. In a dark corner of the latrine a pearl embedded in a little piece of chewing gum in the house of one Abdul Mohammed. He and his sons have been interrogated. At first they denied, but at last they have confessed. A carload of six people said to be from the German archaeological expedition spent a night in his house. Much money was paid, and they were not to mention this to anyone, the excuse being that there was some illicit digging in prospect. Children in the village of El Kaif also have brought in two more pearls. We know now the direction. There is more, *Monsieur le Capitaine.* The hand Fatma has been seen as you foretold. This type here, he will tell you about it."

"This type" was a particularly wild-looking Berber.

"I was with my flocks," he said, "at night and I heard a car. It passed me and as it did so I saw the sign. The hand of Fatma was outlined on one side of it. It gleamed, I tell you, in the darkness."

"The application of phosphorus on a glove can be very efficacious," murmured Leblanc. "I congratulate you, *mon cher,* on that idea."

"It's effective," said Jessop, "but it's dangerous. It's too easily noticed by the fugitives themselves, I mean."

Leblanc shrugged his shoulders.

"It could not be seen in daylight."

"No, but if there was a halt and they alighted from the car in the darkness—"

"Even then—it is a notable Arab superstition. It is painted often on carts and wagons. It would only be thought that some pious Moslem had painted it in luminous paint on his vehicle."

"True enough. But we must be on our guard. For if our enemies did notice it, it is highly possible that they will lay a false trail for us, of hands of Fatma in phosphorous paint."

"Ah, as to that I agree with you. One must indeed be on one's guard. Always, always on one's guard."

On the following morning Leblanc had another exhibit of three false pearls arranged in a triangle, stuck together by a little piece of chewing gum.

"This should mean," said Jessop, "that the next stage of the journey was by plane."

He looked inquiringly at Leblanc.

"You are absolutely right," said the other. "This was found on a disused army airfield, in a remote and desolate place. There were signs that a plane landed and left there not long ago." He shrugged his shoulders. "An unknown plane," he said, "and once again they took off for a destination unknown. That brings us once more to a halt and we do not know where next to take up the trail."

15

"IT'S INCREDIBLE," THOUGHT Hilary to herself, "incredible that I've been here ten days!" The frightening thing in life, Hilary thought, was how easily you adapted yourself. She remembered once being shown in France some peculiar torture arrangement of the Middle Ages, an iron cage wherein a prisoner had been confined and in which he could neither lie, stand nor sit. The guide had recounted how the last man imprisoned there had lived in it for eighteen years, had been released and had lived for another twenty after that, before dying, an old man. That adaptability, thought Hilary, was what differentiated man from the animal world. Man could live in any climate and on any food and under any conditions. He could exist slave or free.

She had felt first, when introduced into the Unit, a blinding panic, a horrible feeling of imprisonment and frustration, and the fact that the imprisonment was camouflaged in circumstances of luxury had somehow made it seem all the more horrible to her. And yet now, already, even after a week here she had begun insensibly to accept the conditions of her life as natural. It was a queer, dreamlike existence. Nothing seemed particularly real, but already she had the feeling that the dream had gone on a long time and would go on for a long time more. It would, perhaps, last forever. . . . She would always live here in the Unit, this was life, and there was nothing outside.

This dangerous acceptance, she thought, came partly from the fact that she was a woman. Women were adaptable by nature. It was their strength and their weakness. They examined their environment, accepted it, and like realists settled down to make the best of it. What interested her most were the reactions of the people who had arrived here with her. Helga Needheim she hardly ever saw except sometimes at meals. When they met, the German woman vouchsafed her a curt nod, but no more. As far as she could judge,

Helga Needheim was happy and satisfied. The Unit obviously lived up to the picture she had formed in her mind of it. She was the type of woman absorbed by her work, and was comfortably sustained by her natural arrogance. The superiority of herself and her fellow scientists was the first article of Helga's creed. She had no views of a brotherhood of man, of an era of peace, of liberty of mind and spirit. For her the future was narrow but all conquering. The super race, herself a member of it; the rest of the world in bondage, treated, if they behaved, with condescending kindness. If her fellow workers expressed different views, if their ideas were Communist rather than Fascist, Helga took little notice. If their work was good they were necessary, and their ideas would change.

Dr. Barron was more intelligent than Helga Needheim. Occasionally Hilary had brief conversations with him. He was absorbed in his work, deeply satisfied with the conditions provided for him, but his inquiring Gallic intellect led him to speculate and ponder on the media in which he found himself.

"It was not what I expected. No, frankly," he said one day, *"entre nous,* Mrs. Betterton, I do not care for prison conditions. And these *are* prison conditions, though the cage, let us say, is heavily gilded."

"There is hardly the freedom here that you came to seek?" Hilary suggested.

He smiled at her, a quick, rueful smile.

"But no," he said, "you are wrong. I did not really seek liberty. I am a civilized man. The civilized man knows there is no such thing. Only the younger and cruder nations put the word *Liberty* on their banner. There must always be a planned framework of security. And the essence of civilization is that the way of life should be a moderate one. The middle way. Always one comes back to the middle way. No. I will be frank with you. I came here for money."

Hilary in her turn smiled. Her eyebrows rose.

"And what good is money to you here?"

"It pays for very expensive laboratory equipment," said Dr. Barron. "I am not obliged to put my hand into my own pocket, and so I can serve the cause of science and satisfy my own intellectual curiosity. I am a man who loves his work, true, but I do not love it for the sake of humanity. I have usually found that those who do so are somewhat woolly headed, and often incompetent workers. No, it is the pure intellectual joy of research that I appreciate. For the rest, a large sum of money was paid to me before I left France. It is safely banked under another name and in due course, when all this comes to an end, I shall have it to spend as I choose."

"When all this comes to an end?" Hilary repeated. "But why should it come to an end?"

"One must have the common sense," said Dr. Barron, "nothing is permanent, nothing endures. I have come to the conclusion that this place is run by a madman. A madman, let me tell you, can be very logical. If you are rich and logical and also mad, you can succeed for a very long time in living out your illusion. But in the end—" he shrugged, "—in the end this will break up. Because, you see, it is not reasonable, what happens here! That which is not reasonable must always pay the reckoning in the end. In the meantime—" again he shrugged his shoulders, "—it suits me admirably."

Torquil Ericsson, whom Hilary expected to be violently disillusioned, appeared to be quite content in the atmosphere of the Unit. Less practical than the Frenchman, he existed in a single-minded vision of his own. The world in which he lived was one so unfamiliar to Hilary that she could not even understand it. It engendered a kind of austere happiness, an absorption in mathematical calculations, and an endless vista of possibilities. The strange, impersonal ruthlessness of his character frightened Hilary. He was the kind of young man, she thought, who in a moment of idealism could send three quarters of the world to their death in order that the remaining quarter should participate in an impractical Utopia that existed only in Ericsson's mind.

With the American, Andy Peters, Hilary felt herself far more in accord. Possibly, she thought, it was because Peters was a man of talents but not a genius. From what others said, she gathered he was a first-class man at his job, a careful and skilled chemist, but not a pioneer. Peters, like herself, had at once hated and feared the atmosphere of the Unit.

"The truth is that I didn't know where I was going," he said. "I thought I knew, but I was wrong. The Party has got nothing to do with this place. We're not in touch with Moscow. This is a lone show of some kind—a Fascist show possibly."

"Don't you think," said Hilary, "that you go in too much for labels?"

He considered this.

"Maybe you're right," he said. "Come to think of it, these words we throw around don't mean much. But I do know this. I want to get out of here and I mean to get out of here."

"It won't be easy," said Hilary, in a low voice.

They were walking together after dinner near the splashing fountains of the roof garden. With the illusion of darkness and the starlit sky they might have been in the private gardens of some sultan's palace. The functional concrete buildings were veiled from their sight.

"No," said Peters, "it won't be easy, but nothing's impossible."

"I like to hear you say that," said Hilary. "Oh, how I like to hear you say that!"

He looked at her sympathetically.

"Been getting you down?" he asked.

"Very much so. But that's not what I'm really afraid of."

"No? What then?"

"I'm afraid of getting used to it," said Hilary.

"Yes." He spoke thoughtfully. "Yes, I know what you mean. There's a kind of mass suggestion going on here. I think perhaps you're right about that."

"It would seem to me much more natural for people to rebel," said Hilary.

"Yes. Yes, I've thought the same. In fact I've wondered once or twice whether there's not a little hocus-pocus going on."

"Hocus-pocus? What do you mean by that?"

"Well, to put it frankly, dope."

"Do you mean a drug of some kind?"

"Yes. It might be possible, you know. Something in the food or drink, something that induces—what shall I say—docility?"

"But is there such a drug?"

"Well, that's not really my line of country. There are things that are given to people to soothe them down, to make them acquiescent before operations and that. Whether there is anything that can be administered steadily over a long period of time—and which at the same time does not impair efficiency— that I don't know. I'm more inclined to think now that the effect is produced mentally. I mean that I think some of these organizers and administrators here are well-versed in hypnosis and psychology and that, without our being aware of it, we are continually being offered suggestions of our well being, of our attaining our ultimate aim (whatever it is), and that all this *does* produce a definite effect. A lot can be done that way, you know, if it's done by people who know their stuff."

"But we mustn't acquiesce," cried Hilary, hotly. "We mustn't feel for one moment that it's a good thing to be here."

"What does your husband feel?"

"Tom? I—oh, I don't know. It's so difficult. I—" she lapsed into silence.

The whole fantasy of her life as she lived it she could hardly communicate to the man who was listening to her. For ten days now she had lived in an apartment with a man who was a stranger to her. They shared a bedroom and when she lay awake at night she could hear him breathing in the other bed. Both of them accepted the arrangement as inevitable. She was an impostor, a spy, ready to play any part and assume any personality. Tom Betterton she quite frankly did not understand. He seemed to her a terrible example of what could happen to a brilliant young man who had lived for some months in the enervating atmosphere of the Unit. At any rate there was in him no calm acceptance of his destiny. Far from taking pleasure in his work, he was, she thought, increasingly worried by his inability to concentrate on it. Once or twice he had reiterated what he had said on that first evening.

"I can't think. It's just as though everything in me has dried up."

Yes, she thought, Tom Betterton, being a real genius, needed liberty more than most. Suggestion had failed to compensate him for the loss of freedom. Only in perfect liberty was he able to produce creative work.

He was a man, she thought, very close to a serious nervous breakdown. Hilary herself he treated with curious inattention. She was not a woman to him, not even a friend. She even doubted whether he realized and suffered from the death of his wife. The thing that preoccupied him incessantly was the problem of confinement. Again and again he had said,

"I must get away from here. I must, I must." And sometimes, "I didn't know. I'd no idea what it was going to be like. How *am* I going to get out of here? How? I've got to. I've simply got to."

It was in essence very much what Peters had said. But it was said with a great deal of difference. Peters had spoken as a young, energetic, angry, disillusioned man, sure of himself and determined to pit his wits against the brains of the establishment in which he found himself. But Tom Betterton's rebellious utterances were those of a man at the end of his tether, a man almost crazed with the need for escape. But perhaps, Hilary thought suddenly, that was where she and Peters would be in six months' time. Perhaps what began as healthy rebellion and a reasonable confidence in one's own ingenuity, would turn at last into the frenzied despair of a rat in a trap.

She wished she could talk of all this to the man beside her. If only she could say: "Tom Betterton isn't my husband. I know nothing about him. I don't know what he was like before he came here and so I'm in the dark. I can't help him, for I don't know what to do or say." As it was she had to pick her words carefully. She said,

"Tom seems like a stranger to me now. He doesn't—tell me things. Sometimes I think the confinement, the sense of being penned up here, is driving him mad."

"It's possible," said Peters dryly, "it could act that way."

"But tell me—you speak so confidently of getting away. How *can* we get away—what earthly chance is there?"

"I don't mean we can walk out the day after tomorrow, Olive. The thing's got to be thought out and planned. People have escaped, you know, under the most unpromising conditions. A lot of our people, and a lot your side of the Atlantic, too, have written books about escape from fortresses in Germany."

"That was rather different."

"Not in essence. Where there's a way in there's a way out. Of course tunneling is out of the question here, so that knocks out a good many methods. But as I say, where there's a way in, there's a way out. With ingenuity, camouflage, playing a part, deception, bribery and corruption, one ought to manage it. It's the sort of thing you've got to study and think about. I'll tell you this. I *shall* get out of here. Take it from me."

"I believe you will," said Hilary, then she added, "but shall I?"

"Well, it's different for you."

His voice sounded embarrassed. For a moment she wondered what he meant. Then she realized that presumably her own objective had been attained. She had come here to join the man she had loved, and having joined him her own personal need for escape should not be so great. She was almost tempted to tell Peters the truth—but some instinct of caution forbade that.

She said goodnight and left the roof.

16

"GOOD EVENING, MRS. Betterton."

"Good evening, Miss Jennsen."

The thin spectacled girl was looking excited. Her eyes glinted behind the thick lenses.

"There will be a Reunion this evening," she said. "The *Director himself* is going to address us!"

She spoke in an almost hushed voice.

"That's good," said Andy Peters who was standing close by. "I've been waiting to catch a glimpse of this Director."

Miss Jennsen threw him a glance of shocked reproof.

"The Director," she said austerely, "is a very wonderful man."

As she went away from them down one of the inevitable white corridors, Andy Peters gave a low whistle.

"Now did I, or did I not, catch a hint of the Heil Hitler attitude there?"

"It certainly sounded like it."

"The trouble in this life is that you never really know where you're going. If I'd known when I left the States all full of boyish ardor for the good old Brotherhood of Man that I was going to land myself in the clutches of yet another Heavenborn Dictator—" he threw out his hands.

"You don't know that yet," Hilary reminded him.

"I can smell it—in the air," said Peters.

"Oh," cried Hilary, "how glad I am that you're here."

She flushed, as he looked at her quizzically.

"You're so nice and ordinary," said Hilary desperately.

Peters looked amused.

"Where I come from," he said, "the word ordinary doesn't have your meaning. It can stand for being just plain mean."

"You know I didn't mean it that way. I mean you're like everybody else. Oh dear, that sounds rude, too."

"The common man, that's what you're asking for? You've had enough of the genius?"

"Yes, and you've changed, too, since you came here. You've lost that streak of bitterness—of hatred."

But immediately his face grew rather grim.

"Don't count on that," he said. "It's still there—underneath. I can still hate. There are things, believe me, that *should* be hated."

The Reunion, as Miss Jennsen had called it, took place after dinner. All members of the Unit assembled in the large lecture room.

The audience did not include what might be called the technical staff: the laboratory assistants, the corps de ballet, the various service personnel, and

578

the small assembly of handsome prostitutes who also served the Unit as purveyors of sex to those men who had no wives with them and had formed no particular attachments with the female workers.

Sitting next to Betterton, Hilary awaited with keen curiosity the arrival on the platform of that almost mythical figure, the Director. Questioned by her, Tom Betterton had given unsatisfactory, almost vague answers, about the personality of the man who controlled the Unit.

"He's nothing much to look at," he said. "But he has tremendous impact. Actually I've only seen him twice. He doesn't show up often. He's remarkable, of course, one feels that, but honestly I don't know *why.*"

From the reverent way Miss Jennsen and some of the other women spoke about him, Hilary had formed a vague mental figure of a tall man with a golden beard wearing a white robe—a kind of godlike abstraction.

She was almost startled when, as the audience rose to their feet, a dark rather heavily built man of middle age came quietly onto the platform. In appearance he was quite undistinguished, he might have been a businessman from the Midlands. His nationality was not apparent. He spoke to them in three languages, alternating one with the other, and never exactly repeating himself. He used French, German and English, and each was spoken with equal fluency.

"Let me first," he began, "welcome our new colleagues who have come to join us here."

He then paid a few words of tribute to each of the new arrivals.

After that he went on to speak of the aims and beliefs of the Unit.

Trying to remember his words later, Hilary found herself unable to do so with any accuracy. Or perhaps it was that the words, as remembered, seemed trite and ordinary. But listening to them was a very different thing.

Hilary remembered once being told by a friend who had lived in Germany in the days before the war, how she had gone to a meeting in mere curiosity to listen "to that absurd Hitler"—and how she had found herself crying hysterically, swept away by intense emotion. She had described how wise and inspiring every word had seemed, and how, afterward, the remembered words in their actuality had seemed commonplace enough.

Something of the same kind was happening now. In spite of herself, Hilary was stirred and uplifted. The Director spoke very simply. He spoke primarily of Youth. With Youth lay the future of mankind.

"Accumulated Wealth, Prestige, influential Families—those have been the forces of the past. But today, power lies in the hands of the young. Power is in Brains. The brains of the chemist, the physicist, the doctor . . . From the laboratories comes the power to destroy on a vast scale. With that power you can say "Yield—or perish!" That power should not be given to this or that nation. Power should be in the hands of those who create it. This Unit is a gathering place for the Power of all the world. You come here from all parts of the globe, bringing with you your creative scientific knowledge. And with you, you bring *Youth!* No one here is over forty-five. When the day comes, we shall create a Trust. The Brains Trust of Science. And we shall administer world affairs. We shall issue our orders to Capitalists and Kings and Armies and Industries. We shall give the World the *Pax Scientifica.*"

There was more of it—all the same heady intoxicating stuff—but it was not the words themselves—it was the power of the orator that carried away an assembly that could have been cold and critical had it not been swayed by that nameless emotion about which so little is known.

When the Director had ended abruptly:

"Courage and Victory! Goodnight!" Hilary left the Hall, half stumbling in a kind of exalted dream, and recognized the same feeling in the faces around her. She saw Ericsson in particular, his pale eyes gleaming, his head tossed back in exultation.

Then she felt Andy Peters' hand on her arm and his voice said in her ear:

"Come up on the roof. We need some air."

They went up in the lift without speaking and stepped out among the palm trees under the stars. Peters drew a deep breath.

"Yes," he said. "This is what we need. Air to blow away the clouds of glory."

Hilary gave a deep sigh. She still felt unreal.

He gave her arm a friendly shake.

"Snap out of it, Olive."

"Clouds of glory," said Hilary. "You know—it *was* like that!"

"Snap out of it, I tell you. Be a woman! Down to earth and basic realities! When the effects of the Glory Gas poisoning pass off you'll realize that you've been listening to the same old Mixture as Before."

"But it was fine—I mean a fine ideal."

"Nuts to ideals. Take the facts. Youth and Brains—glory glory Alleluia! And what are the youth and brains? Helga Needheim, a ruthless egoist. Torquil Ericsson, an impractical dreamer. Dr. Barron who'd sell his grandmother to the knacker's yard to get equipment for his work. Take me, an ordinary guy, as you've said yourself, good with the test-tube and the microscope but with no talent whatever for efficient administration of an office, let alone a World! Take your own husband—yes, I'm going to say it—a man whose nerves are frayed to nothing and who can think of nothing but the fear that retribution will catch up with him. I've given you those people we know best—but they're all the same here—or all that I've come across. Geniuses, some of them, damned good at their chosen jobs—but as Administrators of the Universe—hell, don't make me laugh! Pernicious nonsense, that's what we've been listening to."

Hilary sat down on the concrete parapet. She passed a hand across her forehead.

"You know," she said. "I believe you're right . . . But the clouds of glory are still trailing. How does he do it? Does he believe it himself? He must."

Peters said gloomily,

"I suppose it always comes to the same thing in the end. A madman who believes he's God."

Hilary said slowly,

"I suppose so. And yet—that seems curiously unsatisfactory."

"But it happens, my dear. Again and again throughout history it happens. And it gets one. It nearly got me, tonight. It *did* get you. If I hadn't whisked you up here—" his manner changed suddenly. "I suppose I shouldn't have done that. What will Betterton say? He'll think it odd."

"I don't think so. I doubt if he'll notice."

He looked at her questioningly.

"I'm sorry, Olive. It must be all pretty fair hell for you. Seeing him go down the hill."

Hilary said passionately,

"We must get out of here. We must. We must."

"We shall."

"You said that before—but we've made no progress."

"Oh yes we have. I've not been idle."

She looked at him in surprise.

"No precise plan, but I've initiated subversive activities. There's a lot of dissatisfaction here, far more than our godlike Herr Director knows. Amongst the humbler members of the Unit, I mean. Food and money and luxury and women aren't everything, you know. I'll get you out of here yet, Olive."

"And Tom, too."

Peters' face darkened.

"Listen, Olive, and believe what I say. Tom will do best to stay on here. He's—" he hesitated, "—safer here than he would be in the outside world."

"Safer? What a curious word."

"Safer," said Peters. "I use the word deliberately."

Hilary frowned.

"I don't really see what you mean. Tom's not—you don't think he's becoming mentally unhinged?"

"Not in the least. He's het up, but I'd say Tom Betterton's as sane as you or I."

"Then why are you saying he'd be safer here?"

Peters said slowly,

"A cage, you know, is a very safe place to be."

"Oh no," cried Hilary. "Don't tell me you're going to believe that too. Don't tell me that mass hypnotism, or suggestion, or whatever it is, is working on you. Safe, tame, content! We *must* rebel still! We must want to be free!"

Peters said slowly,

"Yes, I know. But—"

"Tom, at any rate, wants desperately to get away from here."

"Tom mayn't know what's good for him."

Suddenly Hilary remembered what Tom had hinted at to her. If he had disposed of secret information he would be liable, she supposed, to prosecution under the Official Secrets Act— That, no doubt, was what Peters was hinting at in his rather embarrassed way—but Hilary was clear in her own mind. Better to serve a prison sentence even than remain on here. She said, obstinately,

"Tom must come, too."

She was startled when Peters said suddenly, in a bitter tone,

"Have it your own way. I've warned you. I wish I knew what the hell makes you care for that fellow so much?"

She stared at him in dismay. Words sprang to her lips, but she checked them. She realized that what she wanted to say was, "I don't care for him. He's nothing to me. He was another woman's husband and I've a responsibility to her." She wanted to say, "You fool, if there's anybody I care about, it's *you* . . ."

ii

"Been enjoying yourself with your tame American?"

Tom Betterton threw the words at her as she entered their bedroom. He was lying on his back on his bed, smoking.

Hilary flushed slightly.

"We arrived here together," she said, "and we seem to think alike about certain things."

He laughed.

"Oh! I don't blame you." For the first time he looked at her in a new and appraising way. "You're a good-looking woman, Olive," he said.

From the beginning Hilary had urged him always to call her by his wife's name.

"Yes," he continued, his eyes raking her up and down. "You're a damned good-looking woman. I'd have noticed that once. As it is, nothing of that kind seems to register with me any more."

"Perhaps it's just as well," said Hilary dryly.

"I'm a perfectly normal man, my dear, or I used to be. God knows what I am now."

Hilary sat down by him.

"What *is* the matter with you, Tom?" she said.

"I tell you. I can't concentrate. As a scientist I'm shot to pieces. This place—"

"The others—or most of them—don't seem to feel like you?"

"Because they're a damned insensitive crowd, I suppose."

"Some of them are temperamental enough," said Hilary, dryly. She went on, "If only you had a friend here—a real friend."

"Well, there's Murchison. Though he's a dull dog. And I've seen a good deal of Torquil Ericsson lately."

"Really?" For some reason Hilary felt surprised.

"Yes. My God, he's brilliant. I wish I had *his* brains."

"He's an odd sort of person," said Hilary. "I always find him rather frightening."

"Frightening? Torquil? He's as mild as milk. Like a child in some ways. No knowledge of the world."

"Well *I* find him frightening," repeated Hilary obstinately.

"Your nerves must be getting upset, too."

"Not yet. I suspect they will, though. Tom—don't get too friendly with Torquil Ericsson."

He stared at her.

"Whyever not?"

"I don't know. It's a feeling I have."

17

LEBLANC SHRUGGED HIS shoulders.

"They have left Africa, it is certain."

"Not *certain.*"

"The probabilities point that way." The Frenchman shook his head. "After all, we know, do we not, for where they are bound?"

"If they are bound for where we think, why start the journey from Africa? Anywhere in Europe would be simpler."

"That is true. But there is the other side of it. No one would expect them to assemble and start from here."

"I still think there's more to it than that." Jessop was gently insistent. "Besides, only a small plane could have used that airfield. It would have to come down and refuel before crossing the Mediterranean. And where they refueled some trace should have been left."

"*Mon cher,* we have instituted the most searching inquiries—everywhere there has been—"

"The men with the Geiger counters must get results in the end. The number of planes to be examined is limited. Just a trace of radioactivity and we shall know that is the plane we are looking for—"

"If your agent has been able to use the spray. Alas! Always so many 'ifs' . . ."

"We shall get there," said Jessop obstinately. "I wonder—"

"Yes?"

"We have assumed they are going *north*—toward the Mediterranean—suppose instead, they flew *south.*"

"Doubled back on their tracks? But where, then, could they be flying *to?* There are the mountains of the High Atlas—and after that the desert sands."

ii

"Sidi, you swear to me that it will be as you have promised? A petrol station in America, in Chicago? It is certain?"

"It is certain, Mohammed, if we get out of here, that is."

"Success depends on the will of Allah."

"Let us hope, then, that it is the will of Allah that you should have a petrol station in Chicago. Why Chicago?"

"Sidi, the brother of my wife went to America, and he has there a petrol pump in Chicago. Do I want to remain in a backward part of the world all my days? Here there is money and much food and many rugs and women— but it is not modern. It is not America."

Peters looked thoughtfully into the dignified black face. Mohammed in his white robes was a magnificent sight. What strange desires rose in the human heart!

"I don't know that you're wise," he said with a sigh, "but so be it. Of course, if we are found out—"

A smile on the black face revealed beautiful white teeth.

"Then it is death—for me certainly. Perhaps not for you, Sidi, since you are valuable."

"They deal out death rather easily here, do they?"

The shoulders of the other man rose and fell contemptuously.

"What is death? That, too, is the will of Allah."

"You know what you have to do?"

"I know, Sidi. I am to take you to the roof after dark. Also I am to put in your room clothing such as I and the other servants wear. Later—there will be other things."

"Right. You'd better let me out of the lift now. Somebody may notice we're riding up and down. It may give them ideas."

iii

There was dancing going on. Andy Peters was dancing with Miss Jennsen. He held her close to him, and seemed to be murmuring in her ear. As they revolved slowly near where Hilary was standing he caught her eye and immediately gave her an outrageous wink.

Hilary, biting her lip to avoid a smile, averted her eyes quickly.

Her glance fell on Betterton who was standing just across the room talking to Torquil Ericsson. Hilary frowned a little as she watched them.

"Have a turn with me, Olive?" said Murchison's voice at her elbow.

"Yes, of course, Simon."

"Mind you, I'm not very hot at dancing," he warned her.

Hilary concentrated on keeping her feet where he could not possibly tread on them.

"It's exercise, that's what I say," said Murchison, panting slightly. He was an energetic dancer.

"Awfully jolly frock you've got on, Olive."

His conversation seemed always to come out of an old-fashioned novel.

"I'm glad you like it," said Hilary.

"Get it out of the Fashion Department?"

Resisting the temptation to reply: "Where else?" Hilary merely said, "Yes."

"Must say, you know," panted Murchison as he capered perseveringly round the floor, "they do you jolly well here. Said so to Bianca only the other day. Beats the Welfare State every time. No worries about money, or income tax—or repairs or upkeep. All the worrying done for you. Must be a wonderful life for a woman, I should say."

"Bianca finds it so, does she?"

"Well, she was restless for a bit, but now she's managed to get up a few committees and organize one or two things—debates, you know, and lectures. She's complaining that you don't take as much part as you might in things."

"I'm afraid I'm not that kind of person, Simon. I've never been very public spirited."

"Yes, but you girls have got to keep yourselves amused one way or another. At least I don't mean *amused* exactly—"

"Occupied?" suggested Hilary.

"Yes—I mean the modern woman wants to get her teeth into something. I quite realize that women like you and Bianca have made a definite sacrifice coming here—you're neither of you scientists, thank goodness—really, these scientific women! Absolutely the limit, most of them! I said to Bianca, 'Give Olive time, she's got to get tuned in.' It takes a little time getting used to this place. To begin with, one gets a kind of claustrophobic feeling. But it wears off—it wears off . . ."

"You mean—one can get used to anything?"

"Well, some people feel it more than others. Tom, now, seems to take it hard. Where's old Tom tonight? Oh yes, I see, over there with Torquil. Quite inseparable, those two."

"I wish they weren't. I mean, I shouldn't have thought they had very much in common."

"Young Torquil seems fascinated by your husband. He follows him round everywhere."

"I've noticed it. I wondered—why?"

"Well, he's always got some outlandish theory to get off his chest—it's beyond my power to follow him—his English isn't too good, as you know. But Tom listens and manages to take it all in."

The dance ended. Andy Peters came up and claimed Hilary for the next one.

"I observed you suffering in a good cause," he said. "How badly did you get trampled?"

"Oh, I was fairly agile."

"You noticed me doing my stuff?"

"With the Jennsen?"

"Yes. I think I may say without undue modesty that I have made a hit, a palpable hit in that quarter. These plain angular shortsighted girls respond immediately when given the treatment."

"You certainly gave the impression of having fallen for her."

"That was the idea. That girl, Olive, properly handled, can be very useful. She's in the know about all the arrangements here. For instance, tomorrow there's a party of various V.I.P.'s due here. Doctors and a few Government officials and a rich patron or two."

"Andy—do you think there might be a chance . . ."

"No, I don't. I bet *that's* going to be taken care of. So don't cherish false hopes. But it will be valuable because we'll get an idea of the procedure. And on the next occasion—well, there might be something doing. So long as I can keep the Jennsen eating out of my hand, I can get a lot of miscellaneous information out of her."

"How much do the people who are coming know?"

"About *us*—the Unit, I mean—nothing at all. Or so I gather. They just inspect the settlement and the medical research laboratories. This place has been deliberately built like a labyrinth, just so that nobody coming into it can possibly guess its extent. I gather there are kinds of bulkheads that close, and that shut off our area."

"It all seems so incredible."

"I know. Half the time one feels one must be dreaming. One of the unreal things here is never seeing any children about. Thank goodness there aren't! You must be thankful you haven't got a child."

He felt the sudden stiffening of her body.

"Here—I'm sorry—I said the wrong thing!" He led her off the dance floor and to a couple of chairs.

"I'm very sorry," he repeated. "I hurt you, didn't I?"

"It's nothing—no, really not your fault. I did have a child—and it died—that's all."

"You had a child?—" he stared, surprised. "I thought you'd only been married to Betterton six months?"

Olive flushed. She said quickly,

"Yes, of course. But I was—married before. I divorced my first husband."

"Oh, I see. That's the worst of this place. One doesn't know anything about people's lives before they came here, and so one goes and says the wrong thing. It's odd to realize sometimes that I don't know anything about you at all."

"Or I anything about you. How you were brought up—and where—your family—"

"I was brought up in a strictly scientific atmosphere. Nourished on test tubes, you might say. Nobody ever thought or talked of anything else. But I was never the bright boy of the family. Genius lay elsewhere."

"Where exactly?"

"A girl. She was brilliant. She might have been another Madame Curie. She could have opened up new horizons . . ."

"She—what happened to her?"

He said shortly:

"She was killed."

Hilary guessed at some wartime tragedy. She said gently,

"You cared for her?"

"More than I have ever cared for anybody."

He roused himself suddenly.

"What the heck—we've got enough troubles in the present, right here and now. Look at our Norwegian friend. Apart from his eyes, he always looks as though he were made from wood. And that wonderful little stiff bow of his— as though you'd pulled a string."

"It's because he's so very tall and thin."

"Not so very tall. About my height—five foot eleven or six foot, not more."

"Height is deceptive."

"Yes, it's like descriptions on passports. Take Ericsson. Height six foot, fair hair, blue eyes, face long, demeanour wooden, nose medium, mouth ordinary. Even add what a passport wouldn't—speaks correctly but pedantically—you still wouldn't have the first idea what Torquil really looked like. What's the matter?"

"Nothing."

She was staring across the room at Ericsson. That description of Boris Glydr! Almost word for word as she had heard it from Jessop. Was *that* why she had always felt nervous of Torquil Ericsson? Could it possibly be that— Turning abruptly to Peters she said,

"I suppose he *is* Ericsson? He couldn't be someone else?"

Peters looked at her in astonishment.

"Someone else? Who?"

"I mean—at least I think I mean—could he have come here pretending to be Ericsson?"

Peters considered.

"I suppose—no, I don't think that would be feasible. He'd have to be a scientist . . . and anyway, Ericsson is quite well known."

"But nobody here seems ever to have met him before—or I suppose he could be Ericsson, but be someone else as well."

"You mean Ericsson could have been leading some kind of double life? That's possible, I suppose. But it's not very likely."

"No," said Hilary. "No, of course it isn't likely."

Of course Ericsson was not Boris Glydr. But why should Olive Betterton have been so insistent on warning Tom against Boris? Could it have been because she knew that Boris was on his way to the Unit? Supposing the man who had come to London calling himself Boris Glydr was not Boris Glydr at all? Supposing that he was really Torquil Ericsson. The description fit. Ever since he arrived at the Unit, he had focused his attention on Tom. Ericsson, she was sure, was a dangerous person,—you didn't know what went on behind those pale dreamy eyes . . .

She shivered.

"Olive—what's the matter? What is it?"

"Nothing. Look. The Deputy Director is going to make an announcement."

Dr. Neilson was holding up his hand for silence. He spoke into the microphone on the platform of the Hall.

"Friends and colleagues. Tomorrow you are asked to remain in the Emergency Wing. Please assemble at 11:00 A.M. when there will be roll call. Emergency orders are for twenty-four hours only. I much regret the inconvenience. A notice had been pasted on the board."

He retired smiling. The music began again.

"I must pursue the Jennsen again," said Peters. "I see her looking earnest by a pillar. I want to hear just what these Emergency quarters consist of."

He moved away. Olive sat thinking. Was she an imaginative fool? Torquil Ericsson? Boris Glydr?

iv

Roll call was in the big lecture room. Everyone was present and answered to his or her name. Then they were marshaled into a long column and marched off.

The route was, as usual, through a maze of winding corridors. Olive, walking by Peters, knew that he had concealed in his hand, a tiny compass. From this, unobtrusively, he was calculating their direction.

"Not that it helps," he observed ruefully in a low tone. "Or at any rate it doesn't help at the moment. But it may do—some time."

At the end of the corridor they were following was a door and there was a momentary halt as the door was opened.

Peters took out his cigarette case—but immediately Van Heiden's voice was raised peremptorily.

"No smoking, please. That has already been told you."

"Sorry, sir."

Peters paused with the cigarette case in his hand. Then they all went forward again.

"Just like sheep," said Olive disgustedly.

"Cheer up," Peter murmured. "Baa, baa, black sheep is among the flock, thinking up devilry hard."

She flashed him a grateful glance and smiled.

"Women's dormitory to the right," said Miss Jennsen. She shepherded the women off in the direction indicated.

The men were fallen off to the left.

The dormitory was a large room of hygienic appearance rather like a hospital ward. It had beds along the walls with curtains of plastic material that could be pulled for privacy. There was a locker by each bed.

"You will find arrangements rather simple," said Miss Jennsen, "but not too primitive. The bathroom accommodation is through there to the right. The communal living room is through the door at the end."

The communal living room where they all met again was plainly furnished rather like an airport waiting room—there was a bar and snack counter at one side. Along the other side was a row of bookshelves.

The day passed quite agreeably. There were two cinema performances shown on a small portable screen.

The lighting was of the daylight type which tended to obscure the fact that there were no windows. Toward evening a fresh set of bulbs came on—soft and discreet night lighting.

"Clever," said Peters appreciatively. "It all helps to minimize the feeling of being walled up alive."

How helpless they all were, thought Hilary. Somewhere, quite near them, were a party from the outside world. And there was no means of communicating with them, of appealing for help. As usual, everything had been ruthlessly and efficiently planned.

Peters was sitting with Miss Jennsen. Hilary suggested to the Murchisons that they should play bridge. Tom Betterton refused. He said he couldn't concentrate, but Dr. Barron made a fourth.

Oddly enough, Hilary found the game enjoyable. It was half past eleven when their third rubber came to an end, with herself and Dr. Barron the winners.

"I enjoyed that," she said. She glanced at her watch. "It's quite late. I suppose the V.I.P.s will have left now—or do they spend the night here?"

"I don't really know," said Simon Murchison. "I believe one or two of the specially keen medicos stay over. Anyway, they'll all have gone by tomorrow midday."

"And that's when we're put back in circulation?"

"Yes. About time, too. It upsets all one's routine, this sort of thing."

"But it is well arranged," said Bianca with approval.

She and Hilary got up and said goodnight to the two men.

Hilary stood back a little to allow Bianca to precede her into the dimly lit dormitory. As she did so, she felt a soft touch on her arm.

She turned sharply to find one of the tall dark-faced servants standing beside her.

He spoke in a low urgent voice in French.

"*S'il vous plait, Madame,* you are to come."

"Come? Come where?"

"If you will please follow me."

She stood irresolute for a moment.

Bianca had gone on into the dormitory. In the communal living room the few persons left were engaged in conversation with each other.

Again she felt that soft urgent touch on her arm.

"You will follow me please, Madame."

He moved a few steps and stood, looking back, beckoning to her. A little doubtfully Hilary followed him.

She noticed that this particular man was far more richly dressed than most of the native servants. His robes were embroidered heavily with gold thread.

He led her through a small door in a corner of the communal living room, then once more along the inevitable anonymous white corridors. She did not think it was the same way by which they had come to the Emergency Wing, but it was always difficult to be sure because of the similarity of the passages. Once she turned to ask a question but the guide shook his head impatiently and hurried on.

He stopped finally at the end of a corridor and pressed a button in the wall. A panel slid back disclosing a small lift. He gestured her in, followed her, and the lift shot upward.

Hilary said sharply:

"Where are you taking me?"

The dark eyes held hers in a kind of dignified reproof.

"To the Master, Madame. It is for you a great honor."

"To the Director, you mean?"

"To the Master . . ."

The lift stopped. He slid back the doors and motioned her out. Then they walked down another corridor and arrived at a door. Her guide rapped on the door and it was opened from inside. Here again were white robes, gold embroidery and a black, impassive face.

The man took Hilary across the small red-carpeted anteroom and drew aside some hangings at the further side. Hilary passed through. She found herself, unexpectedly, in an almost oriental interior. There were low couches, coffee tables, one or two beautiful rugs hanging on the walls. Sitting on a low divan was a figure at whom she stared with complete incredulity. Small, yellow, wrinkled, old, she stared unbelievingly into the smiling eyes of Mr. Aristides.

18

"*ASSEYEZ-VOUS, CHÈRE Madame,*" said Mr. Aristides.

He waved a small clawlike hand, and Hilary came forward in a dream and sat down upon another low divan opposite him. He gave a gentle little cackle of laughter.

"You are surprised," he said. "It is not what you expected, eh?"

"No, indeed," said Hilary. "I never thought—I never imagined—"

But already her surprise was subsiding.

With her recognition of Mr. Aristides, the dream world of unreality in which she had been living for the past weeks shattered and broke. She knew now that the Unit had seemed unreal to her—because it *was* unreal. It had never been what it pretended to be. The Herr Director with his spellbinder's voice had been unreal too—a mere figurehead of fiction set up to obscure the truth. The truth was here in this secret oriental room. A little old man sitting there and laughing quietly. With Mr. Aristides in the center of the picture, everything made sense—hard, practical everyday sense.

"I see now," said Hilary. "This—is all yours isn't it?"

"Yes, Madame."

"And the Director? The so-called Director?"

"He is very good," said Mr. Aristides appreciatively. "I pay him a very high salary. He used to run Revivalist meetings."

He smoked thoughtfully for a moment or two. Hilary did not speak.

"There is Turkish Delight beside you, Madame. And other sweetmeats if you prefer them." Again there was a silence. Then he went on, "I am a philanthropist, Madame. As you know, I am rich. One of the richest men—possibly the richest man in the world today. With my wealth I feel under the obligation to serve humanity. I have established here, in this remote spot, a colony of lepers and a vast assembly of research into the problem of the cure of leprosy. Certain types of leprosy are curable. Others, so far, have proved incurable. But all the time we are working and obtaining good results. Leprosy is not really such an easily communicated disease. It is not half so infectious or so contagious as smallpox or typhus or plague or any of these other things. And yet, if you say to people, "a leper colony" they will shudder and give it a wide berth. It is an old, old fear that. A fear that you can find in the Bible, and which has existed all down through the years. The horror of the leper. It has been useful to me in establishing this place."

"You established it for that reason?"

"Yes. We have here also a Cancer Research department, and important work is being done on tuberculosis. There is virus research, also—for curative reasons, *bien entendu*—biological warfare is not mentioned. All humane, all acceptable, all redounding greatly to my honor. Well-known physicians, surgeons and research chemists come here to see our results from time to time as they have come today. The building has been cunningly constructed in such a way that a part of it is shut off and unapparent even from the air. The more secret laboratories have been tunneled right into the rock. In any case, I am above suspicion." He smiled and added simply: "I am so very rich, you see."

"But why?" demanded Hilary. "Why this urge for destruction?"

"I have no urge for destruction, Madame. You wrong me."

"But then—I simply don't understand."

"I am a businessman," said Mr. Aristides simply. "I am also a collector. When wealth becomes oppressive, that is the only thing to do. I have collected many things in my time. Pictures—I have the finest art collection in Europe. Certain kinds of ceramics. Philately—my stamp collection is famous. When a collection is fully representative, one goes on to the next thing. I am an old man, Madame, and there was not very much more for me to collect. So I came at last to collecting brains."

"Brains?" Hilary queried.

He nodded gently.

"Yes, it is the most interesting thing to collect of all. Little by little, Madame, I am assembling here all the brains of the world. The young men, those are the ones I am bringing here. Young men of promise, young men of achievement. One day the tired nations of the world will wake up and realize that their scientists are old and stale, and that the young brains of the world —the doctors, the research chemists, the physicists, the surgeons, are all here in my keeping. And if they want a scientist, or a plastic surgeon, or a biologist, they will have to come and buy him from me!"

"You mean . . ." Hilary leaned forward, staring at him. "You mean that this is all a gigantic financial operation?"

Again Mr. Aristides nodded gently.

"Yes," he said. "Naturally. Otherwise—it would not make sense, would it?"

Hilary gave a deep sigh.

"No," she said. "That's just what I've felt."

"After all, you see," said Mr. Aristides almost apologetically, "it is my profession. I am a financier."

"And you mean there is no political side to this at all? You don't want World Power—?"

He threw up his hand in rebuke.

"I do not want to be God," he said. "I am a religious man. That is the occupational disease of Dictators: wanting to be God. So far I have not contracted that disease." He reflected a moment and said: "It may come. Yes, it may come . . . But as yet, mercifully—no."

"But how do you get all these people to come here?"

"I buy them, Madame. In the open market. Like any other merchandise. Sometimes I buy them with money. More often, I buy them with ideas. Young men are dreamers. They have ideals. They have beliefs. Sometimes I buy them with safety—those that have transgressed the law."

"That explains it," said Hilary. "Explains, I mean, what puzzled me so on the journey here."

"Ah! It puzzled you on the journey, did it?"

"Yes. The difference in aims. Andy Peters, the American, seemed completely Left Wing. But Ericsson was a fanatical believer in the Superman. And Helga Needheim was a Fascist of the most arrogant and Pagan kind. Dr. Barron—" she hesitated.

"Yes, he came for money," said Aristides. "Dr. Barron is civilized and cynical. He has no illusions, but he has a genuine love of his work. He wanted unlimited money, so as to pursue his researches further." He added: "You are intelligent, Madame. I saw that at once in Fez."

He gave a gentle little cackle of laughter.

"You did not know it, Madame, but I went to Fez simply to observe you— or rather I had you brought to Fez in order that I might observe you."

"I see," said Hilary.

She noted the oriental rephrasing of the sentence.

"I was pleased to think that you would be coming here. For, if you understand me, I do not find many intelligent people in this place to talk to." He made a gesture. "These scientists, these biologists, these research chemists, they are not interesting. They are geniuses perhaps at what they do, but they are uninteresting people with whom to converse."

"Their wives," he added thoughtfully, "are usually very dull, too. We do not encourage wives here. I permit wives to come for only one reason."

"What reason?"

Mr. Aristides said dryly,

"In the rare cases where a husband is unable to do his work properly because he is thinking too much of his wife. That seemed to be the case with your husband, Thomas Betterton. Thomas Betterton is known to the world as a young man of genius, but since he has been here he has done only mediocre and second-class work. Yes, Betterton has disappointed me."

"But don't you find that constantly happening? These people are, after all, in prison here. Surely they rebel? At first, at any rate?"

"Yes," Mr. Aristides agreed. "That is only natural and inevitable. It is so when you first cage a bird. But if the bird is in a big enough aviary; if it has all that it needs; a mate, seed, water, twigs, all the material of life, it forgets in the end that it was ever free."

Hilary shivered a little.

"You frighten me," she said. "You really frighten me."

"You will grow to understand many things here, Madame. Let me assure you that though all these men of different ideologies arrive here and are disillusioned and rebellious, they will all toe the line in the end."

"You can't be sure of that," said Hilary.

"One can be absolutely sure of nothing in this world. I agree with you there. But it is a ninety-five per cent certainty all the same."

Hilary looked at him with something like horror.

"It's dreadful," she said. "It's like a typists' pool! You've got a pool here of brains."

"Exactly. You put it very justly, Madame."

"And from this pool, you intend, one day, to supply scientists to whoever pays you best for them?"

"That is, roughly, the general principle, Madame."

"But you can't send out a scientist just as you can send out a typist."

"Why not?"

"Because once your scientist is in the free world again, he could refuse to work for his new employer. He would be free again."

"True up to a point. There may have to be a certain—conditioning, shall we say?"

"Conditioning—what do you mean by that?"

"You have heard of lobotomy, Madame?"

Hilary frowned.

"That's a brain operation, isn't it?"

"But yes. It was devised originally for the curing of melancholia. I put it to you not in medical terms, Madame, but in such terms as you and I understand. After the operation the patient has no more desire to commit suicide, no further feelings of guilt. He is carefree, conscienceless and in most cases obedient."

"It hasn't been a hundred per cent success, has it?"

"In the past, no. But here we have made great strides in the investigation of the subject. I have here three surgeons: one Russian, one Frenchman and an Austrian. By various operations of grafting and delicate manipulation of the brain, they are arriving gradually at a state where docility can be assured and the will can be controlled without necessarily affecting mental brilliance. It seems possible that we may in the end so condition a human being that while his powers of intellect remain unimpaired, he will exhibit perfect docility. Any suggestion made to him he will accept."

"But that's horrible," cried Hilary. "Horrible!"

He corrected her serenely.

"It is useful. It is even in some ways beneficent. For the patient will be happy, contented, without fears or longings or unrest."

"I don't believe it will ever happen," said Hilary defiantly.

"*Chère, Madame,* forgive me if I say you are hardly competent to speak on the subject."

"What I mean is," said Hilary, "that I do not believe a contented, suggestible animal will ever produce creative work of real brilliance."

Aristides shrugged his shoulders.

"Perhaps. You are intelligent. You may have something there. Time will show. Experiments are going on all the time."

"Experiments! On human beings, do you mean?"

"But certainly. That is the only practical method."

"But—what human beings?"

"There are always the misfits," said Aristides. "The ones who do not adapt themselves to life here, who will not cooperate. They make good experimental material."

Hilary dug her fingers into the cushions of the divan. She felt a deep horror of this smiling, yellow-faced little man with his inhuman outlook. Everything he said was so reasonable, so logical and so businesslike, that it made the horror worse. Here was no raving madman, just a man to whom his fellow creatures were so much raw material.

"Don't you believe in God?" she said.

"Naturally I believe in God." Mr. Aristides raised his eyebrows. His tone was almost shocked. "I have told you already. I am a religious man. God has blessed me with supreme power. With money and opportunity."

"Do you read your Bible?" asked Hilary.

"Certainly, Madame."

"Do you remember what Moses and Aaron said to Pharaoh? *'Let my people go.'*"

He smiled.

"So—I am Pharaoh?—And you are Moses and Aaron in one? Is that what you are saying to me, Madame? To let these people go, all of them, or just— one special case?"

"I'd like to say—all of them," said Hilary.

"But you are well aware, *chère, Madame,*" he said, "that that would be a waste of time. So instead, is it not your husband for whom you plead?"

"He is no good to you," said Hilary. "Surely by now you must realize that."

"Perhaps, it is true what you say, Madame. Yes, I am very much disappointed in Thomas Betterton. I hoped that your presence here might restore him to his brilliance, for undoubtedly he has brilliance. His reputation in America leaves no doubt as to that. But your coming seems to have had little or no effect. I speak not of my own knowledge, of course, but from the reports of those fitted to know. His brother scientists who have been working with him." He shrugged his shoulders. "He does conscientious, mediocre work. No more."

"There are birds that cannot sing in captivity," said Hilary. "Perhaps there are scientists who cannot attain creative thought under certain circumstances. You must admit that that is a reasonable possibility."

"It may be so. I do not deny it."

"Then write off Thomas Betterton as one of your failures. Let him return to the outer world."

"That would hardly do, Madame. I am not yet prepared to have knowledge of this place broadcast to the globe."

"You could swear him to secrecy. He would swear never to breathe a word."

"He would swear—yes. But he would not keep that word."

"He would! Oh, indeed, he would!"

"There speaks a wife! One cannot take the word of wives on this point. Of course," he leaned back in his chair, and brought the tips of his yellow fingers together, "of course, he might leave a hostage behind him, and that might tie his tongue."

"You mean?"

"I mean you, Madame. . . . If Thomas Betterton went, and you remained as a hostage, how would that bargain strike you? Would you be willing?"

Hilary stared past him into the shadows. Mr. Aristides could not know the pictures that rose before her eyes. She was back in a hospital room, sitting by a dying woman. She was listening to Jessop and memorizing his instructions. If there was a chance, now, that Thomas Betterton might go free, while she remained, would not that be the best way to fulfill her mission? For she knew (what Mr. Aristides did not), that there would be no hostage in the usual meaning of the word, left behind. She herself meant nothing to Thomas Betterton. The wife he had loved was already dead.

She raised her head and looked across at the little old man on the divan.

"I should be willing," she said.

"You have courage, Madame, and loyalty and devotion. They are good qualities. For the rest—" He smiled. "We will talk of it again some other time."

"Oh no, no!" Hilary suddenly buried her face in her hands. Her shoulders shook. "I can't bear it! I can't bear it! It's all too inhuman."

"You must not mind so much, Madame." The old man's voice was tender, almost soothing. "It has pleased me tonight to tell you my aims and my aspirations. It has been interesting to me to see the effect upon a mind totally unprepared. A mind like yours, well balanced, sane and intelligent. You are horrified. You are repulsed. Yet I think that to shock you in this way is a wise plan. At first you repel the idea, then you think of it, you reflect on it, and in the end it will seem to you natural; as though it has always existed, a commonplace."

"Never that!" cried Hilary. "Never that! Never! Never!"

"Ah," said Mr. Aristides. "There speaks the passion and the rebellion that go with red hair. My second wife," he added reflectively, "had red hair. She was a beautiful woman, and she loved me. Strange, is it not? I have always admired red-haired women. Your hair is very beautiful. There are other things I like about you. Your spirit, your courage; the fact that you have a mind of your own." He sighed. "Alas! Women as women interest me very little nowadays. I have a couple of young girls here who please me sometimes, but it is the stimulus of mental companionship that I now prefer. Believe me, Madame, your company has refreshed me greatly."

"Supposing I repeat all that you have told me to—my husband?"

Aristides smiled indulgently.

"Ah yes, supposing you do? But will you?"

"I don't know. I—oh, I don't know."

"Ah!" said Mr. Aristides. "You are wise. There is some knowledge women should keep to themselves. But you are tired—and upset. From time to time, when I pay my visits here, you shall be brought to me, and we will discuss many things."

"Let me leave this place—" Hilary stretched her hands out to him. "Oh, let me go away. Let me leave with you when you go. Please! Please!"

He shook his head gently. His expression was indulgent, but there was a faint touch of comtempt behind it.

"Now you are talking like a child," he said reprovingly. "How could I let you go? How could I let you spread the story round the world of what you have seen here?"

"Wouldn't you believe me if I swore I wouldn't say a word to anyone?"

"No indeed, I should not believe you," said Mr. Aristides. "I should be very foolish if I believed anything of the kind."

"I don't want to be here. I don't want to stay here in this prison. I want to get out."

"But you have your husband. You came here to join him, deliberately, of your own free will."

"But I didn't know what I was coming to. I'd no idea."

"No," said Mr. Aristides, "you had no idea. But I can assure you this particular world you have come to is a much pleasanter world than the life beyond the Iron Curtain. Here you have everything you need! Luxury, a beautiful climate, distractions . . ."

He got up and patted her gently on the shoulder.

"You will settle down," he said, confidently. "Ah yes, the red-headed bird in the cage will settle down. In a year, in two years certainly, you will be very happy! Though possibly," he added thoughtfully, "less interesting."

19

HILARY AWOKE THE following night with a start. She raised herself on her elbow, listening.

"Tom, do you hear?"

"Yes. Aircraft—flying low. Nothing in that. They come over from time to time."

"I wondered—" She did not finish her sentence.

She lay awake thinking, going over and over that strange interview with Aristides.

The old man had got some kind of capricious liking for her.

Could she play upon that?

Could she in the end prevail upon him to take her with him, out into the world again?

Next time he came, if he sent for her, she would lead him on to talk of his dead red-haired wife. It was not the lure of the flesh that would captivate him. His blood ran too coldly now in his veins for that. Besides he had his "young girls." But the old like to remember, to be urged on to talk of times gone by . . .

Uncle George, who had lived at Cheltenham . . .

Hilary smiled in the darkness, remembering Uncle George.

Were Uncle George and Aristides, the man of millions, really very different under the skin? Uncle George had had a housekeeper—"such a nice safe woman, my dear, not flashy or sexy or anything like that. Nice and plain and safe." But Uncle George had upset his family by marrying that nice plain woman. She had been a very good listener . . .

What had Hilary said to Tom? "I'll find a way of getting out of here?" Odd, if the way should prove to be Aristides . . .

ii

"A message," said Leblanc. "A message at last."

His orderly had just entered and, after saluting, had laid a folded paper before him. He unfolded it, then spoke excitedly.

"This is a report from one of our reconnaissance pilots. He has been operating over one of the selected squares of territory. When flying over a certain position in a mountainous region he observed a signal being flashed. It was in Morse and was twice repeated. Here it is."

He laid the enclosure before Jessop.

C.O.G.L.E.P.R.O.S.I.E.S.L.

He separated off the last two letters with a pencil.

"SL—that is our code for 'Do not acknowledge.' "

"And COG with which the message starts," said Jessop, "is our recognition signal."

"Then the rest is the actual message." He underlined it. "LEPROSIE." He surveyed it dubiously.

"Leprosy?" said Jessop.

"And what does that mean?"

"Have you any important Leper Settlements? Or unimportant ones for that matter?"

Leblanc spread out a large map in front of him. He pointed with a stubby forefinger stained with nicotine.

"Here," he marked it off, "is the area over which our pilot was operating. Let me see now. I seem to recall . . ."

He left the room. Presently he returned.

"I have it," he said. "There is a very famous medical Research station, founded and endowed by well known philanthropists and operating in that area—a very deserted one, by the way. Valuable work has been done there in the study of Leprosy. There is a Leper Settlement there of about two hundred people. There is also a Cancer Research station, and a Tubercular Sanatorium. But understand this, it is all of the highest authenticity. Its reputation is of the highest. The President of the Republic himself is its Patron."

"Yes," said Jessop appreciatively. "Very nice work, in fact."

"But it is open to inspection at any time. Medical men who are interested in these subjects visit there."

"And see nothing they ought not to see! Why should they? There is no better camouflage for dubious business, than an atmosphere of the highest respectability."

"It could be," Leblanc said dubiously, "I suppose, a halting place, for parties of people bound on a journey. One or two of the mid-European doctors, perhaps, have managed to arrange something like that. A small party of people, like the one we are tracking, could lie *perdu* there for a few weeks before continuing their journey."

"I think it might be something more than that," said Jessop. "I think it might be—Journey's End."

"You think it is something—big?"

"A Leper Settlement seems to me very suggestive . . . I believe, under modern treatment, leprosy nowadays is treated at home."

"In civilized communities, perhaps. But one could not do that in this country."

"No. But the word Leprosy still has its association with the Middle Ages when the Leper carried his bell to warn away people from his path. Idle curiosity does not bring people to a Leper Settlement; the people who come are, as you say, the medical profession, interested only in the medical research done there, and possibly the social worker, anxious to report on the conditions under which the Lepers live—all of which are no doubt admirable. Behind that façade of philanthropy and charity—anything might go on. Who, by the way, owns the place? Who are the philanthropists who endowed it and set it up?"

"That is easily ascertained. A little minute."

He turned shortly, an official reference book in his hand.

"It was established by private enterprise. By a group of philanthropists of whom the chief is Aristides. As you know, he is a man of fabulous wealth, and gives generously to charitable enterprises. He has founded hospitals in Paris and also in Seville. This is, to all intents and purposes, his show—the other benefactors are a group of his associates."

"So—it's an Aristides enterprise. And Aristides was in Fez when Olive Betterton was there."

"Aristides!" Leblanc savored the full implication. *Mais—c'est colossal!*"

"Yes."

"C'est fantastique!"

"Quite."

"Enfin—c'est formidable!"

"Definitely."

"But do you realize how formidable it is?" Leblanc shook an excited fore-finger in the other's face. "This Aristides, he has a finger in every pie. He is behind nearly everything. The banks, the Government, the manufacturing industries, armaments, transport! One never sees him, one hardly hears of him! He sits in a warm room in his Spanish castle, smoking, and sometimes he scrawls a few words on a little piece of paper and throws it on the ground, and a secretary crawls forward and picks it up, and a few days later an important banker in Paris blows his brains out! It is like that!"

"How wonderfully dramatic you are, Leblanc. But it is really not very surprising. Presidents and Ministers make important pronouncements, bankers sit back behind their sumptuous desks and roll out opulent statements—but one is never surprised to find out that behind the importance and magnificence there is somewhere some scrubby little man who is the real motive power. It is really not at all surprising to find that Aristides is behind all this disappearing business—in fact if we'd had any sense we'd have thought of it before. The whole thing's a vast commercial ramp. It's not political at all. The question is," he added, "what are we going to do about it?"

Leblanc's face grew gloomy.

"It is not going to be easy, you understand. If we are wrong—I dare not think of it! And even if we are right—we have got to prove we are right. If we make investigations—those investigations can be called off—at the highest level, you understand? No, it is not going to be easy. . . . But," he wagged an emphatic stubby forefinger, "it will be done."

20

THE CARS SWEPT up the mountain road and stopped in front of the great gate set in the rock. There were four cars. In the first car was a French Minister and the American Ambassador, in the second car was the British Consul, a Member of Parliament and the Chief of Police. In the third car were two members of a former Royal Commission and two distinguished journalists. The complement of these three cars was made up with the necessary satellites. The fourth car contained certain people not known to the general public, but sufficiently distinguished in their own sphere. They included Captain Leblanc and Mr. Jessop. The chauffeurs, immaculately garbed, were now opening car doors and bowing as they assisted the distinguished visitors to alight.

"One hopes," murmured the Minister, apprehensively, "that there will be no possibility of a contact of any kind."

One of the satellites immediately made soothing noises.

"*Du tout, M. le Ministre.* Every suitable precaution is taken. One inspects only from a distance."

The Minister, who was elderly and apprehensive, looked relieved. The Ambassador said something about the better understanding and treatment of these diseases nowadays.

The great gates were flung open. On the threshold stood a small party bowing to welcome them. The Director, dark, thickset, the Deputy Director big and fair, two distinguished doctors and a distinguished Research Chemist. The greetings were French, florid and prolonged.

"And *ce cher* Aristides," demanded the Minister. "I sincerely hope ill health has not prevented him from fulfilling his promise to meet us here."

"M. Aristides flew from Spain yesterday," said the Deputy Director. "He awaits you within. Permit me, Your Excellency—M. le Ministre, to lead the way."

The party followed him. M. le Ministre, who was slightly apprehensive, glanced through the heavy railings to his right. The lepers were drawn up to attention in a serried row as far as possible from the grating. The Minister looked relieved. His feelings about leprosy were still medieval.

In the well furnished modern lounge Mr. Aristides was awaiting his guests. There were bows, compliments, introductions. Aperitifs were served by the dark-faced servants dressed in their white robes and turbans.

"It's a wonderful place you have here, sir," said one of the younger journalists to Aristides.

The latter made one of his Oriental gestures.

"I am proud of this place," he said. "It is, as you might say, my swan song. My final gift to humanity. No expense has been spared."

"I'll say that's so," said one of the doctors on the staff, heartily. "This place is a professional man's dream. We do pretty well in the States, but what I've seen since I came here . . . and we're getting results! Yes, sir, we certainly are getting results."

His enthusiasm was of a contagious kind.

"We must make all acknowledgments to private enterprise," said the Ambassador, bowing politely to Mr. Aristides.

Mr. Aristides spoke with humility.

"God has been very good to me," he said.

Sitting hunched up in his chair he looked like a small yellow toad. The Member of Parliament murmured to the member of the Royal Commission who was very old and deaf, that he presented a very interesting paradox.

"That old rascal has probably ruined millions of people," he murmured, "and having made so much money, he doesn't know what to do with it, so he pays it back with the other hand."

The elderly judge to whom he spoke, murmured,

"One wonders to what extent results justify increased expenditure. Most of the great discoveries that have benefited the human race have been discovered with quite simple equipment."

"And now," said Aristides, when the civilities were accomplished and the aperitifs drunk, "you will honor me by partaking of a simple repast which awaits you. Dr. Van Heidem will act as your host. I myself am on a diet and eat very little these days. After the repast you will start on your tour of our building."

Under the leadership of the genial Dr. Van Heidem, the guests moved enthusiastically into the dining room. They had had two hours' flight followed by an hour's drive by car and they were all sharp set. The food was delicious and was commented on with special approval by the Minister.

"We enjoy our modest comforts," said Van Heidem. "Fresh fruit and vegetables are flown to us twice a week, arrangements are made for meat and chicken and we have, of course, substantial deep freezing units. The body must claim its due from the resources of science."

The meal was accompanied by choice vintages. After it Turkish coffee was served. The party was then asked to start on its tour of inspection. The tour took two hours and was most comprehensive. The Minister, for one, was glad when it finished. He was quite dazed by the gleaming laboratories, the endless white, shining corridors, and still more dazed by the mass of scientific detail handed out to him.

Though the Minister's interest was perfunctory, some of the others were more searching in their inquiries. Some curiosity was displayed as to the living conditions of the personnel and various other details. Dr. Van Heidem showed himself only too willing to show the guests all there was to see. Leblanc and Jessop, the former in attendance on the Minister and the latter accompanying the British Consul, fell a little behind the others as they all returned to the lounge.

"There is no trace here, nothing," murmured Leblanc in an agitated manner.

"Not a sign."

"*Mon cher,* if we have, as your saying is, barked up the wrong tree, what a catastrophe. After the weeks it has taken to arrange all this! As for me—it will finish my career."

"We're not licked yet," said Jessop. "Our friends are here, I'm sure of it."

"There is no trace of them."

"Of course there is no trace. They could not afford to have a trace of them. For these official visits everything is prepared and arranged."

"Then how are we to get our evidence? I tell you, without evidence no one will move in the matter. They are skeptical, all of them. The Minister, the American Ambassador, the British Consul—they say all of them, that a man like Aristides is above suspicion."

"Keep calm, Leblanc, keep calm. I tell you we're not licked yet."

Leblanc shrugged his shoulders.

"You have the optimism, my friend," he said. He turned for a moment to speak to one of the immaculately arrayed moon-faced young men who formed part of the *entourage,* then turned back to Jessop and asked suspiciously: "Why are you smiling?"

"Heard of a Geiger counter?"

"Naturally. But I am not a scientist, you understand."

"No more am I. It is a very sensitive detector of radioactivity."

"And so?"

"Our friends are here. The Geiger counter tells me that. It imparts a message to say that our friends are here. This building has been purposely built in a confusing manner. All the corridors and the rooms so resemble each other that it is difficult to know where one is or what the plan of the building can be. There is a part of this place that we have not seen. It has not been shown to us."

"But you deduce that it is there because of some radioactive indication?"

"Exactly."

"In fact, it is the pearls of Madame all over again?"

"Yes. We're still playing Hansel and Gretel, as you might say. But the signs left here cannot be so apparent or so crude as the beads of a pearl necklace, or a hand of phosphoric paint. They cannot be seen, but they can be sensed . . . by our radioactive detector—"

"But, *mon Dieu,* Jessop, is that enough?"

"It should be," said Jessop. "What one is afraid of . . ." He broke off. Leblanc finished the sentence for him.

"What you mean is that these people will not want to believe. They have been unwilling from the start. Oh yes, that is so. Even your British Consul is a man of caution. Your government at home is indebted to Aristides in many ways. As for our government," he shrugged his shoulders. "M. le Ministre, I know, will be exceedingly hard to convince."

"We won't put our faith in governments," said Jessop. "Governments and diplomats have their hands tied. But we've got to have them here, because they're the only ones with authority. But as far as believing is concerned, I'm pinning my faith elsewhere."

"And on what in particular do you pin your faith, my friend?"

Jessop's solemn face suddenly relaxed into a grin.

"There's the press," he said. "Journalists have a nose for news. They don't want it hushed up. They're ready always to believe anything that remotely can be believed. The other person I have faith in," he went on, "is that very deaf old man."

"Aha, I know the one you mean. The one who looks as though he crumbles to his grave."

"Yes, he's deaf and infirm and semiblind. But he's interested in truth. He's a former Lord Chief Justice, and though he may be deaf and blind and shaky on his legs, his mind's as keen as ever—he's got that keen sense that legal luminaries acquire—of knowing when there's something fishy about and someone's trying to prevent it being brought into the open. He's a man who'll listen, and will want to listen, to evidence."

They had arrived back now in the lounge. Both tea and aperitifs were provided. The Minister congratulated Mr. Aristides in well-rounded periods. The American Ambassador added his quota. It was then that the Minister, looking round him, said in a slightly nervous tone of voice,

"And now, gentlemen, I think the time has come for us to leave our kind host. We have seen all there is to see . . ." his tone dwelt on those last words with some significance, "all here is magnificent. An establishment of the first class! We are most grateful for the hospitality of our kind host, and we congratulate him on the achievement here. So we say our farewells now and depart. I am right, am I not?"

The words were, in a sense, conventional enough. The manner, too, was conventional. The glance that swept round the assembly of guests might have been no more than courtesy. Yet in actuality the words were a plea. In effect, the Minister was saying, "You've seen, gentlemen, there is nothing here, nothing of what you suspected and feared. That is a great relief and we can now leave with a clear conscience."

But in the silence a voice spoke. It was the quiet, deferential, well-bred English voice of Mr. Jessop. He spoke to the Minister in a Britannic though idiomatic French.

"With your permission, Sir," he said, "and if I may do so, I would like to ask a favor of our kind host."

"Certainly, certainly. Of course, Mr.—ah—Mr. Jessop—yes, yes?"

Jessop addressed himself solemnly to Dr. Van Heidem. He did not look ostensibly to Mr. Aristides.

"We've met so many of your people," he said, "Quite bewildering. But there's an old friend of mine here that I'd rather like to have a word with. I wonder if it could be arranged before I go?"

"A friend of yours?" Dr. Van Heidem said politely, surprised.

"Well, two friends really," said Jessop. "There's a woman, Mrs. Betterton. Olive Betterton. I believe her husband's working here. Tom Betterton. Used to be at Harwell and before that in America. I'd very much like to have a word with them both before I go."

Dr. Van Heidem's reactions were perfect. His eyes opened in wide and polite surprise. He frowned in a puzzled way.

"Betterton—Mrs. Betterton—no, I'm afraid we have no one of that name here."

"There's an American, too," said Jessop. "Andrew Peters. Research chemistry, I believe, is his line. I'm right, sir, aren't I?" He turned deferentially to the American Ambassador.

The Ambassador was a shrewd, middle-aged man with keen blue eyes. He was a man of character as well as diplomatic ability. His eyes met Jessop's. He took a full minute to decide, and then he spoke.

"Why, yes," he said. "That's so. Andrew Peters. I'd like to see him."

Van Heidem's polite bewilderment grew. Jessop unobtrusively shot a quick glance at Aristides. The little yellow face betrayed no knowledge of anything amiss, no surprise, no disquietude. He looked merely uninterested.

"Andrew Peters? No, I'm afraid, Your Excellency, you've got your facts wrong. We've no one of that name here. I'm afraid I don't even know the name."

"You know the name of Thomas Betterton, don't you?" said Jessop.

Just for a second Van Heidem hesitated. His head turned very slightly toward the old man in the chair, but he caught himself back in time.

"Thomas Betterton," he said. "Why, yes, I think—"

One of the gentlemen of the press spoke up quickly on that cue.

"Thomas Betterton," he said. "Why, I should say he was pretty well big news. Big news six months ago when he disappeared. Why, he's made headlines in the papers all over Europe. The police have been looking for him here, there and everywhere. Do you mean to say he's been here in this place all the time?"

"No." Van Heidem spoke sharply. "Someone, I fear, has been misinforming you. A hoax, perhaps. You have seen today all our workers at the Unit. You have seen everything."

"Not quite everything I think," said Jessop, quietly. "There's a young man called Ericsson, too," he added, "and Dr. Louis Barron, and possibly Mrs. Calvin Baker."

"Ah." Dr. Van Heidem seemed to receive enlightenment. "But those people were killed in Morocco—in a plane crash. I remember it perfectly now. At least I remember Ericsson was in the crash and Dr. Louis Barron. Ah, France sustained a great loss that day. A man such as Louis Barron is hard to replace." He shook his head. "I do not know anything about a Mrs. Calvin Baker, but I do seem to remember that there was an English or American woman on that plane. It might well perhaps have been this Mrs. Betterton, of whom you speak. Yes, it was all very sad." He looked across inquiringly at Jessop. "I do not know, Monsieur, why you should suppose that these people were coming here. It may possibly be that Dr. Barron mentioned at one time that he hoped to visit our settlement here while he was in North Africa. That may possibly have given rise to a misconception."

"So you tell me," said Jessop, "that I am mistaken? That these people are none of them here."

"But how can they be, my dear sir, since they were all killed in this plane accident. The bodies were recovered, I believe."

"The bodies recovered were too badly charred for identification." Jessop spoke the last words with deliberation and significance.

There was a little stir behind him. A thin, precise, very attenuated voice said,

"Do I understand you to say that there was no precise identification?" Lord Alverstoke was leaning forward, his hand to his ear. Under bushy, overhanging eyebrows his small keen eyes looked into Jessop's.

"There could be no formal identification, my lord," said Jessop, "and I have reason to believe these people survived that accident."

"Believe?" said Lord Alverstoke, with displeasure in his thin, high voice.

"I should have said I had evidence of survival."

"Evidence? Of what nature, Mr.—er—er—Jessop."

"Mrs. Betterton was wearing a choker of false pearls on the day she left Fez for Marrakesh," said Jessop. "One of these pearls was found at a distance of half a mile from the burnt out plane."

"How can you state positively that the pearl found actually came from Mrs. Betterton's necklace?"

"Because all the pearls of that necklace had had a mark put upon them invisible to the naked eye, but recognizable under a strong lens."

"Who put that mark on them?"

"I did, Lord Alverstoke, in the presence of my colleague, here, Monsieur Leblanc."

"You put those marks—you had a reason in marking those pearls in that special fashion?"

"Yes, my lord. I had reason to believe that Mrs. Betterton would lead me to her husband, Thomas Betterton, against whom a warrant is out," Jessop continued. "Two more of these pearls came to light. Each on stages of a route between where the plane was burnt out and the settlement where we now are. Inquiries in the places where these pearls were found resulted in a description of six people, roughly approximating to those people who were supposed to have been burnt in the plane. One of these passengers had also been supplied with a glove impregnated with luminous, phosphorous paint. That mark was found on a car which had transported these passengers part of the way here."

Lord Alverstoke remarked in his dry, judicial voice,

"Very remarkable."

In the big chair Mr. Aristides stirred. His eyelids blinked once or twice rapidly. Then he asked a question.

"Where were the last traces of this party of people found?"

"At a disused airfield, sir." He gave precise location.

"That is many hundreds of miles from here," said Mr. Aristides. "Granted that your very interesting speculations are correct, that for some reason the accident was faked, these passengers, I gather, then took off from this disused airport for some unknown destination. Since that airport is many hundreds of miles from here, I really cannot see on what you base your belief that these people are here. Why should they be?"

"There are certain very good reasons, sir. A signal was picked up by one of our searching airplanes. The signal was brought to Monsieur Leblanc here. Commencing with a special code recognition signal, it gave the information that the people in question were at a Leper Settlement."

"I find this remarkable," said Mr. Aristides. "Very remarkable. But it seems to me that there is no doubt that an attempt has been made to mislead you. These people are not here." He spoke with a quiet, definite decision. "You are at perfect liberty to search the settlement if you like."

"I doubt if we should find anything, sir," said Jessop, "not, that is, by a superficial search, although," he added deliberately, "I am aware of the area at which the search should begin."

"Indeed! And where is that?"

"In the fourth corridor from the second laboratory turning to the left at the end of the passage there."

There was an abrupt movement from Dr. Van Heidem. Two glasses crashed from the tables to the floor. Jessop looked at him, smiling.

"You see, Doctor," he said, "we are well informed."

Van Heidem said sharply, "It's preposterous. Absolutely preposterous! You are suggesting that we are detaining people here against their will. I deny that categorically."

The Minister said uncomfortably,

"We seem to have arrived at an *impasse.*"

Mr. Aristides said gently,

"It has been an interesting theory. But it is only a theory." He glanced at his watch. "You will excuse me, gentlemen, if I suggest that you should leave now. You have a long drive back to the airport, and there will be alarm felt if your plane is overdue."

Both Leblanc and Jessop realized that it had come now to the showdown. Aristides was exerting all the force of his considerable personality. He was daring these men to oppose his will. If they persisted, it meant that they were willing to come out into the open against him. The Minister, as per his instructions, was anxious to capitulate. The Chief of Police was anxious only to be agreeable to the Minister. The American Ambassador was not satisfied, but he, too, would hesitate for diplomatic reasons to insist. The British Consul would have to fall in with the other two.

The journalists—Aristides considered the journalists—the journalists could be attended to! Their price might come high but he was of the opinion that they could be bought. And if they could not be bought—well, there were other ways.

As for Jessop and Leblanc, they knew. That was clear, but they could not act without authority. His eyes went on and met the eyes of a man as old as himself, cold, legal eyes. This man, he knew, could not be bought. But after all . . . His thoughts were interrupted by the sound of that cold, clear, far away little voice.

"I am of the opinion," said the voice, "that we should not unduly hurry our departure. For there is a case here that it seems to me would bear further inquiry. Grave allegations have been made and should not, I consider, be allowed to drop. In fairness every opportunity should be given to rebut them."

"The onus of proof," said Mr. Aristides, "is on you." He made a graceful gesture toward the company. "A preposterous accusation has been made, unsupported by any evidence."

"Not unsupported."

Dr. Van Heidem swung round in surprise. One of the Moroccan servants had stepped forward. He was a fine figure of a man in white embroidered robes with a white turban surrounding his head, his face gleamed black and oily.

What caused the entire company to gaze at him in speechless astonishment was the fact that from his full rather Negroid lips a voice of purely trans-Atlantic origin was proceeding.

"Not unsupported," that voice said, "you can take my evidence here and now. These gentlemen have denied that Andrew Peters, Torquil Ericsson, Mr. and Mrs. Betterton and Dr. Louis Barron are here. That's false. They're all here—and I speak for them." He took a step forward toward the American Ambassador. "You may find me a bit difficult to recognize at the moment, sir," he said, "but I am Andrew Peters."

A very faint, sibilant hiss issued from Aristides' lips; then he settled back in his chair, his face impassive once more.

"There's a whole crowd of people hidden away here," said Peters. "There's Schwartz of Munich; there's Helga Needheim; there are Jeffreys and David-son, the English scientists; there's Paul Wade from the U.S.A.; there are the Italians, Ricochetti and Bianco; there's Murchison. They're all right here in this building. There's a system of closing bulkheads that's quite impossible to detect by the naked eye. There's a whole network of secret laboratories cut right down into the rock."

"God bless my soul," ejaculated the American Ambassador. He looked searchingly at the dignified African figure, and then he began to laugh. "I wouldn't say I'd recognize you even now," he said.

"That's the injection of paraffin in the lips, sir, to say nothing of black pigment."

"If you're Peters, what's the number you go under in the F.B.I.?"

"813471, sir."

"Right," said the Ambassador, "and the initials of your other name?"

"B.A.B.D.G., sir."

The Ambassador nodded.

"This man is Peters," he said. He looked toward the Minister.

The Minister hesitated, then cleared his throat.

"You claim," he demanded of Peters, "that people are being detained here against their will?"

"Some are here willingly, Excellence, and some are not."

"In that case," said the Minister, "statements must be taken—er—yes, yes, statements must certainly be taken."

He looked at the Prefect of Police. The latter stepped forward.

"Just a moment, please." Mr. Aristides raised a hand. "It would seem," he said, in a gentle, precise voice, "that my confidence here has been greatly abused." His cold glance went from Van Heidem to the Director and there was implacable command in it. "As to what you have permitted yourselves to do, gentlemen, in your enthusiasm for science, I am not as yet quite clear. My endowment of this place was purely in the interests of research. I have taken no part in the practical application of its policy. I would advise you, Monsieur le Directeur, if this accusation is borne out by facts, to produce immediately those people who are suspected of being detained here unlawfully."

"But, Monsieur, it is impossible. I—it will be—"

"Any experiment of that kind," said Mr. Aristides, "is at an end." His calm, financier's gaze swept over his guests. "I need hardly assure you, Messieurs," he said, "that if anything illegal is going on here, it has been no concern of mine."

It was an order, and understood as such because of his wealth, because of his power and because of his influence. Mr. Aristides, that world-famous figure, would not be implicated in this affair. Yet, even though he himself escaped unscathed, it was nevertheless defeat. Defeat for his purpose, defeat for that brains pool from which he had hoped to profit so greatly. Mr. Aristides was unperturbed by failure. It had happened to him occasionally in the course of his career. He had always accepted it philosophically and gone on to the next *coup*.

He made an oriental gesture of his hand.

"I wash my hands of this affair," he said.

The Prefect of Police bustled forward. He had had his cue now, he knew what his instructions were and he was prepared to go ahead with the full force of his official position.

"I want no obstructions," he said. "It is my duty."

His face very pale, Van Heidem stepped forward.

"If you will come this way," he said, "I will show you our reserve accommodation."

21

"OH, I FEEL as if I'd woken up out of a nightmare," sighed Hilary.

She stretched her arms wide above her head. They were sitting on the terrace of the hotel in Tangier. They had arrived there that morning by plane. Hilary went on,

"Did it all happen? It can't have!"

"It happened all right," said Tom Betterton, "but I agree with you, Olive, it was a nightmare. Ah well, I'm out of it now."

Jessop came along the terrace and sat down beside them.

"Where's Andy Peters?" asked Hilary.

"He'll be here presently," said Jessop. "He has a bit of business to attend to."

"So Peters was one of your people," said Hilary, "and he did things with phosphorus and a lead cigarette case that squirted radioactive material. I never knew a thing about that."

"No," said Jessop, "you were both very discreet with each other. Strictly speaking, though, he isn't one of my people. He represents the U.S.A."

"That's what you meant by saying that if I actually reached Tom here, you hoped I should have protection? You meant Andy Peters."

Jessop nodded.

"I hope you're not blaming me," said Jessop in his most owllike manner, "for not providing you with the desired end of your experience."

Hilary looked puzzled. "What end?"

"A more sporting form of suicide," he said.

"Oh, that!" She shook her head incredulously. "That seems just as unreal as anything else. I've been Olive Betterton so long now that I'm feeling quite confused to be Hilary Craven again."

"Ah," said Jessop, "there is my friend, Leblanc. I must go and speak to him."

He left them and walked along the terrace. Tom Betterton said, quickly,

"Do one more thing for me, will you Olive? I call you Olive still—I've got used to it."

"Yes, of course. What is it?"

"Walk along the terrace with me, then come back here and say that I've gone up to my room to lie down."

She looked at him questioningly.

"Why? What are you—"

"I'm off, my dear, while the going's good."

"Off, where?"

"Anywhere."

"But why?"

"Use your head, my dear girl. I don't know what the status is here. Tangier is an odd sort of place not under the jurisdiction of any particular country. But I know what'll happen if I come with the rest of you to Gibraltar. The first thing that'll happen when I get there, I shall be arrested."

Hilary looked at him with concern. In the excitement of their escape from the Unit, she had forgotten Tom Betterton's troubles.

"You mean the Official Secrets Act, or whatever they call it? But you can't really hope to get away can you, Tom? Where can you go?"

"I've told you. Anywhere."

"But is that feasible nowadays? There's money and all sorts of difficulties."

He gave a short laugh.

"The money's all right. It's salted away where I can get at it under a new name."

"So you did take money?"

"Of course I took money."

"But they'll track you down."

"They'll find it hard to do that. Don't you realize, Olive, that the description they'll have of me is quite unlike my present appearance. That's why I was so keen on this plastic surgery business. That's been the whole point, you see. To get away from England, bank some money, have my appearance altered in such a way that I'm safe for life."

Hilary looked at him doubtfully.

"You're wrong," she said. "I'm sure you're wrong. It'd be far better to go back and face the music. After all, it's not wartime. You'd only get a short term of imprisonment, I expect. What's the good of being hounded for the rest of your life?"

"You don't understand," he said. "You don't understand the first thing about it all. Come on, let's get going. There's no time to lose."

"But how are you going to get away from Tangier?"

"I'll manage. Don't you worry."

She got up from her seat and walked with him slowly along the terrace. She felt curiously inadequate and tongue tied. She had fulfilled her obligations to Jessop and also to the dead woman, Olive Betterton. Now there was no more to do. She and Tom Betterton had shared weeks of the closest association and yet she felt they were still strangers to each other. No bond of fellowship or friendship had grown up between them.

They reached the end of the terrace. There was a small side door there through the wall which led out on to a narrow road which curved down the hill to the port.

"I shall slip out this way," Betterton said, "nobody's watching. So long."

"Good luck to you," said Hilary slowly.

She stood there watching Betterton as he went to the door and turned its handle. As the door opened he stepped back a pace and stopped. Three men stood in the doorway. Two of them entered and came toward him. The first spoke formally.

"Thomas Betterton, I have here a warrant for your arrest. You will be held here in custody whilst extradition proceedings are taken."

Betterton turned sharply, but the other man had moved quickly round the other side of him. Instead, he turned back with a laugh.

"It's quite all right," he said, "except that I'm not Thomas Betterton."

The third man moved in through the doorway, came to stand by the side of the other two.

"Oh yes, you are," he said. "You're Thomas Betterton."

Betterton laughed.

"What you mean is that for the last month you've been living with me and hearing me called Thomas Betterton and hearing me call myself Thomas Betterton. The point is that I'm not Thomas Betterton. I met Betterton in Paris, I came on and took his place. Ask this lady if you don't believe me," he said. "She came to join me, pretending to be my wife, and I recognized her as my wife. I did, didn't I?"

Hilary nodded her head.

"That," said Betterton, "was because not being Thomas Betterton, naturally I didn't know Thomas Betterton's wife from Adam. I thought she was Thomas Betterton's wife. Afterwards I had to think up some sort of explanation that would satisfy her. But that's the truth."

"So that's why you pretended to know me," cried Hilary. "When you told me to play up—to keep up the deception!"

Betterton laughed again, confidently.

"I'm not Betterton," he said. "Look at any photograph of Betterton and you'll see I'm speaking the truth."

Peters stepped forward. His voice when he spoke was totally unlike the voice of the Peters that Hilary had known so well. It was quiet and implacable.

"I've seen photographs of Betterton," he said, "and I agree I wouldn't have recognized you as the man. But you are Thomas Betterton all the same, and I'll prove it."

He seized Betterton with a sudden strong grasp and tore off his jacket.

"If you're Thomas Betterton," he said, "you've got a scar in the shape of a Z in the crook of your right elbow."

As he spoke he ripped up the shirt and bent back Betterton's arm.

"There you are," he said, pointing triumphantly. "There are two lab assistants in the U.S.A. who'll testify to that. I know about it because Elsa wrote and told me when you did it."

"Elsa?" Betterton stared at him. He began to shake nervously. "Elsa? What about Elsa?"

"Ask what the charge is against you?"

The police official stepped forward once more.

"The charge," he said, "is murder in the first degree. Murder of your wife, Elsa Betterton."

22

"I'M SORRY, OLIVE. You've got to believe I'm sorry. About you, I mean. For your sake I'd have given him one chance. I warned you that he'd be safer to stay in the Unit and yet I'd come halfway across the world to get him, and I meant to get him for what he did to Elsa."

"I don't understand. I don't understand anything. Who are you?"

"I thought you knew that. I'm Boris Andrei Pavlov Glydr, Elsa's cousin. I was sent over to America from Poland, to the University there to complete my education. And the way things were in Europe my uncle thought it best for me to take out American citizenship. I took the name of Andrew Peters. Then, when the war came, I went back to Europe. I worked for the Resistance. I got my uncle and Elsa out of Poland and they got to America. Elsa— I've told you about Elsa already. She was one of the first-class scientists of our time. It was Elsa who discovered ZE fission. Betterton was a young Canadian who was attached to Mannheim to help him in his experiments. He knew his job, but there was no more to him than that. He deliberately made love to Elsa and married her so as to be associated with her in the scientific work she was doing. When her experiments neared completion and he realized what a big thing ZE fission was going to be, he deliberately poisoned her."

"Oh, no, no."

"Yes. There were no suspicions at the time. Betterton appeared heart-broken, threw himself with renewed ardor into his work and then announced the ZE fission discovery as his own. It brought him what he wanted. Fame and the recognition of being a first-class scientist. He thought it prudent after that to leave America and come to England. He went to Harwell and worked there.

"I was tied up in Europe for some time after the war ended. Since I had a good knowledge of German, Russian and Polish, I could do very useful work there. The letter that Elsa had written to me before she died disquieted me. The illness from which she was suffering and from which she died seemed to me mysterious and unaccounted for. When at last I got back to the U.S.A. I started instituting inquiries. We won't go into it all, but I found what I was looking for. Enough, that is, to apply for an Order of Exhumation of the body. There was a young fellow in the District Attorney's office who had been a great friend of Betterton. He was going over on a trip to Europe about that time, and I think that he visited Betterton and in the course of his visit mentioned the exhumation. Betterton got the wind up. I imagine that he'd been already approached by agents of our friend, Mr. Aristides. Anyway he now saw that there lay his best chance to avoid being arrested and tried for murder. He accepted the terms, stipulating that his facial appearance was to be completely changed. What actually happened, of course, was that he found himself in a very real captivity. Moreover, he found himself in a dangerous position there since he was quite unable to deliver the goods—the scientific goods, that is to say. He was not and never had been, a man of genius."

"And you followed him?"

"Yes. When the newspapers were full of the sensational disappearance of the scientist, Thomas Betterton, I came over to England. A rather brilliant scientist friend of mine had had certain overtures made to him by a woman, a Mrs. Speeder, who worked for UNO. I discovered on arriving in England that she had had a meeting with Betterton. I played up to her, expressing Left Wing views, rather exaggerating perhaps my scientific abilities. I thought, you see, that Betterton had gone behind the Iron Curtain where no one could

reach him. Well, if nobody else could reach him, I was going to reach him."
His lips set in a grim line. "Elsa was a first-class scientist, and she was a
beautiful and gentle woman. She'd been killed and robbed by the man whom
she loved and trusted. If necessary I was going to kill Betterton with my own
hands."

"I see," said Hilary, "oh, I see now."

"I wrote to you," said Peters, "when I got to England. Wrote to you, that
is, in my Polish name, telling you the facts." He looked at her. "I suppose you
didn't believe me. You never answered." He shrugged his shoulders. "Then I
went to the Intelligence people. At first I went there putting on an act. Polish
officer. Stiff, foreign and correctly formal. I was suspicious just then of everybody. However, in the end Jessop and I got together." He paused. "This
morning my quest has come to an end. Extradition will be applied for, Betterton will go to the U.S.A. and will stand his trial there. If he's acquitted, I
have no more to say." He added grimly, "But he won't be acquitted. The
evidence is too strong."

He paused, staring down over the sunlit gardens toward the sea.

"The hell of it is," he said, "that you came out there to join him and I met
you and fell in love with you. It has been hell, Olive. Believe me. So there we
are. I'm the man who's responsible for sending your husband to the electric
chair. We can't get away from it. It's a thing that you'll never be able to forget
even if you forgave it." He got up. "Well, I wanted to tell you the whole story
from my own lips. This is goodbye." He turned abruptly as Hilary stretched
out a hand.

"Wait," she said, "wait. There is something you don't know. I'm not Betterton's wife. Betterton's wife, Olive Betterton, died at Casablanca. Jessop
persuaded me to take her place."

He wheeled round staring at her.

"You're not Olive Betterton?"

"No."

"Good Lord," said Andy Peters. "Good Lord!" He dropped heavily into a
chair beside her. "Olive," he said, "Olive, my darling."

"Don't call me Olive. My name's Hilary. Hilary Craven."

"Hilary?" He said it questioningly. "I'll have to get used to that." He put
his hand over hers.

At the other end of the terrace Jessop, discussing with Leblanc various
technical difficulties in the present situation, broke off in the middle of a
sentence.

"You were saying?" he asked absently.

"I said, *mon cher,* that it does not seem to me that we are going to be able
to proceed against this animal of an Aristides."

"No, no. Aristides always wins. That is to say he always manages to
squirm out from under. But he'll have lost a lot of money, and he won't like
that. And even Aristides can't keep death at bay forever. I should say he'll be

coming up before the Supreme Justice before very long, from the look of him."

"What was it attracting your attention, my friend?"

"Those two," said Jessop. "I sent Hilary Craven off on a journey to a destination unknown, but it seems to me that her journey's end is the usual one after all."

Leblanc looked puzzled for a moment then he said,

"Aha! Yes! Your Shakespeare!"

"You Frenchmen are so well read," said Jessop.

PASSENGER
TO
FRANKFURT

To
MARGARET GUILLAUME

"Leadership, besides being a great creative force, can be diabolical. . . ."

JAN SMUTS

Introduction

THE AUTHOR SPEAKS:

The first question put to an author, personally, or through the post, is:
"Where do you get your ideas from?"

The temptation is great to reply: "I always go to Harrods," or "I get them mostly at the Army & Navy Stores," or, snappily, "Try Marks and Spencer."

The universal opinion seems firmly established that there is a magic source of ideas which authors have discovered how to tap.

One can hardly send one's questioners back to Elizabethan times, with Shakespeare's:

> *Tell me, where is fancy bred,*
> *Or in the heart or in the head,*
> *How begot, how nourished?*
> *Reply, reply.*

You merely say firmly: "My own head."

That, of course, is no help to anybody. If you like the look of your questioner, you relent and go a little further.

"If one idea in particular seems attractive, and you feel you could do something with it, then you toss it around, play tricks with it, work it up, tone it down, and gradually get it into shape. Then, of course, you have to start writing it. That's not nearly such fun—it becomes hard work. Alternatively, you can tuck it carefully away, in storage, for perhaps using in a year or two years' time."

A second question—or rather a statement—is then likely to be:

"I suppose you take most of your characters from real life?"

An indignant denial to that monstrous suggestion.

"No, I don't. I invent them. They are *mine*. They've got to be *my* characters—doing what I want them to do, being what I want them to be—coming

619

alive for me, having their own ideas sometimes, but only because I've made them become real."

So the author has produced the ideas, and the characters—but now comes the third necessity—the setting. The first two come from inside sources, but the third is outside—it must be there—waiting—in existence already. You don't invent that—it's there—it's real.

You have been perhaps for a cruise on the Nile—you remember it all—just the setting you want for this particular story. You have had a meal at a Chelsea café. A quarrel was going on—one girl pulled out a handful of another girl's hair. An excellent start for the book you are going to write next. You travel on the Orient Express. What fun to make it the scene for a plot you are considering. You go to tea with a friend. As you arrive, her brother closes a book he is reading—throws it aside, says: "Not bad, but why on earth didn't they ask Evans?"

So you decide immediately a book of yours shortly to be written will bear the title, *Why Didn't They Ask Evans?*

You don't know yet who Evans is going to be. Never mind. Evans will come in due course—the title is fixed.

So, in a sense, you don't invent your settings. They are outside you, all around you, in existence—you have only to stretch out your hand and pick and choose. A railway train, a hospital, a London hotel, a Caribbean beach, a country village, a cocktail party, a girls' school.

But one thing only applies—they must be there—in existence. Real people, real places. A definite place in time and space. If here and now—how shall you get full information—apart from the evidence of your own eyes and ears? The answer is frighteningly simple.

It is what the press brings to you everyday, served up in your morning paper under the general heading of News. Collect it from the front page. What is going on in the world today? What is everyone saying, thinking, doing? Hold up a mirror to 1970 in England.

Look at that front page every day for a month, make notes, consider and classify.

Every day there is a killing.

A girl is strangled.

Elderly woman attacked and robbed of her meager savings.

Young men or boys—attacking or attacked.

Buildings and telephone kiosks smashed and gutted.

Drug smuggling.

Robbery and assault.

Children missing and children's murdered bodies found not far from their homes.

Can this be England? Is England *really* like this? One feels—no—not yet, *but it could be.*

Fear is awakening—fear of what may be. Not so much because of actual happenings but because of the possible causes behind them. Some known, some unknown, but *felt.* And not only in our own country. There are smaller paragraphs on other pages—giving news from Europe—from Asia—from the Americas—worldwide news.

Hijacking of planes.

Kidnapping.

Violence.

Riots.

Hate.

Anarchy—all growing stronger.

All seeming to lead to worship of destruction, pleasure in cruelty.

What does it all mean? Again an Elizabethan phrase echoes from the past, speaking of life:

> *. . . it is a tale*
> *Told by an idiot, full of sound and fury,*
> *Signifying nothing.*

Not yet one knows—of one's own knowledge—how much goodness there is in this world of ours—the kindnesses done, the goodness of heart, the acts of compassion, the kindness of neighbor to neighbor, the helpful actions of girls and boys.

Then why this fantastic atmosphere of daily news—of things that happen —that are actual *facts?*

To write a story in this year of Our Lord 1970—you must come to terms with your background. If the background is fantastic, then the story must accept its background. It, too, must be a fantasy—an extravaganza. The setting must include the fantastic facts of daily life.

Can one envisage a fantastic cause? A secret Campaign for Power? Can a maniacal desire for destruction create a new world? Can one go a step further and suggest deliverance by fantatic and impossible-sounding means?

Nothing is impossible; science has taught us that.

This story is in essence a fantasy. It pretends to be nothing more.

But most of the things that happen in it are happening, or giving promise of happening in the world of today.

It is not an impossible story—it is only a fantastic one.

Contents

BOOK III
AT HOME AND ABROAD

BOOK I

Interrupted Journey

1

Passenger to Frankfurt

"FASTEN YOUR SEAT belts, please." The diverse passengers in the plane were slow to obey. There was a general feeling that they couldn't possibly be arriving at Geneva yet. The drowsy groaned and yawned. The more than drowsy had to be gently roused by an authoritative stewardess.

"Your seat belts, please."

The dry voice came authoritatively over the intercom. It explained in German, in French, and in English that a short period of rough weather would shortly be experienced. Sir Stafford Nye opened his mouth to its full extent, yawned and pulled himself upright in his seat. He had been dreaming very happily of fishing an English river.

He was a man of forty-five, of medium height, with a smooth, olive, clean-shaven face. In dress he rather liked to affect the bizarre. A man of excellent family, he felt fully at ease indulging any such sartorial whims. If it made the more conventionally dressed of his colleagues wince occasionally, that was merely a source of malicious pleasure to him. There was something about him of the eighteenth-century buck. He liked to be noticed.

His particular kind of affectation when traveling was a kind of bandit's cloak which he had once purchased in Corsica. It was of a very dark, purply blue, had a scarlet lining and a kind of burnoose hanging down behind which he could draw up over his head when he wished to, so as to obviate draughts.

Sir Stafford Nye had been a disappointment in diplomatic circles. Marked out in early youth by his gifts for great things, he had singularly failed to fulfill his early promise. A peculiar and diabolical sense of humor was wont to afflict him in what should have been his most serious moments. When it came to the point, he found that he always preferred to indulge his delicate Puckish malice to boring himself. He was a well-known figure in public life without ever having reached eminence. It was felt that Stafford Nye, though definitely brilliant, was not—and presumably never would be—a safe man. In these days of tangled politics and tangled foreign relations, safety, especially if one were to reach ambassadorial rank, was preferable to brilliance. Sir Stafford Nye was relegated to the shelf, though he was occasionally entrusted with such missions as needed the art of intrigue, but were not of too important or public a nature. Journalists sometimes referred to him as the dark horse of diplomacy.

Whether Sir Stafford himself was disappointed with his own career, nobody ever knew. Probably not even Sir Stafford himself. He was a man of a certain vanity, but he was also a man who very much enjoyed indulging his own proclivities for mischief.

He was returning now from a commission of inquiry in Malaya. He had found it singularly lacking in interest. His colleagues had, in his opinion, made up their minds beforehand what their findings were going to be. They saw and they listened, but their preconceived views were not affected. Sir Stafford had thrown a few spanners into the works, more for the hell of it than from any pronounced convictions. At all events, he thought, it had livened things up. He wished there were more possibilities of doing that sort of thing. His fellow members of the commission had been sound, dependable fellows, and remarkably dull. Even the well-known Mrs. Nathaniel Edge, the only woman member, well known as having bees in her bonnet, was no fool when it came down to plain facts. She saw, she listened and she played safe.

He had met her before on the occasion of a problem to be solved in one of the Balkan capitals. It was there that Sir Stafford Nye had not been able to refrain from embarking on a few interesting suggestions. In that scandal-loving periodical *Inside News* it was insinuated that Sir Stafford Nye's presence in that Balkan capital was intimately connected with Balkan problems, and that his mission was a secret one of the greatest delicacy. A kind friend had sent Sir Stafford a copy of this with the relevant passage marked. Sir Stafford was not taken aback. He read it with a delighted grin. It amused him very much to reflect how ludicrously far from the truth the journalists were on this occasion. His presence in Sofiagrad had been due entirely to a blameless interest in the rarer wild flowers and to the urgencies of an elderly friend of his, Lady Lucy Cleghorn, who was indefatigable in her quest for these shy floral rarities, and who at any moment would scale a rock cliff or leap joyously into a bog at the sight of some flowerlet, the length of whose Latin name was in inverse proportion to its size.

A small band of enthusiasts had been pursuing this botanical search on the slopes of mountains for about ten days when it occurred to Sir Stafford that it was a pity the paragraph was not true. He was a little—just a little—tired of wild flowers and, fond as he was of dear Lucy, her ability, despite her sixty-odd years, to race up hills at top speed easily outpacing him, sometimes annoyed him. Always just in front of him he saw the seat of those bright royal-blue trousers and Lucy, though scraggy enough elsewhere, goodness knows, was decidedly too broad in the beam to wear royal-blue corduroy trousers. A nice little international pie, he had thought, in which to dip his fingers, in which to play about . . .

In the airplane the metallic intercom voice spoke again. It told the passengers that owing to heavy fog at Geneva, the plane would be diverted to Frankfurt airport and proceed from there to London. Passengers to Geneva would be re-routed from Frankfurt as soon as possible. It made no difference to Sir Stafford Nye. If there was fog in London, he supposed they would re-route the plane to Prestwick. He hoped that would not happen. He had been to Prestwick once or twice too often. Life, he thought, and journeys by air were really excessively boring. If only—he didn't know—if only—*what?*

It was warm in the Transit Passenger Lounge at Frankfurt, so Sir Stafford Nye slipped back his cloak, allowing its crimson lining to drape itself spectacularly round his shoulders. He was drinking a glass of beer and listening with half an ear to the various announcements as they were made.

"Flight 4387. Flying to Moscow. Flight 2381 bound for Egypt and Calcutta."

Journeys all over the globe. How romantic it ought to be. But there was something about the atmosphere of a passengers' lounge in an airport that chilled romance. It was too full of people, too full of things to buy, too full of similarly colored seats, too full of plastic, too full of human beings, too full of crying children. He tried to remember who had said:

> *I wish I loved the Human Race;*
> *I wish I loved its silly face.*

Chesterton perhaps? It was undoubtedly true. Put enough people together and they looked so painfully alike that one could hardly bear it. An interesting face now, thought Sir Stafford. What a difference it would make. He looked disparagingly at two young women, splendidly made-up, dressed in the national uniform of their country—England, he presumed—of shorter and shorter mini skirts, and another young woman, even better made-up—in fact quite good-looking—who was wearing what he believed to be called a culotte suit. She had gone a little further along the road of fashion.

He wasn't very interested in nice-looking girls who looked like all the other nice-looking girls. He would like someone to be different. Someone sat down beside him on the plastic-covered artificial leather settee on which he was sitting. Her face attracted his attention at once. Not precisely because it was different; in fact, he almost seemed to recognize it as a face he knew. Here was someone he had seen before. He couldn't remember where or when, but it was certainly familiar. Twenty-five or -six, he thought, possibly, as to age. A delicate high-bridged aquiline nose, a black heavy bush of hair reaching to her shoulders. She had a magazine in front of her, but she was not paying attention to it. She was in fact looking, with something that was almost eagerness, at him. Quite suddenly she spoke. It was a deep contralto voice, almost as deep as a man's. It had a very faint foreign accent. She said:

"Can I speak to you?"

He studied her for a moment before replying. No—not what one might have thought—this wasn't a pickup. This was something else.

"I see no reason," he said, "why you should not do so. We have time to waste here, it seems."

"Fog," said the woman, "fog in Geneva, fog in London, perhaps. Fog everywhere. I don't know what to do."

"Oh, you mustn't worry," he said reassuringly; "they'll land you somewhere all right. They're quite efficient, you know. Where are you going?"

"I was going to Geneva."

"Well, I expect you'll get there in the end."

"I have to get there *now*. If I can get to Geneva, it will be all right. There is someone who will meet me there. I can be safe."

"Safe?" He smiled a little.

She said, "Safe is a four-letter word, but not the kind of four-letter word that people are interested in nowadays. And yet it can mean a lot. It means a lot to me." Then she said, "You see, if I can't get to Geneva, if I have to leave this plane here, or go on in this plane to London with no arrangements made, I shall be killed." She looked at him sharply. "I suppose you don't believe that."

"I'm afraid I don't."

"It's quite true. People can be. They are, every day."

"Who wants to kill you?"

"Does it matter?"

"Not to me."

"You can believe me if you wish to believe me. I am speaking the truth. I want help. Help to get to London safely."

"And why should you select me to help you?"

"Because I think that you know something about death. You have known of death, perhaps seen death happen."

He looked sharply at her and then away again.

"Any other reason?" he said.

"Yes. This." She stretched out her narrow olive-skinned hand and touched the folds of the voluminous cloak. "This," she said.

For the first time his interest was aroused.

"Now what do you mean by that?"

"It's unusual—characteristic. It's not what everyone wears."

"True enough. It's one of my affectations, shall we say?"

"It's an affectation that could be useful to me."

"What do you mean?"

"I am asking you something. Probably you will refuse, but you might not refuse because I think you are a man who is ready to take risks. Just as I am a woman who takes risks."

"I'll listen to your project," he said with a faint smile.

"I want your cloak to wear. I want your passport. I want your boarding ticket for the plane. Presently, in twenty minutes or so, say, the flight for London will be called. I shall have your passport, I shall wear your cloak. And so I shall travel to London and arrive safely."

"You mean you'll pass yourself off as me? My dear girl."

She opened a handbag. From it she took a small square mirror.

"Look there," she said. "Look at me and then look at your own face."

He saw then, saw what had been vaguely nagging at his mind. His sister, Pamela, who had died about twenty years ago. They had always been very alike, he and Pamela. A strong family resemblance. She had had a slightly masculine type of face. His face, perhaps, had been, certainly in early life, of a slightly effeminate type. They had both had the high-bridged nose, the tilt of eyebrows, the slightly sideways smile of the lips. Pamela had been tall, five foot eight, he himself five foot ten. He looked at the woman who had tendered him the mirror.

"There is a facial likeness between us, that's what you mean, isn't it? But my dear girl, it wouldn't deceive anyone who knew me or knew you."

"Of course it wouldn't. Don't you understand? It doesn't need to. I am traveling wearing slacks. You have been traveling with the hood of your cloak drawn up round your face. All I have to do is to cut off my hair, wrap it up in a twist of newspaper, throw it in one of the litter baskets here. Then I put on your burnoose, I have your boarding card, ticket, and passport. Unless there is someone who knows you well on this plane, and I presume there is not or they would have spoken to you already, then I can safely travel as you. Showing your passport when it's necessary, keeping the burnoose and cloak drawn up so that my nose and eyes and mouth are about all that are seen. I can walk out safely when the plane reaches its destination because no one will know I have traveled by it. Walk out safely and disappear into the crowds of the city of London."

"And what do I do?" asked Sir Stafford, with a slight smile.

"I can make a suggestion if you have the nerve to face it."

"Suggest," he said. "I always like to hear suggestions."

"You get up from here, you go away and buy a magazine or a newspaper, or a gift at the gift counter. You leave your cloak hanging here on the seat. When you come back with whatever it is, you sit down somewhere else—say at the end of that bench opposite here. There will be a glass in front of you, this glass still. In it there will be something that will send you to sleep. Sleep in a quiet corner."

"What happens next?"

"You will have been presumably the victim of a robbery," she said. "Somebody will have added a few knockout drops to your drink, and will have stolen your wallet from you. Something of that kind. You declare your identity, say that your passport and things are stolen. You can easily establish your identity."

"You know who I am? My name, I mean?"

"Not yet," she said. "I haven't seen your passport yet. I've no idea who you are."

"And yet you say I can establish my identity easily."

"I am a good judge of people. I know who is important or who isn't. You are an important person."

"And why should I do all this?"

"Perhaps to save the life of a fellow human being."

"Isn't that rather a highly colored story?"

"Oh, yes. Quite easily not believed. Do you believe it?"

He looked at her thoughtfully. "You know what you're talking like? A beautiful spy in a thriller."

"Yes, perhaps. But I am not beautiful."

"And you're not a spy?"

"I might be so described, perhaps. I have certain information. Information I want to preserve. You will have to take my word for it, it is information that would be valuable to your country."

"Don't you think you're being rather absurd?"

"Yes, I do. If this was written down, it would look absurd. But so many absurd things are true, aren't they?"

He looked at her again. She was very like Pamela. Her voice, although foreign in intonation, was like Pamela's. What she proposed was ridiculous, absurd, quite impossible, and probably dangerous. Dangerous to him. Unfortunately, though, that was what attracted him. To have the nerve to suggest such a thing to him! What would come of it all? It would be interesting, certainly, to find out.

"What do I get out of it?" he said. "That's what I'd like to know."

She looked at him consideringly. "Diversion," she said. "Something out of the everyday happenings? An antidote to boredom, perhaps. We've not got very long. It's up to you."

"And what happens to *your* passport? Do I have to buy myself a wig, if they sell such a thing at the counter? Do I have to impersonate a female?"

"No. There's no question of exchanging places. You have been robbed and drugged, but you remain yourself. Make up your mind. There isn't long. Time is passing very quickly. I have got to do my own transformation."

"You win," he said. "One mustn't refuse the unusual, if it is offered to one."

"I hoped you might feel that way, but it was a toss-up."

From his pocket Stafford Nye took out his passport. He slipped it into the outer pocket of the cloak he had been wearing. He rose to his feet, yawned, looked round him, looked at his watch, and strolled over to the counter where various goods were displayed for sale. He did not even look back. He bought a paperback book and fingered some small woolly animals, a suitable gift for some child. Finally he chose a panda. He looked round the lounge, came back to where he had been sitting. The cloak was gone and so was the girl. A half glass of beer was on the table still. Here, he thought, is where I take the risk. He picked up the glass, moved away a little, and drank it. Not quickly. Quite slowly. It tasted much the same as it had tasted before.

"Now I wonder," said Sir Stafford. "Now I wonder."

He walked across the lounge to a far corner. There was a somewhat noisy family sitting there, laughing and talking together. He sat down near them, yawned, let his head fall back on the edge of the cushion. A flight was announced leaving for Teheran. A large number of passengers got up and went to queue by the requisite numbered gate. The lounge still remained half full. He opened his paperback book. He yawned again. He was really sleepy now, yes, he was very sleepy. . . . He must just think out where it was best for him to go off to sleep. Somewhere where he could remain. . . .

Trans-European Airways announced the departure of their plane, Flight 309 for London.

Quite a good sprinkling of passengers rose to their feet to obey the summons. By this time, though, more passengers had entered the transit lounge waiting for other planes. Announcements followed as to fog at Geneva and other disabilities of travel. A slim man of middle height wearing a dark blue cloak with its red lining showing and with a hood drawn up over a close-cropped head, not noticeably more untidy than many of the heads of young men nowadays, walked across the floor to take his place in the queue for the plane. Showing a boarding ticket, he passed out through gate No. 9.

More announcements followed. Swissair flying to Zurich. BEA to Athens and Cyprus— And then a different type of announcement.

"Will Miss Daphne Theodofanous, passenger to Geneva, kindly come to the flight desk. Plane to Geneva is delayed owing to fog. Passengers will travel by way of Athens. The airplane is now ready to leave."

Other announcements followed dealing with passengers to Japan, to Egypt, to South Africa, airlines spanning the world. Mr. Sidney Cook, passenger to South Africa, was urged to come to the flight desk where there was a message for him. Daphne Theodofanous was called for again.

"This is the last call before the departure of Flight 309."

In a corner of the lounge a little girl was looking up at a man in a dark suit who was fast asleep, his head resting against the cushion of the red settee. In his hand he held a small woolly panda.

The little girl's hand stretched out toward the panda. Her mother said, "Now, Joan, don't touch that. The poor gentleman's asleep."

"Where is he going?"

"Perhaps he's going to Australia, too," said her mother, "like we are."

"Has he got a little girl like me?"

"I think he must have," said her mother.

The little girl sighed and looked at the panda again. Sir Stafford Nye continued to sleep. He was dreaming that he was trying to shoot a leopard. A very dangerous animal, he was saying to the safari guide who was accompanying him. "A very dangerous animal, so I've always heard. You can't trust a leopard."

The dream switched at that moment, as dreams have a habit of doing, and he was having tea with his Great-Aunt Matilda, and trying to make her hear. She was deafer than ever! He had not heard any of the announcements except the first one for Miss Daphne Theodofanous. The little girl's mother said,

"I've always wondered, you know, about a passenger that's missing. Nearly always, whenever you go anywhere by air, you hear it. Somebody they can't find. Somebody who hasn't heard the call or isn't on the plane or something like that. I always wonder who it is and what they're doing, and why they haven't come. I suppose this Miss What's-a-name or whatever it is will just have missed her plane. What will they do with her then?"

Nobody was able to answer her question because nobody had the proper information.

2

London

Sir Stafford Nye's flat was a very pleasant one. It looked out upon Green Park. He switched on the coffee percolator and went to see what the post had left him this morning. It did not appear to have left him anything very interesting. He sorted through the letters, a bill or two, a receipt and letters with rather uninteresting postmarks. He shuffled them together and placed them on the table where some mail was already lying, accumulating from the last two days. He'd have to get down to things soon, he supposed. His secretary would be coming in some time or other this afternoon.

He went back to the kitchen, poured coffee into a cup and brought it to the table. He picked up the two or three letters that he had opened late last night when he arrived. One of them he referred to, and smiled a little as he read it.

"Eleven-thirty," he said. "Quite a suitable time. I wonder now. I expect I'd better just think things over, and get prepared for Chetwynd."

Somebody pushed something through the letter box. He went out into the hall and got the morning paper. There was very little news in the paper. A political crisis, an item of foreign news which might have been disquieting, but he didn't think it was. It was merely a journalist letting off steam and trying to make things rather more important than they were. Must give the people something to read. A girl had been strangled in the park. Girls were always being strangled. One a day, he thought callously. No child had been kidnapped or raped this morning. That was a nice surprise. He made himself a piece of toast and drank his coffee.

Later, he went out of the building, down into the street, and walked through the park in the direction of Whitehall. He was smiling to himself. Life, he felt, was rather good this morning. He began to think about Chetwynd. Chetwynd was a silly fool if there ever was one. A good façade, important-seeming, and a nicely suspicious mind. He'd rather enjoy talking to Chetwynd.

He reached Whitehall a comfortable seven minutes late. That was only due to his own importance compared with that of Chetwynd, he thought. He walked into the room. Chetwynd was sitting behind his desk and had a lot of papers on it and a secretary there. He was looking properly important, as he always did when he could make it.

"Hullo, Nye," said Chetwynd, smiling all over his impressively handsome face. "Glad to be back? How was Malaya?"

"Hot," said Stafford Nye.

"Yes. Well, I suppose it always is. You meant atmospherically, I suppose, not politically?"

"Oh, purely atmospherically," said Stafford Nye.

He accepted a cigarette and sat down.

"Get any results to speak of?"

"Oh, hardly. Not what you'd call results. I've sent in my report. All a lot of talky-talky as usual. How's Lazenby?"

"Oh, a nuisance as he always is. He'll never change," said Chetwynd.

"No, that would seem too much to hope for. I haven't served on anything with Bascombe before. He can be quite fun when he likes."

"Can he? I don't know him very well. Yes. I suppose he can."

"Well, well, well. No other news, I suppose?"

"No, nothing. Nothing I think that would interest you."

"You didn't mention in your letter quite why you wanted to see me."

"Oh, just to go over a few things, that's all. You know, in case you'd brought any special dope home with you. Anything we ought to be prepared for, you know. Questions in the House. Anything like that."

"Yes, of course."

"Came home by air, didn't you? Had a bit of trouble, I gather."

Stafford Nye put on the face he had been determined to put on beforehand. It was slightly rueful, with a faint tinge of annoyance.

"Oh, so you heard about that, did you?" he said. "Silly business."

"Yes. Yes, must have been."

"Extraordinary," said Stafford Nye, "how things always get into the press. There was a paragraph in the stop press this morning."

"You'd rather they wouldn't have, I suppose?"

"Well, makes me look a bit of an ass, doesn't it?" said Stafford Nye. "Got to admit it. At my age, too!"

"What happened exactly? I wondered if the report in the paper had been exaggerating."

"Well, I suppose they made the most of it, that's all. You know what these journeys are. Damn boring. There was fog at Geneva, so they had to reroute the plane. Then there was two hours' delay at Frankfurt."

"Is that when it happened?"

"Yes. One's bored stiff in these airports. Planes coming, planes going. Intercom going full steam ahead. Flight 302 for Hong Kong, Flight 109 going to Ireland. This, that, and the other. People getting up, people leaving. And you just sit there yawning."

"What happened exactly?" said Chetwynd.

"Well, I'd got a drink in front of me, Pilsner as a matter of fact, then I thought I'd got to get something else to read. I'd read everything I'd got with me, so I went over to the counter and bought some wretched paperback or other. Detective story, I think it was, and I bought a woolly animal for one of my nieces. Then I came back, finished my drink, opened my paperback and then I went to sleep."

"Yes, I see. You went to sleep."

"Well, a very natural thing to do, isn't it? I suppose they called my flight, but if they did, I didn't hear it. I didn't hear it apparently for the best of reasons. I'm capable of going to sleep in an airport any time, but I'm also capable of hearing an announcement that concerns me. This time I didn't. When I woke up, or came to, however you like to put it, I was having a bit of medical attention. Somebody apparently had dropped a Mickey Finn or something or other in my drink. Must have done it when I was away getting the paperback."

"Rather an extraordinary thing to happen, wasn't it?" said Chetwynd.

"Well, it's never happened to me before," said Stafford Nye. "I hope it never will again. It makes you feel an awful fool, you know. Besides having a hangover. There was a doctor and some nurse creature, or something. Anyway, there was no great harm done apparently. My wallet had been pinched with some money in it and my passport. It was awkward, of course. Fortunately, I hadn't got much money. My traveler's checks were in an inner pocket. There always has to be a bit of red tape and all that if you lose your passport. Anyway, I had letters and things and identification was not difficult. And in due course things were squared up and I resumed my flight."

"Still, very annoying for you," said Chetwynd. "A person of your status, I mean." His tone was disapproving.

"Yes," said Stafford Nye. "It doesn't show me in a very good light, does it? I mean not as bright as a fellow of my—er—status ought to be." The idea seemed to amuse him.

"Does this often happen, did you find out?"

"I don't think it's a matter of general occurrence. It could be. I suppose any person with a pickpocket trend could notice a fellow asleep and slip a hand into a pocket, and if he's accomplished in his profession, get hold of a wallet or a pocketbook or something like that, and hope for some luck."

"Pretty awkward to lose a passport."

"Yes, I shall have to put in for another one now. Make a lot of explanations, I suppose. As I say, the whole thing's a damn silly business. And let's face it, Chetwynd, it doesn't show me in a very favorable light, does it?"

"Oh, not your fault, my dear boy, not your fault. It could happen to anybody, anybody at all."

"Very nice of you to say so," said Stafford Nye, smiling at him agreeably. "Teach me a sharp lesson, won't it?"

"You don't think anyone wanted *your* passport specially?"

"I shouldn't think so," said Stafford Nye. "Why should they want my passport? Unless it was a matter of someone who wished to annoy me, and that hardly seems likely. Or somebody who took a fancy to my passport photo—and that seems even less likely!"

"Did you see anyone you knew at this—where did you say you were— Frankfurt?"

"No, no! Nobody at all."

"Talk to anyone?"

"Not particularly. Said something to a nice fat woman who'd got a small child she was trying to amuse. Came from Wigan, I think. Going to Australia. Don't remember anybody else."

"You're sure?"

"There was some woman or other who wanted to know what she did if she wanted to study archaeology in Egypt. Said I didn't know anything about that. I told her she'd better go and ask the British Museum. And I had a word or two with a man who I think was an antivivisectionist. Very passionate about it."

"One always feels," said Chetwynd, "that there might be something *behind* things like this."

"Things like what?"

"Well, things like what happened to you."

"I don't see what can be behind this," said Sir Stafford. "I daresay journalists could make up some story, they're so clever at that sort of thing. Still, it's a silly business. For goodness' sake, let's forget it. I suppose now it's been mentioned in the press, all my friends will start asking me about it. How's old Leyland? What's he up to nowadays? I heard one or two things about him out there. Leyland always talks a bit too much."

The two men talked amiable shop for ten minutes or so, then Sir Stafford got up and went out.

"I've got a lot of things to do this morning," he said. "Presents to buy for my relations. The trouble is that if one goes to Malaya, all one's relations expect you to bring exotic presents to them. I'll go round to Liberty's, I think. They have a nice stock of Eastern goods there."

He went out cheerfully nodding to a couple of men he knew in the corridor outside. After he had gone, Chetwynd spoke through the telephone to his secretary.

"Ask Colonel Munro if he can come to me."

Colonel Munro came in, bringing another tall middle-aged man with him. "Don't know whether you know Horsham," he said, "in Security."

"Think I've met you," said Chetwynd.

"Nye's just left you, hasn't he?" said Colonel Munro. "Anything in this story about Frankfurt? Anything, I mean, that we ought to take any notice of?"

"Doesn't seem so," said Chetwynd. "He's a bit put out about it. Thinks it makes him look a silly ass. Which it does, of course."

The man called Horsham nodded his head. "That's the way he takes it, is it?"

"Well, he tried to put a good face upon it," said Chetwynd.

"All the same, you know," said Horsham, "he's not really a silly ass, is he?"

Chetwynd shrugged his shoulders. "These things happen," he said.

"I know," said Colonel Munro, "yes, yes, I know! All the same, well, I've always felt in some ways that Nye is a bit unpredictable. That in some ways, you know, he mightn't be really *sound* in his views."

The man called Horsham spoke. "Nothing against him," he said. "Nothing at all as far as *we* know."

"Oh, I didn't mean there was. I didn't mean that at all," said Chetwynd. "It's just—how shall I put it?—he's not always very serious about things."

Mr. Horsham had a mustache. He found it useful to have a mustache. It concealed moments when he found it difficult to avoid smiling.

"He's not a stupid man," said Munro. "Got brains, you know. You don't think that—well, I mean you don't think there could be anything at all doubtful about this?"

"On his part? It doesn't seem so."

"You've been into it all, Horsham?"

"Well, we haven't had very much time yet. But as far as it goes, it's all right. But his passport *was* used."

"Used? In what way?"

"It passed through Heathrow."

"You mean someone represented himself as Sir Stafford Nye?"

"No, no," said Horsham, "not in so many words. We could hardly hope for that. It went through with other passports. There was no alarm out, you know. He hadn't even woken up, I gather, at that time, from the dope or whatever it was he was given. He was still at Frankfurt."

"But someone could have stolen that passport and come on the plane and so got into England?"

"Yes," said Munro, "that's the presumption. Either someone took a wallet which had money in it and a passport, or else someone wanted a passport and settled on Sir Stafford Nye as a convenient person to take it from. A drink was waiting on a table, put a pinch in that, wait till the man went off to sleep, take the passport and chance it."

"But after all, they look at a passport. Must have seen it wasn't the right man," said Chetwynd.

"Well, there must have been a certain resemblance, certainly," said Horsham. "But it isn't as though there was any notice of his being missing, any special attention drawn to that particular passport in any way. A large crowd comes through on a plane that's overdue. A man looks reasonably like the photograph in his passport. That's all. Brief glance, handed back, pass it on. Anyway, what they're looking for usually is the foreigners that are coming in, not the British lot. Dark hair, dark blue eyes, clean-shaven, five foot ten or whatever it is. That's about all you want to see. Not on a list of undesirable aliens or anything like that."

"I know, I know. Still, you'd say if anybody wanted merely to pinch a wallet or some money or that, they wouldn't use the passport, would they? Too much risk."

"Yes," said Horsham. "Yes, that is the interesting part of it. Of course," he said, "we're making investigations, asking a few questions here and there."

"And what's your own opinion?"

"I wouldn't like to say yet," said Horsham. "It takes a little time, you know. One can't hurry things."

"They're all the same," said Colonel Munro, when Horsham had left the room. "They never will tell you anything, those damned Security people. If they think they're on the trail of anything, they won't admit it."

"Well, that's natural," said Chetwynd, "because they might be wrong."

It seemed a typically political view.

"Horsham's a pretty good man," said Munro. "They think very highly of him at headquarters. He's not likely to be wrong."

3

The Man from the Cleaner's

SIR STAFFORD NYE returned to his flat. A large woman bounced out of the small kitchen with welcoming words.

"See you got back all right, sir. Those nasty planes. You never know, do you?"

"Quite true, Mrs. Worrit," said Sir Stafford Nye. "Two hours late, the plane was."

"Same as cars, aren't they?" said Mrs. Worrit. "I mean, you never know, do you, what's going to go wrong with them. Only it's more worrying, so to speak, being up in the air, isn't it? Can't just draw up to the curb, not the same way, can you? I mean, there you are. I wouldn't go by one myself, not if it was ever so." She went on, "I've ordered in a few things. I hope that's all right. Eggs, butter, coffee, tea—" She ran off the words with the loquacity of a Near Eastern guide showing a Pharaoh's palace. "There," said Mrs. Worrit, pausing to take breath, "I think that's all as you're likely to want. I've ordered the French mustard."

"Not Dijon, is it? They always try and give you Dijon."

"I don't know who *he* was, but it's Esther Dragon, the one you like, isn't it?"

"Quite right," said Sir Stafford; "you're a wonder."

Mrs. Worrit looked pleased. She retired into the kitchen again, as Sir Stafford Nye put his hand on his bedroom door handle preparatory to going into the bedroom.

"All right to give your clothes to the gentleman what called for them, I suppose, sir? You hadn't said or left word or anything like that."

"What clothes?" said Sir Stafford Nye, pausing.

"Two suits, it was, the gentleman said as called for them. Twiss and Bonywork it was, think that's the same name as called before. We'd had a bit of a dispute with the White Swan Laundry, if I remember rightly."

"Two suits?" said Sir Stafford Nye. "Which suits?"

"Well, there was the one you traveled home in, sir. I made out that would be one of them. I wasn't quite so sure about the other, but there was the blue pinstripe that you didn't leave no orders about when you went away. It could do with cleaning, and there was a repair wanted doing to the right-hand cuff, but I didn't like to take it on myself while you were away. I never likes to do that," said Mrs. Worrit with an air of palpable virtue.

638

"So the chap, whoever he was, took those suits away?"

"I hope I didn't do wrong, sir." Mrs. Worrit became worried.

"I don't mind the blue pinstripe. I daresay it's all for the best. The suit I came home in, well—"

"It's a bit thin, that suit, sir, for this time of year, you know, sir. All right for those parts as you've been in where it's hot. And it could do with a clean. He said as you'd rung up about them. That's what the gentleman said as called for them."

"Did he go into my room and pick them out himself?"

"Yes, sir. I thought that was best."

"Very interesting," said Sir Stafford. "Yes, very interesting."

He went into his bedroom and looked around it. It was neat and tidy. The bed was made, the hand of Mrs. Worrit was apparent, his electric razor was on charge, the things on the dressing table were neatly arranged.

He went to the wardrobe and looked inside. He looked in the drawers of the highboy that stood against the wall near the window. It was all quite tidy. It was tidier indeed than it should have been. He had done a little unpacking last night, and what little he had done had been of a cursory nature. He had thrown underclothing and various odds and ends in the appropriate drawer, but he had not arranged them neatly. He would have done that himself either today or tomorrow. He would not have expected Mrs. Worrit to do it for him. He expected her merely to keep things as she found them. Then, when he came back from abroad, there would be a time for rearrangements and readjustments because of climate and other matters. So someone had looked around here, someone had taken out drawers, looked through them quickly, hurriedly, had replaced things, partly because of his hurry, more tidily and neatly than he should have done. A quick careful job, and he had gone away with two suits and a plausible explanation. One suit obviously worn by Sir Stafford when traveling and a suit of thin material which might have been one taken abroad and brought home. So why?

"Because," said Sir Stafford thoughtfully to himself, "because somebody was looking for something. But what? And who? And also perhaps why?" Yes, it was interesting.

He sat down in a chair and thought about it. Presently his eyes strayed to the table by the bed on which sat, rather pertly, a small furry panda. It started a train of thought. He went to the telephone and rang a number.

"That you, Aunt Matilda?" he said. "Stafford here."

"Ah, my dear boy, so you're back. I'm so glad. I read in the paper they'd got cholera in Malaya yesterday, at least I think it was Malaya. I always get so mixed up with those places. I hope you're coming to see me soon? Don't pretend you're busy. You can't be busy all the time. One really only accepts that sort of thing from tycoons, people in industry, you know, in the middle of mergers and takeovers. I never know what it all really means. It used to mean doing your work properly, but now it means things all tied up with atom bombs and factories in concrete," said Aunt Matilda rather wildly.

"And those terrible computers that get all one's figures wrong, to say nothing of making them the wrong shape. Really, they have made life so difficult for us nowadays. You wouldn't believe the things they've done to my bank account. And to my postal address, too. Well, I suppose I've lived too long."

"Don't you believe it! All right if I come down next week?"

"Come down tomorrow if you like. I've got the vicar coming to dinner, but I can easily put him off."

"Oh, look here, no need to do that."

"Yes, there is every need. He's a most irritating man and he wants a new organ, too. This one does quite well as it is. I mean the trouble is with the organist, really, not the organ. An absolutely abominable musician. The vicar's sorry for him because he lost his mother, whom he was very fond of. But really, being fond of your mother doesn't make you play the organ any better, does it? I mean, one has to look at things as they are."

"Quite right. It will have to be next week—I've got a few things to see to. How's Sybil?"

"Dear child! Very naughty, but such fun."

"I brought her home a woolly panda," said Sir Stafford Nye.

"Well, that was very nice of you, dear."

"I hope she'll like it," said Sir Stafford, catching the panda's eye and feeling slightly nervous.

"Well, at any rate, she's got very good manners," said Aunt Matilda, which seemed a somewhat doubtful answer, the meaning of which Sir Stafford did not quite appreciate.

Aunt Matilda suggested likely trains for next week with the warning that they very often did not run, or changed their plans, and also commanded that he should bring her down a Camembert cheese and half a Stilton.

"Impossible to get anything down here now. Our own grocer—such a nice man, so thoughtful and such good taste in what we all liked—turned suddenly into a supermarket, six times the size, all rebuilt, baskets and wire trays to carry round and try to fill up with things you don't want and mothers always losing their babies, and crying and having hysterics. Most exhausting. Well, I'll be expecting you, dear boy." She rang off.

The telephone rang again at once.

"Hullo? Stafford? Eric Pugh here. Heard you were back from Malaya— what about dining tonight?"

"Like to very much."

"Good—Limpits Club—eight-fifteen?"

Mrs. Worrit panted into the room as Sir Stafford replaced the receiver.

"A gentleman downstairs wanting to see you, sir," she said. "At least I mean, I suppose he's that. Anyway, he said he was sure you wouldn't mind."

"What's his name?"

"Horsham, sir, like the place on the way to Brighton."

"Horsham." Sir Stafford Nye was a little surprised.

He went out of his bedroom, down a half flight of stairs that led to the big sitting room on the lower floor. Mrs. Worrit had made no mistake. Horsham it was, looking as he had looked half an hour ago—stalwart, trustworthy, cleft chin, rubicund cheeks, bushy gray mustache and a general air of imperturbability.

"Hope you don't mind," he said agreeably, rising to his feet.

"Hope I don't mind what?" said Sir Stafford Nye.

"Seeing me again so soon. We met in the passage outside Mr. Gordon Chetwynd's door—if you remember?"

"No objections at all," said Sir Stafford Nye.

He pushed a cigarette box along the table.

"Sit down. Something forgotten, something left unsaid?"

"Very nice man, Mr. Chetwynd," said Horsham. "We've got him quietened down, I think. He and Colonel Munro. They're a bit upset about it all, you know. About you, I mean."

"Really?"

Sir Stafford Nye sat down, too. He smiled, he smoked, and he looked thoughtfully at Henry Horsham. "And where do we go from here?" he asked.

"I was just wondering if I might ask, without undue curiosity, where you're going from here?"

"Delighted to tell you," said Sir Stafford Nye. "I'm going to stay with an aunt of mine, Lady Matilda Cleckheaton. I'll give you the address if you like."

"I know it," said Henry Horsham. "Well, I expect that's a very good idea. She'll be glad to see you've come home safely all right. Might have been a near thing, mightn't it?"

"Is that what Colonel Munro thinks and Mr. Chetwynd?"

"Well, you know what it is, sir," said Horsham. "You know well enough. They're always in a state, gentlemen in that department. They're not sure whether they trust you or not."

"Trust me?" said Sir Stafford Nye in an offended voice. "What do you mean by that, Mr. Horsham?"

Mr. Horsham was not taken aback. He merely grinned.

"You see," he said, "you've got a reputation for not taking things seriously."

"Oh. I thought you meant I was a fellow traveler or a convert to the wrong side. Something of that kind."

"Oh, no, sir, they just don't think you're serious. They think you like having a bit of a joke now and again."

"One cannot go entirely through life taking oneself and other people seriously," said Sir Stafford Nye disapprovingly.

"No. But you took a pretty good risk, as I've said before, didn't you?"

"I wonder if I know in the least what you are talking about."

"I'll tell you. Things go wrong, sir, sometimes, and they don't always go wrong because people have made them go wrong. What you might call the

Almighty takes a hand, or the other gentleman—the one with the tail, I mean."

Sir Stafford Nye was slightly diverted.

"Are you referring to fog at Geneva?" he said.

"Exactly, sir. There was fog at Geneva and that upset people's plans. Somebody was in a nasty hole."

"Tell me all about it," said Sir Stafford Nye. "I really would like to know."

"Well, a passenger was missing when that plane of yours left Frankfurt yesterday. You'd drunk your beer and you were sitting in a corner snoring nicely and comfortably by yourself. One passenger didn't report and they called her and they called her again. In the end, presumably, the plane left without her."

"Ah. And what had happened to her?"

"It would be interesting to know. In any case, your passport arrived at Heathrow even if you didn't."

"And where is it now? Am I supposed to have got it?"

"No. I don't think so. That would be rather too quick work. Good reliable stuff, that dope. Just right, if I may say so. It put you out and it didn't produce any particularly bad effects."

"It gave me a very nasty hangover," said Sir Stafford.

"Ah, well, you can't avoid that. Not in the circumstances."

"What would have happened," Sir Stafford asked, "since you seem to know all about everything, if I had refused to accept the proposition that may—I will only say may—have been put up to me?"

"It's quite possible that it would have been curtains for Mary Ann."

"Mary Ann? Who's Mary Ann?"

"Miss Daphne Theodofanous."

"That's the name I do seem to have heard—being summoned as a missing traveler?"

"Yes, that's the name she was traveling under. We call her Mary Ann."

"Who is she—just as a matter of interest?"

"In her own line she's more or less the tops."

"And what is her line? Is she ours or is she theirs, if you know who theirs is? I must say I find a little difficulty myself when making my mind up about that."

"Yes, it's not so easy, is it? What with the Chinese and the Russkies and the rather queer crowd that's behind all the student troubles and the new Mafia and the rather odd lot in South America. And the nice little nest of financiers who seem to have got something funny up their sleeves. Yes, it's not so easy to say."

"Mary Ann," said Sir Stafford Nye thoughtfully. "It seems a curious name to have for her if her real one is Daphne Theodofanous."

"Well, her mother's Greek, her father was an Englishman, and her grandfather was an Austrian subject."

"What would have happened if I hadn't made her a—loan of a certain garment?"

"She might have been killed."

"Come, come. Not really?"

"We're worried about the airport at Heathrow. Things have happened there lately—things that need a bit of explaining. If the plane had gone via Geneva as planned, it would have been all right. She'd have had full protection all arranged. But this other way—there wouldn't have been time to arrange anything and you don't know who's who always, nowadays. Everyone's playing a double game or a treble or a quadruple one."

"You alarm me," said Sir Stafford Nye. "But she's all right, is she? Is that what you're telling me?"

"I hope she's all right. We haven't heard anything to the contrary."

"If it's any help to you," said Sir Stafford Nye, "somebody called here this morning while I was out talking to my little pals in Whitehall. He represented that I telephoned a firm of cleaners and he removed the suit that I wore yesterday, and also another suit. Of course it may have been merely that he took a fancy to the other suit, or he may have made a practice of collecting various gentlemen's suitings who have recently returned from abroad. Or—well, perhaps you've got an 'or' to add?"

"He might have been looking for something."

"Yes, I think he was. Somebody's been looking for something. All very nice and tidily arranged again. Not the way I left it. All right, he was looking for something. What was he looking for?"

"I'm not sure myself," said Horsham slowly. "I wish I was. There's something going on—somewhere. There are bits of it sticking out, you know, like a badly done up parcel. You get a peep here and a peep there. One moment you think it's going on at the Bayreuth Festival and the next minute you think it's tucking out of a South American estancia and then you get a bit of a lead in the U.S.A. There's a lot of nasty business going on in different places, working up to something. Maybe politics, maybe something quite different from politics. It's probably money." He added, "You know Mr. Robinson, don't you? Or rather Mr. Robinson knows you, I think he said."

"Robinson?" Sir Stafford Nye considered. "Robinson. Nice English name." He looked across to Horsham. "Large, yellow face?" he said. "Fat? Finger in financial pies generally?" He asked: "Is he, too, on the side of the angels—is that what you're telling me?"

"I don't know about angels," said Henry Horsham. "He's pulled us out of a hole in this country more than once. People like Mr. Chetwynd don't go for him much. Think he's too expensive, I suppose. Inclined to be a mean man, Mr. Chetwynd. A great one for making economies in the wrong place."

"One used to say, 'Poor but honest,' " said Sir Stafford Nye thoughtfully. "I take it that you would put it differently. You would describe our Mr. Robinson as expensive but honest. Or shall we put it honest but expensive." He sighed. "I wish you could tell me what all this is about," he said plaintively. "Here I seem to be mixed up in something and no idea what it is." He looked at Henry Horsham hopefully, but Horsham shook his head.

"None of us knows. Not exactly," he said.

"What am I supposed to have got hidden here that someone comes fiddling and looking for?"

"Frankly, I haven't the least idea, Sir Stafford."

"Well, that's a pity, because I haven't either."

"As far as *you* know you haven't got anything. Nobody gave you anything to keep, to take anywhere, to look after?"

"Nothing whatsoever. If you mean Mary Ann, she said she wanted her life saved, that's all."

"And unless there's a paragraph in the evening papers, you *have* saved her life."

"It seems rather the end of the chapter, doesn't it? A pity. My curiosity is rising. I find I want to know very much what's going to happen next. All you people seem very pessimistic."

"Frankly, we are. Things are going badly in this country. Can you wonder?"

"I know what you mean. I sometimes wonder myself—"

4

Dinner with Eric

"Do you mind if I tell you something, old man?" said Eric Pugh.

Sir Stafford Nye looked at him. He had known Eric Pugh for a good many years. They had not been close friends. Old Eric, or so Sir Stafford thought, was rather a boring friend. He was, on the other hand, faithful. And he was the type of man who, though not amusing, had a knack of knowing things. People said things to him and he remembered what they said and stored them up. Sometimes he could push out a useful bit of information.

"Come back from that Malay Conference, haven't you?"

"Yes," said Sir Stafford.

"Anything particular turn up there?"

"Just the usual," said Sir Stafford.

"Oh. I wondered if something had—well, you know what I mean. Anything had occurred to put the cat among the pigeons."

"What, at the Conference? No, just painfully predictable. Everyone said just what you thought they'd say, only they said it unfortunately at rather greater length than you could have imagined possible. I don't know why I go on these things."

Eric Pugh made a rather tedious remark or two as to what the Chinese were really up to.

"I don't think they're really up to anything," said Sir Stafford. "All the usual rumors, you know, about the diseases poor old Mao has got and who's intriguing against him and why."

"And what about the Arab-Israeli business?"

"That's proceeding according to plan also. Their plan, that is to say. And anyway, what's that got to do with Malaya?"

"Well, I didn't really mean so much Malaya."

"You're looking rather like the Mock Turtle," said Sir Stafford Nye. " 'Soup of the evening, beautiful soup.' Wherefore this gloom?"

"Well, I just wondered if you'd—you'll forgive me, won't you?—I mean you haven't done anything to blot your copybook, have you, in any way?"

"Me?" said Sir Stafford, looking highly surprised.

"Well, you know what you're like, Staff. You like giving people a jolt sometimes, don't you?"

"I have behaved impeccably of late," said Sir Stafford. "What have you been hearing about me?"

"I hear there was some trouble about something that happened in a plane on your way home."

"Oh? Who did you hear that from?"

"Well, you know, I saw old Cartison."

"Terrible old bore. Always imagining things that haven't happened."

"Yes, I know. I know he is like that. But he was just saying that somebody or other—Winterton, at least—seemed to think you'd been up to something."

"Up to something? I wish I had," said Sir Stafford Nye.

"There's some espionage racket going on somewhere and he got a bit worried about certain people."

"What do they think I am—another Philby, something of that kind?"

"You know you're very unwise sometimes in the things you say, the things you make jokes about."

"It's very hard to resist sometimes," his friend told him. "All these politicians and diplomats and the rest of them. They're so bloody solemn. You'd like to give them a bit of a stir-up now and again."

"Your sense of fun is very distorted, my boy. It really is. I worry about you sometimes. They wanted to ask you some questions about something that happened on the flight back and they seem to think that you didn't, well—that perhaps you didn't exactly speak the truth about it all."

"Ah, that's what they think, is it? Interesting. I think I must work that up a bit."

"Now don't do anything rash."

"I must have my moments of fun sometimes."

"Look here, old fellow, you don't want to go and ruin your career just by indulging your sense of humor."

"I am quickly coming to the conclusion that there is nothing so boring as having a career."

"I know, I know. You are always inclined to take that point of view, and you haven't got on as far as you ought to have, you know. You were in the running for Vienna at one time. I don't like to see you muck up things."

"I am behaving with the utmost sobriety and virtue, I assure you," said Sir Stafford Nye. He added, "Cheer up, Eric. You're a good friend, but really, I'm not guilty of fun and games."

Eric shook his head doubtfully.

It was a fine evening. Sir Stafford walked home across Green Park. As he crossed the road in Birdcage Walk, a car leaping down the street missed him by a few inches. Sir Stafford was an athletic man. His leap took him safely onto the pavement. The car disappeared down the street. He wondered. Just for a moment he could have sworn that that car had deliberately tried to run him down. An interesting thought. First his flat had been searched, and now he himself might have been marked down. Probably a mere coincidence. And yet, in the course of his life, some of which had been spent in wild neighborhoods and places, Sir Stafford Nye had come in contact with danger. He knew, as it were, the touch and feel and smell of danger. He felt it now. Someone, somewhere was gunning for him. But why? For what reason? As far as he knew, he had not stuck his neck out in any way. He wondered.

He let himself into his flat and picked up the mail that lay on the floor inside. Nothing much. A couple of bills and a copy of *Lifeboat* periodical. He threw the bills onto his desk and put a finger through the wrapper of *Lifeboat*. It was a cause to which he occasionally contributed. He turned the pages without much attention because he was still absorbed in what he was thinking. Then he stopped the action of his fingers abruptly. Something was taped between two of the pages. Taped with adhesive tape. He looked at it closely. It was his passport returned to him unexpectedly in this fashion. He tore it free and looked at it. The last stamp on it was the arrival stamp at Heathrow the day before. She had used his passport, getting back here safely, and had chosen this way to return it to him. Where was she now? He would like to know.

He wondered if he would ever see her again. Who was she? Where had she gone and why? It was like waiting for the second act of a play. Indeed, he felt the first act had hardly been played yet. What had he seen? An old-fashioned curtain raiser perhaps. A girl who had ridiculously wanted to dress herself up and pass herself off as of the male sex, who had passed the passport control of Heathrow without attracting suspicion of any kind to herself and who had now disappeared through that gateway into London. No, he would probably never see her again. It annoyed him. But why, he thought, why do I want to? She wasn't particularly attractive; she wasn't anything. No, that wasn't quite true. She was something, or someone, or she could not have induced him, with no particular persuasion, with no overt sex stimulation, nothing except a plain demand for help, to do what she wanted. A demand from one human being to another human being because, or so she had intimated, not precisely in words, but nevertheless it was what she *had* intimated, she knew people and she recognized in him a man who was willing to take a risk to help another human being. And he had taken a risk, too, thought Sir Stafford Nye. She could have put anything in that beer glass of his. He could have been found, if she had so willed it, found as a dead body in a seat tucked away in the corner of a departure lounge in an airport. And if she had, as no doubt she must have had, a knowledgeable recourse to drugs, his death might have been passed off as an attack of heart trouble due to altitude or difficult pressurizing—something or other like that. Oh, well, why think about it? He wasn't likely to see her again, and he was annoyed.

Yes, he was annoyed, and he didn't like being annoyed. He considered the matter for some minutes. Then he wrote out an advertisement, to be repeated three times. *"Passenger to Frankfurt. November 3rd. Please communicate with fellow traveler to London."* No more than that. Either she would or she wouldn't. If it ever came to her eyes, she would know by whom that advertisement had been inserted. She had had his passport, she knew his name. She could look him up. He might hear from her. He might not. Probably not. If not, the curtain raiser would remain a curtain raiser, a silly little play that received early arrivals to the theater and diverted them until the real business of the evening began. Very useful in prewar times. In all probability, though, he would not hear from her again, and one of the reasons might be that she might have accomplished whatever it was she had come to do in London, and have now left the country once more, flying abroad to Geneva, or the Middle East, or to Russia or to China or to South America or to the United States. And why, thought Sir Stafford, do I include South America? There must be a reason. She had not mentioned South America. Nobody had mentioned South America. Except Horsham, that was true. And even Horsham had only mentioned South America among a lot of other mentions.

On the following morning as he walked slowly homeward, after handing in his advertisement, along the pathway across St. James's Park his eye picked out, half unseeing, the autumn flowers. The chrysanthemums looking by now stiff and leggy with their button tops of gold and bronze. Their smell came to him faintly, a rather goatlike smell, he had always thought, a smell that reminded him of hillsides in Greece. He must remember to keep his eye on the Personal Column. Not yet. Two or three days at least would have to pass before his own advertisement was put in and before there had been time for anyone to put in one in answer. He must not miss it if there was an answer because, after all, it was irritating not to know—not to have any idea what all this was about.

He tried to recall not the girl at the airport but his sister Pamela's face. A long time since her death. He remembered her. Of course he remembered her, but he could not somehow picture her face. It irritated him not to be able to do so. He had paused just when he was about to cross one of the roads. There was no traffic except for a car jigging slowly along with the solemn demeanor of a bored dowager. An elderly car, he thought. An old-fashioned Daimler limousine. He shook his shoulders. Why stand here in this idiotic way, lost in thought?

He took an abrupt step to cross the road and suddenly with surprising vigor the dowager limousine, as he had thought of it in his mind, accelerated —accelerated with a sudden astonishing speed. It bore down on him with such swiftness that he only just had time to leap across onto the opposite pavement. It disappeared with a flash, turning round the curve of the road further on.

"I wonder," said Sir Stafford to himself. "Now I wonder. Could it be that there *is* someone that doesn't like me? Someone following me, perhaps, watching me make my way home, waiting for an opportunity?"

Colonel Pikeaway, his bulk sprawled out in his chair in the small room in Bloomsbury where he sat from ten to five, with a short interval for lunch, was surrounded as usual by an atmosphere of thick cigar smoke; with his eyes closed, only an occasional blink showed that he was awake and not asleep. He seldom raised his head. Somebody had said that he looked like a cross between an ancient Buddha and a large blue frog, with perhaps, as some impudent youngster had added, just a touch of a bar sinister from a hippopotamus in his ancestry.

The gentle buzz of the intercom on his desk roused him. He blinked three times and opened his eyes. He stretched forth a rather weary-looking hand and picked up the receiver.

"Well," he said.

His secretary's voice spoke.

"The minister is here waiting to see you."

"Is he now?" said Colonel Pikeaway. "And what minister is that? The Baptist minister from the church round the corner?"

"Oh, no, Colonel Pikeaway, it's Sir George Packham."

"Pity," said Colonel Pikeaway, breathing asthmatically. "Great pity. The Reverend McGill is far more amusing. There's a splendid touch of hellfire about him."

"Shall I bring him in, Colonel Pikeaway?"

"I suppose he will expect to be brought in at once. Undersecretaries are far more touchy than secretaries of state," said Colonel Pikeaway gloomily. "All these ministers insist on coming in and having kittens all over the place."

Sir George Packham was shown in. He coughed and wheezed. Most people did. The windows of the small room were tightly closed. Colonel Pikeaway reclined in his chair, completely smothered in cigar ash. The atmosphere was almost unbearable, and the room was known in official circles as the "small cathouse."

"Ah, my dear fellow," said Sir George, speaking briskly and cheerfully in a way that did not match his ascetic and sad appearance. "Quite a long time since we've met, I think."

"Sit down, sit down do," said Pikeaway. "Have a cigar?"

Sir George shuddered slightly.

"No, thank you," he said; "no, thanks very much."

He looked hard at the windows. Colonel Pikeaway did not take the hint. Sir George cleared his throat and coughed again before saying:

"Er—I believe Horsham has been to see you."

"Yes, Horsham's been and said his piece," said Colonel Pikeaway, slowly allowing his eyes to close again.

"I thought it was the best way. I mean that he should call upon you here. It's most important that things shouldn't get round anywhere."

"Ah," said Colonel Pikeaway, "but they will, won't they?"

"I beg your pardon?"

"They will," said Colonel Pikeaway.

"I don't know how much you—er—well, know about this last business."

"We know everything here," said Colonel Pikeaway. "That's what we're for."

"Oh—oh, yes, yes, certainly. About Sir S.N.—you know who I mean?"

"Recently a passenger from Frankfurt," said Colonel Pikeaway.

"Most extraordinary business. Most extraordinary. One wonders—one really does not know, one can't begin to imagine . . ."

Colonel Pikeaway listened kindly.

"What is one to think?" pursued Sir George. "Do you know him personally?"

"I've come across him once or twice," said Colonel Pikeaway.

"One really cannot help wondering—"

Colonel Pikeaway subdued a yawn with some difficulty. He was rather tired of Sir George's thinking, wondering, and imagining. He had a poor opinion anyway of Sir George's process of thoughts. A cautious man, a man who could be relied upon to run his department in a cautious manner. Not a man of scintillating intellect. Perhaps, thought Colonel Pikeaway, all the better for that. At any rate, those who think and wonder and are not quite sure are reasonably safe in the place where God and the electors have put them.

"One cannot quite forget," continued Sir George, "the disillusionment we have suffered in the past."

Colonel Pikeaway smiled kindly.

"Charleston, Conway and Courtauld," he said. "Fully trusted, vetted and approved of. All beginning with C, all crooked as sin."

"Sometimes I wonder if we can trust anyone," said Sir George unhappily.

"That's easy," said Colonel Pikeaway, "you can't."

"Now take Stafford Nye," said Sir George. "Good family, excellent family, knew his father, his grandfather."

"Often a slip-up in the third generation," said Colonel Pikeaway.

The remark did not help Sir George.

"I cannot help doubting—I mean, sometimes he doesn't really seem serious."

"Took my two nieces to see the châteaux of the Loire when I was a young man," said Colonel Pikeaway unexpectedly. "Man fishing on the bank. I had my fishing rod with me, too. He said to me, *'Vous n'êtes pas un pêcheur sérieux? Vous avez des femmes avec vous.'* "

"You mean you think Sir Stafford—?"

"No, no, never been mixed up with women much. Irony's his trouble. Likes surprising people. He can't help liking to score off people."

"Well, that's not very satisfactory, is it?"

"Why not?" said Colonel Pikeaway. "Liking a private joke is much better than having some deal with a defector."

"If one could feel that he was really sound. What would you say—your personal opinion?"

"Sound as a bell," said Colonel Pikeaway. "If a bell is sound. It makes a sound, but that's different, isn't it?" he smiled kindly. "Shouldn't worry, if I were you," he said.

Sir Stafford Nye pushed aside his cup of coffee. He picked up the newspaper, glancing over the headlines, then he turned it carefully to the page which gave Personal advertisements. He'd looked down that particular column for seven days now. It was disappointing but not surprising. Why on earth should he expect to find an answer? His eye went slowly down miscellaneous peculiarities which had always made that particular page rather fascinating in his eyes. They were not so strictly personal. Half of them or even more than half were disguised advertisements or offers of things for sale or wanted for sale. They should perhaps have been put under a different heading, but they had found their way here, considering that they were more likely to catch the eye that way. They included one or two of the hopeful variety.

> "Young man who objects to hard work and who would like an easy life would be glad to undertake a job that would suit him."

> "Girl wants to travel to Cambodia. Refuses to look after children."

> "Firearm used at Waterloo. What offers."

> "Glorious fun fur coat. Must be sold immediately. Owner going abroad."

> "Do you know Jenny Capstan? Her cakes are superb. Come to 14 Lizzard Street, S.W.3."

For a moment Stafford Nye's finger came to a stop. Jenny Capstan. He liked the name. Was there any Lizzard Street? He supposed so. He had never heard of it. With a sigh, the finger went down the column and almost at once was arrested once more.

"Passenger from Frankfurt, Thursday Nov. 11th, Hungerford Bridge 7:20."

Thursday, November 11th. That was—yes, that was today. Sir Stafford Nye leaned back in his chair and drank more coffee. He was excited, stimulated. Hungerford. Hungerford Bridge. He got up and went into the kitchenette. Mrs. Worrit was cutting potatoes into strips and throwing them into a large bowl of water. She looked up with some slight surprise.

"Anything you want, sir?"

"Yes," said Sir Stafford Nye. "If anyone said Hungerford Bridge to you, where would you go?"

"Where should I go?" Mrs. Worrit considered. "You mean if I wanted to go, do you?"

"We can proceed on that assumption."

"Well, then, I suppose I'd go to Hungerford Bridge, wouldn't I?"

"You mean you would go to Hungerford in Berkshire?"

"Where is that?" said Mrs. Worrit.

"Eight miles beyond Newbury."

"I've heard of Newbury. My old man backed a horse there last year. Did well, too."

"So you'd go to Hungerford near Newbury?"

"No, of course I wouldn't," said Mrs. Worrit. "Go all that way—what for? I'd go to Hungerford Bridge, of course."

"You mean—?"

"Well, it's near Charing Cross. You know where it is. Over the Thames."

"Yes," said Sir Stafford Nye. "Yes, I do know where it is quite well. Thank you, Mrs. Worrit."

It had been, he felt, rather like tossing a penny heads or tails. An advertisement in a morning paper in London meant Hungerford Railway Bridge in London. Presumably, therefore, that is what the advertiser meant, although about this particular advertiser Sir Stafford Nye was not at all sure. Her ideas, from the brief experience he had had of her, were original ideas. They were not the normal responses to be expected. But still, what else could one do? Besides, there were probably other Hungerfords, and possibly they would also have bridges, in various parts of England. But today, well, today he would see.

It was a cold, windy evening with occasional bursts of thin misty rain. Sir Stafford Nye turned up the collar of his mackintosh and plodded on. It was not the first time he had gone across Hungerford Bridge, but it had never seemed to him a walk to take for pleasure. Beneath him was the river, and crossing the bridge were large quantities of hurrying figures like himself.

Their mackintoshes pulled round them, their hats pulled down, and on the part of one and all of them an earnest desire to get home and out of the wind and rain as soon as possible. It would be, thought Sir Stafford Nye, very difficult to recognize anybody in this scurrying crowd. Seven-twenty. Not a good moment to choose for a rendezvous of any kind. Perhaps it was Hungerford Bridge in Berkshire. Anyway, it seemed very odd.

He plodded on. He kept an even pace, not overtaking those ahead of him, pushing past those coming the opposite way. He went fast enough not to be overtaken by the others behind him, though it would be possible for them to do so if they wanted to. A joke, perhaps, thought Stafford Nye. Not quite his kind of joke, but someone else's.

And yet—not her brand of humor either, he would have thought. Hurrying figures passed him again, pushing him slightly aside. A woman in a mackintosh was coming along, walking heavily. She collided with him, slipped, dropped to her knees. He assisted her up.

"All right?"

"Yes, thanks."

She hurried on, but as she passed him, her wet hand, by which he had held her as he pulled her to her feet, slipped something into the palm of his hand, closing the fingers over it. Then she was gone, vanishing behind him, mingling with the crowd. Stafford Nye went on. He couldn't overtake her. She did not wish to be overtaken, either. He hurried on and his hand held something firmly. And so, at long last, it seemed, he came to the end of the bridge on the Surrey side.

A few minutes later he had turned into a small café and sat there behind a table, ordering coffee. Then he looked at what was in his hand. It was a very thin oilskin envelope. Inside it was a cheap quality white envelope. That, too, he opened. What was inside surprised him. It was a ticket.

A ticket for the Festival Hall for the following evening.

5

Wagnerian Motif

SIR STAFFORD NYE adjusted himself more comfortably in his seat and listened to the persistent hammering of the Nibelungen, with which the program began. Though he enjoyed Wagnerian opera, *Siegfried* was by no means his favorite of the operas composing the Ring. *Rheingold* and *Götterdämmerung* were his two preferences. The music of the young Siegfried, listening to the songs of the birds, had always for some strange reason irritated him instead of filling him with melodic satisfaction. It might have been because he went to a performance in Munich in his young days which had displayed a magnificent tenor of unfortunately overmagnificent proportions, and he had been too young to divorce the joy of music from the visual joy of seeing a young Siegfried that looked even passably young. The fact of an outsized tenor rolling about on the ground in an excess of boyishness had revolted him. He was also not particularly fond of birds and forest murmurs. No, give him the Rhine Maidens every time, although in Munich even the Rhine Maidens in those days had been of fairly solid proportions. But that mattered less. Carried away by the melodic flow of water and the joyous impersonal song, he had not allowed visual appreciation to matter.

From time to time he looked about him casually. He had taken his seat fairly early. It was a full house, as it usually was. The intermission came. Sir Stafford rose and looked about him. The seat beside his had remained empty. Someone who was supposed to have arrived had not arrived! Was that the answer, or was it merely a case of being excluded because someone had arrived late, which practice still held on the occasions when Wagnerian music was listened to?

He went out, strolled about, drank a cup of coffee, smoked a cigarette, and returned when the summons came. This time as he drew near, he saw that the seat next to his was filled. Immediately his excitement returned. He regained his seat and sat down. Yes, it was the woman of the Frankfurt air lounge. She did not look at him; she was looking straight ahead. Her face in profile was as clean-cut and pure as he remembered it. Her head turned slightly, and her eyes passed over him but without recognition. So intent was that nonrecognition that it was as good as a word spoken. This was a meeting that was not to be acknowledged. Not now, at any event. The lights began to dim. The woman beside him turned.

"Excuse me; could I look at your program? I have dropped mine, I'm afraid, coming to my seat."

"Of course," he said.

He handed over the program and she took it from him. She opened it, studied the items. The lights went lower. The second half of the program began. It started with the overture to *Lohengrin*. At the end of it she handed back the program to him with a few words of thanks.

"Thank you so much. It was very kind of you."

The next item was the *Siegfried* forest murmur music. He consulted the program she had returned to him. It was then that he noticed something faintly penciled at the foot of a page. He did not attempt to read it now. Indeed, the light would have not been sufficient. He merely closed the program and held it. He had not, he was quite sure, written anything there himself. Not, that is, in his own program. She had, he thought, had her own program ready, folded perhaps in her handbag, and had already written some message ready to pass to him. Altogether, it seemed to him, there was still that atmosphere of secrecy, of danger. The meeting on Hungerford Bridge and the envelope with the ticket forced into his hand. And now the silent woman who sat beside him. He glanced at her once or twice with the quick, careless glance that one gives to a stranger sitting next to one. She lolled back in her seat; her high-necked dress was of dull black crêpe, an antique torque of gold encircled her neck. Her dark hair was cropped closely and shaped to her head. She did not glance at him or return any look. He wondered. Was there someone in the seats of the Festival Hall watching her—or watching him? Noting whether they looked or spoke to each other? Presumably there must be, or there must be at least the possibility of such a thing. She had answered his appeal in the newspaper advertisement. Let that be enough for him. His curiosity was unimpaired, but he did at least know now that Daphne Theodofanous—alias Mary Ann—was here in London. There were possibilities in the future of his learning more of what was afoot. But the plan of campaign must be left to her. He must follow her lead. As he had obeyed her in the airport, so he would obey her now and—let him admit it—life had become suddenly more interesting. This was better than the boring conferences of his political life. Had a car really tried to run him down the other night? He thought it had. Two attempts—not only one. It was easy enough to imagine that one was the target of assault, people drove so recklessly nowadays that you could easily fancy malice aforethought when it was not so. He folded his program, did not look at it again. The music came to its end. The woman next to him spoke. She did not turn her head or appear to speak to him, but she spoke aloud, with a little sigh between the words as though she was communing with herself or possibly to her neighbor on the other side.

"The young Siegfried," she said, and sighed again.

The program ended with the March from *Die Meistersinger.* After enthusiastic applause, people began to leave their seats. He waited to see if she would give him any lead, but she did not. She gathered up her wrap, moved out of the row of chairs, and with a slightly accelerated step, moved along with other people and disappeared in the crowd.

Stafford Nye regained his car and drove home. Arrived there, he spread out the Festival Hall program on his desk and examined it carefully, after putting the coffee to percolate.

The program was disappointing, to say the least of it. There did not appear to be any message inside. Only on one page, above the list of the items, were the pencil marks that he had vaguely observed. But they were not words or letters or even figures. They appeared to be merely a musical notation. It was as though someone had scribbled a phrase of music with a somewhat inadequate pencil. For a moment it occurred to Stafford Nye there might perhaps be a secret message he could bring out by applying heat. Rather gingerly, and in a way rather ashamed of his melodramatic fancy, he held it toward the bar of the electric fire, but nothing resulted. With a sigh he tossed the program back onto the table. But he felt justifiably annoyed. All this rigmarole, a rendezvous on a windy and rainy bridge overlooking the river! Sitting through a concert by the side of a woman of whom he yearned to ask at least a dozen questions—and at the end of it? Nothing! No further on. Still, she had met him. But why? If she didn't want to speak to him, to make further arrangements with him, why had she come at all?

His eyes passed idly across the room to his bookcase, which he reserved for various thrillers, works of detective fiction and an occasional volume of science fiction; he shook his head. Fiction, he thought, was infinitely superior to real life. Dead bodies, mysterious telephone calls, beautiful foreign spies in profusion! However, this particular elusive lady might not have done with him yet. Next time, he thought, he would make some arrangements of his own. Two could play at the game that she was playing.

He pushed aside the program and drank another cup of coffee and went to the window. He had the program still in his hand. As he looked out toward the street below, his eyes fell back again on the open program in his hand and he hummed to himself, almost unconsciously. He had a good ear for music and he could hum the notes that were scrawled there quite easily. Vaguely they sounded familiar as he hummed them. He increased his voice a little. What was it now? Tum, tum, tum tum ti-tum. Tum. Tum. Yes, definitely familiar.

He started opening his letters.

They were mostly uninteresting. A couple of invitations, one from the American Embassy, one from Lady Athelhampton, a charity variety performance which Royalty would attend and for which it was suggested five guineas would not be an exorbitant fee to obtain a seat. He threw them aside lightly. He doubted very much whether he wished to accept any of them. He decided that instead of remaining in London he would without more ado go and see his Aunt Matilda, as he had promised. He was fond of his Aunt Matilda, though he did not visit her very often. She lived in a rehabilitated apartment consisting of a series of rooms in one wing of a large Georgian manor house in the country, which she had inherited from his grandfather. She had a large, beautifully proportioned sitting room, a small oval dining room, a new kitchen made from the old housekeeper's room, two bedrooms for guests, a large comfortable bedroom for herself with an adjoining bathroom, and adequate quarters for a patient companion who shared her daily life. The remains of a faithful domestic staff were well provided for and housed. The rest of the house remained under dust sheets, with periodical cleaning. Stafford Nye was fond of the place, having spent holidays there as a boy. It had been a gay house then. His eldest uncle had lived there with his wife and their two children. Yes, it had been pleasant there then. There had been money and a sufficient staff to run it. He had not specially noticed in those days the portraits and pictures. There had been large-sized examples of Victorian art occupying pride of place—overcrowding the walls, but there had been other masters of an older age. Yes, there had been some good portraits there. A Raeburn, two Lawrences, a Gainsborough, a Lely, two rather dubious Vandykes. A couple of Turners, too. Some of them had had to be sold to provide the family with money. He still enjoyed, when visiting there, strolling about and studying the family pictures.

His Aunt Matilda was a great chatterbox, but she always enjoyed his visits. He was fond of her in a desultory way, but he was not quite sure why it was that he had suddenly wanted to visit her now. And what was it that had brought family portraits into his mind? Could it have been because there was a portrait of his sister Pamela by one of the leading artists of the day twenty years ago? He would like to see that portrait of Pamela and look at it more closely. See how close the resemblance had been between the stranger who had disrupted his life in this really outrageous fashion and his sister.

He picked up the Festival Hall program again with some irritation and began to hum the penciled notes. Tum, tum, ti-tum— Then it came to him and he knew what it was. It was the *Siegfried* motif. Siegfried's horn. The Young Siegfried motif. That was what the woman had said last night. Not apparently to him, not apparently to anybody. But it had been the message, a message that would have meant nothing to anyone around, since it would have seemed to refer to the music that had just been played. And the motif had been written on his program also in musical terms. The Young Siegfried. It must have meant something. Well, perhaps further enlightenment would come. The Young Siegfried. What the hell did that mean? Why and how and when and what? Ridiculous! All those questioning words.

He rang the telephone and obtained Aunt Matilda's number.

"But of course, Staffy dear, it will be lovely to have you. Take the four-thirty train. It still runs, you know, but it gets here an hour and a half later. And it leaves Paddington later—five-fifteen! That's what they mean by improving the railways, I suppose. Stops at several most absurd stations on the way. All right. Horace will meet you at King's Marston."

"He's still there then?"

"Of course he's still there."

"I suppose he is," said Sir Stafford Nye.

Horace, once a groom, then a coachman, had survived as a chauffeur, and apparently was still surviving. "He must be at least eighty," said Sir Stafford. He smiled to himself.

6

Portrait of a Lady

"YOU LOOK VERY nice and brown, dear," said Aunt Matilda, surveying him appreciatively. "That's Malaya, I suppose. If it *was* Malaya you went to? Or was it Siam or Thailand? They change the names of all these places and really it makes it very difficult. Anyway, it wasn't Vietnam, was it? You know, I don't like the sound of Vietnam *at all.* It's all very confusing, North Vietnam and South Vietnam and the Viet-Cong and the Viet—whatever the other thing is and all wanting to fight each other and nobody wanting to stop. They won't go to Paris or wherever it is and sit round tables and talk sensibly. Don't you think really, dear—I've been thinking it over and I thought it would be a very nice solution—couldn't you make a lot of football fields and then they could all go and fight each other there, but with less lethal weapons. Not that nasty palm burning stuff. You know. Just hit each other and punch each other and all that. They'd enjoy it, everyone would enjoy it, and you could charge admission for people to go and see them do it. I do think, really, that we don't understand giving people the things they really want."

"I think it's a very fine idea of yours, Aunt Matilda," said Sir Stafford Nye as he kissed a pleasantly perfumed, pale pink wrinkled cheek. "And how are you, my dear?"

"Well, I'm old," said Lady Matilda Cleckheaton. "Yes, I'm old. Of course you don't know what it is to be old. If it isn't one thing, it's another. Rheumatism or arthritis or a nasty bit of asthma or a sore throat or an ankle you've turned. Always something, you know. Nothing very important. But there it is. Why have you come to see me, dear?"

Sir Stafford was slightly taken aback by the directness of the query.

"I usually come and see you when I return from a trip abroad."

"You'll have to come one chair nearer," said Aunt Matilda. "I'm just that bit deafer since you saw me last. You look different. . . . Why do you look different?"

"Because I'm more sunburnt. You said so."

"Nonsense, that's not what I mean at all. Don't tell me it's a girl at last."

"A girl?"

"Well, I've always felt it might be one someday. The trouble is you've got too much sense of humor."

"Now why should you think that?"

"Well, it's what people do think about you. Oh, yes, they do. Your sense of humor is in the way of your career, too. You know, you're all mixed up with all these people. Diplomatic and political. What they call younger statesmen and elder statesmen and middle statesmen, too. And all those different parties. Really, I think it's too silly to have too many parties. First of all those awful, awful Labour people." She raised her Conservative nose into the air. "Why, when I was a girl, there wasn't such a thing as a *Labour* Party. Nobody would have known what you meant by it. They'd have said 'nonsense.' Pity it wasn't nonsense, too. And then there's the Liberals, of course, but they're terribly wet. And then there are the Tories, or the Conservatives, as they call themselves again now."

"And what's the matter with them?" asked Stafford Nye, smiling slightly.

"Too many earnest women. Makes them lack gaiety, you know."

"Oh, well, no political party goes in for gaiety much nowadays."

"Just so," said Aunt Matilda. "And then of course that's where you go wrong. You want to cheer things up. You want to have a little gaiety and so you make a little gentle fun at people and of course they don't like it. They say, *'Ce n'est pas un garçon sérieux,'* like that man in the fishing story."

Sir Stafford Nye laughed. His eyes were wandering round the room.

"What are you looking at?" said Lady Matilda.

"Your pictures."

"You don't want me to sell them, do you? Everyone seems to be selling their pictures nowadays. Old Lord Grampion, you know. He sold his Turners and he sold some of his ancestors as well. And Geoffrey Gouldman. All those lovely horses of his. By Stubbs, weren't they? Something like that. Really, the prices one gets!

"But I don't want to sell my pictures. I like them. Most of them in this room have a real interest because they're ancestors. I know nobody wants ancestors nowadays, but then I'm old-fashioned. I like ancestors. My own ancestors, I mean. What are you looking at? Pamela?"

"Yes, I was. I was thinking about her the other day."

"Astonishing how alike you two are. I mean, it's not even as though you were twins, though they say that different sex twins, even if they are twins, can't be identical, if you know what I mean."

"So Shakespeare must have made rather a mistake over Viola and Sebastian."

"Well, ordinary brothers and sisters can be alike, can't they? You and Pamela were always very alike—to look at, I mean."

"Not in any other way? Don't you think we were alike in character?"

"No, not in the least. That's the funny part of it. But of course you and Pamela have what I call the family face. Not a Nye face. I mean the Baldwen-White face."

Sir Stafford Nye had never quite been able to compete when it came down to talking on a question of genealogy with his great-aunt.

"I've always thought that you and Pamela both took after Alexa," she went on.

"Which was Alexa?"

"Your great-great—I think one more great—grandmother. Hungarian. A Hungarian countess or baroness or something. Your great-great-great-grandfather fell in love with her when he was at Vienna in the Embassy. Yes. Hungarian. That's what she was. Very sporting, too. They are sporting, you know, Hungarians. She rode to hounds, rode magnificently."

"Is she in the picture gallery?"

"She's on the first landing. Just over the head of the stairs, a little to the right."

"I must go and look at her when I go to bed."

"Why don't you go and look at her now and then you can come back and talk about her."

"I will if you like." He smiled at her.

He ran out of the room and up the staircase. Yes, she had a sharp eye, old Matilda. That was the face. That was the face that he had seen and remembered. Remembered not for its likeness to himself, not even for its likeness to Pamela, but for a closer resemblance still to this picture here. A handsome girl brought home by his ambassador great-great-great-grandfather if that was enough greats. Aunt Matilda was never satisfied with only a few. About twenty she had been. She had come here and been high-spirited and rode a horse magnificently and danced divinely and men had fallen in love with her. But she had been faithful, so it was always said, to his great-great-great-grandfather, a very steady and sober member of the Diplomatic Service. She had gone with him to foreign embassies and returned here and had had children—three or four children, he believed! Through one of those children the inheritance of her face, her nose, the turn of her neck had been passed down to him and to his sister Pamela. He wondered if the young woman who had doped his beer and forced him to lend her his cloak and who had depicted herself as being in danger of death unless he did what she asked, had been possibly related as a fifth or sixth cousin removed, a descendant of the woman pictured on the wall at which he looked. Well, it could be. They had been of the same nationality, perhaps. Anyway, their faces had resembled each other a good deal. How upright she'd sat at the concert, how straight that profile, the thin, slightly arched aquiline nose. And the atmosphere that hung about her.

"Find it?" asked Lady Matilda when her nephew returned to the white drawing room, as her sitting room was usually called. "Interesting face, isn't it?"

"Yes, quite handsome, too."

"It's much better to be interesting than handsome. But you haven't been in Hungary or Austria, have you? You wouldn't meet anyone like her out in Malaya? She wouldn't be sitting round a table there making little notes or correcting speeches or things like that. She was a wild creature, by all accounts. Lovely manners and all the rest of it. But wild. Wild as a wild bird. She didn't know what danger was."

"How do you know so much about her?"

"Oh, I agree I wasn't a contemporary of hers. I wasn't born until several years after she was dead. All the same, I've always been interested in her. She was adventurous, you know. Very adventurous. Very queer stories were told about her, about things she was mixed up in."

"And how did my great-great-great-grandfather react to that?"

"I expect it worried him to death," said Lady Matilda. "They say he was devoted to her, though. By the way, Staffy, did you ever read *The Prisoner of Zenda?*"

"*Prisoner of Zenda?* Sounds very familiar."

"Well, of course it's familiar, it's a book."

"Yes, yes, I realize it's a book."

"You wouldn't know about it, I expect. After your time. But when I was a girl—that's about the first taste of romance we got. Not pop singers or Beatles. Just a romantic novel. We weren't allowed to read novels when I was young. Not in the morning, anyway. You could read them in the afternoon."

"What extraordinary rules," said Sir Stafford. "Why is it wrong to read novels in the morning and not in the afternoon?"

"Well, in the mornings, you see, girls were supposed to be doing something useful. You know, doing the flowers or cleaning the silver photograph frames. All the things we girls did. Doing a bit of studying with the governess—all that sort of thing. In the afternoon we were allowed to sit down and read a storybook, and *The Prisoner of Zenda* was usually one of the first ones that came our way."

"A very nice, respectable story, was it? I seem to remember something about it. Perhaps I did read it. All very pure, I suppose. Not too sexy?"

"Certainly not. We didn't have sexy books. We had romance. *The Prisoner of Zenda* was very romantic. One fell in love, usually, with the hero, Rudolf Rassendyll."

"I seem to remember that name, too. Bit florid, isn't it?"

"Well, I still think it was rather a romantic name. Twelve years old, I must have been. It made me think of it, you know, your going up and looking at that portrait. Princess Flavia," she added.

Stafford Nye was smiling at her.

"You look young and pink and very sentimental," he said.

"Well, that's just what I'm feeling. Girls can't feel like that nowadays. They're swooning with love, or they're fainting when somebody plays the guitar or sings in a very loud voice, but they're not sentimental. But I wasn't in love with Rudolf Rassendyll. I was in love with the other one—his double."

"Did he have a double?"

"Oh, yes, a king. The King of Ruritania."

"Ah, of course, now I know. That's where the word Ruritania comes from: one is always throwing it about. Yes, I think I did read it, you know. The King of Ruritania, and Rudolf Rassendyll was stand-in for the King and fell in love with Princess Flavia, to whom the King was officially betrothed."

Lady Matilda gave some more deep sighs.

"Yes. Rudolf Rassendyll had inherited his red hair from an ancestress, and

somewhere in the book he bows to the portrait and says something about the
—I can't remember the name now—the Countess Amelia or something like
that from whom he inherited his looks and all the rest of it. So I looked at you
and thought of you as Rudolf Rassendyll and you went out and looked at a
picture of someone who might have been an ancestress of yours, and saw
whether she reminded you of someone. So you're mixed up in a romance of
some kind, are you?"

"What on earth makes you say that?"

"Well, there aren't so many patterns in life, you know. One recognizes
patterns as they come up. It's like a book on knitting. About sixty-five different fancy stitches. Well, you know a particular stitch when you see it. Your
stitch, at the moment, I should say, is the romantic adventure." She sighed.
"But you won't tell me about it, I suppose."

"There's nothing to tell," said Sir Stafford.

"You always were quite an accomplished liar. Well, never mind. You bring
her to see me sometime. That's all I'd like, before the doctors succeed in
killing me with yet another type of antibiotic that they've just discovered. The
different colored pills I've had to take by this time! You wouldn't believe it."

"I don't know why you say 'she' and 'her'—"

"Don't you? Oh, well, I know a she when I come across a she. There's a
she somewhere dodging about in your life. What beats me is how you found
her. In Malaya, at the conference table? Ambassador's daughter or minister's
daughter? Good-looking secretary from the embassy pool? No, none of it
seems to fit. Ship coming home? No, you don't use ships nowadays. Plane,
perhaps."

"You are getting slightly nearer," Sir Stafford Nye could not help saying.

"Ah!" She pounced. "Air hostess?"

He shook his head.

"Ah, well. Keep your secret. I shall find out, mind you. I've always had a
good nose for things going on where you're concerned. Things generally as
well. Of course I'm out of everything nowadays, but I meet my old cronies
from time to time and it's quite easy, you know, to get a hint or two from
them. People are worried. Everywhere—they're worried."

"You mean there's a general kind of discontent—upset?"

"No, I didn't mean that at all. I mean the high-ups are worried. Our awful
governments are worried. The dear old sleepy Foreign Office is worried.
There are things going on, things that shouldn't be. Unrest."

"Student unrest?"

"Oh, student unrest is just one flower on the tree. It's blossoming everywhere and in every country, or so it seems. I've got a nice girl who comes,
you know, and reads the papers to me in the mornings. I can't read them
properly myself. She's got a nice voice. Takes down my letters and she reads
things from the papers and she's a good, kind girl. She reads the things I want
to know, not the things that she thinks are right for me to know. Yes, every-

one's worried, as far as I can make out, and this, mind you, came more or less from a very old friend of mine."

"One of your old military cronies?"

"He's a major general, if that's what you mean, retired a good many years ago but still in the know. Youth is what you might call the spearhead of it all. But that's not really what's so worrying. They—whoever *they* are—work through youth. Youth in every country. Youth urged on. Youth chanting slogans—slogans that sound exciting, though they don't always know what they mean. So easy to start a revolution. That's natural to youth. All youth has always rebelled. You rebel, you pull down, you want the world to be different from what it is. But you're blind, too. There are bandages over the eyes of youth. They can't see where things are taking them. What's going to come next? What's in front of them? And who it is behind them, urging them on? That's what's frightening about it. You know, someone holding out the carrot to get the donkey to come along and at the same time there is someone behind the donkey urging it on with a stick."

"You've got some extraordinary fancies."

"They're not only fancies, my dear boy. That's what people said about Hitler. Hitler and Hitler Youth. But it was a long, careful preparation. It was a war that was worked out in detail. It was a fifth column being planted in different countries all ready for the supermen. The supermen were to be the flower of the German nation. That's what they thought and believed in passionately. Somebody else is perhaps believing something like that now. It's a creed that they'll be willing to accept—if it's offered cleverly enough."

"Who are you talking about? Do you mean the Chinese or the Russians? What do you mean?"

"I don't know. I haven't the faintest idea. But there's something somewhere, and it's running on the same lines. Pattern again, you see. Pattern! The Russians? Bogged down by Communism, I should think they're considered old-fashioned. The Chinese? I think they've lost their way. Too much Chairman Mao, perhaps. I don't know who these people are who are doing the planning. As I said before, it's why and where and when and *who.*"

"Very interesting."

"It's so frightening, this same idea that always recurs. History repeating itself. The young hero, the golden superman that all must follow." She paused, then said, "Same idea, you know. The young Siegfried."

7

Advice from Great-Aunt Matilda

GREAT-AUNT MATILDA looked at him. She had a very sharp and shrewd eye. Stafford Nye had noticed that before. He noticed it particularly at this moment.

"So you've heard that term before," she said. "I see."

"What does it mean?"

"You don't know?" She raised her eyebrows.

"Cross my heart and wish to die," said Sir Stafford, in nursery language.

"Yes, we always used to say that, didn't we?" said Lady Matilda. "Do you really mean what you're saying?"

"I don't know anything about it."

"But you'd heard the term before."

"Yes. Someone said it to me."

"Anyone important?"

"It could be. I suppose it could be. What do you mean by 'anyone important'?"

"Well, you've been involved in various government missions lately, haven't you? You've represented this poor, miserable country as best you could, which I shouldn't wonder wasn't rather better than many others could do, sitting round a table and talking. I don't know whether anything's come of all that."

"Probably not," said Stafford Nye. "After all, one isn't optimistic when one goes into these things."

"One does one's best," said Lady Matilda correctively.

"A very Christian principle. Nowadays if one does one's worst one often seems to get on a good deal better. What does all this mean, Aunt Matilda?"

"I don't suppose *I* know," said his aunt.

"Well, you very often do know things."

"Not exactly. I just pick up things here and there."

"Yes?"

"I've got a few old friends left, you know. Friends who are in the know. Of course most of them are either practically stone-deaf or half blind or a little bit gone in the top story or unable to walk straight. But something still functions. Something, shall we say, up here." She hit the top of her neatly arranged white head. "There's a good deal of alarm and despondency about. More than usual. That's one of the things I've picked up."

663

"Isn't there always?"

"Yes, yes, but this is a bit more than that. Active instead of passive? as you might say. For a long time, as I have noticed from the outside, and you, no doubt from the inside, we have felt that things are in a mess. A rather bad mess. But now we've got to a point where we feel that perhaps something might have been done about the mess. There's an element of danger in it. Something is going on—something is brewing. Not just in one country. In quite a lot of countries. They've recruited a service of their own, and the danger about that is that it's a service of young people. And the kind of people who will go anywhere, do anything, unfortunately believe anything, and so long as they are promised a certain amount of pulling down, wrecking, throwing spanners in the works, then they think the cause must be a good one and that the world will be a different place. They're not creative, that's the trouble—only destructive. The creative young write poems, write books, probably compose music, paint pictures just as they always have done. They'll be all right—but once people learn to love destruction for its own sake, evil leadership gets its chance."

"You say 'they' or 'them.' Who do you mean?"

"Wish I knew," said Lady Matilda. "Yes, I wish I knew. Very much indeed. If I hear anything useful, I'll tell you. Then you can do something about it."

"Unfortunately, *I* haven't got anyone to tell, I mean to pass it on to."

"Yes, don't pass it on to just anyone! You can't trust people. Don't pass it on to any one of those idiots in the government, or connected with government or hoping to be participating in government after this lot runs out. Politicians don't have time to look at the world they're living in. They see the country they're living in and they see it as one vast electoral platform. That's quite enough to put on their plates for the time being. They do things which they honestly believe will make things better, and then they're surprised when they don't make things better because they're not the things that people want to have. And one can't help coming to the conclusion that politicians have a feeling that they have a kind of divine right to tell lies in a good cause. It's not really so very long ago since Mr. Baldwin made his famous remark—'If I had spoken the truth, I should have lost the election.' Prime ministers still feel like that. Now and again we have a great man, thank God. But it's rare."

"Well, what do you suggest ought to be done?"

"Are you asking my advice? Mine? Do you know how old I am?"

"Getting on for ninety," suggested her nephew.

"Not quite as old as that," said Lady Matilda, slightly affronted. "Do I look it, my dear boy?"

"No, darling. You look a nice, comfortable sixty-six."

"That's better," said Lady Matilda. "Quite untrue. But better. If I get a tip of any kind from one of my dear old admirals or an old general or even possibly an air marshal—they do hear things, you know—they've got cronies still and the old boys get together and talk. And so it gets around. There's always been the grapevine and there still is a grapevine, no matter how elderly the people are. The young Siegfried. We want a clue to just what that means. I don't know if he's a person or a password or the name of a club or a new Messiah or a pop singer. But that term covers *something*. There's the musical motif, too. I've rather forgotten my Wagnerian days." Her aged voice croaked out a partially recognizable melody. "Siegfried's horn call, isn't that it? Get a recorder, why don't you? Do I mean a recorder? I don't mean a record that you put on a gramophone—I mean the things that schoolchildren play. They have classes for them. Went to a talk the other day. Our vicar got it up. Quite interesting. You know, tracing the history of the recorder and the kind of recorders there were from the Elizabethan age onwards. Some big, some small, all different notes and sounds. Very interesting. Interesting hearing in two senses. The recorders themselves. Some of them give out lovely noises. And the history. Yes. Well, what was I saying?"

"You told me to get one of these instruments, I gather."

"Yes. Get a recorder and learn to blow Siegfried's horn call on it. You're musical: you always were. You can manage that, I hope?"

"Well, it seems a very small part to play in the salvation of the world, but I daresay I could manage that."

"And have the thing ready. Because, you see—" she tapped on the table with her spectacle case—"you might want it to impress the wrong people sometime. Might come in useful. They'd welcome you with open arms and then you might learn a bit."

"You certainly have ideas," said Sir Stafford admiringly.

"What else can you have when you're my age?" said his great-aunt. "You can't get about. You can't meddle with people much; you can't do any gardening. All you *can* do is sit in your chair and have ideas. Remember that when you're forty years older."

"One remark you made interested me."

"Only one?" said Lady Matilda. "That's rather poor measure, considering how much I've been talking. What was it?"

"You suggested that I might be capable of impressing the wrong people with my recorder. Did you mean that?"

"Well, it's one way, isn't it? The right people don't matter. But the wrong people—well, you've got to find out things, haven't you? You've got to permeate things. Rather like a death-watch beetle," she said thoughtfully.

"So I should make significant noises in the night?"

"Well, that sort of thing, yes. We had a death-watch beetle in the east wing here once. Very expensive it was to put it right. I daresay it will be just as expensive to put the world right."

"In fact, a good deal more expensive," said Stafford Nye.

"That won't matter," said Lady Matilda. "People never mind spending a great deal of money. It impresses them. It's when you want to do things nice and economically, they won't play. We're the same people, you know. In this country, I mean. We're the same people we always were."

"What do you mean by that?"

"We're capable of doing big things. We were good at running an empire. We weren't good at *keeping* an empire running, but then you see we didn't need an empire anymore. And we recognized that. Too difficult to keep up. Robbie made me see that," she added.

"Robbie?" It was faintly familiar.

"Robbie Shoreham. Robert Shoreham. He's a very old friend of mine. Paralyzed down the left side. But he can talk still and he's got a moderately good hearing aid."

"Besides being one of the most famous physicists in the world," said Stafford Nye. "So he's another of your old cronies, is he?"

"Known him since he was a boy," said Lady Matilda. "I suppose it surprises you that we should be friends, have a lot in common and enjoy talking together?"

"Well, I shouldn't have thought that—"

"That we had much to talk about? It's true I could never do mathematics. Fortunately, when I was a girl, one didn't even try. Mathematics came easily to Robbie when he was about four years old, I believe. They say nowadays that that's quite natural. He's got plenty to talk about. He liked me always because I was frivolous and made him laugh. And I'm a good listener, too. And really, he says some very interesting things sometimes."

"So I suppose," said Stafford Nye dryly.

"Now don't be superior. Molière married his housemaid, didn't he, and made a great success of it—if it *is* Molière I mean. If a man's frantic with brains, he doesn't really want a woman who's also frantic with brains to talk to. It would be exhausting. He'd much prefer a lovely nitwit who can make him laugh. I wasn't bad-looking when I was young," said Lady Matilda complacently. "I know I have no academic distinctions. I'm not in the least intellectual. But Robert has always said that I've got a great deal of common sense, of intelligence."

"You're a lovely person," said Sir Stafford Nye. "I enjoy coming to see you and I shall go away remembering all the things you've said to me. There are a good many more things, I expect, that you could tell me, but you're obviously not going to."

"Not until the right moment comes," said Lady Matilda, "but I've got your interests at heart. Let me know what you're doing from time to time. You're dining at the American Embassy, aren't you, next week?"

"How did you know that? I've been asked."

"And you've accepted, I understand."

"Well, it's all in the course of duty." He looked at her curiously. "How do you manage to be so well informed?"

"Oh, Milly told me."

"Milly?"

"Milly Jean Cortman. The American Ambassador's wife. A most attractive creature, you know. Small and rather perfect-looking."

"Oh, you mean Mildred Cortman?"

"She was christened Mildred, but she preferred Milly Jean. I was talking to her on the telephone about some charity matinée or other—she's what we used to call a pocket Venus."

"A most attractive term to use," said Stafford Nye.

8

An Embassy Dinner

As Mrs. Cortman came to meet him with outstretched hand, Stafford Nye recalled the term his great-aunt had used. Milly Jean Cortman was a woman of between thirty-five and forty. She had delicate features, big blue-gray eyes, a very perfectly shaped head with bluish-gray hair tinted to a particularly attractive shade which fitted her with a perfection of grooming. She was very popular in London. Her husband, Sam Cortman, was a big, heavy man, slightly ponderous. He was very proud of his wife. He himself was one of those slow, rather overemphatic talkers. People found their attention occasionally straying when he was elucidating at some length a point which hardly needed making.

"Back from Malaya, aren't you, Sir Stafford? It must have been quite interesting to go out there, though it's not the time of year I'd have chosen. But I'm sure we're all glad to see you back. Let me see now. You know Lady Aldborough and Sir John, and Herr von Roken? Frau von Roken. Mr. and Mrs. Staggenham."

They were all people known to Stafford Nye in more or less degree. There was a Dutchman and his wife whom he had not met before, since they had only just taken up their appointment. The Staggenhams were the Minister of Social Security and his wife. A particularly uninteresting couple, he had always thought.

"And the Countess Renata Zerkowski. I think she said she'd met you before."

"It must be about a year ago. When I was last in England," said the Countess.

And there she was, the passenger from Frankfurt again. Self-possessed, at ease, beautifully turned out in faint gray-blue with a touch of chinchilla. Her hair dressed high (a wig?) and a ruby cross of antique design round her neck.

"Signor Gasparo, Count Reitner, Mr. and Mrs. Arbuthnot."

About twenty-six in all. At dinner, Stafford Nye sat between the dreary

Mrs. Staggenham and Signora Gasparo on the other side of him. Renata Zerkowski sat exactly opposite him.

An embassy dinner. A dinner such as he so often attended, holding much of the same type of guests. Various members of the Diplomatic Corps, junior ministers, one or two industrialists, a sprinkling of socialites usually included because they were good conversationalists, natural, pleasant people to meet, though one or two, thought Stafford Nye, one or two were maybe different. Even while he was busy sustaining his conversation with Signora Gasparo, a charming person to talk to, a chatterbox, slightly flirtatious, his mind was roving in the same way that his eye also roved, though the latter was not very noticeable. As it roved round the dinner table, you would not have said that he was summing up conclusions in his own mind. He had been asked here. Why? For any reason or for no reason in particular. Because his name had come up automatically on the list that the secretaries produced from time to time with checks against such members as were due for their turn. Or as the extra man or the extra woman required for the balancing of the table. He had always been in request when an extra was needed.

"Oh, yes," a diplomatic hostess would say, "Stafford Nye will do beautifully. You will put him next to Madame So-and-so, or Lady Somebody-else."

He had been asked perhaps to fill in for no further reason than that. And yet, he wondered. He knew by experience that there were certain other reasons. And so his eye, with its swift social amiability, its air of not looking really at anything in particular, was busy.

Among these guests there was someone perhaps who for some reason mattered, was important. Someone who had been asked—not to fill in—on the contrary—someone who had had a selection of other guests invited to fit in round him—or her. Someone who mattered. He wondered—he wondered which of them it might be.

Cortman knew, of course. Milly Jean, perhaps. One never really knew with wives. Some of them were better diplomats than their husbands. Some of them could be relied upon merely for their charm, for their adaptability, their readiness to please, their lack of curiosity. Some again, he thought ruefully to himself, were, as far as their husbands were concerned, disasters. Hostesses who, though they may have brought prestige or money to a diplomatic marriage, were yet capable at any moment of saying or doing the wrong thing, and creating an unfortunate situation. If that was to be guarded against, it would need one of the guests, or two or even three of the guests, to be what one might call professional smoothers-over.

Did the dinner party this evening mean anything but a social event? His quick and noticing eye had by now been round the dinner table, picking out one or two people whom so far he had not entirely taken in. An American businessman. Pleasant, not socially brilliant. A professor from one of the universities of the Middle West. A married couple, the husband German, the wife predominantly, almost aggressively American. A very beautiful woman, too. Sexually highly attractive, Sir Stafford thought. Was one of them important? Initials floated through his mind. FBI. CIA. The businessman perhaps a CIA man, there for a purpose. Things were like that nowadays. Not as they used to be. How had the formula gone? Big brother is watching you. Yes, well, it went further than that now. Transatlantic Cousin is watching you. High Finance Middle Europe is watching you. A diplomatic difficulty has been asked here for *you* to watch *him*. Oh, yes. There was often a lot behind things nowadays. But was that just another formula, just another fashion? Could it really mean more than that, something vital, something real? How did one talk of events in Europe nowadays? The Common Market. Well, that was fair enough, that dealt with trade, with economics, and with the interrelationships of countries.

That was the stage to set. But behind the stage. Backstage. Waiting for the cue. Ready to prompt if prompting were needed. What was going on? Going on in the big world and behind the big world? He wondered.

Some things he knew, some things he guessed at, some things, he thought to himself, I know nothing about and nobody wants me to know anything about them.

His eyes rested for a moment on his vis-à-vis, her chin tilted upward, her mouth just gently curved in a polite smile, and their eyes met. Those eyes told him nothing, the smile told him nothing. What was she doing here? She was in her element, she fitted in, she knew this world. Yes, she was at home here. He could find out, he thought, without much difficulty where she figured in the diplomatic world, but would that tell him where she really had her place?

The young woman in the slacks who had spoken to him suddenly at Frankfurt had had an eager, intelligent face. Was that the real woman, or was this casual social acquaintance the real woman? Was one of those personalities a part being played? And if so, which one? And there might be more than just those two personalities. He wondered. He wanted to find out.

Or had the fact that he had been asked to meet her been pure coincidence? Milly Jean was rising to her feet. The other ladies rose with her. Then suddenly an unexpected clamor arose. A clamor from outside the house. Shouts. Yells. The crash of breaking glass in a window. Shouts. Sounds—surely pistol shots. Signora Gasparo spoke, clutching Stafford Nye's arm.

"What again!" she exclaimed. *"Dio!*—again it is those terrible students. It is the same in our country. Why do they attack embassies? They fight, resist the police—go marching, shouting idiotic things, lie down in the streets. *Si, si.* We have them in Rome—in Milan—we have them like a pest everywhere in Europe. Why are they never happy, these young ones? What do they want?"

Stafford Nye sipped his brandy and listened to the heavy accents of Mr. Charles Staggenham, who was being pontifical and taking his time about it. The commotion had subsided. It would seem that the police had marched off some of the hotheads. It was one of those occurrences which once would have been thought extraordinary and even alarming but which were now taken as a matter of course.

"A larger police force. That's what we need. A larger police force. It's more than these chaps can deal with. It's the same everywhere, they say. I was talking to Herr Lurwitz the other day. They have their troubles, so have the French. Not quite so much of it in the Scandinavian countries. What do they all want—just trouble? I tell you, if I had my way—"

Stafford Nye removed his mind to another subject while keeping up a flattering pretense as Charles Staggenham explained just what his way would be, which in any case was easily to be anticipated beforehand.

"Shouting about Vietnam and all that. What do any of them know about Vietnam? None of them have ever been there, have they?"

"One would think it very unlikely," said Sir Stafford Nye.

"Man was telling me earlier this evening, they've had a lot of trouble in California. In the universities— If we had a sensible policy . . ."

Presently the men joined the ladies in the drawing room. Stafford Nye, moving with that leisurely grace, that air of complete lack of purpose he found so useful, sat down by a golden-haired, talkative woman whom he knew moderately well, and who could be guaranteed seldom to say anything worth listening to as regards ideas or wit, but who was excessively knowledgeable about all her fellow creatures within the bounds of her acquaintance. Stafford Nye asked no direct questions but presently, without the lady being even aware of the means by which he had guided the subject of conversation, he was hearing a few remarks about the Countess Renata Zerkowski.

"Still very good-looking, isn't she? She doesn't come over here very often nowadays. Mostly New York, you know, or that wonderful island place. You know the one I mean. Not Minorca. One of the other ones in the Mediterranean. Her sister's married to that soap king, at least I think it's a soap king. Not the Greek one. He's Swedish, I think. Rolling in money. And then, of course, she spends a lot of time in some castle place in the Dolomites—or near Munich—very musical, she always has been. She said you'd met before, didn't she?"

"Yes. A year or two years ago, I think."

"Oh, yes, I suppose when she was over in England before. They say she was mixed up in the Czechoslovakian business. Or do I mean the Polish trouble? Oh, dear, it's so difficult, isn't it? All the names, I mean. They have so many z's and k's. Most peculiar, and so hard to spell. She's very literary. You know, gets up petitions for people to sign. To give writers asylum here, or whatever it is. Not that anyone really pays much attention. I mean, what else can one think of nowadays except how one can possibly pay one's own taxes? The travel allowance makes things a little better, but not much. I mean, you've got to get the money, haven't you, before you can take it abroad? I don't know how anyone manages to have money now, but there's a lot of it about. Oh, yes, there's a lot of it about."

She looked down in a complacent fashion at her left hand, on which were two solitaire rings, one a diamond and one an emerald, which seemed to prove conclusively that a considerable amount of money had been spent upon her at least.

The evening drew on to its close. He knew very little more about his passenger from Frankfurt than he had known before. He knew that she had a façade, a façade it seemed to him, very highly faceted, if you could use those two alliterative words together. She was interested in music. Well, he had met her at the Festival Hall, had he not? Fond of outdoor sports. Rich relations who owned Mediterranean islands. Given to supporting literary charities. Somebody, in fact, who had good connections, was well related, had entries to the social field. Not apparently highly political and yet, quietly perhaps, affiliated to some group. Someone who moved about from place to place and country to country. Moving among the rich, among the talented, about the literary world.

He thought of espionage for a moment or two. That seemed the most likely answer. And yet he was not wholly satisfied with it.

The evening drew on. It came at last to be his turn to be collected by his hostess. Milly Jean was very good at her job.

"I've been longing to talk to you for ages. I wanted to hear about Malaya. I'm so stupid about all these places in Asia, you know. I mix them up. Tell me, what happened out there? Anything interesting or was everything terribly boring?"

"I'm sure you can guess the answer to that one."

"Well, I should guess it was very boring. But perhaps you're not allowed to say so."

"Oh, yes, I can think it, and I can say it. It wasn't really my cup of tea, you know."

"Why did you go then?"

"Oh, well, I'm always fond of traveling; I like seeing countries."

"You're such an intriguing person in many ways. Really, of course, all diplomatic life is very boring, isn't it? *I* oughtn't to say so. I only say it to you."

Very blue eyes. Blue like bluebells in a wood. They opened a little wider and the black brows above them came down gently at the outside corners while the inside corners went up a little. It made her face look like a rather beautiful Persian cat. He wondered what Milly Jean was really like. Her soft voice was that of a southerner. The beautifully shaped little head, her profile with the perfection of a coin—what was she really like? No fool, he thought. One who could use social weapons when needed, who could charm when she wished to, who could withdraw into being enigmatic. If she wanted anything from anyone, she would be adroit in getting it. He noticed the intensity of the glance she was giving him now. Did she want something from him? He didn't know. He didn't think it could be likely. She said, "Have you met Mr. Staggenham?"

"Ah, yes. I was talking to him at the dinner table. I hadn't met him before."

"He is said to be very important," said Milly Jean. "He's the president of P.B.F., as you know."

"One should know all those things," said Sir Stafford Nye. "P.B.F. and D.C.V. L.Y.H. And all the world of initials."

"Hateful," said Milly Jean. "Hateful. All these initials, no personalities, no *people* anymore. Just initials. What a hateful world! That's what I sometimes think. What a hateful world. I want it to be different—quite, quite different—"

Did she mean that? He thought for one moment that perhaps she did. Interesting . . .

Grosvenor Square was quietness itself. There were traces of broken glass still on the pavements. There were even eggs, squashed tomatoes, and fragments of gleaming metal. But above, the stars were peaceful. Car after car drove up to the embassy door to collect the home-going guests. The police were there in the corners of the square but without ostentation. Everything was under control. One of the political guests leaving spoke to one of the police officers. He came back and murmured, "Not too many arrests. Eight. They'll be up at Bow Street in the morning. More or less the usual lot. Petronella was here, of course, and Stephen and his crowd. Ah, well. One would think they'd get tired of it one of these days."

"You live not very far from here, don't you?" said a voice in Sir Stafford Nye's ear. A deep contralto voice. "I can drop you on my way."

"No, no. I can walk perfectly. It's only ten minutes or so."

"It will be no trouble to me, I assure you," said the Countess Zerkowski. She added, "I'm staying at the St. James's Tower."

The St. James's Tower was one of the newer hotels.

"You are very kind."

It was a big, expensive-looking rented car that waited. The chauffeur opened the door, the Countess Renata got in, and Sir Stafford Nye followed her. It was she who gave Sir Stafford Nye's address to the chauffeur. The car drove off.

"So you know where I live?" he said.

"Why not?"

He wondered just what that answer meant: Why not?

"Why not indeed," he said. "You know so much, don't you?" He added, "It was kind of you to return my passport."

"I thought it might save certain inconveniences. It might be simpler if you burnt it. You've been issued with a new one, I presume—"

"You presume correctly."

"Your bandit's cloak you will find in the bottom drawer of your highboy. It was put there tonight. I believed that perhaps to purchase another one would not satisfy you, and indeed that to find one similar might not be possible."

"It will mean more to me now that it has been through certain—adventures," said Stafford Nye. He added, "It has served its purpose."

The car purred through the night.

The Countess Zerkowski said:

"Yes. It has served its purpose since I am here—alive. . . ."

Sir Stafford Nye said nothing. He was assuming, rightly or not, that she wanted him to ask questions, to press her, to know more of what she had been doing, of what fate she had escaped. She wanted him to display curiosity, but Sir Stafford Nye was not going to display curiosity. He rather enjoyed not doing so. He heard her laugh very gently. Yet he fancied, rather surprisingly, that it was a pleased laugh, a laugh of satisfaction, not of stalemate.

"Did you enjoy your evening?" shc said.

"A good party, I think, but Milly Jean always gives good parties."

"You know her well then?"

"I knew her when she was a girl in New York before she married. A pocket Venus."

She looked at him in faint surprise.

"Is that your term for her?"

"Actually, no. It was said to me by an elderly relative of mine."

"Yes, it isn't a description that one hears given often of a woman nowadays. It fits her, I think, very well. Only—"

"Only what?"

"Venus is seductive, is she not? Is she also ambitious?"

"You think Milly Jean Cortman is ambitious?"

"Oh, yes. That above all."

"And you think to be the wife of the Ambassador to St. James's is insufficient to satisfy ambition?"

"Oh, no," said the Countess. "That is only the beginning."

He did not answer. He was looking out through the car window. He began to speak, then stopped himself. He noted her quick glance at him, but she, too, was silent. It was not till they were going over a bridge with the Thames below them that he said:

"So you are not giving me a lift home and you are not going back to the St. James's Tower. We are crossing the Thames. We met there once before, crossing a bridge. Where are you taking me?"

"Do you mind?"

"I think I do."

"Yes, I can see you might."

"Well, of course you are quite in the mode. Hijacking is the fashion nowadays, isn't it? You have hijacked me. Why?"

"Because, like once before, I have need of you." She added, "And others have need of you."

"Indeed."

"And that does not please you."

"It would please me better to be asked."

"If I had asked, would you have come?"

"Perhaps yes, perhaps no."

"I am sorry."

"I wonder."

They drove on through the night in silence. It was not a drive through lonely country; they were on a main road. Now and then the lights picked up a name or a signpost so that Stafford Nye saw quite clearly where their route lay. Through Surrey and through the first residential portions of Sussex. Occasionally he thought they took a detour or a side road which was not the most direct route, but even of this he could not be sure. He almost asked his companion whether this was being done because they might possibly have been followed from London. But he had determined rather firmly on his policy of silence. It was for her to speak, for her to give information. He found her, even with the additional information he had been able to get, an enigmatic character.

They were driving to the country after a dinner party in London. They were, he was pretty sure, in one of the more expensive types of rented car. This was something planned beforehand. Reasonable; nothing doubtful or unexpected about it. Soon, he imagined, he would find out where it was they were going. Unless, that is, they were going to drive as far as the coast. That also was possible, he thought. Haslemere, he saw on a signpost. Now they were skirting Godalming. All very plain and aboveboard. The rich country-side of moneyed suburbia. Agreeable woods, handsome residences. They took a few side turns and then as the car finally slowed, they seemed to be arriving at their destination. Gates. A small white lodge by the gates. Up a drive, well-kept rhododendrons on either side of it. They turned round a bend and drew up before a house. "Stockbroker Tudor," murmured Sir Stafford Nye under his breath. His companion turned her head inquiringly.

"Just a comment," said Stafford Nye. "Pay no attention. I take it we are now arriving at the destination of your choice?"

"And you don't admire the look of it very much."

"The grounds seem well kept up," said Sir Stafford, following the beam of the headlights as the car rounded the bend. "Takes money to keep these places up and in good order. I should say this was a comfortable house to live in."

"Comfortable but not beautiful. The man who lives in it prefers comfort to beauty, I should say."

"Perhaps wisely," said Sir Stafford. "And yet in some ways he is very appreciative of beauty, of some kinds of beauty."

They drew up before the well-lighted porch. Sir Stafford got out and tendered an arm to help his companion. The chauffeur had mounted the steps and pressed the bell. He looked inquiringly at the woman as she ascended the steps.

"You won't be requiring me again tonight, m'lady?"

"No. That's all for now. We'll telephone down in the morning."

"Good night. Good night, sir."

There were footsteps inside and the door was flung open. Sir Stafford had expected some kind of butler, but instead there was a tall grenadier of a parlormaid. Gray-haired, tight-lipped, eminently reliable and competent, he thought. An invaluable asset and hard to find nowadays. Trustworthy, capable of being fierce.

"I am afraid we are a little late," said Renata.

"The master is in the library. He asked that you and the gentleman should come to him there when you arrived."

9

The House near Godalming

SHE LED THE way up the broad staircase and the two of them followed her. Yes, thought Stafford Nye, a very comfortable house. Jacobean paper, a most unsightly carved oak staircase, but pleasantly shallow treads. Pictures nicely chosen but of no particular artistic interest. A rich man's house, he thought. A man, not of bad taste, a man of conventional tastes. Good thick pile carpet of an agreeable plum-colored texture.

On the first floor, the grenadierlike parlormaid went to the first door along it. She opened it and stood back to let them go in, but she made no announcement of names. The Countess went in first and Sir Stafford Nye followed her. He heard the door shut quietly behind him.

There were four people in the room. Sitting behind a large desk which was well covered with papers, documents, an open map or two and presumably other papers which were in the course of discussion, was a large, fat man with a very yellow face. It was a face Sir Stafford Nye had seen before, though he could not for the moment attach the proper name to it. It was a man whom he had met only in a casual fashion, and yet the occasion had been an important one. He should know, yes, definitely he should know. But why—why wouldn't the name come?

With a slight struggle, the figure sitting at the desk rose to his feet. He took the Countess Renata's outstretched hand.

"You've arrived," he said; "splendid."

"Yes. Let me introduce you, though I think you already know him. Sir Stafford Nye, Mr. Robinson."

Of course. In Sir Stafford Nye's brain something clicked like a camera. That fitted in, too, with another name, Pikeaway. To say that he knew all about Mr. Robinson was not true. He knew about Mr. Robinson all that Mr. Robinson permitted to be known. His name, as far as anyone knew, *was* Robinson, though it might have been any name of foreign origin. No one had ever suggested anything of that kind. Recognition came also of his personal appearance. The high forehead, the melancholy dark eyes, the large generous mouth, and the impressive large white teeth—false teeth, presumably, but at any rate teeth of which it might have been said, like in Red Ridinghood, "the better to eat you with, child!"

He knew, too, what Mr. Robinson stood for. Just one simple word described it. Mr. Robinson represented Money with a capital M. Money in its every aspect. International money, worldwide money, private home finances, banking, foreign governments. Industrial projects. He represented money not in the way that the average person looked at it. You never thought of him as a very rich man. Undoubtedly he was a very rich man, but that wasn't the important thing. He was one of the arrangers of money, the great clan of bankers. His personal tastes might even have been simple, but Sir Stafford Nye doubted if they were. A reasonable standard of comfort, even luxury, would be Mr. Robinson's way of life. But not more than that. So behind all this mysterious business there was the power of money.

"I heard of you just a day or two ago," said Mr. Robinson, as he shook hands, "from our friend Pikeaway, you know."

That fitted in, thought Stafford Nye, because now he remembered that on the solitary occasion before that he had met Mr. Robinson, Colonel Pikeaway had been present. Horsham, he remembered, had spoken of Mr. Robinson. So now there was Mary Ann (or the Countess Zerkowski?) and Colonel Pikeaway sitting in his own smoke-filled room with his eyes half closed either going to sleep or just waking up, and there was Mr. Robinson with his large, yellow face, and so there was money at stake somewhere, and his glance shifted to the three other people in the room because he wanted to see if he knew who they were and what they represented, or if he could guess.

In two cases at least he didn't need to guess. The man who sat in the tall porter's chair by the fireplace, an elderly figure framed by the chair as a picture frame might have framed him, was a face that had been well known all over England. Indeed, it still *was* well known, although it was very seldom seen nowadays. A sick man, an invalid, a man who made very brief appearances, and then, it was said, at physical cost to himself in pain and difficulty. Lord Altamount. A thin emaciated face, outstanding nose, gray hair which receded just a little from the forehead, and then flowed back in a thick gray mane; somewhat prominent ears that cartoonists had used in their time, and a deep, piercing glance that not so much observed as probed. Probed deeply into what it was looking at. At the moment it was looking at Sir Stafford Nye. He stretched out a hand as Stafford Nye went toward him.

"I don't get up," said Lord Altamount. His voice was faint, an old man's voice, a faraway voice. "My back doesn't allow me to. Just come back from Malaya, haven't you, Stafford Nye?"

"Yes."

"Was it worth your going? I expect you think it wasn't. You're probably right, too. Still, we have to have these excrescences in life, these ornamental trimmings to adorn the better kind of diplomatic lies. I'm glad you could come here or were brought here tonight. Mary Ann's doing, I suppose?"

So that's what he calls her and thinks of her as, thought Stafford Nye to himself. It was what Horsham had called her. She was in with them then, without a doubt. As for Altamount, he stood for—what did he stand for nowadays? Stafford Nye thought to himself: He stands for England. He still stands for England until he's buried in Westminster Abbey or a country mausoleum, whatever he chooses. He has *been* England, and he knows England, and I should say he knows the value of every politician and government official in England pretty well, even if he's never spoken to them.

Lord Altamount said:

"This is our colleague, Sir James Kleek."

Stafford Nye didn't know Kleek. He didn't think he'd even heard of him. A restless, fidgety type. Sharp, suspicious glances that never rested anywhere for long. He had the contained eagerness of a sporting dog awaiting the word of command. Ready to start off at a glance from his master's eye.

But who was his master? Altamount or Robinson?

Stafford's eye went round to the fourth man. He had risen to his feet from the chair where he had been sitting close to the door. Bushy mustache, raised eyebrows, watchful, withdrawn, managing in some way to remain familiar yet almost unrecognizable.

"So it's you," said Sir Stafford Nye. "How are you, Horsham?"

"Very pleased to see you here, Sir Stafford."

Quite a representative gathering, Stafford Nye thought, with a swift glance round.

They had set a chair for Renata not far from the fire and Lord Altamount. She had stretched out a hand—her left hand, he noticed—and he had taken it between his two hands, holding it for a minute, then dropping it. He said:

"You took risks, child; you take too many risks."

Looking at him, she said, "It was you who taught me that, and it's the only way of life."

Lord Altamount turned his head toward Sir Stafford Nye.

"It wasn't I who taught you to choose your man. You've got a natural genius for that." Looking at Stafford Nye, he said, "I know your great-aunt, or your great-great-aunt is she?"

"Great-Aunt Matilda," said Stafford Nye immediately.

"Yes. That's the one. One of the Victorian tours de force of the nineties. She must be nearly ninety herself now."

He went on:

"I don't see her very often. Once or twice a year perhaps. But it strikes me every time—that sheer vitality of hers that outlives her bodily strength. They have the secret of that, those indomitable Victorians and some of the Edwardians as well."

Sir James Kleek said, "Let me get you a drink, Nye? What will you have?"

"Gin and tonic, if I may."

The Countess refused with a small shake of the head.

James Kleek brought Nye his drink and set it on the table near Mr. Robinson. Stafford Nye was not going to speak first. The dark eyes behind the desk lost their melancholy for a moment. They had quite suddenly a twinkle in them.

"Any questions?" he said.

"Too many," said Sir Stafford Nye. "Wouldn't it be better to have explanations first, questions later?"

"Is that what you'd like?"

"It might simplify matters."

"Well, we start with a few plain statements of facts. You may or you may not have been asked to come here. If not, that fact may rankle slightly."

"He prefers to be asked always," said the Countess. "He said as much to me."

"Naturally," said Mr. Robinson.

"I was hijacked," said Stafford Nye. "Very fashionable, I know. One of our more modern methods."

He kept his tone one of light amusement.

"Which invites, surely, a question from you," said Mr. Robinson.

"Just one small word of three letters. Why?"

"Quite so. Why? I admire your economy of speech. This is a private committee—a committee of inquiry. An inquiry of worldwide significance."

"Sounds interesting," said Sir Stafford Nye.

"It is more than interesting. It is poignant and immediate. Four different ways of life are represented in this room tonight," said Lord Altamount. "We represent different branches. I have retired from active participation in the affairs of this country, but I am still a consulting authority. I have been consulted and asked to preside over this particular inquiry as to what is going on in the world in this particular year of our Lord, because something *is* going on. James here has his own special task. He is my right-hand man. He is also our spokesman. Explain the general set-out, if you will, Jamie, to Sir Stafford here."

It seemed to Stafford Nye that the gun dog quivered. At last! his eagerness seemed to be saying. At last! At last I can speak and get on with it! He leaned forward a little in his chair.

"If things happen in the world, you have to look for a cause for them. The outward signs are always easy to see, but they're not, or so the chairman"—he bowed to Lord Altamount—"and Mr. Robinson and Mr. Horsham believe, important. It's always been the same way. You take a natural force, a great fall of water that will give you turbine power. You take the discovery of uranium from pitchblende, and that will give you in due course nuclear power that had not been dreamt of or known. When you found coal and minerals, they gave you transport, power, energy. There are forces at work always that give you certain things. But behind each of them there is *someone who controls it*. You've got to find who's controlling the powers that are slowly gaining ascendancy in practically every country in Europe, further afield still in parts of Asia. Less, possibly, in Africa, but again in the American continents both north and south. You've got to get behind the things that are happening and find out the motive force that's making them happen. One thing that makes things happen is *money.*"

He nodded toward Mr. Robinson.

"Mr. Robinson, there, knows as much about money as anybody in the world, I suppose."

"It's quite simple," said Mr. Robinson. "There are big movements afoot. There has to be money behind them. We've got to find out where that money's coming from. Who's operating with it? Where do they get it from? Where are they sending it to? Why? It's quite true what James says: I know a lot about money! As much as any man alive knows today. Then there are what you might call trends. It's a word we use a good deal nowadays! Trends or tendencies—there are innumerable words one uses. They mean not quite the same thing, but they're in relationship with each other. A tendency, shall we say, to rebellion shows up. Look back through history. You'll find it coming again and again, repeating itself like a periodic table, repeating a pattern. A desire for rebellion. A feeling for rebellion, the means of rebellion, the form the rebellion takes. It's not a thing particular to any particular country. If it arises in one country, it will arise in other countries in less or more degrees. That's what you mean, sir, isn't it?" He half turned toward Lord Altamount. "That's the way you more or less put it to me."

"Yes, you're expressing things very well, James."

"It's a pattern, a pattern that arises and seems inevitable. You can recognize it where you find it. There was a period when a yearning toward crusades swept countries. All over Europe people embarked in ships, they went off to deliver the Holy Land. All quite clear, a perfectly good pattern of determined behavior. But *why* did they go? That's the interest of history, you know. Seeing why these desires and patterns arise. It's not always a materialistic answer either. All sorts of things can cause rebellion—a desire for freedom, freedom of speech, freedom of religious worship, again a series of closely related patterns. It led people to embrace emigration to other countries, to formation of new religions very often as full of tyranny as the forms of religion they had left behind. But in all this, if you look hard enough, if you make enough investigations, you can see what started the onset of these and many other—I'll use the same word—patterns. In some ways it's like a virus disease. The virus can be carried—round the world, across seas, up mountains. It can go and infect. It goes apparently without being set in motion. But one can't be sure, even now, that that was always really true. There could have been causes. Causes that made things happen. One can go a few steps further. There are *people.* One person—ten persons—a few hundred persons who are capable of being and setting in motion a cause. So it is not the *end process* that one has to look at. It is the first people who set the cause in motion. You have your crusaders, you have your religious enthusiasts, you have your desires for liberty, you have all the other patterns, but you've got to go further back still. Further back to a hinterland. Behind the materialistic results, there are ideas. Visions, dreams. The prophet Joel knew it when he wrote, 'Your old men shall dream dreams, your young men shall see visions.' And of those two visions, which are the more powerful? Dreams are not destructive. But visions can open new worlds to you—and visions can also destroy the worlds that already exist. . . ."

James Kleek turned suddenly toward Lord Altamount.

"I don't know if it connects up, sir," he said, "but you told me a story once of somebody in the embassy at Berlin. A woman."

"Oh, that? Yes, I found it interesting at the time. Yes, it has a bearing on what we are talking about now. One of the embassy wives, clever, intelligent woman, well educated. She was very anxious to go personally and hear the Führer speak. I am talking, of course, of a time immediately preceding the nineteen thirty-nine war. She was curious to know what oratory could do. Why was everyone so impressed? And so she went. She came back and said, 'It's extraordinary. I wouldn't have believed it. Of course I don't understand German very well, but I was carried away, too. And I see now why everyone is. I mean, his ideas were wonderful. . . . They inflamed you. The things he said. I mean, you just felt there *was* no other way of thinking, that a whole new world would happen if only one followed him. Oh, I can't explain properly. I'm going to write down as much as I can remember, and then if I bring it to you to see, you'll see better than my just trying to tell you the effect it had.'

"I told her that was a very good idea. She came to me the next day and she said, 'I don't know if you'll believe this. I started to write down the things I'd heard, the things Hitler had said. What they'd *meant*—but—it was frightening—*there wasn't anything to write down at all. I didn't seem able to remember a single stimulating or exciting sentence.* I have some of the words, but it doesn't seem to mean the same things as when I wrote them down. They are just—oh, they are just *meaningless.* I don't understand.'

"That shows you one of the great dangers one doesn't always remember, *but it exists.* There are people capable of communicating to others a wild enthusiasm, a kind of vision of life and of happening. They can do that though it is not really by what they *say,* it is not the *words* you *hear,* it is not even the idea described. It's something else. It's the magnetic power that a very few men have of starting something, of producing and creating a vision. By their personal magnetism perhaps, a tone of voice, perhaps some emanation that comes forth straight from the *flesh.* I don't know, *but it exists.*

"Such people have power. The great religious teachers had this power, and so has an evil spirit power also. Belief can be created in a certain movement, in certain things to be done, things that will result in a new heaven and a new earth, and people will believe it and work for it and fight for it and even die for it."

He lowered his voice as he said: "Jan Smuts put it in a phrase. He said, 'Leadership, besides being a great creative force, can be diabolical.'"

Stafford Nye moved in his chair.

"I understand what you mean. It is interesting what you say. I can see perhaps that it might be true."

"But you think it's exaggerated, of course."

"I don't know that I do," said Stafford Nye. "Things that sound exaggerated are very often not exaggerated at all. They are only things that you haven't heard said before or thought about before. And therefore they come to you as so unfamiliar that you can hardly do anything about them except accept them. By the way, may I ask a simple question? What *does* one do about them?"

"If you come across the suspicion that this sort of thing is going on, you must find out about them," said Lord Altamount. "You've got to go like Kipling's mongoose: Go and find out. Find out where the money comes from and where the ideas are coming from, and where, if I may say so, the *machinery* comes from. Who is directing the machinery? There's a chief of staff, you know, as well as a commander in chief. That's what we're trying to do. We'd like you to come and help us."

It was one of the rare occasions in his life when Sir Stafford Nye was taken aback. Whatever he may have felt on some former occasions, he had always managed to conceal the fact. But this time it was different. He looked from one to the other men in the room. At Mr. Robinson, impassively yellow-faced, with his mouthful of teeth displayed; to Sir James Kleek, a somewhat brash talker, Sir Stafford Nye had considered him, but nevertheless he had obviously his uses; master's dog, he called him in his own mind. He looked at Lord Altamount, the hood of the porter's chair framed round his head. The lighting was not strong in the room. It gave him the look of a saint in a niche in a cathedral somewhere. Ascetic. Fourteenth-century. A great man. Yes, Altamount had been one of the great men of the past. Stafford Nye had no doubt of that, but he was now a very old man. Hence, he supposed, the necessity for Sir James Kleek, and Lord Altamount's reliance on him. He looked past them to the enigmatic, cool creature who had brought him here, the Countess Renata Zerkowski, alias Mary Ann, alias Daphne Theodofanous. Her face told him nothing. She was not even looking at him. His eyes came round last to Mr. Henry Horsham of Security.

With faint surprise he observed that Henry Horsham was grinning at him.

"But look here," said Stafford Nye, dropping all formal language and speaking rather like the schoolboy of eighteen he had once been. "Where on earth do I come in? What do *I* know? Quite frankly, I'm not distinguished in any way in my own profession, you know. They don't think very much of me at the F.O. Never have."

"We know that," said Lord Altamount.

It was Sir James Kleek's turn to grin, and he did so.

"All the better perhaps," he remarked, and added apologetically as Lord Altamount frowned at him, "Sorry, sir."

"This is a committee of investigation," said Mr. Robinson. "It is not a question of what you have done in the past, of what other people's opinions of you may be. What we are doing is to recruit a committee to investigate. There are not very many of us at the moment forming this committee. We ask you to join it because we think that you have certain qualities which may help in an investigation."

Stafford Nye turned his head toward the Security man. "What about it, Horsham?" he said. "I can't believe you'd agree with that?"

"Why not?" said Henry Horsham.

"Indeed? What are my 'qualities,' as you call them? I can't, quite frankly, believe in them myself."

"You're not a hero worshipper," said Horsham. "That's why. You're the kind who sees through humbug. You don't take anyone at their own or the world's valuation. You take them at your own valuation."

Ce n'est pas un garçon sérieux. The words floated through Sir Stafford Nye's mind. A curious reason for which to be chosen for a difficult and exacting job.

"I've got to warn you," he said, "that my principal fault, and one that's been frequently noticed about me and which has cost me several good jobs is, I think, fairly well known. I'm not, I should say, a sufficiently serious sort of chap for an important job like this."

"Believe it or not," said Mr. Horsham, "that's one of the reasons why they want you. I'm right, my lord, aren't I?" He looked toward Lord Altamount.

"Public service!" said Lord Altamount. "Let me tell you that very often one of the most serious disadvantages in public life is when people in a public position take themselves too seriously. We feel that you won't. Anyway," he said, "Mary Ann thinks so."

Sir Stafford Nye turned his head. So here she was, no longer a countess. She had become Mary Ann again.

"You don't mind my asking," he said, "but who are you really? I mean, are you a real countess?"

"Absolutely. *Geboren,* as the Germans say. My father was a man of pedigree, a good sportsman, a splendid shot, and had a very romantic but somewhat dilapidated castle in Bavaria. It's still there, the castle. As far as that goes, I have connections with that large portion of the European world which is still heavily snobbish as far as birth is concerned. A poor and shabby countess sits down first at the table while a rich American with a fabulous fortune in dollars in the bank is kept waiting."

"What about Daphne Theodofanous? Where does she come in?"

"A useful name for a passport. My mother was Greek."

"And Mary Ann?"

It was almost the first smile Stafford Nye had seen on her face. Her eyes went to Lord Altamount and from him to Mr. Robinson.

"Perhaps," she said, "because I'm a kind of maid-of-all-work, going places, looking for things, taking things from one country to another, sweeping under the mat, do anything, go anywhere, clear up the mess." She looked toward Lord Altamount again. "Am I right, Uncle Ned?"

"Quite right, my dear. Mary Ann you are and always will be to us."

"Were you taking something on that plane? I mean taking something important from one country to another?"

"Yes. It was known I was carrying it. If you hadn't come to my rescue, if you hadn't drunk possibly poisoned beer and handed over your bandit cloak of bright colors as a disguise, well, accidents happen sometimes. I shouldn't have got here."

"What were you carrying—or mustn't I ask? Are there things I shall never know?"

"There are a lot of things you will never know. There are a lot of things you won't be allowed to ask. I think that question of yours I shall answer. A bare answer of fact. If I am allowed to do so."

Again she looked at Lord Altamount.

"I trust your judgment," said Lord Altamount. "Go ahead."

"Give him the dope," said the irreverent James Kleek.

Mr. Horsham said, "I suppose you've got to know. *I* wouldn't tell you, but then I'm Security. Go ahead, Mary Ann."

"One sentence. *I was bringing a birth certificate. That's all.* I don't tell you any more and it won't be any use your asking any more questions."

Stafford Nye looked round the assembly.

"All right. I'll join. I'm flattered at your asking me. Where do we go from here?"

"You and I," said Renata, "leave here tomorrow. We go to the Continent. You may have read, or know, that there's a Musical Festival taking place in Bavaria. It is something quite new which has only come into being in the last two years. It has a rather formidable German name meaning 'The Company of the Youthful Singers' and is supported by the governments of several different countries. It is in opposition to the traditional festivals and productions of Bayreuth. Much of the music given is modern—new young composers are given the chance of their compositions being heard. While thought of highly by some, it is utterly repudiated and held in contempt by others."

"Yes," said Sir Stafford, "I have read about it. Are we going to attend it?"

"We have seats booked for two of the performances."

"Has this festival any special significance in our investigation?"

"No," said Renata. "It is more in the nature of what you might call an exit-and-entry convenience. We go there for an ostensible and true reason, and we leave it for our next step in due course."

He looked round. "Instructions? Do I get any marching orders? Am I to be briefed?"

"Not in your meaning of those terms. You are going on a voyage of exploration. You will learn things as you go along. You will go as yourself, knowing only what you know at present. You go as a lover of music, as a slightly disappointed diplomat who had perhaps hoped for some post in his own country which he has not been given. Otherwise, you will know nothing. It is safer so."

"But that is the sum of activities at present? Germany, Bavaria, Austria, the Tyrol—that part of the world?"

"It is one of the centers of interest."

"It is not the only one?"

"Indeed, not even the principal one. There are other spots on the globe, all of varying importance and interest. How much importance each one holds is what we have to find out."

"And I don't know, or am not to be told, anything about these other centers?"

"Only in cursory fashion. One of them, we think the most important one, has its headquarters in South America. There are two with headquarters in the United States of America, one in California, the other in Baltimore. There is one in Sweden, there is one in Italy. Things have become very active in the latter in the last six months. Portugal and Spain also have smaller centers. Paris, of course. There are further interesting spots just 'coming into production,' you might say. As yet not fully developed."

"You mean Malaya, or Vietnam?"

"No. No, all that lies rather in the past. It was a good rallying cry for violence and student indignation and for many other things.

"What is being promoted, you must understand, is the growing organization of youth everywhere against their mode of government; against their parental customs, against very often the religions in which they have been brought up. There is the insidious cult of permissiveness, there is the increasing cult of violence. Violence not as a means of gaining money, but violence for the love of violence. That particularly is stressed, and the reasons for it are to the people concerned one of the most important things and of the utmost significance."

"Permissiveness, is that important?"

"It is a way of life, no more. It lends itself to certain abuses but not unduly."

"What about drugs?"

"The cult of drugs has been deliberately advanced and fomented. Vast sums of money have been made that way, but it is not, or so we think, entirely activated for the money motive."

All of them looked at Mr. Robinson, who slowly shook his head.

"No," he said, "it *looks* that way. There are people who are being apprehended and brought to justice. Pushers of drugs will be followed up. But there is more than just the drug racket behind all this. The drug racket is a means, and an evil means, of making money. But there is more to it than that."

"But who—" Stafford Nye stopped.

"Who and what and why and where? The four W's. That is your mission, Sir Stafford," said Mr. Robinson. "That's what you've got to find out. You and Mary Ann. It won't be easy, and one of the hardest things in the world, remember, is to keep one's secrets."

Stafford Nye looked with interest at the fat yellow face of Mr. Robinson. Perhaps the secret of Mr. Robinson's domination in the financial world was just that. His secret was that he kept his secret. Mr. Robinson's mouth showed its smile again. The large teeth gleamed.

"If you know a thing," he said, "it is always a great temptation to show that you know it; to talk about it, in other words. It is not that you want to give information, it is not that you have been offered payment to give information. It is that you want to show how important you are. Yes, it's just as simple as that. In fact," said Mr. Robinson, and he half closed his eyes, "everything in this world is so very, *very* simple. That's what people don't understand."

The Countess got to her feet and Stafford Nye followed her example.

"I hope you will sleep well and be comfortable," said Mr. Robinson. "This house is, I think, moderately comfortable."

Stafford Nye murmured that he was quite sure of that, and on that point he was shortly to be proved to have been quite right. He laid his head on the pillow and went to sleep immediately.

BOOK II
Journey to Siegfried

SIEGFRIED THE HERO

10
The Woman in the Schloss

THEY CAME OUT of the Festival Youth Theater to the refreshing night air. Below them in a sweep of the ground was a lighted restaurant. On the side of the hill was another, smaller one. The restaurants varied slightly in price, though neither of them was inexpensive. Renata was in evening dress of black velvet, Sir Stafford Nye was in white tie and full evening dress.

"A very distinguished audience," murmured Stafford Nye to his companion. "Plenty of money there. A young audience, on the whole. You wouldn't think they could afford it."

"Oh! that can be seen to—it *is* seen to."

"A subsidy for the élite of youth? That kind of thing?"

"Yes."

They walked toward the restaurant on the high side of the hill.

"They give you an hour for the meal. Is that right?"

"Technically an hour. Actually an hour and a quarter."

"That audience," said Sir Stafford Nye, "most of them, nearly all of them, I should say, are real lovers of music."

"Most of them, yes. It's important, you know."

"What do you mean—important?"

"That the enthusiasm should be genuine. At both ends of the scale," she added.

"What did you mean exactly by that?"

"Those who practice and organize violence must love violence, must want it, must yearn for it. The seal of ecstasy in every movement of slashing, hurting, destroying. And the same thing with the music. The ears must appreciate every moment of the harmonies and beauties. There can be no pretending in this game."

"Can you double the roles—do you mean you can combine violence *and* a love of music or a love of art?"

"It is not always easy, I think, but yes. There are many who can. It is safer, really, if they don't have to combine roles."

"It's better to keep it simple, as our fat friend Mr. Robinson would say? Let the lovers of music love music, let the violent practitioners love violence. Is that what you mean?"

"I think so."

"I am enjoying this very much. The two days that we have stayed here, the two nights of music that we have enjoyed. I have not enjoyed all the music, because I am not perhaps sufficiently modern in my taste. I find the clothes very interesting."

"Are you talking of the stage production?"

"No, no, I was talking of the audience, really. You and I, the squares, the old-fashioned. You, Countess, in your society gown, I in my white tie and tails. Not a comfortable get-up, it never has been. And then the others, the silks and the velvets, the ruffled shirts of the men, real lace, I noticed, several times—and the plush and the hair and the luxury of *avant-garde,* the luxury of the eighteen hundreds or, you might almost say, of the Elizabethan age or of Van Dyck pictures."

"Yes, you are right."

"I'm no nearer, though, to what it all means. I haven't *learned* anything. I haven't found out anything."

"You mustn't be impatient. This is a rich show, supported, asked for, demanded perhaps by youth and provided by—"

"By whom?"

"We don't know yet. We shall know."

"I'm so glad you are sure of it."

They went into the restaurant and sat down. The food was good though not in any way ornate or luxurious. Once or twice they were spoken to by an acquaintance or a friend. Two people who recognized Sir Stafford Nye expressed pleasure and surprise at seeing him. Renata had a bigger circle of acquaintances, since she knew more foreigners—well-dressed women, a man or two, mostly German or Austrian, Stafford Nye thought, one or two Americans. Just a few desultory words. Where people had come from or were going to, criticism or appreciation of the musical fare. Nobody wasted much time, since the interval for eating had not been very long.

They returned to their seats for the two final musical offerings. A Symphonic Poem, "Disintegration in Joy," by a new young composer, Solukonov, and then the solemn grandeur of the March of the Meistersinger.

They came out again into the night. The car which was at their disposal every day was waiting there to take them back to the small but exclusive hotel in the village street. Stafford Nye said good night to Renata. She spoke to him in a lowered voice.

"Four A.M.," she said. "Be ready."

She went straight into her room and shut the door and he went to his.

The faint scrape of fingers on his door came precisely at three minutes to four the next morning. He opened the door and stood ready.

"The car is waiting," she said. "Come."

They lunched at a small mountain inn. The weather was good, the mountains beautiful. Occasionally Stafford Nye wondered what on earth he was doing here. He understood less and less of his traveling companion. She spoke little. He found himself watching her profile. Where was she taking him? What was her real reason? At last, as the sun was almost setting, he said:

"Where are we going? Can I ask?"

"You can ask, yes."

"But you do not reply."

"I could reply. I could tell you things, but would they mean anything? It seems to me that if you come to where we are going without my preparing you with explanations (which cannot in the nature of things mean anything), your first impressions will have more force and significance."

He looked at her again thoughtfully. She was wearing a tweed coat trimmed with fur, smart traveling clothes, foreign in make and cut.

"Mary Ann," he said thoughtfully.

There was a faint question in it.

"No," she said, "not at the moment."

"Ah. You are still the Countess Zerkowski."

"At the moment I am still the Countess Zerkowski."

"Are you in your own part of the world?"

"More or less. I grew up as a child in this part of the world. For a good portion of each year we used to come here in the autumn to a Schloss not very many miles from here."

He smiled and said thoughtfully, "What a nice word it is. A *Schloss*. So solid-sounding."

"Schlösser are not standing very solidly nowadays. They are mostly disintegrated."

"This is Hitler's country, isn't it? We're not far, are we, from Berchtesgaden?"

"It lies over there to the northeast."

"Did your relations, your friends—did they accept Hitler, believe in him? Perhaps I ought not to ask things like that."

"They disliked him and all he stood for. But they said, 'Heil Hitler.' They acquiesced in what had happened to their country. What else could they do? What else could anybody do at that date?"

"We are going toward the Dolomites, are we not?"

"Does it matter where we are, or which way we are going?"

"Well, this is a voyage of exploration, is it not?"

"Yes, but the exploration is not geographical. We are going to see a personality."

"You make me feel"—Stafford Nye looked up at the landscape of swelling mountains reaching up to the sky—"as though we were going to visit the famous Old Man of the Mountain."

"The Master of the Assassins, you mean, who kept his followers under drugs so that they died for him wholeheartedly, so that they killed, knowing that they themselves would also be killed, but believing, too, that that would transfer them immediately to the Moslem paradise—beautiful women, hashish and erotic dreams—perfect and unending happiness."

She paused a minute and then said:

"Spellbinders! I suppose they've always been there throughout the ages. People who make you believe in them so that you are ready to die for them. Not only Assassins. The Christians died also."

"The holy martyrs? Lord Altamount?"

"Why do you say Lord Altamount?"

"I saw him that way—suddenly—that evening. Carved in stone—in a thirteenth-century cathedral perhaps."

"One of us may have to die. Perhaps more."

She stopped what he was about to say.

"There is another thing I think of sometimes. A verse in the New Testament—Luke, I think. Christ at the Last Supper saying to his followers: 'You are my companions and my friends, *yet one of you is a devil.*' So in all probability is one of *us* a devil."

"You think it possible?"

"Almost certain. Someone we trust and know, but who goes to sleep at night, not dreaming of martyrdom, but of thirty pieces of silver, and who wakes with the feel of them in the palm of his hand."

"The love of money?"

"Ambition covers it better. How does one recognize a devil? How would one *know?* A devil would stand out in a crowd, would be exciting—would advertise himself—would exercise leadership."

She was silent a moment and then said in a thoughtful voice:

"I had a friend once in the Diplomatic Service who told me how she had said to a German woman how moved she herself had been at the performance of the Passion Play at Oberammergau. But the German woman said scornfully: 'You do not understand. *We* Germans have no need of a Jesus Christ!

We have our Adolf Hitler here with us. He is greater than any Jesus that ever lived.' She was quite a nice ordinary woman. But that is how she felt. Masses of people felt it. Hitler was a spellbinder. He spoke and they listened—and accepted the sadism, the gas chambers, the tortures of the Gestapo."

She shrugged her shoulders and then said in her normal voice, "All the same, it's odd that you should have said what you did just now."

"What was that?"

"About the Old Man of the Mountain. The head of the Assassins."

"Are you telling me there *is* an Old Man of the Mountain here?"

"No. Not an Old Man of the Mountain, but there might be an Old Woman of the Mountain."

"An Old Woman of the Mountain. What's she like?"

"You'll see this evening."

"What are we doing this evening?"

"Going into society," said Renata.

"It seems a long time since you've been Mary Ann."

"You'll have to wait till we're doing some air travel again."

"I suppose it's very bad for one's morale," Stafford Nye said thoughtfully, "living high up in the world."

"Are you talking socially?"

"No. Geographically. If you live in a castle on a mountain peak overlooking the world below you, well, it makes you despise the ordinary folk, doesn't it? You're the top one, you're the grand one. That's what Hitler felt in Berchtesgaden, that's what many people feel perhaps who climb mountains and look down on their fellow creatures in valleys below."

"You must be careful tonight," Renata warned him. "It's going to be ticklish."

"Any instructions?"

"You're a disgruntled man. You're one that's against the Establishment, against the conventional world. You're a rebel, but a secret rebel. Can you do it?"

"I can try."

The scenery had grown wilder. The big car twisted and turned up the roads, passing through mountain villages, sometimes looking down on a bewilderingly distant view where lights shone on a river, where the steeples of churches showed in the distance.

"Where are we going, Mary Ann?"

"To an eagle's nest."

The road took a final turn. It wound through a forest. Stafford Nye thought he caught glimpses now and again of deer or of animals of some kind. Occasionally, too, there were leather-jacketed men with guns. Keepers, he thought. And then they came finally to a view of an enormous Schloss standing on a crag. Some of it, he thought, was partially ruined, though most of it had been restored and rebuilt. It was both massive and magnificent, but there

was nothing new about it or in the message it held. It was representative of
past power—power held through bygone ages.

"This was originally the Grand Duchy of Liechtenstolz. The Schloss was
built by the Grand Duke Ludwig in seventeen ninety," said Renata.

"Who lives there now? The present Grand Duke?"

"No. They're all gone and done with. Swept away."

"And who lives here now then?"

"Someone who has present-day power," said Renata.

"Money?"

"Yes. Very much so."

"Shall we meet Mr. Robinson, flown on ahead by air to greet us?"

"The last person you'll meet here will be Mr. Robinson, I can assure you."

"A pity," said Stafford Nye. "I like Mr. Robinson. He's quite something,
isn't he? Who is he really—what nationality is he?"

"I don't think anybody has ever known. Everyone tells one something
different. Some people say he's a Turk, some that he's an Armenian, some
that he's Dutch, some that he's just plain English. Some say that his mother
was a Circassian slave, a Russian grand duchess, an Indian begum, and so on.
Nobody knows. One person told me that his mother was a Miss McLellan
from Scotland. I think that's as likely as anything."

They had drawn up beneath a large portico. Two menservants in livery
came down the steps. Their bows were ostentatious as they welcomed the
guests. The luggage was removed; they had a good deal of luggage with them.
Stafford Nye had wondered to begin with why he had been told to bring so
much, but he was beginning to understand now that from time to time there
was need for it. There would, he thought, be need for it this evening. A few
questioning remarks and his companion told him that this was so.

They met before dinner, summoned by the sound of a great resounding
gong. As he paused in the hall, he waited for her to join him coming down the
stairs. She was in full elaborate evening dress tonight, wearing a dark red
velvet gown, rubies round her neck, and a ruby tiara on her head. A manservant stepped forward and conducted them. Flinging open the door, he
announced:

"The Gräfin Zerkowski, Sir Stafford Nye."

"Here we come, and I hope we look the part," said Sir Stafford Nye to
himself.

He looked down in a satisfied manner at the sapphire and diamond studs in
the front of his shirt. A moment later he had drawn his breath in an astonished gasp. Whatever he had expected to see, it had not been this. It was an
enormous room, rococo in style, chairs and sofas and hangings of the finest
brocades and velvets. On the walls there were pictures that he could not
recognize all at once, but where he noted almost immediately—for he was
fond of pictures—what was certainly a Cézanne, a Matisse, possibly a Renoir.
Pictures of inestimable value.

Sitting on a vast chair, thronelike in its suggestion, was an enormous woman. A whale of a woman, Stafford Nye thought, there really was no other word to describe her. A great, big, cheesy-looking woman, wallowing in fat. Double, treble, almost quadruple chins. She wore a dress of stiff orange satin. On her head was an elaborate crownlike tiara of precious stones. Her hands, which rested on the brocaded arms of her chair, were also enormous. Great, big, fat hands with great, big, fat, shapeless fingers. On each finger, he noticed, was a solitaire ring. And in each ring, he thought, was a genuine solitaire stone. A ruby, an emerald, a sapphire, a diamond, a pale green stone which he did not know, a chrysoprase, perhaps, a yellow stone which, if not a topaz, was a yellow diamond. She was horrible, he thought. She wallowed in her fat. A great, white, creased, slobbering mass of fat was her face. And set in it, rather like currants in a vast currant bun, were two small black eyes. Very shrewd eyes, looking on the world, appraising it, appraising him, not appraising Renata, he thought. Renata she knew. Renata was here by command, by appointment. However you liked to put it. Renata had been told to bring *him* here. He wondered why. He couldn't really think why, but he was quite sure of it. It was at him she was looking. She was appraising *him,* summing *him* up. Was he what she wanted? Was he, yes, he'd rather put it this way, was he what the customer had ordered?

I'll have to make quite sure that I know what it is she does want, he thought. I'll have to do my best, otherwise . . . Otherwise he could quite imagine that she might raise a fat ringed hand and say to one of the tall, muscular footmen: "Take him and throw him over the battlements." It's ridiculous, thought Stafford Nye. Such things can't happen nowadays. Where am I? What kind of a parade, a masquerade or a theatrical performance am I taking part in?

"You have come very punctual to time, child."

It was a hoarse, asthmatic voice which had once had an undertone, he thought, of strength, possibly even of beauty. That was over now. Renata came forward, made a slight curtsy. She picked up the fat hand and dropped a courtesy kiss upon it.

"Let me present to you Sir Stafford Nye. The Gräfin Charlotte von Waldsausen."

The fat hand was extended toward him. He bent over it in the foreign style. Then she said something that surprised him.

"I know your great-aunt," she said.

He looked astounded, and he saw immediately that she was amused by that, but he saw, too, that she had expected him to be surprised by it. She laughed a rather queer, grating laugh. Not attractive.

"Shall we say, I used to know her. It is many, many years since I have seen her. We were in Switzerland together, at Lausanne, as girls. Matilda. Lady Matilda Baldwen-White."

"What a wonderful piece of news to take home with me," said Stafford Nye.

"She is older than I am. She is in good health?"

"For her age, in very good health. She lives in the country quietly. She has arthritis, rheumatism."

"Ah, yes, all the ills of old age. She should have injections of procaine. That is what the doctors do here in this altitude. It is very satisfactory. Does she know that you are visiting me?"

"I imagine that she has not the least idea of it," said Sir Stafford Nye. "She knew only that I was going to this festival of modern music."

"Which you enjoyed, I hope?"

"Oh, enormously. It is a fine Festival Opera Hall, is it not?"

"One of the finest. Pah! It makes the old Bayreuth Festival Hall look like a comprehensive school! Do you know what it cost to build that Opera House?"

She mentioned a sum in millions of marks. It quite took Stafford Nye's breath away, but he was under no necessity to conceal that. She was pleased with the effect it made upon him.

"With money," she said, "if one knows, if one has the ability, if one has the discrimination, what is there that money cannot do? It can give one the best."

She said the last two words with a rich enjoyment, a kind of smacking of the lips which he found both unpleasant and at the same time slightly sinister.

"I see that here," he said, as he looked round the walls.

"You are fond of art? Yes, I see you are. There, on the east wall, is the finest Cézanne in the world today. Some say that the—ah, I forget the name of it at the moment, the one in the Metropolitan in New York—is finer. That is not true. The best Matisse, the best Cézanne, the best of all that great school of art are here. Here in my mountain aerie."

"It is wonderful," said Sir Stafford. "Quite wonderful."

Drinks were being handed round. The Old Woman of the Mountain, Sir Stafford Nye noticed, did not drink anything. It was possible, he thought, that she feared to take any risks over her blood pressure with that vast weight.

"And where did you meet this child?" asked the mountainous dragon.

Was it a trap? He did not know, but he made his decision.

"At the American Embassy, in London."

"Ah, yes, so I heard. And how is—ah, I forget her name now—ah, yes, Milly Jean, our southern heiress? Attractive, did you think?"

"Most charming. She has a great success in London."

"And poor dull Sam Cortman, the United States Ambassador?"

"A very sound man, I'm sure," said Stafford Nye politely.

She chuckled.

"Aha, you're tactful, are you not? Ah, well, he does well enough. He does what he is told, as a good politician should. And it is enjoyable to be Ambassador in London. She could do that for him, Milly Jean. Ah, she could get him an embassy anywhere in the world, with that well-stuffed purse of hers. Her father owns half the oil in Texas, he owns land, gold fields, everything. A coarse, singularly ugly man— But what does she look like? A gentle little aristocrat. Not blatant, not rich. That is very clever of her, is it not?"

"Sometimes it presents no difficulties," said Sir Stafford Nye.

"And you? You are not rich?"

"I wish I was."

"The Foreign Office nowadays, it is not, shall we say, very rewarding?"

"Oh, well, I would not put it like that. . . . After all, one goes places, one meets amusing people, one sees the world, one sees something of what goes on."

"Something, yes. But not everything."

"That would be very difficult."

"Have you ever wished to see what—how shall I put it—what goes on behind the scenes in life?"

"One has an idea sometimes." He made his voice noncommittal.

"I have heard it said that that is true of you, that you have sometimes ideas about things. Not perhaps the conventional ideas?"

"There have been times when I've been made to feel the bad boy of the family," said Stafford Nye, and laughed.

Old Charlotte chuckled.

"You don't mind admitting things now and again, do you?"

"Why pretend? People always know what you're concealing."

She looked at him.

"What do you want out of life, young man?"

He shrugged his shoulders. Here again, he had to play things by ear.

"Nothing," he said.

"Come now, come now, am I to believe that?"

"Yes, you can believe it. I am not ambitious. Do I look ambitious?"

"No, I will admit that."

"I ask only to be amused, to live comfortably, to eat, to drink in moderation, to have friends who amuse me."

The old woman leaned forward. Her eyes snapped open and shut three or four times. Then she spoke in a rather different voice. It was like a whistling note.

"Can you hate? Are you capable of hating?"

"To hate is a waste of time."

"I see. I see. There are no lines of discontent in your face. That is true enough. All the same, I think you are ready to take a certain path which will lead you to a certain place, and you will go along it smiling, as though you did not care, but all the same, in the end, if you find the right advisers, the right helpers, you might attain what you want, if you are capable of wanting."

"As to that," said Stafford Nye, "who isn't?" He shook his head at her very gently. "You see too much," he said. "Much too much."

Footmen threw open a door.

"Dinner is served."

The proceedings were properly formal. They had indeed almost a royal tinge about them. The big doors at the far end of the room were flung open, showing through to a brightly lighted ceremonial dining room with a painted ceiling and three enormous chandeliers. Two middle-aged women approached the Gräfin, one on either side. They wore evening dress, their gray hair was carefully piled on their heads, each wore a diamond brooch. To Sir Stafford Nye, all the same, they brought a faint flavor of wardresses. They were, he thought, not so much security guards as perhaps high-class nursing attendants in charge of the health, the toilet and other intimate details of the Gräfin Charlotte's existence. After respectful bows, each one of them slipped an arm below the shoulder and elbow of the sitting woman. With the ease of long practice aided by the effort which was obviously as much as she could make, they raised her to her feet in a dignified fashion.

"We will go in to dinner now," said Charlotte.

With her two female attendants, she led the way. On her feet she looked even more a mass of wobbling jelly, yet she was still formidable. You could not dispose of her in your mind as just a fat old woman. She was somebody, knew she was somebody, intended to be somebody. Behind the three of them he and Renata followed.

As they entered through the portals of the dining room, he felt it was almost more a banquet hall than a dining room. There was a bodyguard here. Tall, fair-haired, handsome young men. They wore some kind of uniform. As Charlotte entered, there was a clash as one and all drew their swords. They crossed them overhead to make a passageway, and Charlotte, steadying herself, passed along that passageway, released by her attendants and making her progress solo to a vast carved chair with gold fittings and upholstered in golden brocade at the head of the long table. It was rather like a wedding procession, Stafford Nye thought. A naval or military one. In this case surely, military, strictly military—but lacking a bridegroom.

They were all young men of super physique. None of them, he thought, was older than thirty. They had good looks, their health was evident. They did not smile, they were entirely serious, they were—he thought of a word for it—yes, dedicated. Perhaps not so much a military procession as a religious one. The servitors appeared, old-fashioned servitors belonging, he thought, to the Schloss's past, to a time before the 1939 war. It was like a super production of a period historic play. And queening over it, sitting in the chair or the throne or whatever you liked to call it, at the head of the table, was not a queen or an empress but an old woman noticeable mainly for her avoirdupois weight and her extraordinary and intense ugliness. Who was she? What was she doing here? Why?

Why all this masquerade, why this bodyguard, a security bodyguard perhaps? Other diners came to the table. They bowed to the monstrosity on the presiding throne and took their places. They wore ordinary evening dress. No introductions were made.

Stafford Nye, after long years of sizing up people, assessed them. Different types. A great many different types. Lawyers, he was certain. Several lawyers. Possibly accountants or financiers; one or two army officers in plain clothes. They were of the household, he thought, but they were also in the old-fashioned feudal sense of the term those who "sat below the salt."

Food came. A vast boar's head pickled in aspic, venison, a cool refreshing lemon sorbet, a magnificent edifice of pastry—a super *millefeuille* that seemed of unbelievable confectionery richness.

The vast woman ate—ate greedily, hungrily, enjoying her food. From outside came a new sound. The sound of the powerful engine of a super sports car. It passed the windows in a white flash. There came a cry inside the room from the bodyguard. A great cry of "Heil! Heil! Heil Franz!"

The bodyguard of young men moved with the ease of a military maneuver known by heart. Everyone had risen to their feet. Only the old woman sat without moving, her head lifted high, on her dais. And, so Stafford Nye thought, a new excitement now permeated the room.

The other guests, or the other members of the household, whatever they were, disappeared in a way that somehow reminded Stafford of lizards disappearing into the cracks of a wall. The golden-haired boys formed a new figure, their swords flew out, they saluted their patroness, she bowed her head in acknowledgment, their swords were sheathed and they turned, permission given, to march out through the door of the room. Her eyes followed them, then went first to Renata, and then to Stafford Nye.

"What do you think of them?" she said. "My boys, my youth corps, my children. Yes, my children. Have you a word that can describe them?"

"I think so," said Stafford Nye. "Magnificent." He spoke to her as to Royalty. "Magnificent, ma'am."

"Ah!" She bowed her head. She smiled, the wrinkles multiplying all over her face. It made her look exactly like a crocodile.

A terrible woman, he thought; a terrible woman, impossible, dramatic. Was any of this happening? He couldn't believe it was. What could this be but yet another festival hall in which a production was being given?

The door clashed open again. The yellow-haired band of the young supermen marched as before through it. This time they did not wield swords; instead, they sang. Sang with unusual beauty of tone and voice.

After a good many years of pop music, Stafford Nye felt an incredulous pleasure. Trained voices, these. Not raucous shouting. Trained by masters of the singing art. Not allowed to strain their vocal cords, to be off key. They might be the new heroes of a new world, but what they sang was not new music. It was music he had heard before. An arrangement of the Preislied, there must be a concealed orchestra somewhere, he thought, in a gallery round the top of the room. It was an arrangement or adaptation of various Wagnerian themes. It passed from the Preislied to the distant echoes of the Rhine music.

The élite corps made once more a double lane where somebody was expected to make an entrance. It was not the old empress this time. She sat on her dais awaiting whoever was coming.

And at last he came. The music changed as he came. It gave out that motif which by now Stafford Nye had got by heart. The melody of the Young Siegfried. Siegfried's horn call, rising up in its youth and its triumph, its mastery of a new world which the young Siegfried came to conquer.

Through the doorway, marching up between the lines of what were clearly his followers, came one of the handsomest young men Stafford Nye had ever seen. Golden-haired, blue-eyed, perfectly proportioned, conjured up as it were by the wave of a magician's wand? He came forth out of the world of myth. Myth, heroes, resurrection, rebirth—it was all there. His beauty, his strength, his incredible assurance and arrogance.

He strode through the double lines of his bodyguard, until he stood before the hideous mountain of womanhood that sat there on her throne; he knelt on one knee, raised her hand to his lips, and then rising to his feet, he threw up one arm in salutation and uttered the cry that Stafford Nye had heard from the others. "Heil!" His German was not very clear, but Stafford Nye thought he distinguished the syllables "Heil to the great mother!"

Then the handsome young hero looked from one side to the other. There was some faint recognition, though an uninterested one, of Renata, but when his gaze turned to Stafford Nye, there was definite interest and appraisal. Caution, thought Stafford Nye. Caution! He must play his part right now. Play the part that was expected of him. Only—what the hell was that part? What was he doing here? What were he or the girl supposed to be doing here? Why had they come?

The hero spoke.

"So," he said, "we have guests!" And he added, smiling with the arrogance of a young man who knows that he is vastly superior to any other person in the world, "Welcome, guests, welcome to you both."

Somewhere in the depths of the Schloss, a great bell began tolling. It had no funeral sound about it, but it had a disciplinary air—the feeling of a monastery summoned to some holy office.

"We must sleep now," said old Charlotte. "Sleep. We will meet again tomorrow morning at eleven o'clock."

She looked toward Renata and Sir Stafford Nye.

"You will be shown to your rooms. I hope you will sleep well."

It was the Royal dismissal.

Stafford Nye saw Renata's arm fly up in the Fascist salute, but it was addressed not to Charlotte, but to the golden-haired boy. He thought she said: "Heil Franz Joseph." He copied her gesture and he, too, said "Heil!"

Charlotte spoke to them.

"Would it please you tomorrow morning to start the day with a ride through the forest?"

"I should like it of all things," said Stafford Nye.

"And you, child?"

"Yes, I, too."

"Very good then. It shall be arranged. Good night to you both. I am glad to welcome you here. Franz Joseph—give me your arm. We will go into the Chinese Boudoir. We have much to discuss, and you will have to leave in good time tomorrow morning."

The menservants escorted Renata and Stafford Nye to their apartments. Nye hesitated for a moment on the threshold. Would it be possible for them to have a word or two now? He decided against it. As long as the castle walls surrounded them, it was well to be careful. One never knew—each room might be wired with microphones.

Sooner or later, though, he *had* to ask questions. Certain things aroused a new and sinister apprehension in his mind. He was being persuaded, inveigled into something. But what? And whose doing was it?

The bedrooms were handsome, yet oppressive. The rich hangings of satin and velvets, some of them antique, gave out a faint perfume of decay, tempered by spices. He wondered how often Renata had stayed here before.

11

The Young and the Lovely

AFTER BREAKFASTING ON the following morning in a small breakfast room downstairs, Stafford Nye found Renata waiting for him. The horses were at the door.

Both of them had brought riding clothes with them. Everything they could possibly require seemed to have been intelligently anticipated.

They mounted and rode away down the castle drive. Renata spoke with the groom at some length.

"He asked if we would like him to accompany us, but I said no. I know the tracks round here fairly well."

"I see. You have been here before?"

"Not very often of late years. Early in my life I knew this place very well."

He gave her a sharp look. She did not return it. As she rode beside him, he watched her profile—the thin, aquiline nose, the head carried so proudly on the slender neck. She rode a horse well, he saw that.

All the same, there was a sense of ill ease in his mind this morning. He wasn't sure why. . . .

His mind went back to the airport lounge. The woman who had come to stand beside him. The glass of Pilsner on the table . . . Nothing in it that there shouldn't have been—neither then, nor later. A risk he had accepted. Why, when all that was long over, should it rouse uneasiness in him now?

They had a brief canter following a ride through the trees. A beautiful property, beautiful woods. In the distance he saw horned animals. A paradise for a sportsman, a paradise for the old way of living, a paradise that contained—what? A serpent? As it was in the beginning—with Paradise went a serpent. He drew rein and the horses fell to a walk. He and Renata were alone —no microphones, no listening walls— The time had come for his questions.

"Who is she?" he said urgently. "What is she?"

"It's easy to answer. So easy that it's hardly believable."

"Well?" he said.

"She's oil. Copper. Gold mines in South Africa. Armaments in Sweden. Uranium deposits in the north. Nuclear development, vast stretches of cobalt. She's all those things."

"And yet, I hadn't heard about her, I didn't know her name, I didn't know—"

"She has not wanted people to know."

"Can one keep such things quiet?"

"Easily, if you have enough copper and oil and nuclear deposits and armaments and all the rest of it. Money can advertise, or money can keep secrets, can hush things up."

"But who *actually* is she?"

"Her grandfather was American. He was mainly railways, I think. Possibly Chicago hogs in those times. It's like going back into history, finding out. He married a German woman. You've heard of her, I expect. Big Belinda, they used to christen her. Armaments, shipping, the whole industrial wealth of Europe. She was her father's heiress."

"Between those two, unbelievable wealth," said Sir Stafford Nye. "And so —power. Is that what you're telling me?"

"Yes. She didn't just inherit things, you know. She made money as well. She'd inherited brains, she was a big financier in her own right. Everything she touched multiplied itself. Turned to incredible sums of money, and she invested them. Taking advice, taking other people's judgment, but in the end always using her own. And always prospering. Always adding to her wealth so that it was too fabulous to be believed. Money creates money."

"Yes, I can understand that. Wealth *has* to increase if there's a superfluity of it. But—what did *she* want? What has *she* got?"

"You said it just now. Power."

"And she lives here? Or does she—?"

"She visits America and Sweden. Oh, yes, she visits places, but not often. This is where she prefers to be, in the center of a web like a vast spider controlling all the threads. The threads of finance. Other threads, too."

"When you say other threads—"

"The arts. Music, pictures, writers. Human beings—young human beings."

"Yes. One might know that. Those pictures, a wonderful collection."

"There are galleries of them upstairs in the Schloss. There are Rembrandts and Giottos and Raphaels and there are cases of jewels—some of the most wonderful jewels in the world."

"All belonging to one ugly, gross old woman. Is she satisfied?"

"Not yet, but well on the way to being."

"Where is she going, what does she want?"

"She loves youth. That is her mode of power. To control youth. The world is full of rebellious youth at this moment. That's been helped on. Modern philosophy, modern thought, writers and others whom she finances and controls."

"But how can—?" He stopped.

"I can't tell you because I don't know. It's an enormous ramification. She's behind it in one sense, supports rather curious charities, earnest philanthropists and idealists, raises innumerable grants for students and artists and writers."

"And yet you say it's not—"

"No, it's not yet complete. It's a great upheaval that's being planned. It's believed in, it's the new heaven and the new earth. That's what's been promised by leaders for thousands of years. Promised by religions, promised by those who support Messiahs, promised by those who come back to teach the law, like the Buddha. Promised by politicians. The crude heaven of an easy attainment such as the Assassins believed in, and the Old Man of the Assassins promised his followers and, from their point of view, gave to them."

"Is she behind drugs as well?"

"Yes. Without conviction, of course. Only a means of having people bent to her will. It's one way, too, of destroying people. The weak ones. The ones she thinks are no good, although they had once shown promise. She'd never take drugs herself—she's strong. But drugs destroy weak people more easily and naturally than anything else."

"And force? What about force? You can't do everything by propaganda."

"No, of course not. Propaganda is the first stage, and behind it there are vast armaments piling up. Arms that go to deprived countries and then on elsewhere. Tanks and guns and nuclear weapons that go to Africa and the South Seas and South America. In South America there's a lot building up. Forces of young men and women drilling and training. Enormous arms dumps—means of chemical warfare—"

"It's a nightmare! How do you know all this, Renata?"

"Partly because I've been told it; from information received, partly because I have been instrumental in proving some of it."

"But *you*. You and *she?*"

"There's always something idiotic behind all great and vast projects." She laughed suddenly. "Once, you see, she was in love with my grandfather. A foolish story. He lived in this part of the world. He had a castle a mile or two from here."

"Was he a man of genius?"

"Not at all. He was just a very good sportsman. Handsome, dissolute and attractive to women. And so, because of that, she is in a sense my protectress. And I am one of her converts or slaves! I work for her. I find people for her. I carry out her commands in different parts of the world."

"Do you?"

"What do you mean by that?"

"I wondered," said Sir Stafford Nye.

He did wonder. He looked at Renata and he thought again of the airport. He was working *for* Renata, he was working *with* Renata. She had brought him to this Schloss. Who had told her to bring him here? Big, gross Charlotte in the middle of her spider's web? He had had a reputation, a reputation of being unsound in certain diplomatic quarters. He could be useful to these people perhaps, but useful in a small and rather humiliating way. And he thought suddenly, in a kind of fog of question marks: Renata??? I took a risk with her at Frankfurt airport. But I was right. It came off. Nothing happened to me. But all the same, he thought, who is she? *What* is she? I don't know. I can't be *sure*. One can't in the world today be sure of *anyone*. Anyone at all. She was told perhaps to get me. To get me into the hollow of her hand, so that business at Frankfurt might have been cleverly thought out. It fitted in with my sense of risk, and it would make me sure of her. It would make me trust her.

"Let's canter again," she said. "We've walked the horses too long."

"I haven't asked you what *you* are in all this?"

"I take orders."

"From whom?"

"There's an opposition. There's always an opposition. There are people who have a suspicion of what's going on, of how the world is going to be made to change, of how with money, wealth, armaments, idealism, great trumpeting words of power, of what's going to happen. There are people who say it shall *not* happen."

"And you are with them?"

"I say so."

"What do you mean by that, Renata?"

She said, "I *say so.*"

He said, "That young man last night—"

"Franz Joseph?"

"Is that his name?"

"It is the name he is known by."

"But he has another name, hasn't he?"

"Do you think so?"

"He is, isn't he, the young Siegfried?"

"You saw him like that? You realized that's what he was, what he stands for?"

"I think so. Youth. Heroic youth. Aryan youth. It has to be Aryan youth in this part of the world. There is still that point of view. A super race, the superman. They must be of Aryan descent."

"Oh, yes, it's lasted on from the time of Hitler. It doesn't always come out into the open much and, in other places all over the world, it isn't stressed so much. South America, as I say, is one of the strongholds. And Peru and South Africa also."

"What does the young Siegfried do? What does he do besides look handsome and kiss the hand of his protectress?"

"Oh, he's quite an orator. He speaks and his following would follow him to death."

"Is that true?"

"He believes it."

"And you?"

"I think I might believe it." She added: "Oratory is very frightening, you know. What a voice can do, what words can do, and not particularly convincing words at that. The *way* they are said. His voice rings like a bell, and women cry and scream and faint away when he addresses them—you'll see that for yourself.

"You saw Charlotte's bodyguard last night all dressed up—people do love dressing up nowadays. You'll see them all over the world in their own chosen get-up, different in different places, some with their long hair and their beards, and girls in their streaming white nightgowns, talking of peace and beauty, and the wonderful world that is the world of the young which is to be theirs when they've destroyed enough of the old world. The original Country of the Young was west of the Irish Sea, wasn't it? A very simple place, a different Country of the Young from what we're planning now—It was silver sands, and sunshine and singing in the waves. . . .

"But now we want anarchy, and breaking down and destroying. Only anarchy can benefit those who march behind it. It's frightening, it's also wonderful—because of its violence, because it's bought with pain and suffering—"

"So that is how you see the world today?"

"Sometimes."

"And what am *I* to do next?"

"Come with your guide. I'm your guide. Like Virgil with Dante, I'll take you down into hell, I'll show you the sadistic films partly copied from the old SS, show you cruelty and pain and violence worshipped. And I'll show you the great dreams of paradise in peace and beauty. You won't know which is which and what is what. But you'll have to make up your mind."

"Do I trust you, Renata?"

"That will be your choice. You can run away from me if you like, or you can stay with me and see the new world—the new world that's in the making."

"Pasteboard," said Sir Stafford Nye violently.

She looked at him inquiringly.

"Like Alice in Wonderland. The cards, the pasteboard cards all rising up in the air. Flying about. Kings and queens and knaves. All sorts of things."

"You mean—what do you mean exactly?"

"I mean it isn't real. It's make-believe. The whole damn thing is make-believe."

"In one sense, yes."

"All dressed up playing parts, putting on a show. I'm getting nearer, aren't I, to the meaning of things?"

"In a way, yes, and in a way, no—"

"There's one thing I'd like to ask you because it puzzles me. Big Charlotte ordered you to bring me to see her—why? What did she know about me? What use did she think she could make of me?"

"I don't quite know—possibly a kind of Éminence Grise—working behind a façade. That would suit you rather well."

"But she knows nothing whatever about me!"

"Oh, *that!*" Suddenly Renata went into peals of laughter. "It's so ridiculous, really—the same old nonsense all over again."

"I don't understand you, Renata."

"No—because it's so simple. Mr. Robinson would understand."

"Would you kindly explain what you are talking about?"

"It's the same old business—*'It's not what you are. It's who you know.'* Your Great-Aunt Matilda and big Charlotte were at school together—"

"You actually mean—"

"Girls together."

He stared at her. Then he threw his head back and roared with laughter.

12

Court Jester

THEY LEFT THE Schloss at midday, saying good-by to their hostess. Then they had driven down the winding road, leaving the Schloss high above them, and they had come at last, after many hours of driving, to a stronghold in the Dolomites—an amphitheater in the mountains where meetings, concerts and reunions of the various youth groups were held.

Renata had brought him there, his guide, and from his seat on the bare rock he had watched what went on and had listened. He understood a little more what she had been talking about earlier that day. This great mass gathering, animated as all mass gatherings can be whether they are called by an evangelistic religious leader in Madison Square Garden, New York, or in the shadow of a Welsh church or in a football crowd or in the super demonstrations that marched to attack embassies and police and universities and all the rest of it.

She had brought him there to show him the meaning of that one phrase: "The Young Siegfried."

Franz Joseph, if that was really his name, had addressed the crowd. His voice, rising, falling, with its curious exciting quality, its emotional appeal, had held sway over that groaning, almost moaning crowd of young women and young men. Every word that he had uttered had seemed pregnant with meaning, had held incredible appeal. The crowd had responded like an orchestra. His voice had been the baton of the conductor. And yet, what had the boy said? What had been the young Siegfried's message? There were no words that he could remember when it came to an end, but he knew that he had been moved, promised things, roused to enthusiasm. And now it was over. The crowd had surged round the rocky platform, calling, crying out. Some of the girls had been screaming with enthusiasm. Some of them had fainted. What a world it was nowadays, he thought. Everything used the whole time to arouse emotion. Discipline? Restraint? None of those things counted for anything anymore. Nothing mattered but to *feel*.

What sort of world, thought Stafford Nye, could that make?

His guide had touched him on the arm and they had disentangled themselves from the crowd. They had found their car and the driver had taken them by roads with which he was evidently well acquainted, to a town and an inn on a mountainside where rooms had been reserved for them.

They walked out of the inn presently and up the side of a mountain by a well-trodden path until they came to a seat. They sat there for some moments in silence. It was then that Stafford Nye had said again, "Pasteboard."

For some five minutes or so they sat looking down the valley, then Renata said, "Well?"

"What are you asking me?"

"What you think so far of what I have shown you?"

"I'm not convinced," said Stafford Nye.

She gave a sigh, a deep, unexpected sigh.

"That's what I hoped you would say."

"It's none of it true, is it? It's a gigantic show. A show put on by a producer —a complete group of producers, perhaps.

"That monstrous woman pays the producer, hires the producer. We've not seen the producer. What we've seen today is the star performer."

"What do you think of him?"

"He's not real either," said Stafford Nye. "He's just an actor. A first-class actor, superbly produced."

A sound surprised him. It was Renata laughing. She got up from her seat. She looked suddenly excited, happy, and at the same time faintly ironical.

"I knew it," she said. "I knew you'd see. I knew you'd have your feet on the ground. You've always known, haven't you, about everything you've met in life? You've known humbug, you've known everything and everyone for what they really are.

"No need to go to Stratford and see Shakespearean plays to know what part you are cast for—the kings and the great men have to have a jester—the king's jester, who tells the king the truth, and talks common sense, and makes fun of all the things that are taking in other people."

"So that's what I am, is it? A court jester?"

"Can't you feel it yourself? That's what we want—That's what we need. 'Pasteboard,' you said. 'Cardboard.' A vast well-produced splendid *sham!* And how right you are. But people are taken in. They think something's wonderful, or they think something's devilish, or they think it's something terribly important. Of course it isn't—only—only one's got to find out just how to *show* people—that the whole thing, all of it, is just *silly*. Just damn *silly*. That's what you and I are going to do."

"Is it your idea that in the end we debunk all this?"

"It seems wildly unlikely, I agree. But you know once people are shown that something isn't real, that it's just one enormous leg pull—well—"

"Are you proposing to preach a gospel of common sense?"

"Of course not," said Renata. "Nobody'd listen to that, would they?"

"Not just at present."

"No. We'll have to give them evidence—facts—truth."

"Have we got such things?"

"Yes—what I brought back with me via Frankfurt—what you helped to bring safely into England—"

"I don't understand—"

"Not yet— You will know later. For now we've got a part to play. We're ready and willing, fairly panting to be indoctrinated. We worship youth. We're followers and believers in the young Siegfried."

"*You* can put that over, no doubt. I'm not so sure about myself. I've never been very successful as a worshipper of anything. The king's jester isn't. He's the great debunker. Nobody's going to appreciate that very much just now, are they?"

"Of course they're not. No. You don't let that side of yourself show. Except, of course, when you're talking about your masters and betters, politicians and diplomats, Foreign Office, the Establishment, all the other things. Then you can be embittered, malicious, witty, slightly cruel."

"I still don't see my role in the world crusade."

"That's a very ancient one, the one that everybody understands and appreciates. Something in it for you. That's your line. You haven't been appreciated in the past, but the young Siegfried and all he stands for will hold out the hope of reward to you. Because you give him all the inside dope he wants about your own country, he will promise you places of power in that country in the good times to come."

"You insinuate that this is a world movement. Is that true?"

"Of course it is. Rather like one of those hurricanes, you know, that have names. Flora or Little Annie. They come up out of the south or the north or the east or the west, but they come up from nowhere and destroy everything. That's what everyone wants. In Europe and Asia and America. Perhaps Africa, though there won't be so much enthusiasm there. They're fairly new to power and graft and things. Oh, yes, it's a world movement, all right. Run by youth and all the intense vitality of youth. They haven't got knowledge and they haven't got experience, but they've got vision and vitality, and they're backed by money. Rivers and rivers of money pouring in. There's been too much materialism, so we've asked for something else, and we've got it. But as it's based on hate, it can't get anywhere. It can't move off the ground. Don't you remember in nineteen nineteen everyone going about with a rapt face saying Communism was the answer to everything. That Marxist doctrine would produce a new heaven brought down to a new earth. So many noble ideas flowing about. But then, you see, whom have you got to work out the ideas with? After all, only the same human beings you've always had. You can create a third world now, or so everyone thinks, but the third world will have the same people in it as the first world or the second world or whatever names you like to call things. And when you have the same human beings running things, they'll run them the same way. You've only got to look at history."

"Does anybody care to look at history nowadays?"

"No. They'd much rather look forward to an unforeseeable future. Science was once going to be the answer to everything. Freudian beliefs and unrepressed sex would be the next answer to human misery. There'd be no more people with mental troubles. If anyone had said that mental homes would be even fuller as the result of shutting out repressions, nobody would have believed him."

Stafford Nye interrupted her:

"I want to know something," said Sir Stafford Nye.

"What is it?"

"Where are we going next?"

"South America. Possibly Pakistan or India on the way. And we must certainly go to the U.S.A. There's a lot going on there that's very interesting indeed. Especially in California—"

"Universities?" Sir Stafford sighed. "One gets very tired of universities. They repeat themselves so much."

They sat silent for some minutes. The light was failing, but a mountain peak showed softly red.

Stafford Nye said in a nostalgic tone:

"If we had some more music *now*—this moment—do you know what I'd order?"

"More Wagner? Or have you torn yourself free from Wagner?"

"No—you're quite right—more Wagner. I'd have Hans Sachs sitting under his elder tree, saying of the world: 'Mad, mad, all mad'—"

"Yes—that expresses it. It's lovely music, too. But *we're* not mad. We're sane."

"Eminently sane," said Stafford Nye. "That is going to be the difficulty. There's one more thing I want to know."

"Well?"

"Perhaps you won't tell me. But I've got to know. Is there going to be any fun to be got out of this mad business that we're attempting?"

"Of course there is. Why not?"

"Mad, mad, all mad—but we'll enjoy it all very much. Will our lives be long, Mary Ann?"

"Probably not," said Renata.

"That's the spirit. I'm with you, my comrade and my guide. Shall we get a better world as a result of our efforts?"

"I shouldn't think so, but it might be a kinder one. It's full of beliefs without kindness at present."

"Good enough," said Stafford Nye. "Onward!"

BOOK III
At Home and Abroad

13
Conference in Paris

IN A ROOM in Paris five men were sitting. It was a room that had seen historic meetings before. Quite a number of them. This meeting was in many ways a meeting of a different kind, yet it promised to be no less historic.

Monsieur Grosjean was presiding. He was a worried man doing his best to slide over things with facility and a charm of manner that had often helped him in the past. He did not feel it was helping him so much today. Signor Vitelli had arrived from Italy by air an hour before. His gestures were feverish, his manner unbalanced.

"It is beyond anything," he was saying; "it is beyond anything one could have imagined."

"These students," said Monsieur Grosjean, "do we not all suffer?"

"This is more than students. It is beyond students. What can one compare this to? A swarm of bees. A disaster of nature intensified. Intensified beyond anything one could have imagined. They march. They have machine guns. Somewhere they have acquired planes. They propose to take over the whole of North Italy. But it is madness, that! They are children—nothing more. And yet they have bombs, explosives. In the city of Milan alone they outnumber the police. What can we do, I ask you? The military? The army, too—it is in revolt. They say they are with *les jeunes*. They say there is no hope for the world except in anarchy. They talk of something they call the Third World, but this cannot just happen."

Monsieur Grosjean sighed. "It is very popular among the young," he said, "the anarchy. A belief in anarchy. We know that from the days of Algeria, from all the troubles from which our country and our colonial empire have

708

suffered. And what can we do? The military? In the end they back the students."

"The students, ah, the students," said Monsieur Poissonier.

He was a member of the French government to whom the word "student" was anathema. If he had been asked, he would have admitted to a preference for Asian flu or even an outbreak of bubonic plague. Either was preferable in his mind to the activities of students. A world with no students in it! That was what Monsieur Poissonier sometimes dreamed about. They were good dreams, those. They did not occur often enough.

"As for magistrates," said Monsieur Grosjean, "what has happened to our judicial authorities? The police—yes, they are loyal still, but the judiciary, they will not impose sentences, not on young men who are brought before them, young men who have destroyed property, government property, private property—every kind of property. And why not, one would like to know? I have been making inquiries lately. The Préfecture have suggested certain things to me. An increase is needed, they say, in the standard of living among judiciary authorities, especially in the provincial areas."

"Come, come," said Monsieur Poissonier, "you must be careful what you suggest."

"*Ma foi,* why should I be careful? Things need bringing into the open. We have had frauds before, gigantic frauds, and there is money now circulating around. Money, and we do not know where it comes from, but the Préfecture have said to me—and I believe it—that they begin to get an idea of where it is *going.* Do we contemplate, can we contemplate a corrupt state subsidized from some outside source?"

"In Italy, too," said Signor Vitelli, "in Italy, ah, I could tell you things. Yes, I could tell you things of what we suspect. But who is corrupting our world? A group of industrialists, a group of tycoons? How could such a thing be so?"

"This business has got to stop," said Monsieur Grosjean. "Action must be taken. Military action. Action from the Air Force. These anarchists, these marauders, they come from every class. It must be put down."

"Control by tear gas has been fairly successful," said Poissonier dubiously.

"Tear gas is not enough," said Monsieur Grosjean "The same result could be got by setting students to peel bunches of onions. Tears would flow from their eyes. It needs more than that."

Monsieur Poissonier said in a shocked voice:

"You are not suggesting the use of nuclear weapons?"

"Nuclear weapons? *Quel blague!* What can we do with nuclear weapons? What would become of the soil of France, of the air of France, if we use nuclear weapons? We can destroy Russia, we know that. We also know that Russia can destroy us."

"You're not suggesting that groups of marching and demonstrating students could destroy our authoritarian forces?"

"That is exactly what I am suggesting. I have had a warning of such things.

Of stockpiling of arms, and various forms of chemical warfare and of other things. I have had reports from some of our eminent scientists. Secrets are known. Stores—held in secret—weapons of warfare have been stolen. What is to happen next? I ask you. What is to happen next?".

The question was answered unexpectedly and with more rapidity than Monsieur Grosjean could possibly have calculated. The door opened and his principal secretary approached his master, his face showing urgent concern. Monsieur Grosjean looked at him with displeasure.

"Did I not say I wanted no interruptions?"

"Yes, indeed, Monsieur le Président, but this is somewhat unusual—" He bent toward his master's ear. "The Marshal is here. He demands entrance."

"The Marshal? You mean—"

The secretary nodded his head vigorously several times to show that he did mean. Monsieur Poissonier looked at his colleague in perplexity.

"He demands admission. He will not take refusal."

The two other men in the room looked first at Grosjean and then at the agitated Italian.

"Would it not be better," said Monsieur Coin, the Minister for Home Affairs, "if—?"

He paused at the "if" as the door was once more flung open and a man strode in. A very well-known man. A man whose word had been not only law, but above law in the country of France for many past years. To see him at this moment was an unwelcome surprise for those sitting there.

"Ah, I welcome you, dear colleagues," said the Marshal. "I come to help you. Our country is in danger. Action must be taken—immediate action! I come to put myself at your service. I take over all responsibility for acting in this crisis. There may be danger. I know there is, but honor is above danger. The salvation of France is above danger. They march this way now. A vast herd of students, of criminals who have been released from jails, some of them who have committed the crime of homicide. Men who have committed incendiarism. They shout names. They sing songs. They call on the names of their teachers, of their philosophers, of those who have led them on this path of insurrection. Those who will bring about the doom of France unless something is done. You sit here, you talk, you deplore things. More than that must be done. I have sent for two regiments. I have alerted the Air Force, special coded wires have gone out to our neighboring ally, to my friends in Germany, for she is our ally now in this crisis!

"Riot must be put down. Rebellion! Insurrection! The danger to men, women and children, to property. I go forth now to quell the insurrection, to speak to them as their father, their leader. These students, these criminals even, they are my children. They are the youth of France. I go to speak to them of that. They shall listen to me, governments will be revised, their studies can be resumed under their own auspices. Their grants have been insufficient, their lives have been deprived of beauty, of leadership. I come to promise all this. I speak in my own name. I shall speak also in your name, the name of the Government, you have done your best, you have acted as well as you know how. But it needs higher leadership. It needs *my* leadership. I go now. I have lists of further coded wires to be sent. Such nuclear deterrents as can be used in unfrequented spots can be put into action in such a modified form that though they may bring terror to the mob, we ourselves shall know that there is no real danger in them. I have thought out everything. My plan will go. Come, my loyal friends, accompany me."

"Marshal, we cannot allow—you cannot imperil yourself. We must . . ."

"I listen to nothing you say. I embrace my doom, my destiny."

The Marshal strode to the door.

"My staff is outside. My chosen bodyguard. I go now to speak to these young rebels, this young flower of beauty and terror, to tell them where their duty lies."

He disappeared through the door with the grandeur of a leading actor playing his favorite part.

"Bon dieu, he means it!" said Monsieur Poissonier.

"He will risk his life," said Signor Vitelli. "Who knows? It is brave, he is a brave man. It is gallant, yes, but what will happen to him? In the mood *les jeunes* are in now, they might kill him."

A pleasurable sigh fell from Monsieur Poissonier's lips. It might be true, he thought. Yes, it might be true.

"It is possible," he said. "Yes, they might kill him."

"One cannot wish that, of course," said Monsieur Grosjean carefully.

Monsieur Grosjean did wish it. He hoped for it, though a natural pessimism led him to have the second thought that things seldom fell out in the way you wanted them to. Indeed, a much more awful prospect confronted him. It was quite possible, it was within the traditions of the Marshal's past, that somehow or other he might induce a large pack of exhilarated and bloodthirsty students to listen to what he said, trust in his promises, and insist on restoring him to the power that he had once held. It was the sort of thing that had happened once or twice in the career of the Marshal. His personal magnetism was such that politicians had before now met their defeat when they least expected it.

"We must restrain him," he cried.

"Yes, yes," said Signor Vitelli, "he cannot be lost to the world."

"One fears," said Monsieur Poissonier. "He has too many friends in Germany, too many contacts, and you know they move very quickly in military matters in Germany. They might leap at the opportunity."

"Bon dieu, bon dieu," said Monsieur Grosjean, wiping his brow. "What shall we do? What can we do? What is that noise? I hear rifles, do I not?"

"No, no," said Monsieur Poissonier consolingly. "It is the canteen coffee trays you hear."

"There is a quotation I could use," said Monsieur Grosjean, who was a great lover of the drama, "if I could only remember it. A quotation from Shakespeare. 'Will nobody rid me of this—' "

" '—turbulent priest,' " said Monsieur Poissonier. "From the play *Becket.*"

"A madman like the Marshal is worse than a priest. A priest should at least be harmless, though indeed even His Holiness the Pope received a delegation of students only yesterday. He *blessed* them. He called them his children."

"A Christian gesture, though," said Monsieur Coin dubiously.

"One can go too far even with Christian gestures," said Monsieur Grosjean.

14

Conference in London

IN THE CABINET Room at 10 Downing Street, Mr. Cedric Lazenby, the Prime Minister, sat at the head of the table and looked at his assembled Cabinet without any noticeable pleasure. The expression on his face was definitely gloomy, which in a way afforded him a certain relief. He was beginning to think that it was only in the privacy of his cabinet meetings that he could relax his face into an unhappy expression, and could abandon that look which he presented usually to the world, of a wise and contented optimism which had served him so well in the various crises of political life.

He looked round at Gordon Chetwynd, who was frowning; at Sir George Packham, who was obviously worrying, thinking, and wondering as usual; at the military imperturbability of Colonel Munro; at Air Marshal Kenwood, a tight-lipped man who did not trouble to conceal his profound distrust of politicians. There was also Admiral Blunt, a large formidable man, who tapped his fingers on the table and bided his time until his moment should come.

"It is not too good," the Air Marshal was saying. "One has to admit it. Four of our planes hijacked within the last week. Flew 'em to Milan. Turned the passengers out and flew them on somewhere else. Actually Africa. Had pilots waiting there. Black men."

"Black Power," said Colonel Munro thoughtfully.

"Or Red Power?" suggested Lazenby. "I feel, you know, that all our difficulties might stem from Russian indoctrination. If one could get into touch with the Russians—I really think a personal visit at top level—".

"You stick where you are, Prime Minister," said Admiral Blunt. "Don't you start arseing around with the Russkies again. All *they* want at present is to keep out of all this mess. They haven't had as much trouble there with their students as most of us have. All they mind about is keeping an eye on the Chinese to see what they'll be up to next."

"I do think that personal influence—"

"You stay here and look after your own country," said Admiral Blunt. True to his name, and as was his wont, he said it bluntly.

"Hadn't we better hear—have a proper report of what's actually been happening?" Gordon Chetwynd looked toward Colonel Munro.

"Want facts? Quite right. They're all pretty unpalatable. I presume you want, not particulars of what's been happening here so much, as the general world situation?"

"Quite so."

"Well, in France the Marshal's in hospital still. Two bullets in his arm. Hell's going on in political circles. Large tracts of the country are held by what they call the Youth Power troops."

"You mean they've got arms?" said Gordon Chetwynd in a horrified voice.

"They've got a hell of a lot," said the Colonel. "I don't know really where they've got them from. There are certain ideas as to that. A large consignment of arms was sent from Sweden to West Africa."

"What's that got to do with it?" said Mr. Lazenby. "Who cares? Let them have all the arms they want in West Africa. They can go on shooting each other."

"Well, there's something a little curious about it as far as our Intelligence reports go. Here is a list of the armaments that were sent to West Africa. The interesting thing is they were sent there, but they were sent out again. They were accepted, delivery was acknowledged, payment may or may not have been made, but they were sent out of the country again before five days had passed. They were sent out, re-routed elsewhere."

"But what's the idea of that?"

"The idea seems to be," said Munro, "that they were never really intended for West Africa. Payments were made and they were sent on somewhere else. It seems possible that they went on from Africa to the Near East. To the Persian Gulf, to Greece and to Turkey. Also, a consignment of planes were sent to Egypt. From Egypt they were sent to India, from India they were sent to Russia."

"I thought they were sent *from* Russia."

"—and from Russia they went to Prague. The whole thing's mad."

"I don't understand," said Sir George; "one wonders—"

"Somewhere there seems to be some central organization which is directing the supplies of various things. Planes, armaments, bombs, both explosive and those that are used in germ warfare. All these consignments are moving in unexpected directions. They are delivered by various cross-country routes to trouble spots, and used by leaders and regiments—if you like to call them that —of the Youth Power. They mostly go to the leaders of young guerrilla movements, professed anarchists who preach anarchy, and accept—though one doubts if they ever pay for—some of the latest, most up-to-date models."

"Do you mean to say we're facing something like war on a world scale?" Cedric Lazenby was shocked.

The mild man with the Asiatic face who sat lower down at the table, and had not yet spoken, lifted up his face with the Mongolian smile, and said:

"That is what one is now forced to believe. Our observations tell us—"

Lazenby interrupted.

"You'll have to stop observing. UNO will have to take arms itself and put all this down."

The quiet face remained unmoved.

"That would be against our principles," he said.

Colonel Munro raised his voice and went on with his summing up.

"There's fighting in some parts of every country. Southeast Asia claimed independence long ago and there are four, five different divisions of power in South America, Cuba, Peru, Guatemala, and so on. As for the United States, you know Washington was practically burnt out—the West is overrun with Youth Power Armed Forces—Chicago is under martial law. You know about Sam Cortman? Shot last night on the steps of the American Embassy here."

"He was to attend here today," said Lazenby. "He was going to have given us his views of the situation."

"I don't suppose that would have helped much," said Colonel Munro. "Quite a nice chap—but hardly a live wire."

"But who's *behind* all this?" Lazenby's voice rose fretfully.

"It could be the Russians, of course—" He looked hopeful. He still envisaged himself flying to Moscow.

Colonel Munro shook his head. "Doubt it," he said.

"A personal appeal," said Lazenby. His face brightened with hope. "An entirely new sphere of influence. The Chinese . . . ?"

"Nor the Chinese," said Colonel Munro. "But you know there's been a big revival in Neo-Fascism in Germany."

"You don't really think the Germans could possibly . . ."

"I don't think they're behind all this necessarily, but when you say possibly —yes, I think possibly they easily could. They've done it before, you know. Prepared things years before, planned them, everything ready, waiting for the word GO. Good planners, very good planners. Staff work excellent. I admire them, you know. Can't help it."

"But Germany seemed to be so peaceful and well run."

"Yes, of course it is up to a point. But do you realize, South America is practically alive with Germans, with young Neo-Fascists, and they've got a big Youth Federation there. Call themselves the Super-Aryans, or something of that kind. You know, a bit of the old stuff still, swastikas and salutes, and someone who's running it, called the Young Wotan or the Young Siegfried or something like that. Lot of Aryan nonsense."

There was a knock on the door and the secretary entered.

"Professor Eckstein is here, sir."

"We'd better have him in," said Cedric Lazenby. "After all, if anyone can tell us what our latest research weapons are, he's the man. We may have something up our sleeve that can soon put an end to all this nonsense." Besides being a professional traveler to foreign parts in the role of peacemaker, Mr. Lazenby had an incurable fund of optimism seldom justified by results.·

"We could do with a good secret weapon," said the Air Marshal hopefully.

Professor Eckstein, considered by many to be Britain's top scientist, when you first looked at him seemed supremely unimportant. He was a small man with old-fashioned mutton-chop whiskers and an asthmatic cough. He had the manner of one anxious to apologize for his existence. He made noises like "ah," "hrrumph," "mrrh," blew his nose, coughed asthmatically again and shook hands in a shy manner as he was introduced to those present. A good many of them he already knew, and these he greeted with nervous nods of the head. He sat down on the chair indicated and looked round him vaguely. He raised a hand to his mouth and began to bite his nails.

"The heads of the services are here," said Sir George Packham. "We are very anxious to have your opinion as to what can be done."

"Oh," said Professor Eckstein, "done? Yes, yes, done?"

There was a silence.

"The world is fast passing into a state of anarchy," said Sir George.

"Seems so, doesn't it? At least, from what I read in the paper. Not that I trust to that. Really, the things journalists think up. Never any accuracy in their statements."

"I understand you've made some most important discoveries lately, Professor," said Cedric Lazenby encouragingly.

"Ah, yes, so we have. So we have." Professor Eckstein cheered up a little. "Got a lot of very nasty chemical warfare fixed up. If we ever wanted it. Germ warfare, you know, biological stuff, gas laid on through normal gas outlets, air pollution and poisoning of water supplies. Yes, if you wanted it, I suppose we could kill half the population of England given about three days to do it in." He rubbed his hands. "That what you want?"

"No, no, indeed. Oh, dear, of course not." Mr. Lazenby looked horrified.

"Well, that's what I mean, you know. It's not a question of not having enough lethal weapons. We've got too much. Everything we've got is too lethal. The difficulty would be in keeping anybody alive, even ourselves. Eh? All the people at the top, you know. Well—*us,* for instance." He gave a wheezy, happy little chuckle.

"But that isn't what we want," Mr. Lazenby insisted.

"It's not a question of what you *want;* it's a question of what we've *got.* Everything we've got is terrifically lethal. If you want everybody under thirty wiped off the map, I expect you could do it. Mind you, you'd have to take a lot of the older ones as well. It's difficult to segregate one lot from the other, you know. Personally, I should be against that. We've got some very good young research fellows. Bloody-minded, but clever."

"What's gone wrong with the world?" asked Kenwood suddenly.

"That's the point," said Professor Eckstein. "We don't know. We don't know up at our place in spite of all we *do* know about this, that and the other. We know a bit more about the moon nowadays, we know a lot about biology, we can transplant hearts and livers; brains, too, soon, I expect, though I don't know how *that*'ll work out. But we don't know who is doing *this.* Somebody is, you know. It's a sort of high-powered background stuff. Oh, yes, we've got it cropping up in different ways. You know, crime rings, drug rings, all that sort of thing. A high-powered lot, directed by a few good, shrewd brains behind the scenes. We've had it going on in this country or that country, occasionally on a European scale. But it's going a bit farther now, other side of the globe—Southern Hemisphere. Down to the Antarctic Circle before we've finished, I expect." He appeared to be pleased with his diagnosis.

"People of ill will—"

"Well, you could put it like that. Ill will for ill will's sake, or ill will for the sake of money or power. Difficult, you know, to get at the point of it all. The poor dogsbodies themselves don't know. They want violence and they like violence. They don't like the world, they don't like our materialistic attitude. They don't like a lot of our nasty ways of making money, they don't like a lot of the fiddles we do. They don't like seeing poverty. They want a better world. Well, you could make a better world, perhaps, if you thought about it long enough. But the trouble is, if you insist on taking away something first, you've got to put something back in its place. Nature won't have a vacuum—an old saying, but true. Dash it all, it's like a heart transplant. You take one heart away but you've got to put another one there. One that works. And you've got to arrange about the heart you're going to put there *before* you take away the faulty heart that somebody's got at present. Matter of fact, I think a lot of those things are better left alone altogether, but nobody would listen to me, I suppose. And, anyway, it's not my subject."

"A gas?" suggested Colonel Munro.

Professor Eckstein brightened.

"Oh, we've got all sorts of gases in stock. Mind you, some of them are reasonably harmless. Mild deterrents, shall we say. We've got all *those.*" He beamed like a complacent hardware dealer.

"Nuclear weapons?" suggested Mr. Lazenby.

"Don't you monkey with *that!* You don't want a radioactive England, do you, or a radioactive continent, for that matter?"

"So you can't help us," said Colonel Munro.

"Not until somebody's found out a bit more about all this," said Professor Eckstein. "Well, I'm sorry. But I must impress upon you that most of the things we're working on nowadays are *dangerous*—" He stressed the word. *"Really* dangerous."

He looked at them anxiously as a nervous uncle might look at a group of children left with a box of matches to play with, and who might quite easily set the house on fire.

"Well, thank you, Professor Eckstein," said Mr. Lazenby. He did not sound particularly thankful.

The Professor, gathering correctly that he was released, smiled all round and trotted out of the room.

Mr. Lazenby hardly waited for the door to close before venting his feelings.

"All alike, these scientists," he said bitterly. "Never any practical good. Never come up with anything sensible. All they can do is split the atom—and then tell *us* not to mess about with it!"

"Just as well if we never had," said Admiral Blunt, again bluntly. "What we want is something homely and domestic, like a kind of selective weedkiller which would—" He paused abruptly. "Now what the devil—?"

"Yes, Admiral?" said the Prime Minister politely.

"Nothing—just reminded me of something. Can't remember what—"

The Prime Minister sighed.

"Any more scientific experts waiting on the mat?" asked Gordon Chetwynd, glancing hopefully at his wrist watch.

"Old Pikeaway is here, I believe," said Lazenby. "Got a picture—or a drawing—or a map or something or other he wants us to look at—"

"What's it all about?"

"I don't know. It seems to be all bubbles," said Mr. Lazenby vaguely.

"Bubbles? Why bubbles?"

"I've no idea. Well," he sighed, "we'd better have a look at it."

"Horsham's here, too—"

"He may have something new to tell us," said Chetwynd.

Colonel Pikeaway stumped in. He was supporting a rolled-up burden which with Horsham's aid was unrolled and which with some difficulty was propped up so that those sitting round the table could look at it.

"Not exactly drawn to scale yet, but it gives you a rough idea," said Colonel Pikeaway.

"What does it mean, if anything?"

"Bubbles?" murmured Sir George. An idea came to him. "Is it a gas? A new gas?"

"You'd better deliver the lecture, Horsham," said Pikeaway. "You know the general idea."

"I only know what I've been told. It's a rough diagram of an association of world control."

"By whom?"

"By groups who own or control the sources of power—the raw materials of power."

"And the letters of the alphabet?"

"Stand for a person or a code name for a special group. They are intersecting circles that by now cover the globe.

"That circle marked 'A' stand for armaments. Someone, or some group, is in control of armaments. All types of armaments. Explosives, guns, rifles. All over the world armaments are being produced according to plan, dispatched ostensibly to underdeveloped nations, backward nations, nations at war. But they don't remain where they are sent. They are rerouted almost immediately elsewhere. To guerrilla warfare in the South American continent—in rioting and fighting in the U.S.A.—to depots of Black Power—to various countries in Europe.

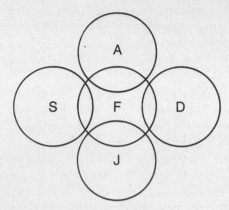

" 'D' represents drugs—a network of suppliers run them from various de- pots and stockpiles. All kinds of drugs, from the more harmless varieties up to the true killers. The headquarters seem likely to be situated in the Levant, and to pass out through Turkey, Pakistan, India, and Central Asia."

"They make money out of it?"

"Enormous sums of money. But it's more than just an association of push- ers. It has a more sinister side to it. It's being used to finish off the weaklings among the young, shall we say, to make them complete slaves. Slaves so that they cannot live and exist or do jobs for their employers without a supply of drugs."

Kenwood whistled.

"That's a bad show, isn't it? Don't you know at all who those drug pushers are?"

"Some of them, yes. But only the lesser fry. Not the real controllers. Drug headquarters are, so far as we can judge, in Central Asia, and the Levant. They get delivered from there in the tires of cars, in cement, in concrete, in all kinds of machinery and industrial goods. They're delivered all over the world and passed on as ordinary trade goods to where they are meant to go.

" 'F' stands for finance. Money! A money spider's web in the center of it all. You'll have to go to Mr. Robinson to tell you about money. According to a memo here, money is coming very largely from America and there's also a headquarters in Bavaria. There's a vast reserve in South Africa, based on gold and diamonds. Most of the money is going to South America. One of the principal controllers, if I may so put it, of money, is a very powerful and talented woman. She's old now—must be near to death. But she is still strong, and active. Her name was Charlotte Krapp. Her father owned the vast Krapp yards in Germany. She was a financial genius herself and operated in Wall Street. She accumulated fortune after fortune by investments in all parts of the world. She owns transport, she owns machinery, she owns industrial concerns. All these things. She lives in a vast castle in Bavaria—from there she directs a flow of money to different parts of the globe.

" 'S' represents science—the new knowledge of chemical and biological warfare—Various young scientists have defected—There is a nucleus of them in the U.S., we believe, vowed and dedicated to the cause of anarchy."

"Fighting for anarchy? A contradiction in terms. Can there be such a thing?"

"You believe in anarchy if you are young. You want a new world, and to begin with, you must pull down the old one—just as you pull down a house before you build a new one to replace it. But if you don't know where you are going, if you don't know where you are being lured to go, or even pushed to go, what will the new world be like, and where will the believers be when they get it? Some of them slaves, some of them blinded by hate, some by violence and sadism, both preached and practiced. Some of them—and God help those—still idealistic, still believing as people did in France at the time of the French Revolution that that revolution would bring prosperity, peace, happiness, contentment to its people."

"And what are *we* doing about all this? What are we proposing to do about it?" It was Admiral Blunt who spoke.

"What are we doing about it? All that we can. I assure you, all you who are here, we are doing all that we can. We have people working for us in every country. We have agents, inquirers, those who gather information and bring it back here—"

"Which is very necessary," said Colonel Pikeaway. "First we've got to *know*—know who's who, who's with us and who's against us. And after that, we've got to see what, if anything, can be done."

"Our name for this diagram is The Ring. Here's a list of what we know about The Ring leaders. Those with a query mean that we know only the name they go by—or alternatively we only suspect that they are the ones we want."

THE RING

F	Big Charlotte	—Bavaria
A	Eric Olafsson	—Sweden, Industrialist, Armaments
D	Said to go by the name of Demetrios	—Smyrna, Drugs
S	Dr. Sarolensky	—Colorado, U.S.A., Physicist-Chemist. Suspicion only
J		—A woman. Goes by code name of Juanita. Said to be dangerous. No knowledge of her real name.

15

Aunt Matilda Takes a Cure

"A CURE OF some kind, I thought?" Lady Matilda hazarded.

"A cure?" said Dr. Donaldson. He looked faintly puzzled for a moment, losing his air of medical omniscience, which, of course, so Lady Matilda reflected, was one of the slight disadvantages attached to having a younger doctor attending one rather than the older specimen to whom one has been accustomed for several years.

"That's what we used to call them," Lady Matilda explained. "In my young days, you know, you went for the cure. Marienbad, Carlsbad, Baden-Baden, all the rest of it. Just the other day I read about this new place in the paper. Quite new and up to date. Said to be all new ideas and things like that. Not that I'm really sold on new ideas, but I wouldn't really be afraid of them. I mean, they would probably be all the same things all over again. Water tasting of bad eggs and the latest sort of diet and walking to take the cure, or the waters, or whatever they call them now, at a rather inconvenient hour in the morning. And I expect they give you massage or something. It used to be seaweed. But this place is somewhere in the mountains. Bavaria or Austria or somewhere like that. So I don't suppose it would be seaweed. Shaggy moss, perhaps—sounds like a dog. And perhaps quite a nice mineral water as well as the eggy sulfury one, I mean. Superb buildings, I understand. The only thing one is nervous about nowadays is that they never seem to put banisters in any up-to-date modern buildings. Flights of marble steps and all that, but nothing to hang on to."

"I think I know the place you mean," said Dr. Donaldson. "It's been publicized a good deal in the press."

"Well, you know what one is at my age," said Lady Matilda. "One likes trying new things. Really, I think it is just to amuse one. It doesn't really make one feel one's health would be any better. Still, you don't think it would be a bad idea, do you, Dr. Donaldson?"

Dr. Donaldson looked at her. He was not so young as Lady Matilda labeled him in her mind. He was just approaching forty and he was a tactful and kindly man and willing to indulge his elderly patients as far as he considered it desirable, without any actual danger of their attempting something obviously unsuitable.

"I'm sure it wouldn't do you any harm at all," he said. "Might be quite a good idea. Of course travel's a bit tiring, though one flies to places very quickly and easily nowadays."

"Quickly, yes. Easily, no," said Lady Matilda. "Ramps and moving staircases and in and out of buses from the airport to the plane, and the plane to another airport and from the airport to another bus. All that, you know. But I understand one can have wheelchairs in the airports."

"Of course you can. Excellent idea. If you promise to do that and not think you can walk everywhere . . ."

"I know, I know," said his patient, interrupting him. "You do understand. You're really a very understanding man. One has one's pride, you know, and while you can still hobble around with a stick or a little support, you don't really want to look absolutely a crock or bedridden or something. It'd be easier if I was a man," she mused. "I mean, one could tie up one's leg with one of those enormous bandages and padded things as though one had the gout. I mean, gout is all right for the male sex. Nobody thinks anything the worse of them. Some of their older friends think they've been tucking into the port too much, because that used to be the old idea, though I believe that is not really true at all. Port wine does *not* give you gout. Yes, a wheelchair, and I could fly to Munich or somewhere like that. One could arrange for a car or something at the other end."

"You will take Miss Leatheran with you, of course."

"Amy? Oh, of course. I couldn't do without her. Anyway, you think no harm would be done?"

"I think it might do you a world of good."

"You really are a nice man."

Lady Matilda gave him the twinkle from her eyes with which now he was becoming familiar.

"You think it'll amuse me and cheer me up to go somewhere new and see some new faces, and of course you're quite right. But I like to think that I'm taking a cure, though really there's nothing for me to be cured of. Not really, is there? I mean, except old age. Unfortunately old age doesn't get cured, it only gets more so, doesn't it?"

"The point is really, will you enjoy yourself? Well, I think you will. When you get tired, by the way, when doing anything, stop doing it."

"I shall still drink glasses of water if the water tastes of rotten eggs. Not because I like them or because frankly I think they do me any good. But it has a sort of mortifying feeling. It's like old women in our village always used to be. They always wanted a nice, strong medicine either colored black or purple or deep pink, heavily flavored with peppermint. They thought that did much more good than a nice little pill or a bottle that only appeared to be full of ordinary water without any exotic coloring."

"You know too much about human nature," said Dr. Donaldson.

"You're very nice to me," said Lady Matilda. "I appreciate it. Amy!"

"Yes, Lady Matilda?"

"Get me an atlas, will you? I've lost track of Bavaria and the countries round it."

"Let me see now. An atlas. There'll be one in the library, I suppose. There must be some old atlases about, dating back to about nineteen twenty or thereabouts, I suppose."

"I wondered if we had anything a little more modern."

"Atlas," said Amy, deep in reflection.

"If not, you can buy one and bring it along tomorrow morning. It's going to be very difficult because all the names are different, the countries are different, and I shan't know where I am. But you'll have to help me with that. Find a big magnifying glass, will you? I have an idea I was reading in bed with one the other day and it probably slipped down between the bed and the wall."

Her requirements took a little time to satisfy, but the atlas, the magnifying glass and an older atlas by which to check were finally produced and Amy, nice woman that she was, Lady Matilda thought, was extremely helpful.

"Yes, here it is. It still seems to be called Monbrügge or something like that. It's either in the Tyrol or Bavaria. Everything seems to have changed places and got different names—"

ii

Lady Matilda looked round her bedroom in the Gasthaus. It was well appointed. It was very expensive. It combined comfort with an appearance of such austerity as might lead the inhabitant to identify herself with an ascetic course of exercises, diet, and possibly painful courses of massage. Its furnishings, she thought, were interesting. They provided for all tastes. There was a large framed Gothic script on the wall. Lady Matilda's German was not as good as it had been in her girlhood, but it dealt, she thought, with the golden and enchanting idea of a return to youth. Not only did youth hold the future in its hands, but the old were being nicely indoctrinated to feel that they themselves might know such a second golden flowering.

Here there were gentle aids so as to enable one to pursue the doctrine of any of the many paths in life which attracted different classes of people. (Always presuming that they had enough money to pay for it.) Beside the bed was a Gideon Bible such as Lady Matilda when traveling in the United States had often found by her bedside. She picked it up approvingly, opened it at random, and dropped a finger on one particular verse. She read it, nodding her head contentedly, and made a brief note of it on a note pad that was lying on her bed table. She had often done that in the course of her life—it was her way of obtaining divine guidance at short notice.

I have been young and now am old, yet have I not seen the righteous forsaken.

She made further researches of the room. Handily placed but not too apparent was an *Almanach de Gotha,* modestly situated on a lower shelf of the bedside table. A most invaluable book for those who wished to familiarize themselves with the higher stratas of society reaching back for several hundred years and which were still being observed and noted and checked by those of aristocratic lineage or interested in the same. It will come in handy, she thought. I can read up a good deal on that.

Near the desk, by the stove of period porcelain, were paperback editions of certain preachings and tenets by the modern prophets of the world. Those who were now or had recently been crying in the wilderness were here to be studied and approved by young followers with haloes of hair, strange raiment, and earnest hearts. Marcuse, Guevara, Lévi-Strauss, Fanon.

In case she was going to hold any conversations with golden youth, she had better read up a little on that also.

At that moment there was a timid tap on the door. It opened slightly and the face of the faithful Amy came round the corner. Amy, Lady Matilda thought suddenly, would look exactly like a sheep when she was ten years older. A nice, faithful, kindly sheep. At the moment, Lady Matilda was glad to think, she looked still like a very agreeable plump lamb with nice curls of hair, thoughtful and kindly eyes, and able to give kindly baas rather than to bleat.

"I do hope you slept well."

"Yes, my dear, I did, excellently. Have you got that thing?"

Amy always knew what she meant. She handed it to her employer.

"Ah, my diet sheet. I see." Lady Matilda perused it, then said, "How incredibly unattractive! What's this water like one's supposed to drink?"

"It doesn't taste very nice."

"No, I don't suppose it would. Come back in half an hour. I've got a letter I want you to post."

Moving aside her breakfast tray, she moved over to the desk. She thought for a few minutes and then wrote her letter. "It ought to do the trick," she murmured.

"I beg your pardon, Lady Matilda. What did you say?"

"I was writing to the old friend I mentioned to you."

"The one you said you haven't seen for about fifty or sixty years?"

Lady Matilda nodded.

"I do hope—" Amy was apologetic. "I mean—I—it's such a long time. People have short memories nowadays. I do hope that she'll remember all about you and everything."

"Of course she will," said Lady Matilda. "The people you don't forget are the people you knew when you were about ten to twenty. They stick in your mind forever. You remember what hats they wore, and the way they laughed, and you remember their faults and their good qualities and everything about them. Now anyone I met twenty years ago, shall we say, I simply can't remember who they are. Not if they're mentioned to me, and not if I saw them even. Oh, yes, she'll remember about *me*. And all about Lausanne. You get that letter posted. I've got to do a little homework."

She picked up the *Almanach de Gotha* and returned to bed, where she made a serious study of such items as might come in useful. Some family relationships and various other kinships of the useful kind. Who had married whom, who had lived where, what misfortunes had overtaken others. Not that the person whom she had in mind was herself likely to be found in the *Almanach de Gotha*. But she lived in a part of the world, had come there deliberately to live in a Schloss belonging to originally noble ancestors, and she had absorbed the local respect and adulation for those above all of good breeding. To good birth, even impaired with poverty, she herself, as Lady Matilda well knew, had no claim whatever. She had had to make do with money. Oceans of money. Incredible amounts of money.

Lady Matilda Cleckheaton had no doubt at all that she herself, the daughter of an eighth duke, would be bidden to some kind of festivity. Coffee, perhaps, and delicious creamy cakes.

iii

Lady Matilda Cleckheaton made her entrance into one of the grand reception rooms of the Schloss. It had been a fifteen-mile drive. She had dressed herself with some care, though somewhat to the disapproval of Amy. Amy seldom offered advice, but she was so anxious for her principal to succeed in whatever she was undertaking that she had ventured this time on a moderate remonstrance.

"You don't think your red dress is really a little *worn,* if you know what I mean. I mean just beneath the arms, and, well, there are two or three very shiny patches—"

"I know, my dear, I know. It is a shabby dress but it is nevertheless a Patou model. It is old, but it was enormously expensive. I am not trying to look rich or extravagant. I am an impoverished member of an aristocratic family. Anyone of under fifty, no doubt, would despise me. But my hostess is living and has lived for some years in a part of the world where the rich will be kept waiting for their meal while the hostess will be willing to wait for a shabby, elderly woman of impeccable descent. Family traditions are things that one does not lose easily. One absorbs them, even, when one goes to a new neighborhood. In my trunk, by the way, you will find a feather boa."

"Are you going to put on a feather boa?"

"Yes, I am. An ostrich feather one."

"Oh, dear, that must be years old."

"It is, but I've kept it very carefully. You'll see, Charlotte will recognize what it is. She will think one of the best families in England was reduced to wearing her old clothes that she had kept carefully for years. And I'll wear my sealskin coat, too. That's a little worn, but such a magnificent coat in its time."

Thus arrayed, she set forth. Amy went with her as a well-dressed though only quietly smart attendant.

Matilda Cleckheaton had been prepared for what she saw. A whale, as Stafford had told her. A wallowing whale, a hideous old woman sitting in a room surrounded with pictures worth a fortune. Rising with some difficulty from a thronelike chair which could have figured on a stage representing the palace of some magnificent prince from any age from the Middle Ages down.

"Matilda!"

"Charlotte!"

"Ah! After all these years. How strange it seems!"

They exchanged words of greeting and pleasure, talking partly in German and partly in English. Lady Matilda's German was slightly faulty. Charlotte spoke excellent German, excellent English though with a strong guttural accent, and occasionally English with an American accent. She was really, Lady Matilda thought, quite splendidly hideous. For a moment she felt a fondness almost dating back to the past although, she reflected the next moment, Charlotte had been a most detestable girl. Nobody had really liked her and she herself had certainly not done so. But there is a great bond, say what we will, in the memories of old schooldays. Whether Charlotte had liked her or not, she did not know. But Charlotte, she remembered, had certainly— what used to be called in those days—sucked up to her. She had had visions, possibly, of staying in a ducal castle in England. Lady Matilda's father, though of most praiseworthy lineage, had been one of the most impecunious of English dukes. His estate had only been held together by the rich wife he had married, whom he had treated with the utmost courtesy, and who had enjoyed bullying him whenever able to do so. Lady Matilda had been fortunate enough to be his daughter by a second marriage. Her own mother had been extremely agreeable and also a very successful actress, able to play the part of looking a duchess far more than any real duchess could do.

They exchanged reminiscences of past days, the tortures they had inflicted on some of their instructors, the fortunate and unfortunate marriages that had occurred to some of their schoolmates. Matilda made a few mentions of certain alliances and families culled from the pages of the *Almanach de Gotha,* "but of course that must have been a terrible marriage for Elsa. One of the Bourbons de Parme, was it not? Yes, yes, well, one knows what that leads to. Most unfortunate."

Coffee was brought, delicious coffee, plates of *mille-feuille* pastry and delicious cream cakes.

"I should not touch any of this," cried Lady Matilda. "No, indeed. My doctor, he is most severe. He said that I must adhere strictly to the cure while I was here. But after all, this is a day of holiday, is it not? Of renewal of youth. That is what interests me so much. My great-nephew who visited you not long ago—I forget who brought him here, the Countess—ah, it began with a Z, I cannot remember her name."

"The Countess Renata Zerkowski—"

"Ah, that was the name, yes. A very charming young woman, I believe. And she brought him to visit you. It was most kind of her. He was so impressed. Impressed, too, with all your beautiful possessions. Your way of living and, indeed, the wonderful things which he had heard about you. How you have a whole movement of—oh, I do not know how to give the proper term. A Galaxy of Youth. Golden, beautiful youth. They flock round you. They worship you. What a wonderful life you must live. Not that I could support such a life. I have to live very quietly. Rheumatoid arthritis. And also the financial difficulties. Difficulty in keeping up the family house. Ah, well, you know what it is for us in England—our taxation troubles."

"I remember that nephew of yours, yes. He was agreeable, a very agreeable man. The Diplomatic Service, I understand?"

"Ah, yes. But it is—fell, you know. I cannot feel that his talents are being properly recognized. He does not say much. He does not complain, but he feels that he is—well, he feels that he has not been appreciated as he should. The powers that be, those who hold office at present, what are they?"

"Canaille!" said Big Charlotte.

"Intellectuals with no savoir-faire in life. Fifty years ago it would have been different," said Lady Matilda, "but nowadays his promotion has been not advanced as it should. I will even tell you, in confidence, of course, that he has been distrusted. They suspect him, you know, of being in with—what shall I call it?—rebellious, revolutionary tendencies. And yet one must realize what the future could hold for a man who could embrace more advanced views."

"You mean he is not, then, how do you say it in England, in sympathy with the Establishment, as they call it?"

"Hush, hush, we must not say these things. At least *I* must not," said Lady Matilda.

"You interest me," said Charlotte.

Matilda Cleckheaton sighed.

"Put it down, if you like, to the fondness of an elderly relative. Staffy has always been a favorite of mine. He has charm and wit. I think also he has ideas. He envisages the future, a future that should differ a good deal from what we have at present. Our country, alas, is politically in a very sad state. Stafford seems to be very much impressed by things you said to him or showed to him. You've done so much for music, I understand. What we need I cannot but feel is the ideal of the super race."

"There should and could be a super race. Adolf Hitler had the right idea," said Charlotte. "A man of no importance in himself, but he had artistic elements in his character. And undoubtedly he had the power of leadership."

"Ah, yes. Leadership, that is what we need."

"You had the wrong allies in the last war, my dear. If England and Germany now had arrayed themselves side by side, if they had had the same ideals, of youth, strength, two Aryan nations with the right ideals. Think where your country and mine might have arrived today. Yet perhaps even that is too narrow a view to take. In some ways the communists and the others have taught us a lesson. Workers of the world, unite? But that is to set one's sights too low. Workers are only our material. It is, 'Leaders of the world, unite!' Young men with the gift of leadership, of good blood. And we must start, not with the middle-aged men set in their ways, repeating themselves like a gramophone record that has stuck. We must seek among the student population, the young men with brave hearts, with great ideas, willing to march, willing to be killed but willing also to kill. To kill without any compunction—because it is certain that without aggressiveness, without violence, without attack—there can be no victory. I must show you something—"

With somewhat of a struggle she succeeded in rising to her feet. Lady Matilda followed suit, underlining a little her difficulty, which was not quite as much as she was making out.

"It was in May nineteen forty," said Charlotte, "when Hitler Youth went on to its second stage. When Himmler obtained from Hitler a charter. The charter of the famous SS. It was formed for the destruction of the eastern peoples, the slaves, the appointed slaves of the world. It would make room for the German master race. The SS executive instrument came into being." Her voice dropped a little. It held for a moment a kind of religious awe.

Lady Matilda nearly crossed herself by mistake.

"The Order of the Death's Head," said Big Charlotte.

She walked slowly and painfully down the room and pointed to where on the wall hung, framed in gilt and surmounted with a skull, the Order of the Death's Head.

"See, it is my most cherished possession. It hangs here on my wall. My golden youth band, when they come here, salute it. And in our archives in the castle here are folios of its chronicles. Some of them are only reading for strong stomachs, but one must learn to accept these things. The deaths in gas chambers, the torture cells, the trials at Nuremberg speak venomously of all those things. But it was a great tradition. Strength through pain. They were trained young, the boys, so that they should not falter or turn back or suffer from any kind of softness. Even Lenin, preaching his Marxist doctrine, declared, 'Away with softness!' It was one of his first rules for creating a perfect state. But we were too narrow. We wished to confine our great dream only to the German master race. But there are other races. They, too, can attain masterhood through suffering and violence and through the considered practice of anarchy. We must pull down, pull down all the soft institutions. Pull down the more humiliating forms of religion. There is a religion of strength, the old religion of the Viking people. And we have a leader, young as yet, gaining in power every day. What did some great man say? Give me the tools and I will do the job. Something like that. Our leader has already the tools. He will have more tools. He will have the planes, the bombs, the means of chemical warfare. He will have the men to fight. He will have the transport. He will have shipping and oil. He will have what one might call the Aladdin's creation of genii. You rub the lamp and the genie appears. It is all in your hands. The means of production, the means of wealth and our young leader, a leader by birth as well as by character. He has all this."

She wheezed and coughed.

"Let me help you."

Lady Matilda supported her back to her seat. Charlotte gasped a little as she sat down.

"It's sad to be old, but I shall last long enough. Long enough to see the triumph of a new world, a new creation. That is what you want for your nephew. I will see to it. Power in his own country, that is what he wants, is it not? You would be ready to encourage the spearhead there?"

"I had influence once. But now—" Lady Matilda shook her head sadly. "All that is gone."

"It will come again, dear," said her friend. "You were right to come to me. I have a certain influence."

"It is a great cause," said Lady Matilda. She sighed and murmured, "The Young Siegfried."

"I hope you enjoyed meeting your old friend," said Amy as they drove back to the Gasthaus.

"If you could have heard all the nonsense I talked, you wouldn't believe it," said Lady Matilda Cleckheaton.

16

Pikeaway Talks

"THE NEWS FROM France is very bad," said Colonel Pikeaway, brushing a cloud of cigar ash off his coat. "I heard Winston Churchill say that in the last war. There was a man who could speak in plain words and no more than needed. It was very impressive. It told us what we needed to know. Well, it's a long time since then, but I say it again today. The news from France is very bad."

He coughed, wheezed and brushed a little more ash off himself.

"The news from Italy is very bad," he said. "The news from Russia, I imagine, could be very bad if they let much out about it. They've got trouble there, too. Marching bands of students in the street, shop windows smashed, embassies attacked! News from Egypt is very bad. News from Jerusalem is very bad. News from Syria is very bad. That's all more or less normal, so we needn't worry too much. News from Argentina is what I'd call peculiar. Very peculiar indeed. Argentina, Brazil, Cuba, they've all got together. Call themselves the Golden Youth Federated States, or something like that. It's got an army, too. Properly drilled, properly armed, properly commanded. They've got planes, they've got bombs, they've got God-knows-what. And most of them seem to know what to do with them, which makes it worse. There's a singing crowd as well, apparently. Pop songs, old local folk songs, and bygone battle hymns. They go along rather like the Salvation Army used to do—no blasphemy intended—I'm not crabbing the Salvation Army. Jolly good work they did always. And the girls—pretty as Punch in their bonnets."

He went on:

"I've heard that something's going on in that line in the civilized countries, starting with *us*. Some of us can be called civilized still, I suppose? One of our politicians the other day, I remember, said we were a splendid nation, chiefly because we were permissive, we had demonstrations, we smashed things, we beat up anyone if we hadn't anything better to do, we got rid of our high spirits by showing violence and our moral purity by taking most of our clothes off. I don't know what he thought he was talking about—politicians seldom do—but they can make it sound all right. That's why they are politicians."

He paused and looked across at the man he was talking to.

"Distressing—sadly distressing," said Sir George Packham. "One can hardly believe—one worries—if one could only— Is that all the news you've got?" he asked plaintively.

"Isn't it enough? You're hard to satisfy. World anarchy well on its way— that's what we've got. A bit wobbly still—not fully established yet, but very near to it—very near indeed."

"But action can surely be taken against all this?"

"Not so easy as you think. Tear gas puts a stop to rioting for a while and gives the police a break. And naturally we've got plenty of germ warfare and nuclear bombs and all the other pretty bags of tricks. What do you think would happen if we started using those? Mass massacre of all the marching girls and boys, and the housewives' shopping circle, and the old-age pensioners at home, and a good quota of our pompous politicians as they tell us we've never had it so good, and in addition you and me—Ha ha!

"And anyway," added Colonel Pikeaway, "if it's only news you're after, I understand you've got some hot news of your own arriving today. Top secret from Germany, Herr Heinrich Spiess himself."

"How on earth did you hear that? It's supposed to be strictly—"

"We know everything here," said Colonel Pikeaway, using his pet phrase— "That's what we're for."

"Bringing some tame doctor, too, I understand," he added.

"Yes, a Dr. Reichardt—a top scientist, I presume—"

"No. Medical doctor. Loony bins—"

"Oh, dear—a psychologist?"

"Probably. The ones that run loony bins are mostly that. With any luck he'll have been brought over so that he can examine the heads of some of our young firebrands. Stuffed full they are of German philosophy, Black Power philosophy, dead French writers' philosophy, and so on and so forth. Possibly they'll let him examine some of the heads of our legal lights who preside over our judicial courts here saying we must be very careful not to do anything to damage a young man's ego, because he might have to earn his living. We'd be a lot safer if they sent them all round to get plenty of National Assistance to live on and then they could go back to their rooms, not do any work, and enjoy themselves reading more philosophy. However, I'm out of date. I know that. You nccdn't tell me so."

"One has to take into account the new modes of thought," said Sir George Packham. "One feels, I mean one hopes—well, it's difficult to say—"

"Must be very worrying for you," said Colonel Pikeaway. "Finding things so difficult to say."

His telephone rang. He listened, then handed it to Sir George.

"Yes?" said Sir George. "Yes? Oh, yes. Yes. I agree. I suppose—No—no—not the Home Office. No. Privately, you mean. Well, I suppose we'd better use —er—" Sir George looked round him cautiously.

"This place isn't bugged," said Colonel Pikeaway amiably.

"Code word Blue Danube," said Sir George Packham in a loud, hoarse whisper. "Yes, yes. I'll bring Pikeaway along with me. Oh, yes, of course. Yes, yes. Get on to him. Yes, say you particularly want him to come, but to remember our meeting has got to be strictly private."

"We can't take my car then," said Pikeaway. "It's too well known."

"Henry Horsham's coming to fetch us in the Volkswagen."

"Fine," said Colonel Pikeaway. "Interesting, you know, all this."

"You don't think—?" said Sir George, and hesitated.

"I don't think what?"

"I meant just really—well, I—mean, if you wouldn't mind my suggesting —a clothesbrush?"

"Oh, this." Colonel Pikeaway hit himself lightly on the shoulder and a cloud of cigar ash flew up and made Sir George choke.

"Nanny," Colonel Pikeaway shouted. He banged a buzzer on his desk.

A middle-aged woman came in with a clothesbrush, appearing with the suddenness of a genie summoned by Aladdin's lamp.

"Hold your breath, please, Sir George," she said. "This may be a little pungent."

She held the door open for him and he retired outside while she brushed Colonel Pikeaway, who coughed and complained:

"Damned nuisance these people are. Always wanting you to get fixed up like a barber's dummy."

"I should not describe your appearance as quite like that, Colonel Pikeaway. You ought to be used to my cleaning you up nowadays. And you know the Home Secretary suffers from asthma."

"Well, that's his fault. Not taking proper care to have pollution removed from the streets of London.

"Come on, Sir George, let's hear what our German friend has come over to say. Sounds as though it's a matter of some urgency."

17

Herr Heinrich Spiess

HERR HEINRICH SPIESS was a worried man. He did not seek to conceal the fact. He acknowledged, indeed, without concealment, that the situation which these five men had come together to discuss was a serious situation. At the same time, he brought with him that sense of reassurance which had been his principal asset in dealing with the recently difficult political life in Germany. He was a solid man, a thoughtful man, a man who could bring common sense to any assemblies he attended. He gave no sense of being a brilliant man, and that in itself was reassuring. Brilliant politicians had been responsible for about two thirds of the national states of crisis in more countries than one. The other third of trouble had been caused by those politicians who were unable to conceal the fact that although duly elected by democratic governments, they had been unable to conceal their remarkably poor powers of judgment, common sense and, in fact, any noticeable brainy qualities.

"This is not in any sense an official visit, you understand," said the Chancellor.

"Oh, quite, quite."

"A certain piece of knowledge has come to me which I thought is essential we should share. It throws a rather interesting light on certain happenings which have puzzled as well as distressed us. This is Dr. Reichardt."

Introductions were made. Dr. Reichardt was a large and comfortable-looking man with the habit of saying "Ach, so" from time to time.

"Dr. Reichardt is in charge of a large establishment in the neighborhood of Karlsruhe. He treats there mental patients. I think I am correct in saying that you treat there between five and six hundred patients, am I not right?"

"Ach, so," said Dr. Reichardt.

"I take it that you have several different forms of mental illness?"

"Ach, so. I have different forms of mental illness, but nevertheless, I have a special interest in, and treat almost exclusively, one particular type of mental trouble." He branched off into German, and Herr Spiess presently rendered a brief translation in case some of his English colleagues should not understand. This was both necessary and tactful. Two of them did in part, one of them definitely did not, and the two others were truly puzzled.

"Dr. Reichardt has had," explained Herr Spiess, "the greatest success in his treatment of what as a layman I describe as megalomania. The belief that you are someone other than you are. Ideas of being more important than you are. Ideas that if you have persecution mania—"

"Ach, no!" said Dr. Reichardt. "Persecution mania, *no,* that I do not treat. There is no persecution mania in my clinic. Not among the group with whom

I am specially interested. On the contrary, they hold the delusions that they do because they wish to be happy. And they are happy, and I can keep them happy. But if I cure them, see you, they will not be happy. So I have to find a cure that will restore sanity to them, and yet they will be happy just the same. We call this particular state of mind—"

He uttered a long and ferociously sounding German word of at least eight syllables.

"For the purposes of our English friends, I shall still use my term of megalomania, though I know," continued Herr Spiess rather quickly, "that that is not the term you use nowadays, Dr. Reichardt. So, as I say, you have in your clinic six hundred patients."

"And at one time, the time to which I am about to refer, I had eight hundred."

"Eight hundred!"

"It was interesting—most interesting."

"You have such persons—to start at the beginning—"

"We have God Almighty," explained Dr. Reichardt. "You comprehend?" Mr. Lazenby looked slightly taken aback.

"Oh—er—yes—er—yes. Very interesting, I am sure."

"There are one or two young men, of course, who think they are Jesus Christ. But that is not so popular as the Almighty. And then there are the others. I had at the time I am about to mention twenty-four Adolf Hitlers. This you must understand was at the time when Hitler was alive. Yes, twenty-four or twenty-five Adolf Hitlers—" He consulted a small notebook which he took from his pocket. "I have made some notes here, yes. Fifteen Napoleons. Napoleon, he is always popular; ten Mussolinis; five reincarnations of Julius Caesar; and many other cases, very curious and very interesting. But that I will not weary you with at this moment. Not being specially qualified in the medical sense, it would not be of any interest to you. We will come to the incident that matters."

Dr. Reichardt spoke again at rather shorter length, and Herr Spiess continued to translate.

"There came to him one day a government official. Highly thought of at that time—this was during the war, mind you—by the ruling government. I will call him for the moment Martin B. You will know who I mean. He brought with him his chief. In fact he brought with him—well, we will not beat about the bush—he brought the Führer himself."

"Ach, so," said Dr. Reichardt.

"It was a great honor, you understand, that he should come to inspect," went on the doctor. "He was gracious, mein Führer. He told me that he had heard very good reports of my successes. He said that there had been trouble lately. Cases from the army. There, more than once there had been men believing they were Napoleon, sometimes believing they were some of Napoleon's marshals and sometimes, you comprehend, behaving accordingly, giving out military orders and causing therefore military difficulties. I would have been happy to have given him any professional knowledge that might be useful to him, but Martin B., who accompanied him, said that that would not be necessary. Our great Führer, however," said Dr. Reichardt, looking at Herr Spiess slightly uneasily, "did not want to be bothered with such details. He said that no doubt it would be better if medically qualified men with some experience as neurologists should come and have a consultation. What he wanted was to—ach, well, he wanted to see round, and I soon found what he was really interested to see. It should not have surprised me. Oh, no, because, you see, it was a symptom that one recognizes. The strain of his life was already beginning to tell on the Führer."

"I suppose he was beginning to think he was God Almighty himself at that time," said Colonel Pikeaway unexpectedly, and he chuckled.

Dr. Reichardt looked shocked.

"He asked me to let him know certain things. He said that Martin B. had told him that I actually had a large number of patients thinking, not to put too fine a point on it, that they were themselves Adolf Hitler. I explained to him that this was not uncommon, that naturally with the respect, the worship they paid to Hitler, it was only natural that the great wish to be like him should end eventually by them identifying themselves with him. I was a little anxious when I mentioned this, but I was delighted to find that he expressed great signs of satisfaction. He took it, I am thankful to say, as a compliment, this passionate wish to find identity with himself. He next asked if he could meet a representative number of these patients with this particular affliction. We had a little consultation. Martin B. seemed doubtful, but he took me aside and assured me that Herr Hitler actually wished to have this experience. What he himself was anxious to insure was that Herr Hitler did not meet— well, in short, that Herr Hitler was not to be allowed to run any risks. If any of these so-called Hitlers, believing passionately in themselves as such, were inclined to be a little violent or dangerous . . . I assured him that he need have no worry. I suggested that I should collect a group of the most amiable of our Führers and assemble them for him to meet. Herr B. insisted that the Führer was very anxious to interview and mingle with them without my accompanying him. The patients, he said, would not behave naturally if they saw the chief of the establishment there, and if there was no danger . . . I assured him again that there was no danger. I said, however, that I should be glad if Herr B. would wait upon him. There was no difficulty about that. It was arranged. Messages were sent to the Führers to assemble in a room for a very distinguished visitor, who was anxious to compare notes with them.

"Ach, so. Martin B. and the Führer were introduced into the assembly. I retired, closing the door, and chatted with the two A.D.C.'s who had accompanied them. The Führer, I said, was looking in a particularly anxious state. He had no doubt had many troubles of late. This I may say was very shortly before the end of the war when things, quite frankly, were going badly. The Führer himself, they told me, had been greatly distressed of late but was convinced that he could bring the war to a successful close if the ideas which he was continually presenting to his general staff were acted upon, and accepted promptly."

"The Führer, I presume," said Sir George Packham, "was at that time—I mean to say—no doubt he was in a state that—"

"We need not stress these points," said Herr Spiess. "He was completely beyond himself. Authority had to be taken for him on several points. But all that you will know well enough from the researches you have made in my country."

"One remembers that at the Nuremberg trials—"

"There's no need to refer to the Nuremberg trials, I'm sure," said Mr. Lazenby decisively. "All that is far behind us. We look forward to a great future in the Common Market with your government's help, with the government of Monsieur Grosjean and your other European colleagues. The past is the past."

"Quite so," said Herr Spiess, "and it is of the past that we now talk. Martin B. and Herr Hitler remained for a very short time in the assembly room. They came out again after seven minutes. Herr B. expressed himself to Dr. Reichardt as very well satisfied with their experience. Their car was waiting and he and Herr Hitler must proceed immediately to where they had another appointment. They left very hurriedly."

There was a silence.

"And then?" asked Colonel Pikeaway. "Something happened? Or had already happened?"

"The behavior of one of our Hitler patients was unusual," said Dr. Reichardt. "He was a man who had a particularly close resemblance to Herr Hitler, which had given him always a special confidence in his own portrayal. He insisted now more fiercely than ever that he *was* the Führer, that he must go immediately to Berlin, that he must preside over a council of the General Staff. In fact, he behaved with no signs of the former slight amelioration which he had shown in his condition. He seemed so unlike himself that I really could not understand this change taking place so suddenly. I was relieved, indeed, when two days later, his relations called to take him home for future private treatment there."

"And you let him go," said Herr Spiess."

"Naturally I let him go. They had a responsible doctor with them, he was a voluntary patient, not certified, and therefore he was within his rights. So he left."

"I don't see—" began Sir George Packham.

"Herr Spiess has a theory—"

"It's not a theory," said Spiess. "What I am telling you is fact. The Russians concealed it, we've concealed it. Plenty of evidence and proof has come in. Hitler, our Führer, *remained in the asylum by his own consent* that day and a man with the nearest resemblance to the real Hitler departed with Martin B. It was that patient's body which was subsequently found in the bunker. I will not beat about the bush. We need not go into unnecessary details."

"We all have to know the truth," said Lazenby.

"The real Führer was smuggled by a prearranged underground route to the Argentine and lived there for some years. He had a son there by a beautiful Aryan girl of good family. Some say she was an English girl. Hitler's mental condition worsened, and he died insane, believing himself to be commanding his armies in the field. It was the only plan possibly by which he could ever have escaped from Germany. He accepted it."

"And you mean that for all these years nothing has leaked out about this, nothing has been known?"

"There have been rumors, there are always rumors. If you remember, one of the Czar's daughters in Russia was said to have escaped the general massacre of her family."

"But that was—" George Packham stopped. "False—quite false."

"It was proved false by one set of people. It was accepted by another set of people, both of whom had known her. That Anastasia was indeed Anastasia, or that Anastasia, Grand Duchess of Russia, was really only a peasant girl. Which story was true? Rumors! The longer they go on, the less people believe them, except for those who have romantic minds, who go on believing them. It has often been rumored that Hitler was alive, not dead. There is no one who has ever said with certainty that they have examined his dead body. The Russians declared so. They brought no proofs, though."

"Do you really mean to say—Dr. Reichardt, do *you* support this extraordinary story?"

"Ach," said Dr. Reichardt. "You ask me, but I have told you my part. It was certainly Martin B. who came to my sanatorium. It was Martin B. who brought with him the Führer. It was Martin B. who treated him as the Führer, who spoke to him with the deference with which one speaks to the Führer. As for me, I lived already with some hundreds of Führers, of Napoleons, of Julius Caesars. You must understand that the Hitlers who lived in my sanatorium, they looked alike, they could have been, nearly all of them *could* have been, Adolf Hitler. They themselves could never have believed in themselves with the passion, the vehemence with which they knew that they were Hitler, unless they had had a basic resemblance, with makeup, clothing, continual acting, playing of the part. I had had no personal meeting with Herr Adolf Hitler at any previous time. One saw pictures of him in the papers, one knew roughly what our great genius looked like, but one knew only the pictures that he wished shown. So he came, he was the Führer, Martin B. the man best to be believed on that subject said he was the Führer. No, I had no doubts. I obeyed orders. Herr Hitler wished to go alone into a room to meet a selection of his—what shall one say?—his plaster copies. He went in. He came out. An exchange of clothing could have been made, not very different clothing, in any case. Was it he himself or one of the self-appointed Hitlers who came out? Rushed out quickly by Martin B. and driven away while the real man could have stayed behind, could have enjoyed playing his part, could have known that in this way and in this way only could he manage to escape from the country which at any moment might surrender. He was already disturbed in mind, mentally affected by rage and anger that the orders he gave, the wild fantastic messages sent to his staff, what they were to do, what they were to say, the impossible things they were to attempt, were not, as of old, immediately obeyed. He could feel already that he was no longer in supreme command. But he had a small faithful two or three and they had a plan for him, to get him out of this country, out of Europe, to a place where he could rally round him in a different continent his Nazi followers, the young ones who believed so passionately in him. The swastika would rise again there. He played his part. No doubt, he enjoyed it. Yes, that would be in keeping with a man whose reason was already tottering. He would show these others that he could play the part of Adolf Hitler better than they did. He laughed to himself occasionally, and my doctors, my nurses, they would look in, they would see some slight change. One patient who seemed unusually mentally disturbed, perhaps. Pah, there was nothing in that. It was always happening with the Napoleons, with the Julius Caesars, with all of them. Some days, as one would say if one was a layman, they are madder than usual. That is the only way I can put it. So now it is for Herr Spiess to speak."

"Fantastic!" said the Home Secretary.

"Yes, fantastic," said Herr Spiess patiently, "but fantastic things can happen, you know. In history, in real life, no matter how fantastic."

"And nobody suspected, nobody knew?"

"It was very well planned. It was well planned, well thought out. The escape route was ready, the exact details of it are not clearly known, but one can make a pretty good recapitulation of them. Some of the people who were concerned, who passed a certain personage on from place to place under different disguises, under different names, some of those people, on our looking back and making inquiries, we find did not live as long as they might have done."

"You mean in case they should give the secret away or should talk too much?"

"The SS saw to that. Rich rewards, praise, promises of high positions in the future and then—death is a much easier answer. And the SS were used to death. They knew the different ways of it, they knew means of disposing of bodies—Oh, yes, I will tell you that, this has been inquired into for some time now. The knowledge has come little by little to us, and we have made inquiries, documents have been acquired, and the truth has come out. Adolf Hitler certainly reached South America. It is said that a marriage ceremony was performed—that a child was born. The child was branded in the foot with the mark of the swastika. Branded as a baby. I have seen trusted agents whom I can believe. They have seen that branded foot in South America. There that child was brought up, carefully guarded, shielded, prepared—prepared as the

Dalai Lama might have been prepared for his great destiny. For that was the idea behind the fanatical young, the idea was greater than the idea that they had started out with. This was not merely a revival of the new Nazis, the new German super race. It was that, yes, but it was many more things besides. It was the young of many other nations, the super race of the young men of nearly every country in Europe, to join together, to join the ranks of anarchy, to destroy the old world, the materialistic world, to usher in a great new band of killing, murdering, violent brothers. Bent first on destruction and then on rising to power. And they had now their leader. A leader with the right blood in his veins and a leader who, though he grew up with no great likeness to his dead father, was—no, *is* a golden-haired fair Nordic boy, taking presumably after the looks of his mother. A golden boy. A boy whom the whole world could accept. The Germans and the Austrians first because it was the great article of their faith of their music, the Young Siegfried. So he grew up as the Young Siegfried who would command them all, who would lead them into the promised land. Not the promised land of the Jews, whom they despised, where Moses led his followers. The Jews were dead under the ground, killed or murdered in the gas chambers. This was to be a land of their own, a land gained by their own prowess. The countries of Europe were to be banded together with the countries of South America. There already they had their spearhead, their anarchists, their prophets, their Guevaras, the Castros, the Guerrillas, their followers, a long arduous training in cruelty and torture and violence and death, and after it, glorious life. Freedom. As rulers of the New World State. The appointed conquerors."

"Absurd nonsense," said Mr. Lazenby. "Once all this is put a stop to—the whole thing will collapse. This is all quite ridiculous. What *can* they do?" Cedric Lazenby sounded merely querulous.

Herr Spiess shook his heavy, wise head.

"You may ask. I tell you the answer, which is—*they do not know.* They don't know where they're going. They don't know what is going to be done with them."

"You mean they're not the real leaders?"

"They are the young marching heroes, treading their path to glory, on steppingstones of violence, of pain, of hatred. They have now their following not only in South America and Europe. The cult has traveled north. In the United States, there too the young men riot, they march, they follow the banner of the Young Siegfried. They are taught his ways, they are taught to kill, to enjoy pain, they are taught the rules of the Death's Head, the rules of Himmler. They are being trained, you see. They are being secretly indoctrinated. They do not know what they're being trained for. But we do, some of us at least. And you? In this country?"

"Four or five of us, perhaps," said Colonel Pikeaway.

"In Russia they know, in America they have begun to know. They know that there are the followers of The Young Hero, Siegfried, based on the Norse legends, and that a young Siegfried is the leader. That that is their new religion. The religion of the glorious boy, the golden triumph of youth. In him the old Nordic gods have risen again.

"But that, of course," said Herr Spiess, dropping his voice to a commonplace tone, "that, of course, is not the simple prosaic truth. There are some powerful personalities behind this. Evil men with first-class brains. A first-class financier, a great industrialist, someone who controls mines, oil, stores of uranium, who owns scientists of the top class, and those are the ones, a committee of men, who themselves do not look particularly interesting or extraordinary, but nevertheless have got control. They control the sources of power, and control through certain means of their own the young men who kill and the young men who are slaves. By control of drugs they acquire slaves. Slaves in every country who little by little progress from soft drugs to hard drugs and who are then completely subservient, completely dependent on men whom they do not even know but who secretly own them body and soul. Their craving need for a particular drug makes them slaves, and in due course, these slaves prove to be no good, because of their dependence on drugs, they will only be capable of sitting in apathy dreaming sweet dreams, and so they will be left to die, or even helped to die. They will not inherit that kingdom in which they believe. Strange religions are being deliberately introduced to them. The gods of the old days disguised."

"And permissive sex also plays its part, I suppose?"

"Sex can destroy itself. In old Roman times the men who steeped themselves in vice, who were oversexed, who ran sex to death until they were bored and weary of sex, sometimes fled from it and went out into the desert and became anchorites like St. Simeon Stylites. Sex will exhaust itself. It does its work for the time being, but it cannot rule you as drugs rule you. Drugs and sadism and the love of power and hatred. A desire for pain for its own sake. The pleasures of inflicting it. They are teaching themselves the pleasures of evil. Once the pleasures of evil get a hold on you, you cannot draw back."

"My dear Chancellor—I really can't believe you—I mean, well—I mean if there are these tendencies, they must be put down by adopting strong measures. I mean, really, one—one can't go on pandering to this sort of thing. One must take a firm stand—a firm stand."

"Shut up, George." Mr. Lazenby pulled out his pipe, looked at it, put it back in his pocket again. "The best plan, I think," he said, his *idée fixe* reasserting itself, "would be for me to fly to Russia. I understand that—well, that these facts are known to the Russians."

"They know sufficient," said Herr Spiess. "How much they will admit they know—" he shrugged his shoulders—"that is difficult to say. It is never easy to get the Russians to come out in the open. They have their own troubles on the Chinese border. They believe perhaps less in the far-advanced stage into which this movement has got than we do."

"I should make mine a special mission, I should."

"I should stay here if I were you, Cedric."

Lord Altamount's quiet voice spoke from where he leaned rather wearily back in his chair. "We need you here, Cedric," he said. There was gentle authority in his voice. "You are the head of our Government—you must remain here. We have our trained agents—our own emissaries who are qualified for foreign missions."

"Agents?" Sir George Packham dubiously demanded. "What can agents do at this stage? We must have a report from—Ah, Horsham, there you are—I did not notice you before. Tell us—what agents have we got? and what can they possibly do?"

"We've got some very good agents," said Henry Horsham quietly. "Agents bring you information. Herr Spiess also has brought you information. Information which *his* agents have obtained for *him*. The trouble is—always has been (you've only got to read about the last war)—nobody wishes to believe the news the agents bring."

"Surely—Intelligence—"

"Nobody wants to accept that the agents *are* intelligent! But they are, you know. They are highly trained and their reports, nine times out of ten, are true. What happens then? The high ups refuse to believe it, don't want to believe it, go further and refuse to act upon it in any way."

"Really, my dear Horsham, I can't—"

Horsham turned to the German.

"Even in your country, sir, didn't that happen? True reports were brought in, but they weren't always acted upon. People don't want to know—if the truth is unpalatable."

"I have to agree—that can and does happen—not often, of that I assure you—But yes—sometimes—"

Mr. Lazenby was fidgeting again with his pipe.

"Let us not argue about information. It is a question of dealing—of acting upon the information we have got. This is not merely a national crisis—it is an international crisis. Decisions must be taken at top level—we must act. Munro, the police must be reinforced by the Army—military measures must be set in motion. Herr Spiess, you have always been a great military nation—rebellions must be put down by armed forces before they get out of hand. You would agree with that policy, I am sure—"

"The policy, yes. But these insurrections are already what you term 'out of hand.' They have tools, rifles, machine guns, explosives, grenades, bombs, chemical and other gases—"

"But with our nuclear weapons—a mere threat of nuclear warfare—and—"

"These are not just disaffected schoolboys. With this Army of Youth there are scientists—young biologists, chemists, physicists. To start—or to engage in nuclear warfare in Europe—" Herr Spiess shook his head. "Already we have had an attempt to poison the water supply at Cologne—Typhoid."

"The whole position is incredible—" Cedric Lazenby looked round him hopefully—"Chetwynd—Munro—Blunt?"

Admiral Blunt was, somewhat to Lazenby's surprise, the only one to respond.

"I don't know where the Admiralty comes in—not quite our pigeon. I'd advise you, Cedric, if you want to do the best thing for yourself, to take your pipe and a big supply of tobacco, and get as far out of range of any nuclear warfare you are thinking of starting as you can. Go and camp in the Antarctic, or somewhere where radioactivity will take a long time catching up with you. Professor Eckstein warned us, you know, and he knows what he's talking about."

18

Pikeaway's Postscript

THE MEETING BROKE up at this point. It split into a definite rearrangement.

The German Chancellor with the Prime Minister, Sir George Packham, Gordon Chetwynd and Dr. Reichardt departed for lunch at Downing Street.

Admiral Blunt, Colonel Munro, Colonel Pikeaway and Henry Horsham remained to make their comments with more freedom of speech than they would have permitted themselves if the VIPs had remained.

The first remarks made were somewhat disjointed.

"Thank goodness they took George Packham with them," said Colonel Pikeaway. "Worry, fidget, wonder, surmise—gets me down sometimes."

"You ought to have gone with them, Admiral," said Colonel Munro. "Can't see Gordon Chetwynd or George Packham being able to stop our Cedric from going off for a top-level consultation with the Russians, the Chinese, the Ethiopians, the Argentinians or anywhere else the fancy takes him."

"I've got other kites to fly," said the Admiral gruffly. "Going to the country to see an old friend of mine." He looked with some curiosity at Colonel Pikeaway.

"Was the Hitler business really a surprise to you, Pikeaway?"

Colonel Pikeaway shook his head.

"Not really. We've known all about the rumors of our Adolf turning up in South America and keeping the swastika flying for years. Fifty-to-fifty chance of its being true. Whoever the chap was, madman, play-acting impostor, or the real thing, he passed in his checks quite soon. Nasty stories about that, too—he wasn't an asset to his supporters."

"Whose body was it in the bunker? is still a good talking point," said Blunt. "Never been any definite identification. Russians saw to that."

He got up, nodded to the others, and went toward the door.

Munro said thoughtfully, "I suppose Dr. Reichardt knows the truth—though he played it cagey."

"What about the Chancellor?" said Munro.

"Sensible man," grunted the Admiral, turning his head back from the doorway. "He was getting his country the way he wanted it, when this youth business started playing fun and games with the civilized world. Pity!"

He looked shrewdly at Colonel Munro.

"What about the golden-haired wonder? Hitler's son? Know all about him?"

"No need to worry," said Colonel Pikeaway unexpectedly.

The Admiral let go of the door handle and came back and sat down.

"All my eye and Betty Martin," said Colonel Pikeaway. "Hitler never had a son."

"You can't be sure of that."

"We *are* sure—Franz Joseph, the Young Siegfried, the idolized leader, is a common or garden fraud, a rank impostor. He's the son of an Argentinian carpenter and a good-looking blond, a small-part German opera singer—inherited his looks and his singing voice from his mother. He was carefully chosen for the part he was to play, groomed for stardom. In his early youth he was a professional actor—he was branded in the foot with a swastika—a story made up for him full of romantic details. He was treated like a dedicated Dalai Lama."

"And you've proof of this?"

"Full documentation," Colonel Pikeaway grinned. "One of my best agents got it. Affidavits, photostats, signed declarations, including one from the mother, and medical evidence as to the date of the scar, copy of the original birth certificate of Karl Aguileros—and signed evidence of his identity with the so-called Franz Joseph. The whole bag of tricks. My agent got away with it just in time. They were after her—might have got her if she hadn't had a bit of luck at Frankfurt."

"And where are these documents now?"

"In a safe place. Waiting for the right moment for a spectacular debunking of a first-class impostor—"

"Do the Government know this?—the Prime Minister?"

"I never tell all I know to politicians—not until I can't avoid it, or until I'm quite sure they'll do the right thing."

"You *are* an old devil, Pikeaway," said Colonel Munro.

"Somebody has to be," said Colonel Pikeaway sadly.

19

Sir Stafford Nye Has Visitors

SIR STAFFORD NYE was entertaining guests. They were guests with whom he had previously been acquainted except for one of them whom he knew fairly well by sight. They were good-looking young men, serious-minded and intelligent, or so he should judge. Their hair was controlled and stylish, their clothes were well-cut, though not unduly old-fashioned. Looking at them, Stafford Nye was unable to deny that he liked the look of them. At the same time he wondered what they wanted with him. One of them he knew was the son of an oil king. Another of them, since leaving the university, had interested himself in politics. He had an uncle who owned a chain of restaurants. The third one was a young man with beetle brows, who frowned and to whom perpetual suspicion seemed to be second nature.

"It's very good of you to let us come and call upon you, Sir Stafford," said the one who seemed to be the blond leader of the three.

His voice was very agreeable. His name was Clifford Bent.

"This is Roderick Ketelly and this is Jim Brewster. We're all anxious about the future. Shall I put it like that?"

"I suppose the answer to that is, aren't we all?" said Sir Stafford Nye.

"We don't like things the way they're going," said Clifford Bent. "Rebellion, anarchy, all that. Well, it's all right as a philosophy. Frankly, I think we may say that we all seem to go through a phase of it, but one does come out the other side. We want people to be able to pursue academic careers without their being interrupted. We want a good sufficiency of demonstrations, but not demonstrations of hooliganism and violence. We want intelligent demonstrations. And what we want, quite frankly, or so I think, is a new political party. Jim Brewster here has been paying serious attention to entirely new ideas and plans concerning trade union matters. They've tried to shout him down and talk him out, but he's gone on talking, haven't you, Jim?"

"Muddle-headed old fools, most of them," said Jim Brewster.

"We want a sensible and serious policy for youth, a more economical method of government. We want different ideas to obtain in education, but nothing fantastic or high-falutin. And we shall want, if we win seats, and if we are able finally to form a government—and I don't see why we shouldn't —to put these ideas into action. There are a lot of people in our movement. We stand for youth, you know, just as well as the violent ones do. We stand for moderation, and we mean to have a sensible government, with a reduction in the number of M.P.'s, and we're noting down, looking for the men already in politics no matter what their particular persuasion is, if we think they're men of sense. We've come here to see if we can interest you in our aims. At the moment they are still in a state of flux, but we have got as far as knowing the men we want. I may say that we don't want the ones we've got at present, and we don't want the ones who might be put in instead. As for the third party, it seems to have died out of the running, though there are one or two good people there who suffer now for being in a minority, but I think they would come over to our way of thinking. We want to interest you. We want, one of these days, perhaps not so far distant as you might think—we want someone who'd understand and put out a proper, successful foreign policy. The rest of the world's in a worse mess than we are now. Washington's razed to the ground. Europe has continual military actions, demonstrations, wrecking of airports. Oh, well, I don't need to write you a news letter of the past six months, but our aim is not so much to put the world on its legs again as to put England on its legs again. To have the right men to do it. We want young men, a great many young men, and we've got a great many young men who aren't revolutionary, who aren't anarchistic, who will be willing to try and make a country run profitably. And we want some of the older men—I don't mean men of sixty-odd, I mean men of forty or fifty—and we've come to you because, well, we've heard things about you. We know about you and you're the sort of man we want."

"Do you think you are wise?" said Sir Stafford.

"Well, we think we are."

The second young man laughed slightly.

"We hope you'll agree with us there."

"I'm not sure that I do. You're talking in this room very freely."

"It's your sitting room."

"Yes, yes, it's my flat and it's my sitting room. But what you are saying, and in fact what you might be going to say, might be unwise. That means both for you as well as me."

"Oh! I think I see what you're driving at."

"You are offering me something. A way of life, a new career, and you are suggesting a breaking of certain ties. You are suggesting a form of disloyalty."

"We're not suggesting your becoming a defector to any other country, if that's what you mean."

"No, no, this is not an invitation to Russia or an invitation to China or an invitation to other places mentioned in the past, but I think it is an invitation connected with some foreign interests." He went on: "I've recently come back from abroad. A very interesting journey. I have spent the last three weeks in South America. There is something I would like to tell you. I have been conscious since I returned to England that I have been followed."

"Followed? You don't think you imagined it?"

"No, I don't think I've imagined it. Those are the sort of things I have learned to notice in the course of my career. I have been in some fairly far-distant and—shall we say?—interesting parts of the world. You chose to call upon me to sound me as to a proposition. It might have been safer, though, if we had met elsewhere."

He got up, opened the door into the bathroom and turned the tap.

"From the films I used to see some years ago," he said, "if you wished to disguise your conversation when a room was bugged, you turned on taps. I have no doubt that I am somewhat old-fashioned and that there are better methods of dealing with these things now. But at any rate perhaps we could speak a little more clearly now, though even then I still think we should be careful. South America," he went on, "is a very interesting part of the world. The federation of South American countries (Spanish Gold has been one name for it), comprising by now Cuba, the Argentine, Brazil, Peru, one or two others not quite settled and fixed but coming into being. Yes. Very interesting."

"And what are your views on the subject?" the suspicious-looking Jim Brewster asked. "What have you got to say about things?"

"I shall continue to be careful," said Sir Stafford. "You will have more dependence on me if I do not talk unadvisedly. But I think that can be done quite well after I turn off the bath water."

"Turn it off, Jim," said Cliff Bent.

Jim grinned suddenly and obeyed.

Stafford Nye opened a drawer at the table and took out a recorder. "Not a very practiced player yet," he said.

He put it to his lips and started a tune. Jim Brewster came back, scowling.

"What's this? A bloody concert we're going to put on?"

"Shut up," said Cliff Bent. "You ignoramus, you don't know anything about music."

Stafford Nye smiled.

"You share my pleasure in Wagnerian music, I see," he said. "I was at the Youth Festival this year and enjoyed the concerts there very much."

Again he repeated the tune.

"Not any tune I know," said Jim Brewster. "It might be the *Internationale* or the *Red Flag* or *God Save the King* or *Yankee Doodle* or the *Star-Spangled Banner*. What the devil is it?"

"It's a *motif* from an opera," said Ketelly. "And shut your mouth. We know all we want to know."

"The horn call of a young Hero," said Stafford Nye.

He brought his hand up in a quick gesture, the gesture from the past meaning "Heil Hitler." He murmured very gently:

"The new Siegfried."

All three rose.

"You're quite right," said Clifford Bent. "We must all, I think, be very careful."

He shook hands.

"We are glad to know that you will be with us. One of the things this country will need in its future—its great future, I hope—will be a first-class Foreign Minister."

They went out of the room. Stafford Nye watched them, through the slightly open door, go into the lift and descend. He gave a curious smile, shut the door, glanced up at the clock on the wall and sat down in an easy chair— to wait . . .

His mind went back to the day, a week ago now, when he and Mary Ann had gone their separate ways from Kennedy Airport. They had stood there, both of them finding it difficult to speak. Stafford Nye had broken the silence first.

"Do you think we'll ever meet again? I wonder . . ."

"Is there any reason why we shouldn't?"

"Every reason, I should think."

She looked at him, then quickly away again.

"These partings have to happen. It's—part of the job."

"The job! It's always the job with you, isn't it?"

"It has to be."

"You're a professional. I'm only an amateur. You're—" He broke off. "What are you? Who are you? I don't really know, do I?"

"No."

He looked at her then. He saw sadness, he thought, in her face. Something that was almost pain.

"So I have to—wonder . . . You think I ought to trust you, I suppose?"

"No, not that. That is one of the things that I have learned, that life has taught me. There is nobody that one can trust. Remember that—always."

"So that is your world? A world of distrust, of fear, of danger."

"I wish to stay alive. I am alive."

"I know."

"And I want *you* to stay alive."

"*I* trusted you—in Frankfurt . . ."

"You took a risk."

"It was a risk well worth taking. You know that as well as I do."

"You mean because—?"

"Because we have been together. And now— That is my flight being called. Is this companionship of ours which started in an airport to end here in another airport? You are going where? To do what?"

"To do what I have to do. To Baltimore, to Washington, to Texas. To do what I have been told to do."

"And I? I have been told nothing. I am to go back to London—and do what there?"

"Wait."

"Wait for what?"

"For the advances that almost certainly will be made to you."

"And what am I to do then?"

She smiled at him with the sudden gay smile that he knew so well.

"Then you play it by ear. You'll know how to do it, none better. You'll like the people who approach you. They'll be well chosen. It's important, Very important, that we should know who they are."

"I must go. Good-by, Mary Ann."

"*Auf wiedersehen.*"

In the London flat, the telephone rang. At a singularly apposite moment, Stafford Nye thought, bringing him back from his past memories just at that moment of their farewell. "*Auf wiedersehen,*" he murmured as he rose to his feet and crossed to take the receiver off, "let it be so."

A voice spoke whose wheezy accents were quite unmistakable.

"Stafford Nye?"

He gave the requisite answer: "No smoke without fire."

"My doctor says I should give up smoking. Poor fellow," said Colonel Pikeaway, "he might as well give up hope of that. Any news?"

"Oh, yes. Thirty pieces of silver. Promised, that is to say."

"Damned swine!"

"Yes, yes, keep calm."

"And what did you say?"

"I played them a tune. Siegfried's horn motif. I was following an elderly aunt's advice. It went down very well."

"Sounds crazy to me!"

"Do you know a song called *Juanita?* I must learn that too, in case I need it."

"Do you know who Juanita is?"

"I think so."

"H'm, I wonder—heard of in Baltimore last."

"What about your Greek girl, Daphne Theodofanous? Where is she now, I wonder?"

"Sitting in an airport somewhere in Europe waiting for you, probably," said Colonel Pikeaway.

"Most of the European airports seem to be closed down because they've been blown up or more or less damaged. High explosives, hijackers, high jinks.

> *Boys and girls come out to play,*
> *The moon doth shine as bright as day—*
> *Leave your supper and leave your sleep*
> *And shoot your playfellow in the street.*

"The Children's Crusade à la mode."

"Not that I really know much about it. I only know the one that Richard Coeur de Lion went to. But in a way this whole business is rather like the Children's Crusade. Starting with idealism, starting with ideas of the Christian world delivering the holy city from pagans, and ending with death,

death, and again death. Nearly all the children died. Or were sold into slavery. This will end the same way unless we can find some means of getting
them out of it. . . ."

20

The Admiral Visits
an Old Friend

"THOUGHT YOU MUST all be dead here," said Admiral Blunt with a snort.

His remark was addressed not to the kind of butler which he would have
liked to see opening this front door, but to the young woman whose surname
he could never remember but whose Christian name was Amy.

"Rung you up at least four times in the last week. Gone abroad, that's what
they said."

"We have been abroad. We've only just come back."

"Matilda oughtn't to go rampaging about abroad. Not at her time of life.
She'll die of blood pressure or heart failure or something in one of these
modern airplanes. Cavorting about, full of explosives put in them by the
Arabs or the Israelis or somebody or other. Not safe at all any longer."

"Her doctor recommended it to her."

"Oh, well, we all know what doctors are."

"And she has really come back in very good spirits."

"Where's she been, then?"

"Oh, taking a cure. In Germany or—I never can quite remember whether
it's Germany or Austria. That new place, you know, the Golden Gasthaus."

"Ah, yes, I know the place you mean. Costs the earth, doesn't it?"

"Well, it's said to produce very remarkable results."

"Probably only a different way of killing you quicker," said Admiral Blunt.
"How did *you* enjoy it?"

"Well, not really very much. The scenery was very nice, but—"

An imperious voice sounded from the floor above.

"Amy. Amy! What are you doing, talking in the hall all this time? Bring
Admiral Blunt up here. I'm waiting for him."

"Gallivanting about," said Admiral Blunt, after he greeted his old friend.
"That's how you'll kill yourself one of these days. You mark my words—"

"No, I shan't. There's no difficulty at all in traveling nowadays."

"Running about all those airports, ramps, stairs, buses."

"Not at all. I had a wheelchair."

"A year or two ago when I saw you, you said you wouldn't hear of such a thing. You said you had too much pride to admit you needed one."

"Well, I've had to give up some of my pride, nowadays, Philip. Come and sit down here and tell me why you wanted to come and see me so much all of a sudden. You've neglected me a great deal for the last year."

"Well, I've not been so well myself. Besides, I've been looking into a few things. You know the sort of thing. Where they ask your advice but don't mean in the least to take it. They can't leave the Navy alone. Keep on wanting to fiddle about with it, drat them."

"You look quite well to me," said Lady Matilda.

"You don't look so bad yourself, my dear. You've got a nice sparkle in your eye."

"I'm deafer than when you saw me last. You'll have to speak up more."

"All right. I'll speak up."

"What do you want, gin and tonic or whiskey or rum?"

"You seem ready to dispense strong liquor of any kind. If it's all the same to you, I'll have a gin and tonic."

Amy rose and left the room.

"And when she brings it," said the Admiral, "get rid of her again, will you? I want to talk to you. Talk to you particularly is what I mean."

Refreshment brought, Lady Matilda made a dismissive wave of the hand, and Amy departed with the air of one who is pleasing herself, not her employer. She was a tactful young woman.

"Nice girl," said the Admiral, "very nice."

"Is that why you asked me to get rid of her and see she shut the door? So that she mightn't overhear you saying something nice about her?"

"No. I wanted to consult you."

"What about? Your health or where to get some new servants or what to grow in the garden?"

"I want to consult you very seriously. I thought perhaps you might be able to remember something for me."

"Dear Philip, how touching that you should think I can remember *anything*. Every year my memory gets worse. I've come to the conclusion one only remembers what's called the 'friends of one's youth.' Even horrid girls one was at school with one remembers, though one doesn't want to. That's where I've been now, as a matter of fact."

"Where've you been now? Visiting schools?"

"No, no, no, I went to see an old school friend whom I haven't seen for thirty—forty—fifty—that sort of time."

"What was she like?"

"Enormously fat and even nastier and horrider than I remembered her."

"You've got very queer tastes, I must say, Matilda."

"Well, go on, tell me. Tell me what it is you want me to remember."

"I wondered if you remembered another friend of yours. Robert Shoreham."

"Robbie Shoreham? Of course I do."

"The scientist feller. Top scientist."

"Of course. He wasn't the sort of man one would ever forget. I wonder what put him into your head."

"Public need."

"Funny you should say that," said Lady Matilda. "I thought the same myself the other day."

"You thought what?"

"That he was needed. Or someone like him—if there is anyone like him."

"There isn't. Now listen, Matilda. People talk to you a bit. They tell you things. I've told you things myself."

"I've always wondered why, because you can't believe that I'll understand them or be able to describe them. And that was even more the case with Robbie than with you."

"I don't tell you naval secrets."

"Well, he didn't tell me scientific secrets. I mean, only in a very general way."

"Yes, but he used to talk to you about them, didn't he?"

"Well, he liked saying things that would astonish me sometimes."

"All right, then, here it comes. I want to know if he ever talked to you, in the days when he could talk properly, poor devil, about something called Project B."

"Project B." Matilda Cleckheaton considered thoughtfully. "Sounds vaguely familiar," she said. "He used to talk about Project this or that sometimes, or Operation that or this. But you must realize that none of it ever made any kind of *sense* to me, and he knew it didn't. But he used to like—oh, how shall I put it?—astonishing me rather, you know. Sort of describing it the way that a conjurer might describe how he takes three rabbits out of a hat without your knowing how he did it. Project B? Yes, that was a good long time ago. . . . He was wildly excited for a bit. I used to say to him sometimes, 'How's Project B going on?'"

"I know, I know, you've always been a tactful woman. You can always remember what people were doing or interested in. And even if you don't know the first thing about it, you'd show an interest. I described a new kind of naval gun to you once and you must have been bored stiff. But you listened as brightly as though it was the thing you'd been wanting to hear about all your life."

"As you tell me, I've been a tactful woman and a good listener, even if I've never had much in the way of brains."

"Well, I want to hear a little more what Robbie said about Project B."

"He said—well, it's very difficult to remember now. He mentioned it after talking about some operation that they used to do on people's brains. You know, the people who were terribly melancholic and who were thinking of suicide and who were so worried and neurasthenic that they had awful anxiety complexes. Stuff like that, the sort of thing people used to talk of in connection with Freud. And he said that the side effects were impossible. I mean, the people were quite happy and meek and docile and didn't worry anymore, or want to kill themselves, but they—well, I mean they didn't worry enough, and therefore they used to get run over and all sorts of things like that because they weren't thinking of any danger and didn't notice it. I'm putting it badly, but you do understand what I mean. And anyway, he said, that was going to be the trouble, he thought, with Project B."

"Did he describe it at all more closely than that?"

"He said I'd put it into his head," said Matilda Cleckheaton unexpectedly.

"What? Do you mean to say a scientist—a top-flight scientist like Robbie actually said to you that you had put something into his scientific brain? You don't know the first thing about science."

"Of course not. But I used to try and put a little common sense into people's brains. The cleverer they are, the less common sense they have. I mean, really, the people who matter are the people who thought of simple things like perforations on postage stamps, or like somebody Adam, or whatever his name was—no—McAdam in America, who put black stuff on roads so that farmers could get all their crops from farms to the coast and make a better profit. I mean, they do much more good than all the high-powered scientists do. Scientists can only think of things for destroying you. Well, that's the sort of thing I said to Robbie. Quite nicely, of course, as a kind of joke. He'd been just telling me that some splendid things had been done in the scientific world about germ warfare and experiments with biology and what you can do to unborn babies if you get at them early enough. And also some peculiarly nasty and very unpleasant gases and saying how silly people were to protest against nuclear bombs because they were really a kindness compared to some of the other things that had been invented since then. And so I said it'd be much more to the point if Robbie, or someone clever like Robbie, could think of something really sensible. And he looked at me with that, you know, little twinkle he has in his eye sometimes and said, 'Well, what would you consider sensible?' And I said, 'Well, instead of inventing all these germ warfares and these nasty gases, and all the rest of it, why don't you just invent something that makes people feel happy?' I said it oughtn't to be any more difficult to do. I said, 'You've talked about this operation where, I think you said, they took out a bit of the front of your brain or maybe the back of your brain. But anyway it made a great difference in people's dispositions. They'd become quite different. They hadn't worried anymore or they hadn't wanted to commit suicide. But,' I said, 'well, if you can change people like that just by taking a little bit of bone or muscle or nerve or tinkering up a gland, or taking out a gland or putting in more of a gland,' I said, 'if you can make all that difference in people's dispositions, why can't you invent something that will make people pleasant or just sleepy perhaps? Supposing you had something, not a sleeping draught, but just something that people sat down in a chair and had a nice dream. Twenty-four hours or so and just woke up to be fed now and again.' I said it would be a much better idea."

"And is that what Project B was?"

"Well, of course he never told me what it was exactly. But he was excited with an idea and he said I'd put it into his head, so it must have been something rather pleasant I'd put into his head, mustn't it? I mean, I hadn't suggested any ideas to him of any nastier ways for killing people and I didn't want people even—you know—to cry, like tear gas or anything like that. Perhaps laughing—yes, I believe I mentioned laughing gas. I said well, if you have your teeth out, they give you three sniffs of it and you laugh, well, surely, surely you could invent something that's as useful as that but would last a little longer. Because I believe laughing gas only lasts about fifty seconds, doesn't it? I know my brother had some teeth out once. The dentist's chair was very near the window and my brother was laughing so much, when he was unconscious, I mean, that he stretched his leg right out and put it through the dentist's window and all the glass fell in the street, and the dentist was very cross about it."

"Your stories always have such strange sidekicks," said the Admiral. "Anyway, this is what Robbie Shoreham had chosen to get on with, from your advice."

"Well, I don't know what it was exactly. I mean, I don't think it was sleeping or laughing. At any rate, it was *something*. It wasn't really Project B. It had another name."

"What sort of a name?"

"Well, he did mention it once, I think, or twice. The name he'd given it. Rather like Benger's Food," said Aunt Matilda, considering thoughtfully.

"Some soothing agent for the digestion?"

"I don't think it had anything to do with the digestion. I rather think it was something you sniffed or something, perhaps it was a gland. You know we talked of so many things that you never quite knew what he was talking about at the moment. Benger's Food. Ben—Ben—it did begin Ben. And there was a pleasant word associated with it."

"Is that all you can remember about it?"

"I think so. I mean, this was just a talk we had once and then, quite a long time afterwards, he told me I'd put something into his head for Project Ben something. And after that, occasionally, if I remembered, I'd ask him if he was still working on Project Ben and then sometimes he'd be very exasperated and say no, he'd come up against a snag and he was putting it all aside now because it was in—in—well, I mean the next eight words were pure jargon and I couldn't remember them and you wouldn't understand them if I said them to you. But in the end, I think—oh, dear, oh, dear, this is all about eight or nine years ago—in the end he came one day and he said, 'Do you remember Project Ben?' I said, 'Of course I remember it. Are you still working on it?' And he said no, he was determined to lay it all aside. I said I was sorry. Sorry if he'd given it up and he said, 'Well, it's not only that I can't get what I was trying for. I know now that it *could* be got. I know where I went wrong. I know just what the snag was. I know just how to put that snag right again. I've got Lisa working on it with me. Yes, it could work. It'd require experimenting on certain things, but it could work.' 'Well,' I said to him, 'what are you worrying about?' And he said, 'Because I don't know what it would really do to people.' I said something about his being afraid it would kill people or maim them for life or something. 'No,' he said, 'it's not like that.' He said, it's a— Oh, of course, now I remember. He called it Project Benvo. Yes. And that's because it had to do with *benevolence."*

"Benevolence!" said the Admiral, highly surprised. "Benevolence? Do you mean charity?"

"No, no, no. I think he meant simply that you could make people benevolent. *Feel* benevolent."

"Peace and good will toward men?"

"Well, he didn't put it like that."

"No, that's reserved for religious leaders. They preach that to you, and if you did what they preach, it'd be a very happy world. But Robbie, I gather, was not preaching. He proposed to do something in his laboratory to bring about this result by purely physical means."

"That's the sort of thing. And he said you can never tell when things *are* beneficial to people or when they're not. They are in one way, but they're not in another. And he said things about—oh, penicillin and sulfonamides and heart transplants and things like pills for women, though we hadn't got 'The Pill' then. But you know, things that seem all right and they're wonder drugs or wonder gases or wonder something or other, and then there's something about them that makes them go wrong as well as right, and then you wish they weren't there and had never been thought of. Well, that's the sort of thing that he seemed to be trying to get over to me. It was all rather difficult to understand. I said: 'Do you mean you don't like to take the risk?' and he said: 'You're quite right. I don't like to take the risk. That's the trouble because, you see, I don't know in the least what the risk will be. That's what happens to us poor devils of scientists. We take the risks and the risks are not in what we've discovered. It's the risks of what the people we'll have to tell about it will do with what we've discovered.' I said: 'Now you're talking about nuclear weapons again and atom bombs,' and he said: 'Oh, to hell with nuclear weapons and atomic bombs. We've gone far beyond that.'

" 'But if you're going to make people nice-tempered and benevolent,' I said, 'what have you got to worry about?' And he said, 'You don't *understand,* Matilda. You'll never understand. My fellow scientists in all probability would not understand either. And no politicians would ever understand. And so, you see, it's too big a risk to be taken. At any rate one would have to think for a long time.'

" 'But,' I said, 'you could bring people out of it again, just like laughing gas, couldn't you? I mean, you could make people benevolent just for a short time, and then they'd get all right again—or all wrong again—it depends which way you look at it, I should have thought.' And he said, 'No. This will be, you see, permanent. Quite permanent because it affects the—' and then he went into jargon again. You know, long words and numbers. Formulas, or molecular changes—something like that. I expect, really, it must be something like what they do to cretins. You know, to make them stop being cretins, like giving them thyroid or taking it away from them. I forget which it is. Something like that. Well, I expect there's some nice little gland somewhere and if you take it away or smoke it out, or do something rather drastic to it— But then, the people are permanently—"

"Permanently *benevolent?* You're sure that's the right word? Benevolence?"

"Yes, because that's why he nicknamed it *Benvo.*"

"But what did his colleagues think, I wonder, about his backing out?"

"I don't think he had many who knew. Lisa what's-her-name, the Austrian girl; she'd worked on it with him. And there was one young man called Leadenthal or some name like that, but he died of tuberculosis. And he rather spoke as though the other people who worked with him were merely assistants who didn't know exactly what he was doing or trying for. I see what you're getting at," said Matilda suddenly. "I don't think he ever told anybody, really. I mean, I think he destroyed his formulas or notes or whatever they were and gave up the whole idea. And then he had his stroke and got ill, and now, poor dear, he can't speak very well. He's paralyzed on one side. He can hear fairly well. He listens to music. That's his whole life now."

"His life's work's ended, you think?"

"He doesn't even see friends. I think it's painful to him to see them. He always makes some excuse."

"But he's alive," said Admiral Blunt. "He's alive still. Got his address?"

"It's in my address book somewhere. He's still in the same place. North Scotland somewhere. But—oh, do understand—he was such a wonderful man once. He isn't now. He's just—almost dead. For all intents and purposes."

"There's always hope," said Admiral Blunt. "And belief," he added. "Faith."

"And benevolence, I suppose," said Lady Matilda.

21

Project Benvo

PROFESSOR JOHN GOTTLIEB sat in his chair looking very steadfastly at the handsome young woman sitting opposite him. He scratched his ear with a rather monkeylike gesture which was characteristic of him. He looked rather like a monkey anyway. A prognathous jaw, a high mathematical head, which make a slight contrast in terms, and a small wizened frame.

"It's not every day," said Professor Gottlieb, "that a young lady brings me a letter from the President of the United States. However," he said cheerfully, "presidents don't always know exactly what they're doing. What's this all about? I gather you're vouched for on the highest authority."

"I've come to ask you what you know or what you can tell me about something called Project Benvo."

"Are you really Countess Renata Zerkowski?"

"Technically, possibly, I am. I'm more often known as Mary Ann."

"Yes, that's what they wrote me under separate cover. And you want to know about Project Benvo. Well, there was such a thing. Now it's dead and buried and the man who thought of it also, I expect."

"You mean Professor Shoreham."

"That's right. Robert Shoreham. One of the greatest geniuses of our age. Einstein, Niels Bohr and some others. But Robert Shoreham didn't last as long as he should. A great loss to science—what is it Shakespeare says of Lady Macbeth?—*'She should have died hereafter.'* "

"He's not dead," said Mary Ann.

"Oh. Sure of that? Nothing's been heard of him for a long time."

"He's an invalid. He lives in the north of Scotland. He is paralyzed, can't speak very well, can't walk very well. He sits most of the time listening to music."

"Yes, I can imagine that. Well, I'm glad about that. If he can do that, he won't be too unhappy. Otherwise it's a pretty fair hell for a brilliant man who isn't brilliant anymore. Who's, as it were, dead in an invalid chair."

"There *was* such a thing as Project Benvo?"

"Yes, he was very keen about it."

"He talked to you about it?"

"He talked to some of us about it in the early days. You're not a scientist yourself, young woman, I suppose?"

"No, I'm—"

"You're just an agent, I suppose. I hope you're on the right side. We still have to hope for miracles these days, but I don't think you'll get anything out of Project Benvo."

"Why not? You said he worked on it. It would have been a very great invention, wouldn't it? Or discovery, or whatever you call these things?"

"Yes, it would have been one of the greatest discoveries of the age. I don't know just what went wrong. It's happened before now. A thing goes along all right, but in the last stages, somehow, it doesn't click. Breaks down. Doesn't do what's expected of it and you give up in despair. Or else you do what Shoreham did."

"What was that?"

"He destroyed it. Every damn bit of it. He told me so himself. Burnt all the formulas, all the papers concerning it, all the data. Three weeks later he had his stroke. I'm sorry. You see, I can't help you. I never knew any details about it, nothing but its main idea. I don't even remember that now, except for one thing. Benvo stood for Benevolence."

22

Juanita

LORD ALTAMOUNT WAS dictating.

The voice that had once been ringing and dominant was now reduced to a gentleness that had still an unexpectedly special appeal. It seemed to come gently out of the shadows of the past, but to be emotionally moving in a way that a more dominant tone would not have been.

James Kleek was taking down the words as they came, pausing every now and then when a moment of hesitation came, allowing for it and waiting gently himself.

"Idealism," said Lord Altamount, "can arise and indeed usually does so when moved by a natural antagonism to injustice. That is a natural revulsion from crass materialism. The natural idealism of youth is fed more and more by a desire to destroy those two phases of modern life, injustice and crass materialism. That desire to destroy what is evil sometimes leads to a love of destruction for its own sake. It can lead to a pleasure in violence and in the infliction of pain. All this can be fostered and strengthened from outside by those who are gifted by a natural power of leadership. This original idealism arises in a non-adult stage. It should and could lead on to a desire for a new world. It should lead also toward a love of all human beings, and of good will toward them. But those who have once learned to love violence for its own sake will never become adult. They will be fixed in their own retarded development and will so remain for their lifetime."

The buzzer went. Lord Altamount gestured and James Kleek lifted it up and listened.

"Mr. Robinson is here."

"Ah, yes. Bring him in. We can go on with this later."

James Kleek rose, laying aside his notebook and pencil.

Mr. Robinson came in. James Kleek set a chair for him, one sufficiently widely proportioned to receive his form without discomfort. Mr. Robinson smiled his thanks and arranged himself by Lord Altamount's side.

"Well," said Lord Altamount. "Got anything new for us? Diagrams? Circles? Bubbles?"

He seemed faintly amused.

"Not exactly," said Mr. Robinson imperturbably. "It's more like plotting the course of a river—"

"River?" said Lord Altamount. "What sort of a river?"

"A river of money," said Mr. Robinson in the slightly apologetic voice he was wont to use when referring to his specialty. "It's really just like a river, money is—coming from somewhere and definitely going to somewhere. Really very interesting—that is, if you are interested in these things. It tells its own story, you see—"

James Kleek looked as though he didn't see, but Altamount said, "I understand. Go on."

"It's flowing from Scandinavia—from Bavaria—from the U.S.A.—from Southeast Asia—fed by lesser tributaries on the way—"

"And going—where?"

"Mainly to South America—meeting the demands of the now securely established Headquarters of Militant Youth—"

"And representing four of the five intertwined circles You showed us— Armaments, Drugs, Scientific and chemical warfare missiles as well as Finance?"

"Yes—we think we know now fairly accurately who controls these various groups—"

"What about circle J—Juanita?" asked James Kleek.

"As yet we cannot be sure."

"James has certain ideas as to that," said Lord Altamount. "I hope he may be wrong—yes, I hope so. The initial J is interesting. What does it stand for— Justice? Judgment—?"

"A dedicated killer," said James Kleek. "The female of the species is more deadly than the male."

"There are historical precedents," admitted Altamount. "Jael setting butter in a lordly dish before Sisera—and afterwards driving the nail through his head. Judith executing Holofernes, and applauded for it by her countrymen. Yes, you may have something there."

"So you think you know who Juanita is, do you?" said Mr. Robinson. "That's interesting."

"Well, perhaps I'm wrong, sir, but there have been things that made me think—"

"Yes," said Mr. Robinson, "we have all had to think, haven't we? Better say who you think it is, James."

"The Countess Renata Zerkowski."

"What makes you pitch upon her?"

"The places she's been, the people she's been in contact with. There's been too much coincidence about the way she has been turning up in different places, and all that. She's been in Bavaria. She's been visiting Big Charlotte there. What's more, she took Stafford Nye with her. I think that's significant—"

"You think they're in this together?" asked Altamount.

"I wouldn't like to say that. I don't know enough about him, but . . ." he paused.

"Yes," said Lord Altamount, "there have been doubts about him. He was suspected from the beginning."

"By Henry Horsham?"

"Henry Horsham for one, perhaps. Colonel Pikeaway isn't sure, I imagine. He's been under observation. Probably knows it, too. He's not a fool."

"Another of them," said James Kleek savagely. "Extraordinary, how we can breed them, how we trust them, tell 'em our secrets, let them know what we're doing, go on saying: 'If there's one person I'm absolutely sure of, it's— oh, Mclean, or Burgess, or Philby, or any of the lot.' And now—Stafford Nye."

"Stafford Nye, indoctrinated by Renata alias Juanita," said Mr. Robinson.

"There was that curious business at Frankfurt airport," said Kleek, "and there was the visit to Charlotte. Stafford Nye, I gather, has since been in South America with her. As for she herself—do we know where she is now?"

"I daresay Mr. Robinson does," said Lord Altamount. "Do you, Mr. Robinson?"

"She's in the United States. I've heard that after staying with friends in Washington or near it, she was in Chicago, then in California and that she went from Austin to visit a top-flight scientist. That's the last I've heard."

"What's she doing there?"

"One would presume," said Mr. Robinson in his calm voice, "that she is trying to obtain information."

"What information?"

Mr. Robinson sighed.

"That is what one wishes one knew. One presumes that it is the same information that *we* are anxious to obtain, and that she is doing it on our behalf. But one never knows—it may be for the other side."

He turned to look at Lord Altamount.

"Tonight, I understand, you are traveling to Scotland. Is that right?"

"Quite right."

"I don't think he ought to, sir," said James Kleek. He turned an anxious face to his employer. "You've not been so well lately, sir. It'll be a very tiring journey whichever way you go. Air or train. Can't you leave it to Munro and Horsham?"

"At my age it's a waste of time to take care," said Lord Altamount. "If I can be useful, I would like to die in harness, as the saying goes."

He smiled at Mr. Robinson.

"You'd better come with us, Robinson."

23

Journey to Scotland

THE SQUADRON LEADER wondered a little what it was all about. He was accustomed to being left only partly in the picture. That was Security's doing, he supposed. Taking no chances. He'd done this sort of thing before more than once. Flying a plane of people out to an unlikely spot, with unlikely passengers, being careful to ask no questions except such as were of an entirely factual nature. He knew some of his passengers on this flight, but not all of them. Lord Altamount he recognized. An ill man, a very sick man, he thought, a man who, he judged, kept himself alive by sheer will power. The keen hawk-faced man with him was his special guard dog, presumably. Seeing not so much to his safety as to his welfare. A faithful dog who never left his side. He would have with him restoratives, stimulants, all the medical box of tricks. The Squadron Leader wondered why there wasn't a doctor also in attendance. It would have been an extra precaution. Like a death's-head, the old man looked. A noble death's-head. Something made of marble in a museum. Henry Horsham the Squadron Leader knew quite well. He knew several of the Security lot. And Colonel Munro, looking slightly less fierce than usual, rather more worried. Not very happy on the whole. There was also a large, yellow-faced man. Foreigner, he might be. Asiatic? What was he doing, flying in a plane to the north of Scotland? The Squadron Leader said deferentially to Colonel Munro:

"Everything laid on, sir? The car is here waiting."

"How far exactly is the distance?"

"Seventeen miles, sir; roughish road, but not too bad. There are extra rugs in the car."

"You have your orders? Repeat, please, if you will, Squadron Leader Andrews."

The Squadron Leader repeated and the Colonel nodded satisfaction. As the car finally drove off, the Squadron Leader looked after it, wondering to himself why on earth those particular people were here on this drive over the lonely moor to a venerable old castle where a sick man lived as a recluse without friends or visitors in the general run of things. Horsham knew, he supposed. Horsham must know a lot of strange things. Oh, well, Horsham wasn't likely to tell him anything.

The car was well and carefully driven. It drew up at last over a gravel driveway and came to a stop before the porch. It was a turreted building of heavy stone. Lights hung at either side of the big door. The door itself opened before there was any need to ring a bell or demand admittance.

An old Scottish woman of sixty-odd, with a stern, dour face, stood in the doorway. The chauffeur helped the occupants out.

James Kleek and Horsham helped Lord Altamount to alight, and supported him up the steps. The old Scottish woman stood aside and dropped a respectful curtsy to him. She said:

"Good evening, y'r lordship. The master's waiting for you. He knows you're arriving; we've got rooms prepared and fires for you in all of them."

Another figure had arrived in the hall now. A tall lean woman between fifty and sixty, a woman who was still handsome. Her black hair was parted in the middle, she had a high forehead, an aquiline nose and a tanned skin.

"Here's Miss Neumann to look after you," said the Scottish woman.

"Thank you, Janet," said Miss Neumann. "Be sure the fires are kept up in the bedrooms."

"I will that."

Lord Altamount shook hands with her.

"Good evening, Miss Neumann."

"Good evening, Lord Altamount. I hope you are not too tired by your journey."

"We had a very good flight. This is Colonel Munro, Miss Neumann. This is Mr. Robinson, Sir James Kleek and Mr. Horsham, of the Security Department."

"I remember Mr. Horsham from some years ago, I think."

"I hadn't forgotten," said Henry Horsham. "It was at the Leveson Foundation. You were already, I think, Professor Shoreham's secretary at that time?"

"I was first his assistant in the laboratory, and afterwards his secretary. I am still, as far as he needs one, his secretary. He also has to have a hospital nurse living here more or less permanently. There have to be changes from time to time—Miss Ellis, who is here now, took over from Miss Bude only two days ago. I have suggested that she should stay near at hand to the room in which we ourselves shall be. I thought you would prefer privacy, but that she ought not to be out of call in case she was needed."

"Is he in very bad health?" asked Colonel Munro.

"He doesn't actually suffer," said Miss Neumann, "but you must prepare yourself, if you have not seen him, that is, for a long time. He is only what is left of a man."

"Just one moment before you take us to him. His mental processes are not too badly depleted? He can understand what one says to him?"

"Oh, yes, he can understand perfectly, but as he is semiparalyzed, he is unable to speak with much clarity, though that varies, and is unable to walk without help. His brain, in my opinion, is as good as ever it was. The only difference is that he tires very easily now. Now, would you like some refreshment first?"

"No," said Lord Altamount. "No, I don't want to wait. This is a rather urgent matter on which we have come, so if you will take us to him now—he expects us, I understand?"

"He expects you, yes," said Lisa Neumann.

She led the way up some stairs, along a corridor and opened a room of medium size. It had tapestries on the wall, the heads of stags looked down on them; the place had been a one-time shooting box. It had been little changed in its furnishing or arrangements. There was a big record player on one side of the room.

The tall man sat in a chair by the fire. His head trembled a little; so did his left hand. The skin of his face was pulled down one side. Without beating about the bush, one could only describe him one way—as a wreck of a man. A man who had once been tall, sturdy, strong. He had a fine forehead, deep-set eyes, and a rugged, determined-looking chin. The eyes, below the heavy eyebrows, were intelligent. He said something. His voice was not weak, it made fairly clear sounds, but not always recognizable ones. The faculty of speech had only partly gone from him; he was still understandable.

Lisa Neumann went to stand by him, watching his lips, so that she could interpret what he said if necessary.

"Professor Shoreham welcomes you. He is very pleased to see you here, Lord Altamount, Colonel Munro, Sir James Kleek, Mr. Robinson and Mr. Horsham. He would like me to tell you that his hearing is reasonably good. Anything you say to him he will be able to hear. If there is any difficulty, I can assist. What he wants to say to you he will be able to transmit through me. If he gets too tired to articulate, I can lip-read and we also converse in a perfected sign language if there is any difficulty."

"I shall try," said Colonel Munro, "not to waste your time and to tire you as little as possible, Professor Shoreham."

The man in the chair bent his head in recognition of the words.

"Some questions I can ask of Miss Neumann."

Shoreham's hand went out in a faint gesture toward the woman standing by his side. Sounds came from his lips, again not quite recognizable to them, but she translated quickly.

"He says he can depend on me to transcribe anything you wish to say to him or I to you."

"You have, I think, already received a letter from me," said Colonel Munro.

"That is so," said Miss Neumann. "Professor Shoreham received your letter and knows its contents."

A hospital nurse opened the door just a crack—but she did not come in. She spoke in a low whisper:

"Is there anything I can get or do, Miss Neumann? For any of the guests or for Professor Shoreham?"

"I don't think there is anything, thank you, Miss Ellis. I should be glad, though, if you could stay in your sitting room just along the passage, in case we should need anything."

"Certainly—I quite understand." She went away, closing the door softly.

"We don't want to lose time," said Colonel Munro. "No doubt Professor Shoreham is in tune with current affairs."

"Entirely so," said Miss Neumann, "as far as he is interested."

"Does he keep in touch with scientific advancements and such things?"

Robert Shoreham's head shook slightly from side to side. He himself answered.

"I have finished with all that."

"But you know roughly the state the world is in? The success of what is called the Revolution of Youth. The seizing of power by youthful fully equipped forces."

Miss Neumann said, "He is in touch entirely with everything that is going on—in a political sense, that is."

"The world is now given over to violence, pain, revolutionary tenets, a strange and incredible philosophy of rule by an anarchic minority."

A faint look of impatience went across the gaunt face.

"He knows all that," said Mr. Robinson, speaking unexpectedly. "No need to go over a lot of things again. He's a man who knows everything."

He said:

"Do you remember Admiral Blunt?"

Again the head bowed. Something like a smile showed on the twisted lips.

"Admiral Blunt remembered some scientific work you had done on a certain project—I think project is what you call these things? Project Benvo."

They saw the alert look which came into the eyes.

"Project Benvo," said Miss Neumann. "You are going back quite a long time, Mr. Robinson, to recall that."

"It was *your* project, wasn't it?" said Mr. Robinson.

"Yes, it was his project." Miss Neumann now spoke more easily for him, as a matter of course.

"We cannot use nuclear weapons, we cannot use explosives or gas or chemistry, but *your* project, Project Benvo, we *could* use."

There was silence and nobody spoke. And then again the queer distorted sounds came from Professor Shoreham's lips.

"He says, of course," said Miss Neumann, "Benvo *could* be used successfully in the circumstances in which we find ourselves—"

The man in the chair had turned to her and was saying something to her.

"He wants me to explain it to you," said Miss Neumann. "Project B, later called Project Benvo, was something that he worked upon for many years but which at last he laid aside for reasons of his own."

"Because he had failed to make his project materialize?"

"No, he had not failed," said Lisa Neumann. "We had not failed. I worked with him on this project. He laid it aside for certain reasons, but he did not fail. He succeeded. He was on the right track, he developed it, he tested it in various laboratory experiments, and it worked." She turned to Professor Shoreham again, made a few gestures with her hand, touching her lips, ear, mouth in a strange kind of code signal.

"I am asking if he wants me to explain just what Benvo does."

"We do want you to explain."

"And he wants to know how you learned about it."

"We learned about it," said Colonel Munro, "through an old friend of yours, Professor Shoreham. Not Admiral Blunt; he could not remember very much, but the other person to whom you had once spoken about it, Lady Matilda Cleckheaton."

Again Miss Neumann turned to him, and watched his lips. She smiled faintly.

"He says he thought Matilda was dead years ago."

"She is very much alive. It is she who wanted us to know about this discovery of Professor Shoreham's."

"Professor Shoreham will tell you the main points of what you want to know, though he has to warn you that this knowledge will be quite useless to you. Papers, formulae, accounts and proofs of this discovery were all destroyed. But since the only way to satisfy your questions is for you to learn the main outline of Project Benvo, I can tell you fairly clearly of what it consists. You know the uses and purpose of tear gas as used by the police in controlling riot crowds, violent demonstrations, and so on. It induces a fit of weeping, painful tears and sinus inflammation."

"And this is something of the same kind?"

"No, it is not in the least of the same kind, but it can have the same purpose. It came into the heads of scientists that one can change not only man's principal reactions and feeling, but also mental characteristics. You can change a man's character. The qualities of an aphrodisiac are well known. They lead to a condition of sexual desire. There are various drugs or gases or glandular operations—any of these things can lead to a change in your mental vigor, increased energy as by alterations to the thyroid gland, and Professor Shoreham wishes to tell you that there is a certain process—he will not tell you now whether it is glandular, or a gas that can be manufactured, but there is something that can change a man in his outlook on life—his reaction to people and to life generally. He may be in a state of homicidal fury, he may be pathologically violent, and yet, by the influence of Project Benvo, he turns into something, or rather *someone*, quite different. He becomes, there is only one word for it, I believe, which is embodied in its name

—he becomes *benevolent*. He wishes to benefit others. He exudes kindness. He has a horror of causing pain or inflicting violence. Benvo can be released over a big area, it can affect hundreds, thousands of people if manufactured in big enough quantities and if distributed successfully."

"How long does it last?" said Colonel Munro. "Twenty-four hours? Longer?"

"You don't understand," said Miss Neumann. "It is *permanent.*"

"Permanent? You've changed a man's nature, you've altered a component, a physical component, of course, of his being which has produced the effect of a permanent change in his nature. And you cannot go back on that? You cannot put him back to where he was again. It has to be accepted as a permanent change?"

"Yes. It was, perhaps, a discovery more of medical interest at first, but Professor Shoreham had conceived of it as a deterrent to be used in war, in mass risings, riotings, revolutions, anarchy. He didn't think of it as merely medical. It does not produce happiness in the subject, only a great wish for others to be happy. That is an effect, he says, that everyone feels in their life at one time or another. They have a great wish to make someone, one person or many people—to make them comfortable, happy, in good health, all these things. And since people can and do feel these things, there is, we both believed, a component that controls that desire in their bodies, and if you once put that component in operation, it can go on in perpetuity."

"Wonderful," said Mr. Robinson.

He spoke thoughtfully rather than enthusiastically.

"Wonderful. What a thing to have discovered. What a thing to be able to put into action if— But why?"

The head resting toward the back of the chair turned slowly toward Mr. Robinson. Miss Neumann said:

"He says you understand better than the others."

"But it's the answer," said James Kleek. "It's the *exact* answer! It's wonderful." His face was enthusiastically excited.

Miss Neumann was shaking her head.

"Project Benvo," she said, "is not for sale and not for a gift. It has been relinquished."

"Are you telling us the answer is no?" said Colonel Munro incredulously.

"Yes. Professor Shoreham says the answer is no. He decided that it was against—" She paused a minute and turned to look at the man in the chair. He made quaint gestures with his head, with one hand, and a few guttural sounds came from his mouth. She waited and then she said, "He will tell you himself; he was afraid. Afraid of what science has done in its time of triumph. The things it has found out and known, the things it has discovered and given to the world. The wonder drugs that have not always been wonder drugs, the penicillin that has saved lives and the penicillin that has taken lives, the heart transplants that have brought disillusion and the disappointment of a death not expected. He has lived in the period of nuclear fission; new weapons that have slain. The tragedies of radioactivity; the pollutions that new industrial discoveries have brought about. He has been afraid of what science could do, used indiscriminately."

"But this is a benefit. A benefit to everyone," cried Munro.

"So have many things been. Always greeted as great benefits to humanity, as great wonders. And then come the side effects, and worse than that, the fact that they have sometimes brought not benefit but disaster. And so he decided that he would give up. He says"—she read from a paper she held, while beside her he nodded agreement from his chair—"*I am satisfied that I have done what I set out to do, that I made my discovery. But I decided not to put it into circulation. It must be destroyed. And so it has been destroyed. And so the answer to you is no. There is no benevolence on tap. There could have been once, but now all the formulae, all the know-how, my notes and my account of the necessary procedure are gone—burnt to ashes—I have destroyed my brain child.*"

Robert Shoreham struggled into raucous difficult speech.

"I have destroyed my brain child and nobody in the world knows how I arrived at it. One man helped me, but he is dead. He died of tuberculosis a year after we had come to success. You must go away again. I cannot help you."

"But this knowledge of yours means you could save the world!"

The man in the chair made a curious noise. It was laughter. Laughter of a crippled man.

"Save the world. Save the world! What a phrase! That's what your young people are doing, they think! They're going ahead in violence and hatred to save the world. But they don't know how! They will have to do it themselves, out of their own hearts, out of their own minds. We can't give them an artificial way of doing it. No. An artificial goodness? An artificial kindness? None of that. It wouldn't be *real.* It wouldn't *mean* anything. It would be against nature." He said slowly: "*Against God.*"

The last two words came out unexpectedly, clearly enunciated.

He looked round at his listeners. It was as though he pleaded with them for understanding, yet at the same time had no real hope of it.

"I had a right to destroy what I had created—"

"I doubt it very much," said Mr. Robinson; "knowledge is knowledge. What you have given birth to—what you have made to come to life, you should not destroy."

"You have a right to your opinion—but the fact you will have to accept."

"No." Mr. Robinson brought the word out with force.

Lisa Neumann turned on him angrily.

"What do you mean by 'No'?"

Her eyes were flashing. A handsome woman, Mr. Robinson thought. A woman who had been in love with Robert Shoreham all her life probably. Had loved him, worked with him, and now lived beside him, ministering to him with her intellect, giving him devotion in its purest form without pity.

"There are things one gets to know in the course of one's lifetime," said Mr. Robinson. "I don't suppose mine will be a long life. I carry too much weight to begin with." He sighed as he looked down at his bulk. "But I do know some things. I'm right, you know, Shoreham. You'll have to admit I'm right, too. You're an honest man. You wouldn't have destroyed your work. You couldn't have brought yourself to do it. You've got it somewhere still, locked away, hidden away, not in this house, probably. I'd guess, and I'm only making a guess, that you've got it somewhere in a safe deposit or a bank. She knows you've got it there, too. You trust her. She's the only person in the world you do trust."

Shoreham said, and this time his voice was almost distinct:

"Who are *you*? Who the devil are you?"

"I'm just a man who knows about money," said Mr. Robinson, "and the things that branch off from money, you know. People and their idiosyncrasies and their practices in life. If you liked to, you could lay your hand on the work that you've put away. I'm not saying that you could do the same work now, but I think it's all there somewhere. You've told us your views, and I wouldn't say they were all wrong," said Mr. Robinson.

"Possibly you're right. Benefits to humanity are tricky things to deal with. Poor old Beveridge, freedom from want, freedom from fear, freedom from whatever it was, he thought he was making a heaven on earth by saying that and planning for it and getting it done. But it hasn't made heaven on earth and I don't suppose your Benvo or whatever you call it (sounds like a patent food), will bring heaven on earth either. Benevolence has its dangers just like everything else. What it will do is save a lot of suffering, pain, anarchy, violence, slavery to drugs. Yes, it'll save quite a lot of bad things from happening, and it *might* save something that was important. It might—just *might* —make a difference to people. Young people. This Benvoleo of yours—now I've made it sound like a patent cleaner—is going to make people benevolent, and I'll admit perhaps that it's also going to make them condescending, smug and pleased with themselves, but there's just a chance, too, that if you change people's natures by force and they have to go on using that particular kind of nature until they die, one or two of them—not many—might discover that they had a natural vocation, in humility, not pride, for what they were being forced to do. *Really* change themselves, I mean, before they died. Not be able to get out of a new habit they'd learned."

Colonel Munro said, "I don't understand what the hell you're all talking about."

Miss Neumann said, "He's talking nonsense. You have to take Professor Shoreham's answer. He will do what he likes with his own discoveries. You can't coerce him."

"No," said Lord Altamount. "We're not going to coerce you or torture you, Robert, or force you to reveal your hiding places. You'll do what you think right. That's agreed."

"Edward?" said Robert Shoreham. His speech failed him slightly again, his hands moved in gesture, and Miss Neumann translated quickly.

"Edward? He says you are Edward Altamount?"

Shoreham spoke again and she took the words from him.

"He asks you, Lord Altamount, if you are definitely, with your whole heart and mind, asking him to put Project Benvo in your jurisdiction. He says—" she paused, watching, listening—"he says you are the only man in public life that he ever trusted. If it is *your* wish—"

James Kleek was suddenly on his feet. Anxious, quick to move like lightning, he stood by Lord Altamount's chair.

"Let me help you up, sir. You're ill. You're not well. Please stand back a little, Miss Neumann. I—I must get to him. I—I have his remedies here. I know what to do—"

His hand went into his pocket and came out again with a hypodermic syringe.

"Unless he gets this at once, it'll be too late—" He had caught up Lord Altamount's arm, rolling up his sleeve, pinching up the flesh between his fingers. He held the hypodermic ready.

But someone else moved. Horsham was across the room, pushing Colonel Munro aside; his hand closed over James Kleek's as he wrenched the hypodermic away. Kleek struggled, but Horsham was too strong for him. And Munro was now there, too.

"So it's been *you,* James Kleek," he said. "You who've been the traitor, a faithful disciple who wasn't a faithful disciple."

Miss Neumann had gone to the door—had flung it open and was calling. "Nurse! Come quickly. Come."

The nurse appeared. She gave one quick glance to Professor Shoreham, but he waved her away and pointed across the room to where Horsham and Munro still held a struggling Kleek. Her hand went into the pocket of her uniform.

Shoreham stammered out, "It's Altamount. A heart attack."

"Heart attack, my foot," roared Munro. "It's attempted murder." He stopped.

"Hold the chap," he said to Horsham, and leaped across the room.

"Mrs. Cortman? Since when have you entered the nursing profession? We'd rather lost sight of you since you gave us the slip in Baltimore."

Milly Jean was still wrestling with her pocket. Now her hand came out with the small automatic in it. She glanced toward Shoreham, but Munro blocked her, and Lisa Neumann was standing in front of Shoreham's chair.

James Kleek yelled, "Get Altamount, Juanita. Quick—get Altamount."

Her arm flashed up and she fired.

James Kleek said, "Damned good shot!"

Lord Altamount had had a classical education. He murmured faintly, looking at James Kleek, "Jamie? *Et tu, Brute?*" and collapsed against the back of his chair."

Dr. McCulloch looked round him, a little uncertain of what he was going to do or say next. The evening had been a somewhat unusual experience for him.

Lisa Neumann came to him and set a glass by his side.

"A hot toddy," she said.

"I always knew you were a woman in a thousand, Lisa." He sipped appreciatively.

"I must say I'd like to know what all this has been about—but I gather it's the sort of thing that's so hush-hush that nobody's going to tell me anything."

"The Professor—he's all right, isn't he?"

"The Professor?" He looked at her anxious face kindly. "He's fine. If you ask me, it's done him a world of good."

"I thought perhaps the shock—"

"I'm quite all right," said Shoreham. "Shock treatment is what I needed. I feel—how shall I put it?—*alive* again." He looked surprised.

McCulloch said to Lisa, "Notice how much stronger his voice is? It's apathy really that's the enemy in these cases. What he wants is to work again—the stimulation of some brain work. Music is all very well—it's kept him soothed and able to enjoy life in a mild way. But he's really a man of great intellectual power—and he misses the mental activity that was the essence of life to him. Get him started on it again if you can."

He nodded encouragingly at her as she looked doubtfully at him.

"I think, McCulloch," said Colonel Munro, "that we owe you a few explanations of what happened this evening, even though, as you surmise, the powers-that-be will demand a hush-hush policy. Lord Altamount's death—" he hesitated.

"The bullet didn't actually kill him," said the doctor. "Death was due to shock. That hypodermic would have done the trick—strychnine. The young man—"

"I only just got it away from him in time," said Horsham.

"Been the Indian in the woodpile all along?" asked the doctor.

"Yes—regarded with trust and affection for over seven years. The son of one of Lord Altamount's oldest friends—"

"It happens. And the lady—in it together, do I understand?"

"Yes. She got the post here by false credentials. She is also wanted by the police for murder."

"Murder?"

"Yes. Murder of her husband, Sam Cortman, the American Ambassador. She shot him on the steps of the embassy—and told a fine tale of young men, masked, attacking him."

"Why did she have it in for him? Political or personal?"

"He found out about some of her activities, we think."

"I'd say he suspected infidelity," said Horsham. "Instead he discovered a hornets' nest of espionage and conspiracy, and his wife running the show. He didn't know quite how to deal with it. Nice chap, but slow-thinking—and she had the sense to act quickly. Wonderful how she registered grief at the memorial service."

"Memorial—" said Professor Shoreham.

Everyone, slightly startled, turned round to look at him.

"Difficult word to say, memorial—but I mean it. Lisa, you and I are going to have to start work again."

"But, Robert—"

"I'm alive again. Ask the doctor if I ought to take things easy."

Lisa turned her eyes inquiringly on McCulloch.

"If you do, you'll shorten your life and sink back into apathy—"

"There you are," said Shoreham. "Fash-fashion—medical fashion today. Make everyone, even if they're—at death's door—go on working—"

Dr. McCulloch laughed and got up.

"Not far wrong. I'll send you some pills along to help."

"I shan't take them."

"You'll do."

At the door the doctor paused. "Just want to know—how did you get the police along so quickly?"

"Squadron Leader Andrews," said Munro, "had it all in hand. Arrived on the dot. We knew the woman was around somewhere, but had no idea she was in the house already."

"Well—I'll be off. Is all you've told me true? Feel I shall wake up any minute, having dropped off to sleep halfway through the latest thriller. Spies, murders, traitors, espionage, scientists—"

He went out.

There was a silence.

Professor Shoreham said slowly and carefully, "Back to work—"

Lisa said as women have always said, "You must be *careful,* Robert—"

"Not—not careful. Time might be short."

He said again, "Memorial—"

"What do you mean? You said it before."

"Memorial? Yes. To Edward. His memorial! Always used to think he had the face of a martyr."

Shoreham seemed lost in thought.

"I'd like to get hold of Gottlieb. May be dead. Good man to work with. With him and with you, Lisa. Get the stuff out of the bank—"

"Professor Gottlieb is alive—in the Baker Foundation, Austin, Texas," said Mr. Robinson.

"What are you talking of doing?" said Lisa.

"Benvo, of course! Memorial to Edward Altamount. He died for it, didn't he? Nobody should die in vain."

Epilogue

Sir Stafford Nye wrote out a telegraph message for the third time.

ZP 354XB 91 DEP S.Y.
HAVE ARRANGED FOR MARRIAGE CEREMONY TO BE PER-
FORMED ON THURSDAY OF NEXT WEEK AT ST. CHRISTOPHERS
IN THE VALE LOWER STAUNTON 2:30 PM STOP ORDINARY
CHURCH OF ENGLAND SERVICE IF R.C. OR GREEK ORTHODOX
DESIRED PLEASE WIRE INSTRUCTIONS STOP WHERE ARE YOU
AND WHAT NAME DO YOU WISH TO USE FOR MARRIAGE CER-
EMONY STOP NAUGHTY NIECE OF MINE FIVE YEARS OLD AND
HIGHLY DISOBEDIENT WISHES TO ATTEND AS BRIDESMAID
RATHER SWEET REALLY NAME OF SYBIL STOP LOCAL HONEY-
MOON AS THINK WE HAVE TRAVELED ENOUGH LATELY STOP
SIGNED PASSENGER TO FRANKFURT.

TO STAFFORD NYE BXY42698
ACCEPT SYBIL AS BRIDESMAID SUGGEST GREAT AUNT MA-
TILDA AS MATRON OF HONOR STOP ALSO ACCEPT PROPOSAL
OF MARRIAGE THOUGH NOT OFFICIALLY MADE STOP C OF E
QUITE SATISFACTORY ALSO HONEYMOON ARRANGEMENTS
STOP INSIST PANDA SHOULD ALSO BE PRESENT STOP NO GOOD
SAYING WHERE AM AS SHANT BE WHEN THIS REACHES YOU
STOP SIGNED MARY ANN

"Do I look all right?" asked Stafford Nye nervously, twisting his head to look in the glass.

He was having a dress rehearsal of his wedding clothes.

"No worse than any other bridegroom," said Lady Matilda. "They're always nervous. Not like brides, who are usually quite blatantly exultant."

"Suppose she doesn't come?"

"She'll come."

"I feel—I feel—rather queer inside."

"That's because you would have a second helping of pâté de foie gras. You've just got bridegroom's nerves. Don't fuss so much, Staffy. You'll be all right on the night—I mean you'll be all right when you get to the church."

"That reminds me—"

"You haven't forgotten to buy the ring?"

"No, no—it's just I forgot to tell you that I've got a present for you, Aunt Matilda."

"That's very nice of you, dear boy."

"You said the organist had gone—"

"Yes, thank goodness."

"I've brought you a new organist."

"Really, Staffy, what an extraordinary idea! Where did you get him?"

"Bavaria—he sings like an angel—"

"We don't need him to sing. He'll have to play the organ."

"He can do that, too—he's a very talented musician."

"Why does he want to leave Bavaria and come to England?"

"His mother died."

"Oh, dear! That's what happened to our organist. Organists' mothers seem to be very delicate. Will he require mothering? I'm not very good at it."

"I daresay some grandmothering or great-grandmothering would do."

The door was suddenly flung open and an angelic-looking child in pale pink pajamas, powdered with rosebuds, made a dramatic entrance—and said in dulcet tones as of one expecting a rapturous welcome—

"It's me."

"Sybil, why aren't you in bed?"

"Things aren't very pleasant in the nursery."

"That means you've been a naughty girl, and Nannie isn't pleased with you. What did you do?"

Sybil looked at the ceiling and began to giggle.

"It was a caterpillar—a furry one. I put it on her and it went down *here.*"

Sybil's finger indicated a spot in the middle of her chest which in dressmaking parlance is referred to as "the cleavage."

"I don't wonder Nannie was cross—ugh," said Lady Matilda.

Nannie entered at this moment, said that Miss Sybil was overexcited, wouldn't say her prayers, and wouldn't go to bed.

Sybil crept to Lady Matilda's side.

"I want to say my prayers with you, Tilda—"

"Very well—but then you go straight to bed."

"Oh, yes, Tilda."

Sybil dropped on her knees, clasped her hands, and uttered various peculiar noises which seemed to be a necessary preliminary to approaching the Almighty in prayer. She sighed, groaned, grunted, gave a final catarrhal snort, and launched herself:

"Please, God, bless Daddy and Mummy in Singapore, and Aunt Tilda, and Uncle Staffy, and Amy and Cook and Ellen, and Thomas, and all the dogs, and my pony Grizzle, and Margaret and Diana, my best friends, and Joan, the last of my friends, and make me a good girl for Jesus' sake, amen. And please, God, make Nannie nice."

Sybil rose to her feet, exchanged glances with Nannie with the assurance of having won a victory, and said good night and disappeared.

"Someone must have told her about Benvo," said Lady Matilda. "By the way, Staffy, who's going to be your best man?"

"Forgot all about it. Have I got to have one?"

"It's usual."

Sir Stafford Nye picked up a small furry animal.

"Panda shall be my best man—please Sybil please Mary Ann— And why not? Panda's been in it from the beginning—ever since Frankfurt. . . ."

About the Author

AGATHA CHRISTIE's enormous success as a detective story writer and the excellence of her work caused her to be honored by Queen Elizabeth of England as a Dame of the British Empire in 1971.

She knew, and described with humor and deadly accuracy, the world of culture, wealth, and breeding, laying bare, with devastating effectiveness, the passions that dwelt there, turning otherwise attractive men and women into killers. Her devilishly complex and daring plots have baffled and delighted mystery fans throughout the world for more than half a century.

After her marriage to the archaeologist Max Mallowan, she spent part of each year in the Middle East, which provided the exotic settings for several of her popular mysteries.

At the time of her death in 1976, Agatha Christie had written a total of 87 published works, over fifty of them mysteries, and had been translated more widely than any other British author, not excepting Shakespeare.